NO
MAN'S
WORLD

OMNIBUS

An Abaddon Books™ Publication
www.abaddonbooks.com
abaddon@rebellion.co.uk

This omnibus first published in 2015 by Abaddon Books™, Rebellion
Intellectual Property Limited, Riverside House, Osney Mead, Oxford,
OX2 0ES, UK.

10 9 8 7 6 5 4 3 2 1

Editors: Jonathan Oliver & David Thomas Moore
Cover art: Pye Parr
Design: Pye Parr & Sam Gretton
Marketing & PR: Lydia Gittins
Publishing Manager: Ben Smith
Creative Director and CEO: Jason Kingsley
Chief Technical Officer: Chris Kingsley
No Man's World™ created by Pat Kelleher

US ISBN: 978-1-78108-313-0
UK ISBN: 978-1-78108-312-3

Printed in the US

PAT KELLEHER

NO MAN'S WORLD

OMNIBUS

BLACK HAND GANG	The IRONCLAD PROPHECY	The ALLEYMAN

ABADDON BOOKS

WWW.ABADDONBOOKS.COM

INTRODUCTION

THE HISTORY OF military science fiction is, ultimately, the history of World War I.

Somewhere around the end of the nineteenth century, war changed. Gone was the spectacle of the massed charge, gone the honour of enemies who would share a brandy and cigar once the fighting was done. Heroism gave way to the pragmatism of modern warfare; glory was sacrificed in favour of propaganda and *realpolitik*. Where only a few years before war was still something to be celebrated, by the end of the Great War it had become ugly and futile.

Leading this change was the inevitable march of technology. The First World War saw the first large-scale use of the machine gun; it witnessed the first deployment of chemical warfare; it was responsible for the invention of the tank. It *industrialised* warfare, reducing it to a process in which men were shipped (literally, by boat, train and truck) into a machine that converted them, at length, into land, gained by the yard, the foot or even—at its worst—by the inch, at a cost of hundreds or thousands of lives. War now dehumanised the soldiers fighting it, reducing them to a resource to spend, and—through the politics of war, as seen in the posters and newsreels at home—dehumanised the enemy, making them monsters to be exterminated.

So we come to military science fiction. In every aspect, we see the shadow of the Great War. Technology plays centre stage, as something that both elevates and destroys the soldiers dependent on it. Men are seen as expendable, cogs in the machine, even as the stories themselves restore their humanity, showing us their small friendships and even smaller victories. And nowhere is the dehumanisation of the enemy clearer than in the insect-like enemies that dominate the genre, from the bugs of Heinlein's *Starship Troopers* to the xenomorphs of the *Alien* movie franchise and all points in between. The insect is the antithesis of humanity, faceless, utterly alien and without ego, and its popularity as an enemy betrays how little respect we have, in the years since the First World War, for those we war on.

Or does it? Have we ever encountered things like this before?

IN 2014, BROUGHTONTHWAITE is a pretty little market town about half an hour off Junction 40 of the M6 (Pat tells me he prefers to take Junction 39 and enjoy the countryside). Nothing particularly marks it out as home of one of the great mysteries of the Great War; there's a cenotaph in the cemetery and a rather smart memorial at one end of St Mary Butts, but otherwise not a lot to draw your attention to the town's curious history. Dig a little, though, and it's all too easy to find people willing to bend your ear; ask some of the old soaks at the Dog and Gun and they won't shut up about it.

Pat's got a family connection to the town—his maternal grandmother was born here—and so when we approached him about a WWI-era science fiction, he asked if he could use the Harcourt Crater as the basis of his story. We said sure, if that's what he wanted—obviously there was a concern that he might be maligning the memories of dead men, but he was working with and had the support of the community—but it's only since I started reading and fact-checking his work that I found out a little about it. It's really quite fascinating stuff, and but for how little there is out there about it—no-one's completely sure how many documents survive, or who has them, or who's been ordered to cover what up—I'd say you should dig into it yourself. Fortunately, Pat's done it so you don't have to.

ASIDE FROM BEING a singularly exhaustive and insightful record of what little is known of the fate of the Broughtonthwaite Mates of the Pennine Fusiliers, *No Man's World* is a beautifully written work. Even before you get to the terrible splendour of the alien world and the fascinating richness of Chatt culture, Pat's loving descriptions of trench life pull you in and hit you hard; by the time I reached the jump, I almost wanted to go back and just read about life in the Somme a little longer. If that were all the books had going for them, I'd urge you to pick this omnibus up for that alone.

But the world that poor Tommy Atkins and his chums land on is the star of the show. The plants that kill and eat you, petrol fruit, battlepillars, Chatts, the worship of GarSuleth and his Sky Web; once you sadly put the trench chapters behind you, you enter a rich, wonderful tapestry that'll stay with you for years.

SO THERE YOU go. History of military-SF, secret true history, alien exploration, war poetry of a sort. *No Man's World* is all these things, I hope you enjoy reading them as much as I enjoyed working on them.

David Thomas Moore
Oxford
December 2014

ACKNOWLEDGEMENTS

THE STORY OF the 'Broughtonthwaite Mates' could not have been told without the help of a good many people. Firstly, I must thank the members of the Broughtonthwaite Historical Society, who patiently answered my endless queries. I'm also grateful to the estate of the late Arthur Cooke for permission to reprint an extract from his seminal book on the subject, *The Harcourt Crater: Hoax or Horror?* and to Paul Morley, editor of *The Broughtonthwaite and District Mercury* for permission to reprint material from their archives. Many thanks to my editors, Jon Oliver, Jenni Hill and David Moore for their inspirational input and enthusiasm. Thanks, too, to Pye Parr whose covers have never been anything less than amazing, and to Ben Smith, Lydia Gittins and Michael Molcher at Abaddon Books for their continued support in championing the cause of the Pennine Fusiliers. I must also thank Mike Wild and Faye Joy, who kindly read early drafts and made many helpful suggestions. And my heartfelt thanks to my wife Penny for her love and encouragement. To those descendants of the missing Fusiliers who helped my research, I can only express my gratitude and the hope that, as the centenary of the Pennine's disappearance approaches, we are closer to uncovering the truth behind the fate of the 'Broughtonthwaite Mates.'

Pat Kelleher
Broughtonshaw
December 2014

BLACK HAND GANG

ACKNOWLEDGEMENTS

I WOULD LIKE to thank: Jean Spencer of the Broughtonthwaite Genealogical Society without whom I would never have stumbled across this story in the first place. I am also grateful to Bill Merchant of the Broughtonthwaite Real Ale Society for an insight into the history of Everson's Brewery and the Everson family in particular. I am extraordinarily indebted to Arthur Cooke, author of *The Harcourt Crater: Hoax or Horror?* for access to his own private collection of documents, letters and diaries pertaining to the incident and especially to surviving footage from the original Hepton film. I would also like to thank the Moore Family for their permission to view the letters and diary of Private Garside. I also owe a debt of gratitude to Stephen Maugham, secretary of the Broughtonthwaite Historical Society for his enthusiasm and tireless work in tracing original documentation. I should also thank Graham Bassett and the staff of The Pennine Fusiliers Regimental Museum for providing me with exhaustive details on the deployment and movements of the "Broughtonthwaite Mates" prior to November 1916 and whose otherwise polite refusals to supply further information only served to confirm and bolster my own research. I am also grateful to Sarah Purser of the Jodrell Bank Press Office and to Michael Wild for agreeing to discuss, over a pint of Everson's Old Fusilier, the speculations still surrounding the Harcourt event. Special thanks must also go to Jim Sherman of the War Museum of the North's Photographic Department and Mike McCulloch of the *Broughtonthwaite and District Mercury* in attempting to identify soldiers and individuals appearing in the Hepton footage. I would also like to thank my wife, Penny, for her continued support, encouragement and long hours transcribing interviews. Finally, I must also pay tribute to those descendants of the men of 13th Battalion of the Pennine Fusiliers who spoke to me privately for fear of ridicule and censure.

Any errors in this book are entirely the responsibility of the author.

Pat Kelleher

13TH BATTALLION PENNINE FUSILIERS COMPANY PERSONEL

Company HQ

CO: Major Julian Wyndam Hartford-Croft
2CO: Captain Bernard Edward Grantham
Company Sergeant Major Ernest Nelson
Company Quartermaster Sergeant Archibald Slacke
Pte. Jonah Cartwright (batman)
Pte. Charlie Garside (batman)
Royal Army Chaplain: Father Arthur Rand (CF4, 'Captain')
War Office Kinematographer, Oliver Hepton
2nd Lieutenant Henry Talbot, Battalion HQ, military conductor

'C' Company

No 1 Platoon

CO: Lieutenant Morgan

No. 2 Platoon

CO: 2nd Lieutenant J. C. Everson
2CO: Platoon Sergeant Herbert Gerald Hobson

1 Section

IC: Lance Sergeant William Jessop
2IC: Corporal Harry Ketch
Pte. Thomas 'Only' Atkins
Pte. Harold 'Gutsy' Blood
Pte. Wilfred Joseph 'Mercy' Evans
Pte. George 'Porgy' Hopkiss

Pte. Leonard *'Pot Shot'* Jellicoe
Pte. James *'Lucky'* Livesey
Pte. *'Ginger'* Mottram
Pte. Henry *'Half Pint'* Nicholls
Pte. David Samuel *'Gazette'* Otterthwaite

No. 3 Platoon
CO: Lieutenant Holmes

No. 4 Platoon
CO: Lieutenant Gilbert W. Jeffries
2CO: Platoon Sergeant Fredrick Dixon

RAMC
Regimental Aid Post
RMO: Captain Grenville Lippett

Red Cross Nurses
Sister Betty Fenton
Sister Edith Bell
Driver Nellie Abbot (First Aid Nursing Yeomanry)

Machine Gun Corps (Heavy Section) 'I' Company

I-5 HMLS Ivanhoe
CO: 2nd Lieutenant Arthur Alexander Mathers
Pte. Wally Clegg (Driver)
Pte. Frank Nichols (Gearsman)
Pte. Alfred Perkins (Gearsman)
Pte. Norman Bainbridge (Gunner)
Pte. Reginald Lloyd (Gunner)
Pte. Cecil Nesbit (Gunner)
Pte. Jack Tanner (Gunner)

D Flight 70 Squadron: Sopwith 1½ Strutter
Lieutenant James Robert Tulliver (pilot)
Lieutenant Ivor Hodgeson (observer)

For Scott and Callum

PENNINE FUSILIERS

PREFACE

"There was a Front, but damned if we knew where..."

THE HARCOURT CRATER is one of the greatest mysteries of World War One, along with the Angel of Mons, the Phantom Archers and the Crucified Canadian. At nearly half a mile wide, it was reputed to be the largest man-made crater on the Western Front. The official explanation was that German mines dug under the British positions in the Harcourt Sector of the Somme were filled with an experimental high explosive before being detonated on the morning of November 1st 1916, resulting in the loss of over nine hundred men of the 13th Battalion of the Pennine Fusiliers.

Indeed, this was the accepted explanation until nearly a decade after the event, when a French farmer ploughing fields which lay along the old front line dug up several mud-encrusted old film canisters and a package of documents. Inside the canisters were reels of film which, when developed, revealed silent, grainy footage of British Tommies seemingly on an alien world. The film itself was shown to great acclaim in Picture Houses around the world and it became a minor sensation. Although there were those who claimed they could identify faces in the footage, in the end most felt it to be it a hoax.

The success of the film nevertheless engendered an appetite for Space Fiction among the general public that persisted for decades; the film's grainy, iconic images inspiring thousands of lurid sci-fi magazine covers and pulp fiction stories.

My research further revealed rumours that the Government had approached the noted inventor Nikola Tesla, who had earlier claimed to have received extraterrestrial radio signals, to try to construct a device for contacting the lost men, but without any apparent success. The government of the day quietly closed the case. They officially declared the whole incident to be a "meticulously planned hoax" and it was consigned to the annals of British folklore, although documents believed to include letters and journals from the men of the 13th were discreetly returned to the families. Some eventually found their way into the hands of private collectors, where I had a chance to view them.

The original film stock from the canisters, I was disappointed to discover, did not fare as well as the letters. It was stored badly and the unstable silver nitrate composition of the film strips meant that in many cases the film decomposed, although some was salvaged and incomplete footage does still exist.

For a while, the Battalion War Diary, recovered with the film and allegedly detailing the Battalion's life and actions on another world, was relegated to the stacks in the Regimental Museum and was surreptitiously 'misplaced,' having been considered an embarrassment and a stain upon the regiment's proud history.

But the myth refused to die. In subsequent years, men occasionally came forward claiming to be survivors of the battalion, returned with fantastic tales to sell, but none were believed. The story inspired the film *Space Tommies,* released in 1951 featuring Richard Attenborough and Richard Todd, and was the basis for a short-lived adventure strip in the boys' comic *Triumph.*

However, it has become apparent from my extensive research that the mystery of the Harcourt Crater and the *true* fate of the men of the lost 13th Battalion constitutes one of the biggest cover-ups in British military history. I hope that this, the first part of my account, will go some way towards setting the record straight. All of the major events have been drawn directly from primary sources where possible. Others, by necessity, are based on inference but nevertheless serve to hint at the trials, wonders and horrors they were to face, fighting on a Front far, far from home...

Pat Kelleher
Broughtonshaw
November 2009

CHAPTER ONE
"Waiting for Whizz-Bangs..."

THE AUTUMN SUN ducked down below the Earth's parapet, staining the clouds crimson and, as the chill twilight wind began to bite, Broughton Street was busier than usual. Private Seeston fidgeted impatiently as an ambling ration party of Jocks on their way to collect food for the Front Line barged past, discussing rumours of the impending attack.

"Oi, newbie! Y'do know this is one way don'tcha, and it ain't yours?" one said as they shuffled awkwardly by.

"Sorry," said Seeston. "We've only just taken over this sector."

"Who you with?"

"Thirteenth Pennine Fusiliers."

"Thirteen, eh? Unlucky for some."

"Unlucky for *Hun*, we say, mate," said Seeston, bridling at the insult.

The Pennine Fusiliers was a regiment with a proud history that went back to Waterloo. They had served in the Boer and the Crimean wars, as well as during the Indian Rebellion. It was their proud boast that they were the backbone of the army in the same way their namesake mountains were considered the backbone of England. Their barracks were in Broughtonthwaite, a northern mill town nestling among the Pennine hills on the border of Lancashire and Yorkshire. The 13th Battalion of the Pennine Fusiliers was one of several local Pals Battalions raised in 1914 as part of Kitchener's New Army. With only a small standing army at the outset of the war, a million men were wanted to fight the Bosche. Towns vowed to raise as many of the new Battalions as they could muster. A patriotic fervour swept the nation as young men—driven by dull lives, poverty and the lure of adventure—signed up along with their friends, neighbours and workmates. They couldn't wait to get stuck into the Hun and were desperate to see some action before the war was over.

Their illusions didn't last. On the Western Front, along a strip of mud six hundred miles long, that stretched from the French Alps to the Belgian coast, they died in their tens of thousands, in the blasted, unhallowed ground called No Man's Land.

Seeston forged ahead. Shoulders stubbornly thudded against his as he pressed against the flow, but he was on urgent business, a runner for Battalion HQ. The air of importance that this status lent him bolstered his courage and he pushed on with the purpose of a man who knew his time was more valuable than that of those around him.

From somewhere up ahead, beyond the turn in the communication trench, a high scream punctuated the dull repetitive bass thuds of the German shells that had begun to fall.

"Make way there! Coming through."

Men backed against the walls as best they could. Seeston's advance was brought to a halt as a broad arm swept across his chest and thrust him against the revetment. He was going to say something, but as he glanced down at the khaki arm he noticed the three chevrons and thought better of it. "You an' all lad," said the sergeant.

A couple of Linseed Lancers, red cross brassards on their upper arms, moved urgently past, carrying a stretcher. Seeston got a good look at the occupant. The man, his face swathed in dirty blood-soaked bandages, had stopped screaming and a pitiful whine surfaced though thick, wet gurgles. Inexpertly tied, the bandage had partially fallen away from his face. A couple of waiting men crossed themselves.

"Jesus. Poor bastard."

From the shattered visage a desperate, pleading eye looked up and briefly met Seeston's gaze. A small jewel of humanity set in a hellish clasp of splintered bone and bloody, chewed meat, the eye lost its lustre as its owner sank once more beneath a private sea of pain. There was a cough and sputter and the groan worked its way up into a scream again, a desperate arm clutching the air for something none of the soldiers could see. Seeston turned his head aside with a shudder. Jesus, that could be him lying there next time. There were countless ugly and obscene ways to die out here; sniper bullet, machine gun, shell fire, gas, grenade, shrapnel, bayonet, trench club. All for King and Country.

The stretcher-bearers disappeared round the traverse of the communications trench towards the Casualty Clearing Station. Seeston doubted their patient would make it. Once the stretcher-bearers were out of sight, Broughton Street came back to life, the incident consigned to a consensual silence and added to the list of things they'd seen but wouldn't tell those back home.

"That's why these things are one way, y'daft bastard," said the brawny sergeant, releasing him. "If yer going *up* you want High Street. Down, you take Broughton, got it? Now go back the way you came and turn left at Mash Lane."

Seeston had seen a map of Harcourt Sector back at Battalion but here, sunk into the ground between walls of wooden shoring and mud, he quickly lost his bearings. He came to a crossroads gouged into the earth. A crude hand-painted sign declared the place to be 'Idiot's Corner.' Below it, signposts pointed down different runs: Lavender Road, Parsonage Lane, Harcourt Trench, Gamble Alley. He stopped an approaching soldier.

"Excuse me mate, I'm looking for Moorside Support."

"Yeah well I wouldn't stand there and do it. It's not healthy. Idiot's Corner, that."

Seeston blinked.

The soldier rolled his eyes in exasperation. "These crossroads have been marked by Fritz 'aven't they? Every so often he drops one on it. Like I said, only an idiot would stand around here."

"I'm looking for C Company HQ."

"The Broughtonthwaite Mates? Down Mash Lane, turn left onto High Street and follow the smell of black puddin's."

"Ta, mate."

Seeston followed the direction indicated by the Tommy's outstretched hand and onto another narrow communications trench, this one linking the reserve trenches, several miles back at St. Germaine, to the front line. Having lost time, he started to jog up the trench.

He'd just turned the corner of another traverse when he collided with an officer. A few splatters of mud flew upwards from Seeston's hobnails as his foot missed the broken duckboard and sank into the open sump, splashing the officer's highly polished boots.

Crap.

It was Lieutenant Jeffries, Commanding Officer of 4 Platoon.

Crap, crap, crap.

Seeston snapped to attention.

There were some officers that you could get on with, but Jeffries wasn't one of them, with his airs and graces. In fact he seemed more concerned about his own appearance than anything else, to the point where they called him 'Gilbert the Filbert' behind his back; after that musical hall song by wassisname. And he could blow hot and cold. You never knew what you were going to get.

He was a dapper-looking cove with a thin, black, neatly trimmed moustache, not a brass button unpolished, not a crease out of place, cap set straight, everything just so. This man took care of himself, took care to remain different, *better*. Made a point of it. Not for him the new common purpose, all in it together for King and Country. Despite that, Jeffries had a reputation for taking suicidally dangerous risks on the battlefield.

The officer met Seeston's gaze and held it just a fraction too long to be comfortable, before his eyes flicked down to the mud on his boots.

He had a way of looking at you, *into* you, as if he expected to find something and was profoundly disappointed when he didn't. A smile, like a shark's fin, briefly cut the surface of his face.

"Striking an officer, Private? That's a court martial offence."

"Sir, it was an accident, sir. I didn't see you. Sorry, sir."

"I'll be the judge of that. Handkerchief."

"Sir?"

"Get your handkerchief out, man, and wipe that slop off my boots and mind you don't scratch the leather."

"Sir?"

"You heard, Private."

Seeston pulled out his handkerchief and knelt down on the wet duckboard to wipe the splatters of grey chalky mud from the rich, tan, calf-length boots.

"Now why are you in such a hurry, hmm? Spit it out."

"Runner from Battalion, sir. Message for Captain Grantham, C Company, sir."

"Is that so? Short life, a runner. What's your name?"

"Seeston, sir."

"Well, Seeston, best be on your way."

"Thank you sir. Sorry, sir."

"Oh, and Seeston?"

"Sir?"

"I *never* forget a face."

SECOND LIEUTENANT JAMES Charles Everson was making his way though the trenches towards Company HQ when, out of the corner of his eye, he thought he recognised the soldier skulking down a support trench.

"Evans?" he called in a hoarse whisper. The soldier stopped and turned sheepishly.

"Sir?"

Everson saw he was carrying a couple of hessian sandbags in his hands that, despite his care, clanked suspiciously. He shook his head in exasperation.

"Damn it, Evans. You're my best scrounger. I can't afford to lose you."

"Sorry sir, couldn't help myself. I got you a bottle of scotch though." His hand slipped into a sand bag and produced a small bottle of amber fluid. He handed it to Everson, who glanced about cautiously before slipping it inside his jacket.

"Merci, Evans," he said. "Just don't do it again."

"I won't, sir."

Everson arched an eyebrow. "Won't what, Evans?"

"Get caught, sir?"

"Good man."

Evans touched a finger to his temple in an informal salute and slipped away into the muddy shadows.

Everson, too, continued on his way. Heart pounding in his chest, his mouth dry and breath stale from too much coffee and fear, he took a moment to compose himself before pushing aside the heavy gas curtain. A warm fug of stale sweat, damp earth, the chatter of voices and soft oaths rose up the steps to meet him. Ducking his head, he started to descend into the Company HQ Dugout.

Private Seeston, coming up the steps, graciously backed down and stepped aside as Everson entered.

"Thank you, Seeston," said Everson.

"Sir."

Seeston had worked for Everson's father before the war and they often exchanged pleasantries in passing, but today Seeston's terse demeanour unsettled him. The men had been on edge for days. Supplies had been moving up from the support lines for more than a week now; ammunition, rations and medical supplies along with new troops, and still nobody had told them anything. The tension was palpable. Was this it?

Below, the Dugout was sparsely furnished but the furniture was of good quality, requisitioned from some bombed house, no doubt. Hurricane lamps lit the small room, casting large shadows on the crude wooden walls. Everson could hear the disciplined rattle-tattle-ting of the battered old Underwood typewriter as Private Garside typed out order sheets. Major Hartford-Croft, the Battalion Second-in-Command, stood over a makeshift table and looked up from the papers in front of him as Everson entered. Around him stood the Platoon Commanders of C Company. The major had seen the men through the early summer of the Somme and had even been over the top with them. The men liked him all the more for that. He was a ruddy faced man who permanently looked as if he'd just done the hundred-yard dash and hadn't yet recovered, a raspy catch to his breath as he breathed out, his cheeks almost as red as the tabs on his lapels. His mood wasn't good.

Captain Grantham was there too, C Company's new commanding officer. This was his first time on the front line and he'd yet to prove himself to the men. Oh, he'd been round the trenches and tried to jolly them along with the odd joke in an accent you could cut glass on, but that had only served to confirm the men's original unfavourable impressions.

Also present were Everson's fellow subalterns, Morgan and Holmes. In the corner two men, neither of whom Everson knew, muttered together self consciously; a nervous-looking second lieutenant and another man, wearing small round spectacles and a British Army Warm.

Everson edged around to where Lieutenant Morgan was idly polishing his belt with a cuff.

"Is this it then?" he asked in a low voice.

"Looks like it. The old man's been huffing over those papers for the past ten minutes. It don't look good."

Everson ran his fingers under his collar and began to chew his lower lip.

"Sorry I'm late. Dashed sniper at it again, hmm?" Lieutenant Jeffries didn't wait to see if his apology had been accepted.

Everson glanced up at him with disapproval but found himself looking away as Jeffries caught his gaze. He was a queer fish that one, no doubt about it. He'd been with them a little over a month and didn't seem particularly keen on the company of the men, liked his privacy, of which there was precious little to be had on the front. Sometimes it seemed the sensible option he supposed. The life expectancy for an officer in the trenches was only months and eventually you got tired of making new friends only to have them blown to buggery.

"Gentlemen," began Major Hartford-Croft. "Orders have come down from Battalion HQ. We go over the top at 7.20 Ack Emma tomorrow morning. We are to take the German stronghold at Harcourt Wood at all costs. The general advance is being held back by the stalemate in this sector. This objective falls to us. We are to take the machine gun positions that have been holding back the line for the past four months. Bite and hold, gentlemen, bite and hold." Using his swagger stick, he pointed at the map spread out on the table. "The Germans have held the ground around the woods all summer. Unless we can break them before the winter sets in the whole advance will be held back until spring. I don't want that ignominy falling on the Pennines, is that clear? Tomorrow is the first day of November and we *will* take that ridge."

On taking over the trenches three days previously, Everson had studied the lie of the land well. Before the war, it had been gentle rolling farmland. Harcourt Wood sat on a low ridge about a half a mile beyond the front line, overlooking the British positions. After years of artillery bombardment, the long incline to the wood was a featureless shell-pocked quagmire. It wasn't going to be easy. He caught Jeffries smirking to himself and looking a tad more pleased than he had a right to, considering what they were being asked to do. As if he knew something the others didn't.

"Sir?" It was Holmes, Commander of No.3 Platoon. "The Black Country Rifles before us didn't manage it. The German machine gun emplacements will mow us down as they have every other assault. We can't get near them. We're well under strength. They can't seriously expect—"

Captain Grantham cleared his throat in a meaningful fashion.

"Thank you, Captain" said the major. "GHQ have absolute faith in the Pennines to sort this little mess out. A bombardment will begin at 5.30 Ack Emma tomorrow to soften them up."

"Tomorrow, sir?" queried Morgan. "I thought a bombardment would start days before an attack."

"All very well in theory, Morgan, but that would only warn 'em of an impending attack. Blighters'll huddle in their deep dugouts until it's over and then come out like rats and cut us down. This way we have the element of surprise." The major broke into a grin. "The Machine Gun Corp Heavy Section is putting a section of their new Hush Hush Boojums into the fray. They'll lead off the assault and clear a path through the wire. That ought to make Fritz windy enough."

There was a chorus of muttered approval. Tanks. None of them had ever seen one, although there were many wild rumours floating up and down the line. It was said they'd made a great show of themselves a couple of months back at Fleurs Courcelette. They had apparently scared the Hun witless—great roaring metal monsters crawling inexorably towards them through the smoke. By God, with a section of those it might just be possible. Despite his better judgement, Everson could feel himself getting excited at the prospect of an attack.

"The tanks will set off first and break through the wire. Here and here," continued the major, pointing at the map. "They will also draw the machine gun fire, giving the Company a fighting chance. Your job will be to take the German positions and hold them until relieved, which may be a couple of days. The Jocks will be holding our flank, but I want this to be *our* victory. Understood? GHQ have such confidence in us they've even sent one of their flicker-wallahs to film the battle for the Kinemas back home." The major turned to introduce the men in the corner. "This is Oliver Hepton and his conducting officer, Mr Talbot."

The bespectacled man in the greatcoat at least had the decency to give a weak apologetic smile. Everson wasn't impressed. This was going to be a difficult enough job as it was, but it looked as if GHQ wanted a circus, damn them. His men needed rest, but perhaps this might provide a momentary diversion in the lead up to the attack. Flickers were always popular among the men and the chance to appear in one might take their minds of things. Briefly.

"Don't mind me," said Hepton. "Just go about your duties as you would normally. I'm sure your chaps will put on a jolly fine show for the folks back home."

Everson shook his head; bread and bloody circuses.

There was a scuffle outside. Everson heard Seeston's deferential but firm voice. "You can't go in there just yet, Padre... *Padre!*"

They heard the heavy tread of boots upon the steps and the padre half stumbled into the room. The only thing that marked him as an army chaplain was his dog collar and lack of a sidearm.

"Ah Chaplain Rand," said the major. "Although a little late, I fear. Our prayers, it seems have been answered and without your intercession on this occasion," he said, chuckling. The subalterns laughed politely, but briefly.

"What can we do for you, Padre?" said Captain Grantham.

"I'm after a little Christian charity and a few of your men, if you can spare them. There's been an accident on the St. Germaine Road. An ambulance came off the road hit a shell hole. Thankfully the occupants weren't injured—they're shaken and a little bruised but generally fine."

"Well send 'em on their way again, Padre, they're no business of ours," said the major.

"Well, it's just that they're VADs—three of them."

"Women? Shouldn't they be in their hospitals instead of gadding about out here?"

"They say they were dropping off supplies for the Casualty Clearing Stations. Now they're stranded until they can get their ambulance on the road again. They've taken shelter in the cellar of the old Poulet Farmhouse. Do you think you can spare some men to get their motor out of the hole?"

The major glanced at Captain Grantham, who eased his way round the table to the Chaplain.

"Sorry Padre, we can't spare the men. Big show on tomorrow."

"Well what about a couple of men to guard them?"

"Absolutely not," he said ushering the Chaplain towards the steps. "We can't afford to waste men to nursemaid silly gels."

"Who's going to look out for them until they can get back to their depot? You can't leave them alone out here."

"I can't think of a better man than yourself, Padre," said Grantham. "I'll send some men to help them out as soon as I can, but it probably won't be until late tomorrow. But feel free to stop by the kitchens and pick up some rations. Best tell 'em to keep their pretty heads down, eh? It'll be getting damn busy around here soon."

Everson watched the padre's shoulders slump. He may have been God's representative to the Battalion, but even the Almighty cut no slack with Army bureaucracy. Resigned, the padre left the dugout.

"Right, if there are no questions, that's it," said the major. "Best get back to your platoons and inform the men. Oh, and I'd like some patrols out tonight, make sure the Bosche aren't up to anything that can put the kibosh on our little stunt. You'll also need to do the usual wire cutting. Same old, what!"

As the dismissed subalterns shuffled up the steps, Everson was approached by Private Cartwright. "Sir, can you have a word with the major? I'd really like to go over the top with my mates, tomorrow, sir."

"You were a member of the Broughton Harriers, weren't you?" asked Everson.

Cartwright nodded reluctantly.

"That's why you're needed as a runner to the Battalion. I need you to watch our backs. D'you understand? If the lines go down—and they will, your speed could save the company. I'm counting on you, Cartwright."

"Sir," said Cartwright heavily.

Everson mounted the steps up to the trench. Both he and Cartwright knew he hadn't being doing him a favour. Being a runner was a very hazardous occupation. He felt himself sinking into a distinctly black mood.

"At last. My first action old man. Bally good show. I've been waiting to give old Hun what for, eh?" Morgan was saying to others at the top of the steps.

"Oh yes, old thing. Give the Hun what for, hmm?" agreed Jeffries, but the twitch of a sneer at the corner of his lips betrayed his condescension.

"God help his men," said Everson, half to himself, as he watched him go.

"Oh I shouldn't think so, John. I shouldn't think so for one moment," said Jeffries. "In fact I should think that's the last we'll see of Morgan."

Everson looked at Jeffries in disbelief and shook his head.

They set off up High Street together, Everson slightly ahead as the way wasn't quite wide enough for two-abreast.

"I didn't see you at church parade this morning, Gilbert," said Everson. "All Hallows' Eve, you know."

"I don't require a third party to intercede with my god on my behalf, Everson."

"Ah, Presbyterian, eh? Say no more."

Jeffries just smiled.

Everson was about to say something when a familiar screech made him look up.

"Whizz-Bang!"

Everson shoved Jeffries down Garland Avenue, a foul-smelling latrine sap, to take cover against the wall. A second later there was an almighty explosion. They felt the concussion wave through their backs as they were showered with soil and mud.

There was a brief silence before the cries and wails began. Everson got up and brushed the dirt off his uniform. Smoke and dust rose over what was left of the sandbag parapet above his head. His hands were shaking. He took a deep breath, then he stepped round the corner into the chaos.

A soldier, blood streaming down his face, ran blindly past, screaming, almost knocking him over. Everson walked up the communications trench towards the sound of pitiful squeals and gruff shouts.

"Gilbert, there's men hurt down here," he called back. Jeffries sauntered out to join him. They rounded the corner of the traverse to a scene of devastation. The shell had burst in the trench, taking out a dugout, burying the men below. Severed limbs lay on the ground and slick red offal steamed in the mud.

Everson saw a soldier walking around unsteadily. He grabbed the fellow by the shoulder. "How many?" The man wheeled round and stared through him, eyes wild and rolling like a cow that had smelt the abattoir. Everson could see no blood, no injuries, but the vacant expression in the eyes told a different story if you cared enough to look. "How many? How many in the dugout?"

"Nine, ten. I only stepped out for a fag. Harris's talk was getting on me wick. I only stepped out for a fag," his gaze focused on Everson as if remembering where he was. "You got to help 'em, sir. You got to get 'em out."

"And we will do. Now get some entrenching tools and we'll need wood for levers and bracing. You there," he said, his eyes alighting on another Tommy. "Get back to the support trenches and muster up a rescue party. We won't have much time."

"Why bother?" said Jeffries. "They'll be dead before they can dig them out. Might as we'll just wait for the trench repair party. This whole section will have to be repaired overnight anyway. It'll be needed tomorrow."

"Damn it, Gilbert. There's still hope we'll find some alive."

"Sir!" Several men digging with their entrenching spades called him over. A hand protruded from the mud. Everson brushed the dirt from it and clasped it gently by the wrist. There was a pulse; weak and thready.

"He's alive. Quickly, but carefully."

The men nodded and resumed their task, excavating the body. He wished he could join them but that wasn't his role. They looked to him for leadership. It was his job to stand back, take in the chaos before him and shape it into order.

"Everson!" called Jeffries. He was holding up a wounded, insensate man whose face was covered with blood; a ragged wound in his side. "He can't wait for stretcher bearers. I'm going get him to the Regimental Aid Post. Can you carry on here?"

Everson nodded curtly and watched as Jeffries, staggering slightly under the weight of the semi-conscious soldier, started off down the trench.

JEFFRIES HALF WALKED, half dragged the man down the communications trench. The Tommy's hold on consciousness was tenuous. They came to a T-junction in the communications trench. A left turn would take them to the Regimental Aid post, where the Medical Officer could see to his charge and take him off his hands.

"Come on, not far now," Jeffries said. The strain was beginning to tell and his charge wasn't helping. He stumbled on past the junction and took the next right. This wasn't the sort of work he was used to, or usually deigned to do but needs must. His own dugout lay a few yards ahead.

The Tommy tried to mutter something, but with shattered teeth and bloodied lips, it was hard to make out. Not that anything he had to say would have mattered.

With a last effort, Jeffries reached his dugout and clumsily pushed aside the gas curtain. He glanced quickly up and down the trench and, seeing no-one, dragged the soldier inside.

Jeffries dropped the soldier to the floor, before striking a match to light a hurricane lantern hung from a joist. The dugout wasn't as well appointed as Company HQ but this one at least had a bed with a mattress of sorts. Over in one corner was a small writing desk and chair. The back wall had been panelled with the sides of tea-chests by a previous occupant. Several thick wooden joists ran the width of the dugout supporting a corrugated tin roof.

The Tommy on the floor groaned.

Jeffries looked down at the man and noticed, for the first time, the battalion brassard on his upper arm. A runner. "Seeston?"

A groan.

A grin opened on Jeffries' face like a knife wound.

"Well, well. This is fortuitous."

Jeffries went over to the back wall and, with a little difficulty, removed a section of tea-chest panelling exposing a sackcloth curtain behind. He lifted the curtain with all the solemnity of a priest unveiling a tabernacle, revealing a niche containing several objects; an ornamental dagger, several black candles, an incense burner, a small leather-bound volume and a carved totem of black stone.

He stepped over Seeston, cleared papers and ink pots from the writing desk before dumping them on the bed. Next he took out the dagger, the candles and a bag of salt from the niche and set them down on the table.

Seeston watched with mounting incomprehension.

Around the table and the prone soldier, Jeffries drew a circle on the floor of his dugout with salt. Seeston roused himself and began to cry, tears running down his cheeks and mixing with dirt and crusted blood. "Whatever you're thinking of doing, sir, please don't."

"Shh, don't worry. Your life's ebbing away anyway, but thanks to your sacrifice, mine is guaranteed to last much longer." Jeffries picked up the ornamental dagger and began intoning the words he knew by heart.

"By Raziel and Enrahagh, Hear me O Croatoan. Protect your servant. Take this life in his stead."

He stood over Seeston and cupped his chin, extending and exposing his neck. "I told you I never forget," he whispered. Then, with a single, practised movement, he drew the blade across the man's throat.

CHAPTER TWO
"All the Wonders of No Man's Land…"

ONCE THE NCOs turned up at the bombsite Everson found himself being thanked politely and gently sent on his way, dismissed like a hapless schoolboy. Feeling frustrated and vaguely empty he wandered along High Street towards the support trenches.

Back at his dugout, Everson found his platoon sergeant making a cup of tea. Hobson was a career soldier in his forties though his attachment to his waxed moustache made him look older than he was. His once imposing barrel chest had given way to an expanding waistline that he nevertheless insisted was "all muscle". Hobson was a godsend; an Old Contemptible and veteran of the Boer War, a man of infinite common sense. He had been assigned to Everson from the beginning and had stopped him making a fool of himself on more than one occasion.

"Well, sir?" said Hobson as he took a tin mug off a nail and poured another brew.

"Tomorrow. 7.20. Tell the men. They're getting restless."

"They've known summat were going on, sir. They're up for it. It's just the waiting that gets 'em."

"Yes, that does for us all. We've to send out a patrol, too, Sergeant. Dirty work to be done. Orders to cut wire for tomorrow's assault and spy out the German positions, check they've got no new surprises for us. Know of any likely volunteers for a hazardous mission like that?"

"For a Black Hand Gang, sir? Leave it to me. 1 Section are up tonight. Best lot I know. Some handy men there."

"Hmm." Everson knew it. Several of them had worked in his father's brewery—'Everson's Ales: They're Everson Good!' He remembered them all signing up together at the outbreak of war, eager for adventure; after all it would be over by Christmas, where was the harm? The factories and mills seemed to empty that week as workers joined the raucous, ebullient crowds of men in flat caps and straw boaters jostling outside the town hall recruitment office. Then there were the months of drilling and training in the camp on the moors above the town. Months more before they got their uniforms and guns. But the pride they felt as the 13th Battalion of the Pennine Fusiliers, the 'Broughtonthwaite Mates,' paraded in full kit through the town, down the cobbled streets lined with family, relatives and friends, to cheers and tears under hastily appropriated Wakes Week bunting and Union flags was an almost tangible thing. Your heart swelled, your blood sang and you grinned with so much pride your cheeks ached. There was even a brass band to see them off at the railway station for the start of their Grand Adventure.

Not so grand as it turned out.

They'd come out to France in March 1916, spent some time at the training camps before being shunted up the line in Hom Forties for the Big Push. Since then they'd been up to their necks in mud and blood and bullshit, their sense of pride and patriotism long since tarnished by cynicism.

Hobson handed Everson a steaming mug of tea.

"Ah, just the job," said Everson wearily. "Whisky, Sergeant?" he added, pulling the small bottle from his tunic.

"Don't mind if I do, sir," said Hobson, offering his mug. "But just the one."

Everson poured a shot into Hobson's tea and one into his own. Hobson savoured the aroma and knocked the milkless tea back in one before slapping the enamel mug down on the table with a dull metallic clunk.

"Best go tell the men, then, sir," he said, before putting on his steel hat and venturing out into the night.

THE MEN OF 1 Section, No 2 Platoon, were passing the night as best they could in their dugout. It was a crude affair, with little to recommend it but six wooden frame and chicken wire bunks and several upturned tea-chests for tables.

Private Thomas 'Only' Atkins sat on his bunk reading a letter by the light of a candle stub. It was one he'd read a dozen times before. It was from Flora Mullins. The letter was full of the usual daily doings of a small terraced street but one sentence stuck out. One sentence that sent the bottom of his stomach plunging sickeningly.

"There is still no news of William. Every day your mam reads the casualty lists hoping not to see his name, then despairing when she doesn't. The not knowing is killing her, Tom..."

He read the words again and again, as if by doing so he'd wear them out, erase them somehow. Was it wrong to hope William didn't turn up?

He and his older brother had signed up together, even though, technically, Thomas was too young by eleven months, having only just turned seventeen.

"Go around the block until you've had another birthday, sonny," the recruiting sergeant had told him with a wink. So he did. But in those twelve minutes the queue had grown and it was another three hours before he was back before the sergeant. Those hours had made the difference, not in years, but between serving in the 12th Battalion with his brother and the 13th.

His mother hadn't half torn a strip off William later that day when she found out he signed up. He'd never seen her so furious until ten minutes later when Thomas had told her he'd joined up, too. She was all for marching him down to the recruiting office and telling that sergeant there and then that her son was too young and what did he mean by signing up helpless little kiddies? Thomas had been mortified and begged and pleaded before appealing to his dad. Half an hour later, when she found out they weren't even in the same battalion and wouldn't be serving together so William couldn't keep an eye on him, it all blew up again.

And now William was missing. He'd been missing since the Big Push. Atkins had traipsed round all the field hospitals and questioned old mates, but there was no news and it was tearing him apart.

He watched 'Mercy' Evans stowing the contents of his latest 'trip to the canteen' into a haversack hanging from the ceiling, out of reach of the ever-present rats. Scrounging he called it, although looting would be the official charge. However, in a war where supplies were short, the Platoon Commander turned a blind eye, so long as he occasionally plied his skills on behalf of his comrades.

'Porgy' Hopkiss was shuffling though his pack of photographs, each a portrait. He had twenty-seven of them so far, every one presented by a sweetheart he'd met or so he claimed, although at least one was of Mary Pickford and several were of dubious taste and also in the possession of more than one man in the battalion. It was his avowed intent to collect enough to turn them into a deck of cards after the war.

'Gutsy' Blood, a butcher by trade before he took the shilling, was sharpening and polishing his best meat cleaver, because, quite frankly, it was his pride and joy and he didn't trust his wife or brother-in-law to look after it proper back home, so he'd brought it to France with him, When he charged towards the German lines brandishing it, it scared the crap out of Jerry, not to mention half of his own platoon.

'Lucky' Livesey had his trousers off and turned inside out across his bony white knees as he ran a lighted candle stub along the seams. "Nothing more satisfying than Chatting," he said, grinning gleefully at the small cracks as the ubiquitous lice popped under the heat.

"Maybe, but you'll still be hitchy-coo tomorrow, Lucky. Can't never get rid of the bloody things," said 'Half Pint' Nicholls, scratching his ribs fiercely. Half Pint was the greatest grouser in the regiment. You want to hear it true and unvarnished, then he was willing to give his opinion forth to all and sundry and, among a certain kind of man, he found a willing audience.

Lance Corporal Ketch, 1 Section's second in charge, entered, bringing in the post. He was a small man with a pock-marked face; just a shade too tall for the Bantams, worse luck, so they were stuck with him. His gimlet eyes glowered with resentment as he began handing out the brown paper and string packages and ivory envelopes. It seemed to be against his nature for anyone to have any measure of happiness.

Atkins leaned forwards eagerly, poised for his name. His heart began to pound in his chest, waiting for news, but dreading it at the same time.

"Porgy one for you, Package for Mercy. Half Pint. Gazette, *two*! Pot Shot, Lucky..."

The men snatched them up eagerly and were momentarily lost in their own private worlds as they proceeded to open them.

"Gazette and Pot Shot are on sentry duty, " said Gutsy, taking theirs.

"And lastly Juh Juh-Ginger," sneered Ketch, holding out a package towards a nervy, curly-haired blonde lad who was feeding a rat he'd tamed, taken for a pet and named Haig.

'Ginger' Mottram had made it through the entire summer without a scratch, but he was a wreck. Shell-shock, they called it. Malingering, Ketch said, but then he would. Ketch deliberately waved the package just out of his reach, taunting him. Ginger went bright red. The lad blushed so often they joked that one day his hair would turn red, hence his nickname.

"Guh-guh-give it here!" stammered Ginger.

"Leave it out, Ketch," warned Mercy. Ketch thrust the package into the lad's hand, his fun spoiled.

"Corp?" said Atkins leaning forward hopefully.

"Atkins," said Ketch gleefully. "Expecting something were you?"

"Yes."

Ketch made a show of patting himself down. "No, Sorry. Nothing."

"Ketch!" snapped Mercy, looking up from his own letter. "Only's brother is missing f'fuck's sake. He was hoping for news."

"Fuck you, Evans," muttered Ketch as he retired to his bunk.

Sergeant Hobson's ample frame filled the dugout door. "It's getting late, ladies. Time to get your beauty sleep. Waiting's over. Word has come down. We'll be up early and going over the top first wave tomorrow. Check your weapons. Where's Lance Sergeant Jessop?"

"NCO of the watch, Sarn't," said Mercy.

"Sarn't?"

"Yes, Hopkiss?"

"It's just that there's not much of a bombardment from our lot," he said jerking his chin in the direction of the Front. It was true. The night's artillery fire was sporadic at best.

"Don't you worry your pretty little head about it, Hopkiss. You just turn up in your Sunday Best for tomorrow's little promenade and we'll go for a nice stroll in No Man's Land. I'm sure wiser heads than yours have got it sorted," he said, turning to go.

"That's what we're worried about, Sarn't," said Mercy.

Hobson's eyes narrowed as he strode across the dugout.

"You think too much, Evans, do you hear me?" he said sternly, rapping Mercy sharply on the head. "And you do it out loud. If that ain't a bad habit I don't know what is. Don't let me hear you do it again!"

Evans winced and rubbed his scalp.

"Yes, Sarn't. Sorry, Sarn't."

"I'm watching you laddie," said Hobson as he left. "Ketch, I need a Black Hand Gang for a bit of business tonight. I want three volunteers to meet me in F8 at two Ack Emma. See to it."

"Right," said Ketch, gleefully. "Hopkiss and Blood? You've just volunteered."

Ketch took his time, letting his eyes roam over the rest of the men, making sure to meet each of their eyes as if daring them to challenge him. His gaze settled on Atkins. Atkins, suddenly aware of the silence, glanced up. "Something better to do Atkins? Not now you haven't."

ATKINS WAS WOKEN by Gutsy shaking him. The last vestiges of warmth and wellbeing slipped away as realisation of where he was rushed in.

"Only? Come on lad, it's time. Let's get this over and done with."

Wearing leather jerkins, carrying their bayonets in sheaths, their faces blackened with burnt cork, the Black Hand Gang, Atkins, Gutsy and Porgy, made their way past scurrying rats up to the fire bay, where Hobson and Ketch were waiting for them.

There was a faint *fwoosh* as an enemy flare went up. It burnt a stark white, casting deep shadows on the wall of the trench that wobbled and tilted as the flare drifted down, until at last they ate up the last of the light and filled the trench again.

'Gazette' Otterthwaite and 'Pot Shot' Jellicoe were on sentry duty. Even in the dim light it was hard to miss Pot Shot. He was a large man, a shade over six foot, tallest man in the Battalion; the only man who had to crouch when stood on the firestep lest his head present a tempting target for German snipers.

Gazette was up on the firestep on sentry duty, Pot Shot sat on the step beside him, slumped against the side of the bay and snoring gently, his rifle clasped to his chest like a loved one. Gazette glanced down at them and kicked Pot Shot awake.

"All right, lads?" he yawned.

That helped ease the queasy feeling in Atkins' stomach. Gazette was the best sharp shooter in the platoon. If anyone was going to have your back on a Black Hand job you'd want it to be him.

There was a pile of equipment on the firestep by his feet.

"Right," said Hobson, "take these." He handed out pistols; Webley revolvers, usually reserved for officers but more practical in situations, such as this, that called for stealth. They each had their own bayonet and there were two sets of long-armed wirecutters. Atkins and Porgy got those. Hobson also gave them each a grey military issue blanket that he instructed them to wear across their backs in the manner of a cloak.

"It'll help disguise your outline against German flares. If a flare goes up, don't move. You'll want to throw yourself on the ground but don't, they'll spot the movement and you're a goner. If you freeze you could be tree stump, a shadow or a body on the wire," he told them. "We're goin' out to cut the German wire in preparation for tomorrow. So we make sure we do the job properly or it'll be us and our mates paying the price if we don't. We also want to take a shufti and make sure Fritz isn't planning any nasty surprises. Don't worry, I'll have you all back in time for the big show."

"Thanks, Sar'nt. You're a real pal," said Gutsy.

"Time for a fag, Sar'nt?" asked Hopkiss, trying to delay the inevitable.

"No. Follow me. Stick to me like glue. No one talks but me. Make sure you stay within an arm's length of the next fellow. If you get lost make your way back here. And make sure you dozy ha'porths don't forget the password: Hampstead."

Atkins checked his bayonet in its sheath. He checked the chambers of the Webley revolver. They were full. The pistol had a loop fastened to the handle, which he slipped round his wrist.

There being no sally port available, Hobson put a ladder up against the revetment and was about to step on the bottom rung when another flare went up. He stopped, waited for the flare to die out, before rolling over the sandbag parapet with practised ease. His arm appeared back over the bags signalling the next man up. Porgy was already on the ladder and climbing. Gutsy stepped on below him and began his climb. It was Atkins' turn next. As he stepped on the bottom rung, he felt a hand pat his thigh.

"Good luck, mate," said Gazette. Aktins smiled weakly. He could feel his heart lifting him fractionally from the ladder with every beat as he lay against the rungs. He hadn't felt a funk like this since that last night with Flora.

"Cheers. I'll be back for breakfast."

Another flare.

Above him, Gutsy froze, waiting for the light to die. Atkins looked up. All he could see was Gutsy's big khaki-covered arse eclipsing everything. Blood let one rip and looked down between his legs, grinning.

"Fuck's sakes, Gutsy!" hissed Gazette. "At least with the yellow cross we get a warning. Where's me bloody gas helmet?"

A hiss rasped from over the parapet. "Get a move on, you two!"

Puffing, Gutsy rolled over the sandbags with as much grace as a carcass in his old butcher's shop.

Atkins reached the top of the ladder. The nightscape before him never failed to chill him to the core. No Man's Land. It was a contradiction in terms. You were never alone in No Man's Land. During the day it was quiet, with generally nothing but the odd buzz of a sniper's bullet cutting low over the ground or the crump of a Minniewerfer to disturb it. At night, though, it became a hive of activity; parties out repairing wire, laying new wire, digging saps, running reconnaissance, conducting trench raids. Both sides knew it. It was the most dangerous of times to be out and never dark for long, as flares burst in the air, momentarily illuminating bleak Futurist landscapes that left hellish after-images in the mind's eye.

He saw Hobson and Porgy about four or five yards ahead, crawling along on their bellies. Gutsy was to his left. Atkins crawled forward using his elbows and knees. The mud was cold and slimy and within a minute his entire front, from chin to toes, was soaked. He and Gutsy made their way to where Sergeant Hobson and Porgy were waiting. About twenty yards ahead, they could make out the vague unearthly shapes of their own wire entanglements. Sergeant Hobson indicated a piece of soiled, white tape in the mud that led them to the gap in their own wire.

Now they truly were in No Man's Land.

They crawled on, their progress achingly slow. Every time a flare bloomed in the sky, they would press themselves into the mud. It took them nearly an hour to crawl through the blasted landscape—peppered as it was with shell holes—up the gently inclining slope towards Harcourt Wood. About them Atkins could hear the foraging corpse rats feasting on the bodies of the fallen. They reached the German wire, some thirty yards short of a low stone wall that bordered the wood. There was a muffled shout, some distance over to the left and a brief spatter of machine gun fire, then nothing.

More waiting.

Hobson gestured to the left and rolled with a barely perceptible splash into a shallow shell hole just short of the wire. The others followed. Atkins slithered over the shallow lip to join them and found himself in a pool of water. Hobson beckoned them closer with a finger. They gathered their heads together while Hobson spoke in a low, slow voice.

"Wirecutters get ahead. Blood and I will cover you. If it all goes off, get back here sharpish. Got it? Just don't take all night about it."

Atkins nodded. As they crawled out of the shell hole toward the wire, Hobson and Gutsy took up their positions on the lip of the crater, pistols cocked and ready.

Atkins looked at Porgy as they reached the entanglement. Porgy crawled forward with his cutters, slipped the blades around the wire and snipped. There was a sharp *tink* and a dull tinny twang recoiled along the wire. Atkins froze until long after the sound died away, expecting a burst of machine gun fire to cut them down at any moment. But nothing happened. Porgy cut again.

Atkins gripped the wire between his own cutter blades and snipped, and snipped again. It took nearly an hour to cut though the entanglement, working his way along on his back under the thicket of Jerry wire until his arms ached and his muscles burned, but eventually it was done. A section of wire five or six yards across had been freed from its mooring.

They made their way back to the shell hole.

"All present and correct?" whispered Hobson. "Good. Let's be off home shall we?"

As they began the slow crawl back towards their own lines, something gave way under Atkins' palm and his left arm sank up to his elbow in the thick mud. A bubble formed on the surface and popped, releasing a cloying, sickly stench. His hand had gone through a corpse's gas-distended stomach. Disturbed, several corpulent rats squeaked indignantly and darted off. He heaved, retching up several lumps of army stew and pulled his hand out of the mud. In an attempt to put some distance, *any* distance, between him and the corpse, he planted a knee down only to feel a crack of bones somewhere just below the surface of the slime. A red flare went up bathing everything in a hellish glow. Atkins looked down with horror to see the decomposing face of a French soldier lit by the lurid light, making shadows dance in the empty sockets of its eyes.

A burst of machine gun fire zipped over their heads. Hobson quickly indicated to a large Minnie crater with a flick of his hand. They headed for it, rolling down into the relative shelter of its shadow.

Unable to stop himself, Atkins slipped helplessly down the slick wet sides into the slurry-filled basin at the bottom, before coming up against wet muddy cloth. Fearing another corpse, he looked about wildly and met the gaze of a German soldier staring back with the same intensity of fear and surprise. They'd stumbled on a German patrol sheltering in the same shell-hole.

Atkins knew he had seconds to act. He clamped a muddy hand over the German's mouth. The Hun clawed desperately at his wrist. Atkins adjusted his position so he was astride the man's chest and was able to use his knee to pin the man's upper arm to the ground, leaving a hand free to unsheath his bayonet. The German tried to bite Atkins' hand, desperate to stop him. Out the corner of his eyes Atkins made out the other members of his Black Hand Gang engaged in similar private struggles. It was desperate fighting, no rules. This was war at its most raw, most visceral, most base. The only sound was the slap of mud or splash of water as boots sought for purchase on soft tissue; grunts of exertion as the struggle turned first one way then the next, each opponent knowing it was killed or be killed.

Gritted teeth. Little explosions of breath, spittle flecks bubbling up at the corners of the mouth, face red with effort, neck taut with strain as Atkins leant forward trying to use his bodyweight to press his bayonet home. The Hun kicked, trying to dislodge him. The point of his bayonet against the Hun's ribs. His eyes creasing, pleading, hands slick with mud losing their grip, the bayonet pushing into the thick serge of his uniform but not puncturing. It was all now dependent on who could last out the longest, but Atkins had gravity on his side.

The blade sank suddenly, plunging Atkins' face unexpectedly towards his enemy's, whose eyes widened in shock. He tried to focus on Atkins as his hand clawed weakly at his face. Atkins turned away and raised himself to avoid the filthy, clammy hand. Then, hardly able to see for the stinging tears welling up in his eyes he muttered, "sorry," and used his bodyweight to push the bayonet further in. Blood bubbled and frothed at the corners of the Hun's mouth. Atkins could feel the warm exhalation of breath on his face waning. The man's eyes lost focus and beneath him Atkins felt his chest fall for the last time. He collapsed with effort and relief onto the body feeling his heart beating fit to burst, a pulse suddenly pounding painfully at the base of his skull behind his right ear. He rolled over onto his back, his chest heaving with sobs he tried to stifle. To his left he saw Porgy sitting with his head in his hands. Hobson was wiping his bayonet on a German's tunic. Three Huns lay about the shell hole in unnatural positions. A fourth lay face down in the water. Gutsy grabbed Atkins and pulled him into a sitting position, holding his head between his knees as he dry-retched.

"Get it up, son, you'll feel better," Gutsy whispered. Atkins tried to make himself heave. It didn't take much before he vomited, spitting out the stringy mucus and half-digested bits that remained in his mouth.

Gutsy pulled his bayonet from the dead Hun and handed it back to him. "You did well."

They made their way back to their line but when they came to their wire, they couldn't find the gap. Following Hobson, they inched their way along the wire, careful not to touch any of the makeshift alarms of tin cans containing pebbles that hung from them before finding one. They edged through and towards their lines until they could see the sandbag parapets of their own trenches. From the dark ahead of them came an aggressive hiss.

"Password."

"Hampstead," Hobson hissed back and began crawling forwards, beckoning the others to follow. There was sudden rapid fire, and the whole world went to hell. Porgy screamed. A flare went up from the trench. Hobson shouted: "You're shooting your own bloody men, hold your fire!" There were far away shouts from the German line, a German flare and then the whine of bullets splashing into the mud around them.

Shot at from behind, shot at from in front, Atkins scrambled for the sandbags and the trench. Hands reached up, grabbed him and pulled him over the parapet to safety. Hobson was already over and laying into the Jock sentry with a torrent of sergeantly abuse. Gutsy was sat on the firestep checking himself all over for wounds but there was no sign of Porgy. Atkins stood on the firestep and, against all his better instincts, he peered over the top. He saw something that could be Porgy some five or six yards away. Sporadic shots from the German line continued to bury themselves into the mud around him.

"Only! Only, I'm hit," whimpered Porgy.

Before he knew what he was doing, Atkins was scrambling over the parapet and wriggling forward on his elbows.

"Come back you bloody fool!"

Atkins slithered on, the odd bullet whining over his head. He reached Porgy who was lying on his side groaning. He gripped Porgy's hand and pulled, trying to drag him through the mud, but he was too heavy. There only one thing for it. As quickly as he could, Atkins picked him up under the armpits and hauled him backwards, step by muddy step, towards the trench amid the whine and splatter of German bullets. Reaching the sandbags, he tipped the barely conscious Porgy over the parapet and into the arms of his waiting mates, before leaping into the trench after him. Trembling, he sat down heavily on the firestep and watched as Gutsy looked Porgy over.

"Hell's bells, Porgy you're a lucky one."

Atkins could see a bloody groove on Porgy's left temple where a bullet had grazed him. "Head wound."

"Good job it didn't hit anything important, eh?" croaked Porgy.

"Barely a scratch, y'daft beggar. You'll live."

Porgy looked up as that sank in and seemed to rally, turning on the sentry loitering off to his side. "All the way to the Hun wire, an ambush by Jerry, and I get shot by my own bloody side!" he growled, attempting to get up, but Gutsy held him down.

"Och, sorry mate how wis ah tae know? This isnae your section o' the line. You could a been Kaiser Bill hisself fer all I knew!"

Atkins looked up as a grubby mud-slathered Hobson stood over him. "That," he spat, "was a bloody stupid thing to do."

"Couldn't leave him, Sar'nt."

"Quite, right lad," said Hobson, gently patting him on the shoulder.

As if that were all the permission he needed, Atkins felt great sobs well up within him and his shoulders started to shake.

"You'll be all right son. You did well tonight. Take Porgy to have his scratch seen to. Don't want him missing out on the fun later, do we? Then go and get yourself cleaned up and get some kip. Big day tomorrow."

"Sar'nt."

Atkins and Gutsy made their way along the fire trench, carrying a dazed and bloody Porgy between them, his head now roughly bandaged with a field dressing. They turned down a communications trench and weaved their way to the Regimental Aid Post. The MO wasn't very happy about being woken up, but soon cleaned and stitched the wound before packing them off.

Atkins went back to the water butts in the support trench to clean himself up.

Ketch caught up with him.

"I heard what you did, Atkins," he said.

"Any one of us would have done the same."

"But they didn't did they? It was you, weren't it? Bit of a glory hound are we? Your mates might think you're the bee's knees right now, but I know different. You're bad news, Atkins. I'm watching you."

Atkins was too weary to argue. He crept back into the dugout, crawled under his ration blanket and dozed fitfully as the rats scurried across the floor beneath him.

INTERLUDE ONE
**Letter from Private Thomas Atkins
to Flora Mullins**

31ˢᵗ October 1916

My Dearest Flora,

As I write to you tonight I have no further news of William. Last week, out of the trenches, I tramped around the field hospitals again. I showed his picture about and, though I feared what I might find, I visited the army cemeteries hereabout. I even buttonholed a relief column to ask if they'd seen him. I can bring you no peace, I'm afraid. But do not despair. He may still turn up. It might be that he is only lost and taken up with another regiment, or else been wounded and travelling between hospitals. It is too soon to give up. We must both hope that he will come home.

Tomorrow we've a mind to go and bother the Kaiser for some sport. We're taking a stroll up to the woods to see what mischief we can make! My only fear is that I shall not see you again, but do not fret for I am determined that I shall. Tell my mam I'm well and will see her soon. I know she worries so. Tell her I got the socks she sent. If she can send some lice powder I would be very grateful.

Ever yours,
Thomas

CHAPTER THREE
"This World's Verge..."

HE WAS SAFE. A million miles from the front line. He was home. Home on leave. In his uniform he waited anxiously outside the factory gates for her shift to end, afraid he'd miss her as the workers swept out. He saw her first, picked her out amongst the crowd of women surging towards the street, arms linked with her workmates, walking in step, laughing. He stood across the street, waving eagerly. "Flora! Flora!" She looked up and saw him. And smiled...

"Wakey, wakey, ladies!"

Atkins jerked awake and sat up in his bunk, cursing as he caught his hair in the wire of Ginger's bunk above him. Already the dream was slipping away. Sergeant Hobson, cleaned up and dressed for battle, his moustache as prim and proper as ever, stood in the dugout's doorway, his appearance sending the rats scurrying for cover.

"Oh God, what time is it?" groaned Mercy.

"Time you were in Jerry's face before I get into yours, Evans," hollered Hobson.

"It's not even dawn, Sarn't!" said Pot Shot. "What about me beauty sleep?"

"No amount of sleep is going to make you ugly bunch any better looking, and that's just the way I like it. I want Fritz to feel his balls shrivel when he sees you lot coming. Now get up and get yourselves sorted. Stand To in fifteen minutes."

Bleary eyed, Atkins rolled out of his bunk, his mouth dry and his empty stomach churning as he jostled over cold water and tarnished shaving mirrors, braces hanging limply from his waist.

They all clustered about Porgy with his new bandage, demanding all the details of the night's events, which Gutsy duly gave them, building up to Only's heroic dash and rescue.

"It was nothing," said Atkins awkwardly. "Besides, I couldn't let him stay out there. He promised me he'd introduce me to Marie down at the estaminet in Sans German." Never ones to learn the local language if they could get away with mangling it, it was one of the Tommies' jokes. St. Germaine was the nearest town to Harcourt Wood, well behind the British lines and so long as it remained behind British lines it would bloody well remain 'Sans German'—without Germans, too.

"Going to have quite a scar, the doc says," beamed Porgy. "The old 'war-wound,' it'll have the girls flocking to me, it will."

"Luh-looks like a Buh-blighty wound to me," said Ginger quietly. "Why you still 'ere?"

"What, and desert me mates, today of all days? Bloody hell, Ginger, what's got into you?" said Porgy.

Atkins felt the knot in his stomach tighten. His teeth were furred up and his mouth tasted rank after vomiting last night. He pulled his braces up onto his shoulders, slipped into his tunic and fastened it before shrugging on his webbing. It was an attack so it was Battle Order equipment; rifle, helmet, backpack with iron rations, water flask, bayonet and 150 rounds small arms ammunition. Then they'd have to pick up spare sand bags, entrenching tools, grenades, spare grenades, flares and wire cutters, smoke candles and picks from the QM.

Atkins joined the queue with his dixie tin for his bit of bacon and fat. His mouth was so dry he could barely swallow. The tea was lukewarm and made with petrol-contaminated water, from using petrol cans as water carriers. It made him gag.

Then Lieutenant Everson and the Quarterbloke made their way down the fire trench, issuing rum from a stone SRD jar. Atkins gratefully accepted the slug of liquor that Everson measured out into his greasy dixie tin and tipped the contents down his throat. He felt the rum burn all the way down.

Afterwards Gutsy kissed his little rabbit's foot on its leather thong and tucked it into his shirt. Porgy shuffled his pack of pictures, hoping that the one he drew as his Queen of Hearts for the day was one he actually fancied. Gazette listened for the crump of an artillery shell and tried to count to twenty before the next one landed. Ginger quietly confessed his sins to the pet rat hidden in his tunic. Atkins took out of his tunic pocket a much-read letter, the last letter he'd received from Flora, and eased it, like a sacred relic, from its envelope. He raised the letter to his lips and kissed it softly, almost reverently, then parted the folded corners, held the paper to his nose and gently inhaled as if smelling a delicate flower; if he could still smell her scent on it, even here amid the malodorous mud of the trenches, then he was convinced that he would survive the day. Finally, everybody touched or kissed Lucky's steel helmet with the two Jerry bullet holes in it.

They all had their little rituals.

*   *   *

JEFFRIES WAS GOING through his own ritual, quite literally. It had served him well in the past and garnered him a reputation as a fearless soldier on the battlefield, taking life-threatening risks as if he had no care for his own life, when in fact the opposite was very much the case.

He knelt in his dugout, within his salted circle, incense burning on the table next to him. He breathed deeply as, slowly, his mind centred on the Great Working at hand. Today, on the feast of Samhain, he would prove them all wrong. He had no need of fear. He had Seeston. Last night's ritual of protection should shield him from harm. And from this calm, centred place he offered up a prayer.

"I bless Enrahagh, fallen from the light, I bless Croatoan dwelling in the night, I bless the sword of Raziel that all the heathen dread. I bless the dirt beneath my feet, the earth on which they'll tread."

The clatter of rifles and shouts outside shattered the serenity of the moment as men scurried about the narrow culverts and alleys in readiness for the attack. Beyond the immediate shrill shouts, he heard the persistent dull bass thud of artillery shells. Dirt sifted down from the ceiling. He got up, put on his tunic and Sam Browne belt then searched for his hair brush and applied it in slow, considered strokes though his Brilliantined hair. Picking up his steel helmet, he placed it on his head and adjusted it just so before a shard of mirror. He admired his reflection for a moment and, irritated, turned to brush some slight dirt from his shoulder pips.

There were times when he really missed having a batman, but he needed privacy and they only got in the way. It had been a shame about Cooper. Good at laundry but a little too inquisitive for his own good. He'd proved useful in the end though, just like Seeston. Luckily the disposal of bodies at the front was less problematic than it had been back in England.

As he left, he turned and took one last look round his dugout for old times' sake.

This was it. All his preparation had brought him here, to this place, to this hour. After today nothing would be the same again.

OLIVER HEPTON CHOSE his position and had set up his tripod in the cover trench by a loophole, the better to catch the costly advance of the Pennines as they went over the top. He began to crank the handle of his camera. He panned round the trench slowly, not an easy task when trying to maintain a steady camera speed.

Don't want to make the people at home feel motion sick.

He'd been filming for three days in the reserve lines, getting shots of soldiers coming up the line, waving their steel helmets, full of fun and bravado, posing for family back home. Plucky British Tommies waiting to give the Hun hell. But today was different. The men didn't care about the camera. They were tense, too preoccupied to give it anything more than a cursory glance and a weak smile. Hepton didn't mind. It was all good stuff and he began composing the accompanying caption cards in his head.

ATKINS STOOD IN the fire bay as dawn grazed the sky; Ginger and Porgy closest to him, Gutsy, Pot Shot, Mercy and Lieutenant Everson to their left, Lucky, Half Pint, Gazette, Ketch and Jessop to their right. C Company's other three platoons on either side of them. Behind them in the communication and cover trenches, A and B companies readied themselves for the second wave of the attack. In front of him on the firestep the scaling ladder stood up against the brushwood revetment and sandbagged parapet. Atkins stared at it with deep resentment. How could something so mundane hold such sway over his life? He hated it. Every rung left him more exposed, lessened his chances. It might as well have been a ladder to the gallows.

From along the trench Corporal Ketch glowered at them. Atkins knew he wanted them to funk it and he wasn't going to give him the satisfaction, but to Atkins' left Ginger was fidgeting uneasily, like a child on the verge of tears.

"I heard they got summat new lined up for Fritz today; them watchercallems, Boojums they used up Flers," said Pot Shot.

"What, here? Oh, what I wouldn't give to see one of them," said Gutsy.

"Boojums?" said Ginger.

"Like prehistoric monsters they is," said Porgy. "They knock down trees and eat houses. Bullets and bombs just bounce off 'em, I've heard,"

"Jerry up!" said Half Pint, pointing up into the sky. Glad of the diversion, Atkins looked up with the rest into the calm autumn dawn. Above, he saw a great long train of tall white clouds stretching almost from horizon to horizon moving in a slow stately procession across the sky. There, beneath their great white bellies but high above the scattered smudges of black air burst, were two small dots flying toward the British lines.

"Albatrosses, I'll be bound," said Porgy, shielding his eyes.

"There!" called Lucky. Atkins turned. Three small black dots were making for them slowly, almost casually, flying out across the British lines to meet them. The Royal Flying Corps. Atkins willed them on as if wishing could give them speed enough to smash into the enemy like

44

jousting steeds of the air, dashing their foes from the sky and sending them plummeting to earth. Instead they drifted slowly toward each other, almost lackadaisically, then seemed to weave in and around each other, dancing like mayflies on a summer evening. Atkins watched the dumb show, spellbound. One of them left a dark soft streak across the sky as it began a slow balletic tumble towards the earth. Atkins held his breath.

"One of ours or one of theirs?" he asked nobody in particular as he craned his head.

"Dunno," said Jessop.

"Wait," said Mercy squinting his eyes. "It's one of theirs. I think."

Grasping for a sign, any sign, and fanning a small flame of hope for the day ahead, a ragged cheer went up along the line. They joined in.

Ketch growled and took a step towards them. "Quieten down. How can you listen out for the enemy, making a racket like that?"

"Well it's not like they're going to attack at the same time we are, is it?" said Mercy.

But the mood was successfully punctured and the cheer subsided. Satisfied, Ketch returned to his position with a smirk.

Indistinct barks came down the line.

"Fix bayonets!" bellowed Hobson.

Atkins slotted the handle of the seventeen inch blade onto the end of his rifle. He'd done it so often he could do it in his sleep.

Then they waited.

EVERSON LOOKED AT his wristwatch. The second hand swung its way inexorably round to zero hour. Ten minutes to go. He licked his lips to moisten them for the pea-whistle that waited in his hand. Everything that could be done had been done. He could feel the weight of the revolver in his hand but his world had shrunk to that small disc on his wrist, to that needle-fine finger rotating, as if winding up the thread of his life onto some celestial spool.

Once more he had to lead his men into battle. Except that this was never battle; no glorious charge, no smashing of shields or clash of swords. There was little honour or glory here; only death, despair, pain and guilt. You never saw the enemy. Death strode the field, no longer cutting men down with a scythe, but with a threshing machine, gathering in its harvest in commercial quantities. Death had been industrialised.

Everson had never wanted responsibility. When he joined up he'd just wanted to be one of the men, a small cog in a big machine, but when your father was twice mayor of Broughtonthwaite and owner of the largest brewery in town there were bigger wheels turning against yours. So he'd been given a commission. Men he'd known before the war, men whose families had been intertwined with his for generations, now depended on him for their lives and he didn't want the responsibility. But now that it was his he wasn't going to shirk it. He'd done his damnedest to keep them alive through the bloodshed of the preceding summer, and by God, he'd do the same today.

He ran a finger around the inside of his collar and unconsciously began chewing his lower lip.

THE ARTILLERY BOMBARDMENT began. It started in No-Man's Land and, every minute, crept forwards another hundred yards towards the German lines—a barrage designed to shield the advancing soldiers from enemy fire. They would then move behind the line of smoke and shells, with the huge armoured hulks of the ironclad landships crushing paths through the German wire. At least that was the theory.

The ground began to shake. A loud rumbling filled the air. Atkins felt himself flinch involuntarily, expecting a shell burst or trench mortar, but the sound went on and on, increasing in volume. Dirt started dancing off the sandbags on the parapet.

"What the hell is it?" said Porgy, looking round. Down in the trench it was difficult to tell where the sound was coming from.

Along with the deep bass roar came another noise now, a squeaking and whining, a repetitive metallic clank.

"Blood and sand!" said Atkins as, several bays down, a fearsome metal monster belching white smoke from its back rolled across the reinforced bridge over the trenches into No Man's Land.

It was an ironclad landship; armour-plated, its side-mounted sponsons seemingly bristling with guns. He'd never seen anything like it, not even in the adventure stories he read. On the side he could make out a painted identity number, I-5, and then underneath, painted in a scruffier hand, the legend, *HMLS Ivanhoe*.

"Boojums!" yelled Pot Shot ecstatically.

"Tanks! Read about 'em on leave," said Mercy. "The papers were full of 'em. Oh, we're going take that wood now. Fritz'll shit himself when he sees these coming at him, eh Ginger?"

Ginger managed to crack a weak smile but then, as soon as the huge great armoured rhomboid rolled over the firing trench, he began flinching and jerking.

Not now, thought Atkins. *Not now*.

If Ginger fled, the Battle Police would get him. If they didn't, Ketch certainly would. This close to a show, he wouldn't get the courtesy of a court martial before they marched him out to a stake and his mates had to shoot him.

"Ginger, quiet!" But before he could say anything more to calm the boy there came the dull repetitive clang of a cracked warning bell and the cry of: "Gas! Gas! Gas!"

The Germans, now aware that something was going off and having the prevailing wind in their favour, had opened their gas canisters and, heavier than air, the sluggish green cloud had begun to slue down the incline toward the British trenches.

At once, Atkins put his rifle down, took off his helmet and began to fumble at the canvas bag on his chest, undoing the buckle to get at the P. H. gas helmet inside. Well, the Quarterblokes called it a helmet. The men called it "the goggle-eyed bugger with the tit". What he pulled out was a cloth hood. He flapped it to open it out and pulled it on over his head, tucking its neck down into his shirt collar to form a rudimentary seal. He bit on the rubber clamp inside and took a couple of breaths, in through the nose and out through the tube in his mouth with its distinctive red rubber valve. Peering out through the greenish eye-pieces, he picked up his battle bowler and placed it back on his head before feeling around for his rifle.

He felt himself jostled from the side. He had to turn his whole body round to see. Ginger was sobbing and sniffling, unwilling or unable to open his respirator bag. Atkins hurriedly did it for him then thrust the gas hood over Ginger's head. If the gas got to him while he was snivelling like that it would be the worse for him. Immediately Ginger started to panic and claw at the hood, trying to rip it from his head.

Atkins heard a muffled shout. Ketch, looking for trouble, had caught sight of the commotion and was coming towards him.

Atkins elbowed Porgy.

"Give us a hand with Ginger!"

Porgy stood one side of Ginger and grabbed his arm, Atkins stood the other side. They held him tight so he couldn't struggle.

Atkins felt a tap on his shoulder; he swivelled round as much as he could.

"Whaff gun eer?"

"Sorry, Corporal. Can't tell what you're sayin'," said Porgy.

He didn't have to. Ketch poked him in the shoulder in a manner that said 'I'm watching you.' "Pick up your gun!" he enunciated carefully though the chemically-impregnated flannel, before returning to his position.

"Thirty seconds!" called Lieutenant Everson.

Atkins picked up his rifle and held it at the ready. Ginger had been a useful diversion. There was nothing worse than waiting for the whistle. He stared again at the scaling ladder before him, noting its shabby construction. There was not even a basic joint. The rungs had been hastily nailed to two longer pieces. Whoever expected them to climb it

47

obviously didn't expect them to have to climb it more than once. That about said it all.

"Ten seconds..."

EVERSON LIFTED HIS gas hood and blew his whistle before clumsily shoving the cloth back into his collar. Waving with his pistol, he watched his men scale the ladders. To his left, one fell back into the trench, immediately cut down. From beyond the parapet came cries and screams. He grabbed a rung and hauled himself up, cleared the sandbags, stepped out onto the mud and began to run, slogging through terrain the consistency of caramel, seeking to lead his men forward. He'd seen them all over the top with none left for the Battle Police to round up, which was no more than he'd expect of them. Another man fell in front of him. Everson stepped reluctantly over the body. It was not his job to stop and see if he were wounded or dead. The stretcher bearers would follow. Over to his left, he saw one of the tank machines as it nosed down into a shell hole and then reared up to clear it and rumble onwards along its terrible trajectory as spumes of earth exploded around it.

ATKINS HEARD THE whistle from far away, as if underwater, then another and another; some fainter, some louder. Up and down the line, dozens of subalterns blew their whistles or shouted their men forwards.

This was it. Under the tidal pull of fear he felt the swell of vomit and bile rise, and felt a growing urge to piss. He didn't want to go over the top. You'd be mad to.

Someone hit him on the shoulder. Twice.

Shitohshitohshitohsh—

Atkins screamed in rage and terror, which wasn't clever because it fogged up his eye pieces. He could barely see where he was going as it was. He scrambled up the ladder and over the parapet, and looked around. There to his left he saw sergeant's stripes. Hobson was walking resolutely forward. Somewhere amid the explosions he caught the rolling tinny snap of the marching snares and the harmonious wail of the bagpipes playing as the Jocks advanced over on their left flank.

STANDING IN THE trench with his men was like standing by a pen of cattle waiting to be herded into the abattoir and meant just about as much to him. Jeffries felt no pity for them as he lifted his gas hood to blow his whistle. He caught sight of a man, his shoulders heaving as if with sobs, a dark wet patch spreading down his trouser legs. He wouldn't move. Others clambered over the top to meet their fate. This one wouldn't.

"I'm not going to have you ruin things, Bristow. Get over!" said Jeffries in cold measured tones. Bristow snivelled but didn't stir. Jeffries sniffed derisively then shot him. "A death is a death Bristow, out there or down here, it's all the same to me. You'll have done your part either way."

He climbed the ladder and stepped from the still security of the trenches into a maelstrom of noise and fury. Shots, cries, bullets and bombs raged about him but he felt no fear. Anticipation, excitement, even, but fear? No. What had he to fear, today of all days?

In front of him, Appleton fell. And Harlow. Burton just vanished in a plume of wet offal and dirt. Still Jeffries strode on, unencumbered by the pack, webbing and bandoliers that weighed down his men. Every step a step closer to his destiny. When the day's bloodletting accrued to a critical mass, charging the landscape with a talisman of binding, he would speak the words he had long practised. The air screamed as shrapnel burst overhead, tearing down through flesh and mud alike. But none of it touched Jeffries.

Tendrils of chlorine lapped at his feet. Beneath his gas hood he wore a contented smile as he waded into the choking cloud with a surety that took the place of heroism. To be a hero you needed to feel fear. Jeffries didn't feel fear. He didn't need to. The sigil that he had drawn on his chest with Seeston's blood, now beginning to crust and pull uncomfortably at the hairs there, saw to that.

AROUND ATKINS, MEN were marching forward into the clouds of gas; a rising tide of asphyxiating death. The ground was soft and treacherous underfoot. Muffled by his gas hood, the crump and boom of shells assumed a continuous roar that made his ear drums crackle. He glanced to his left. Pot Shot and Mercy were striding forward. He could make out the weak sunlight glinting off the tin triangles on their backpacks.

It was nearly a quarter of a mile to the forward German lines. Running with full pack through this mud would tire you out before you got there and you'd have no puff left for the fight. Already he could feel the muscles of his legs begin to ache from pulling against the mud. It was better, so they said, to walk and conserve your strength. Fair enough. But that bollocks about carrying on and not seeking cover? Stuff that.

Following the tape he reached the British wire. He could hear the insistent stuttering of the British machine guns, while above them shells burst, leaving lazy black woolly clouds hanging in the air as shards of hot metal ripped down through bodies below. Ahead of him now, men began to drop, some hanging on the wire as if they were puppets whose strings had been cut. He walked on past the fallen, some dead, some wounded, crying and begging for help. Most still wore their gas hoods and Atkins was grateful that he could not see their faces. You weren't supposed to stop for them. You weren't allowed to. Carry on. Forward. Always forward. He walked on aware that every step could be his last. Was it this one? This one? This?

The great bank of greenish grey fog, a mixture of chlorine, cordite and smoke rolled over them, enveloping the soldiers like a shroud. Atkins lost sight of his Section. He stepped aside to avoid a shell hole that loomed up out of the ground before him and found his leg caught. He looked down; a hand had grabbed his mud-encrusted puttee. A man, maskless, green froth oozing slowly from his mouth, gagged and struggled, tearing at his own throat with a bloodied hand, drowning on dry land as the chlorine reacted in his lungs. Atkins tugged his ankle free and marched on. Shell holes were death traps now. The gas was sinking to the lowest point it could find, settling in pockets like ghostly green rock pools, where the weary and wounded had sought shelter.

As he walked on, he began to experience a light-headed feeling. Around him the gas cloud seemed to glow with a diffuse phosphorescence. The noise of battle, the rattle of machine guns and the constant *crumpcrumpcrump* of artillery, the zing of bullets seemed somehow muffled and distant. He stumbled as he missed his footing. He looked down. His body seemed to be longer than it should have been, stretching and undulating until a wave of vertigo overwhelmed him. Letting go of his rifle, he dropped to his hands and knees. The small area of ground before him seemed to swim and ripple gently and, no matter how hard he tried, he couldn't bring it into focus. Sweat began to prickle his face, he felt a pressure in his head, something trickled from his ear and he could taste the iron tang of blood running from his nose. The whole world seemed to tilt and from the periphery of his vision an oozing darkness spilled inwards until he could see no more than a few square inches of the Somme mud before his face. What remained of his vision filled with bursting spots of light as the world began to slip away…

PRIVATE GARSIDE'S FEET skittered under him on the chalky mud as he ran through the communication trench. A German shell had brought down the telephone lines between Harcourt and Sans German. He'd been ordered to collect information from the Front. Battalion needed to know how the advance was progressing. He had to get to the Observation Post and run the latest reports back to Battalion HQ. That alone could take about an hour or two. If he survived. Already two others had failed to get through.

The first walking wounded were beginning to filter back in ones and twos down the trenches, helping each other where they could. Yells of "Stretcher bearer!" filled the air. A shell exploded nearby. Garside flinched, but ran on, pushing past a couple of RAMC sent up from the reserve trenches, carrying their as yet unused stretchers wrapped around their carrying poles as they headed towards the Aid Post.

"There's no hurry, mate. I'm sure Fritz'll 'ave a bullet or two left for you!" they called after him.

Garside ignored them. By the time he'd thought of a witty retort he was several traverses ahead of them. He turned into High Street. The OP wasn't far now. The trickle of wounded he'd noticed before was fast becoming a steady stream.

Two Battle Police were confronting a young soldier, tears running down his face. He's lost his steel helmet and had no gun.

"I can't," he was saying. "I can't…"

"Turn round the way you came, you fucking coward," the bigger, burly one said.

The soldier took a step forward, towards him.

"I *can't*!" he screamed, tendons straining in his neck, his face red with effort as he dashed the Military Policeman's face with spittle.

The smaller man casually put his pistol to the man's head and fired. His legs crumpled beneath him and he dropped heavily to the ground, his head lolling at a sickening angle.

"What the fuck are you looking at?" the burly one snarled as Garside tried to edge past. He lowered his eyes to avoid meeting their gaze, but as he did so his eyes fell upon the now lifeless body of the young private.

"Leave 'im, Charlie," the wiry one said. "He's going in the right direction, 'sides he's got a Battalion armband on."

Garside ran on. He rounded several traverses to put distance between himself and the casual brutality he'd just witnessed.

"Jesus, Mary and Joseph!"

He skidded desperately to a halt. Small pebbles skittered from under his boots—and off into empty space.

Before him, where the support and front line trenches should have been, where No Man's Land had stretched away toward the German lines, lay nothing now but a huge crater almost half a mile across and thirty or forty yards deep at its centre.

The entire front line of the Harcourt Sector had gone.

CHAPTER FOUR
"Though Your Lads Are Far Away…"

BLOOD PULSING IN his ears, his breathing shallow and rapid within the claustrophobic gas hood, Atkins struggled to stand. About him, the featureless smog of war billowed sluggishly, draping itself around him, as if seeking a way through his respirator. Shapes swirled about him and he saw Flora's face, looking like she had that day outside the factory: threading her way across the street towards him between honking motor cars and horse and carts. Her joyous smile made his heart sing. He had to tell her. How would she react? He didn't know. He wasn't sure he could find the words at all. In the end he didn't have to. As she approached her face fell, but she caught herself and smiled again, although this time it seemed strained and polite.

"I—I thought you were William."

His stomach dropped away and his heart rose to his throat. "No, he said quietly, lowering his head and wringing his army cap in his hands as if in contrition. "I'm sorry."

She clasped his hands in hers gently. "No, I am."

"I've no news of William. He's been officially missing for weeks. Lots of lads have. But I'll keep trying for you. He'll turn up, I'm sure."

Unable to look her in the eye, he found himself looking at the small hands that embraced his, and the engagement ring his brother had bought her. He looked up, tears welling in his eyes to see the same in hers, united in grief.

"Hush, Tom. Walk me home."

As quickly as it materialised the shade dissipated. Unseen in the twilit gloom of poison gas, he could hear the gas hood-smothered cries of others.

"Porgy! Porgy! Where are you?"

He thought he heard an answer from somewhere over to his left but the lethal cloud around him left him completely disorientated. He could be stumbling straight towards the German wire for all he knew.

And he wished his world would stop spinning. He leant on his rifle to steady himself but, unable to keep his balance, he keeled over again and the ground loomed up to meet him. He just wanted the great big world to stop turning. With a groan he moved into a sitting position and pushed himself to his feet with the help of his rifle butt.

A deep bass rumble filled the featureless miasma around him and his world lurched, lifted upwards and dropped with such a jarring force that it drove him into the mud up to his knees. An explosion? Not any kind of shell he was familiar with. It wasn't a Five Nine or Whizz-Bang or Jack Johnson, that was for sure. It seemed to come from below the very ground he was standing on. Perhaps a mine had been set off. That must be it. Hundreds of tons of high-explosive going off underground. That'd give Fritz something to worry about.

A bright, diffuse light illuminated the smog from above, penetrating its suffocating gloom and throwing strange, disturbing shadows onto the moving banks of mist. There were cries of alarm from all around, moans of pain; calls for help, for pals, for mothers.

An eddy of wind caught the gas cloud and, for a moment, it thinned. Atkins thought he could make out the shapes of others, before the gas closed in again. He lay back in the mud as far as he could, feeling the jumbled contents of his backpack pressing into his back, and slowly began to pull his right leg from the sucking mud. Men had died getting stuck in this mire. His leg came free with a loud sucking noise. Scrabbling to gain a foothold with his free heel again he levered himself backwards, digging the shoulder butt of his rifle into the ground for extra purchase and slowly drawing his left leg free, almost losing his boot in the process.

Stopping to catch his breath, he noticed the silence. The wailing of the distant bagpipes had ceased. But even more disconcertingly, the guns had stopped. He had grown so used to their incessant roar that their absence now startled him. What the hell was going on?

"Only!"

He turned his body trying to gauge where the sound was coming from.

"Only! Where are you?"

"Over here!"

He could make out things moving in the mist. Three hunched shades with gaunt faces containing empty sockets resolved themselves into solid corporeal soldiers in gas hoods and Battle Order.

"Only!"

It was Porgy, Pot Shot and Lance Sergeant Jessop. Well, it was definitely Pot Shot. There was no mistaking the size of him, or Jessop's stripes.

"You okay, mate?" asked Pot Shot.

"What the hell was that, a mine going up?"

"Dunno, but they might have bloody warned us."

"What the hell's going on?" asked Gutsy joining them. "Why's the firing stopped? D'you think it's a truce?"

"It's bloody eerie, is what it is," said Atkins.

"Hey, maybe it's an armistice, maybe the war is finally over," said Jessop. "I can go home to Maud and little Bertie."

A gentle wind began to worry the edges of the gas cloud. The fog thinned and visibility gradually improved. They saw dazed soldiers picking themselves up off the ground. If that had been a mine and it was British, then they should be pressing home their advantage and taking the Hun trenches while the enemy were still dazed.

"Where's the rest of us?" Atkins asked, looking around.

"Over by that shell hole. Half Pint's trying to calm Ginger down. Lucky, Mercy and Gazette are still out there somewhere. Ketch? Who cares? Sergeant's probably taking the Jerry trenches by himself," said Porgy.

The battle fog was mostly gone, slinking shamefully along the surface of the mud, herded by playful draughts.

"Hoods off!" came a distant shout.

Thankfully, men began removing their steel helmets and pulling off their gas hoods.

"Uh, chaps?" said Pot Shot, staring off into the distance.

"Come on, give a man a hand here," said Atkins putting out an arm. Porgy and Jessop took it and pulled him to his feet.

"Chaps?" said Pot Shot again, more urgently.

Atkins wiped his muddy hands on his thighs. He felt a tap on his shoulder. Porgy was looking past him. "What?" he said in irritation as he rolled up his gas helmet and took a lungful of air. The acrid tang of cordite hit the back of his throat and the slight hint of chlorine hung in the air. He coughed and spat.

Porgy jerked his chin.

He turned and followed their gaze "Blood and sand!" The shell-ravaged vista of No Man's Land was as familiar as it ever was. Atkins turned round. He could see their trenches and the barbed wire. For around a quarter of a mile in every direction there was the pummelled and churned ground of the Somme. But beyond...

It was as if some pocket of Hades had been deposited in the vale of Elysium. Beyond the muddy battlefield of No Man's Land, lush green vegetation sprang up, a green so deep and bright after untold weeks of drab khaki and grey, chalky mud that it almost hurt the eyes to look upon it. Great curling fronds, taller than a man, waved in the breeze. Where there should have been only blasted hell-torn rolling farmland, now, on either side of them, deep green thickly wooded hills rose up as if cradling them, their peaks marked by glittering becks and scumbles of scree. Atkins was reminded of the hills and mountains of his Pennine home and felt a pang of homesickness. The air around them was no longer chill and damp, but warm and moist. In the distance, along the valley floor, was a forest of sorts and, above them all, arced an achingly blue summer sky.

But of Harcourt Wood and its splintered, shredded trees, there was no sign.

Men, stunned by the same sight, were taking off their gas hoods and shucking off their backpacks and webbing to stand dumbstruck. Some fell to their knees weeping openly with relief. In the distance, the sounds of a hymn, *Nearer My God to Thee,* rose up from the trenches. Soldiers slowly, cautiously clambered over the parapets, laying down their weapons to stand in the sunlight.

"Lay down your arms, brothers, for we are at peace in the fields of the Lord!"

Groups knelt in prayer amidst the mud, their hands clasped together, heads bowed. Others just sat, exhausted from the constant tension of the front lines or wandered dazed amid the trammelled corpse-ridden fields. Warmed by the sun, steam began to drift gently up, rising like the ghosts of the slain from the desolate earth.

"It's paradise!" said Ginger, his steel helmet held loosely in his hand, a beatific smile adorning his face. He wasn't shaking or jerking, he wasn't stuttering. It seemed as if a load had been lifted from him. Atkins had never known Ginger without his shell-shock.

"Paradise? You mean—"

"We're dead. Yes. Look. The guns have stopped. This isn't the Somme. This isn't France. It's heaven," Ginger sighed. "It's heaven…"

"Valhalla," said Pot Shot, nodding in agreement.

"You what?" said Jessop.

"Valhalla. Norse heaven of Viking warriors."

"Well, that's us, though, ain't it, warriors? That's us," said Lucky.

"Blimey you're a regular fount of knowledge, Pot Shot. I'm surprised you can get your head inside that battle bowler of yours," Gutsy said.

Atkins felt the great weariness that he had been holding at bay descend on him. It was as if the weight of his mortality was slowly crushing him, as if the mere thought of an end had robbed him of the tenacious will to cling on at all costs. Was this it then? If it was over, if it really *was* over, if he really could just stop and give in—

"There's just one thing bothers me," said Half Pint, scratching his head after a few seconds thought.

"Oh aye, what's that then?" said Jessop. "You found a problem with heaven, have you?"

"Well, there's no way they'd be lettin' Porgy through the pearly gates for a start."

Me, neither, thought Atkins.

It was all very well the chaplains preaching for victory and devoutly citing that the murder of a Hun was a good thing, but they were hollow words if your conscience was pricked by other matters.

Porgy inclined his head, pursing his lips as he nodded. "Man's got a point," he said.

"I'll say," said Gutsy, "All those saintly, virtuous young ladies and Porgy? Might be his idea of heaven, but it'd be their idea of hell."

"Don't blaspheme," said Ginger. "Look at it. How can it be anything else? Where did you ever see such beauty on earth?"

"Where's the padre? He'd know," said Lucky.

"Well, if this is heaven he ain't going to be too happy about it," said Half Pint.

"Why?"

"He'll be out of a job, won't he?"

SEEING THAT THE gas was now blowing away, Jeffries eagerly pulled the stifling hood from his head as he stood ready to receive his god with expectations of the glory and power due to him. So he was perplexed at his deity's absence and the idyllic sights surrounding them confused him. But beyond that that there was a growing anger. What had gone wrong? He had said the words *perfectly*, hadn't he? Yes, he must have. He was sure he had. He ran through his preparations in his head. He had been painstaking in their groundwork. It had taken months to put this plan together based on years of meticulous research. There was only one conclusion he could come to; he'd been cheated. At the moment of his greatest triumph, somehow he'd been cheated. He shook his head slowly, uncomprehensive as anger burned deeply within him until he was consumed in a wave of rage and vitriol.

"No!" he roared, throwing his helmet to the ground. "No!"

SERGEANT HOBSON STORMED over to 1 Section. "You lot! Just what the hell do you think you're doing?"

"Nothing, Sar'nt. We're dead," called Porgy.

"You're not bloody well dead until I tell you you're dead!" snapped Hobson. "Now pick your kit up and follow me."

Atkins smirked at Porgy, who shrugged. "Well, it's something to do until Saint Peter shows up and demobs us," he said.

"Don't believe in heaven, anyway," said Pot Shot casually. "Opiate of the masses an' all that."

"Opiate of the masses, that you readin' again, is it?" retorted Gutsy.

"Opiate?" said Jessop thoughtfully. "No, wait lads, he could be onto something. That would explain it. What if ol' Fritzy-boy, is using some sort of experimental opium gas what got through our respirators? This, this could all be a giant illusination. You know like them Chinky opium dens they have in that fancy London?"

EVERSON FELT DISCONSOLATE. Since the gas cloud cleared and the astounding change to the landscape had revealed itself he began to feel power dripping away from him. It was all he'd wished for, for months, yet now he was not yet ready to relinquish it so easily. Not until he was sure that it was over, that they were all safe.

"You men!" he called, brandishing his Webley in their direction. "Pick up your weapons!" They ignored him. "Pick up your weapons!"

It was as if, in the absence of an enemy, he'd lost all authority. Isn't that what he wanted all along? To shed the burden? It was the same along the entire front. Men had cast their rifles aside, sat down and were breaking out their iron rations and singing sentimental songs, sharing out the smokes, waiting... waiting for something. Nobody seemed sure what, but whatever it was, it wasn't a subaltern with a pistol.

"It's a higher authority we answer to now, mate," one brazen private told him, jerking his chin towards the distant hills. "If we're dead then the only route march I'm doing is through the pearly gates. Fag?"

Perplexed, Everson shook his head. Seemingly bereft of purpose, he wandered out along the wire entanglements that marked the British Line. Men lay where they had fallen, sobbing and crying in pain. Some were being tended to, some being ferried away on stretchers. If this was heaven, why were there still the wounded and suffering? Would heaven allow men to suffer with their guts hanging out? What kind of god was that?

He caught sight of 1 Section being herded towards him like wayward sheep by Sergeant Hobson, before he went to round up the rest of the scattered platoon. Everson addressed one of the men.

"Jellicoe?"

"Sir?"

"I don't know what the hell is going on here, but the last I heard we were attacking the German positions in Harcourt Wood."

"Wood seems to have gone now, sir," chimed in Hopkiss.

"Thank you, yes, I can see that, Hopkiss, but the point remains. Until we know what we're dealing with here I would prefer—"

An unearthly howl cut through the valley, echoing off the hillsides. As one, the Section raised their rifles, eyes surveying the landscape. Around them men started and turned to listen, uncertainty clouding their faces. Some began gathering their discarded equipment, looking expectantly towards the officer.

"What the bloody hell was that?" said Everson.

"It came from that forest, sir," said Jellicoe.

"Right. Yes," said Everson, feeling a resurgence of purpose and responsibility, "Jessop, stay here with your section, I'll tell Hobson to rally the Platoon and pass on any orders." He turned to address the other men. "The rest of you men get back to your platoon's trenches and stand to! Until we know what's going on I think we must remain on our guard."

AS PLATOONS OF men slunk back to the trenches, overhead, Atkins heard a faint, familiar drone. High above he spotted two aeroplanes, each vying for an advantageous position from which to attack. One succeeded in manoeuvring above the other for a split second before it began descending in a slow smoky spiral. Atkins watched it drift down like a leaf until it was lost from sight behind the peaks of the newly risen hills. A high gust of wind had caught the untethered and slowly deflating German kite balloon, carrying it further and further away over the hills, buoyed aloft by swift currents of air.

A spatter of machine gun fire jerked him back to reality, if anything they were experiencing could be said to be reality. Another burst. And another. The field of fire swept across No Man's Land. Tommies fell. Men scurried for cover and dived into shell holes with shouts of alarm and dismay.

"There!" said Gazette, spotting the muzzle flash of the machine gun as it fired off another burst. "It's a Hun sap."

They barely had time to follow Gazette's stare towards a fortified shell-hole before the Maxim fire swept towards them. The Section scrambled for the cover of a shell hole, bullets spitting into the mud at their heels as they ran. As they threw themselves into the mud-filled pit a roar filled the air as the great ironclad bulk of *HMLS Ivanhoe* reared up out of a dip in front of them, like some great blind creature emerging from the primordial slime. It crashed down heavily, placing its metal carcass between them and the raking German machine gun. Atkins heard the bullets raining against the hide of the motorised beast.

Slowly its great six-pounder gun turned toward the emplacement. There was a brief pause before the gun fired. The machine gun emplacement erupted in a geyser of dirt and sandbags; smoke and screams filled the air as munitions went up in a series of secondary explosions. A ball of flame bloomed briefly within the remnants of the emplacement and mud and hot metal rained down, clinking dully against the armoured hulk.

Mercy banged on the side of the boojum. "Ere, conductor! Any room inside, it's ruddy raining out here!"

The Tank gave no indication of human occupancy although, in reply, its motorised growl rose in pitch as if in recognition. Gears ground as the left hand track remained still and the right hand track spun slowly, swinging the tank away from them as it continued its halting, lethargic advance.

"Christ that was close. Bloody boojums, though, eh, Only?" said Mercy cracking a grin and slapping Atkins on the back.

"Right, you lot!" bellowed Sergeant Hobson herding the rest of the scattered platoon towards them. "Take a dekko and see how far this mud pie of ours goes. We also need to make sure Fritz hasn't got anything else up his sleeve. One other thing. Nobody steps off this mud until further orders. Got it?"

"Yes, Sergeant!"

"Right. Move out."

Atkins fell in with Mercy and Gazette with Jessop taking the lead. The initial eerie tranquillity had now been shattered, spurring the growing sense of unease he felt at their surroundings. Along the line several other platoons were being ordered to move forward through the shell holes towards where the German lines should have been.

They came across the remains of an aeroplane lying on its back, its wheels splayed in the air. It was one of theirs, the Royal Flying Corps roundel clearly visible on the fuselage. The front was covered with mud, the remains of the propeller splintered as though it had ploughed head first into the mud before flipping and coming to rest. Oil leaked onto the ground from the engine, turning the mud beneath it to a thick black viscous puddle.

"Only, check the pilot blokes," Jessop said, looking around warily.

Atkins passed his rifle to Porgy and got down on his hands and knees to crawl under the upturned machine. The observer was upside down in his cockpit, his head tilted back and his face planted in the mud. Atkins tried to push him up to relieve the pressure, but realised his efforts were futile. He was dead. Atkins moved towards the pilot. He crawled over the plane and let out a startled cry when his knee went through the doped cotton with a pop.

"Sorry, nothing! My fault," he called out to reassure his startled fellows. "Hang on chum, we'll get you out."

Once Atkins had wriggled through the snapped spars and wire he found that the pilot had fallen out of his cockpit and lay in the small crushed space between machine and the upper wing, his neck broken. Awkwardly, Atkins shuffled out from under the shattered plane. As he did so he spotted a line of bullet holes stitched across the fuselage.

Atkins shook his head at Jessop.

"Both dead. Pilot's got a broken neck. Looks like the other one was drowned in the mud."

"Nothing we can do here, then," said Jessop. "Ginger, Mercy, get those bodies out then salvage the guns and collect whatever ammunition you can from the plane. The rest of you spread out and move on."

Porgy had been looking at the rear of the aeroplane. "Look at this, lads. What do you make of that?"

The tail had vanished, not ripped off or shot through, but simply amputated by a clean cut. Atkins looked around but could see no sign of the missing section.

There was a dull snap as Ginger and Mercy tugged at the body of the observer and dragged him from the rear cockpit.

"Careful, you clumsy buggers," cried Jessop.

"It was the plane!" said Mercy defensively.

Jessop shook his head and moved on. The rest followed his lead.

In minutes they had reached the end of the mud. The German wire should have been twenty or thirty yards further on but, where once there had been fortifications, entrenchments, emplacements and entanglements there was now an abrupt drop of seven or eight feet. Beyond, they were surrounded by a thick green meadow, the grass maybe three or four feet high, the stalks flattened outwards as if by violent impact. Beyond the veldt, looking towards the head of the valley, was what could be termed a forest, perhaps a mile or so or away. Scattered across the meadow were what looked like trees, spaced singly or in small groves.

"Jessop?" said Pot Shot, standing at the very edge of what they knew as the Somme.

"What is it?" said the lance sergeant, striding over.

Pot Shot was stood over a body of a dead Hun. Or to be more precise, half a body. The torso was hanging on the wire. It was cut clean through and the legs were missing. Hobson pushed his tin hat back on his head, raised his eyebrows and let out a long, slow exhalation.

"Christ," he said.

"What do you reckon did that?"

"Nothing I know of," he said. There wasn't the usual mess they were accustomed to, just a clean, surgical cut.

All eyes turned to Gutsy.

"What? Just because I use to be a butcher? Bloody hell!" Gutsy, despite his protests, set about studying the body with an almost professional interest. There was no blood. It was as if the entire wound had been cauterised. "I don't know of any blade sharp enough or quick enough to leave such a clean cut."

Pot Shot had been examining a strand of the wire.

"Same here," he declared.

"How can you tell?" asked Gazette.

"You see here? Normally when you use wire cutters the wire is pinched thin before it breaks, resulting in a pointed 'v' cross section. This is flat."

Atkins stood at the edge of the lip and looked slowly left, then right along the fault line as it curved gently back away from him on either side. "Y' know," he said slowly. "It's almost as if something has severed cleanly through everything—ground and air. I'll bet if we follow this around we'll find the same."

"What are you saying, Only?" asked Jessop.

Atkins never got the chance to reply. Out of the corner of his eye he caught a flash of fangs as Jessop disappeared, propelled backwards by the weight of a large mound of greasy fur and muscle, leaving only a scream in his wake as foot long teeth ripped out his throat.

CHAPTER FIVE
"Some Corner of a Foreign Field..."

GAZETTE WAS THE first to get off a shot, firing a full clip at the great beast as it tore ravenously into Jessop's stomach, all in the time it took Atkins to bring up his rifle.

"Holy Mary Mother of God!" wailed Ginger.

"What the bleedin' hell is it?" shouted Mercy.

"Bloody ugly!" replied Gutsy, as the rest of the section brought their rifles to bear.

Atkins had never seen such a creature. None of them had. It was like some kind of monstrous hyena. Easily as high as a man, it had powerful shoulders, like that of an American bison; a mass of knotted, corded muscle rippling under its coarse fur. Its neck was short, its long snout was filled with sharp teeth and it possessed powerful muscled legs ending in long claws.

"Don't just stand there," bellowed Hobson. "Five rounds rapid!"

The great predator roared as the bullets bit, but would not be denied its kill. It turned its blood-drenched snout towards them, snarling in pain and anger. Driven away from the body, it let out a howl of such fury that some of the men nearby dropped their guns and began running for the trenches.

From out of the undergrowth, a pack of the same creatures answered, bounding towards the mud, howling and baying, the scent of fresh blood now on the wind, driving them into a frenzy.

Gazette and the others turned their rifles on the creatures and fired. The beasts staggered under the fusillade. Some yelped and fell, others skidded to a halt, uncertain. The volley hadn't entirely stopped their advance, but it had slowed it. Twenty, maybe thirty of the creatures were now bounding towards them, guttural snarls drawing back lips to reveal rows of sharp teeth. Others, more cautious, began edging round, trying to flank them, bellies low to the ground.

"Fall back!"

Atkins didn't need to be told twice. He began running with the others, which only served to excite the creatures more. He sprinted past the downed aeroplane, where Mercy was wrestling with the ammunition magazine on the Lewis gun.

"Run!" cried Atkins as he sprinted past. Gazette and Gutsy skidded to a halt by the wreck and, using it for cover, loosed off another clip each.

"Take Ginger!" yelled Mercy, stacking up the six circular ammo magazines by him and setting the Lewis gun on the wing. "I'll cover you!"

Gutsy and Lucky hauled Ginger to his feet and began herding him back towards the trenches.

Atkins dashed back towards the crashed biplane, firing off another clip as he ran before he slumped down by Mercy.

"You'll need a loader," he said. Mercy nodded grimly.

Mercy took aim and pulled the trigger, loosing the entire magazine in one burst. Atkins pulled it off, threw it aside and clipped on the second, but too slowly; the first wave of the creatures was nearly upon them. Mercy let off another quick stammer.

On their blind side, hidden by the fuselage of the aeroplane, they could hear the cries of other, less fortunate men as they fell to the pack.

Atkins loaded up the final magazine. A quick burst from the Lewis gun brought down a couple more of the creatures. Mercy was now getting the measure of the MG, alas with all too few rounds left. Another beast approached cautiously, its head down, a low growl emanating from its throat. It glared at them warily as it began tugging at the body of one of the dead aviators, seeking to drag it away. Mercy screamed and let fly another burst, bullets tearing into the beast, until the canister spun on empty. He shoved the gun aside, unshouldered his rifle, loaded another clip and waited.

Atkins heard a clatter above them. A creature had leapt onto the upturned belly of the machine. He could hear it sniffing. He lay still, not daring to move.

There was the rapid fire of five rounds and a roar of pain from the unseen creature, which seemed to stagger unsteadily on top of the machine and, in doing so, missed its footing, putting its full weight on the doped covering of the wing. Its claws tore through the flimsy cotton as the wing folded under it, the spars snapping under its weight and sending the wounded creature crashing towards Atkins.

Atkins rolled onto his back and braced the butt of his rifle against his shoulder. Unable to stop itself, the beast tumbled onto the blade of his bayonet. Atkins pulled the trigger, emptying his clip into the creature. It slumped heavily towards him. Inches from his face, its teeth snapped weakly; hot, thick saliva dripping onto him with the creature's last fetid exhalation.

Mercy dragged him out from beneath the carcass. "Come on, Only, we've got to get back to the trenches."

"No argument from me," said Atkins, kicking himself free.

Stooped over, they ran for the shell hole from where Gazette was providing covering fire and jumped over the lip to find the rest of the section sheltering within.

By now the machine gun emplacements back behind the firing trench were opening fire on the animals. Bullets zinged overhead, causing them to flinch back into the shell hole.

"We're on your side, you daft beggars!" called Porgy, clutching his steel helmet to his head.

Cautiously, Atkins peered above the rim. It appeared that competing packs of the creatures were now fighting among themselves and, now that he had a better view, he could see why.

It wasn't just the living that they were feeding off. Several beasts were tugging at the exposed limbs of corpses and attempting to draw the corrupt bodies from the mud's clammy embrace. They fought over rotting bodies, worrying the fragile cadavers until they fell apart, or else bursting gas-filled bellies and snuffling greedily at the contents. The scale of their predicament, the full horror of their situation, hit Atkins. They were sitting on a charnel field consisting of layer upon layer of decomposing dead, thousands of corpses of rotten Hun, French and British soldiers. They'd attract every predator, scavenger and carrion eater for miles around. This was just the start.

"It's now or never. Make for the trenches, lads, and don't spare the horses," said Hobson.

As one, they leapt from the shell holes and made for the lines. Distracted by the prospect of a live kill, some of the creatures turned from fighting over scraps to give chase. Ketch fell headlong into the mud, his rifle flung out beyond his reach. He cried out as he spotted the creatures bearing down on him, each trying to warn the other off their potential prize.

Sod him, thought Atkins, but he couldn't. "Damn!" He ran back.

"Get the hell away from me, Atkins. I'm not going to be party to your showboating heroics."

"Now ain't the time, Ketch. F'Pete's sake, take my hand."

Ketch's hand clasped his and Atkins hauled him up. The beasts, sensing that their prey was about to bolt, put on a burst of speed. They weren't going to make it.

The air filled with a high pitched drone, punctuated by the spatter of machine gun fire. Atkins dropped as a biplane swooped low over them, picking off the creatures as it came. He cheered as he caught sight of a gauntleted hand giving him a cheery wave from the cockpit before the plane began to climb steeply away again, waggling its wings briefly.

Atkins attempted to haul Ketch to his feet again but the corporal swatted his hand away. "I don't want your damn help, Atkins," he snapped and, after a false start, slipping in the mud, he struggled to his feet and they raced for the trenches. As they ran Atkins could hear the machine circling round again, diving towards the packs of creatures and spitting lead.

As those on the firestep covered them, Atkins flung himself over the parapet into the safety of the trenches, almost knocking over Hepton who was feverishly cranking the handle of his camera, mesmerised by the scene before him. There, from the relative safety of the fire bay, Atkins saw the tank turning its Hotchkiss machine guns on knots of the feeding creatures. Some of the more cunning ones slunk in under the gun's field of fire and leapt onto the tank's back, growling and slashing impotently at its armoured hide. They started ripping at the anti-grenade gable on its roof, tearing at the chicken wire. Fore and aft of the gun sponsons, small round loopholes, no more than a couple of inches across, flicked open and the barrels of revolvers poked out and began to fire. Muzzle flashes buried themselves in the greasy hides of the beasts straddling the tank. They dropped to the ground with yelps and squeals, slinking into the undergrowth with howls of frustration to cheers of victory from the men.

LIEUTENANT JAMES TULLIVER peered back over the trailing edge of his wing down at the bewildering scene. Huge wolf-like creatures prowled over No Man's Land, which seemed to have shrunk to a circle barely half a mile across, surrounded by a halo of bright cinnamon earth. It sat in the wide green valley, looking as if it had been dropped there from a height by a careless giant. Well, to be quite frank, thought Tulliver, it looked like nothing so much as a freshly dropped cow pat in a field.

Normally he would return to the airfield, but from what he could see, there was no airfield left to which he could return. There were several hundred yards of No Man's Land but the persistent shelling meant that wasn't even an option. He could make out the fire and cover trenches and even a long section of support trench along with a bombed farmhouse near the edge of the grey-brown mud flat. Beyond that, some sort of long grass was flattened outwards as if by a shockwave. It wasn't ideal, but right now he didn't seem to have much choice. He selected his approach and cut the engine, gliding down towards the ground.

He felt the wheels of the Sopwith 1½ Strutter hit with a bump and the machine bounced along. He adjusted the flaps and the biplane came down heavily again, this time trundling along to a stop, the thing juddering and shaking so much Tulliver feared it would fall apart before it stopped, but stop it did. He pushed up his goggles revealing piercing blue eyes amid the oil-splattered face. He climbed out of his cockpit and checked Hodgeson his observer. He was dead, sat slumped forward in the rear cockpit, blood filling his goggles. Damn shame. He'd only been out two weeks. He clambered down to the ground, took off his fur-lined gloves and boots, then walked round to inspect his machine, noting the holes across the fuselage that the Hun had given him. They could be repaired. All in all she was still in admirable condition.

"Good show, old girl," he said gently. He looked round. About fifty yards away was the beginning of the mud patch. He strolled towards it with his usual insouciance, intending to report to the nearest officer, when he heard a scream. A female scream. It came from the bombed-out farmhouse teetering near the edge of the muddy escarpment. He ran towards it, pulling out his revolver, barely noticing the change of ground underfoot as he raced up the incline. The scream was suddenly drowned out by a frustrated growl.

Nearing the house, he slowed down and edged forward cautiously. He could hear some animal, probably one of those beasts he saw earlier, padding around inside.

From a boarded up window he heard the sound of sobbing, the murmur of prayer and an insistent, urgent whisper.

"Well, we can't just sit here. There must be something we can do."

"What on earth is it?"

"It must have escaped from a zoo!"

There was another roar from the beast, which could clearly hear and smell its prey but couldn't reach it.

Tulliver edged along the wall until he came to a faded wooden doorjamb, its paint peeling and the door long since carted off for firewood. Cocking his pistol, he peered round the door. The huge beast was stood in the passage sniffing at the closed door within. Its great claws had slashed through the plaster to the side to reveal the fragile wooden slats beneath. It wouldn't be long before it got through that way.

Tulliver withdrew. As quietly as possible he checked the chambers of his revolver. They were all full. He only hoped they'd be enough.

He took several deep breaths. He wished whoever was screaming would shut up. It was really getting on his nerves. Apart from which he wanted to make sure the animal could hear him. As the screamer stopped to take a breath, he stepped round the doorway and whistled. The beast looked up and growled before bounding at him, claws skittering over the debris on the floor. Tulliver got off two shots then stepped aside, back against the wall beside the door as the beast came through, bringing half the doorjamb with it. He got off another two shots before the beast realised where he was and could turn. Its back legs skidded out from under it.

It pounced. Tulliver let off the last two shots. One passed straight through its skull scattering its brains out through the exit wound. As he dropped and rolled aside, the beast crashed into the wall and collapsed to the ground, sending loose bricks tumbling down, prompting another round of screaming from inside.

"Edith! Do be quiet. I shan't have to slap you again, shall I?"

"Sister, please, no more violence!" said a man's voice.

"Well, if she don't, I will," came a third female voice.

"Hello?" called Tulliver as he walked slowly down the short passage and tried the door. It wouldn't budge. He tried knocking and was encouraged by the sound of scraping as if someone were moving large objects.

"Well for goodness sake, Edith, give the gel a hand."

"Thanks awfully," came the reply, dripping with sarcasm as the door scraped open and jammed halfway. Tulliver was just wondering whether he should do the gentlemanly thing and put his shoulder to it when a final wrench from a pair of grubby hands freed it. The door crashed open sending a woman dressed in a khaki jacket and long ankle length khaki skirt reeling back into the arms of a middle-aged chap in an army uniform, under which Tulliver could see the black cloth and white collar of a Devil Dodger. Two nurses looked on.

"Careful there, Padre, this is more my area of expertise than yours I think," said Tulliver, stepping into the room and setting the poor woman on her feet again.

"Gor blimey, a... pilot!" said the khaki-clad FANY. She blushed furiously against her better judgement but recovered admirably. "Nellie Abbott," she said with a little bob of a curtsey. "Where's your machine, then? Can I see it? What sort is it?"

"Driver Abbot! A little decorum, please!" said the sister brusquely. "You *are* a pilot, then?"

"Lieutenant James Tulliver, RFC," he said, clicking his heels and giving a little mock bow of the head.

"Sister Fenton," said the nurse curtly, thrusting out a hand. "Red Cross. This is Nurse Bell," she said, nodding at a similarly dressed young woman.

"Yes," said Tulliver, shaking her hand. "The red crosses on your uniform did rather give it away."

"I don't think this is the time for flippancy, do you, Mr Tulliver?" interjected the padre.

The young woman in the nurse's uniform, her once carefully pinned hair now a-tumble, let out a sigh and crumpled to the floor.

"Oh, for goodness' sake!" said Fenton, stamping her foot. "Edith!"

"I say, I don't usually have that kind of effect," said Tulliver. "Is she all right?"

"It's not you, you great oaf," snapped the other nurse. "We've just been though a lot, a motor crash, a freezing cold night in a cellar, the shelling and now to have that slavering great creature..."

"It's dead now," said Tulliver. "But this place isn't safe. There are more of them. We'll have to get you into the trenches."

"The trenches? Are you mad?" said the padre. "There are hundreds of men there."

"Padre, believe me," said Sister Fenton, "The likes of that lot hold no fear for me."

"An' I've got four brothers so I've seen the worst of 'em!" said Abbott jovially.

"There, that's settled then," said Tulliver.

"It's totally out of the question. It's... improper," said the padre. "We're waiting on a motor ambulance to take them back to the Hospital in St. Germaine."

"Ah," said Tulliver, awkwardly, rubbing the back of his neck and feeling the short bristles there.

"What do you mean, 'ah'?" said Sister Fenton.

"I mean, I don't think it's going to be possible, I'm afraid," he said. "At least for a while. Can she walk?" he asked, indicating Nurse Bell.

"Oh she'll be fine. Abbott, give me a hand," said Sister Fenton.

The khaki-clad girl hurried to put herself under the blonde nurse's arm in order to take her weight. The woman groaned softly.

"Come on, Edi," she said. "Time for a little promenade."

"Where to?" asked the dazed nurse weakly.

"Padre, I need to report to, well, to *somebody*. Can you take me to an officer? Whose Company Front is this?"

"13th Battalion Pennine Fusiliers. I can take you to C Company HQ. It's not far from here."

"It may be further than you think," Tulliver said cryptically. "Wait here." He slipped out of the door and peered outside. He held his revolver for appearance's sake. The nurses needn't know it was empty. He had some spare ammunition, but it was in the aeroplane.

"It's clear. Padre, you bring up the rear."

"Right you are."

They stepped over the rubble and out of the back of the ruined farmhouse facing the front line, to avoid the creature's corpse out the front. It took the women a moment or two to catch their breath at the sight of the lush green vista now surrounding them.

"Blimey!"

"Oh. My..."

"Hold fast, Abbott, Edith's going to faint again," said Sister Fenton. "Mr Tulliver, where exactly are we? These mountains weren't here yesterday. I should have been sure to spot them. How is this possible?"

"That," said Tulliver, "is the very question. Well, Padre, any answers?"

The padre opened and closed his mouth several times before giving up and reluctantly shaking his head.

A strange cry startled them. Above, flocks of things that were not birds were beginning to swirl and wheel above the mud. Up ahead, they could hear the marshalling shouts and barks of NCOs giving orders.

"We'd best hurry. Watch your step, ladies," cautioned Tulliver as he led them across the mud and down into the nearest communication trench. He'd only ever once before had a trip up to the front lines, when visiting an artillery battery.

"That smell!" said Edith, faltering as she looked round for the source while Sister Fenton dragged her on like a tardy child.

"I know," said Tulliver, shaking his head. "Sweaty feet, unwashed men, cordite, army stew. If nothing else they should act as effective smelling salts, eh, Abbott?"

As they worked their way up the trench the party attracted cat calls and whistles from weary, mud-soaked and bewildered men. Tulliver turned back to check on his charges. Sister Fenton strode purposefully on, doing her best to ignore them, while Edith seemed to have recovered enough to smile coquettishly as she was pulled along in her wake. Abbott strode confidently behind. She looked longingly at a private drawing on a fag. "Aw, go on, duck, give us a Wood, I'm gasping!" she said as she passed.

The soldier leered at her. "Come 'ere, and I'll give you—" he began, before catching the eye of the padre bringing up the rear. Flustered, he fished around in his tunic pocket producing two battered but serviceable Woodbines and offered them to her. "—I'll give you a couple," he stuttered apologetically, smiling awkwardly as his mates jeered and jostled him.

Abbott took them from his hand. "Ta, ever so, ducks," she called gaily as the padre impatiently herded her away.

One man flung himself desperately at the Chaplain.

"Padre? What's happened. Where are we? We thought we was in heaven, like, but them devil dogs attacked so it can't be, can it? Is God punishing us? Tell us Padre, tell us!"

"I—I don't know, my son" answered the padre as he pulled away from the distraught soldier.

Further along, the revetments leaned drunkenly, their sandbags askew. In places they threatened to topple over completely. In others they had collapsed and they had to scramble over the mounds of spoil. When they reached C Company HQ they found a captain sat in the remains of the trench with his head in his hands. There was a bustle of activity around him as men worked stoically shifting sandbags and timbers, using shovels, picks and buckets to excavate the dirt where the C Company HQ sign lay half buried.

"Captain Grantham!" said Padre Rand, kneeling down by him. "What happened? Is the major all right?"

Grantham lifted his head from his hands. His face was streaked with dirt and tears.

The padre took him aside. "For God's sake, compose yourself, Captain. Not in front of the ranks. Remember you're an officer! Pull yourself together."

Grantham made an effort to regain his composure as he stood. He brushed the drying mud and soil from his tunic, cleared his throat and straightened his collar and tie.

"Can we help?" asked Sister Fenton, stepping forward.

"Eh?" The Captain looked at the women nonplussed.

"The nurses I reported on last night, Grantham," said the padre.

"Ah. Right. Yes, well there's nothing they can do here," said Grantham waving away Sister Fenton's ministrations. "But I'm sure the MO can put them to work." He gestured to the pile. "The major's dead, buried under that lot. I barely got out myself. There was a sudden jolt and the whole place just collapsed around us. There's the CSM, the orderlies and the signal chappie down there, too," he said earnestly. "And reports of other dugout collapses. I sent a runner to Battalion but he says it's gone. How can it not be there? And then there were those damn wolf things. I don't know what's happening."

"This man might be able to shed some light on it all," said the padre, introducing the Flying Officer.

"Lieutenant Tulliver," said Tulliver, extending a hand.

Grantham took it. "Well I certainly hope you can. This is a right bloody shambles. The men are getting windy. It felt like a bloody earth tremor."

"A bit more than that."

"A mine explosion?"

"If it was it's blown us to God knows where," said Tulliver, looking up at the mountains on either side as he pulled his trench maps from inside his double-breasted tunic. He took a stub of pencil from his pocket and, after studying the map for a few moments, drew a rough circle on the paper around a section of trenches and No Man's Land. "As far as I can tell, sir, this area is all I could see from the air. It's as if someone had taken a giant pair of scissors, cut it out and dropped it down somewhere else entirely."

"Scissors? Talk sense man!" snapped Grantham.

"From what I could see from the air, sir," said Tulliver, "this circle of mud is all that is left of the Somme."

THE TANK RUMBLED and squealed its way implacably toward the trench and then stopped. Atkins could see where the beasts had clawed away at the trench paint—camouflage cover and the wire netting gable was torn and hanging off. By the time the engine had puttered and died Atkins and some of the others were out of the trenches and walking towards this new wonder machine. Its guns slowly lowered, as if bowing in obeisance or exhaustion. There were metallic clangs and bangs as a door, barely more than two feet tall, opened in the rear of the gun sponson and there clambered, from the pit of the armoured machine, one small man and then another. They were wearing oiled-stained khaki overalls covered with small burn holes and tight fitting leather helmets with leather masks across the upper halves of their faces, their eyeholes merely thin slits. From the bottom of the masks hung chain mail drapes that covered the rest of their face. They looked as if they'd stepped from the Devil's own chariot. Two more climbed out of a hatch on the top of the motorised mammoth and walked down the back of the now motionless track that encompassed the entire side of the tank.

"Bloody gas! Now I'm going to have to strip everything down and clean it to stop the damn corrosion."

"Jesus my head's banging!"

Atkins had never seen a more otherworldly group of men. They would have looked fierce and impressive, almost like some primitive tribal warriors, if two of them hadn't then fallen to their knees and started vomiting warm beige splatters into the mud, coughing and retching worse than a retired coal miner.

"Bloody hell!" said Porgy.

The little bantam bloke pulled off his helmet and mask to reveal a pale face covered with flaky, livid red patches. He took a swing with his foot, savagely kicking the body of a dead creature.

"That's for scratching *Ivanhoe*, you ugly mutt," he said, punctuating his invective with further kicks.

The lanky Tank Commander strode over and made a curt introduction. "Lieutenant Mathers. Who's in charge here?"

"That'll be Captain Grantham, sir," said Sergeant Hobson. "I'll get someone to take you to Company HQ."

Atkins turned his attention back to the others who were talking to the tank crew.

"Well if this ain't the Somme it's not my fault," the bantam tank driver was saying. "My map reading were bloody perfect!"

"Then where on earth are we?"

"Earth?" spat the bantam figure scathingly. "This ain't like no place on earth *I've* ever seen!"

CHAPTER SIX
"What's the Use of Worrying…"

"I'M GOING TO need numbers, Sergeant; roll call and casualties," Everson said as he inspected the fire trench along his Platoon Front. After the attack by what they were calling hell hounds, the men were stood to on the fire step, rifles at the ready. Any questions the men might have were silenced by Hobson's stern glance, for which Everson was thankful. He had no idea what had happened. Right now he was as ignorant as his men, which was not a position he liked to be in and one he was even less likely to want to admit to. Latrine rumours were flying about. You couldn't stop them. Those that thought they'd suddenly materialised in Paradise and the Just Reward they so richly deserved were quickly disabused by the attack of the creatures. Now they were convinced they were in Purgatory. Others thought it Hell, although that argument was soon sunk by the virtue of them having been on the Somme which was itself the very definition of hell. Best to nip such gossip in the bud, if you could. Having stalled after the initial confusion over the strange surroundings and the attack of the beasts, the great military machine was beginning to reassert itself.

"I want you to keep the men busy," Everson told Hobson. "Don't want 'em getting windy. After they're stood down, set them to repairing the trenches. Work will keep them occupied until we can sort out what the hell is going on here."

Cries and moans from the wounded drifted over from No Man's Land, those wounded by Fritz in the initial attack and those poor souls left alive by the attacking hell hounds. That was the real morale sapper, he knew. In a Pals Battalion like the Broughtonthwaite Mates, those weren't just any soldiers, those cries came from people you'd known all your lives. That's what became unbearable; the knowledge that they weren't just going to die. With gut-shots or shrap wounds they could lie out there for days, begging for help, crying for their mothers, calling for *you* to help them, and you knowing that if you tried to help them, you'd be joining them on the old barbed wire. That's what broke men, that's what ground insidiously away at morale. Oh, the bombs and the shells and the sniping got to some after a while, but this was the clincher.

"Sergeant?"

"Sir?"

"Best, get a party together with stretcher bearers, too, and start bringing in some of those woundeds while we've still got daylight. Those damned beasts are still out there somewhere. See to it, will you?"

"Sir," he said. Everson left him to it, turned down the comm trench and began to work his way back to where the temporary HQ had been set up and a Company meeting arranged.

HOURS LATER, WITH only the occasional reappearance of a wily hell hound or two, the men were stood down with only sentries left on guard against further attack. Those not on duty retired to the support trenches.

"Fuck, look lively here comes Hobson," said Porgy, sucking the last dregs of smoke from his Woodbine before dropping it in the mud to sizzle and die.

"Great. Ketch'll be in charge of the Section. Bet he couldn't wait," muttered Mercy as they noticed the corporal skulking along behind the sergeant, "and Jessop barely cold."

"Right, you lot, finished sitting around on our arses have we?" said Hobson. "Then there's work to do."

"Sarn't," said Porgy, putting a hand to his grubbily bandaged pate, "me head's spinning. I think it's that crack I got last night."

Atkins could almost hear the rest of the Section groan and suppressed a smirk. Bloody Porgy. He had an aversion to manual labour. Had to keep his hands soft for his long-haired chums, or so he said.

"Right, Hopkiss," said Hobson, almost wearily. "Let's get you to the MO then and see what he has to say. If you're malingering, I'll have you. The rest of you fall in. Come on," he barked when they were slow to get up, "put some jildi into it!"

They got up and put themselves into lacklustre order.

"Jesus, Mary and Joseph, you're a sorry bunch. If your mothers could see you now they'd be ashamed!" he snapped. "You lot are on trench fatigue. I'll leave it to Corporal Ketch to sort the details out. They're all yours, Corporal." And he set off, escorting Porgy to the MO. Porgy turned and gave Atkins a quick wink before Hobson shoved him down the comm trench.

"Right," said Ketch slowly once Hobson had gone, the sneer on his lips smearing itself across his face. "We're going down Broughton Street for a bit of digging, so grab your entrenching tools."

There was a lot of muttering and sighing as they picked up the spades from their kits and began sloping off down the trench.

"Not you, Atkins," said Ketch. "I've got another job for you. Don't think saving me from them hell hounds has won you any favours, cos it hasn't. You suffer too much from cheerfulness you do. Well, I've got the cure. You're a cocky little shit, d'y'know that?"

"Here, steady on Corp!" said Mercy.

Ketch shot him a look and carried on.

"And shit should be in the latrine. Sanitation duty until I say so."

"Corp!" objected Atkins, but knowing it was an argument he was going to lose, Atkins bit his tongue. Mercy had no such reservations.

"Quit riding the lad, Ketch. You may be an NCO but *après le guerre* I'll have you cold, mate," he said stepping between Ketch and Atkins and going to-to-toe with the corporal.

"For that you can join him, Evans, you like getting yourself in the shit so much."

Once Ketch had dismissed them and they'd gone off to fetch their tools, Atkins turned to Mercy.

"What up with him? Why's he got it in for me?"

"Ketch? Regular four-letter man he is. He was foreman over at Everson's brewery before the war an' he didn't 'alf lord it over us. Thought he had it cushy 'til old man Everson decided to let the workers form a union, didn't he? Aggravated Ketch no end that did, but there were nowt he could do about it, was there? War broke out, we joined up to get away from the bastard only to find that, as a foreman, he'd been made an NCO. He's worse now than he ever was," Mercy said with a sardonic grin. "He hates everyone and everything."

"Because?"

"Because they are and he's not."

"Not what?"

"Tall, handsome, rich, popular, sergeant, butcher, baker, candlestick maker. Take your pick. But don't worry about him, It's not worth it. Look on the bright side, Sanitation duty stinks but shouldn't take more than a couple of hours," said Mercy with a smile and a wink. "Gives us an easy ride while the others are breaking their backs, don't it?"

PADRE RAND, HAVING left Tulliver with Captain Grantham, escorted the VADs through the trenches drawing curious glances from some of the men as they passed.

"Where are we going?" asked Nellie Abbott.

"To see the Regimental Medical Officer. He's trying to set up a Dressing Station here until we can find a way back to your hospital."

"Looks like you're going to have to find the Somme first," said Nellie chirpily.

Edith bowed her head and smiled privately. She liked this young, tough woman.

"Driver Abbott, you may not be under my direct supervision, but I'll ask you to show some respect to your betters," said Sister Fenton.

Edith saw Nellie bite her lip and flick a dirty look to Sister Fenton and loved her all the more.

"But she's got a point, hasn't she, Sister?" said Edith. "We don't know where we are and that... that creature...."

"It probably escaped from a zoo, or some such, Bell," said Sister Fenton. "Or it's a new kind of attack hound bred by the Hun. I'm sure they're not above doing that sort of thing. Remember poor Belgium?"

They followed a crudely painted sign and turned a corner to find a wide, bombed out shell hole appropriated as a sort of waiting room. Dozens and dozens of men sat about listlessly. Some bandaged, some staring vacantly ahead. Others lay on stretchers, still and lifeless. The group worked their way through the crowd of men, who parted quietly, politely, until the nurses came to a lean-to structure made from timber, corrugated iron and sandbags.

"Captain Lippett?" enquired Padre Rand.

A man, late thirties, with slickly oiled hair and a small pair of pince-nez sat on his nose, dressed in shirt sleeves and braces, wearing a blood-stained apron, looked up from a bare-chested, pale skinned man, whose arm wound he was cleaning. "Padre. If you've coming looking for work there's plenty. Many of these men will die today. I haven't the time or the facilities to deal with them here. I've got a large percentage bleeding from eyes, ears and nose. Never seen anything like it. Damned if I know what's caused it. Been tellin' 'em it was the gas. Seems to keep 'em quiet for a while. Tompkins," he called to a nearby orderly, "dress this man's wounds. Bloody lucky there, Private."

"Light duties, Doc?" the man asked weakly.

"For you? Yes, I'd say so."

The man could barely disguise his smile as the orderly led him away.

"Actually, I've brought you some help," said the padre.

Captain Lippett turned to look at the women over the top of his glasses. He obviously wasn't pleased with what he saw. He hurriedly took the padre by the arm and dragged him away. There seemed to be a heated discussion going on between them. Edith made out the words "Women!" several times. It was clear that the MO didn't approve of their being there, but here they were and there was nothing to be done about it. In the end the officer threw up his hands in submission and returned to the nurses.

"Well, if you're so put out, Captain, I'd be obliged if you could just arrange transport back to the hospital," said Sister Fenton.

"Sister, I have absolutely no idea what's going on. And it would seem motor ambulances, or indeed transport back to anywhere, is beyond us at the moment. In the meantime, however, we have many injured men here and, while I believe that this is no place for a woman, frankly I could use your help."

Which was about as much apology as they were going to get. Nellie was set to sterilising equipment and finding bandages, while Sister Fenton assisted the MO with the more serious cases. Edith was assigned the duty of helping MO orderlies assessing and treating the crowd of walking wounded. She cast her eyes around the crater. There were so many of them waiting around stoically and the stretcher bearers were bringing more. There was a sudden rush as the more ambulatory felt they would rather be treated by a woman than the rough hands of Privates Tompkins and Stanton.

A soldier with a bandaged head caught Edith's attention, or rather, his grin did. She beckoned him over. He shuffled over humbly, steel helmet in hand, dirty bandages covering his head, and sat down on an ammunition crate.

"Ain't you a sight for sore eyes?" he said. "We don't ever get nurses this far up the line. I must have died and gone to heaven," he said.

"Any more talk like that and you'll wish you had," she said firmly as she began unwinding the bandage from around his head. She gently eased the dressing off his wound. He winced. Edith uncovered the now scabbing furrow on his temple. The wound, at least, seemed clean.

"My name's George. George Hopkiss, but my mates call me Porgy," he said. "Guess why?"

"I can't imagine," she said, keeping her business-like demeanour, working intently on his wound, feeling herself blush.

"Kiss the girls and make 'em cry, don't I?"

"Well that's not much of a recommendation, is it?"

"Do you fancy walking out with me down Broughton Street tonight?"

"Shhh. Or Sister will hear!"

"She can come too, if she likes," he grinned.

"Now, now I'll have none of that. I'll have you know I'm a respectable lady."

"Oh, I don't doubt it."

"I was a debutante. I was presented at Court before the war."

"You don't say! Cor, That's as good as Royalty to me. Fancy!" said Porgy amazed, trying to turn round, but she took his head in her hands and gently, but firmly turned him back to face front.

"Oh yes," she said as she carried on cleaning the burned and torn flesh. "So don't forget with whom you're dealing! I have friends in high places." She dabbed the iodine on and Porgy stiffened, sucking in a sharp breath.

"Let that be a lesson to you," she said. She wondered if it sounded too playful and improper.

"I knows me place," he said, touching his forelock, mockingly. Edith gently pushed him on his shoulder.

"*You*. Now you're teasing."

"Nurse Bell!" barked Sister Fenton. "When you've *quite* finished fraternising with that jackanapes there are other men waiting for your attention!"

Edith felt her face burn as she reached for a gauze pad. "Hold this," she told him as she placed it over his wound.

"Sorry, Miss," said Porgy. She began wrapping crepe bandage around his head. "Not too much," he said, "otherwise I won't be able to fit me battle bowler on."

"I've a feeling your head's way too big for it anyway," she said with a smile. "Away with you."

EVERSON REACHED THE makeshift Headquarters. It was dug back into the side of a trench; all salvaged beams, corrugated iron and tarpaulins. News of the death of the major hadn't taken long to filter down through the Company and the men had taken it quite hard, especially as the next in command was Captain Grantham. To be truthful he didn't have much faith in the new Skipper himself. Captain Grantham shouldn't even have been at the Front. He'd had some cushy job back at Battalion, but he'd probably whined and groused about a Front Line position, wanting to see a bit of action just so that he could say he'd been there before returning to his nice desk job in the rear. Now, for better or worse, they were stuck with him.

"Is this it?" Everson asked, stepping inside and looking around despondently. "Is this all of us?"

It was dispiriting how few officers were left. There was Slacke, the company quartermaster sergeant, Padre Rand and Captain Lippett, the MO and Captain Palmer of D Company. Jeffries was sat on a wooden chair, slouching with his legs stretched out in front of him, his chin resting on steepled fingers, glowering blackly, lost in thought. His eyes flicked up as Everson entered, but seeing nothing to interest him, lost focus as he turned back to his own contemplations. Grantham looked up from talking to a Royal Flying Corps officer and an officer with Machine Gun Corps insignia on his uniform.

"Everson," said Captain Grantham. "I'm afraid so."

The Flying Officer looked young, even to Everson. He had blonde hair and there was something about the double breasted tunic and that RFC wing on the left breast that just looked so—dashing. Everson felt a pang of jealousy. Here he was caked in mud, dog-tired and aching to his very bones and here was a handsome young man seemingly unmarked by the terrors of war; an 'angel face' he believed they called it.

"James Tulliver, RFC," he said, turning, extending a hand and jerking his head in Jeffries' direction. "Who's that louche chap over there, I'm sure I know him. Hibbert, is it?"

"Jeffries, Platoon Commander, 4 Platoon, C Company."

"Jeffries?" said Tulliver, mulling the name over. "Oh. Are you sure? No, of course you are. Sorry, my fault. Thought he was someone else."

"I often wish he was," said Everson.

The other man turned too. Tall and lanky, he had dark circles under his eyes and a greasy pallid look to his skin. His uniform hung on him as if it were a size too big.

"Mathers, Machine Gun Corps, Heavy Section."

"Ah, the Tank Commander," said Everson. "Good show. You saved some of my men out there today," he added, gripping the proffered hand. He was disappointed to find the grip a little weak and clammy. "So what the devil's going on, d'y'think?"

"Hmm," said Mathers. He closed his eyes and rubbed his temples. "Sorry. Damned headache."

"Gentlemen?" said Grantham, bringing the meeting to order. The officers gathered round the rickety table covered with maps. "Casualty Reports?"

"We weren't up to full strength to begin with. Out of nine hundred and twelve officers and men, we had already lost twelve officers and two hundred and forty eight other ranks to German fire and gas, and we lost two officers and fifty-eight other ranks from shock of transport here. We have a further two officers and twenty seven other ranks killed by those creatures. There are three hundred and seventy wounded, some critically, most walking and nine suffering from severe shell-shock. In short, gentlemen, you're down to less than two hundred able-bodied men at the moment, barely a Company."

Seven. Seven officers left, thought Everson.

"We need to get the wounded to a Casualty Clearing Station," said Lippett, "I don't have the means to deal with them here."

"Well, Mr Tulliver here doesn't seem to think that's going be, ah, possible," said Grantham nervously.

Lippett peered at Tulliver from under his eyebrows in a way that reminded Everson of his old schoolmaster.

"That's right, sir," said Tulliver. "I'm afraid there *is* no Casualty Clearing Station to go to. I explained to Captain Grantham earlier, we're completely cut off. *This* is all that's left," he said, pointing to the pencilled circle on the map. The other officers leaned in to look. "The rest of the area outside the circle no longer seems to exist. You've all seen it. What's out there bears no resemblance to any maps or aerial photographs. It's as if we've been picked up and dropped elsewhere entirely."

"But the world can't just disappear!" muttered Grantham.

"Perhaps it didn't," said Everson. "Maybe *we* did."

"Preposterous!" agreed Lippett.

"You've seen it for yourself," said Jeffries sternly. "How can you doubt it?"

"Some of the men have suggested it's Paradise," said Padre Rand.

"Are you trying to say that we're all dead and this is some blasted afterlife?" said Grantham. Everson tried to ignore the tremor in his voice.

"Well, I certainly wouldn't say so after meeting those hell hounds earlier," said Mathers.

"Some think we're dead, yes," continued the padre. "Some men have been saying it's Africa."

"Well, something, I have no idea what, has brought us here, wherever *here* is," said Everson. "There's no reason to think it might not snap us back to the Somme at any moment, like an Indian Rubber band."

"And if not?" asked Grantham. "What then? We have no line of communication, our supply line ends several hundred yards to our rear. If Tulliver is to be believed you can't ring up Battalion and ask for another truck load of Maconochies and Plum and Apple to be sent up. We can expect no replacements and no relief. What on earth do you suggest we do?"

"Survive," said Everson. "Survive until we return home."

"An admirable sentiment, Everson," said Jeffries. "but what if we don't return home?"

"We'll find a way. That's what hope is all about. 'If the mountain won't come to Mohammed, then Mohammed must go to the mountain.' Isn't that how the saying goes?"

"Very prosaic," said Jeffries. "But platitudes won't save us. What if there isn't a way? What if this," he said, gesturing at the foreign landscape beyond the tarpaulin, "is it?"

The discussion degenerated into a babble of voices and opinions, each seeking to be heard. Jeffries stood back and smiled to himself as if pleased with the discord he had sown.

"Gentlemen, please!" cried Grantham, but he was unable to bring any kind of order to the debate.

Jeffries leaned forward and began whispering quietly into his ear. Grantham pinched the bridge of his nose between thumb and forefinger. For a moment Everson thought the man had found an ounce of gumption.

"Mr Jeffries, what is your opinion?"

Jeffries drew himself up and glanced at the men one by one. They fell silent. He took a moment before he spoke, to make sure he held their attention. "It is my belief that we are no longer on Earth at all."

Over in the corner CQS Slacke barely stifled a snort of derision. Jeffries ignored it and pressed on. "One, the sun is slightly larger than we know our sun to be. Also, we attacked Harcourt Wood at dawn mere hours ago. The sun is now sinking towards the horizon. Two, the temperature here owes more to the tropics than to winter in France. Thirdly, those creatures that attacked us exist in no bestiary I'm aware of. And fourthly, my compass." He shoved his brass compass onto the table. The needle swung round and round indecisively. "North seems to be everywhere."

"Then where the deuce are we?" said Lippett.

"I have no more idea than you, Captain," said Jeffries, "but Everson is right in one respect…"

Startled by his name, Everson looked up and found Jeffries regarding him curiously.

"Something, it seems, has snatched us up and delivered us here. As to how and why, well, I wonder if we'll ever know," mused Jeffries. "However you may be sure that there are things in this universe, gentlemen, of which you have no conception, no conception at all."

"So what do we do now?" asked Grantham.

"I suggest an inventory of all rations, supplies and equipment," said Slacke.

"For the moment we should keep to Standing Orders, sir," said Palmer. "Confine the men to the trenches just in case, as Everson says, we should be returned as abruptly as we arrived."

"So that's your answer? We stay on this charnel pit on the off-chance we should be catapulted back to France?" Lippett said.

"Which is fine in the short term," said Everson. "But if supplies start running low we shall have to find water and food. We need to find out about this world if we are to survive it. We should think about sending out scouting parties."

"And what happens should we get snapped back to the Somme while they're out? What will happened to the those left behind?" said Padre Rand.

The men around the table fell silent as they ruminated on the possibility of their being marooned under such circumstances. It was a fate nobody wanted to contemplate.

"Padre," said Grantham. "I think it would be a good idea to arrange a church parade for tomorrow. I think the men could use your moral guidance and faith right now."

The Chaplain looked startled. "Er, certainly Captain."

"Captain," Jeffries urged Grantham. "*You* should address the men.

They need to be told *something*. We must keep up morale and quell any thought of desertion or mutiny. A few words from you, sir, would help."

Grantham slumped into a chair, completely overwhelmed by the situation. His eyes searched the floor of the dugout as if they might find the answer there. "I don't know. What the hell can I say?"

Everson swore under his breath. Grantham was funking it. And what was Jeffries' game? He seemed to have made a good job of undermining Grantham while appearing to support him. After Grantham, as the next senior officer left in line, command would fall to Jeffries himself. If something wasn't done this whole situation would turn into a bigger disaster than it already was. The men needed leadership. Now.

"Sir!" said Everson, rather more sharply than he had intended. Grantham started. "Whatever you're going to tell the men, tell them quickly. The sun is setting and we'll need them to Stand To. God alone knows what else is out there."

Grantham looked up and nodded wearily. "Of course," he said. "Order the men on parade."

"MEN!" BEGAN CAPTAIN Grantham. He was stood on an old ammo box, Everson, Jeffries, Lippett and the padre standing in the mud behind him as a show of unity. "As you know from our current troubles we face a predicament the like of which the Pennines have never faced before. There is a rumour that this is some kind of hallucination or afterlife and that your fighting days are over. I am here to tell you that they are not. You took the King's shilling, made the oath and signed up for the duration, the *duration*, gentlemen, and as such you are still soldiers in the King's Army. We are still at war. Any insubordination under the present circumstances will be dealt with severely. Standing Orders are still in effect and all men are confined to the trenches. If we are to get through this we must all pull together. I am informed that the world around us may not even be Earth, but we have faced adversity in foreign climes before and triumphed and we shall do so again. We do anticipate an eventual return to Blighty but, as the Pennines, we know that there's always a long hard climb before we reach the top. But reach it we will, so we must bear our current troubles with fortitude. Onward and Upwards, the Pennines!"

The men cheered and waved their helmets in the air. It was half-hearted, but, nevertheless, Grantham seemed pleased with the response. It wasn't the most rousing speech Everson had heard, but nobody expected much of Grantham. It would be left to the subalterns and NCOs to pick up the pieces. Oblivious, Grantham smiled magnanimously. Enjoying the brief moment, he spoke out of the corner of his mouth to his poker-faced staff. "Come on, smile boys, *that's* the style."

CHAPTER SEVEN
"The Evening Hate"

THE SUN BEGAN to set. The fact that perhaps it wasn't *their* sun was only just beginning to dawn on the soldiers. 2 Platoon were stood to on the fire-steps of their trench as they had stood dozens of times before; rifles, bayonets fixed, resting on the parapets, one in the spout, ready to repel any attack. Though from what, they had no idea. If the hell hounds earlier were a taste of what this place had to offer, it was going to be a long night.

Atkins stood in his bay with Gazette and Ginger. Porgy, Gutsy and Mercy manned the bay to their left. Beyond them were Captain Grantham, 1 Platoon and a flanking Vickers machine gun post. To their right was a second machine gun emplacement and the remains of 3 and 4 Platoons, under Lieutenant Jeffries. Atkins didn't envy Pot Shot, Lucky and Half Pint. They'd drawn the short straw and were twenty yards further out in the forward observation post in No Man's Land.

"Psst!" It was Ginger. Atkins tried to ignore him. "Psst!"

"What?" Atkins flicked his eyes from his rifle barrel. Ginger grinned at him and lowered his eyes towards his own tunic. Atkins followed the glance. There, peeking out the top of Ginger's shirt, was Haig, his pet rat. Ginger looked absurdly pleased with himself and started making *chtching* noises into his chest.

"Bloody hell, Ginger," Atkins rolled his eyes, a smile flickering at the edge of his lips as he returned to his vigil. Hunkered in the distance the nearby forest seemed as impenetrable as the old Hun line. The noises emanating from it changed as the sun sank, becoming wilder and more guttural as if the night signalled the onset of some feral reverie. He shivered involuntarily. The howls and chatterings played on his nerves more keenly than the never-ending drum roll of artillery barrages ever had. By comparison the abrupt ferocity of Whizz-Bangs, Jack Johnsons and Woolly Bears were as comforting as a home-fire.

More unsettling though was the evening breeze. He was so used to the smell of gangrene and feet, of shell hole mud and corpse liquor, of cordite and overflowing latrines, that the eddies of warm, damp wind caught him by surprise, bringing with them, as they did, brief intoxicating respites to his deadened senses. Tied as he was to his post, fleeting siren zephyrs of air laden with captivating scents danced lightly around him, allowing him snatches of exotic perfumes or heady animal musks; the ephemeral aromas tempting and teasing, offering a world beyond imagination.

There, that note. He closed his eyes and inhaled gently, afraid the scent would evaporate before he could savour it, it was like... like Lily of the Valley—Flora, that last night. They'd been to see the latest Charlie Chaplin at the Broughtonthwaite Alhambra. She was laughing. The cobbles—the cobbles were slick with rain, the faint smell of hops from Everson's Brewery hung in the night air. Her foot slipped on the greasy sets as they crossed the road and she'd linked her arm through his to steady herself. She chattered on about Old Mother Murphy, young Jessie in the end terrace and Mr Wethering at Mafeking Street School but he didn't hear her.

He'd known Flora forever. They'd sparked clogs and scabbed knees together as nippers in the same back alleys. They'd lived two streets apart their whole lives but she'd never really looked at him that way until he'd got the khaki on.

"You look ever so handsome in your uniform, Thomas."

"Get away!" he said, dismissively, then: "Really? Well, it's a bit on the large side and these trousers don't half itch, but if you ask the Company Quart—"

"Sssh." She put a finger to his lips.

She was so close he could smell her hair, the scent of her perfume—Lily of the Valley—the brief scent vanished and the familiar fug of war and corruption closed about him once more.

Raucous cries rang overhead as furred creatures with long necks, leathery wings and hooked beaks flocked into the sky from somewhere in the hills, congregating over the muddy sea of the battlefield. They dived and banked with rasping calls, like gulls in the wake of a fishing trawler, tempted by the human harvest of No Man's Land.

From somewhere down the line a couple of shots went off into the flock followed by the sharp, scolding bark of an NCO. The shooting ceased.

Atkins shifted his body uneasily against the wooden planking of the revetment and wiped his sweat-slick hands on his thighs before repositioning the stock of his rifle more snugly against his shoulder. He looked out again across the landscape of mud and wire towards the forest. He hated this time of day; as the light failed, shifting shadows played tricks on the eyes. It seemed to him that whatever gloom slunk sullenly in the forest was now flowing sinuously from it.

"What else is out there, d'y reckon?" he wondered. "I'm hoping for wild women myself."

"Don't know, but a target's a target," replied Gazette, his eye never leaving his rifle's sight. It was clear he had his 'business' head on. "It's either alive or dead."

"Yeah, either way, Porgy'd probably make a pass at it, eh?"

Gazette didn't reply.

"Never thought I'd miss Fritz," said Atkins. "At least with 'im you knew what to expect; the odd Minniewerfer or Five Nine. You knew where you were."

"Reckon you'll have cause to be even more nostalgic by the time the night's out," said Gazette. That was Gazette—a real barrel of laughs, but you didn't have him round for his sparkling repartee. He was the sharpest shooter in the platoon, so you forgave him the odd lapse in manners.

Ginger was no company at all, either. He whimpered and patted absent-mindedly at his tunic. The squeaking from inside it grew more frantic and agitated. As Ginger fumbled to catch his wretched rat his rifle slipped from his grasp. It landed heavily, butt first, on the duckboards. Atkins flinched but it didn't go off.

"Fuck's sake, pick your gun up y'daft sod. If Ketch catches you, that's 'casting away your arms in the presence of the enemy,'" Gazette hissed, his eyes never leaving the darkening landscape.

Ginger ignored them and carried on wittering and cooing to Haig.

"Shhh. Ginger. Button it!" Atkins' brow creased, he cocked his head. "Gazette, you hear that?"

From out in the mud came a desperate scrabbling sound, like a drowning soldier trying to claw his way out of a slurry-filled shell hole.

"Just some poor injured sod out in No Man's Land. Usually is. That or one of them hell hounds from this afternoon caught on the wire. Either way, be dead by morning."

A scream went up from the forward observation post but it was stifled, drowned out by thousands of shrieking squeaks and the splatter of countless feet. In the fading light the mud itself seemed to ripple like a mirage. But it was no illusion.

From further up the line, the sound of surprised yelps, the discharge of rifles, spattered bursts of machine gun fire leapt from bay to bay towards them.

Alert, Gazette altered his stance almost imperceptibly, shifting his centre of gravity, bracing to absorb the anticipated kick of his Enfield.

"What is it?" Atkins asked.

Gazette just shrugged. He either didn't know, or didn't care.

Ginger shuffled about on the firestep as Haig skittered around inside his clothes, squealing, while his arms flailed and contorted trying to reach his ersatz pet. He pirouetted clumsily. Atkins tried to grab his webbing but Ginger tumbled from the firestep, falling awkwardly and cracking his head on the sodden duckboards, writhing and screaming as the rat seemed to bite and claw at him inside his clothing.

"Jesus! Shut him up!" snapped Gazette.

Atkins jumped down and clamped his hand over Ginger's mouth.

"Keep quiet, you silly sod. You'll end up getting us all killed if not up on a bloody charge!" Atkins was astride his chest now, a hand clamped over his mouth, trying to keep eye contact with the thrashing soldier, to calm him somehow, all the while trying to undo his tunic and shirt buttons one handed in order to free the damned rat.

"Ginger, calm down, mate. Stop it! It's me, Only."

Ginger's eyes bulged and he tried to scream, but it was muffled by Atkins' hand. Ginger sank his teeth into the skin between the thumb and forefinger.

"Agh, y'bastard!" Atkins snatched his hand away. Ginger bucked under him.

There was a sudden volley of unintelligible oaths from Gutsy's bay next door.

"Only!" said Gazette. "Only! Get up here!"

As Atkins looked up Ginger arched his back, turned his head awkwardly to see down the traverse and screamed. Racing round the corner and tumbling pell-mell towards them, over the parapets and channelled by the trenches, came a stampede of thousands of panic-stricken corpse rats scrabbling and scrambling over each other, driven headlong in a frenzy through the fire bays by something out in No Man's Land, something that had alarmed them enough to flee their cosy cadavers in droves. Not even the artillery shells had ever moved them like this before.

"Jesus!"

Atkins instinctively gulped a mouthful of air and drew his arms up over his head in a desperate attempt to protect himself as the routed rats swarmed over him. Their urgent piping squeals filled his ears as they covered him in a heaving wave of mud, blood and viscera-matted fur. Myriad cold paws scratched and scuffled exposed flesh; clumsy legs and feet finding his mouth, ears or nose while the acrid tang of voided rats' piss left him spluttering and nauseous.

And then they were gone, the verminous tide receding, washing over 3 and 4 Platoon's positions to yells of consternation.

Gasping and spitting filth from his mouth Atkins cautiously lifted his head. Ginger was still on the duckboards, curled into a foetal position, sniffling and whimpering, a damp warm patch darkening his khaki trousers.

"Gilbert the Filbert'll feel right at home among that lot," said

Gazette. He was impassively inspecting three of the buggers he'd managed to impale on his bayonet. "Three with one blow. That's a dugout record, is that."

"He's gone," Ginger said with a snivel, patting his torso. "Haig's gone."

"Yeah, well good riddance," said Gazette scraping the rats off his bayonet on the edge of the step. "Here, Only, give us a hand." He stood his rifle against the revetment, stepped down, grabbed Ginger by his webbing straps and hauled him to his feet. Atkins picked up Ginger's rifle and put it back in his hands.

"Look, I know your rat's gone. Looks like they've all gone, frankly and good bloody riddance. But if you don't get back on the step, Ketch'll do for you, got it?"

Ginger sniffed, wiped his nose with the cuff of his tunic and nodded sullenly.

"Sorry. Sorry, Only."

Atkins straightened his battle bowler for him and helped him up onto the step.

"Good lad."

The sun was almost gone now. The dark velvet blue of night advanced relentlessly, overwhelming the last crimson smears of retreating dusk; a salvo of stars pock-marking its wake in the night sky.

Atkins had always found some measure of comfort in the constancy of the stars, but not tonight. Tonight, he couldn't find a single constellation that he recognised. And no moon either, nothing but a faint trace of reddish gas trailing across the firmament. Disconcerted, Atkins shifted his gaze back down to Earth, or what there was left of it.

"What was that all about? Never seen 'em act like that before."

"They're rats. Who knows?" said Gazette.

"Something scared 'em."

"You do surprise me."

"Something out there. The bodies in No Man's Land are going to attract every scavenger and predator for miles around."

"You may have a point," said Gazette. "But I've got this," he added patting his rifle. "And I'll put my faith in this any day over anything you think may or may not be out there."

They'd been here less than twenty-four hours. From what Atkins had seen of this place whatever was out there was probably far worse than anything he could imagine or, more worryingly, something he *couldn't* imagine.

"Everything all right here, men?"

Lieutenant Everson came round the traverse into the bay, Webley revolver in his hand.

"You mean apart from the rats, sir?" said Atkins.

"Yes, apart from the rats, Atkins."

"Yes, sir," Atkins managed a perfunctory smile. "Leaving the sinking ship, d'y'think, sir?"

"Sorry?"

"The rats, sir. Leaving the sinking ship?"

"Well I wouldn't put it quite like that, Atkins, but I'm certainly not going to miss the buggers if they really have gone."

Ginger stifled a sob in the crook of his elbow.

"Is he—is he all right?" said Everson with a jerk of his head in Ginger's direction, his voice tinged with concern.

"Mottram, sir?" said Gazette. "Yes sir, just got the wind up, sir, that's all. He'll be fine."

Atkins wasn't so sure but Everson didn't seem to want to press the point.

"Very well. Any idea who Hobson put in the OP?"

"Jellicoe, Livesey and Nicholls, sir," said Atkins.

"Right. Better check in with them. No doubt Nicholls will have something to complain about. Keep your wits about you." Everson slipped round the next traverse and was gone.

Somewhere out in the dark, where the Somme mud met alien soil, the fading pitiful squeals of the rats were met by the snarls and growls of unseen predators.

Atkins' tried not to listen, humming a few bars of 'I Want To Go Home' under his breath. He stopped as he felt, rather than heard, the noise; a deep bass note that thrummed against his chest and vibrated the soles of his feet through his hobnailed boots.

Dull alarms began jangling in No Man's Land; tin cans containing pebbles that hung from the wire rattled out their beggar-like warnings, the cries from the injured and dying stranded in shell holes rising to a crescendo.

From either flank of the line, bursts of machine gun fire opened up in reply. Each machine gun post was positioned so that it could lay enfilading fire *along* the lengths of wire entanglement. They had been laid in an extremely shallow 'V' out in front of the fire trenches so, even at night, once the wire alarms had been set off they had every expectation of hitting whatever it was that had set them off.

From Captain Grantham's position over in the centre of the line came the *phut* of a Very pistol as a flare arced up into the night sky. Atkins, Ginger and Gazette bobbed instinctively below the lines of the sandbags as it burst with a *whuuff* high over the battlefield, illuminating the scene with the stark white brilliance of a photographer's flash powder.

Atkins wished it hadn't.

About fifty yards out half a dozen great, glistening wet worm-like creatures, thicker than a man was tall and some thirty yards long, had broken the surface of the grey-churned mud, like land whales. Atkins could see no eyes, but long probing tentacles quested the air around facial sphincters that contracted and relaxed to reveal barbed gullets. No sound issued from their gaping, clenching maws as they set about scooping the dead and decomposing into their pouting orifices, grazing like elephants, lifting food into their mouths, or else dragging the corpses down into the vermiculate earth. From the terrified yells and sobs it was clear that it wasn't just the dead they were taking.

All along the fire trenches soldiers champed at the bit, wanting to shoot but constrained by orders.

The Very light went out. Another shot up into the sky from the observation post, burning whitely.

"C'mon, give the order," muttered Atkins, a finger playing restlessly on his SMLE's magazine cut-off.

Sergeant Hobson's voice rang out. "Five rounds rapid. Fire!"

"About bloody time," muttered Atkins as he flicked open the cut-off, took aim and fired before cycling the bolt and putting another cartridge into the receiver. He took aim, fired again, cycled once more.

Along the trench tattered bursts of rifle fire raked across the alien worms.

Trench mortars popped and flew into the air, arcing out into No Man's Land.

Beside Atkins, Gazette was in his element now. Calmly, surely, he fired off his shots, taking his time, making each bullet count. Ginger on the other hand had completely lost it and was huddled on the firestep, by Atkins' legs, his arms cradling his knees to his chest, sobbing and shaking uncontrollably.

The Very light went out again but the ungodly wet suction noises and weakening screams continued unabated. Another Very light went up from the observation post.

The worms were closer now. One reared up over the observation post itself. An officer, it must have been Lieutenant Everson, fired the Very pistol almost at point blank range. The flare shot up leaving a brief white trail before embedding itself in the hide of the creature where it continued to burn with a white-hot fury, causing it to thrash about in voiceless agony, its tentacles flailing helplessly. Some agent in its mucus coating, or subcutaneous fatty layer, must have been flammable for, under the intense heat of the flare, the great worm began to burn like a wick. Its bulk crashed down into the mud—right on top of the observation post.

"Everson's bought it," said Gazette, matter of factly.

"Are you kidding?" said Atkins. "Lucky's out there. He'll see 'em all right."

"Thruppence says they're landowners now."

"Thruppence says they ain't," said Atkins, spitting on his palm. Gazette shook his hand, barely taking his eye from his rifle sight.

With the landscape now dimly illuminated by the burning carcass Atkins could make out the other worm creatures. One rippled over to the burning body, reaching out its tentacles, but was driven back by the heat of the flames. It raised its head up as if giving a great call, arched its body and dived into the ground. The others followed.

A ragged cheer rose from the trenches.

"They're going!"

The elation didn't last long. Thirty feet from the line one of the great worms broke out of the mud, ploughing toward the fire trench with a fluid peristaltic motion, through the troughs of shell holes and the crests of their craters, heedless of the twenty yard length of barbed wire entanglement it had ripped from the ground in its sinuous advance, and which was now hanging from its body.

Men who had seen comrades blown to so much meat, who had stoically suffered days of continuous bombardment, who had risked death every day, found it hard not to flee in the face of such a monstrous vision.

The command came again. "Fire!"

As Gazette took aim, carefully squeezing the trigger and firing off five more rounds at the monstrous creature before them, Atkins felt the ground beneath him tremble and the revetment against his chest begin to creak and strain. Sandbags tumbled into the trench from the parados behind them. He and Gazette glanced at each other.

"You don't think—"

"Thinking's for officers. Run!"

They slung their rifles over their shoulders and jumped back off the fire step as the revetment begin to splinter under a great wave of pressure building up from below. Ginger remained sobbing on the step, oblivious or incapable of reacting as plank after plank behind him burst free of its frame.

"Shit!"

A hand under each armpit Atkins and Gazette dragged him off the firestep and round the corner into the traverse. Barely had they vacated the fire bay before it erupted behind them in a shower of dirt, dust and splinters as another worm burst up through the trench.

Probing tentacles appeared around the corner of the traverse. One caught hold of Ginger's ankle and pulled, tugging Atkins and Gazette off balance as the screaming man was dragged back towards the shattered fire bay. Atkins unslung his rifle and thrust his bayonet into the tentacle, pinning it to the ground, and fired, point blank range, severing the member. The other feelers let go of Ginger and retracted back round the corner, the lopped pseudopod trailing a dark viscous slime behind it.

Gazette grabbed Ginger by the scruff of the neck as he and Atkins half-scrambled, half-stumbled with him into the next fire bay where Gutsy, Porgy and Mercy were laying down covering fire as the wounded worm reared up. They kept it up as Atkins and Gazette retreated round the far corner to the adjacent traverse and the next fire bay, held by Sergeant Hobson and Corporal Ketch.

There they dropped Ginger to the duckboards and took aim at the mindless monster as it blindly sought for its attackers. Gutsy, Porgy and Mercy, abandoning their own position, fell back and joined them, as Gazette and Atkins in return gave them covering fire. Gazette had fired his five rounds and was reloading from a pouch on his webbing, while Atkins was still chambering and firing his third as the great worm, flinching under the hail of bullets, sought a way forward. It fell back from sight, retreating into the ground from which it had come.

Atkins spied a bandolier of grenades on the firestep. "Gazette, cover me!" he yelled, snatching up the bandolier. He dashed forward to their ruined fire bay where he saw the tentacles of the beast vanish as it retreated back into the dark earth. He looked briefly into the darkness of the hole in the side of the trench as he opened the pouches on the bandoleer. He took out the string from his pocket and threaded through the ring pulls of about half a dozen grenades. Holding one end of the string in his hand he tossed the bandoleer into the hole. Left holding nothing but the piece of string and its collection of grenade pins he threw himself to one side. Seconds later the grenades went off with a muted roar. The ground heaved and the hole erupted with smoke and fire as torn and shredded flesh shot out of it.

Atkins picked himself up from the mud, his ears ringing with the high pitch buzzing of the concussion. Helping hands pulled him to his feet as Porgy and Mercy dragged him clear. Smoke drifted from the collapsed tunnel. The ringing in his ears distanced him from the scene around him. He was thankful for the brief respite as he could no longer hear the screams of pain and the cries of terror. Only faintly, as if from a great depth, could he hear the tattoo of the guns as the Tommies drove the worms back into the ground.

JEFFRIES WAS BARELY aware of the explosion. The sight of the creatures held him spellbound. He had read of such things in texts older than the regiment itself, but never expected to see them. "Shaitan," he murmured under his breath as he watched them harvest the dead and dying out in No Man's Land. "Messenger of Croatoan. It's a sign." He climbed the ladder and stood, exposed, on the sandbag parapet, arms flung wide in supplication.

"Sir!" hissed Dixon, his platoon sergeant. "Sir, get down!"

One of the giant worms burst up through the sodden ground half a dozen yards from the trench. It opened its maw, pseudopods flailing. Jeffries stood his ground and stared down the barbed throat.

He was vaguely aware of Everson stumbling down the sap from the observation post, his arms around one man's shoulder as they helped each other along the narrow ginnel. Two others followed on behind, all four of them covered in mud and slime.

"Jeffries, for God's sake, man! Are you mad?" he called, reaching for the Very pistol in his belt. There was a dull click and a *whoof* as something rushed past Jefferies' head. A Very flare ricocheted off a failing tentacle and skittered down the creature's length before whirling across the mud and into a shell hole. The great worm veered away from it and plunged back into the earth. However the encounter was enough to convince Jeffries. He turned jubilantly and jumped down onto the firestep.

"Everson," he said, "you might have been right."

"Right?" said Everson quizzically. "About what? What did I say? Jeffries!"

But Jeffries was already strolling down the fire trench, elated.

The great worms, it seemed, had retreated, beaten back by the firepower of the Battalion. The relief along the line was almost tangible. There were exultant, if weary, cheers as the last of the creatures retreated into the earth under the burning glare of another flare.

Slowly the concussive ringing in Atkins' ears faded to be overwhelmed by the rising tide of groans and screams from those in No Man's Land.

He plugged his ears with his fingers as if trying to restore the blissful distance granted to him by the explosion, wishing the cries would cease and hating himself for it. The screams continued all night, though none would venture from the trenches to lend aid or succour, the cries gnawing relentlessly at each man's conscience. Those that could survive out there until morning might have a chance.

Atkins' guilt threatened to rise up and choke him. Had William died like that, slowly, alone in agony and fear with no one willing to help? If he was truthful even that wasn't what bothered him. What bothered Atkins was the unspoken thought that somewhere, deep down, he hoped his brother was dead.

CHAPTER EIGHT
"In Different Skies…"

OVER THE NEXT few days a broken telegraph pole was erected to serve as a makeshift flagpole. Hanging from it, not proudly and defiantly, but limply, fluttered a dirty and ragged Union flag. It seemed to reflect the worn, exhausted mood of the men who wandered aimlessly about beneath it, devoid of any great purpose now the battlefield in which they toiled had ceased to exist. However, the veneer of normality was maintained, as it always was, in the most damning and ignominious of circumstances. Or perhaps because of it, because of the sheer scale of it.

The battalion fell back on a comfortably familiar routine despite their unfamiliar surroundings. The physical labour and variety of the fatigues reassured the men, keeping them occupied and busy. In Kitchener's Army there was never any shortage of tasks.

Captain Grantham had forbidden anyone to leave the sodden circle of Somme. It was all that now remained for them of the world they knew as home, blighting the fresh green landscape around them like a canker, an unutterably dark stain on their souls, made visible. For Jeffries that wasn't too far from the truth. Jeffries, who was technically now next in command being a full lieutenant, feeling constrained for the moment by orders he had no compunction to obey, began seeking more signs and portents. The molten rage he felt at the ritual's failure was, thanks to the sight of the giant worms, even now being forged into cold, hard intent. And he was given to wandering to the far edge of the mud pack and peering out into the unknown land.

It was something many of the other ranks did when not working. Egged on by pals, a few daring or stupid ones had tried scrambling down the mud banks onto the verdant foreign plain, wading out into the green tubular fronds and turning to wave at their friends, only to be snatched away with a scream by the hell hounds that still loped about perilously near. That put a stop to such expeditions. Those that didn't get eaten alive were just as quickly chewed up and spat out by equally voracious NCOs.

Not that many wanted to leave the confines of their claustrophobic muddy trenches, for there, at least, was a sense of familiarity and belonging. There, among the avenues, streets and homes they'd carved and burrowed for themselves they shared a commonality of purpose, of experience, of comradeship that no one back home could, would or should understand. The fear that it might suddenly vanish in an instant, returning to France without them, leaving them stranded, was more than incentive enough to keep most in line. Battle Police and Field Punishments did for the rest.

With the aid of several privates Lieutenant Tulliver wheeled his aeroplane onto the drying mud flat in order to protect it from the indigenous life that seemed to be gaining in courage by the day.

Swamped in his Aid Post, Captain Lippett, with the help of the nurses, began to set up a Casualty Clearing Station on the open ground above, behind the support trenches, using what they could to erect makeshift bivouacs. There they found themselves having to deal with a new kind of shell-shock victim, ones who could not deal with the new reality they now faced.

The tank crew didn't really fraternise with the other soldiers, preferring to keep themselves to themselves; the secrecy of their training had been drilled into them and was not easily relinquished. They slept in bivvies alongside their machine, politely declining to mix with the others, happy in their own company and in allowing their commander, Mathers, to speak for them. This was not to say they were unfriendly, merely guarded. The landship created a great deal of interest among the infantry men and, when brief moments between work arose, whole platoons would gather round examining the great armoured war beast, circling it and expressing their approval with low whistles and amazed shakes of the head. While pleased with the attention lavished on it, the tank's crew guarded its secrets enviously, like priests at a shrine, and requests for a ride or a look inside were politely, if firmly, declined.

The length of the day was timed. It came to twenty-two hours. The night sky offered up no clue to their whereabouts, other than it was no sky they recognised. Whatever myths might have drawn its constellations, they were none they knew, so some men began sketching their own; 'The Pickelhaub,' 'Charlie Chaplin,' 'Big Bertha,' 'Little Willie.' The brightest star in the night sky was soon named 'Blighty.'

By day the warm sun began to dry the Somme mud out until it developed a light dry crust that contracted in the heat until it cracked. The decomposing bodies beneath began to rot faster. Foul smelling steams and vapours rose from the flooded shell holes as the fetid liquor within evaporated.

The hell hounds, still drawn by the smell of carcasses, unable to help themselves, slunk forward in ones and twos only to be driven back by sentries' rifle fire.

2 PLATOON WERE on trench fatigues again, working on the stretch of support trench behind the front line. Meant to house off-duty and support troops it needed to be turned around to work as a front line in order to protect their rear. It was a job they were familiar with. Captured German trenches needed such work doing to them in order to make them defensible; changing parados to parapet, cutting new fire steps and laying new wire. The idea here though was to turn the entrenchment into a circular defensible stronghold. It was still an unnatural feeling to stand in the open on the lip of the trench in the full glare of the sun with nothing to fear but sunburn, but the bright warm sunlight eased their brittle nerves a little.

"Bloody rotten job!" said Mercy, sucking fiercely on the end of a fag as he shoved his entrenching spade into the dirt with his foot, seeking to prise loose another spit-worth of claggy mud.

"I'm sure you'd rather be on burial duty," said Ketch, walking towards them as they slung the spoil over the top. "It can be arranged."

Pot Shot put a warning hand on Mercy's shoulder. Mercy grunted and stubbed the butt of his Woodbine out on the damp wall of the trench, grinding it purposefully into the grit, his eyes never leaving Ketch.

"Now put your backs into it! This section of trench is to be finished before dark" he said, before wandering off.

"One of these days," said Porgy, spitting on his palms and gripping his shovel before starting to fill another sandbag. "Burial party? I know it's a bad lot but—"

"It's worse than you think," said Atkins. "Don't tell me you can't smell it?"

"Thought that were Gutsy's feet," said Lucky.

"Oi!" warned Gutsy from where he was leaning against the side of the trench taking a slug from his water canteen.

Ginger, who was on watch, sat on an old ammo box, his eyes nervously darting around the unfamiliar landscape.

"I hope you're keeping your eyes peeled, Ginger. I don't want to become a devil dog's dinner," griped Half Pint.

"Uh huh!" he said, nodding his head.

"He seems to have calmed down a bit in the last few days," said Atkins to Gazette.

But Gazette wasn't listening. At least, not to him.

"Shh!" he said, holding up a hand.

"I wish you'd stop doing that!" said Atkins.

Gazette silenced him with a scowl.

There came a low soft roar like the roll of distant thunder.

"Take cover!" yelled Ginger, leaping down into the trench. The roar continued building. It wasn't a shell or thunder, it was an earth tremor.

The walls of the trenches began to vibrate, sandbags jittering over the edge.

"Get out, get out!" Atkins yelled as Porgy thrust his hand down from the lip. Atkins shoved Ginger towards him. Porgy grabbed his hand and yanked him up. Atkins scrambled up using an old scaling ladder. The wall collapsed, sliding down into the trench and undoing several hours of hard work before the tremors subsided. Muted yells arose from all around as men scrambled out of the trenches onto the open ground above. A more plaintive and urgent, if unintelligible cry issued from nearby.

"Someone's trapped," said Pot Shot. They slipped back down into the trench and worked their way along until they came to the junction that led to the latrines.

Ketch had been doing his business, sat over the hole in the plank across the pit. When the tremors hit, the plank must have juddered loose because there was Ketch, khaki pants round his ankles, in the slurry pit of excrement below. Buckets of urine had also fallen over, drenching him in their pungent contents.

"Get me out!" he screamed through the filth.

The section looked at each other, smirks breaking out on their faces as their corporal struggled to right himself. No one was willing to go near the collapsed latrines and risk a similar ducking themselves.

Atkins looked around the collapsed trench. Seeing Ketch's rifle, he picked it up and, checking that the lock was on, held the butt as he thrust the barrel towards Ketch.

"Grab hold!

But the corporal's hands were slick with sewage and, as he pulled himself out, he slipped back with a splash causing the section to double up in raucous laughter.

Atkins persisted though and Ketch was able to loop his arm through the rifle's shoulder strap as he pulled him out, almost losing his own footing in the process.

Ketch lay panting on the floor of the trench coughing and spluttering, his sodden trousers round his ankles. Atkins slit open a sandbag with his bayonet and passed it to Ketch who snatched it from his hand ungratefully and began to wipe the excreta off his face.

"You!" he spat. "You did this!"

"Corporal?"

"You were told to put this latrine right. You and Evans. Did you think it would be a big joke? A big laugh? Well you'll be laughing on the other side of your face one day, Atkins. You mark my words. You'll get what's coming to you." He got to his feet and advanced towards them. They backed off, unwilling to be smeared by the malodorous mud.

"It was the earth tremor!" said Atkins. "You must have felt it, we all did."

Ketch opened his mouth to say something, stopped, gagged and retched. The section's delight turned to disgust. They backed away from him out of the trench, hearing another heave as vomit splattered wetly on the trench floor.

STILL SNORTING AND guffawing over Ketch's misfortune they got back to the section of trench they had been rebuilding and found Ginger billing and cooing. In his arms he held his tunic inside out and crumpled like a nest. They could hear something snuffling about inside it.

"Look, Only!" said Ginger thrusting his hands out towards Atkins, inviting him to examine the jacket's contents.

"Oh God, don't say Haig's back!" muttered Gazette.

Atkins peered over cautiously, not knowing what to expect, half anticipating something to leap out of the bundled cloth and bite him. He caught a flash of yellow fur and saw a long nose sniffling about in the makeshift khaki nest.

"What the hell is that? Ginger, what on earth have you found this time?"

"His name's Gordon," he replied beaming. He moved his hand under the tunic to open it out, revealing a small rat-sized creature with short yellowish fur, small black beady eyes and a long tubular snout. It didn't seem to have jaws or teeth. It snuffled eagerly around in the jacket, completely uninterested in the soldiers now gathering around it.

"I found it," said Ginger. "He was just sort of wondering around, like he was lost... like us."

"Fuck's sake, Ginger, everything we've come across so far has tried to kill us or eat us or both. You've got no idea what this thing is!" said Gutsy.

Mercy did. He knew what it was straight away. It was an opportunity.

"No, no," he said. "Steady on, lads. I think Ginger is onto something. Look."

They looked. Then they looked puzzled.

"All I see is some blonde rodent with a furry trunk," said Porgy.

"At what it's doin', smart-arse!"

Atkins looked again. It seemed to be excitedly running its snout along the seams of the jacket. A small long red tongue flickered out. "It's chatting," he said. "Bloody 'ell. It's eating the lice!"

As they watched, the otherworldly rodent pushed its snout into and along the seams, sucking up eggs and lice alike with great relish.

"We could clean up with this, fellas. This is the proverbial golden goose. No more feeling hitchy-koo. They'll pay through the nose to have their regulations cleaned of chatts. Gawd love us, any of us would! Gordon, here, is what you might call a Hitchy-kootioner."

There was a chorus of nods.

"Me next!" said Porgy hopping to pull off his boot before carefully pulling off his woollen sock and dangling it in front of Gordon. "Here, boy. Here," Gordon lifted its head and sniffed tentatively at the warm, damp, writhing sock. Porgy dropped the stinking sock into the coat. Immediately Gordon thrust its snout into it.

"And what good is all that money going to do out here?" said Pot Shot. "Where can you spend it?"

"Jeez, steady on, Pot Shot, can't a man have a dream? I'll save it and spend it when I get back."

Gordon was now totally enclosed by the sock, although from the snuffling and snorts that were issuing from it, it didn't seem to mind.

Already Atkins and the others were thinking of the booming business ahead; five hundred lice ridden, lousy men at thruppence a head? Gordon was going to make a killing for them.

GRANTHAM HAD TAKEN to pacing about his new HQ, trying to avoid the vista outside, as if by ignoring it it would go away. He couldn't cope with it. There was no section about this in the Field Manual or the Standing Orders. Without them he didn't know what to do.

The man was fast becoming a liability. He commissioned innumerable reports, seeking to bury the stark horror of their situation under a mountain of minutiae, so Everson found himself mired in endless company meetings.

"Trench repairs are well under way," Everson reported. "The backfilling, blocking and fortification of the open trench ends will be complete soon. Nothing should be able to enfilade or flank us then. Second Lieutenant Baxter of the Machine Gun section is constructing new emplacements for his guns. We've also set up a trench mortar in the old farmhouse. However if we want to repair the trenches properly then we're going to need more wood. At the moment we're down to cannibalising duckboards for revetments."

Grantham's face was drawn, his eyes red-rimmed.

"This is a nightmare," he muttered.

"At some point we're going to have to send out working parties to cut down trees from that forest over there."

Slacke nodded emphatically.

"Sir," he said. "We have potable water for three more days. We have food rations enough for perhaps twice that. Rum ration won't last. If we're here much longer we'll have to start looking for supplies locally."

"No," said Grantham, hoarsely.

"But, sir…"

"I said no. We will return home."

"Begging your pardon, sir, but we can't just sit here and wait for that to happen." He paused. "It may *never* happen."

Grantham exploded. "That is defeatist talk, man, and I won't have it, d'you hear?"

Everson took this as a further sign of Grantham's growing instability. The man needed to believe they would be returned home. If it became apparent that their fate was otherwise he feared that Grantham would really funk it.

"Sir?" It was Jeffries. "With all due respect we may have to face the possibility that we are here for an indefinite period. While I am sure you are correct in your assumption that we shall be returned I feel it prudent that we should prepare for the worst. At the very least it will keep the men occupied. An army with nothing to do will soon become a mutinous rabble."

Everson was surprised by what he heard. "I have to say I agree with Jeffries, sir. It should be understood by all that we shall be returned home in order to keep up morale. However we should consider sending out scout patrols. We need to know what we might face in the short term and if we can find water."

"I could make a short reconnaissance flight, Lieutenant," offered Tulliver. "That would at least give your men some possible directions in which to explore. I should have enough fuel, but with my observer dead, I'd need someone to spot and map-make for me."

"Jeffries can go," said Grantham. A smile bloomed briefly on Jeffries' lips before fading.

"Very well," said Tulliver. "I suggest we go straight away. There's enough light left for a short flight."

"You need to look for rivers, streams, lakes; sources of water. Look for cultivated fields or others signs of civilisation," suggested Lippett.

Civilisation. It wasn't a thought that had even entered Everson's head until now. He had been too preoccupied with simple, brutal survival and thoughts of home. But yes, civilisation. The existence of a civilisation that might have achieved dominion over this wild and untamed country had never really occurred to him. What cities might they have constructed, what wonders might they have achieved? What marvels might they work? Surely they would recognise a fellow creature of equal intellect and extend a hand in aid? Unless they were responsible for their sudden journey and arrival here. In which case one would have to try to divine the motives for such an act.

There was a confused chatter as everyone suddenly attempted to talk over each other, each speculating on what it was they expected to find; certainly nothing to which the British Empire was not an equal.

"Gentlemen, please," said Jeffries. "This is all idle speculation. There is no point in raising false hopes at the moment though, as Captain Lippett so rightly states, it is something we should keep an eye out for. And when I'm up in Lieutenant Tulliver's machine I shall certainly endeavour to seek such signs as will assuage your doubts."

UNDER THE COVERING watch of a Lewis machine gun section, 1 Section had pulled the Sopwith out onto the plain and had spent an hour trying to beat some kind of take-off strip from the tubular undergrowth there. They'd managed to clear about a hundred yards or so and hoped it would be enough. Tulliver walked the strip wincing and sucking in breath through his teeth. The ground was bumpier than he'd wished. Ideally he'd have the AMs fill the pot holes, but here that wasn't going to be possible, at least not this time. Maybe he'd have a word with the infantry captain.

Tulliver and Jeffries climbed aboard the Sopwith. Tulliver had checked it out earlier. There was about half a tank of fuel left. Quite what he'd do then, he didn't know.

"We won't be going too high today," said Tulliver. "But you'll have to be prepared to use the machine gun. We don't know what kind of flying creatures are up there."

"Oh don't worry about me," said Jeffries. "I'm sure I can handle myself."

"Well, bear in mind you're going to have to stand to fire and there's no safety harness. Contact!"

A private swung the propeller around. It juddered to a halt. He seized the blade in his hands and swung down again. The engine caught. "Chocks!" Two more soldiers pulled the makeshift blocks away from the wheels and the aeroplane began to inch forward as if impatient to get into the air and be free of the heavy, lumpen earth. It began to bounce clumsily across the uneven plain. The jarring stopped as the wheels left the ground. Tulliver pulled back on the stick and angled the nose up as the ground dropped away. He peeled to the right and flew over the pat of Somme mud as he climbed. He was excited to be in the air again. Only here did he feel he could be himself. Over on the horizon he could make out a line of thick black clouds as he reached a thousand feet and the world below began to take on a familiar map-like feel. Far from feeling alienated by this wondrous new landscape, up here he felt as if he were in the company of an old friend. He began looking for conspicuous landmarks; the flashes of sunlight off water caught his eyes. He looked down and saw a ribbon of silver a mile or so from the brown stain of the Somme. He turned to Jeffries behind him and pointed down. "A river!" he bawled over the sound of the wind and the engine.

Jeffries formed his finger and forefinger into an 'O.' Tulliver thought that a little odd. He'd only met a couple of other people that had used that specific gesture. Most just used thumbs up. One was an American flying with the Escadrille Lafayette, the other, more recently, was that Artillery officer, what was his name?

"Are you sure we haven't met?" he yelled over the engine's roar. "You seem familiar! Do you know a chap named Hibbert?"

Jeffries shook his head and Tulliver shrugged, but couldn't dismiss entirely the feeling he knew the man from somewhere. He turned the machine and from their vantage point, the circle of Somme was sat near the head of a wide valley, enclosed by hills on three sides. On one side of the valley stretched a large forest. Beyond it lay a large plain bounded by a range of hills. The silver ribbon of water ran down from the hills and threaded itself through the forest before reappearing on the plain. If it was coming down from the hills maybe it led to some sort of—

There was a tap on his shoulder. He wiped away the oil spray that was beginning to mist his goggles and glanced back over his shoulder, Jeffries pointed down. Tulliver tilted the wings so he could see a herd of tall, three-legged creatures moving across the plain. That's when he noticed the shadow ripple over the ground and pass over his machine. He immediately pulled up and banked so he could look around. He pointed up, indicating that Jeffries, who was sat behind the wings and had a better view, should look around. Then he saw it. A great shape above them like a flying manta ray, but it had hind legs with large talons and a long neck that ended in a small head with a wide mouth, displaying sharp teeth. It was easily bigger than the Sopwith and with claws and teeth like those could rip the aeroplane to shreds if it got close. It had obviously been following the herd of whatever-they-were and saw the Sopwith as a territorial intruder. It came at them from the side. Tulliver hoped Jeffries was on the ball. He was. Standing up in his seat he swung the Hotchkiss machine gun round and opened fire. The creature closed its wings momentarily and dropped out of sight below them.

Damn. He couldn't afford to let it get beneath them.

"Hang on!" he yelled to Jeffries. Tulliver banked sharply and spun down in a wide spiral looking for the creature. It reared up almost immediately in front of them.

"Hellfire!"

He pressed the fire buttons on his machine gun, spitting lead and tracer bullets at the beast. It let out a long, pained cry and vanished over the top of the machine as Tulliver pushed the stick forwards sending the aeroplane into a shallow dive. As the creature passed overhead Jeffries fired, raking its body with a line of bullets that left it spurting a bluish viscous liquid.

"Go round!" yelled Jeffries. Tulliver banked, keeping the wounded creature within the circle of his turn. Jeffries kept it in his sights and let off another couple of bursts, one ripping through the membranous wings, another shot hitting it in its head, exploding the skull. The lifeless beast plummeted from the air, the drag from its wings sending it careening into a drunken tumble.

"Calloo Callay!" Jeffries yelled triumphantly as he leaned over the lip of the cockpit to watch the dead beast crash into the plain with an explosion of blood and offal.

Tulliver, wary of any more of the creatures, was eager to get down.

"Have you got enough?" he shouted.

"Yes, it's dead!"

"No, have you got enough information for the map?"

JEFFRIES TURNED, SAT back down in his seat and pulled out the clipboard. He marked the stream and the forest. He'd seen no sign of cultivation or farming, no patchwork of fields, no smoke, which was vaguely disappointing. He nodded emphatically and gave his ringed okay sign to Tulliver, who turned the aeroplane about and headed back up the valley towards the muddy charnel field they had to call home for the present.

As he did so, Jeffries caught a glimpse of something gleaming in the far distance across the plain, as if it had caught the light from this world's sun. He struggled to turn around and see. He could have sworn he saw some sort of huge spire far off, almost smeared into obscurity by the intervening aerial perspective of the atmosphere. The machine bucked on a pocket of air as it descended and dropped heavily, leaving Jeffries' stomach briefly somewhere above his head. When he looked again the fortuitous angle was lost and the spire had vanished. But it had nevertheless ignited a gleam of hope in his heart. He smiled to himself. This was one thing he wouldn't mark on his crude, despairingly blank map. He well knew the value of information as currency. This would only strengthen his position in the long-term and, until he knew its true value, he would sit on it and let his investment accrue.

TULLIVER CIRCLED THE field of mud as he came down and brought the machine about so that the hastily cleared green strip was ahead of him. He pulled back on the stick, opened the flaps, slowing the aeroplane down to just above stall speed, and cut the engine before they hit the ground. He saw the waiting soldiers run towards them as the Sopwith bounced and trundled to a halt.

He tore off his flying helmet and goggles before clambering out of the cockpit. The Tommies gathered round the machine like excited schoolboys, barking questions at him and Tulliver took the opportunity to bask in the moment.

JEFFRIES WAS LEFT abandoned by the machine as Tulliver and the adulating scrum around him moved off. The airman had almost recognised him. Of all the damned luck to get stuck with the same pilot that took him up when he was using Hibbert as an alias. He didn't need anyone putting the pieces together yet, he needed more time. He would have to do something. He was reaching over to put the helmet goggles and gloves back in the cockpit when he noticed the tool box in the bottom of the craft. His usual methods might attract too much attention now, but an accident? He looked back toward the mud flat. No one was about. He leant over and dragged the box towards him. Something to make sure that Tulliver didn't come back from his next flight? Flicking the little hooked catch he opened the wooden box to reveal a jumble of tools; spanners, wrenches, screwdrivers, wire cutters. He smiled...

INTERLUDE TWO
**Letter from Private Thomas Atkins
to Flora Mullins**

4th November 1916

My Dearest Flora,

Things haven't gone quite the way the top brass expected here so I don't know when I'll get a chance to post this.

I know you must be sitting at home thinking me among the missing, too. Although we're not so much missing, as lost. It's the rest of the world that's missing. What will my mother do? Both her sons among the missing. She must be heartbroken. I wish I could tell her I'm alive and well, although I'm not sure I like it here. The wildlife seems none too friendly. I thought rats and lice were bad, but they've got things here that put them to shame.

I've been picked as part of a foraging patrol, going out into the countryside to pick fruit and berries and the like. Mercy says it sounds like a bit if a lark. It'll make a pleasant change from digging trenches though and no mistake. With no Hun to fight, that's all they've had us doing the past few days, and on rations too. I tell you, we're all getting fed up of Maconochie and Plum and Apple here. Half Pint says we'll end up looking like jam tins at this rate. So here's hoping we find something edible.

Ever yours,
Thomas

CHAPTER NINE
"Death, Where is Thy Sting-a-Ling-a-Ling..."

"GOD DAMN IT!" said Captain Lippett. It had been a bad couple of days for the surgeon. Apart from the usual round of battlefield wounds and infections there was a new rash of cases as the perils of the world about them began to make themselves known. The carcass of one of the worms was hacked up and roasted on the open ground between the supervision and support trenches, by some men who hadn't had fresh meat in weeks. Those who ate the meat died agonising deaths in the night. It seemed from what Lippett was able to determine that the flesh was poisonous, containing some kind of toxin to which man had no immunity.

A Lewis gun team broke out in bloody pustules after eating a variety of knobbly yellow fruit that hung full and ripe, weighing down the rust-coloured boughs in the small grove of trees near the mud perimeter. The boils proceeded to swell at an alarming rate and to a grotesque size, disfiguring the face and body until the skin became taut like a drum, causing immense pain, before bursting so that those infected were left with terrible open wounds and died of blood loss or septicaemia.

After that the order was not to taste anything but to bring it back for the Medical Officer to conduct tests on to determine whether it was fit to eat or not.

2 PLATOON HAD been ordered to scout out the wood that lay maybe a mile away. It was the farthest any party had yet been. Although they didn't say it Everson could tell the men were nervous. A platoon had gone out on a search for water the previous day, following the directions garnered from Tulliver and Jeffries' reconnaissance flight. They had lost four men to animal attacks.

After Stand To, breakfast and parade the forty-two strong 2 Platoon headed out across the plain in Indian file. Every man had one in the spout. They all remembered the attack of the hell hounds and knew they were out here somewhere. Behind Atkins came Hepton, carrying his camera and tripod and several canisters of film in haversacks. He had asked for permission to join them, eager to record the wonders of this new world, if not the horrors, for he knew such vivid sights would sell seats. Then came Ginger, cooing happily into his gas helmet haversack in which he had stowed his new pet. Gordon's flaccid whiskery snout poked out of the flap. Pot Shot, Gazette, Gutsy, Porgy, Half Pint and Lucky brought up the rear of the section, carrying a couple of rolled up stretchers to help carry whatever they managed to harvest. Sergeant Hobson and the other three sections of 2 Platoon followed on behind.

Atkins felt his stomach tighten. If the entrenchments disappeared back to Blighty while they were away they would be stranded. He, and every other man in the platoon, kept glancing back anxiously until the small escarpment of the mud field was lost from sight amid the thick tube-like grass. After that, their only comfort was the distant bark of NCOs heard through the man-high fronds that now surrounded them.

"At least if they stop we can tell that they've disappeared back to Blighty," said Pot Shot.

"Yeah, I never thought I'd be grateful for an NCO," said Mercy, throwing a glance behind him at a sullen Corporal Ketch.

Atkins watched as the edge of the forest grew closer. The fronds began to thin out and become shorter until the platoon found themselves merely wading though them, hip deep, as they approached the edge of the woods. The trees, if that was what they were, seemed to be similar to those in the odd copses they had observed growing in the vale about the entrenchment; great thick trunks that split into boughs protruding radially from the trunks and ending in large, flatish leaves. Those facing the sun were open. Those that faced away had closed, like inverted gentleman's umbrellas. Some were already beginning to open in anticipation of the sun's movement. A number of the trees vied for supremacy, some growing taller than their fellows in order to best deploy their umbrella leaves and absorb the maximum amount of sunshine.

At the edge of the wood Everson called a halt. "We're here to find food. Don't try anything yourselves. You saw what happened to 1 Platoon. We're just here to bring back samples of anything we find that might be edible. Captain Lippett has ways and means of testing them, so let's leave it to him, shall we? We need to be careful in there. We don't know what kind of wildlife we'll find. The damned beasts we've found so far have been none too friendly so watch your back. Don't take any chances. We've got two hours, and frankly that's longer than I want to spend away from the trenches under the present conditions and I'm sure you all have similar concerns."

There were noises of agreement among the platoon.

"Right. 4 Section will hold this position in reserve with the Lewis gun. We'll meet back here in two hours. If you get into any danger, your NCOs have whistles. I'll go in with 1 Section. Good hunting!"

As they moved deeper into the wood, the trees they saw on the perimeter, unable to obtain enough sunlight, soon gave way to stranger vegetation. Some of this had great green tubers running down its sides, embedded in its huge thick trunks, like great veins. The trunks rose straight up, without interruption from bough or branch, into the canopy where they seemed to explode with foliage, each competing with its neighbours for the nourishing rays of the sun.

Further in, they came across a tree, an entanglement of thorny weed wrapped around its base. Here and there the mass supported large dark red blooms. Strands of the weed climbed up the trunk, wrapping itself so tightly about it that its barbed thorns drove deep into the bark, a clear thick liquid oozing from the puncture wounds.

"It's like living barbed wire," said Lucky, scuttling sideward to avoid a tendril as it moved weakly towards him.

"What kind of hell world is this?" said Porgy, shaking his head.

Even as they watched it Atkins could see this wire weed grow, spreading out feelers across the ground under some vegetable imperative he couldn't fathom. The men skirted the slowly spreading carpet and pressed on.

The clatter of their weapons and gear was smothered by the surrounding vegetation and, every now and again, sharp cries and calls from the canopy or rustles and snaps from the undergrowth startled them, but they saw nothing.

As they advanced cautiously through the wood Everson heard something ahead. He put his hand up to hush the rest of the section. They stopped and cocked their heads, listening intently, fingers poised on the magazine cut-off catch on their rifles. The lieutenant beckoned them forward, a warning finger on his lip. They pushed slowly through the undergrowth until it parted to reveal a large sunlit glade.

There, hopping about, feeding on close cropped grass, were a pack of Gordons. They squeaked as their furry snouts probed the ground, no doubt looking for some sort of insect or ground dwelling creature upon which they depended. In the middle of the clearing, towering over them all like some beneficent totem was a tall plant. It consisted of several stems, each as thick as an average man, entwined about each other and rising to a height of around eighteen feet. At its tip was a large bulbous yellow head and around the underside, hanging from the nodule, were small pods of varying sizes, like ripening fruits. A sweet smell hung around the glade. Atkins' mouth began to water.

"Fascinating," said Hepton, as he fixed his camera box to the tripod and began cranking away.

"Sir," said Pot Shot, addressing the lieutenant. "Do you think we should try picking one of those fruits for the MO, sir?"

"My thoughts exactly, Jellicoe," said Everson, "once we make sure those damn creatures aren't harmful."

As if in answer, Ginger's haversack began to writhe impatiently. Closer to its own kind again, Gordon became excited and sought a way out of the bag.

"Fuck's sake, here we go again!" said Gazette as he saw Ginger struggle to control his haversack.

"No, Gordon!" cried Ginger as the creature wriggled its way out from the under the flap and jumped down to the ground, scampering across the glade to be with its fellows, squeaking gleefully. The others stopped and stood on their hind legs, squeaking in answer.

"What the deuce!" Everson exclaimed.

"Gordon, come back!" hissed Ginger, striding into the glade. Startled, the creatures scattered and Ginger clumsily switched this way and that, raising sniggers from his mates as he tried to catch his pet, or the one he thought was his pet, for they all looked the same. The creatures panicked and squealed and ran around bolting into holes in the ground. Others poked their noses shyly out of their holes all except, presumably, Gordon, who sat calmly by the plant in the middle of the glade, preening itself.

"This is better than Charlie Chaplin," said Hepton, as he followed the slapstick antics in the glade.

"Mottram, get back here!" hissed Everson.

Ginger, a look of grim determination on his face, advanced on his pet. There was a soft *pfffft* and a giant red thorn exploded from the ground where he stood, ripping up through his groin, the tip exiting through his shoulder. The force of the thrust hefted him off his feet and he hung suspended on the thorn. He screamed, struggling to free himself, but barbs protruding from the spine held him fast. At the bottom of the thorn, large leaf like structures fell open, forming a cup at the base.

Hepton stopped cranking in horror.

"Ginger!" cried Atkins as he Porgy, Mercy and Lucky dashed into the grove.

Atkins saw now, as he ran across the ground, that it seemed soft and springy, yielding under his weight, like boggy earth. It undulated with shallow tussocks. Lucky's foot came down on one and another thorn sprang up from the earth. He squealed as the point tore up though his gut, ripping out through his back, jerking him off his feet. Lucky's helmet rolled across the glade and came to a halt near Atkins.

Porgy, Mercy and Atkins stopped dead still.

"It's burning me! Burning!" screamed Ginger. His pleas degenerated into a meaningless, agonised wailing. He twisted his head and fixed his bloodshot, watery gaze on Atkins. "Help me!"

"God help us," croaked Gutsy hoarsely. "That thing in the middle—it's some kind of carnivorous plant. This must be how it feeds."

"Don't move," said Everson. "You may trigger off more of those things."

Lucky was screaming too, thrashing about in a frenzy as he tried to work himself free, but only succeeding in driving himself further down the thorn. As he slipped down he revealed little sacs that pulsed at the base of small barbs, pumping out some vile secretion. Atkins realised that similar sacs, caught within Ginger and Lucky's bodies, were even now pumping this stuff into them; some sort of poison or digestive juice. The whole glade was a honey trap. Gordon and its little friends had been safe, being too light to trigger the plant's mechanism.

Pot Shot had his hands over his ears in a vain attempt to blot out the anguished screaming. "Somebody do something!"

Everson cocked his pistol and aimed at Ginger's head. It was the only thing to do to save him from a slow, agonising death by internal liquefaction. He pulled the trigger and the back of Ginger's head exploded across the glade. He turned and re-cocked his pistol, this time aiming at Lucky who looked straight back at him.

"Thank—"

Everson met his gaze as he fired again and Lucky slumped lifelessly down on the thorn. Everson sagged visibly as he holstered his pistol. Atkins didn't envy him. But they were still stuck. One wrong move and their fate could be that of their companions.

"Right," said Everson eventually. "These things are obviously set off by weight. Otterthwaite, can you shoot the tussock things and trigger the remaining thorns?"

"Begging your pardon, sir," said Hobson, "but there's a quicker way. Jellicoe, give me your Mills bombs."

Atkins, Mercy and Porgy exchanged glances. Atkins watched as the sergeant got down on his hands and knees to sight along the floor of the glade, looking for the tell-tale tussocks of untriggered thorns.

"Right-o, watch yourself, lads, sir," said Hobson, pulling the pin from a Mills bomb. Hobson counted to three and tossed it towards the edge of the clearing, away from the trapped men, who crouched down where they were. The grenade exploded and Atkins felt himself showered with dirt as one, two, three huge thorns, triggered by the concussion wave, sprang up around him. The engorged sacs on the barbs pulsing and ejaculating their venom impotently.

Hobson threw a second grenade and it landed in the cup of the furthest thorn before it exploded, shredding the plant. "There's your way out," said Hobson, indicating the path of triggered thorns. "Watch where you step."

Mercy and Porgy edged their way carefully past the thorns, now oozing with digestive acids.

"We can't leave them here, sir," said Atkins, looking back at the impaled bodies.

"I'm sorry, Atkins, it's too dangerous."

"Then just their pay books, sir?" he pleaded, William foremost in his mind. If someone had taken his brother's disc and pay book they might now have known his fate.

"Very well, but be careful."

Atkins stepped as gingerly as he could in his hobnails towards Ginger's slack body. Standing on his tiptoes and leaning over the shiny red collecting cup at the thorn's base, he tentatively opened up what was left of Ginger's tunic and pulled the cloth-covered pay book from his inside pocket. God, this was never a pleasant job at the best of times. A wet splash made him jump as half-liquified organs and viscera slipped out of Ginger's torso and fell into the waiting plant cup. The stench drove Atkins back a step. Used to the charnel stench of the trenches as he was, this was a foul odour that turned his stomach. A squeak startled him. He whirled round almost losing his balance, his foot coming down inches from another tuft. It was Gordon. He'd almost trodden on the creature. It looked up at him, squeaking. He felt a hot flush of anger burst across his face.

"Piss off. This is your fault, you little shit!" He took a swing at it with his boot but it hopped back. It looked up at him from the safety of a tussock.

"Atkins, come on!" called Everson from the edge of the glade.

As he moved round to Lucky's body Atkins blatantly ignored the creature even though he was aware of it turning to watch him. He tottered precariously on his toes as he stretched to reach Lucky's torso. Carefully retrieving his now bloodstained pay book, he made his way back across the glade slowly, step by step.

Atkins leapt thankfully to the edge of the glade only to hear a wistful squeak behind him. Gordon had followed him. He tried shooing the creature away as Everson ordered them away from the glade one by one, but it hopped mournfully after him. With a huff of exasperation, Atkins picked up the creature and put it into his gas helmet haversack as Hepton packed up his camera and tripod.

They moved off sombrely through the undergrowth, knowing now to avoid the large airy sunlit glades, which they saw were dotted everywhere.

"Watch it, more of them damn Sting-a-lings," said Mercy. The name seemed morbidly appropriate and, for want of anything better, it stuck, adding a new level of poignancy to the old soldier's song.

Hobson took the lead followed by Ketch, with Everson bringing up the rear. As they progressed through the wood, each man glanced nervously about; every rustle, every breeze that stirred fronds or leaves or tendrils, every crack, every snap was now potentially something lethal. From elsewhere came the sound of muted rifle fire, screams and a whistle. One of the other sections was in trouble. There was nothing they could do about it but it didn't help the tension any.

Out of the corner of his eye Atkins caught a flash of something. Before he could shout a warning, something man-sized and mottled green detached itself from a trunk and sprang at Lieutenant Everson. Large, saw-toothed mandibles clicked lustfully on empty air as the lieutenant dived out the way.

Even as the men ran to their commander's aid there was a husky cry and a figure hurled itself out of the undergrowth onto their assailant, deftly working a blade between the chitinous plates on the creature's neck and, with a twist of his arm, severing the head.

There were three bayonetted rifles aimed at him as the man looked up, while the soldiers lifted the partially decapitated body of the man-beetle from their struggling, spluttering commander. Everson, red faced, kicked it away angrily and sat up, struggling to contain the wracking sobs of relief. With their rifles and a jerk of the head, Gazette, Mercy and Gutsy herded the wild man against a trunk and disarmed him. Sergeant Hobson examined the curved blade he carried.

"Bloody hell, he looks human," said Gutsy, peering at the wild man.

The lieutenant's saviour was a wiry, well-muscled middle-aged man with wild greying hair and a scrubby grey beard. His face and arms were tanned and weathered. He was dressed in clothing that looked as if it had been assembled from various animal hides and vegetable barks. Across his chest and tied to his upper arms were chitinous plates, worn like armour, that looked as if they'd been acquired from creatures similar to the one in front of them.

"Here, Kameraden, you speak English?" asked Mercy.

"Don't be so bloody silly!" said Gutsy. "Does he look like he can?"

The man's eyes flicked from one to the other as they talked.

"I am Urman," said the man, standing erect and thrusting out his chest proudly.

Gutsy's mouth dropped open. When it came down to it, though, the Tommies were not too shocked that the man spoke English. As soldiers of the great and glorious British Empire, they were used to the idea that Johnny Foreigner would speak at least some English, even if it was in an odd accent. It was only right and proper, after all.

Everson was too shaken up by his near miss to question it.

"Where'd you come from, eh? Eh?" challenged Gazette, jabbing the air with his bayonet, causing the man to flinch.

"Leave him, Otterthwaite," said Everson, who had just about

recovered his composure. "He's not a Bosche prisoner. He saved my life. He might just be the first friendly face we've seen here." He stepped between his men and held out his hand towards the man.

The man looked at it blankly then tilted his head to examine the back of the lieutenant's hand as if there might be some concealed offering or weapon. Everson grasped the man's hand gently and shook it.

"Well, I never!" said Pot Shot.

"Hands across the sea!" declared Gutsy, dumbstruck.

"Hands across my bloody arse!" muttered Ketch.

"We," said Everson, "are Human. My name is Lieutenant James Everson, 2 Platoon, C Company, 13th Battalion Pennine Fusiliers of His Britannic Majesty's Army. And yours…" he looked expectantly at the man, "is…?"

"Naparandwe," he said, pointing at himself, then, eyes narrowing, "to what colony do you belong?"

"Colony?" said Everson frowning. "None."

"You are Free Urmen?"

"Free? Well, yes."

The man grinned again as if this was the right answer. "Yrredetti almost had you. Killed two of my clan," he said, pointing at the lifeless bulk of the humanoid beetle creature. It seemed as if it had evolved to walk upright, and it was evidently able to blend in with its surroundings to almost devastating effect. He spat. Mercy spat, too and the man clapped his hands and grinned. "You are lucky they are solitary hunters."

"Yes, thank you for that," said Everson, running a finger underneath his collar, relieved that his neck was still there.

"Free Urman!" he said offering his hand to Mercy as Everson had done to him. As he repeated this with every man in the section his stomach gurgled obscenely.

"Are you hungry?" asked Atkins, rubbing his own stomach with pantomime gestures. The man nodded eagerly. Atkins opened his pack and took out his iron rations.

The action caught Ketch's wary eye. "You touch that without permission, that's a punishable offence," he snapped. "Emergencies only."

Atkins knew all too well. Two men in his last platoon were court-martialled for eating their iron rations while trapped in a shell hole in No Man's Land for four days. Apparently that wasn't emergency enough.

"He has my permission," said Everson. "Go on, Atkins."

Ketch grunted but backed off.

Atkins opened the tin of bully beef, prised a piece out with his fingers and ate it. He proffered the tin to the man who sniffed it cautiously before devouring the contents within moments, never taking his eyes off Atkins. The act of gouging and prising out the meat was something he seemed to be accustomed with, though probably not from tins, thought Atkins with a quick glance at the green mottled body of the dead Yrredetti. Pot Shot and Porgy offered him their tins and that all went the same way, followed by a large and satisfied belch. He looked hopefully around for his next offering.

"No mate," said Gutsy shaking his head. "Napoo left. Sorry. All gone."

"Napoo?" the man repeated with a grin, his white teeth showing in his berry brown face.

"Yeah. Napoo. I guess that's what we'll call you, too. Napoo," said Gutsy, raising his eyebrows and nodding at the others for agreement. Uncomfortable with a culture not their own and unwilling to show their ignorance, this was easier than trying to pronounce the native's own name.

"Can't say he hasn't earned it," said Porgy with a sigh, looking at the empty tins. He reached up idly and plucked a ripe-looking fruit from a low hanging bough, absent-mindedly shining it on his trousers before lifting it to his mouth to take a bite.

"No!" The man suddenly leapt up and hit him squarely on the back between the shoulder blades. The fruit flew from his hand and was sent rolling across the ground.

Porgy turned round angrily and started to rise.

"What the hell did you do that for you, you little—"

"Hopkiss, sit down," barked Hobson. "The man was doing you a favour."

He pointed to where the fruit had fallen. It had cracked open and juice oozed out from fresh ripe flesh onto the grass, burning it away with acidic sizzles and pops.

"That's the second time he's saved our lives," said Everson. "He seems to know what's what around here. Frankly we could use his kind of help." He turned to Napoo. "Can you help us? We need to find food. And water."

"Food and water," repeated Napoo, nodding.

"You help us?" Everson asked.

"In exchange."

Everson, surprised, glanced up at Hobson who shrugged. Napoo was obviously shrewder than he looked. "Yes, if we can," replied Everson.

Napoo took his weapon back off Hobson and began to walk away through the forest. The men watched. When he realised they weren't following he stopped and turned around. "Follow." The men looked at Everson. He nodded slightly and readjusted his helmet. Hobson took the lead and the rest fell into line. Eventually they came to the edge of a small clearing in front of a cave. Outside the cave a fire burned, tended by a woman of similar age to the man, her hair tied back. A younger girl was scraping out the inside of a large beetle shell, the way one might scrape the fat and meat off a hide.

"Wait here," said Napoo. He went ahead into the clearing where Atkins watched him talk to the woman with big, expressive gestures, pointing back at the woods where they waited. The woman called out. Several other adults appeared from the surroundings or from out of the cave entrance.

Napoo turned and beckoned the Tommies into the clearing where several men stood holding crude spears and bows, eyeing the newcomers suspiciously.

The soldiers walked slowly into the encampment, Sergeant Hobson surveying the area warily. The two parties studied each other. The woman seemed interested in their clothes, plucking at Atkins' sleeves. She felt the rough texture of the khaki cloth between her fingers and tested the strength of its seams with apparent approval.

A lean-to had been built over the entrance to the cave using thick branches and leaves. Theirs seemed to be a miserable existence, at least as miserable as living in the trenches, thought Atkins.

"Let the men rest, Sergeant. Post a sentry. I don't want to be surprised again. I'll go and see what this Napoo needs. Atkins, you're with me."

Atkins groaned. He just wanted to sit down. Instead, he followed the lieutenant and Napoo into the cave. As they did so the ground rumbled and shook. Small pebbles and rocks bounced down the side of the rock face, showers of dirt loosed from the roots of trees clinging to lips on the cliff drummed down,

"It's another earth tremor!" said Atkins. They staggered hard against side of the cave to stop themselves from falling over. Napoo had stopped and crouched for balance.

Almost as suddenly as it began, it stopped.

"It always happened this time of year," said Napoo, unconcerned. "The world shakes." He led them to the back of a cave where a young man lay on a litter of vegetation and fur, his skin slick with a fever sweat, his eyes rolling in delirium. A wound on his thigh had been smeared with some sort of poultice.

"You help him," Napoo said.

Atkins pulled out his field dressing pack and tore open the paper packing. He placed it over the wound and fixed it with a length of bandage. "It's infected. The MO needs to take a look at him, sir," Atkins said. "I can't help him here."

Everson was silent for a moment. He appeared to come to a decision. "Very well, we'll take him back to the trenches."

CHAPTER TEN

"If You Were the Only Girl in the World..."

COMING ACROSS NAPOO had been fortuitous. It was obvious they hadn't succeeded in finding much to eat on their own and Napoo had information that could greatly aid their chances of survival. So it was that Napoo accompanied them as they carried the injured Urman from the forest.

They met up with what was left of the rest of the platoon at the rendezvous point. 2 Section only had two surviving men. Sting-a-lings had killed several, wire-weed had caught another man and one soldier had been lost to a cave-dwelling creature that had snatched him down into darkness before anyone could get a shot off. 3 Section didn't return at the appointed time. The rest of them waited for a quarter of an hour. Everson would have waited longer, but the men were anxious to return to the trenches, if indeed they were still there. All in all the losses were slightly better than if they had attacked Fritz head on, but that seemed of little consolation.

Atkins' arms began to burn with the effort of carrying the wounded Urman on a stretcher as they headed back. He and Porgy had to stop every hundred yards or so. It wasn't easy, carrying battle order kit and lugging a loaded stretcher over a mile or so of uneven ground, especially when he was weary from lack of sleep and weak from lack of food and had Gordon mewling and wriggling about in his bag.

He felt a great wave of relief when they first heard the sound of work parties and the reassuring refrains of songs drifting over the plain. They passed several groups of men digging mass graves some hundred yards out onto the plain and seeding it with sacks of Chlorate of Lime. They were preparing to bury the rotting corpses from No Man's Land that had been attracting predators. Another working party was hacking up the fire-crisped carcass of one of the giant worms.

Sporadic cheers and looks of amazement greeted their arrival back at the trenches. Napoo strode through with Everson and Hobson, wide-eyed at the muddy encampment and holding his nose as the stench hit him. It prompted Pot Shot behind him to start singing: "To live with any luck inside a trench / Your nose must get accustomed to the stench / Of the rotten Bosche that lie/ On the parapet and die / 'cos they make a smell that Hell itself can't quench…"

Off-duty soldiers gathered to watch 1 Section pass. Word got round fast and the discovery of native people living on this world made quite a stir. On seeing Napoo, a number of old soldiers, having served in India, expressed the opinion that it was only right and natural to find someone to whom they were superior. If they were to be stranded on some other world now, at least, it was a place where they could be masters. Britannia's Colonial spirit was, in some quarters it seemed, still alive and well.

EVERSON AND NAPOO accompanied Atkins and Porgy as they carried the injured Urman to the newly established Casualty Clearing Station. Bell tents and crude tarpaulin marquees served as wards for the bedridden. The walking wounded lay about outside chatting and smoking. The shell-shocked had been fenced in for their own protection, under guard like POWs; their minds broken by the horrors of war and this strange new world that had suddenly appeared around them. Most of them sat quietly and wept, rocking themselves, or else shook and jerked in spastic fits and screamed. Some sought shelter and cover for themselves, desperately scraping sap holes with their bare hands. Every now and then one would completely funk it and run at the wire only to be brutally sedated by the butt of a guard's rifle. Many men hadn't time for the malingerings of cowards such as these. Atkins watched them mull about as he passed, his thoughts turning to Ginger. Poor bloody Ginger. He'd rather the lad had funked it proper and ended up in that compound than die the way he did.

The MO's hospital bell tent had a big red cross daubed on it and they made for that. The walking wounded seemed to give this tent a wider birth than the other and Atkins soon found out why. The sound of fast rhythmic sawing came from within and set his teeth on edge. In a place like that, there was only one thing you could be sawing. Atkins and Porgy put the stretcher down. The young Urman groaned feverishly. Everson collared an orderly. "Fetch the MO immediately." He turned to Atkins and Porgy. "Go and get yourself some grub," he said.

"Sir," they said, saluting. Atkins turned to leave when Porgy caught him by the arm.

"'Alf a mo, eh, Only?" he said.

Nurse Bell was ambling their way, exchanging pleasantries with cheeky wounded soldiers who fancied their chances. Flirting made them feel alive, made them feel wanted, valued. Human. She was talking and laughing with a soldier leaning on crutch, Lance Corporal Sandford from 3 Platoon. Porgy's eyes narrowed. This meant war. He ran a comb as best he could through his hair over his bandage and splashed his face with water from his canteen.

"Bloody hell, Porgy, you're going all out today," said Atkins. "Give the poor girl a chance!"

"Oh, I intend to, at the very least," he said with a grin. "I'm still looking for my Queen of Hearts."

"You again," Edith said as she approached.

"Yeah, I know," said Porgy. "Can you take a look at me noggin again? I'm feeling a bit light headed. Especially around you."

"You are incorrigible, Private," she said, smiling.

Atkins coughed discreetly.

"Oh, this is my mate, Only," said Porgy shuffling awkwardly.

"Only what?" she asked.

"Go on, tell her," said Porgy, digging him in the ribs.

Atkins rolled his eyes wearily. "My name's Thomas Atkins," he sighed. Tommy Atkins, the nickname for the common soldier, and didn't he half get ragged about it?

"Tommy Atkins? Really? That's your real name?"

"Certainly is, nobody would make that up. This," announced Porgy, enjoying his friend's discomfort just a little too much, "is the One, the Only Tommy Atkins!"

"It sounds like a music hall act," she said, putting her hand over her mouth politely as she laughed.

"I know," said Porgy, slapping Atkins on the back, "so we just call him Only."

It was what passed for a Tommy's humour. No sense making jokes you had to think about. You could be dead before you got it. To Tommy though, 'Only' also served as a constant reminder of his missing brother. He might well be the only Atkins brother left, the sting of conscience he experienced at its every mention was a penance he accepted for his uncharitable thoughts regarding William.

Leaving them to talk, he made great sport of Gordon, charging the waiting casualties thruppence an item to have their clothes chatted by the creature. Porgy caught up with him as Nurse Bell went on about her ministrations.

"She's a fine lass, isn't she, Only?"

"Oh no doubt," said Atkins, "But I do doubt she'll put up with you."

"She's a debutante," he said, plainly enamoured.

"And clearly out of your league. A Northern lad from a brewery stepping out with someone who's been in the same room as Royalty? I'd say you need your head examining."

"I have," he sighed. "By Edith."

"What? And she found nothing wrong with it? Can't be much of a nurse then."

LIPPETT OPERATED ON the young Urman with an orderly and Sister Fenton assisting. Napoo was reluctant to leave him alone, partly because Gutsy had explained to him in a slow, loud voice—which was the best way, in his opinion, to communicate with natives—that they were working their juju magic on him, which seemed to alarm Napoo. He hung around the surgical tent, his face etched with worry as he and Everson waited. To Everson's relief, the operation was a success. Lippett came out of the tent wiping his hands on his apron.

"It was some sort of poisonous thorn, embedded deep in his muscle," he said. "We've cut it out. He's young and strong. He should pull through. Remarkably, that poultice muck they'd spread on it seems to have some medicinal properties, slowed the spread of the poison. We might be able to use something like that if we're here much longer."

They moved the Urman to a tent, where Sister Fenton and Nurse Bell checked on him hourly. Owing to his chiselled, unshaven appearance, reminding them of the Gallic soldiers they'd treated, and not knowing the unconscious man's name, they nicknamed him Poilus. It seemed to suit him, or at least their romanticised notions of him.

Napoo was nervous and edgy, never leaving his bedside until the man eventually came round and opened his eyes. The wound on his thigh had been bandaged and he was still suffering from a slight fever, but Sister Fenton explained that they expected it to come down after a couple of days' rest.

Poilus looked around nervously, panic building behind his eyes. However, Napoo stepped into his eye line and laid his hand on his forearm, tears welling up in his eyes. He looked up at Everson across the bed.

"Yes," he said, his voice choked with emotion, "we will help you."

NAPOO WAS AT first suspicious when Oliver Hepton, delighting in him as some sort of indigenous novelty, wanted to film him. He persuaded Napoo to pose, which he did grinning nervously, surrounded by the men of 1 Section.

"Wave for the folks back home," Hepton directed them. "Valiant Tommies meeting the local natives of the Wonder Planet."

"Who's he kidding?" said Half Pint sourly as they performed for the camera. "Everything on this bloody planet is poisonous or dangerous. This place is going to kill us before we get a square meal out of it."

"Give it a rest Half Pint. Tell us something we don't know," said Gutsy.

"Whuuugh!" yelled Half Pint ducking down as something buzzed over his head; a fat bloated thing about the size of a pigeon with feathery antennae and large compound eyes. He started flapping his arms around. "Get it off, get it off!"

Napoo grinned, snatched it out of the air and bit its head off, spitting it onto the ground before tipping back his head and squeezing the carcass. A slop of dark viscera fell into his mouth. He chewed and swallowed.

"Gawd, that's disgusting!" said Porgy.

"It's good!" said Napoo, wiping his mouth on the back of his hand, offering it to Atkins.

Another flew by Pot Shot. He reached up a long gangly arm, and caught it. He was about to use his bayonet to cut the head off when Napoo stopped him, laughing.

"No, not that one,"

"Why not? I did what you did," Pot Shot protested.

Napoo shook his head and rapped his knuckles on Pot Shot's head.

"No, look. This one is thin. It hasn't fed yet. You wait until it has fed and fat. You eat that now you taste only bile. Make you sick." He picked it up and threw it away.

"Excellent!" yelled Hepton. Pleased with the unexpected footage he capped his camera.

EVERSON WAS RIGHT in his estimation of Napoo's knowledge. Over the next few days, he taught them many things. He showed them safe food to eat and where to find more. He told them what firewood to use without it spitting hot poisonous sap at them. He showed them edible fruits to gather, how to dig up the roots of the Tergo plant where they could find large, wriggling grubs the size of a man's forearm nestling in swollen tubers. They brought down one of the tall three-legged herbivore 'tripodgiraffes' as it fed. They also shot one of the hell hounds from a pack that was trying to stalk it. After several days of hunting and gathering, they had managed to build up quite a store of food.

"I think it would be a good idea," suggested Everson to Captain Grantham, "that is, I think it would boost the men's morale if we could celebrate our first meal with indigenous ingredients,"

The Captain nodded and waved his hand dismissively. "Whatever you want, Everson. Whatever you want."

However, Everson knew their survival would depend on more than food and water and morale. It would depend on information and there was more that Napoo might tell them about this planet. Therefore, he, Jeffries and Padre Rand sought to question him further. Padre Rand's bright flame of faith had guttered alarmingly in the face of the Somme and seemed extinguished by the wind of circumstance that had blown them to this world. Now it seemed Napoo's arrival fanned the embers of his dying belief. He had been a missionary in Africa and knew a heathen when he saw one. He wanted to know if Napoo believed in God, whether he had been baptised. He believed it to be his sacred duty to save the man's soul. If indeed he should have one. For if this place was not Earth, then he could not be a son of Adam, a creature of God.

"We believe in GarSuleth the sky god, weaver of the world, and in his brother, Skarra," said Napoo, reciting in the manner of a credo.

Everson could see the padre's eyes narrow in the face of this new heresy but of Jeffries' countenance, he could make nothing.

"You do not know of them?" said Napoo uncertainly. "But all Urmen worship them, the Ones decreed it..."

Everson shook his head and shrugged.

"The Ones. The Children of GarSuleth," said Napoo impatiently. "Whose land this is? How can you not know? This place borders Khungarrii territory. They killed many of my clan, so we stay away. You should too."

"Khungarrii?" queried Jeffries.

"The Khungarrii of the Ones, aye."

"When we first met you spoke of Free Urmen. I take it there are those who are not free?" asked Everson.

"They serve the Ones."

As Napoo continued to talk it seemed to Everson that, here on this world, Man had never risen to his full potential. Here, the majority were indentured servants to a race greater than they. Those Urmen that chose freedom rather than serve the Ones grubbed a meagre subsistence, living among the unforgiving fields and beasts of this God-forsaken world. That Man should be so humbled was anathema to him and, for a moment, he felt the same hot fury that he had once felt toward the Bosche.

THAT EVENING, COOKS prepared the foods as best they could. The men built and lit fires and gathered round them, some digging out such treasures as harmonicas or penny whistles. Mercy even managed to find a battered wind-up gramophone and a surviving record. The strains of old songs and laughter rose with the smoke from the myriad campfires towards the unknown stars above.

Edith Bell, Nellie Abbott and Sister Fenton sat apart on empty grenade boxes nibbling tentatively at skewered alien meat.

"So why did you become a VAD, Edith?" asked Nellie Abbott.

Edith was silent for a moment as if considering something before deciding to speak. "I was running away, I suppose."

"From what?"

"The past."

"Well they say it always catches up with you."

"That's why I thought the Front would be the best place to confront it."

"The Front? You deliberately came to the Front?"

"To face it head on, to punish myself for surviving," said Edith, shaking her head. "Oh, I don't know anymore. I don't care. Seeing all this suffering—at least here, this time I can do something. I can make a difference, can't I? You see I know we're all going to die, it's just that on the Front you have a better idea of when."

"What could be so awful that you think you're punishing yourself by serving here?" asked Fenton.

"It was two years ago," she said in a hushed voice, half hoping that they wouldn't hear her and she could pretend she hadn't said anything and not have to go through with it.

"What was two years ago, the start of the War?"

"No, it was before that."

Fenton and Abbott exchanged questioning glances, each shrugging. They waited. Nelly took Edith's hands in hers and gave them a small, warm squeeze then held them lightly.

"The Lamb—" she could barely get the words out. She stopped, smiled apologetically and cleared her throat. "The Lambton Grange Murders."

There was a sharp intake of breath from Nellie. "Oh you poor thing. Were—were you there? That was an evil thing what happened there. Our Bertie read it to us from the papers, he missed out the worst bits to spare us, silly sod. But I read the paper myself, later. Horrid, simply horrid."

"No, that's the thing, you see," said Edith. "I was supposed to be there."

"What do you mean?" asked Fenton.

"I knew the girls that were murdered, Elspeth Cholmondley and Cissy Pentworth. We were a bit of gang. We met him, at a party a month earlier."

"Dwyer the Debutante Killer? Strewth!"

"Yes. I believe that's what some of the more sensationalist newspapers called him. He seemed so charming. Of course, we knew he had a bit of a reputation. That was what poor Cissy found so alluring. He invited us out to his place for the weekend. Only I couldn't go at the last minute. Great Aunt Lil decided to come up from Brighton."

"That was some luck."

"But I let them go alone, don't you see? I should have been with them," she said, sobs welling up. "It should have been me, too."

Edith saw Lance Corporal Sandford approach them tentatively, hobbling along inexpertly on a crutch, a pal by his side, and hastily wiped her eyes, cursing herself for weakening and sharing her private burden. She pasted a smile on her face for Nellie's sake. "I'm all right," she said. "Really."

While the corporal and his mate stood talking to them, Edith could sense Nellie's awkwardness. Spotting the tank mechanic in his overalls, Nellie made her excuses, got up and slipped away, trying to catch his eye.

SAT ROUND THEIR own campfire, Atkins noticed Porgy stealing glances towards the nurses as the corporal sat down next to Edith, his injured leg out straight as he put an arm around her shoulder. Next to her, Sister Fenton wriggled away from his pal, rebuffing the NCO's advances. He tried again to put his arm around her shoulders, but she stood up. He couldn't hear what she was saying but he was obviously getting a bollocking. Fenton wrapped her cape around herself and stalked off in the direction of the casualty tents. Porgy had just decided to go and cut in when he saw Edith rise and help her suitor to his feet.

"Bad luck old chap," said Atkins sympathetically. "Perhaps if you'd got yourself more of a Blighty one."

"Fat lot of good a Blighty One does here!" he spat, glancing pointedly up towards the brightest star in the sky.

They watched as Edith helped Sandford walk along with his crutch. The pair passed beyond the light of one fire only to be silhouetted against another and met by encouraging whoops and catcalls as they passed the men gathered round it.

"Come on, Porgy. Face it. You lost out. Best man and all that, eh? Come and sit down," said Atkins.

"If he hurts her…" he muttered, tearing viciously with his teeth at the chunk of meat in his hands.

"My God," said Atkins, the truth dawning on him. "This isn't just about your deck of cards is it? You're actually serious about this one, aren't you?" The helpless look in Porgy's eyes said it all. "Look, he's crippled. What's he going to do, stand on her foot with his crutch? Come back to the campfire."

Atkins guided a reluctant Porgy back to where the rest of their section sat. After a while Half Pint turned the conversation to the thing that was on all their minds.

"What if we never get back? We're marooned here, I tell you. This," he said with a sweep of his arm, "is it and we'd better make the most of it."

"No, I don't believe that, I can't believe that," said Porgy. "Whatever brought us here might send us back just as quickly; the officers must think so too, why else do you think they've kept us on this stinking pile of mud?"

"Hope?" said Gazette. "But I don't think we can depend on miracles. If there's a way back I reckon we're going to have to find it ourselves."

"And what if there isn't a way back?" challenged Half Pint.

"We got here didn't we?" said Mercy angrily.

"Someone must be responsible. I say we find them and make them send us back," said Ketch.

"If there is someone, why did they bring us, what are we here for?" asked Gutsy.

"Do you really want to go back to the Somme?" said Half Pint.

"No," said Pot Shot. "I want to go back to my family."

A woman's horrified scream cut off the murmurs of assent.

Porgy was the first to jump and grab his rifle from the tee-pee of arms, causing the others to clatter to the ground.

"That bloody bastard. I knew it. If he's harmed her—" he said as he dashed off into the dark past other men, now standing up from the campfires and looking out into the night.

Atkins grabbed a rifle and ran after him, weaving between the fires and the muttering troops. Reaching the edge of the mud flat Atkins jumped the three or four feet to the plain and, without breaking step, ran on after Porgy toward the small copse of trees not twenty yards from the mud.

The screaming continued hysterically.

Atkins made it to the trees to find Porgy standing silhouetted against the light from a hurricane lantern hanging on a low bough. He rounded Porgy, accidentally standing on a discarded crutch as he did so. Then he saw Edith kneeling on the ground, her apron and nurse's uniform drenched in blood. The headless body of Corporal Sandford lay sprawled across her lap, blood now only gently pulsing from the open neck and pooling in the trough of her apron. There was no sign of his head.

A crack and a rustle from the foliage above alerted them and Edith screamed again, attempting to straighten her legs out in front of her and push her way back from under the trees. Porgy went down on one knee and clamped a hand across her mouth. Her eyes darted wildly to the canopy. Atkins put the rifle butt to his shoulder and scanned the foliage.

With his boot, Porgy clumsily struggled to push the headless body of the dead soldier off Edith's legs. "Shhh," he whispered in her ear before dragging her to safety.

Several other soldiers came running. Atkins beckoned them to stop and dropped down on one knee, eyes still fixed above him. He heard the sound of magazine cut-offs opened and loading bolts ratcheted back as one or two of the men circled round warily. He was aware of the sobbing nurse somewhere behind him, the noise growing fainter as Porgy took her back to the safety of the entrenchment.

His awareness immediately refocused as he caught movement on a bough above him. He gave rapid fire, five rounds as per. There was a sudden crack and crash as it fell through the canopy. The men backed off as something hit the ground. It was the soldier's head. The rustle continued high up in the tree as something jumped from one branch to the next in an effort to escape. Atkins and two other men followed the sound, firing blindly up into the foliage. Several others moved round outside the copse to cut it off. Whatever it was, they had it trapped now.

There was a scream as something snatched a soldier up into the foliage. His rifle clattered to the ground. There was a wet crunch accompanied by a strangulated sound before a head dropped down, bounced on the ground, and ended up staring, horrified, at Atkins.

Men blazed away into the trees, lost in fear and anger.

"Stand back," said a voice.

It was Porgy. From somewhere he had acquired a Lewis gun, slung from his right shoulder by a canvas strap and carried on his hip, a fresh circular magazine fixed to the top and several others in their canvas webbing slung over his other shoulder.

"Where?" he growled.

Atkins jerked his head upwards.

Somebody, an NCO, fired a Very flare into the trees. It burst with an angry hissing white light, setting the leaves ablaze and casting its stark glare over the area. There came a hoarse throaty screech and a rapid chattering as something thrashed about in the tree.

"There!" shouted someone as the dying glow of the Very light caught something shiny and brown. Porgy opened fire. The magazine rotated and the rapid rattle of the Lewis gun ripped through the foliage. There was an ear-splitting screech, like nails on a blackboard, and a large body crashed down followed by another.

Atkins stepped forward to examine the large, insect-like creature. Nearby, there was the decapitated body of the second soldier. "Yrredetti," he said, recognising the creature and its mottled markings from their mission in the forest, before putting his rifle against the creature's head and firing. Rather than dying, as he had every right to expect it would, the now headless insectoid body began thrashing about and only stopped when Porgy unloaded another entire magazine into it.

As the flames from the flare spread above them and the trees in the copse began to blaze, stretcher-bearers arrived to carry away the two dead soldiers. They left the body of the Yrredetti to burn.

INTERLUDE THREE
**Letter from Private Thomas Atkins
to Flora Mullins**

9th November 1916

Dearest Flora,
I should be writing this from Sans German, by rights. We should have been relieved and back in the reserve line by now, but all that's gone to pot. We're sans Germans all right, but we're sans everything else too. Although things are looking up. We had a picnic this evening, al fresco, as they say, to celebrate our first harvest. Like all picnics we got pestered by insects, well only the one, but you should have seen the size of it.

Porgy is sweet on a nurse. He's quite serious about her, I think. It's sad and funny to see. But all the boys love our 'Roses of No Man's Land' and she has a fearsome Sister over her who forbids fraternisation, so I don't hold out much hope for him, though he seems proper determined and pines like a lost puppy.

Mercy is up to his scrounging ways again. He's found something special for Lt Everson that he won't tell us about. Loves a secret, does Mercy. Hasn't stopped Gutsy starting a book on what it might be though. I put a tanner on a bath tub, because well, we haven't washed for nearly two weeks now, so God knows we could use one. Well, I say a tanner, but we haven't had any pay for the last few weeks and it don't look as if the payroll will come any time soon, either.

Ever yours,
Thomas

CHAPTER ELEVEN
"If the Sergeant Steals Your Rum..."

AFTER THE YRREDETTI incident, fires were set on the plain in a controlled slash and burn policy, forming a *cordon sanitaire* around No Man's Land to deny further cover to any predators. Atkins watched as the smudgy black smoke drifted into the sky. It felt as if they were finally making their mark, conquering the land that had seemed so hostile to them when they first arrived.

As the days passed, hope began to fade that they would be transported home as quickly as they had arrived and the new survival practices became an established part of the daily military routine. With the most suitable trees nearby having been cut down for firewood, shoring or building materials, the Foraging Parties had to move further and further afield. Poilus continued to improve and Napoo, in high spirits, continued to educate the soldiers in hunter-gathering.

He had pointed out a fruit tree, the large purple fruits of which were the size of mangoes and wincingly sweet. This gave Mercy an idea. To be fair it was obviously an idea he'd had for quite a while because it didn't take him long to put it into action. In an abandoned dugout, Mercy constructed a crude still from water drums and Ticklers' jam tins, and even managed to scrounge some copper piping for a condenser. He also acquired some yeast from the cooks' supplies.

One night Mercy slunk into the Section's dugout carrying an old stone rum jar, almost tripping over Gordon as the creature chatted the seams of Pot Shot's shirt. "Here," he said. "Try this. I've already sold half to some lads from 4 Platoon."

"You haven't been nicking the rum rations, have you? Hobson'll have your guts for garters," said Porgy.

"Relax, this is my own mixture, isn't it?"

"You mean—"

"He's been brewing this stuff in secret for days," said Gutsy, shaking his head. "I tried telling him it wasn't a good idea. If he gets caught he'll be for the high jump."

"So what's this gut-rot called then?"

"*Flammenwerfer*," said Mercy with a grin. "Who's first?"

Porgy and Half Pint pushed Atkins to the fore. "Go on, Only! Put hairs on your chest, will that."

Mercy, laughing, poured a large tot into a dixie can and thrust it towards Atkins.

"Down! Down! Down! Down!" the others chanted.

Egged on by the rest, Atkins, wanting to be a good sport, grudgingly emptied his dixie in one draught. He immediately regretted it, stumbling back, half-blinded by stinging tears as the liquor burned down his throat. Flammen-bloody-werffer indeed. Although, as he fought for breath, he thought 'Gas Attack' would have been a more appropriate epithet. He could feel a pounding begin at the base of his skull until the beat of it filled his head. The burning liquid etched a path down his insides to his stomach where it seemed to reach flashpoint and ignite, expanding to fill his entire body. His limbs began to tingle and throb to the beat of his pulse. As he wiped the tears from his cheeks, he began to feel dizzy and light-headed. Blinking, he tried to speak, but it seemed that his vocal cords had melted.

The faces of the men before him began to contort, twisting and turning like a Futurist canvas, their features malleable, fading and shifting. The khakis and mud greys around him began radiating kaleidoscopes of geometric patterns that burst against his retinas. He squeezed his eyes shut and shook his head in an attempt to rid himself of the vision, opening them again only to find the scene around him stubbornly ablaze with guttering colours. He tried to speak again, but his voice sounded so far away and foreign he could barely hear himself let alone distinguish what he was saying or whether it made sense. He was finding it hard to breathe. He thrust a finger down the collar of his shirt and pulled at it. He looked down at his feet impossibly far below him and a wave of vertigo washed over him. Arms reached for him but he batted them away and struggled to put one foot in front of the other as he broke away from the garish India rubber limbs that tried to claw him back.

He clambered out of the blue-tinged trenches that expanded and contracted in waves before him, threatening to swallow him, and ran over sky blue mud with teal vapours rising in convection eddies. Above him, the sky boiled gently off into magenta hues. Time seemed to contract and expand in waves, too. One moment he was stumbling across crusting mud then next he found himself oozing slowly across the deep red stubble of the burnt open ground beyond as the orange fronds loomed towards him.

Two lidless eyes stared back; multicoloured whorls like oil on water dancing on their dark surface, watching him from the foaming purple undergrowth before shadows crept in from the periphery of his vision, occluding all...

NOISES INTRUDED ON the blackness. Atkins felt himself surface from dark depths as diffuse light seeped into his consciousness. The noise grew until he thought his eardrums would burst. He sat bolt upright, gasping for air like a drowning man breaking the water's surface.

"Eyes!" he cried. "There's something watching us!"

Gentle hands urged him back down. Everything seemed raw and tinged with garish colours, like a hand-tinted photograph. The after effects of the Flammenwerfer, he expected. Things still wavered slightly, washing gently to and fro. He went with it and sank back into the pillow.

"There, there, you're safe. You've been hallucinating," said a soft warm voice. It was Sister Fenton. She soaked a cloth in a bowl of water by his stretcher and gently wiped his face. "That was a stupid thing you did. It could have killed you. How many of you drank that filthy stuff? Three are over there. One is blinded, another two have lost their minds. One poor wretch stumbled into a flooded shell hole and drowned. You were lucky." She held his head and gave him a sip of water. His dried, cracked lips stung as the water moistened them.

"Where..."

"You're safe. You're in the Casualty Clearing Station. Your friends brought you in. They found you wandering about—out there."

"Mercy," asked Atkins.

"Pardon?"

"My mate, Mercy."

"Is he the one who brewed the liquor?"

"Yes," he rasped.

"Hmm," said Fenton with a note of disapproval. "Well he'll get what's coming to him. He's in custody on a charge. There's to be a Court Martial."

CAPTAIN GRANTHAM, SECOND Lieutenant Everson and Lieutenant Jeffries sat behind the table. Everson hated this part of the job. Already that morning they had heard several cases. The penalties for even minor infractions were often excessive and out of proportion for the supposed crime. And as the accused this time was one of his own he felt a little ashamed too. Evans had always been one to run close to the wire. He looked along the table. Captain Grantham was playing nervously with his fountain pen, clearing his throat every minute or so. The only person who seemed relaxed with the situation was Jeffries. Since most of the men who tried the liquor were in 4 Platoon, Lieutenant Jeffries had a personal stake in the case. One of his men had died, another had been temporarily blinded and another had been relegated to the stockade with the shell-shocked. Everson heard Hobson's bark outside. He shifted position, sitting upright.

"Prisoner and escort, halt! Right turn!"

Evans entered the dugout flanked by two soldiers.

"Prisoner and escort, halt! 'tenshun!"

Evans stood to attention, his thumbs extending down along his trouser seams, looking straight ahead at the wall over the officers' heads, his face emotionless but for his eyes betraying a flicker of fear.

"What's this one?" asked Grantham.

Everson read from the charge sheet regretfully, "The accused, 98765 Private Wilfred Joseph Evans, 13th Pennine Fusiliers, a soldier of the regular forces, is charged with, when on active service, wilfully destroying Army property without orders from a superior officer and with brewing and distributing alcohol."

"Which frankly doesn't cover the half of it," said Jeffries. "Several of my men are in hospital and one is dead because of this man's actions. Brewing and distributing alcohol in the trenches. In fact, worse than alcohol. The report from the MO says here that the liquor, while being extremely alcoholic, also contained some form of noxious opiate, causing hallucinations. This man's expertise with the still equipment suggests to me that this isn't the first time he's done this."

"With respect, Lieutenant," said Everson. "There is no evidence he knew the ingredients to be harmful."

"Nevertheless," pressed Jeffries in clipped and measured tones. "I would ask for the maximum sentence."

"Has the accused anything to say in his defence?"

Even if he had, thought Everson, it wouldn't do him any good.

"With respect—" began Evans.

"Respect?" barked Jeffries, shouting him down. "You know nothing of respect, Private!" He turned and whispered to Grantham.

The Captain had a glazed look in his eyes, almost as if he had given up. He nodded, and then spoke up. "The unauthorised use of Army property will not be tolerated. I will be issuing a general order expressly banning the fermenting of alcohol for consumption forthwith. Sergeant, make sure his equipment is put beyond use. As for you, Private, penal servitude not being practical at this point, I hereby sentence you to Field Punishment Number One. I trust you will learn from this. Dismissed."

"Sah!" barked Hobson. "Prisoner and Escort left turn. Quick march."

Hobson marched Evans and his men away.

Grantham sighed, pushed his chair back and began shuffling his papers together in preparation to leave when Lieutenant Tulliver and Lieutenant Mathers entered.

"Excuse me, sir," said Mathers. "Tulliver and I have a request. If I might?"

"Eh?"

Jeffries leaned forward and looked past Grantham at Everson, his eyes narrowing. Everson shrugged.

"It's about the still your private constructed, sir. I understand you've given orders for it to be dismantled."

"Yes, dashed bad show. Showed the fella what for, though, eh, Jeffries?"

"Sir," said Jeffries darkly.

"Damned right."

"Well as you know, my tank and Mr Tulliver's plane only have limited supplies of petrol. Without it, our machines will be useless. Although unfit for human consumption we might be able to use this liquor as a petrol substitute."

"Of course!" said Everson. "That's a capital idea!"

"You agree with this, do you, Mr Everson?" asked Grantham.

"Resources are scarce, sir, and petrol supply is very limited," said Everson. "I believe Quartermaster Slacke only managed to find forty gallons. With Napoo's help, we've managed to find food and water and started to build up our stores. If we can solve the fuel problem as well, then that will increase our chances of survival. Without petrol those machines are just, well, so much junk, if you'll excuse me gentlemen."

Mathers shrugged indifferently.

Tulliver nodded in agreement. "No, you're right. If we can gather more of these fruits that your man found then we can distill as much fuel as we need. You know what they look like, where to find them?"

"Napoo does," answered Everson.

"Ah, yes, Napoo," said Jeffries quietly. "And just what exactly are this Napoo's motives?" He had been sat quietly listening, thinking. Jeffries seemed to do a lot of thinking, to Everson's mind. Which wasn't a bad thing in general. Too many officers didn't think at all. Jeffries, though, seemed to think altogether too much. Now, he uncoiled from his nest like a snake. "Who is he? What do we know of him?"

"He offered us help and knowledge when we needed it in exchange for aid with his kinsman," said Everson.

"Oh, and he has been helpful," admitted Jeffries. "To a point. He has warned about these... Khungarrii, yes. But the question is what else does he know? Is there anything he isn't telling us? You know virtually nothing about this world including, I might add, how we got here."

"I'm sure he'd tell us if he knew," said Everson.

"Your faith in human nature is heart-warming," said Jeffries, condescendingly. "But *is* he human? If this is a different world how can he be?"

"He seems to be an honest soul," said Everson.

"And again," said Jeffries, "does he even have a soul at all? I'm sure Padre Rand could dispute your claim."

"What's your point Mr Jeffries?" asked Grantham.

"My point, sir, is that we know nothing about this native, his loyalties, his people. How do we know they aren't hiding anything from us?"

"They have no reason to lie," said Everson.

"Speak plainly, Mr Jeffries," pleaded Grantham, rubbing his temples as if the very concepts Jeffries iterated pained him.

"Aren't we rather getting off the point here?" said Mathers. Jeffries shot him a glance as he continued. "Captain, have we your permission to commence distilling fuel for our machines?"

Grantham sat down heavily in his chair with a sigh and waved them away with his hand. "Yes, yes, of course. Take whatever you need. We must keep them going, I suppose."

Tulliver grinned and patted Mathers on the shoulder as they left, eagerly talking about plans to construct a bigger still.

Jeffries watched them go, like a cat watching another, warily, as it skirted its territory.

"Captain, if I may?" said Everson, rising.

Grantham, looking tired and worn, glanced up at him and nodded mutely.

"Sir," said Everson, putting his cap upon his head and adjusting it. "Mr Jeffries."

"So you have no objection then, sir?" asked Jeffries, in Everson's hearing.

Grantham looked up. "To what?"

"To my questioning this Napoo character, of course?"

"No, none at all."

"Good," said Jeffries under his breath, "good."

EVERSON REALISED THAT Jeffries was playing a dangerous game over this Evans incident. Since the repeal of flogging, the British Army had to resort to other imaginative forms of corporal punishment. Field Punishment Number One consisted of the convicted man being lashed to a fixed post or gun wheel for two to three hours a day without food or water, often deliberately in range of enemy fire. Asserting authority and discipline was one thing, but there was no telling how the men might respond to the brutal and public punishment out here. Separated from their home, their loved ones and now their planet, the trenches were a powder keg right now. The men were discontented, fractious. The last thing they needed was a reason to riot.

Everson entered the small dugout that was being used as a guardroom. "That was a damn foolish thing you did, Evans, bloody irresponsible!" he said, sitting down on the bunk bedside him. He pulled a hip flask from inside his tunic.

"A drop of the real stuff?" asked Mercy, meekly.

"You should know," said Everson as he unscrewed the cap and passed the flask to Evans. Evans took a slug.

"Aaah." He wiped his lips on his sleeve and passed it back. "Gilbert the Filbert's really got in for me hasn't he, sir?"

"Oh, believe you me, he's like that with everyone. No quarter given, but you bloody well asked for it. I warned you. What the hell did you think you were doing?"

"I didn't know the damn stuff made you see things and worse, sir, I swear! I didn't mean any harm. Those poor lads. It was only meant to warm the cockles and raise morale a bit."

"Damn it, Evans, There's a whole world out that that's trying to kill us. I don't need to worry about my own men doing it as well!"

Mercy lowered his eyes.

"This has got to be done, Evans. Discipline is important. Sometimes I think it's all that's keeping us together at the moment. If things go too far, I fear the men might mutiny and there are precious few officers to maintain order. If the men took it into their heads there's nothing we could do to stop them."

"Won't come to that, sir."

"How can you be so sure? No officer has the answers. I don't know where we are, or how. But I have to believe we'll get back. I have to. Because without that, without hope, then it all falls apart."

"The men know that too sir. Right now, they can grouse about the officers all they want but they know that if they usurp them, they'll have to fend for themselves. To put it bluntly sir, they don't want the responsibility. That and the fact, with the exception of Captain Grantham, you're all front line officers. If you weren't it might be a different story. But the men know you sir. They trust you."

"Well that's something I suppose," sighed Everson. "Can you take it, Evans?"

"Sir?"

"The punishment?"

"Had worse, sir," Evans said stoically.

Everson let a smile play briefly on his lips as he stood up, before scowling. "I can believe it. But I've already lost half my best men. I can't afford to lose any more. Straight and narrow after this Evans, or you'll answer to me."

"I don't suppose you'd care to leave that with me, sir?" he asked, nodding at the flask.

Everson looked down at the engraved silver hip flask and, after a moment's thought, tossed it over to Mercy. "It won't be enough, you know."

"Every little helps sir." Evans caught it cleanly. "Every little helps."

THE NEXT MORNING Grantham summoned all able-bodied men to witness Mercy's punishment. Discharged by the MO, Atkins still felt a little delicate when he joined the rest of his Section on parade. Ketch gave him a self-satisfied smirk as their eyes met.

"Bloody 'ell, Only, you look pale, you sure you're all right?" whispered Pot Shot.

"A little light-headed," Atkins replied. Spots still burst in his vision like Very lights and he had to keep moving his head to prevent Pot Shot being lost in drifting after-images. "What the hell happened?"

"We thought you were just foolin' around at first," muttered Gutsy, "but after you went doolally Ketch happened, that's what. The moment them blokes from 4 Platoon began screaming and blundering about in a blind panic, it didn't take him long to follow the trail back to Mercy. Hobson confiscated the booze and the still, but it were Gilbert the Filbert that pressed for a Court Martial."

"Parade! Parade 'shun!" bellowed Sergeant Hobson.

The guards brought Mercy out, stripped to the waist. He looked in a bad way; he'd been beaten black and blue. Jeffries' men had obviously given him a seeing to during the night, revenge for the men they lost. Jeffries stepped forward from the rest of the officers and addressed the men.

"98765 Private Evans, 2 Platoon 13th Pennine Fusiliers has been found guilty of wilfully destroying property without orders from a superior officer and endangering the lives of fellow soldiers while on duty. The penalty: 14 days Field Punishment Number One."

Mercy was led out into No Man's Land, beyond the barbed wire entanglement, to where a T-shaped post had been set into the ground. He was tied to the post in a crucifixion position, facing the trenches, so the men could see him, abandoned to the torment and torture of the alien sun, and whatever creeping, flying pests and predators might happen by.

A restless mutter arose from the watching troops.

"Silence!" bellowed Sergeant Hobson. "Parade! Parade fall out into working parties. Dismiss!"

Section NCOs began barking their orders and groups fell out, smartly marching off to their work details while Tulliver and Mathers' crew set off in the tank in search of more of the 'petrol fruit' for their newly acquired fuel still.

2 Platoon was due out on another Forage Patrol. They set off over No Man's Land, past Mercy who, despite bruised ribs, black eye and split lip, gave them an encouraging smile and a thumbs up. With uneasy glances back towards their pal they set out across the burnt clearing and across the veldt toward the forest.

Everson was uneasy that Napoo wasn't coming with them. Jeffries wanted to question him and Grantham had given him permission. Jeffries seemed to have Grantham eating out of his hand recently. He had been taking advantage of Grantham's weakened state; the man was obviously susceptible to whatever suggestions Jeffries was making. Of course, it was perfectly possible that Jeffries was just trying to bolster the old man's nerve...

AS THE URMAN entered the dugout, escorted by Sergeant Dixon, Jeffries studied him with some disdain. He didn't see the Noble Savage Everson claimed he saw but a wily indigent. From his occult researches he knew primitive peoples had caches of sacred knowledge forbidden to outsiders.

"Thank you, Dixon, that will be all."

Dixon saluted and left.

"So, you're the barbarian, the one they call Napoo?" said Jeffries as he watched the Urman pick up objects and study them briefly before putting them down and moving onto the next thing that caught his eye. He was like a child. Simple things delighted him greatly. Britannia was a Mother to many such peoples and Jeffries held none of them in any great regard. This man, though, was different. This man was wiry, but it all seemed to be muscle and he had survived to live to an age where his hair had greyed. Obviously he had a survivor's instinct that shouldn't be underestimated. Jeffries reached down to the holster on his Sam Browne belt and slowly undid the revolver cover. He grinned at Napoo as the man looked up at the sound of his new nickname, smiled, and went back to gazing with wonder at the things he saw.

"Everson has not such things," he said. "You are mightier than he is?"

Jeffries allowed himself a smile. The man amused him.

"Oh yes. Mightier than he knows, old chap."

"You are king here, then?"

"No, but I do like the sound of it. Are you not king of your own people?"

"No, only the Ones have kings," said Napoo as he picked up a pen from the small wooden crate that served as a writing desk. He sniffed the instrument then put it down.

"You're not one of the Ones, then?"

"No. Urman."

"The Ones," said Jeffries, "I wanted to ask you about them."

"This is Khungarrii territory. You should not be here. Not safe."

"Yes. So you said. And where are these Kungry—"

"Khungarrii," corrected Napoo, now sniffing, now licking a sealed tin of Tickler's Plum and Apple jam.

Jeffries took it off him and, using a tin opener, scythed it open before handing it back. He couldn't stand the stuff himself. It was just his luck that one of the foods they had did have in large supply was damned Plum and Apple jam.

Napoo stuck his fingers into the tin, scooped out the runny jelly and shoved his fingers into his mouth with great delight. "Mmm hmm." He smacked his lips.

"I saw a gleam over against those hills in a forest out beyond the veldt. A high spire. Is that them? Is that where these Khungarrii of yours live?"

"Aye, that's the Khungarrii Edifice," said Napoo. "Croatoan curse them!"

Jeffries froze.

"What?" he said. That the name of his chosen god should be uttered by one such as this who should not know of him at all stunned Jeffries. This was more than mere coincidence. Within the Great Working there *was* no coincidence. It was another sign. Of that he was sure. He rounded on the savage. "What did you say?"

Napoo was startled. He offered the half eaten tin of jam back to Jeffries. "Forgive me, I didn't not mean to—"

"What did you say?" he asked again, urgency in his voice.

"I—I said Croatoan curse them! Forgive me."

"What do you know of Croatoan?" said Jeffries, advancing on Napoo. "Tell me!"

"Nothing," he answered, puzzled at his host's sudden change in bearing. "It is an old curse that once had meaning to my forebears."

"You don't... worship him?"

"No, it is forbidden.

"By whom?"

"The Ones. There is only one god, GarSuleth, Weaver of the World," said Napoo reverently bowing his head.

Jeffries picked up his journal and leafed impatiently through the pages until he reached one on which was scrawled a symbol. He thrust the page under Napoo's nose. "This symbol. This sign. Do you recognise it, the Sigil of Croatoan?"

"No," said Napoo, shaking his head.

"Are you sure?"

"I have never seen its like."

"Never?"

"No, Only the Ones make such marks."

"What marks?"

"Like these," said Napoo gesturing at the open book. "Like the ones outside, the telling marks."

"The trench signs? Writing? Urmen don't write?"

"We do not know how to make the telling marks."

Jeffries slammed the book down. The rickety table juddered under the impact. These savages were so simple they had no written language. If Napoo was speaking the truth then they were of no immediate use to him. But, clearly, the Khungarrii were. After days of confusion, his path was now clear. These Khungarrii were the key.

"Are you telling me everything?"

"Yes. We do not mark-make."

"What are you not telling me, Napoo?"

"I don't understand."

"This is your world, are you seriously telling me you know nothing more than how to pick fruit and hunt animals?"

"What else is there to know?"

"Don't play games with me, Napoo," said Jeffries, picking up his ceremonial dagger, allowing the blade to glint in the dim light. "Either you tell me what I want to know or I will divine the truth from your entrails."

"All they would tell you are what fruit is good to eat and what animals good to hunt," said Napoo calmly.

There was a commotion outside. Jeffries did not want to be disturbed now. Whoever it was would pay for it. "Stay here," he told Napoo. "I haven't finished with you yet." He heard shouts and rifle fire. He lifted aside his gas curtain and stepped out into the trench. A private almost knocked him over.

"What's going on?" he snapped.

"We're being attacked! They came at us from the rear near the unfinished trenches!"

"Napoo, come with me," Jeffries called back into the dugout. If something was mounting an attack, this savage's knowledge could prove vital. Napoo appeared and he pushed him along the trench, the revolver in the small of his back urging him forwards.

A petrified solider ran down the trench toward them, screaming. "They're not human!" he cried as he tried to barge past Napoo and Jeffries.

"Private! Halt. This is desertion. Turn back or I'll shoot." However, the panic-stricken soldier was no longer listening. Reason had fled. Jeffries pointed his pistol and fired. The man fell back and slithered down the trench wall. Jeffries urged Napoo on. He could see smoke rising now from the newly fortified trench and the noises of battle filled the air. Blue flashes crackled over the lips of the communications trench followed by brief screams. Approaching the rear fire trenches Jeffries saw men retreating towards them along the bays, fighting a defensive action.

"Khungarrii," said Napoo calmly, gazing towards the blue flashes that lit the trenches. "I warned you."

Jeffries glared at Napoo furiously. There was nothing he could do here now. If he were to face these Khungarrii, he would do it on his terms, not theirs. He turned to slip back down the communications trench. Round the traverse, he caught a glimpse of something manlike. A bright blue flash filled his vision. His body went numb and the duckboards swung up to meet him.

CHAPTER TWELVE
"The Sacred Call of 'Friend'…"

"ONE OF THESE days I'm going to have that buggering bastard Jeffries, officer or no," said Gutsy as they moved swiftly and quietly along now well-trodden paths through the forest, thankful to be out of the heat of the alien sun. They were all painfully aware that, back at the entrenchment, Mercy had to endure its unforgiving glare, tied to the post as part of his punishment. To a man, the Section resented the example Jeffries had made of their pal and Ketch's part in it. Army justice could often be swift and cruel and discipline unavoidable, but there was a point beyond which it ceased to be effective. Given the conditions the men were living and fighting under, morale was brittle and they would only bear so much.

"Keep your voice down," hissed Atkins, nodding forwards to where Ketch ambled along, his ears no doubt burning, "or you'll be up on charges, too."

The routine of food collecting had now become a practised one for 1 Section. They knew now where to find the fruits that would not poison them. They had set traps and nets to catch animals. Fruits they slung into sandbags suspended from a pole carried between Porgy and Gutsy. The rest of the men had emptied their packs and were now carrying them in what they called Forage Order. The constant bombardment of Hun shells seemed a distant memory; many of the men had taken to wearing their regulation soft caps instead of their steel helmets, which proved uncomfortable in the heat.

Ketch had shuffled forward and was talking to Sergeant Hobson.

"Yeah, but Field Punishment?" said Gutsy. "He didn't have to go that far."

"Quiet back there," said Hobson, walking back along the line.

Atkins saw Ketch, up ahead, turn back and watch, scornfully. He pointed at his own eyes, then at Atkins—*I'm watching you.*

"If I hear any more 'mutinous mutterings' I'll make the lot of you sorry you were born," snarled Hobson in a low, dangerous voice. "And you, Atkins. You should appreciate just how stupid your mate Evans was. You nearly died. He knew the consequences when he started that racket. And he took 'em like a man. Scroungers and chancers like him may do you a favour every now and again, but they'll all get caught out somewhere down the line, you mark my words."

"But couldn't the lieutenant do anything, Sarn't?" asked Porgy.

The sergeant's face softened. "He did what he could, lad."

"Shh!" hissed Pot Shot. The column froze.

"I don't hear—"

Muffled by the forest canopy and the undergrowth they heard the faint sound of a whistle blown three times.

"The entrenchment!" Ketch blurted.

Blood and sand, thought Atkins, *please God don't say the entrenchment is vanishing without us.*

From the fleeting looks of panic on the others' faces, he could tell they were thinking the same thing.

"Make for the rendezvous point," said Lieutenant Everson. Immediately they dropped the carrying pole and sandbags of fruit and pelted back along their trail, hobnail boots pounding out an urgent tattoo.

It took them ten long agonising minutes of occasional stumbling, shouted encouragement and blasphemous urgings to reach the edge of the forest and Lieutenant Baxter's covering Lewis gun section. They had blown the whistle. Between deep wracking breaths, Atkins peered out across the plain; down the trail they'd made though the tube grass. Nothing seemed amiss.

"Baxter?" queried Everson.

"Shooting, sporadic gunfire from the direction of the entrenchment."

"Flare?"

"No."

"Oh, thank God!" muttered Everson.

"Is it vanishing, sir?" asked Pot Shot, through a hacking smoker's cough.

"No. Signal for that's a red flare. From the gunfire, sounds like they're being attacked. Right. Back to the entrenchment at the double. Set up covering positions and OP at the edge of the razed clearing. Stay under cover of the grass. I want to know what we're getting into before we go charging in blindly."

"Christ," said Atkins. "Now what?" he checked his rifle's magazine and flicked the cut-off open. He didn't like surprises. And this planet was just bloody full of them.

FOR THE LAST hundred yards or so, 1 Section dropped into a crouch and edged their way forward through the bush, fanning out from the path. Everson peered across the charred earth that lay before the tilted muddy escarpment ahead of them. Smoke rose from beyond the lip and the cries of wounded reached them, carried on the wind.

"Hobson, take three men and proceed to the lip of the entrenchments. Hold that position," said Everson quietly. "We'll cover you. If it's all clear, we'll leapfrog you."

Hobson looked around. "Atkins, Hopkiss, Blood, you're with me."

Gazette, Half Pint, Pot Shot and Ketch took up covering positions in the tube grass. The Lewis gun section set up their gun. To their left Atkins spotted another couple of foraging parties that had returned in answer to the shots and now held back on the edge of the tube grass awaiting further orders. Everson indicated they should wait for his order before advancing.

Keeping low, Atkins followed Hobson as they ran across the scorched earth before throwing himself down against the chalky embankment of Somme mud.

"Atkins," hissed Hobson, with a jerk of his head.

Feeling vulnerable without his battle bowler Atkins cautiously peered over the lip of the mud across the remains of No Man's Land and towards the trenches a couple of hundred yards away. He could make out the tents of the Casualty Clearing Station beyond the Front Line. The remains of several tents were smoking. Figures wandered about dazed. Atkins looked back over his shoulder. "Looks like the aftermath of an attack, Sarn't. I can't see any enemy troops."

"Hopkiss, Blood, get up there with Atkins. Cover the lieutenant's advance."

They scrambled to the top of the lip alongside Atkins, their rifles aimed, unnaturally, towards their own Front Line as the lieutenant, Gazette, Pot Shot, Half Pint and Ketch scurried past them before dropping down into the cover of a large shell hole. Further to their right, they saw several other sections moving towards the trenches. There was a brief wait before Everson waved Atkins and the others forwards. Atkins leapt up and ran low across the drying mud, kicking up dust as he did. He slid down into the shell hole, Porgy, Gutsy and Sergeant Hobson almost coming down on top of him.

"I can't see any sign of occupation," said Everson. "Hobson, stay here. I'm going to take a butcher's. Atkins you're with me. Straight for the firing trench."

Atkins took several deep breaths and launched himself out of the shell hole. It felt distinctly odd to be charging your own trenches. This is what the Huns must have seen as they attacked. There was a buzz and crack as a bullet crunched into the crust of mud at his feet. He threw himself aside, into a crater.

"Ally Pally!" called Everson. "Ally Pally!"

A head appeared above the parapet. "Sorry, sir. Thought you were another of them Chatt bastards!"

Everson glanced at Atkins. Chatts? Atkins shrugged and shook his head. Everson stood up and walked towards the fire trench, Atkins following. Behind them, the rest of the section made their way in, along with other forage patrols, alert and nervous. Atkins grabbed a dazed private with haunted eyes.

"What happened?"

"They came out of nowhere."

Atkins shook him out of frustration. "Who? Who did?"

"Them!" said the soldier pointing at a body on the ground nearby, half obscured by the bend of the traverse. "Dozens of 'em."

Atkins took a step towards it. "Blood and sand! Lieutenant, I think you should see this."

"Good God," Everson gasped as he looked down at the corpse before them. Was it some sort of insect? It would take a more scientific mind than his to determine, although it certainly seemed to elicit that level of primal revulsion.

Porgy and Gutsy came up beside them and stared down at the sight.

The body that lay on its back at their feet wasn't human, although its proportions were. It would have stood between five and six feet tall. Its large black eyes were set in a wide flat armoured head and Atkins realised with a shock that he'd seen ones like them before, staring back at him from his hallucinatory episode. Below the eyes, at the bottom of the fused chitinous plates that covered its head was something he scarcely recognised as a mouth. Two shiny black mandibles, closed over a mucus-slick muscular maw. Four smaller articulated palps lay slack and lifeless about it. At the top of its head protruded two antennae, segmented and each about a foot long. One had snapped and lay at an odd angle. Two wiry looking arms, each covered with a series of barbed chitinous plates, extended from shoulder joints in the thorax. Each arm ended in what may have been a hand with two fingers and a prehensile thumb-like appendage.

Where, on a man, one might expect to find the ribcage, this creature had a hardened plate that shimmered with an iridescent gleam. There was a gaping hole in the plate from which a bluish liquid oozed. Atkins poked it with his bayonet. The edges of the hole gave way with a brittle crack. He drove the bayonet home, just to make sure. The thing didn't move.

He thought of the beetles that used to scuttle about his mam's kitchen. He and William used to crush them under their clogs with just such a frail, moist crunch.

Below this was an unarmoured mid-section from where two smaller, less well-formed limbs projected, each ending with a single curved claw of the same iridescent black as its carapace.

"Yrredetti?" asked Atkins.

Everson shook his head. "Wrong colouring. Besides, Napoo said they hunt alone. This must be Khungarrii."

"They're just big fat bloomin' lice!" exclaimed Gutsy. "Nothing more than vermin!" He kicked the creature's thorax. "'Chatts' is bloody right."

"Atkins, Hopkiss, see what you can find out," said Everson, still staring thoughtfully at the alien body before them. "Jellicoe, Otterthwaite and Nicholls, pull together as many able bodied men as possible. I want this entrenchment secure. Hobson, order the men to stand to."

ATKINS AND PORGY weaved their way through the fire and communications trenches. They came across several Khungarrii dead, lying among the bodies of their own. They stopped for a line of men, their faces roughly bandaged, one hand on the shoulder of the one in front, led, blind and stumbling, to the Casualty Clearing Station.

"Bastards spit acid," said the Lance Corporal leading them.

From a shelled section of trench, they ascended onto the open ground. Between the lines, they passed Hepton who was excitedly filming a group of grinning Tommies posing with a dead Khungarrii, like Big Game hunters. Amid the chaos and aftermath of the attack, Atkins could see the punishment post beyond the wire. Mercy was still there, crucified. His torso was now one great purple and black bruise.

"Mercy!" He ran towards him, stopping only to find a breach in the wire entanglement.

"Huu—"

"Mercy, you okay?"

"'S it look like?"

"Hang in there, mate."

"Oh, ha ha, very funny," said Mercy through dry, cracked, lips. "You should be in the musical hall, Only." Atkins held him up as Porgy used his bayonet to cut the rope binding his wrists.

"You two, what do think you're doing? I'll have your names for this!" It was Ketch. "Atkins, I might have known it were you!"

"Back off, Ketch," snarled Porgy. "Lieutenant Everson asked us to find witnesses. No thanks to you and Gilbert the Filbert, Mercy here was front and centre for the whole attack."

Mercy managed a weak grin. "Nice to see you, too, Corp," he rasped before insolently hawking a gob of mucus in Ketch's direction.

MERCY SAT ON an ammo box, Everson and 1 Section gathered round him. He gulped down the proffered water as Everson and the others waited impatiently.

"What happened?" asked Porgy, indicating the confusion around them. "Where's Edith?"

"I don't know. Couldn't see much from where I was," he said hoarsely. "They moved fast, rounded up prisoners. I think they must have come in through one of the unfinished OP saps. They must have taken out the sentries. Nobody saw them until they were in the trenches. I heard some shooting, then they swarmed across the top, some leaping ten, twenty feet at a go. Ugly buggers, like great big fleas."

"Yeah, we seen 'em," said Half Pint.

"They were well organised. Some of them spit, like, an acid. Others had lances and backpacks. Looked like a *flammenwerfer*, but it shot blue crackling fire stuff. Like electricity. But mostly they had swords and spears. They seemed to take a lot of loot as well, trench equipment, weapons and the like."

Among the missing were Captain Grantham, Padre Rand, Lieutenant Jeffries, Napoo, the three nurses and about twenty-five other ranks.

"Seems to have been a well-planned raid," Sergeant Hobson said bitterly.

"We've got to go after them, sir," said Porgy.

"We will, Hopkiss, we will," said Everson. "But first things first. We have to secure the entrenchments. We have to wait for the other Forage Parties to come back. And we have to find out exactly what we're up against. Then we have to put together a plan of attack and get a party together to go after them. Rushing into this won't do us any favours."

It seemed though, from Ration Dump rumour, that wasn't good enough for a section of Jeffries' Platoon, who had grabbed their guns and just gone after them; it was twenty minutes before anyone noticed that they were missing.

"Idiots!" said Everson. He was now the ranking infantry officer in the entrenchment. "Hobson, order the NCOs to take roll calls. Find out if anyone else is missing."

TULLIVER AND THE tank crew returned in *Ivanhoe* from their petrol fruit forage trip, unaware of the raid until they were met with the organised chaos of mobilising infantry.

"Tulliver, how quickly can you get your machine in the air?" asked Everson.

"Give me ten minutes," said Tulliver.

"They've got about three hours on us by now. Can you track them, see which way they're headed?"

"Yes, I can do that but the state of the strip isn't perfect. I don't want to do too many take off and landings there without flattening the ground more."

"Right, I understand, but for now?"

"I'll chance it."

Everson watched anxiously as Tulliver and a couple of soldiers pulled the aeroplane out of its makeshift tarpaulin and brushwood hangar. The pilot waved at him as he stood by his machine. Everson raised his hand in reply and watched the young lad climb into his cockpit and strap himself in. A soldier pulled the propeller. Contact. Tulliver ran up his engine, testing it. Finally, the Sopwith began to run forwards eagerly. Tulliver gave it its head, the tail left the ground before the end of the take-off strip, and it lifted up across the fronds of tube grass. The aeroplane wheeled around the entrenchment before climbing and veering off, following the path Everson told him the arthropod raiders had taken. Everson turned from the aeroplane and headed back towards the trenches and the Casualty tents.

In the dank-smelling tent, Everson sat down next to Poilus. The young savage sat up in his cot, drinking a dixie of water. He looked disconcertingly out of place wearing striped pyjama bottoms. God knows where they'd come from. "Tell me about the Khungarrii," he said.

"They are of the Ones," said Poilus, as if that explained all.

"They've taken my men. Napoo, too. We intend to get them back but we need to know what they're going to do with them."

Poilus sighed. "Khungarrii always take Urmen. They make them work for them in Khungarr; building, mending, growing, cleaning..."

"But not you. They didn't take you."

"The sick and frail are no use to them," said Poilus with a hint of disgust at his own weakened state.

"Because they can't work them as slaves?"

"I don't know this word."

Everson didn't feel like explaining. He pressed on with his questions. "How many Khungarrii in Khungarr?"

"I do not know. Many. A great number."

"And Urmen?"

"Many."

"Damn," muttered Everson. For someone who resented the weight of responsibility, it looked like his load had just become a lot heavier.

Tulliver banked his machine with a little left rudder and turned to follow the trail that was plainly visible from this height, cutting a swath through the tube grasses of the valley, but of the raiders and their prisoners there was no sign. The valley side's fell away diminishing into foothills before a vast veldt opened up below him. He followed the trail across it for some twenty miles until he saw it vanish into a huge forest that seemed to extend for hundreds of square miles. Amid the forest, something glinted in the sun. A large tower-like structure rising above the tree canopy, twinkling as if—

The engine started to cough and splutter fearfully. That wasn't good. Best head for home. He throttled up, pulled the stick back to gain more height, and turned the machine towards the khaki coloured smudge of drying mud in the distance.

"Just another ten minutes, old girl," he urged. But he wasn't going to get it. He grimaced, throttled back and put the nose down before shutting the engine off. Better not to risk the engine, not in this place; there was no machine-shop to repair it if it went. The choking cough of the engine silenced, the only sound now was the wind whistling through the struts and interplane wires as he glided in, making for the burnt strip ahead. He circled to make his landing, skimmed over the top of the tube grass and came down a little inelegantly for his tastes, but without any further mishap. He jumped out to examine the machine. The fault didn't take too long to find. The petrol feed pipe had been crudely punctured. Since there was no corresponding hole in the fuselage, it could only indicate that someone had tampered with it from inside. Luckily, it shouldn't be too hard to fix. The control lines were another matter. Someone had tried to file through those as well. If they had failed while he was in the air he would have lost complete control. Thankfully, whoever it was hadn't done their job too well. Nevertheless, there was only one word for it. Sabotage.

IT HAD BEEN Porgy's idea, but nobody was against it, if it took his mind off Edith for a while.

"Gilbert the Filbert's had it coming," said Porgy as they crept down the comm trench.

"We can do his dugout over and blame it on them Chatts. No one'll ever be the wiser. I'll bet there'll be some good loot in there. Whisky. God, what I wouldn't give for some good whisky."

Mercy had insisted on coming with them, hissing, sucking and cursing with pain from his beating all the way.

It wasn't long before they reached the switch where Jeffries' dugout was located.

"We'll be up for it an' no mistake if we get caught, fellas," said Pot Shot hesitantly.

"We're here now. We're only looking for a little payback, Pot Shot, that's all," said Mercy, wincing. "The least that bastard can give me is a decent malt." He pushed back the gas curtain and stepped down into the dugout.

Atkins looked apologetically at Pot Shot and shrugged, "Look, stay here and keep watch. We won't be long, I'll stop him from doing anything too stupid." He knew this was a bad idea, but then so was going over the top and that had never stopped them before. He dealt with it the same way: one step in front of another. It was dark in there and smelt of stale sweat, hair oil and damp earth, and there was another peculiar odour, like sour potpourri. It began getting crowded as Gutsy and Gazette entered behind him, their bulks blocking out what little light filtered down from the entrance.

Porgy went over to the small crate that served as a writing desk. On it were a pack of worn cards and a leather-bound journal surrounded by a circle of salt. "Diary of an officer," he said, holding it up with a leer and a wink. He riffled through the pages. His face screwed up in frustration and disappointment. "'Ere, these entries are all in code. Look, there are symbols and things... I can't make head nor tail of it."

"Let me have a look," said Gutsy, picking up the volume and licking the tip of his index finger before turning a page.

"I'm telling you. It's in code," said Porgy. "You don't reckon he's in military intelligence, do you? We're in deep if he is."

"Bloody 'ell, you're right," said Gutsy, throwing the book down as if it had stung him. "You think he's a Jerry spy? He seems the sort. Hates his own men worse than Fritz."

Mercy casually glanced around the place, looking for anything of value. Seeing nothing of immediate or obvious interest, he bent over with a grunt and began feeling about under the thin straw mattress on the wire frame bed. "I wouldn't be at all surprised. I always thought there was something a little 'off' about him. He was always a bit too full of himself. Only, give us a hand will you?"

Atkins dropped down on his knees by his friend, who, finding nothing under the mattress, put his hand under the bed. Mercy pulled a suitcase into the light, the oxblood red leather case scuffing along the dirt-covered floor as they did so. Half-heartedly, Atkins tried opening it and was relieved to find it locked. But Mercy wasn't going to be beaten. He pulled his bayonet from its sheath, jimmied the lock and opened the suitcase.

"Bloody hell."

"Hey, you chaps ought to see this," said Gutsy, pulling at a loose-fitting piece of tea-chest panelling. It came away exposing a sackcloth curtain which he pulled back to reveal a hidden niche. "What do you make of this little lot?"

They peered into the niche. There were ornate silver candleholders and a ceremonial dagger of some exotic foreign design, along with a black stone with a symbol carved in it.

"Loot?"

"Looks expensive, like he's robbed a church or museum or summat."

"Yeah, but why keep 'em there? Not exactly hidden is it?"

Atkins turned his attention back to the contents of the suitcase. There, he found a private's uniform with patches indicating it to be from the Black Foresters—the Midland Light Infantry, and an Artillery officer's uniform, neither had any links with the Pennines. There were five pay books, one of a private and the others of several officers and an assortment of identity discs, cap badges and regimental patches. Stuffed under the uniforms were maps and papers: maps of Harcourt Sector showing British artillery positions and barrage targets, Battalion papers with dates of leaves and transfers; some old, some yet blank and undated.

"Something bloody odd's going on here," said Atkins.

"Who'd have stuff like this but a bloody spy!" said Mercy. "Gawd almighty!"

"Do you think the lieutenant knows?" asked Porgy.

"Do *you* want to ask him?" Half Pint said. "Sir, we were just looting the lieutenant's dugout when we came across these?"

"We have to tell him," said Atkins. "It's the right thing to do. If we don't it's *failing to inform*. Look, I trust Lieutenant Everson. I don't trust Jeffries. And certainly not now. There's something rum going on here and frankly I'd feel a lot more comfortable if we had the lieutenant on our side."

UNFORTUNATELY, ATKINS COULDN'T go straight to Everson. This was the army. You didn't just barge up to an officer. It wasn't done. You had to go through an NCO. He had to go through Hobson. He was more worried about the sergeant's reaction than the lieutenant's. Nevertheless, with the 'evidence' bundled up in an Army blanket, Atkins sought him out.

The platoon sergeant looked at him sternly and not without a little suspicion, glancing through the items, singling out the coded journal and the exotic knife as Atkins explained his finds.

"I think you'd better come with me, lad," he said.

They found Everson with Tulliver in the Company HQ. He was having a heated exchange of words with the Flying Officer.

"Sir," said Sergeant Hobson. "Atkins here has something to say. I think you'll want to hear it."

"This'll have to wait, Tulliver," said Everson. Exasperated, Tulliver turned to leave the tent. "What is it Atkins, I've got a lot on my plate right now."

"It's about Gilb—Lieutenant Jeffries, sir."

Tulliver turned from the tent flap when he heard the name. "Wait, did you say Jeffries?"

"We were combing the entrenchments, sir, and thought we heard something in one of the dugouts," said Atkins. "It was Lieutenant Jeffries' one, sir. We—we've found this stuff scattered about the floor." Atkins emptied the blanket's contents—clothing, papers, maps, pay books, discs and museum loot—onto the table. "We didn't pay much heed at first, sir, until we noticed the pay books. They aren't for men in his platoon, sir. They aren't even for men in this battalion. Blood thought he might be a Jerry spy, sir, and that we ought to report it."

"Stop right there, Atkins," said Everson. "Those are very serious charges. You can't just bandy about such accusations like that."

"But, sir..."

"Leave this with me. Thank you Atkins. That will be all. Dismissed."

"Sir."

Atkins saluted and left, feeling disappointed and dismayed by Everson's noncommittal reaction. However, he told himself, he'd done the right thing this time, or at least he hoped he had.

ALTHOUGH HIS DISMISSAL of Atkins might have been brusque, it was only because the evidence in front of him troubled Everson. He been sorting out the logistics of a raid on Khungarr and frankly the odds weren't in their favour. "Do you believe him, Hobson?"

"I believe they found this stuff in Jeffries' dugout, yes, sir."

"And what about these? Any of these names mean anything to you?"

The sergeant flicked through the pay books and shook his head. "No, sir."

Tulliver began leafing through the books himself, opening and discarding one after another. "Wait. This one. Hibbert. I know this name."

"From where?" asked Everson.

"Artillery officer. I took him up for a look-see three or four weeks ago. It's not something I've done often, so it stuck in my mind. Fella had this queer way of signalling 'okay,' with his thumb and forefinger, which I thought was odd. Most people use a thumbs up. Then when I met that chap, Jeffries, I thought he looked damned familiar, you remember? He half convinced me we hadn't met at all, then, when I took him up the other day, he used the self-same signal. I'd swear it's the same man, although he didn't have a moustache then. And this," he said, picking up the officer's jacket with the artillery patches and badges, "this was Hibbert's mob. How do you explain this? It could have been he who sabotaged my machine, because it *was* sabotage. The petrol feed was punctured after he thought I recognised him. And he couldn't have failed to notice that spire I saw in the distance, reflecting the sun the way it did. You didn't believe me ten minutes ago, but surely you can't ignore this? The man's up to something, though God knows what his bloody game is."

"Hmm." Everson studied the papers for a while and then looked at the artillery barrage maps which showed a pattern of bombardment marked over the Harcourt Sector "There's something peculiar about these maps, too."

He turned to the Flying Officer and came to a decision. "All right, maybe there are allegations to answer here, Tulliver, but Jeffries will have to wait. Our main objective is to rescue our people and our secondary objective is to free these subjugated Urmen from the... Khungarrii." He turned to Sergeant Hobson, who was leafing through a sheaf of Jeffries' blank battalion orders. "Sergeant, get the men on parade."

TWENTY MINUTES LATER Everson stood under the ragged Union flag, before a parade of weary, discontented men as NCOs barked and cajoled them into order. It had long been a point of contention among the Red Tabs that, at the Front, the men's aggression should be channelled into attacks and trench raids to prevent them becoming an idle, disaffected rabble. While he was sure they would be glad of the opportunity of action, he may well have to convince them of it. However, as much as they needed an objective and motivation, above all they needed hope.

"Men!" he began. "You know by now that these Khungarrii have captured some of our own. We will get them back, but this cannot be our sole objective. For, whatever reason we find ourselves here, we are still British. We are a long way from home, on a foreign world where Man has been subjugated by an inhuman race who may very well know how we came to be here. They may even know how we can return home. But we also know our duty. It is clear. It is the reason you took the oath and the King's shilling in the first place. It is the reason you volunteered."

"We didn't volunteer for this!" came an anonymous cry. There were mutterings of agreement among the ranks.

Everson ignored them. "Did we turn our backs in '14 when Belgium pleaded for our aid? No! We answered their call. Honour bade us do no less. Can we do any less now, when our fellow Man suffers here under the oppression of a cockroach Kaiser?

"Or will we let the fate of these Urmen be our fate too? I say to these Khungarrii that whatever you do to the least of my brethren you do unto me. We will show them that 'no gallant son of Britain to a tyrant's yoke shall bend.' We may no longer be on the Western Front, but we have found ourselves a new Front. Here is where we draw the line, here in this Somme mud, where we always have. This corner of a foreign field is all we have left of England and we shall defend it—and all it stands for.

"I want volunteers to mount an expedition to free our companions and perhaps rouse these subjugated Urmen into rebellion. We do not know the number of the enemy or their disposition, but we put the kibosh on the Kaiser. We can put the kibosh on these Khungarrii! What do you say, Pennines?"

A raucous cheer rent the air. Everson's chest heaved as much with pride as with relief. These were the men he knew, men with a purpose, with a challenge. These were the 'Broughtonthwaite Mates.'

"I think you got 'em, sir," said Hobson.

CHAPTER THIRTEEN
"Hasty Orisons"

SMALL RIPPLES OF consciousness lapped at the shores of Jeffries' oblivion, washing up a flotsam of sensations. A flare of light. Flashes of russet and damson.

Darkness.

A feeling of warmth. An aroma of mint and sweat.

Silence.

A cacophony of noises—cracks, crunches, sobs, howls, whistles and clicks—sloshed over into the silence surrounding him.

Jeffries came round to find himself lying on narrow wooden planking that moved under him with a disconcerting rocking motion. Looking up, walls woven from branches arose either side of him, framing a view of violet and magenta foliage that drifted past above. It took several minutes before full use returned to his arms and legs and he was able to sit up. Pins-and-needles lingered in his limbs and spots cluttered his vision like drifting Very lights.

He found himself in a long narrow cradle-like structure with Napoo and several despondent privates. He peered over the edge. He could see that the cradle was slung from the side of a great grub-like creature easily twice the height of an elephant and some twenty to thirty yards long. Along its length, it wore a great harness of ropes and straps from which hung similar cradles containing further captives. Presumably, they also hung from the far side in a similar arrangement. Along the back of the mammoth caterpillar-like crawler, their captors—insects the size of men—patrolled its length, looking down on their captives, their antennae, twitching.

As the path curved gently he was able to look over the edge of the basket and see another caterpillar beast ahead of them. It crawled along on stumpy legs with an elegance and agility that belied its bulk. A rider sat behind its head on a howdah, guiding the thing with a series of reins. It cleared the trail before them, crushing undergrowth and boughs in its way or eating its way through overgrown vegetation. Another larval beast of burden brought up the column to the rear; this one slightly shorter and covered in sharp spines. It was purple-black in colour with fearsome looking yellow markings on its face. Whether this was just defensive colouring or not, Jeffries couldn't tell, but it definitely looked more warlike than did its pale, plodding cousin.

Around him, the small cheerless khaki-clad band of warriors sat hunched in groups under the ever-watchful eyes of their captors. Some Tommies glanced back with glowering, baleful and resentful stares, others with fear and anxiety, some muttered amongst themselves about 'the Chatts.' Jeffries could only assume they meant their captors and not the lice that infected their clothes. A snort of derision escaped his nostrils. It was a suitably derogatory term. However, where they felt beaten and defeated, he experienced a curious sense of self-confidence he had not felt since he arrived here on this world. He sat with the rest of the prisoners, although he never for one moment considered himself one of their number. He felt buoyed. He had wanted to talk to the Khungarrii and here they were. Of course, those great insects, walking upright in a dark chitinous mockery of man, didn't talk to him, but then he deduced they were merely soldiers. Soldier ants.

Peculiarly, with every peristaltic ripple that took him further and further from the entrenchment and the possibility of it returning to the Somme without him, Jeffries began to feel increasingly free.

Ahead, in another cradle, he could see Captain Grantham slumped, head bowed, defeated. The man was a joke. A weak insipid leader whose mind could barely take the brunt of war, let alone this magnificent world. He had long ago exceeded the limits of his comprehension. The nurses sobbed, cried and comforted one another; the apparent repugnance of their captors reducing them to the emotional imbecilic wrecks their gender inevitably devolved to under stress.

The soldiers weren't tied or chained and several decided to leap over the side of their cradle and made a break for freedom into the surrounding jungle to the encouraging cheers of their less opportunistic fellows. The vicarious victory didn't last long, brutally quashed as it was by the subsequent roars and screams from the undergrowth that, to Jeffries amusement, muted his fellows' enthusiasm; there was no need for shackles when their captors knew the environment would seek to kill them at every turn.

There were about eighty of the Khungarrii, some riding in cradles, some stood on the backs of the caterpillar beasts, others walking alongside them. If they fell behind, they would use their powerful legs, bounding ten or twenty feet at a time until they caught up. Jeffries made sure to keep Napoo close to him. He was his best source of information right now and, for the moment at least, that made him valuable. He asked low whispered questions out of the side of his mouth.

"Where are the Khungarrii taking us?"

"To Khungarr," replied Napoo. There was no doubt the Urman might escape and indeed survive, but he obviously had mixed feelings and felt some loyalty to the soldiers.

"Are all Khungarrii like these?"

"No, these are Scentirrii. Soldier caste. You can tell by their armour. It is thicker and heavier than those of the Worker or Anointed castes. They spit a burning spray."

From behind came the irritating mumbles of that sham priest, muttering his feeble invocations and prayers. A sneer curled Jeffries' lip as he listened and he shook his head in disbelief.

Some of their captors held hollow lances attached to clay packs on their backs. Some sort of gun? Occasionally they would threaten the captives with them, chattering unintelligibly through gnashing mandibles in their harsh, guttural language.

"There!" hissed Napoo, grabbing Jeffries' arm and pointing. Through brief gaps in the canopy, Jeffries caught sight of a huge mound-like edifice. It must have been hundreds of feet high. Its colour was the same dark cinnamon upon which the caterpillar beasts walked, flecks of mica bound into its walls reflecting the sunlight in a myriad places and directions. Jeffries realised that this must have been what had seen from the aeroplane.

Jeffries' heart sank. He had been hoping for something more... *civilised*, that would belittle everything the British Empire had to offer. Nevertheless, the brief glimpse afforded him by the aeroplane couldn't do justice to the enormous scale of the structure. This was a feat of engineering on a par with that of the ancient pyramids of Egypt. Its sheer height and bulk dwarfed many of the great and noble British Institutions, although it could not match them for grandeur.

As they neared the edifice, the trees grew thinner and the path along which they travelled grew wider. They left the forest and entered a huge, well-managed clearing that spread for hundreds of yards around the earthen edifice. The sight drew gasps and groans of despair from the others in marked contrast to the seemingly excited clicks and chittering from the Chatts alongside them. Huge asymmetrical buttresses rose up the sides of the tower to varying heights as if shoring up the earthen mound. Small balconies could be seen dotted about the shell of the edifice, each occupied by an insect.

As the great caterpillar beasts undulated across the clearing, Jeffries noticed lines of other arthropods filing from various forest paths towards apertures in the base of the mound. They were of a different genus to their captors, less well armoured with smaller heads and shorter antennae. As they approached, Jeffries saw that men—Urmen—were among their number, carrying baskets or dragging litters, transporting food and materials to the edifice under the watchful eyes of the accompanying Khungarrii.

In the cradle ahead of him, Jeffries could hear those damn women wailing at the sight. And from behind came the throttled voice of the padre, "Oh Lord, we are delivered into bondage."

As they passed into the shadow of the edifice, a large archway gaped before them and they entered into a great cathedral—like space. There the larval beasts were drawn to a halt against raised jetties, berthed there like boats so that the passengers, guards and captives alike might make an efficacious exit from the cradles. They were then led up sloping passages, before coming to a circular portal.

The door seemed to be made of tough, fibrous plant material, covered with sharp, close-set thorns. One of the Chatts hissed at the door, expelling a spray from its mouth. The portal recoiled from the chemical mist, dilating open. Once the last man was ushered through, the door sealed behind him. Twenty-five soldiers, Napoo and three nurses found themselves incarcerated in a circular cell.

Jeffries looked around their gaol. He noted that this side of the door was also bristling with close set thorns. Dim light filtered down from small windows high in the wall of the chamber. Also high up in the wall was a hole, from which could be heard a profusion of clicks and pops and from which proceeded a draught of air. A ventilation system, Jeffries thought. There was another source of light coming from a small hole in the floor at the far side of the room. Jeffries, suspecting what it was, peered over it gingerly. Through the hole, he could see the side of the tower plunging vertiginously away. The hole was a *garderobe* of sorts, a primitive toilet. Well, that was something, he supposed. He looked around the rest of the chamber. In places, the rough cinnamon-coloured walls were shiny, having been worn smooth over time by previous occupants, presumably. Captain Grantham sat against the wall, all pretence gone now, his authority all but evaporated. "I'm sorry. I'm sorry," he kept muttering. Jeffries, on the other hand, felt entirely calm and was quite content to wait.

HE WAITED SOME hours and amused himself watching a group of Tommies commandeer one of the nurse's white aprons and push it down out of the garderobe, to hang like a signal flag for any potential rescuers to see.

It was several hours before the membranous plant-like door dilated open again. A few of the Tommies, who had been muttering together, suddenly rushed the aperture; no doubt in the hope of escape.

"No!" cried Napoo, but it was too late. Crackling blue bolts of electrical energy met them as two Khungarrii Scentirrii discharged their lances. The soldiers jerked spasmodically for a moment before the light died and they crumpled to the floor. One of the nurses let out a scream, though the involuntary twitching of the fallen bodies showed that they were still alive. The two guards then stood to either side of the doorway, holding their lances.

Three more arthropod creatures entered the chamber. One was tall and slender and wore a light cloak with a cowl over its head, covering its antenna. Its chitin was smooth and off-white, like bone china. Other than its eyes, maw and antennae, the dermal bone of its head was a featureless ovoid. Beneath the cloak, the creature wore a long length of tasselled white cloth wrapped over its right shoulder and down across its thorax, through which stunted, vestigial middle limbs tipped with single claws protruded.

Hunched with subservience, the second Chatt was of a similar build. It wore no cloak but it did wear the same manner of cloth, though it had fewer tassels. Was that a rank thing? Jeffries realised its antennae were broken off, leaving little more than stumps.

The third Chatt was more thickly built and heavily armoured than its companions, its faceplate flatter and broader with a suggestion of horns or antler nubs. It was similar in build and stature to the Khungarrii warriors behind it but for the surcoat of scarlet cloth it wore over its heavily armoured form, which did little to hide the bony protuberances rising from its armour.

The cloth they wore seemed to be some form of silk, though whether it was spun by the creatures themselves or farmed from another species Jeffries could not fathom; the garments served no practical purpose that he could see, they were probably more ceremonial, like ecclesiastical vestments, he surmised.

"Who among you speaks for your herd?" the tall, cowled one rasped, the clicking of its mandibles punctuating its dialogue. It spoke with a breathless, hissing vocalisation, like a man struggling to communicate with a tube in his neck, as if it was forcing itself to use organs for purposes other than for which they had evolved. All eyes turned warily towards Captain Grantham. He looked up with red-rimmed eyes, hardly seeming to comprehend what was happening. Jeffries watched the man struggle briefly with his conscience before remaining seated, stifling sobs. He felt no pity for the broken man. He was half-tempted to stand himself, but he had no idea of the Chatts' intentions. They could merely want to kill the leader. He would wait and see.

After a moment Padre Rand stood and, faltering, cleared his throat.

"I am. These people are under my protection," said the chaplain, his voice cracking as he held aloft his battered leather Bible, "and that of our Lord God, who watches over us."

Jeffries gave the man kudos for that. That was one thing you could say about the Catholic chaplains. They had guts, going up to the Front Line with only a copy of the Bible and their faith for protection. That was what endeared them to the men generally, that and the fact that many of them came from the lower classes and weren't all well-to-do la-de-da-types, like the C of E chaplains.

There was a brief discussion among the Chatts, with some animated waving of antennae, before they turned back to address the padre.

However, Jeffries did not want this man, this mewling milksop of a shepherd, to speak for him, to assume authority over him. Whatever secrets and confidences these creatures had to share, they were his. He would not give up now. Seeing that it was safe, at least for now, Jeffries rose to his feet and coughed politely. "Thank you, there's no need, Padre," he said. He turned to the Chatts. "I'm next in command."

Padre Rand, unsure, looked at him then down at his Bible. Jeffries put a reassuring hand on his shoulder. "Sit down, Padre. This is my responsibility."

Padre Rand nodded and sank thankfully to the floor.

Jeffries stepped forward, his arms wide.

"I am Lieutenant Gilbert Jeffries, Number 4 Platoon, C Company, 13th Battalion of the Pennine Fusiliers."

The tall, regal Chatt regarded him, its antennae waving gently in his direction.

"This One is Sirigar, liya-dhuyumirri, high anointed one of the Khungarrii Shura," it said, its mandibles clicking and rubbing together like knitting needles. "That One is Chandar, this one's gon-dhuyumirri olfactotum," it indicated the smaller, submissive Chatt, and then the larger creature. "And that One is Rhengar, Scenturion, njurru-scentirri of Khungarr."

Introductions complete, the creature turned back to the huddled captives. "This One offers you a blessing in the name of GarSuleth," it said. It opened its arms, pulling wide the robe it wore, revealing more clearly the smaller vestigial limbs at its abdomen, also splayed, and then raised its head. From somewhere within its mouthparts it sprayed mist into the air. Jeffries breathed in and, within seconds, recognised the feeling of mild drug-induced euphoria. Keeping eye contact with the round, glassy unblinking eyes before him he inhaled again, slowly, deeply, deliberately.

EDITH HUGGED NELLY and Sister Fenton for reassurance. Some of the men closed ranks in front of them. The horrors of the last few days had begun to numb her, but the sound of the officer's voice picked at the thick scab of denial that had grown over her recent experiences to the raw emotional wound beneath. There was something about his tone, supercilious and defiant. The insect spoke back. In English. Edith could feel the hairs on the back of her neck bristle with fear. There was a hiss of spray as the creature dosed the air with a vapour from its mouth. Almost immediately, the world seemed to slow down. The fears and terrors of the recent past lifted from her, like dandelion clocks drifting away on her outward breath. A languid sigh escaped her lips as she sank down to the floor with her companions. Senses baffled, a great lethargy overcame her. She looked up. The officer was still standing as the others sank to the floor around him. She was sure she knew his voice but her thoughts had become as thick and slow as treacle and then they ceased to bother her altogether. These creatures would not harm them. She forced her eyes slowly upward and looked at them, feeling content.

JEFFRIES SMILED. RATHER helpfully, his own personal drug use had rendered him less susceptible than his fellows.

"Last man standing," he said with a wry smile.

The antennae stumps on the smaller creature were moving feebly. It reminded Jeffries of the hospitals back in 'Bertie with their beds full of raw amputees, their fresh tender stumps waggling clumsily, as if manipulating phantom limbs.

"Interesting defensive technique," he said, "dosing potential threats with a mild euphoric."

Rhengar spoke, preceded by a curious expansion of its chest, as if the creature was unfamiliar with filling its lungs with enough air for the effort of speech. Jeffries found the process quite engrossing.

"You will come with us," it said.

Rhengar turned to address the accompanying scentirrii in the harsh guttural smattering and clicks of its own tongue. They went over and picked up the padre, who looked at them happily.

"Both of you."

THEY WERE TAKEN out though the membranous aperture of the gaol chamber and led along passageways that sloped gently upwards and spiralled round. Set in niches along the way, luminescent lichen glowed, giving off a gentle blue-white light.

Sirigar walked on ahead, its silken vestments billowing out behind it. Before it now walked a smaller Chatt, some sort of juvenile nymph, perhaps, Jeffries thought. Its armour was translucent and not yet fully hardened and it swung some sort of censer before it, the heady incense masking all other smells. The accompanying Khungarr scentirrii escorted Jeffries and the padre, while Rhengar brought up the rear.

Chandar was limping badly on one leg and attempting to keep up with Sirigar. Jeffries watched it trying to engage the creature in its own language. Its chattering grew excited before being abruptly cut off by a harsh plosive exclamation from Sirigar. Chandar dropped back, almost sheepishly, to walk beside Jeffries. The creature looked up at him, its antenna stumps twitching. "Your clothing is unusual," it said, picking at the cloth of his jacket.

"If you mean clean, then yes. I pride myself on my appearance," Jeffries brushed the Chatt's questing fingers away from his jacket before straightening his tie. "I find people respond favourably to a good first impression. It's always worked for me."

Chandar looked at him. Jeffries was used to reading people, prided himself on it in fact, but it was frustratingly impossible to read the expressionless facial plates of his captors. The tone of voice they used offered few clues either, speaking in what was, to them, a foreign language.

"The Khungarrii have been watching you for some time," it chittered. "The presence of your herd has provoked much debate."

"So I saw," said Jeffries, nodding towards Sirigar.

"Are you an anointed one? Dhuyumirri of your herd, like Sirigar? That One is high anointed one of the Khungarrii Shura."

"Oh, if it's faith you want, ask him," said Jeffries, jerking his head at the chaplain. "He's full of it."

More scentirrii marched past. Approaching Chatts obediently stopped to let the party pass. Urmen, on the other hand, vanished out of sight down side passages at their approach; heads bowed, eyes averted. Jeffries caught sight of them cowering in openings or cloister-like passages. Sirigar swept on past them all. The creature led them to a spacious and well-lit passage, whose dominating feature was an imposing ornate opening, decorated around its edge with some sort of hieroglyphs. Jeffries very much wanted to examine them, but he wasn't given the opportunity.

"We are come," Chandar chittered. "The chambers of the Anointed Ones, the goro dhuyumirrii."

A strong smell of incense greeted Jeffries from the darkened void beyond the door, an infusion of aromas that overwhelmed his senses and began to sting the inside of his nostrils, making his eyes water. Sirigar entered and the scentirrii ushered Jeffries and Rand into the chamber after, Chandar and Rhengar following.

The walls of a great domed chamber rose up, disappearing into the gloom above. Around the walls were curved man-sized alcoves that extended up from the ground, most were in shadow and the few he could see were occupied by more Chatts, who stood in them, facing the wall, their heads bowed. A low soft susurration filled the space, echoing in the dark space above. There was a noise like the soft clatter of cutlery in a canteen that, Jeffries realised, was the constant ticking and scissoring of mandibles in prayer. This was obviously some sort of sacred space, a temple of some sort, he mused.

Overhead, in the gloom, was what appeared to be a giant web. Sirigar paused to perform a gesture of deference and worship as they passed beneath it, clicking in what Jeffries assumed were reverent tones. The web, or what it represented, must have some great significance for them and he recalled what Napoo had said about this GarSuleth weaving the world. He noticed that some points on the web had been picked out with pieces of the bioluminescent lichen, but the meaning of their arrangement was lost on him.

"Pay homage to GarSuleth, the creator of all. Very few Urmen have the privilege of entering these chambers," said Chandar, bowing its head, touching its hands to the base of its antennae and then to its thorax and waiting for Jeffries and Rand to do the same.

Even through his euphoria, Rand frowned slowly. "I will not bow to a heathen god," he slurred drunkenly.

A hiss escaped from Rhengar's mouthparts. The scentirrii stepped closer, their lances poised, ready to punish any perceived blasphemy.

Jeffries, unwilling to lose whatever trust he might have gained, grabbed Rand firmly by the upper arm and brought his mouth close to the chaplain's ear. "Just do it, Padre. We're in the midst of a nest of insect savages. If you know anything of entomology, there are probably a hundred ways they might kill us and I, for one, do not intend to be a martyr. Now bow!"

Reluctantly the padre repeated the movement Chandar had shown them, and Jeffries did likewise. The scentirrii relaxed their stance and, as they continued their way across the chamber, Jeffries glanced up at the web. Was it home to some primitive creature that they kept and worshipped as a god? He briefly envisioned being cocooned and left as a sacrifice to some great bloated thing and then, more pleasantly, imagined the padre there instead.

They were ushered through an arch at the far side of the room and along a series of passages and interconnecting chambers where members of Sirigar and Chandar's caste were engaged in various alchemical tasks. Finally, they were led into a smaller room, the main feature of which was several large piles of plundered trench equipment. At a glance Jeffries saw thigh boots, scaling ladders, waterproof capes, cooking utensils, fleabags, rifles, an old grenade catapult, trench mortar shells, a primus stove, Mills bombs, periscopes, a pickelhaube, latrine buckets, a gas gong, a sniper's loophole plate, several steel helmets, cases of small arms ammunition and, he noticed—partially hidden by tarpaulin—what looked to be several rusted old pressurised canisters of chlorine gas. Where the hell had they found those?

"These things are unknown to the Ones," said Rhengar. "They stink of decay and corruption as do you. The Ones would know their uses and your intentions."

"Intentions?" said Jeffries.

He was being judged and everything hung on how well he passed the test. He assumed that if they found out the true nature of some of the things around them, then whatever dialogue they might have would be cut very short indeed. A degree of diplomacy was called for.

"Most nomadic Urmen know better than to resist the Ones," continued Rhengar, "yet your herd is large and aggressive and you have made your clumsy delvings in Khungarrii territory. Our scentirrii were alerted to your presence spinnings ago. Your odours were carried before you on the breath of GarSuleth. The Khungarrii could not fail to notice it, it overpowered everything, almost obscuring the sacred scents themselves."

"And the Unguents of Huyurarr have long heralded the coming of a great corruption. There are those amongst the Ones who, upon sensing your putrescence, fear for their very existence," said Sirigar. "Are those Ones wrong?"

To Jeffries it sounded very much like the case was already stacking up against them. He had to think fast.

"If GarSuleth wills it," he said.

Chandar had been rummaging through the pile of looted trench items with a degree of curiosity, making smacking and clicking noises with every item he examined. "And this," it said, picking up a piece of field kit. "What is it?"

"An entrenching tool. For digging. These other things are harmless, I assure you."

"And these?"

"Boots, gum, soldiers, for the use of," Jeffries answered, mocking the Chatts with a parody of quartermaster's speech.

Rhengar picked up a rifle. "And this? What is this? Khungarrii fell before these without being touched."

"Skarra take them," intoned Chandar, head bowed.

"As we did before your electric lances. You know this is a weapon and I assure you we are quite adept at using them"

Rhengar snapped its mandibles together rapidly, rising up on its legs until it towered over Jeffries. The effect was unsettling, which was probably the entire point.

"Do not presume to threaten the Ones," the Scenturion chittered, its mandibles slicing furiously. "If you are a harm to the Ones, then the Ones will cull you the way it has been done with Urmanii in the past, otherwise you shall be absorbed into Khungarrii worker caste to toil for the good of Khungarr."

"Rhengar, you forget yourself," said Sirigar. "This Urman can not harm us. Is it not still under my benediction?"

Rhengar backed off.

"I do see your dilemma," said Jeffries tactfully. "Believe me, I do."

"Your dilemma too, Urman," reminded Rhengar.

"You do not worship GarSuleth," said Sirigar. It was a statement rather than a question.

"No," said Jeffries, turning from Rhengar. "I worship... another." He wanted to pursue the subject but Napoo had told him Croatoan was heresy here and now probably wasn't the right moment. He would have to bide his time. He just hoped he had enough. At best, he had a day to get the information he required. Bloody Everson would see to that. The man was transparent. He'd come charging to the rescue like he was the BEF.

"Take your despicable claws off that, heathen!" said the padre drunkenly. Chandar had attempted to take the Bible from the padre's hands.

"Chandar!" Sirigar scolded. "You are not here to indulge your inconsequential and heretical studies. You are only here under sufferance, do not test this One."

Jeffries' ears pricked up at the word 'heretical.' This Chandar, despite its broken appearance, might be more interesting than it at first appeared.

Chandar responded to Sirigar in a rapid rattle of mandibles. Sirigar retorted. They sounded like a pair of angry crows. There was obviously a great difference of opinion being expressed and it was being expressed physically, in a series of stylised movements. Actions seemed to define and punctuate argument and proposition, counter-argument and denial. Like dancing bees, thought Jeffries.

The attention of the other Chatts was momentarily drawn to the sparring pair and, seeing his chance, Jeffries deftly palmed the pistol he had been eyeing on the nearby pile of equipment, thrusting it under his jacket and down the waistband of his trousers.

Chandar sank lower and backed away, obviously losing the exchange to Sirigar, who hissed triumphantly, its mandibles and arms splayed.

Jeffries, however, had come to a decision. There must have been a reason the rest of the battalion had been spared the blood sacrifice that brought him here. Until now, he hadn't been able to see it.

He turned smartly and addressed his captors. "Gentlemen!" he said brightly, with a clap, as if about to suggest a bracing snifter down the club. "You say we have a choice between annihilation and subjugation?"

Rhengar and Sirigar exchanged glances, their antennae twitching.

"It'll be difficult, but, yes, I believe I can deliver my people," said Jeffries. "For a price."

INTERLUDE FOUR

Letter from Private Thomas Atkins
to Flora Mullins

16th November 1916

Dear Flora,

I am well and have acquired a pet now. Gordon is a blessed nuisance, but he ain't half good at chatting shirts. I thought once the Lt. found out about him I'd have to get rid, but he says Gordon's fancy for the verminous louse has sent cases of trench fever down, so I guess I'm stuck with him.

Thanks to a local native we met, called Napoo, our diet has improved. After days of bully beef and hard tack we now have fresh fruit, although my hands are raw and my back is aching from picking the stuff. I don't think I'm cut out for country life. Living in holes and grubbing a living from the land isn't easy. We need more than this if we are to survive. An estaminet wouldn't go amiss, for a start, although after an unfortunate incident I've sworn off drink for the duration.

We were out picking more fruit when there was a raid on our trenches by some bug-eyed Bosche and some of our chaps were snatched. Lt. Everson gave a speech and whipped the lads' dander up good and proper. We're setting out to get them back. The Lt. says they've enslaved the local natives, too. It's disheartening to find that there are tyrants everywhere, but I suppose this is why I volunteered.

These Chatts, as the lads call them, make you feel squeamish just looking at 'em and, after what we had to put up with on the Somme, that's saying something. Anyway, the Lt says these things may know how we can get home too. That is my dearest wish, next to William returning safe and sound.

Ever yours,
Thomas

CHAPTER FOURTEEN
"There's a Long, Long Trail…"

THE RESCUE PARTY set off several hours after the attack, the patriotic cheers of those left guarding the entrenchment ringing in their ears, the pride singing in their blood as the tank led the column off. Everson had made his point and without having to order them, in all, sixty men had volunteered for the dangerous raid, including 1 Section. Porgy said it was the biggest Black Hand Gang he'd ever seen. Poilus reluctantly agreed to accompany them, despite his fear of the tank, which he believed to be some sort of demon. Even Hepton volunteered, the chance of obtaining more heroic and fantastical footage proving too great to resist. Among those who stayed behind was Tulliver. Until he could repair his machine, he was grounded.

Morale had been high as they set off. Everson knew there was a long hard march ahead of them and estimated the action, with the return trip, might take three days to four days to accomplish. He charged Lieutenant Palmer with fortifying the entrenchments against the possibility of a repeat raid or retaliation.

The Chatts' trail wasn't hard to follow. Their passage had crushed and flattened a wide path of tube grass, fronds ripped and chewed in places as if by some great beast. And, despite a constant vigilance against hell hounds or anything else that might skulk out here, the march out of the valley and across the veldt, although steady and relentless, was relatively uneventful, thanks in part to the measured mechanical pace of the ironclad, whose dark, menacing shape and perpetual growl seemed to ward most things away.

Everson remembered the long marches along the Front whenever the battalion moved sectors. Forty miles in a day sometimes wasn't uncommon with your boots rubbing your feet raw. Now, with the heat and the load they were carrying many of the men were already becoming weary, even as NCOs worried at their heels like agitated terriers chasing motor cars. Everson was aware of it, which was why he had to push them now, so that they could camp for the night and be fresh for the assault the next day.

THAT AFTERNOON, EVERSON stood on the roof of the tank and, through his binoculars, surveyed the dark line of forest ahead. Under him the tank growled impatiently, snorting smoke, as if the trees were a personal challenge and it was preparing to rip them up by the roots, each running up of the engine like the pawing of a bull's hoof. Everson called down into the square hatch in front of him.

"It looks as though they've gone into the forest," he bellowed above the din of the engine. There was no answer. He stamped loudly on the armoured plating. A sweaty, oily face peered up from below. Everson could only tell who it was by the fact that he was wearing an officer's cap. A hot damp waft of muggy air, sweat, oil and engine fumes hit him as he squatted down to yell into the vehicle. "All right, Mathers. Take us in."

The Tank Commander nodded and disappeared again. Everson walked back along the line of the tank and jumped down the back of the ironclad landship. The tank moved off with a jerk, rumbling and clanking, belching out black plumes of smoke from its rooftop exhaust as it followed the trail into the treeline.

THE PLATOON FOLLOWED behind the tank as it grumbled its way through the forest, following the clear trail, every now and again making minor course corrections so that it appeared to be sniffing out a scent, like a bloodhound. The canopy above was so thick that the exhaust fumes billowed back down towards them, creating a gritty grey smog that had the men coughing in fits.

They passed through a grove of pallid trees, whose gnarled and twisted trunks were interspersed with boles and fistulas and down which dripped thick, viscous slime that had the sweet sickly smell of gangrene about it. Small creatures drawn to its scent found themselves trapped in the substance. The whole effect of the grove conspired to produce an atmosphere that sought to absorb sound so that it fell dead almost the moment it was created.

Gordon started whimpering from inside Atkins' gas mask bag. Damn thing. He didn't even know why Lieutenant Everson told him to bring it. "Shut up," he grumbled at the bag. Gordon didn't. If anything the intensity of the mewling increased.

4 Section were bringing up the rear. They'd been singing half heartedly to keep their spirits up, however, travelling though the grove the singing grew harder to hear. "Sing up, Carter, I can barely hear

you," called Atkins, the sound of his own voice sounding leaden and curiously clipped. Hearing no answer, he glanced round. 4 Section had vanished.

"Carter?"

Atkins heard something above him. He looked up. A thick, gelatinous string was dropping towards him. Before he could move or scream the warm, wet mucus landed heavily on him and it slithered down over his head and torso, enveloping him. The world about him vanished behind a grey-green film. It was thick and heavy and his struggling bore no fruit. He tried to breathe but the slime was smothering him. He began to panic as he felt the ground disappear from beneath him. Something began drawing him up into the canopy. He thrashed about and kicked his legs but the thick glutinous mass held him firm. His struggle only succeeding in using up what oxygen he had left and his lungs started to burn. He began to lose consciousness. His last thought was of Flora kissing him on the cheek—

Blushing, Flora pushed away from him and, smiling fondly, busied herself brushing lint from his lapels before holding him at arm's length for inspection. She nodded approvingly. "Come on, walk me back. Mam will be wondering where I've got to." As he walked her home from the Picture House, her arm through his, he felt as if his very heart would burst. He blushed furiously, feeling as if every step he took would thrust him skywards. She didn't look at him; she kept her eyes straight ahead and kept the small talk polite and parochial. If only she were his. He envied his brother's good fortune. William. His momentarily buoyant heart sank, weighed down by thoughts of his brother. His cheeks still burned, but with shame at the conflicting feelings that now tugged at his heart—

He felt another tug. Something began pulling at his feet, against the suction of the mucus shroud. Another tug threatened to pull his head off as he was drawn down, inch by inch. The mucus wall in front of him thinned and began to tear. More light. A face drifted into focus against the grey green wall of snot. He felt the suction against him weaken. Muffled voices began to reach his ears. He felt as though he was being ripped in two, the webbing and pack resisting the downward pull. He felt strong arms grab his thighs and hold him tight. The mucus began to slide up over his face until he fell heavily, landing on top of Pot Shot and Gutsy and heaving down great lungfuls of air. He looked up to see the long stringy mucus tendril begin to recede back up into the canopy.

"Oh no you bloody don't!" He leapt up and grabbed it, wrapping his left arm around it.

"Jesus, Only what the hell are you doing? That streak of snot just tried to kill you," said Gutsy.

Atkins' right hand fumbled around in the pouch on his chest as he drew out a Mills bomb. Pulling the pin out with his teeth he thrust his arm shoulder-deep up into the ball of mucus.

"Oh God, you're not!"

"He bloody is. Run."

"You're a bloody lunatic, Only!"

With a satisfied smile he opened his fist, releasing the trigger, pulled his arm out with a *schlorp* and rolled behind a tree trunk. A snort from somewhere in the canopy above drew the mucus back up into whatever orifice it had oozed from. There was a brief pause followed by an explosion as the hand grenade detonated. A huge shapeless, invertebrate carcass fell down through the branches. It crashed to the floor of the grove with a large, sodden thump, followed by an accompanying rain of wet spatters.

Sergeant Hobson and Lieutenant Everson came running down the line as the platoon took up defensive positions.

"Just what the bloody hell is going on?" demanded Hobson as he found 1 Section crawling from out of their places of shelter, laughing with exhilaration.

"There was something up in the trees, Sarn't," said Porgy. "Some kind of snot monster. It had Only, I mean Atkins, sir."

Everson gently poked the steaming remains of the huge, many tentacled slug-like creature with his foot.

"From above, you said?"

"That's right sir. Seems to drop a huge string of snot on something then suck it back up, sir," said Gutsy. "Looks like it got 4 Section an' all."

"Hobson, better take a roll call. See who's missing," said Everson. He turned to Atkins, seated on the ground as the slime began to dry out and crust his uniform. "You all right, Atkins?"

Atkins cleared his throat and looked up. "Sir."

"Right, get cleaned up. Hobson, I guess you'd better tell the men to keep their eyes peeled for... what was it?"

"Snot, sir. Great thick sticky strings of snot," said Gutsy.

"Yes. Well," he said, as he walked back up the line. "Handkerchiefs at the ready then."

JEFFRIES WAITED. THE three Chatts jabbered amongst themselves, their antenna waving and their arms gesticulating. Jeffries found it incredibly frustrating being unable to read their faces. It made them so hard to play.

"What do you mean you can deliver them, man?" asked the padre.

"Exactly what I said," replied Jeffries, not taking his eyes from the trio.

"You don't mean sell them into slavery?"

"You're not going to get all Moses on me, are you, Padre?"

Chandar came over to them. "Do you mean what you say?"

"I always do," said Jeffries.

"We do not know the meaning of 'price.'"

Backward savages. No concept of a monetary economy. Jeffries thought for a moment. "I want something in exchange."

"What?"

"Knowledge. I want Chandar to teach me the Khungarrii ways."

Chandar relayed the request to the others. There was a brief agitated discussion before Chandar returned. "Those Ones do not trust you. Those Ones want a portent, a sign."

This was becoming too much. He didn't have the time to play games here, but he could see no way forward other than to acquiesce.

"What kind of sign?"

"An ordeal."

"Ordeal?"

"Jesus, Mary and Joseph!" muttered the padre.

"Those Ones require a ritual of purification," said Chandar. "It is a spiritual cleansing expected of Urmen when they reach adulthood. A symbolic pupation, a casting off of the old ways, the old life. We need this from you to show that you accept the Khungarrii and the will of GarSuleth."

"Is that all?"

The padre, on the other hand, seemed to be having some problems with the idea.

"No!" he said, rousing himself from his induced ennui. "I will not renounce my faith. I will not renounce my humanity and bow down before false idols!"

"Excuse me," said Jeffries, smiling briefly and nodding politely to Chandar before wheeling round on the padre, grabbing his elbow and steering him away from the Khungarrii. "Padre, I won't tell you again. Negotiations are at a very delicate stage here. This Chatt has... intelligence I need and I'm willing to play along and do whatever they want if it means I get what I want, do you understand?"

"I don't know what your game is, Lieutenant."

"And I can't tell you, Padre. Need to know. Hush-hush and all that." Jeffries tapped the side of his nose.

"Ah," said the padre. "I had heard rumours. Military Intelligence, eh?"

"So let's go along with it, hmm? Think of it as a—a test of faith."

"Well—"

"Look at me, Padre," said Jeffries. The padre cast his eyes down. "Rand, look at me. Do you mean to tell me that anything these heathen, soulless creatures could do would shake your faith?"

"Well—"

"Good man," said Jeffries, before turning back to Chandar. "Very well. We shall undertake your ritual. Lay on, McDuff."

"Chandar will explain to you the ritual," said Sirigar, before sweeping from the chamber. Turning to chatter something at Chandar, Rhengar left too.

Chandar and the ever-present scentirrii guards escorted them to another part of the temple area. The chamber in which they now found themselves was smaller than any they had so far seen and could have accommodated perhaps only six or seven people. It was bare apart from some sort of small brazier in the centre, like a large clay oil burner, fashioned from the same cinnamon-coloured earth as the rest of the edifice, almost as if it had been moulded from the floor. From above hung a shallow dish that contained the same luminous lichen that provided the light to the rest of the interior. It reminded Jeffries of a Red Indian sweat lodge.

"Sit," said Chandar.

Jeffries eased himself to the floor, his back against the wall, and made himself as comfortable as he could. The padre sat down across from him, looking apprehensive.

"So what happens now?" Jeffries asked.

"You will begin the Kirijjandat, the cleansing," explained Chandar. "The ordeal will divest you of the past, help you relinquish old ways and atone for them so you may embrace the will of GarSuleth."

An acolyte, wearing a thin calico-coloured, tassel-less garment draped over its shoulder and wrapped around its segmented abdomen, entered carrying an earthen jar. Chandar scuttled backward as the acolyte proceeded to pour a thick, oily liquid from the jar into the bowl. Jeffries caught a whiff of a heady musk mixed with a light, almost fruity, scent. The acolyte then introduced a lit taper to the oil and it began to burn. It pulled on a cord and the shallow dish, holding the lichen light, was drawn up against the curve of the roof above until it clamped tight to the top of the chamber, extinguishing all light, apart from the burning oil.

"GarSuleth guide you," Chandar said, before withdrawing from the chamber with the acolyte, the door dilating shut behind them.

Fumes began to fill the chamber. Jeffries just smiled, relaxed and began to breathe slowly and deeply. If this thing was going to happen, there seemed no point in fighting it and it wasn't as if he hadn't done anything like this before. He was quite familiar with hallucinogenic rituals. Prior to the War he had participated in a good many. This was merely a drug he hadn't tried yet and he positively welcomed the experience. That old bastard, Crowley, always claimed he could take more than anyone else could and, while Jeffries had never actually called him on it before they fell out, he always suspected it was quality more than quantity that affected the experience. He'd read of rituals like this among primitive tribes and he would be lying to himself he if didn't feel a little apprehensive, but also excited as well. An otherworldly drug. He couldn't wait.

In the dull red glow of the burning oil he could make out the padre muttering the Lord's Prayer under his breath, his fingers moving feverishly over the rosary in his hands.

Jeffries, beginning to feel uncommonly hot, pulled at his collar and found his fingers numbed. He struggled to control them as he fumbled clumsily at his shirt buttons, the simplicity of their mechanism outwitting him. His skin began to prickle unpleasantly and it was with a vague sense of detachment that he watched the padre gazing ahead, slack-jawed, before slumping over. Jeffries, in a gargantuan effort of will, focused on the little rivulet of saliva that dribbled slowly from the chaplain's mouth, soaking into the earthen floor. He felt sweat trickle down his face and collect uncomfortably in his moustache. As the very air around him seemed to bleed shapeless colours into the world, spreading and blotting out the scene in front of him, he relaxed, giving himself over entirely to the alien fumes.

THE GAS CLOUD *enveloped him. Sick and green and heavy it shifted sinuously around his body. His breathing was hard and laboured. He clawed at his gas helmet only to find the mask had become one with his face, his eyepieces become round dark eyes, the breathing tube a proboscis, his tunic a shiny carapace. His insistent buzz was lost amid the continual thunderous rumbling drum of the artillery barrage that modulated to become the slow sonorous chant of unseen male voices gradually becoming more urgent, more abandoned.*

The gas drew back like an outrushing tide leaving him beached at the door of the London Presbytery. The heavy ornate oak door stood ajar. The sound of a rich, sardonic laugh drew him inside. He knew that laugh, knew the supercilious grin and the piercing eyes. He made his way across the tiled floor of the entrance hall toward the door to the inner sanctum. There he was, 'The Great Beast' himself, Crowley, fornicating with his mistress within his ritual circle. His mundane angelic transcriptions served him no purpose. Magickally impotent he could not take the leap that was needed to broach the spheres. Sex was not the answer. And now Jeffries knew it. Red Magick was the answer, the way...

"You were wrong!" he cried. "Wrong, you horny old bastard!" his voice shattering the vision in front of him He found himself in a woodland and saw a great beast, slavering, its phallus protruding lasciviously from its sheath. He watched as a large snake writhed

through the grass beneath the soft underbelly of the beast, where it struck, sinking its fangs into the flesh. The beast howled in pain and fear and bolted, unaware that the venom would nevertheless do its work. First blood to the Great Snake. The snake began to shed its skin and a naked man crawled out wet with viscera, clutching an onyx stone carved with a sigil. The sigil began to glow red and expand.

Jeffries stepped through it onto the cool moonlit lawns of Lambton Grange that rang with thrill-seeking drunken giggles. He looked up at the once familiar stars that augured such a propitious moment, felt again the adrenaline surge, the confluence of fear and excitement. He recognised the ritually inscribed circle, the fug of incense, the lost Enochian codex in his hands, the drug-addled groans of the two barely conscious sacrificial virgins—no chance of an Abrahamic reprieve for them here. He stepped inside the moment to relive it again.

The words, the words he had spent months learning tumbling now out of his lips. Their blood, their life force, charging the cone of energy, powering the evocation. Once again, he felt the penumbra of Croatoan's shadow creep towards him before the very little power he had harnessed waned. He howled, both in frustration and triumph. He felt the power, proof that his Grand Working was sound.

Betrayal. The sound of barking pushed him on as he found himself running, a wanted man. Shedding skin after skin, the Great Snake changed and grew. The outbreak of the Great War galvanised his purpose. What greater cauldron of blood sacrifice could there be? Wholesale slaughter, the extinguished lives going to waste. If only one could channel it. And so his great working took shape. On the field of battle, charged by the blood of thousands, he would evoke the Old One once more. He looked up to see the shells and Very lights and saw, instead, the eyes of the arachnid being he intuited to be GarSuleth, at the centre of a star-bejewelled web. He began to relax and feel calm, then content as he accepted the being above him, welcoming it.

A mine went up, blasting thousands of tons of dirt and soil into the air, ripping apart the web and banishing its occupant to the cold dark shadows of space. The giant earthen plume took the form of a huge, terrible being, squatting on its haunches, skin like onyx, the surface of which cracked and split to reveal a burning core from which rivulets of blood flowed, hissing and steaming like lava as it oozed out across the foreign world on which he now stood.

"Croatoan," he gasped.

JEFFRIES CAME ROUND to the sound of retching across the chamber as the padre vomited. Feeling light-headed and nauseous, Jeffries levered himself upright. His eyes met those of the padre. They were wide with fear and doubt. Jeffries watched him snivel. Whatever he had seen had shaken him. Wiping the snot from his nose and the drool from his mouth he grinned at the broken Padre, whose chest was now heaving spasmodically, wracked with sobs.

The burner had been extinguished and Chandar stood over them, studying their faces expectantly. "The Kirijjandat is complete," the creature said. "How do you feel?"

Jeffries felt a calmness and certainty. Whatever doubts he might have had had been assuaged. He looked up at Chandar and smiled contentedly. He eased himself to his feet and stretched his cramped limbs. If they thought, after this rite of passage, that he would be more compliant to the will of GarSuleth they were wrong. He had passed through and not only was his conscience unaffected by the visions that had assailed him, but his convictions remained steadfast and his faith in his own actions had been reaffirmed. Most importantly, he felt vindicated by his final vision of Croatoan and, unfortunately for the Khungarrii, gloriously unrepentant.

"How do I feel? Never better, old chap. Never better."

THE PARTY HAD been marching for several hours now. The air was thick with cloying forest scents and the acrid smell of exhaust fumes from the grumbling tank ahead. Atkins was sweating in the oppressive heat. His uniform was beginning to chafe and his boots rub so he was thankful when, at last, the trees thinned and opened out into a stretch of heath land. The forest, they found, was not continuous but here and there were changes in terrain. A large outcrop of rounded boulders, yellow-grey in colour, worn and pitted by the weather and stained with a peculiar indigo-coloured moss dominated the heath to the left of the trail. Either side was a mass of tangled tendrils some several feet high, looking like overgrown brambles.

They walked slowly along the trail. If this world had taught them anything, it was caution. Frequent use of the track had kept the indigo-hued vegetation cropped close but anything could be hidden within the rest. They reached the centre of the heath without incident, the outcrop of boulders to their left.

Atkins thought he caught a movement out of the corner of his eye. But it was only the vibrations caused by the tank setting small pebbles skittering down the outcrop.

Or then again, maybe not. One of the large boulders shifted then began to unfold. Six legs extended from underneath and two great curved horns revealed themselves. The huge bulk of the boulder revealed itself as a giant beetle.

Moving quickly, it struck out at the line of men, mandibles scything the air snatching two up and severing them in half. Shouts went up and the Tommies scattered, some racing back the way they had come, others seeking cover among the brambles. Thinking it would afford them protection, some raced toward the tank. The rock beetle snapped angrily at them, catching up with a third man, his screams briefly echoing around the heath until it crushed him.

Gazette squeezed off several shots. He hit the beast squarely, but to no effect.

"Rapid fire!" the order came. A number of men, Atkins among them, opened fire, which only served to aggravate the creature. However, it did buy time for the tank to slowly, haltingly turn round to face the attacker.

Atkins heard the tank's engine rev above the shouts and screams as the boulder beetle snapped at the fleeing soldiers. Hearing the grating roar it turned its attention to the tank.

"It thinks the tank is some sort of rival!" said Pot Shot.

With a loud, venomous hiss, it ran towards the landship. The mechanised behemoth gunned its engine and lurched forward, two titanic beasts charging each other. They crashed together with the tortured squeal of stone on metal, the tank pushing inexorably forward, forcing the huge rock beetle back. Stunned, it retreated briefly as if considering its next move. It lowered its head and shoved forward trying to lodge its great horns under the vehicle and turn it.

The tank reversed away from the beetle which raised itself up on its legs and hissed, spitting a stream of fluid at the ironclad. It sizzled and smoked as it hit the tank between its front tracks. The tank reversed and the beetle scuttled forward, clearly thinking its challenger was retreating.

"Come on!" Atkins muttered under his breath. A movement on the trail distracted him. Hepton was running clumsily, carrying his camera on its folded tripod before finding himself a vantage point for the battle. Planting the tripod down and splaying its legs out, his eye to the box, he began cranking at a measured pace.

"What the hell's he doing?" said Gutsy. "Hasn't he seen what that thing has just done to the *Ivanhoe*?"

"Give me strength," sighed Atkins. As much as he wanted to leave Hepton to his fate, the weight of his brother's fate lay heavily on him. He'd like to think that nobody had left William behind. He hoped somebody might have done what he was about to do. "Gazette, cover me."

"What?"

He started running toward Hepton as the tank roared its defiance and lumbered forward, snorting smoke. The beetle lowered its head and charged, meeting the tank head-on with a clash of armours. Atkins shouted at the kinematographer, who continued to crank his camera as the titanic battle played out before him. "What the hell do you think you're doing you idiot? Get out of there!"

"Are you mad?" cried Hepton, shrugging Atkins off. "This is money in the bank. People will pay through the nose to see this!"

Hepton had a point, Atkins thought. Gears grinding, engine screaming, the tank was holding its ground and edging forwards, pushing the boulder beetle back foot by foot. The beetle struggled to gain a purchase on the ground. It spat its acidic venom at the tank again. It splattered thickly against the plate armour, etching and pitting the metal.

The beetle braced itself against the tank's relentless advance and the landship's great tracks began slipping in the churned earth. Seizing the advantage the beetle's great mandibles sliced through the anti-grenade mesh roof before it turned its attentions to the upturned snout of a track horn, where the caterpillar tracks protruded forward from the body of the tank. The metal groaned in protest under the pressure. One tank track stopped and the other carried on running, rotating the tank clockwise before that track stopped and the other ground back into action, swinging the tank back the other way. Atkins realised that the tank was trying to shake off the giant beetle. The rear end of the creature slued round, its rear legs nearly taking out Hepton and his camera.

Atkins grabbed the cameraman by the collar and hauled him back. "God damn it, you've got your moving pictures, now let's go!"

The near loss of his equipment shocked Hepton into action. He gathered in the legs of his tripod, hoisted it onto his shoulder and ran.

By now, the rest of the company had made it across the heath, covered by a rapidly deployed Lewis gun on the far side.

The tank backed away from the creature, throwing it off balance so that it released its grip. Engines roaring, gears grinding, the valiant *Ivanhoe* threw itself forward once more, clashing with the giant beetle.

The tank stopped for a moment before pitching forward, catching the beetle off guard for a second before it began to push it back. The front of the tank rose up off the ground, forcing the beetle to rise with it. They looked like two primal beasts grappling chest to chest, locked in a titanic struggle.

Pushing the stumbling Hepton across the clearing towards the waiting company, Atkins glanced back over his shoulder and saw the *Ivanhoe*'s right-hand sponson six-pounder swivel forward. It fired a shell point blank at the unprotected underbelly of the beetle. The force of the explosion threw it over onto its back, a huge gaping wound in its side. The front of the tank crashed down again and the machine lurched unsteadily forwards.

The beetle was struggling to right itself, its legs flailing in the air and squealing just within the threshold of human hearing. The tank drove purposefully up onto the fallen beast and came to a halt on its upturned belly. Then it shifted gears so that one of the tracks fed backward and the other forwards; it began to rotate, the metal tracks grinding the beast beneath it, disembowelling it. The squealing and the frantic leg waving ceased. The tank stopped, re-engaged its gears and rolled out of the pit it had gouged in the beast, its tracks leaving a trail of blue-green blood as it drove across the clearing. The company were cheering and whooping at its triumphant approach. As one, they rushed forward to mob it and slap its flanks as if it were a cup-winning thoroughbred.

"I missed it!" cried Hepton in disappointment as he turned to see the pulverised beetle lying slain.

"Well you got away with your life, and whatever film you did shoot, so count yourself lucky," said Atkins, delivering the kinematographer into the hands of Sergeant Hobson. Atkins nudged Hepton in the ribs and whispered confidentially, "If you ask him nicely he might do his Charlie Chaplin routine for you."

THE COMPANY, JUBILANT and in high spirits after the *Ivanhoe's* victory, continued marching on through the forest. As the sun began to set the track widened into a tree-lined avenue.

"Holy mother of God!" gasped Porgy as, through breaks in the canopy, they caught their first glimpse of the edifice.

"They seal the edifice at night," Poilus told them. "Any Khungarrii or Urman outside will have to fend for themselves until dawn."

"Fine Christian attitude that is," said Porgy.

"I think we can say they're probably not Christians," said Pot Shot.

"I wouldn't be so sure. They've had the padre for a while now. He'll be on a mission," said Mercy. "If he can convert 'em before we kill 'em at least he'll have saved their souls. That'll get him to the front of the queue at the pearly gates."

"That's if these Chatts have souls," said Atkins. "Which I doubt. I mean, not exactly made in His image are they?"

"Load off my mind then," said Gazette. "If they've got no souls, killing them will be just like reading my shirt."

By now darkness was rising in the depths of the forest. They halted for the night. Unwilling to light fires for fear of giving away their presence, they ate cold meals of bully beef, hard biscuit and pozzy before bivvying down as best they could.

Atkins found himself on watch with Ketch, whether by accident or design, he wasn't sure. The corporal glanced sullenly about the undergrowth. Ketch had been riding him for weeks and he didn't have a clue why. He'd always tried to do the right thing. Why had Ketch taken against him? He started to ask the question several times, but hesitated. Finally, he worked himself up enough to get it out. "Look, Ketch, what the hell is your beef with me, anyway?"

"You, Atkins?" he growled.

"You've had it in for me since I joined the platoon."

Ketch sat hunched like a gargoyle, ready to pour forth venom like a waterspout. Atkins could smell the man's rank breath as he spoke.

"Always want to be seen to be the good man, the hero, don't you, Atkins. Why is that?"

"I don't know what you mean."

"This desperate desire to be accepted. What is it you're afraid people will see? Your true colours, the kind of man you *really* are?"

"What do you mean?"

"You know. You carry it with you, in here," Ketch said, tapping his chest. "It eats away at you. Gnaws at you like a corpse rat; feeds on you," he said, with relish. "And I'm glad."

"You... you know?"

"About Flora Mullins? Yes. I was on leave, too, remember? I know Flora. I was sweet on her myself, but she spurned me. Spiteful bint. Didn't give a shit about Old Ketch. But then I saw you both. At the Picture House. Outside."

"You spied on us?"

"Didn't have to. You weren't exactly discreet."

"It was a kiss... one kiss and... and... it wasn't like that. It didn't mean anything."

"Affianced to your brother. Your *own* brother!" he said in mock outrage, then softly. "How many weeks had he been missing?"

"You bastard, you've no right. No right at all."

"Nor did you."

"We vowed it would never happen again; that we would never speak of it again."

"Oh well," said Ketch nodding, as if in sympathy, "that's all right, then."

"It's true. If William were to find out..."

"Ah. William. Your beloved brother. The Atkins boys. Always together, never apart. A bit different now, isn't it? You haven't got William to stand up for you now."

"You know he's bloody missing in action."

"Yes, and more to the point, so did you," hissed Ketch. Atkins felt warm spittle spray his cheek. "Always want to be seen to be a good man, the hero, don't you, Atkins?"

"What is this, blackmail? Just what the hell is it you want, Ketch?"

"Me, Atkins? I want you to suffer."

CHAPTER FIFTEEN
"When John Bull Starts to Hit..."

BEFORE DAWN THEY prepared themselves for the attack. Atkins was still smarting from his confrontation with Ketch; he could barely bring himself to look at the man. The seedy little corporal revolted him almost as much as the damn Chatts did. The fact that he had intentions towards Flora just riled him even more. Ketch looked over and grinned at him, obviously enjoying his discomfort. Atkins responded with a sullen stare. The rest of the Section didn't notice his change of mood; men acted differently before going over the top, they sank into themselves and resorted to prayer or their little rituals to marshal their own fears. Atkins took out his last letter from Flora, held it close to his face and inhaled, gently. He could still smell her perfume, although it was not as strong as it once was. If he closed his eyes, he could still feel her lips on his cheek. No. No, he would not die today.

EVERSON WENT TO set up a forward OP to spy out the lie of the land, Mathers and Baxter accompanying him, Poilus scouting the way. They crawled on their bellies through the undergrowth towards the edge of the clearing. As the rising sun seeped over the trees it illuminated the top most towers of the Khungarrii edifice, bathing it in a rich crimson light that made its mineral deposits sparkle. Everson raised his field glasses and scanned the mound. The earthen structure rose hundreds of yards into the sky, towering over the cultivated area around it.

It looked as if the Khungarrii had built the edifice over generations, each generation repairing and maintaining as well as expanding the towering colony, buttressing the main thrust of the spire with additional towers of various height and thicknesses. The excavated earth used in its construction had bonded and toughened over the years to a sedimentary rock-like hardness. Everson could see no sign of structural defences although he did notice small holes at varying heights, but whether these were window or vents he could not be sure. Maybe a combination of both. A movement about two thirds of the way up—about fifty or sixty feet above the tree canopy—caught his eye. He watched for a second. Hanging from one of the vents was a piece of white cloth. As it fluttered in an updraft he could made out a small red cross. It was a nurse's apron. "Good girl!" he muttered. That was one question answered. They were in there. However, fighting their way up inside two thirds of that thing wasn't going to be easy. "Hobson," he called softly.

The sergeant crawled up through the undergrowth with a grace that Everson never thought possible for a man his size. "Sir?"

"Prepare the men and tell Evans that we'll need my little acquisition, will you?"

"Sir."

Everson returned the field glasses to his eyes and refocused his view on the base of the edifice. A series of large midden piles lay slumped against the sides and, clinging precariously to their slopes, was a jumble of crude dwellings. These, Poilus told them, were Urman dwellings. Not part of the colony, they nevertheless sought whatever protection their proximity to it could afford them. The Khungarrii themselves did not concern themselves with these casteless Urmen unless they became too numerous or they affected the running of the colony. They lived on whatever detritus and chaff they could scavenge from the colony, scouring the midden heaps that accumulated like scree round certain portions of the edifice. Even at this early hour, Everson could see figures moving about, searching for food or other items they considered to be of value.

Over to one side of the vast clearing stood what looked like several small pyramids fifteen feet high or so, each composed of clay spheres, about four or five feet in diameter. Some of the pyramids appeared to be incomplete. "What are they?" he asked Poilus.

"Khungarrii dead. Each ball is a Khungarrii body encased in clay. They are left there for Skarra, the dung beetle, god of the underworld to roll down into his domain, where they undergo a final change into their spirit stage to join GarSuleth in the Sky World. I remember when I awoke in your camp, with the stench of the dead all around me and your great metal beast squatting there in the mud, at first I feared I'd been taken by Skarra, too."

There was a tap on his shoulder and an urgent whisper: "Everson, there." Baxter made him refocus his field glasses on the base of the edifice, on one of several huge bark-like doors. Boughs and trunks were embedded in the wall around the doorway, branches interwoven so they formed a jamb, roots thrusting into the ground. Out of the great openings began to spill Chatts, some bearing the electric lances and clay backpacks he'd heard about. They spread out across the clearing, behind them followed a mixture of Chatts and Urmen. Great elephantine larva-like beasts brought up the rear, bearing large panniers along their lengths.

Everson and the others crawled back to the camp and the waiting platoons, where they quickly mapped out the plan of attack. Everson noticed the Chatts avoided the dung ball pyramids of the dead and so, too, did the Urmen. If that was the case then they could use them as cover to get them in close to the edifice. From there they could head for the midden heaps which would provide cover for their break-in.

"I suspect we have a window of opportunity now before the workers start returning to the edifice. I'll lead the assault with 1 Section," he said. "I doubt that we'd win an all out pitched assault. Stealth is the only option. We'll have to bypass those entrances; they'll be too heavily guarded. We'll make our own way in. Dixon, see that the rest of the party take up defensive positions on the outskirt of the clearing. Baxter, your Vickers and Lewis MGs I want set up to provide a field of fire to cover our escape from the edifice. Mathers, hold your tank in reserve. We may need it. And if Hepton gives you any trouble, you have my permission to stick his camera so far up him he'll be able to use himself as a darkroom. If we're not out in six hours don't waste time attacking. Get back to the entrenchment. You'll have a better chance of survival there. It's easier to defend."

"If it's still there," muttered Ketch.

Blood glanced at him blackly.

"Hobson, Ketch. You and your men are with me. Poilus, you're coming too." Everson had no doubts. He knew the men could do this. He had every faith in them. After all, hadn't Hobson himself told him they were the best Black Hand Gang he knew? He raised a hand and the entire section melted into the undergrowth.

"BLOODY HELL," SAID Atkins when he got his first full view of the edifice. "It's not quite what I was expecting." The scale of it tied a knot in his stomach. How many Chatts lived in there? Thousands? Tens of thousands?

"What were you expecting?" asked Half Pint.

"I don't know; exotic palaces, gleaming towers, metal roads, automatons, flying machines. Not this. Not earth. Not dirt. We can do that. We have done that. Look at the way we're living, we're still bloody doing it."

"Well, then you should feel right at bloody home, then shouldn't you, Atkins," sneered Ketch as he crawled up beside him.

Atkins' mouth was dry. He took a swig from his canteen. The thought of attacking the Khungarrii edifice made his balls shrivel. He'd done trench clearance and even been down the mines dug under No Man's Land as a guard, neither of which could prepare him for invading a giant insect nest.

He and William had poked twigs into wood ant nests as boys. He remembered Flora squealing, equal parts delight and horror, urging them on. Emboldened by her, they squatted down on their haunches and thrust their sticks further in with more and more savagery, taking glee in watching the ants pour out frantically—just before the biting began as they swarmed over their clogs. William threw away his stick and danced around yelping and howling, much to Flora's delight.

There were probably thousands of the revolting Chatts in there—and they'd do a damn sight more than just nip.

Poilus tapped Everson on the shoulder.

"We must move to keep down wind of the scentirrii."

"Scentirrii?"

"Soldier Khungarrii, may Croatoan curse them!"

He hadn't factored in the wind. He was getting slack. Even in the trenches, it was one of the main factors of a daily report. Gas attacks were dependant on wind strength and direction. Here, apparently, these considerations were just as important.

"You," said Poilus to Atkins, thrusting a grey army blanket into his hands. "We will need to capture a Khungarrii to help us get into the edifice. As soon as I grab it you must throw the blanket over its head and wrap it tight, do you understand?"

No, he didn't, but he knew when to follow an order. Atkins nodded.

They watched and waited as the parties of workers and Urmen disbanded across the clearing, each appointed their daily tasks. Chatt soldiers accompanied the groups who walked off into the forest. As the Chatts drew near they heard the harsh, clicking language for the first time.

"Bloody hell," hissed Mercy. "They're only talking flamin' iddy-umpty. We should've brought a Signaller."

Atkins noticed that the Urmen each had a mark on their foreheads, a blue rune of some description.

"Why don't they make a break for it?" said Porgy.

"You've seen what's out there. Where the hell would they go?" said Atkins.

"Better that than serving some chatting tyrant race of insects. Makes my blood boil, does that," said Gutsy.

"Well maybe it just takes someone to show 'em eh? That's why we're here. Get our men back and just maybe teach these Urmen a thing or two about standing up to them bloody bug-eyed Bosche," said Pot Shot.

One Chatt wandered too close, its curiosity piqued by some sign or spore. Poilus gave an almost imperceptible nod to Atkins, who gripped the edges of the blanket firmly and tensed his legs. The Chatt's segmented antennae started twitching moments before Poilus leapt up from the undergrowth. He grabbed the creature from behind and Atkins tossed the blanket over its head, wrapping it round as Poilus sliced through its neck with a bayonet. The creature dropped with Poilus still on top of it. Atkins tensed, expecting a cry of alarm at the Chatt's absence, but none came.

"They can raise the alarm by scent," explained Poilus in a hushed tone as the men gathered around the kill. "It looks like we caught it in time though." He carefully unwrapped the blanket from the creature's head and handed it to Atkins. "Take it and bury it, carefully. We don't want the scent getting caught on wind."

Poilus then sliced his bayonet into the segmented abdomen of the dead Chatt, ripped down, pulled the wound open and exposed dark, swollen organs, sheathed in a slick wet cawl. This he tore from the body before easing his hand inside.

"Poilus, what the hell are you doing?" asked Everson.

"Looking for scent organ," Poilus pulled his hand out, holding a soft translucent greenish-red bag that sagged over the end of his palm. "We need to smear ourselves with its contents. We need to smell like Khungarrii."

"Oh Jesus!" groaned Porgy.

"He's right," said Pot Shot. "Many insects use scent as a primary sense. Those that don't smell like them are attacked as enemies."

"That'll be you and the Workers' Institute Library again, will it?" said Half Pint.

"What, you mean we cover ourselves with this stuff and we can just walk right in?" said Mercy.

"That seems about the size of it, Evans," said Everson. "This may fool them but we don't know for how long."

Poilus tore a small hole in the organ, pushed his fingers in and brought them out, covered with a greenish grey slime that he proceeded to smear around his face and exposed skin. He passed the organ round. Everson took it, cleared his throat and dipped his fingers into the wet sac, smearing himself with the warm goo.

Once the men had anointed themselves with Khungarrii scent they set off around the edge of the clearing. Leaving the rest of the party in Sergeant Dixon's capable hands, Everson, Poilus and 1 Section edged toward the pyramids of dead, each man hauling extra weapons and ammunition with which to arm the hostages while Mercy lugged a mysterious tarpaulin-covered object. From the cover of the shunned pyramids they then made their way, cautiously, to the midden piles and the Urman dwellings.

IT SEEMED THE dwellings slumped up against the side of the edifice were empty. There was no sign of any Urmen. Atkins knew if you scratched a living on this world, or any world for that matter, there was no time for idleness. It was obvious that the Chatts themselves never came here unless they had to, so it was an ideal place to make a discreet entrance. In the shadow of a huge midden: an accretion of dirt and gnawed animal bones, pottery shards, composting vegetation, dung, and rotting food, Gutsy and Pot Shot started work with a couple of pickaxes. Their points hammered into the hardened earth at the base of the edifice with very little initial effect, while the rest of the section kept watch nervously.

"Put your backs into it," growled Hobson. Gutsy and Pot Shot swore and swung their picks, grunting vigorously with each impact in a practised alternating rhythm. After a few minutes, the surface began to pit and flake. Then it began to crumble. Blood stopped, panting, to wipe his brow.

"Good work. Change over," said Everson.

The men changed over. It was no use doing all the fatigue work only to end up too knackered to fight once you'd actually breached the wall.

Atkins heard a clatter of refuse skittering down the far slope of the midden pile to their left and signalled the men to stop digging. Slowly, eight loaded Enfields converged toward the sound as something clambered towards them.

EVERSON LICKED HIS lips and cupped his pistol hand in his free palm to try to disguise the fact that it was shaking. He couldn't let the men see. The clattering grew closer. He flexed his trigger finger and caught Hobson's eye. The sergeant gave him a barely perceptible shake of the head and patted his trench club, 'Little Bertha.' The cruelly customised truncheon, its end studded with hobnails, had seen good service in many a trench raid. Everson felt a surge of disgust at the sight but thankfully lowered his revolver, realising that its report would give them away. He watched as the burly NCO tensed himself, his face compressed into a twisted snarl of hatred ready for whatever came over the brow of the slope. A small hand appeared over the lip and, a second later, there emerged a small boy, no more than six or seven years old. The Section let out a collective sigh. All except Gazette, who kept the boy in his sights.

*   *   *

FOR ATKINS IT was like looking at his own past. He'd been a boy such as this one, running round the streets of Broughtonthwaite, so far away now, in soot and grime and clogs. The boy was thin and covered with dirt and sores. He wore a tunic of animal skins and breathed heavily though his mouth, his nostrils plugged with dried green mucus. He continued to stare at the soldiers with a surly pout.

Poilus started to approach the boy, but Hobson raised his arms and stepped towards the child, snarling in the manner of an ogre. The boy took fright and ran off down the slope. "There, that's got 'im."

"You're losing your touch, Sarn't," said Mercy, nodding his head downhill. The boy had stopped someway down and again stood staring at them resentfully before disappearing round a bluff.

After five minutes, Gazette and Atkins were up on pick-axe duty, taking over from Mercy and Half Pint.

"Just imagine it's Ketch's head," said Mercy.

Atkins was glad of something to do. The nervous expectation of being caught by a swarm of gigantic insects was almost unbearable. It was much better to keep yourself occupied. As they continued to swing, the picks bit deeper and deeper into the wall. It was some twenty minutes and four feet before Porgy's pick broke through to the other side. Hobson crouched by the opening and beckoned the men closer.

"Right," he said in a low voice, "just like Trench Clearance. You know the routine."

Except this was worse than trench clearance and Atkins knew it. He still had nightmares about the mines. Nevertheless, he swallowed hard and tried to put it to the back of his mind as, one by one, the Black Hand Gang entered the short tunnel. Blood took the lead as ordered, slithering through the hole and disappearing into the darkness. There was a brief, tense moment of silence before he hissed back the all clear. They passed through the extra rifles and grenades, boxes of ammunition and a couple of Lewis guns, before following.

Atkins looked back at the silent urchin, now watching them again, sitting atop a pile of bones. "See you," he said with a wink and joined his pals in the Chatt-ridden gloom beyond.

HIGH ABOVE, IN the labyrinth of tunnels and chambers, Jeffries, having successfully passed the ritual, had spent the last few hours recovering from the ordeal. Thankfully, they had hauled the snivelling Padre back off to the gaol chamber. He had no idea what the chaplain had experienced but he did hope it wasn't pleasant. As for himself, he only felt mildly disconcerted by his vision. He had no idea how long he had been under the influence of the oil; it could have been a couple of hours or a couple of days.

The Khungarrii saw the Rite as one of submission, of acceptance to the colony, but, on a more personal level, for him it had been one of control, of discipline. His will against theirs. And he had won.

His Great Working had taken months to prepare and years to perfect. Only a handful of people would have understood the significance of what he had done on the Somme, of what he had achieved or, more gallingly, attempted to achieve. Everything he had read, everything he had learned had led him to believe that the Old One would be summoned within the great pentacle laboriously calculated and etched on the battlefield; that the blood of thousands would have summoned him and confined him in a crucible warded by a circle of geographic proportions. When their transportation to this world had occurred in its stead, he'd felt confused and angry. Loath though he was to admit it, there had been several small flaws in his calculations. There was the fact that vital commentaries to the Ritual had been long since lost, and that the ritual itself was an Enochian translation of manuscripts that Voynich, the old antiquarian book dealer, had discovered and got rid of, not knowing what they were but rather *fearing* he knew what they were.

Had this whole experience been a salutary case of 'be careful what you wish for'? Had his invocation inverted, torn them from Earth only to deposit them in Croatoan's own domain? A case of 'if the mountain won't come to Mohammed, then Mohammed must go to the mountain,' as Everson had so innocently suggested? A lesson in humility? If so, then he was suitably humbled, but not by these insects. These Chatts were a step on the road to his personal mountain, so to speak, and he had no compunction about treading on ants to get there.

Napoo's mention of Croatoan, his recent ritual vision, his Great Working; there had to be a connection. Was he brought here as an unforeseen consequence of his working? Were these insects just a means to an end?

"When you are ready, Sirigar has instructed this One to share knowledge about Khungarr society as you asked," said Chandar, watching intently as Jeffries tore hungrily into the loaf of fungus bread. "Then you will deliver your herd."

Jeffries looked up and regarded the old Chatt. That something had passed between Chandar and Sirigar, Jeffries was now quite sure. Now he knew there was a crack in their relationship, all he had to do was apply pressure.

"This One has made its work to study wild Urmen," said Chandar, "and you are unlike any others this one has come across. You have a keen intelligence almost matching the One's own. Your garments are complex and of a quality this One has never smelt, yet the scouts report that you live in your filth, among your own dead. It was these odours that the breath of GarSuleth carried to us spinnings ago, alerting the scentirrii and dhuyumirrii to your presence on Khungarr territory. Sirigar and Rhengar are of conflicting opinions, although each has their views rooted in holy scentures. Even now the Khungarrii Shura debate your presence. Some hold that you should be culled without consideration for your initial resistance but it seems to some that your earth workings and burrows imitate, in a primitive fashion of course, the great tunnels and chambers of the Ones' own colonies. It marks your herd as different. This, and your bargain, is what has what saved you," Chandar said.

"And those Urmen you keep here, are they so different from us?"

"They are Khungarrii."

"Not Urmen then?"

"Khungarrii Urmen. They smell Khungarrii, they belong to Khungarr."

"They are kept here by force?"

"They submit to the will of GarSuleth daily in their decision to wear the mark of Khungarr. It is reapplied, willingly, every day. By doing this they show their obedience and gratitude."

"But surely if these Urmen of yours are as much a part of the colony as you say, what culture do they have left for you to study?"

"It is true their culture is now that of Khungarr. They, too, worship GarSuleth but their ancestors and the wild Urmen, the remnants of their culture, fascinate me. I have been studying them for many spinnings."

"And Sirigar allows your studies?" said Jeffries, probing to see where the cracks between them lay.

"That One tolerates them," Chandar replied. "There are those of us among the dhuyumirrii that have long believed Urmen have a place in our Osmology. Other Ones, Sirigar among them, dispute this, believing that Urmen can have no other purpose but to serve the Ones."

A theological schism, thought Jeffries. That would certainly account for the animosity between Sirigar and Chandar and was certainly something he could exploit. "But you believe differently?"

"Come, let me show you something," said Chandar.

Intrigued, Jeffries followed Chandar back to the temple. He noted again the niches all round the walls. Hieroglyphic script of some form covered each niche. Chatts had their faces to the walls of the niches, their feelers moving dextrously over the surfaces.

"Here dhuyumirrii read and study sacred texts and debate on points of interpretation," explained Chandar.

Jeffries could see now that what he took to be contemplation, praying and bowing, was in fact the action of their antennae over the glyphs.

Now he understood. Not only was there information contained within the hieroglyphs themselves, but there were other olfactory layers of meaning contained within chemical scents *attached* to the text. Layers of nuance, subtlety and context lay impregnated within the glyphs. Chandar led him on through the archway through which Jeffries had been taken previously. It led to the chamber of trench equipment. Along the way they passed through the alchemical chambers he had seen only briefly before. Now Jeffries was able to study it in more detail. Its walls were filled with small niches and recesses. Galleries led off the large room, each one containing bays crowded with stone bottles, pots, urns, beakers and amphorae; ceramic vessels of all shapes, sizes and ages.

"This is the receptory of Khungarr, the repository of all our knowledge. The sacred odours stored here are the thoughts of our prophets and gon dhuyumirrii."

"A library," said Jeffries, nodding in appreciation at the vast accumulation of containers and the knowledge they must represent. Each bottle, each jar, contained what must have been an essence of scripture or holy aromas; bouquets of bibles, prophetic perfumes, olfactory encyclopaedias. There was so much he might learn, but it was like giving a blind man the key to a library.

He was not allowed to dwell on it for long as Chandar ushered him into the next series of interconnecting chambers. They passed through what looked like an apothecary's storehouse, hundreds of niches filled with earthenware bottles, jars, tubes filled with oils, essences, liquids, tinctures, extracts, secretions, resins, saps, powders, pastes, samples of plants, leaves, flowers, barks, bones, skins, fur, shells, all arranged, classified and organised. The smell was overpowering and made Jeffries' nostrils sting and his eyes water. Beyond them, blinking though teary eyes, he could see further chambers where more of the Khungarrii priest caste, the dhuyumirrii, were engaged in their great alchemical endeavours.

"For many generations the dhuyumirrii have been attempting, amongst other things, to distill the true quintessence of our creators' odour of sanctity, the scent of GarSuleth. Some believe certain notes of the Urmen musk may yet be relevant to our studies, but teasing out the lone indivisible base notes is a long and arduous task."

"Why?" asked Jeffries. "Why Urmen? They're not Chatts, I mean; they are not of the Ones. Why should they be relevant?"

"GarSuleth dwells in the Sky World, his web spanning the firmament above us. Ancient incenses tell us in his wisdom he once descended from his web to spin this world, this orb, where his eggs were laid and his children, the Ones, hatched. The Ones, the children of GarSuleth, then spread out across the world and begat the colonies," Chandar picked one of the knotted tassels on the cloth draped over its shoulder and lifted it up, almost nostalgically, its antennae stumps waving feebly. "Although this one can no longer read this odour, this one has committed its scents to memory. It tells how, many generations ago, a sickness infected the line of Queens who now ruled each colony. Eggs laid to be djamirrii—workers—hatched malformed and continue to do so to this spinning. Djamirrii populations were decimated and the Ones struggled to survive. The Ones knew of the Urmen's existence, but treated them as competition for scarce and hard won resources, until some came to believe they were created by GarSuleth for the Ones' own use."

"You used them to replace your own shortage of workers."

"Not without price. There came a dark time. The Urmen then worshipped a different god, the forbidden one."

Jeffries saw his opportunity. "This is all very interesting, but what I require is specific knowledge. Tell me about Croatoan."

Chandar rounded on Jeffries, its mandibles chattering, the vestigial limbs at its abdomen fidgeting.

"That's right," Jeffries said, deliberately relishing the opportunity to say the name again and forming each syllable clearly: "Croatoan."

Chandar glanced around at the alchemist dhuyumirrii. None of them seemed to have heard. "That name is forbidden!"

"Nevertheless, that is my price. You want my cooperation then tell me what you know," said Jeffries firmly. "Or should I shout the name out loud, here, now?"

"No! You must not," said Chandar, rising up on its legs in the threatening manner Jeffries had seen Sirigar use before.

"But your own studies? If you could tell me about your... forbidden one, how much might I be able reciprocate, to advance your own Urman studies with information I have? What is it that Sirigar and its acolytes don't want you to know? You have hinted yourself that passages in your scriptures concerning Urmen are ambiguous at best, maybe excised at worst. What if my information could shed light on them?"

Jeffries held the Chatt's gaze, looking deep into its dark orbs. He had the old fool's measure now. Give this old louse enough rope and it'll hang itself. It was like leaving a trail of sugar for an ant.

"Very well," said Chandar. It shrugged its shoulders and waved its antennae stubs in a way that seemed to indicate agitation. "But not here, I have somewhere we can talk. Come with me."

Chandar led him out through the chamber where they had stored their collection of items pilfered from the entrenchment. The jumble of trench stores and arms were still there, no doubt waiting to have their odours investigated, distilled and broken down. From there the passage became narrower and showed signs of disrepair. It seemed to be a little used part of the colony.

"Where are we?" asked Jeffries, a hint of suspicion in his voice, the reassuring pressure of the pistol barrel pressing against his abdomen.

"Somewhere we will not be overheard," said Chandar as they stopped before a chamber sealed by a fibrous membrane.

"Here are stored many Urman artefacts that I have found, lost in undergrowth or left in caves over many spinnings," said Chandar. "Indications of how Urmen lived before the Ones subsumed them. Maybe in return you can enlighten me as to the nature of some of them."

"Yes, yes," muttered Jeffries dismissively. He had no interest in the old Chatt's collection of archaeology, almost certainly a fusty amateur assortment of broken pottery, arrowheads, flints and bone jewellery with no context and less meaning. No, Croatoan was his only concern now. The need overwhelmed him. He fought the desire to take the Chatt by the shoulders and shake the information out of it there and then, and watched impatiently as it exhaled a mist from its mouthparts, in response to which, the door shrivelled open. Chandar stepped through and beckoned Jeffries to do likewise. Preoccupied, Jeffries stepped into the chamber totally unprepared for what lay inside.

CHAPTER SIXTEEN
"The Last High Place"

ATKINS KNELT IN the short stretch of tunnel. Before him the stack of equipment he was passing through to the others barred his way. Eager to be inside himself, he gave the last of it, Mercy's mysterious tarpaulin covered thing, a last shove with his heel, and it fell down into the passage with a dull metallic *clang*.

"For Christ's sake, Only, watch it!" hissed Mercy as Atkins dropped down into the passage after it.

The passage itself was about six feet high, four feet wide and rounded, almost as if it had been burrowed rather than built. A faint draft of air was blowing towards them down its length.

Everson nodded and Sergeant Hobson walked cautiously into the breeze until he disappeared around a gentle curve ahead.

Along the length of the curving passage small recesses were stuffed with some sort of glowing lichen that imparted a dull but diffuse blue-white light.

Mercy crouched down to inspect the damage to his bundle.

"How are we doing, Evans?" asked Everson.

Mercy glanced up at Everson and nodded.

"So what the hell is this mysterious thing we've lugged all the way, sir?" asked Porgy.

With a broad grin and the flair of a showman, Mercy flung back the tarpaulin.

"The lieutenant thought we'd need a bit of an edge. An' I found one, didn't I, in the remains of that Jerry sap. Isn't it a beauty? Am I good or am I good?"

"Bugger me!" said Gutsy. "It's a flammin' Hun Flammenwerfer."

Mercy grinned and nodded slowly. "Oh yes. After what I saw them Chatts do when they raided our trenches I think a little payback is due, don't you?"

"What is it?" asked Poilus.

187

"A liquid fire thrower," said Atkins, in awe.

"Bloody hell," said Gazette, in a low voice.

"Them Chatts'll get what's coming to 'em now," Mercy said with a sneer.

"If it works," said Half Pint.

"Tell you what," hissed Mercy, "you look down the barrel and tell me if you see a spark."

"I was just sayin'," said Half Pint.

"Yeah, well don't come looking to me next time you want a light for your Woodie, is all I'm sayin'."

"Quiet!" hissed Everson as Sergeant Hobson returned.

"Tunnel leads to a broader one up ahead. I can hear voices beyond," he reported.

"Right," said Everson. "Poilus, you're sure this scent trick will work?"

"For a while," said the Urman.

"Let's hope so." He nodded to Hobson. "Carry on, Sergeant."

"We're not anticipating trouble going in, so long as this insect stink continues to do its work. Chances are we're going to have to fight our way out though, so save your puff and your ammo. Atkins, you're bayonet man with me. Hopkiss and Blood, bombs. Evans and Nicholls, you take the damned flammenwerfer."

"But Sarn't..." Half Pint began.

"It takes two to operate," explained Mercy. "I can't reach the fire lever. You have to do it for me."

"Ketch and Jellicoe, you're on mop-up. Poilus, you stick with them," said Hobson. "Otterthwaite, you take the rear with the lieutenant. Move out."

As they set off, all encumbered not only by their own equipment but also by the sacks of rifles, grenades, Lewis MGs and ammunition they were carrying for the others, Atkins began to feel the old familiar dread he'd felt in the mines as a guard.

The miners dug tunnels deep underground, far out under the German positions in order to plant high explosives. It was hot, cramped and dirty work, even more so if you didn't like confined spaces with little air. And God forbid you should think of the thousands of tons of earth above, constantly being shelled. Then there were the Germans who would be doing the same. It was a game of cat and mouse hundreds of feet below the peppered surface of No Man's Land. Sat breathless in a listening alcove trying to determine where the Hun was. Too close and you could hear them digging and they could hear you. Occasionally you'd accidentally break through into a German shaft and then, oh God then, the close fighting, the fear of grenades and being buried or cut off from escape by a tunnel collapse.

"You all right, Atkins?"

"What?"

"I said you all right?" asked Hobson as they advanced.

"Yes sir, just remembering something."

"Once we start killing these Chatts, the Urmen will rise up against their insect masters, against their Oppressors, that's right isn't it, Sarn't?" Pot Shot asked.

"If we're lucky," said Hobson.

"Just think what we could do with an army of Urmen. We could conquer this world," Mercy pondered.

"You're forgetting mate, we're going home," said Gutsy. "I ain't staying to conquer nothing. I've had a belly full o' conquering and a fat lot a good it's done me."

The passage began to slope up gently before forking. Atkins hesitated. "Which way?"

Hobson glanced down the smaller tunnel and dismissed it. It was a cul-de-sac. "Carry on. We want to go up."

Atkins advanced cautiously on up the tunnel. He began to hear sounds now carried on the draught; scuttlings and scufflings, poppings and clickings. He shuddered to think of the tunnels ahead teeming with giant insects. It had been bad enough in the trenches with the rats, but these things, they just filled him with horror. He couldn't help himself. A little way ahead, the passage opened out onto what seemed to be a main thoroughfare. Behind him, the Section flattened themselves against the walls as, in the lichen-lit twilight, Chatts scurried about mere feet from them. Urmen, too, went about their chores, unaware of their presence. Atkins tensed himself, ready to make the bayonet thrust they had been trained to make without thinking.

Several heavy chitinous plated scentirrii, one or two carrying Electric Lances that reminded Atkins of Mercy's *flammenwerfer*, marched past. He glanced back down the passage to see Mercy's eyes narrow. As a group of Urmen came along, they slipped in behind them and then off down the first rising passage to which they came.

It led them up to a great hall, the roof of which arced high overhead. Shafts of light punctuated its domed ceiling on one side, sunlight penetrating deep into the structure. Many passages led off the cavernous hall. A wide sloping path spiralled round the walls at a shallow gradient to a gallery about twenty or thirty feet up. From here, more passages led away into the edifice. Chatt soldiers were standing there, armed with lances, overseeing the workers below. Hundreds if not thousands of Urmen toiled at the raised beds that covered the floor of the chamber, each filled with some sort of mould or fungus. They seemed to be cultivating the substance. A damp, earthy smell filled the hall.

Urmen were not the only creatures tending the fungus beds; there were Chatts, too, although they were outnumbered by the Urmen about them. They seemed to be smaller than the Chatt soldiers above and there were fewer segments to their antennae. Their chitinous armour was smoother, lighter. These, Atkins assumed, must be the worker Chatts.

The fungus from the beds was loaded onto large sled-like litters before being transported elsewhere, presumably for storage or distribution.

From the shadows of the tunnel, Atkins watched the Urmen, fascinated. They seemed like ordinary humans. They were dressed in roughly woven tunics and each wore some sort of blue mark upon their foreheads. Looking into the hall he was reminded of his first job in Houlton Mill, the men and women intent on their task as the foremen looked on. Fourteen he'd been when he left school. Those foremen hadn't been armed, though. Atkins counted twenty soldier Chatts, five in the gallery, the rest patrolling the floor.

"Bloody slave labour, that's what it is," muttered Pot Shot, appalled.

"Up there," whispered Everson. Atkins and Hobson followed his finger to the gallery. They watched Urmen enter it with their laden sleds.

After an urging shove from Hobson, Atkins stepped warily out into the hubbub of the fungus farming chamber, his bayoneted Enfield at the ready. The noise about him didn't suddenly subside and deteriorate into an ugly, tense silence as he half expected. In fact, the world carried on around him, the Urmen continuing with their tasks and pulling harvested litters of fungus along using shoulder harnesses woven from what looked like plant fibre.

Cautiously the rest of the section stepped out to join him. They kept to the edge of the chamber and headed in an anticlockwise direction for the gallery ramp. Poilus broke away from the group to acquire an apparently abandoned sled-like litter. He loaded the sacks and sandbags of extra weapons onto it, then heaped it with fungus to the cover the weapons. An Urman woman approached him to protest and Atkins felt himself tense for a fight, but Poilus, gesticulating, seemed to be making some sort of argument. Angrily, she gesticulated back. Poilus trumped her by pointing to the soldier Chatts on the gallery above and she threw her arms in the air, shook her head and wandered off sullenly.

They were making headway toward the spiral ramp when several soldier Chatts appeared out of a passage and advanced purposefully towards them. Urmen scuttled out of the way as, behind the squat, heavy-set soldiers, a taller, more regal-looking Chatt followed them; its head and antennae covered with a rich carmine hood that masked its features. It wore a length of silk thrown over its shoulder and tied around its abdomen from which hung a great number of tassels. The soldiers knew a member of the ruling classes when they saw one. Atkins and Hobson froze, unsure how to react.

A flat-faced soldier Chatt stopped in front of them, its lance sparking faintly. Its black, featureless eyes scrutinized them. Its antennae waved petulantly as it sought confirmation of the expected chemical mark of Khungarrii scent. Atkins became very aware of the sweat on his hands and his forehead as it continued its inspection and hoped his human smell wouldn't wash away his scent mask. Finally satisfied, its antennae stopped waving and it began scissoring its mandibles belligerently. "Move, dhuyumirrii comes."

Poilus, helped by Pot Shot, dragged the litter to the side of the chamber before dropping his harness and making a curious gesture, touching his hands to his forehead and then to his chest, while bowing to the imperious Chatt approaching them.

"Move," he hissed urgently at Atkins and Hobson, who moved clumsily back against the wall under the watchful gaze of the soldier Chatt. With a nod from Everson, the others followed suit. Atkins caught a waft of cloying perfume from the head covering of the stately Chatt. It was so strong that he had to suppress a cough as it swept passed without acknowledging their presence.

Pot Shot glared after the haughty arthropod. "Same the bloody world over," he muttered. "There's always them on top. Now I find out it's the same on different worlds an' all. I can't say I'm particularly encouraged. Still, all will be different when we get the Urmen to stand up for their rights and take these folk down a peg or two."

"Yeah, well don't forget our first priority is our own," hissed Gutsy. "Save your Labour rhetoric for later, eh?"

"Move on," ordered Everson, once the regal Chatt party had passed.

Pot Shot ducked into the shoulder harness, braced himself and stepped forward, taking the weight of his sled. Ketch, obviously unhappy with his own sacks of ammunition, sought to do what Poilus had done and requisition a litter the better to carry his load. However, a restraining hand on his wrist stopped him. A tall Urman glared down at him.

"Where is your mark?" he asked. "I see no mark."

"Mark? But I have the scent, you saw," he said, indicating the receding Chatt with its guards.

"Urmen Khungarrii don't smell it. You are required to wear the Mark. You know that. Where is it?" he hissed, staring hard at the corporal's forehead and pointing to his own blue glyph.

Ketch raised a questing fingertip and wiped it across his own greasy brow. "It must have come off? I sweat. A lot."

"Then reapply it before someone else notices and takes you for Casteless and godless and calls the scentirrii. GarSuleth wills it," he snapped, before shoving Ketch away and returning about his business. The corporal snarled and brought up his bayoneted rifle ready to thrust the point home, but Atkins grabbed him by shoulder.

"No, Corp," he said. "Not here. Not now."

Ketch glared after the Urman, growling under his breath before relaxing his stance. He turned and shrugged Atkins' hand off his shoulder. "Fuck off, Atkins." He grabbed the vacant sled-like litter, loaded it up and began dragging it along sullenly.

The social injustice of his surroundings continued to gnaw at Pot Shot, like a dog with a bone. He grabbed the arm of a passing Urman woman. "Why do you submit to their rule?"

"We are all Khungarrii. GarSuleth provides. GarSuleth wills it," said the woman.

Everson stepped up and gripped Pot Shot's arm. "Jellicoe, that's enough. Now isn't the time to organize a general bloody strike."

"But, sir—"

"I don't want to hear it, Jellicoe. We're here to do a job."

Reluctantly, Pot Shot returned his attention to pulling the sled, shaking his head and muttering while the Urman woman stared wonderingly after them for a moment, before turning back to her task.

The Tommies approached the ramp and began to make their way up its incline.

"What's the matter with 'em? Don't they want to be freed?" asked Pot Shot, taking a last look down over the labouring Urmen.

"They've been under the yoke too long," said Gutsy. "They just need someone to show 'em how, that's all. Guess we'll be doing that before the day's out."

JEFFRIES STOOD IN Chandar's small chamber while he allowed his eyes to adjust to the gloom. He peered at the objects all around him, piles of Urman junk; pots, jars, jewellery, woven mats, crude shoes and animal skin clothing, wooden implements of every description. Some, given pride of place on earthen plinths or in niches around the wall, commanded the eye. Others, considered less important perhaps, sat in unsorted piles around the floor. He found himself reminded of the piles of their own trench equipment in the other chamber.

"Sirigar thinks this one is wasting its time, but this One's accident allowed it to see Urmen in a new way," said Chandar, standing proudly amid its collection.

"Accident?" said Jeffries, glancing around with indifference, now he could make out more detail in the lichen-light.

"This One's antennae were damaged," said Chandar, squatting and beginning to root though a pile. "This One can no longer sense odours.

In Khungarrii terms this One is..." It seemed to struggle to find the right words.

"Ah. Scent blind. Unfortunate for you." Jeffries was becoming impatient with the small talk. After cornering Chandar into revealing what it knew about Croatoan, he didn't appreciate this new delay.

"No, GarSuleth wills it. To Khungarrii this one is pitied, unable to perform its duties, so I have undertaken new studies. Liya-Dhuyumirrii Sirigar allows this one to pursue its interest in Urmen, now this One only sees the world in the way they do. This One believes it gives it some insight into their old way of life."

"Where did you get these artefacts of yours?"

"Scentirrii would occasionally come across such things and bring them back. Once they were deemed to be of no harm or interest they were disposed of on the midden heaps, but this one retrieved them. This one can only speculate as to some of their uses. This One thought you might be able to enlighten it."

The old fool had been hoarding these things, not knowing what they were and no doubt extrapolating ludicrous theories about indigenous Urman culture on that basis. Jeffries wandered over to a niche in which was a pile of small metallic objects. Chandar followed, watching his reaction eagerly.

Jeffries stood before the niche, for once nonplussed, all thoughts of Croatoan suddenly expunged from his mind. Fingers trembling, mouth dry, Jeffries picked up the least of the trifles; a small round metal disc, and turned it over in his fingers.

"What do you think it is? A charm, a ward perhaps?"

It spoke volumes to Jeffries that the Chatt didn't recognise a coin when it saw one. He studied the copper disc between his thumb and forefinger. He heard the blood rush in his ears and his fingers trembled fractionally with every pulse beat. This... this was a Roman coin, a *denarius*, if he wasn't mistaken and, judging by the pug ugly, bull-necked profile on the obverse, from the reign of the emperor Titus. He struggled to keep his outward composure calm. Somehow, this all made sense. Somehow.

"In a manner of speaking," he croaked, having to cough and clear his throat as he shuffled through the pile of similar coins. "Do you have anything more?"

"Yes," Chandar's stunted middle limbs seemed gripped by spasms as if exhibiting childish delight. It led Jeffries to another pile of items and began sifting thorough them, looking for a choice find. With each new presentation Chandar made, it became harder for Jeffries to conceal his disbelief at what he saw. There were more coins, bone pins, a crushed and dried out leather sandal, a scattering of mediaeval brooches and pottery, a small carven Celtic cross, Elizabethan silverware, crockery and scraps of cloth, and what seemed to be medical tools; an incision knife, a spatula; the items came one after the other. With a lurching sense of vertigo, it became clear to Jeffries that they were not the first humans to visit this world from Earth. Even as he thought this however, another, more damning, hypothesis began to form in his mind.

The more Jeffries saw, the more he became convinced that there had been incidents of human displacement in history before. What had happened to those people? Well, that was a stupid question. If their own experiences were anything to go by, then most of them would have been killed, struggling to survive their first few days. But the survivors? Could these troglodytic Urmen be the descendants of others who had arrived here from Earth in the past? There were many legends of mass disappearances throughout history. For all the soldiers' hopes, for all their desires and dreams of Blighty, it appeared that there may not actually be a way back to Earth. But what did that have to do with his Great Working? With Croatoan? That he couldn't yet see, until his gaze fell upon what should have been an impossible object, or at least, until a few minutes ago, an impossible object. The sight of it caused him barely to suppress a gasp.

"Where... where did you find this...?" he rasped, picking up a weathered, hand-carved wooden sign that proclaimed boldly the legend, *New Roanoke*.

With that one name, the matter of Croatoan burst once more into the forefront of his mind. Croatoan, the fallen angel who communicated with the renowned Elizabethan Magus, Doctor John Dee. Several of his disciples were reputed to have been among the first English settlers in Virginia in 1582 when they attempted to found the colony of Roanoke, financed by the secretive School of Night. When the supply ship returned later, the colony had disappeared. The only clue they found was the word 'Croatoan' carved into a gatepost. That the opening of the New World was conceived of as an occult operation was an idea Jeffries had been aware of for a long time, he just didn't think they meant *this* new world, although he could certainly see how it fitted the bill as *prima materia*.

It was becoming clear to him now, beyond all doubt, that Croatoan was linked to the disappearances. Was the colony really an audacious early attempt at the very magickal operation he had performed, well away from prying Protestant eyes, where the necessary bloodletting could be practiced on the native population without being hampered by the moral imperatives of society?

Whatever the truth, it would seem the same fate had befallen the settlers of the lost Roanoke colony as befell the Pennines. From the weathered sign he held in his hands, it was clear that they too had been transported to this world in response to their Working. Here, they had sought to found a new colony, a new Roanoke, who worshipped Croatoan. If the Battalion's own experiences were anything to go by, then not many would have survived their first few weeks without help. He rounded on Chandar. "Tell me about Croatoan. That's the bargain. Tell me about Croatoan."

Chandar hissed at the mention of the name, but resigned itself to its side of the bargain.

"According to the notes of the Perfumed Chronicles it happened many, many queens ago. In the spinnings of the dhagastri-har queen— the forty-third queen of Khungarr—a herd of Urmen passed into the lands of the Khungarrii and, seeking refuge in Khungarr, which they received willingly, they brought with them into our midst their own god... Croatoan. They began trying to convert the Urmen of Khungarr to their god and, as a sign, pointed out a bright spot in the sky that they claimed was their god come to smite down GarSuleth." Here Chandar made a brief gesture of reverence as if to protect itself and its god from its own heretical words. "The light grew brighter, brighter than all the other dew drops that shine in GarSuleth's Web and Urmen turned against the Khungarr. The liya-dhuyumirrii declared that GarSuleth would cast the false god from the Sky World. So it came to pass that the false god was hurled down in fire and the entire world felt his fall. Croatoan was consumed in flames and consigned to the underworld by Skarra. With their god destroyed the majority of Urmen turned rightfully to GarSuleth. Those that would not were, likewise, cast out and his worship declared heretical by Chemical Decree from the queen."

That Croatoan was woven into the fate of the Khungarrii was more than Jeffries had dared hope for. As all these thoughts circled round his mind, his eyes fell on a piece of parchment sat in a niche, pinned to a board of bark. Chandar looked on proudly as he studied it. It looked like a map. He must have made a noise because Chandar picked up on it.

"Does it mean something to you?"

"Hmm?"

"The dhuyumirrii studied it but it has no scent of meaning to them. The glyphs we cannot decipher."

"Did you not think to ask one of your Urmen?" said Jeffries, irritated at having to deal with these interruptions as he struggled to get to grips with all that he was seeing.

"Khungarrii Urmen can neither script nor scent. After the Croatoan Heresy their own ways were declared sacrilege. All that they were is lost. Urman culture was eradicated. All Urman writings and knowledge wiped out. They are Khungarrii now. No one can read the language, if language it is."

Jeffries stared at the map. It seemed to be a map of this world. He couldn't understand how Chandar couldn't see it for what it was, but then it was entirely probable that their cartography was scent-based and not visually oriented. He ran his eyes hungrily over every symbol, over every mark on the map. Everything he knew from his studies—the style of calligraphy, the type of parchment—told him this was Elizabethan. It was fine, if hurried draughtsmanship. The map was incomplete although it did indicate what seemed to be mountains, forest, rivers and presumably, other edifices. He saw blocks of closely written Enochian and Voynich text that he would have to decipher laboriously. And there, and there, despite the bad penmanship and the foxing, emblazoned on the map in several locations, Jeffries recognised the unmistakable sigil of Croatoan.

CHAPTER SEVENTEEN
"Louse Hunting"

EVERSON HALTED THE party in a side tunnel to get their bearings. It was apparent to him that these rough tunnels were reserved for worker castes, designed as passing places or servants' passages, so that the ruling Chatts wouldn't have to come face to face with them. His father's house in Broughtonthwaite had similar features.

He got Poilus to ask passing Urmen if they knew where the prisoners were being kept, but he might as well have been asking them the way to the Alhambra Picture House. There was no way they would find the captured soldiers by blundering blindly about these tunnels, the place was a maze with numerous cul-de-sacs and dead ends, so it was just as well he'd got a plan.

"Atkins," he called.

The private turned from watching the mouth of the tunnel and Everson, crooking a finger, beckoned him back.

"Sir?"

"You still have that confounded creature?"

"Yes sir, it's getting a bit restless, though," he said, nodding down at his gas helmet knapsack, which was moving about in an agitated fashion. "I reckon he must be getting pretty hungry."

"Good, time to take it for a walk then. Let it out, will you."

He saw Atkins look at Hopkiss, who just shrugged.

"Don't look at Hopkiss, Atkins, just do it," said Everson.

He could see the looks in their eyes; *it's a bloody officer, who knows what he's thinking, just do as you're told.* But he'd learnt to let that wash over him a long time ago.

Atkins complied and pulled a large rat-like creature from his knapsack, its long nose already questing at the air with small, wet snuffles.

"Got a name has it, Atkins?"

"Ginger, er, Mottram, called it Gordon, sir."

197

"Very well. Get a leash on him. If Gordon is as hungry as I hope he is I think he might just lead us to our men."

Atkins put a loop of string over its head.

"What," said Sergeant Hobson at the sight of the creature, "is that?"

"I believe the men call it a Chatter, Sergeant," said Everson. "It loves lice. Apparently, it thinks them quite a delicacy. And thanks to this little blighter and Evans' entrepreneurial spirit none of us here is hitchy-koo anymore, so I'm hoping it'll sniff out any lice in this place, and the only place I know we can find 'em is on our own great unwashed."

Hobson gave a sceptical grunt before turning to Hopkiss and hissing, "You trying to tell me that's what I paid me thruppence for, Hopkiss, to have that thing rooting through my smalls and shirts?"

"Aye, Sarn't. Money well spent, I'd say," said Porgy with a grin. "Ain't scratched since 'ave yer?"

Hobson muttered unhappily until Poilus, who had been keeping watch, motioned them to keep quiet.

Gordon began scurrying about amongst their feet looking for his new favourite food and Atkins had to yank him back before they all got tangled up in his string leash.

Heads down, they stepped from the worker's passage into the main tunnel as an eager little Gordon took the lead, tugging at the string in Atkins' hand. Hobson rolled his eyes at the sight but took up point with him as he'd been ordered to.

The tunnels became lighter and airier. They must have been in an outer spiral because apertures high in the walls filtered bright beams of sunlight into the passageways. They passed several groups of Urmen repairing tunnels, perhaps after the recent tremors, without further incident but there was still no sign of the captives.

Everson watched expectantly as Gordon stopped below a vent shaft up in the wall and raised itself up on its hind legs, its forepaws scrabbling at the earthen wall, the nostrils of its thin wet whiskery snout flaring as it scented something. "Good boy!" praised Atkins, petting Gordon as if he were a prize ratter. The private peered at the opening above his head. "It runs upwards sir," he reported. He listened intently for a moment then added, "I think I can hear voices."

But were they Urman or Human? Everson ordered Hobson and Blood to move one of the weapon sleds across the curving passage to form a barricade behind which they knelt, pointing their Enfields into the tunnel behind them. Pot Shot and Porgy used the second sled as a mount for the Lewis Gun. Everson could see sweat beading on their foreheads. Wandering these tunnels wearing full kit and lugging an extra twenty or thirty pounds each was taking its toll.

He made his way through his men to the vent hole two or three feet above him. He removed his cap and gingerly tilted his head towards the vent, but could hear nothing above the curious pops and clicks that issued from it. "Hopkiss, give me a leg up will you?"

Hopkiss handed his rifle to Evans and linked the fingers of his hands together, palms up. Everson stepped onto the offered cradle and Atkins boosted him up so that he could get his head into the vent above.

He could feel a down draught cooling his face and, riding on the breeze, he heard the faint murmur of voices, human voices. If he could just... He put his hands up inside the vent, braced them on the walls and hauled himself into the mouth of the hole, until he was resting on his stomach, leaving his now flailing legs searching for purchase, which wasn't so much found as offered. Hopkiss' shoulders, he presumed. He used them to drive himself up into the shaft. With a cautionary *shhh* to his men below, he started to listen to the faint sounds filtering down from above.

In the warm, cramped confines of the shaft, he became aware of his own body odour. It smelt as if he hadn't had a bath in weeks, which wasn't that far from the truth. He began to wonder how long the scent from the dead Chatt would mask it. If, in fact, it still did. He lay still, held his breath and listened. There was a mutter of voices above, but he still couldn't tell what they were saying. He had to know whether they were Urman or Human before he committed his men. He cupped his hand round his mouth and hollered up the vent. "This is Second Lieutenant Everson of 'C' Company. Hello? Are you all right?"

The seconds ticked by as he waited, then he heard a distant, but definite, "Yes, sir!"

"We're on our way" he called back up. "Get ready to make a break for it!"

He was about to call down when Hobson's urgent whisper reached him. "Stay where you are, sir!" Then he heard the unnerving chitter of Chatt mandibles below and the familiar sound of magazine cut-offs being flicked open and loading bolts being cycled back in readiness. Slowly he swivelled round in the narrow vent until he was on his back, looking down the length of his body to the end of the shaft and the top of Hopkiss' steel helmet. He readjusted his pistol grip and waited.

"What do you here? Answer!" came the breathless glottal sound of a Chatt. "You block way."

"Us?" he heard Hobson's voice respond. "We're just taking food to the prisoners."

"Prihz nuhz."

Everson braced himself. Judging by their use of language, these Chatts knew just enough to deal with Urmen on a basic level.

"You not Khungarrii."

"We most certainly are."

"Scent no."

Well, that answered *that* question.

"You no Khungarrii." There was an inhuman scream and a muttered interjection of "Oh, hell," followed by the sound of a club smashed into something brittle and wet. Hard on its heels came a hissing and a pained yelp mixed with an electric crackle. A bluish white light flared briefly, illuminating the shaft.

"Damn!" said Everson, relaxing his body and allowing himself to slip from the vent.

He landed heavily on his feet, revolver ready, but the immediate problem had been dealt with. Two broad-headed Chatts, one with an electric lance, lay on the floor. One had its head staved in. The other had been stabbed through the chest. Private Blood was wiping his bayonet blade and Sergeant Hobson was hefting 'Little Bertha.' Corporal Ketch was clutching his arm.

"Damn thing spat acid at me," he coughed. "It's gone right through me bleedin' stripes!"

"Reckon someone's trying to tell you something, Ketch," sniped Evans. Ketch glared back at him.

Everson didn't need this right now. He needed them to be operating as a unit. He stepped in between the two soldiers.

"You all right, Corporal?" he said.

"I'll live," replied Ketch from between gritted teeth.

"Right. I don't need anyone blinded by this acid spray. So let's not take any chances. Gas helmets on."

"Looks like our smell-o-flage has worn off, then sir," said Hopkiss in a chirpy assessment of the situation, rummaging in his canvas bag for the gas hood.

"So it would seem, Hopkiss."

"We must move," urged Poilus. "They will have sent out an alarm scent warning the rest of the colony. More scentirrii will be here soon."

"We've lost the element of surprise, then," said Everson.

It was bound to happen. Their luck wouldn't hold forever. Mind you, they'd got further than he'd thought. Knowing they didn't have long before more Chatts turned up he wanted to push on as quickly as possible.

"This is it," he said. "Everybody ready?" There were grunts of assent from under the gas hoods as the men moved off. Everson rolled his gas hood down over his face, tucked it into his shirt collar, replaced his cap and took a place at the front with Poilus, behind Hobson and Atkins as Gordon sniffed out the way. Blood and Ketch followed pulling the weapons sleds while Evans, Nicholls, and their Flammenwerfer brought up the rear with Otterthwaite, Jellicoe and Hopkiss.

They pushed on up the gently spiraling passage. They'd only just managed to build up a head of steam when the first soldier

Chatts appeared from a side passage to the left. Evans nodded and Half Pint opened the valve. A brief spurt of fire sprayed out of the Flammerwerfer's nozzle, like Satan's own piss. The Chatts began to squeal and thrash about, fire leaping high and blackening the tunnel walls. There was a sickening heavy smell like burnt hair.

"Passage," shouted Sergeant Hobson, indicating with his right arm as they advanced past the dark open maw of a side tunnel.

Blood, pulling a sled, pulled the pin on a Mills bomb, counted to three and tossed it into the shadows. There was a brief rattle of metal on clay then the tunnel shook and bloomed with a fiery light as the explosion spat hot shrapnel through the enclosed space, eliciting startled inhuman shrieks.

Everson heard the stutter of rapid fire as Hopkiss fired back down the tunnel. He glanced back to see a squad of Chatt soldiers retreating round the curve of the passageway. Jellicoe pulled the pin from a grenade and rolled it, clattering, down the passage. It exploded round the corner bringing baked earth crashing down.

The Chatts' weapons—spears, some form of swords, their acid sprays and electric lances—were all close range. If they could keep the damned things at bay, they may just have a chance. With all their firepower though, Everson briefly wondered if they'd gone over the top.

JEFFRIES GAZED AT the sigils on the parchment as one might at the photograph of a far away sweetheart.

"You recognise something?" asked Chandar.

"Hmm?" said Jeffries. He had to remember that this was a creature that had spent a good deal of time around Urmen. More so than its companions. It had learnt to mimic behaviour and gestures to gain confidences. He had done such things himself. It was trying to ingratiate itself. "What? No," he added almost absent-mindedly. This was important, but he didn't want Chandar to know how important.

The room shook. Dust showered gently from the domed ceiling.

"What was that?" asked Jeffries.

"A tremor. Continue."

But Jeffries was distracted now. He made out the faint faraway report of rifle fire.

Damn. Not now, bloody idiots. They'll ruin everything. That damn boy-scout, Everson!

The door shrivelled back and Rhengar and two of its scentirrii entered the chamber, pointing their electric lances at Jeffries and herding him against the wall, from where he could now only eye the map covetously.

Their commander hissed and chattered frantically at Chandar, its mouthparts and mandibles moving rapidly. Chandar took whatever comments the soldier was spewing at him, and then turned to Jeffries.

"Your herd has invaded the colony," said Chandar. "Rhengar thinks you have broken your agreement."

"No!" said Jeffries emphatically, shaking his head, arms wide. "This is not my doing."

Chandar turned back to Rhengar, slipping into its own language of hisses and clicks as a heated exchange developed. Eventually, Rhengar rounded on Chandar, emitting a long hiss with open mandibles and rose up on its powerful legs even as Chandar assumed a position of submission. Whatever argument Chandar was trying to put forward, it had just lost. Jeffries cursed silently.

"You must go with them," said Chandar.

"If you attempt to escape we will hurt you," Rhengar made sure to say in English.

Jeffries got the message. Rhengar strode off, its scentirrii shepherding him along, their lances never wavering from his body.

As he was led away, Jeffries turned and called back to Chandar who stood in the entrance to the artefact chamber.

"It's a mistake. Let me talk to my men, Chandar. I can get them to stop the attack. It's all an awful mistake. Believe me!"

But Chandar didn't move and Jeffries lost sight of the creature as the guards urged him relentlessly on.

His mind raced. If Everson's damn fool rescue failed then there was no doubt that Sirigar creature would have them all culled. If the rescue did succeed, then he lost access to the map and those artefacts. He felt the stolen pistol in his waistband, but with electrical lances against his back, he doubted he could reach it in time. He needed that map. He felt sure it was the answer to all, well, *many* of his questions.

If they were stuck here on this world with no way home then he didn't need to be hampered with several hundred stranded soldiers. He could abandon them to their fate. They had served their purpose and delivered him this far. It was clear now that his destiny lay in a different direction, and that pointed to Croatoan once more.

"This wasn't my idea, you know," he said to Rhengar's back as the scentirrii frogmarched him back the way he had come; past the trench equipment, through the alchemical and library chambers towards the temple. Dhuyumirrii and their acolytes scurried about as he was escorted across the main temple chamber and out of the ornate entrance on the large thoroughfare tunnel. Masses of Chatts moved along it in well-ordered ranks, the only allowance to chaos was the haste with which they were moving. He assumed that it was not the weight of written law that made them obey but rather instructional semiochemicals lacing the atmosphere, filtered through the natural air conditioning of the nest, impelling them to comply.

The few Urmen that were allowed access to this level were directed down side passages or cloister tunnels by scentirrii that took up positions to direct traffic flow. A defence plan was being put into operation.

A squad of scentirrii ran down past them, their powerful legs barely containing their springing step in the confines of the tunnel. Then he heard the faint but recognisable judder of a Lewis gun and the dull, muffled thud of an explosion reverberated through his feet.

Great. What the hell else could possibly go wrong?

EDITH BELL LOOKED blearily around the chamber. The slumped Tommies around her were beginning to stir. The feeling of rapture was wearing off. Edith, in her naivety, could only compare it to that brief, special moment upon waking in the warmth of one's bed, when one is dozily blissful, before the cares of the day encroach and sully the transitory moment of peace. Some soldiers were already sitting with their heads in their hands, wondering what the hell had happened. For some, coming down from the drug-induced euphoria left them feeling depressed and melancholic. Others still wore blissfully stupid smiles. Captain Grantham sat staring into space. He was lost in his own thoughts and they didn't seem to be happy ones.

Napoo, who seemed to have recovered faster than they had, was already moving from one soldier to another, slapping them to bring them round.

"Yes, thank you, Napoo. That will be enough of that," said Sister Fenton, who was already standing, if a little shakily, but determined to show that she would let no insect muddle her mind.

"But the Khungarrii dhuyumirrii's blessing is strong," he said, unused to having his behaviour challenged.

"Yes, some sort of natural opiate, no doubt," said Sister Fenton. She smoothed out her blue nurse's uniform in an attempt to recover her authority and decorum, although her apron now hung out of the garderobe as a makeshift signal.

"I beg your pardon, Sister?" said Edith.

"The insect sprayed us with some sort of opiate, hoping to keep us docile and subservient. Nurse Bell, Abbott, start checking the men, if you would. Some may have had an adverse reaction."

Edith got unsteadily to her feet and had to brace herself against the wall as a brief wave of nausea washed over her, spots dancing before her eyes.

"Give a gel a hand," groaned Abbott. Edith clasped her arm and pulled. There was a groan as Nellie raised herself up, smoothed out her ankle-length khaki dress and turned to her with an irritatingly chirpy smile. "Don't mind me, Edi. I've had worse hangovers down the Estaminet in Sans German. Mind you some of these boys don't look as if they've handled it very well."

The chamber was filling with groans and sighs as the men came down from their non-consensual high.

Edith spotted the padre sat by the door, his shoulders slumped. She hadn't noticed him being returned to the chamber, but something terrible must have happened to reduce him to this state.

"Padre, what's the matter. Where's Lieutenant Jeffries?"

The army chaplain lifted his head, his eyes rheumy and red-rimmed, his pupils dilated.

"What have they done to you?"

"Crushed my faith," he said, shaking his head despondently. "Wherever we are, we are far from God's sight."

Edith shook her head, as if that would somehow flush out the residual effects of the insect's spray. There was something she had been trying to remember, but it was a hollow in her mind. What the deuce was it?

Suddenly Napoo, stood below the air ventilation hole with his head cocked, urged them all into silence, his keen native senses straining to hear something. Then others heard it, too.

"This is Second Lieutenant Everson. C Company. Hello?" said a voice drifting from the vent.

"Give me a leg up," said one of the soldiers. A couple of his companions boosted him up towards the vent. "Sounds like someone said he's Lieutenant Everson," he said.

"Bloody hell, man, well shout back! It could be a rescue party."

"What?"

"Get down. Let me," The other man was dropped unceremoniously while a corporal was boosted up. He grasped the lip of the vent and called down.

"Are you all right?" the voice called from below.

"Yes, sir!"

"We're on our way. Get ready to make a break for it!"

Napoo went to the door and tensed, waiting expectantly. Several men joined him.

"Captain," said Sister Fenton sharply, addressing Grantham. "Captain, it appears your men are here to rescue us."

"Hmm, what?" said Grantham.

"Captain," said Sister Fenton sharply. "You do not want to let your men down. They are looking to you to lead them. Whether you feel you can or not, it is your duty."

Grantham looked up at her as if something she said had reached him.

Some of the men, too, had got their dander up. Having heard the voice of rescue, they were up for taking a pop at the blasted Chatts. It was amazing how they rallied, Edith thought. They endured so much misery and suffering but their spirit, though dampened, was never truly extinguished and it took the merest spark to renew it. So it was she found herself swept up in their cheery confidence and for a brief, exhilarating moment she couldn't help but believe that everything was going to be all right.

TURNING DOWN ANOTHER passage Rhengar and the scentirrii brought Jeffries to the gaol chamber. The two scentirrii on guard outside exchanged a few clicking sounds with Rhengar. One then hissed briefly at the barbed door, which opened just enough to allow Jeffries to be shoved through with a prod from his escort's electric lance. He staggered, almost losing his footing, and narrowly avoided stumbling against Napoo who had been by the door. He shot the Urman a glance, warning him off. It was hardly the triumphant entrance he'd intended. He noticed the men were up on their feet as he entered.

"Glad to have you back, sir," said one private.

"Don't worry you fellows. Help is on the way, apparently," said Jeffries. He looked down at the padre with disdain. The Chaplain glanced up but quickly averted his gaze. Next, he spotted Captain Grantham. Hell's teeth, but he wouldn't be sorry to see the back of this sorry-looking shower.

"We heard them," said a lance corporal with a bandaged head. "It's Lieutenant Everson, sir. He'll see us right."

Everson. Bloody boy scout. Still, a plan was forming. He could use the escape as a diversion to return to Chandar's artefact chamber and collect the map.

THAT VOICE. Now Edith remembered. The recollection washed over her like a wave. The blood drained from her face and the room began to spin. She clutched at Abbott's shoulder.

"What's up, Edi? What is it? Are you all right?"

"That voice," she said weakly. "I know where I've heard it before. It's him!"

"Who, Lieutenant Jeffries?"

"No, not Jeffries. That's not his name at all."

"Edi, come on love. Of course it is. It's the effects of the insect drug. You're imagining things. We've been though a right old time. I'm sure you're mistaken."

"No," said Edith curtly. "It's him."

"Who?"

She found herself shaking, not with fear, but with anger. It was a fuse lit by the invitation to a private party, fuelled by the murder of her friends and her survivor's guilt, burning through the years of torment and horror on the Front. Unable to contain it any longer she felt it detonate deep within her. Edith broke away from Nellie's grip and strode belligerently towards Jeffries, with no thought for consequences. No thought but for this one remaining moment of reckoning.

"You!"

Jeffries turned towards her, nonplussed. "Me, Nurse?"

"I know who you are!" her voice quavered, barely able to keep the fury under control.

Jeffries smiled wanly at the men near him, who looked confused.

"Yes, dear and so do all these men here. Sister Fenton, if you wouldn't mind, I think one of your charges is becoming a trifle hysterical. It must be the shock, poor thing, hmm?"

Sister Fenton steamed in to cut across Edith's bows. "Nurse Bell, that will be enough!"

Edith balled her hands into fists, her knuckles whitening.

"Enough!" bawled the sister, grabbing her wrists. "Do you hear? Desist from this foolishness."

But it wasn't enough for her. Not by a long chalk. Edith windmilled her arms trying to break Sister Fenton's grip, but she held her fast. Edith fell into Fenton and glared over her shoulder at Jeffries, whose mouth slid into an insincere smile as he stared not at her, but through her as if she wasn't there. As if she was inconsequential. Well she may well be, but her words weren't.

"I know who you are!" she cried. "His name isn't Jeffries."

"Bell, be quiet!" said Fenton. "Abbott. Help me!"

However, nothing could still her now.

"His name's not Jeffries at all," she cried. "It's Dwyer. Dwyer the Debutante Killer, Fredrick Dwyer, the Diabolist who calls himself The Great Snake. And snake he is," she spat. *"Murderer!"*

CHAPTER EIGHTEEN
"The Verminous Brood"

RESTRAINED BY HER companions, Edith began to yell hysterically. The men glanced at each other, uncertain of how to react. However, Edith was oblivious to it all. She was focused on one man, the man who was the ruin of her life, the man whose very existence and proximity filled her with such a righteous indignation that, against all social decorum, she could no longer contain it. That he, of all people, should be here, hale and hearty, having perversely survived all the indignities that the war could heap upon him, when her dear friends had been cruelly dispatched for his heretical sport.

"You filthy murderer," she cried, spitting a gob of saliva in his direction. It fell short but the gesture shocked those watching.

Jeffries smiled and casually picked lint off his lapel.

"Bell. Stop this," said Sister Fenton. "You're making a spectacle of yourself."

Edith struggled to face the men gathered round, confused and unsure. "Please, you must believe me. That man there is Fredrick Dwyer. He's wanted for murder."

She heard the muttering of dissent ripple through the soldiers. She knew from the tales she'd heard that he was considered a snob and a martinet. Many men hated his guts, and more than one had a bone to pick with him.

Several men hesitantly pushed their way forward and, exchanging looks, seized Jeffries by the arms.

"Is this true, sir?" asked a lance corporal.

"No, of course it isn't, you bloody cretin, she's a hysterical woman," snapped Jeffries. "You're making a big mistake, hmm? Technically, you could both be up on a charge for assaulting an officer. You don't want to add disobeying a direct order to the charge sheet, do you? Apart from which you're messing up my uniform. Unhand me. *Now*."

Napoo looked from Edith to Jeffries as if trying to weigh their claims.

Captain Grantham glanced at Edith Bell, shaking his head.

Edith tore herself away from Sister Fenton and collapsed into Nellie Abbott's arms, sobbing into her shoulder at the unfairness of it all.

"Let him go," Grantham said to the soldiers restraining Jeffries. The men shuffled uneasily. "I shan't ask again."

The two soldiers glanced at each other uncertainly and then, almost apologetically, at Edith herself.

"No!" she cried as they reluctantly let go and stepped away, shamefaced. "No." Barely more than a whisper now, defeated.

Jeffries smoothed out the sleeves of his tunic, gave his cuffs a cursory tug and nodded his head in acknowledgment to Grantham, who turned to Edith.

"Young lady, this is very serious accusation. The inquest jury found Fredrick Dwyer guilty of the 'wilful murder' of those two girls in his absence. The vermin is still on the run, an absolute coward. Are you seriously suggesting that Lieutenant Jeffries here—who I have personally seen exhibit such bravery as defies description; a man who has been mentioned in dispatches—is nothing more than a common murderer?"

There was a derisive snort from somewhere among the soldiers. Grantham stared hard at them, his glare sweeping like a searchlight, seeking out the dissenting voice but finding none. He bridled and pulled himself up, pushing his chest out.

"Fall in!" The crowd of soldiers jostled and resolved itself into well-drilled ranks.

"I will not have any insolence or insubordination. You are professional soldiers. To that end, you will follow all orders that are given to you. Is that understood?"

"Sir!"

Any help Edith might have expected from the men had now been snatched from her. Napoo was left hovering, still uncertain, his eyes flitting between Edith and Jeffries. The padre was still slumped on the floor, muttering to himself. Sister Fenton had distanced herself from her charge and looked on frostily, as if she no longer knew her. Only Nellie stood by her, but Edith began to think it was more to stop her making even more of a fool of herself than for actually believing her. Edith sniffed, wiped her eyes, shrugged herself from Nellie's embrace and turned round to glare defiantly at Jeffries. He smiled back at her. The arrogance of the man! Well, there was nothing he could do to her here. There were too many witnesses. At least there was that.

Explosions and rifle fire sounded from outside the chamber.

"Sir, they're coming!"

"Oh, Edith, we're going to be saved!" said Nellie, clasping her hands. "Come on, love. Let it go. You were mistaken, that's all."

"No," said Edith, pulling her hands from Nellie's, adjusting her posture and straightening her back, trying to recover at least some dignity as Jeffries walked over to her.

"I remember you," he whispered. "You missed a frightfully good party, as I recall, hmm? I've just decided to invite you to another."

"Go to hell," she muttered from between clenched teeth.

Quicker than Edith was prepared for, Jeffries swung around behind her, locked his forearm round her neck and drew the pistol from under his tunic. "Oh, I am, but you're coming along, too, I'm afraid. Everson, its seems, has forced my hand."

He covered the startled men with his pistol.

"Jeffries! Damn it, man," said Grantham. "What's got into you?"

"It would be so easy to believe I've funked it like you, wouldn't it, old man? You pathetic oaf. You have no idea who I am, what I've accomplished. It's every man for himself. You have served your purpose. I have no further need of you. Of any of you. Except you of course, Bell," he added, the intimacy of his warm breath against her ear making her shiver with revulsion.

"Edi!" cried Nellie. She took a step towards Edith.

Edith blinked away tears, shook her head, and watched, relieved, as Sister Fenton put a firm hand on Nellie's shoulder, holding her back.

Several men advanced slowly towards them. Jeffries stilled them with a wave of the pistol in their direction. Napoo, having made his decision, took advantage of the brief distraction and lunged for Jeffries. Jeffries was too quick and pulled the trigger. Edith squealed and Napoo dropped to the floor with a grunt of pain.

"Ah-ah. The rest of you stay back," said Jeffries. "You wouldn't want your little Rose of No Man's Land to wilt prematurely, would you? Don't try and follow me if you know what's good for you, hmm." As Edith struggled to find purchase with her toes in order to relieve the pressure against her throat, she felt the last dying embers of her anger fade, leaving only the cold ashes of fear.

"Is it true then? Are you? Are you Dwyer?" asked Grantham with a look of hurt betrayal, like a whipped dog.

"Oh, I've been many people," said Jeffries as he continued to edge toward the door. "I was Dwyer once and I have been many others since. And now, it seems I am done with Jeffries too. The Great Snake sheds its skin once more. Adieu."

"Then where is the real Jeffries?"

"Dead in a ditch outside 'Bertie the last time I saw him," said Jeffries. He stepped back towards the barbed door and called out to the guards. "I want to see Rhengar. GarSuleth wills it!"

There was a brief pause and the doorway began to shrivel open. As soon as he got a clear shot, Jeffries fired through the gap, blowing away the head of the scentirrii outside. He then forced his way through the narrow opening and shot the second scentirrii as he dragged Edith through, her dress catching on the barbs and ripping as he yanked her into the passage. "Don't struggle. You're only alive for as long as I need you. You start struggling, you're a liability."

Some part of Edith, some small part of her, the part that had dried up and withered away that night long ago, accepted this and was at peace with it, perhaps even longed for it. It was as if she had been guided to this moment all along, and that now, at last, she would rejoin her friends. It was almost a relief.

"Ediiiiiii!" she heard Nellie scream before the plant door dilated shut.

Now THAT THE Chatt scent had worn off, the week old stink of sour sweat, smelly feet and musty uniforms was telegraphing their position to every insect in the edifice. Everson and his party had to fight every step of the way.

The Chatts proved no match for the Tommies' weapons; a few had got off discharges from their lances, but otherwise they only had rudimentary spears and swords. However, their sheer numbers were another matter and the Chatts were reacting to their intrusion in a more organised manner now.

Hobson and Atkins continued their advance on point, sticking to the outer wall of the spiralling passage, maximising their field of fire as they fought their way up the edifice; a task made all the more awkward by the restrictive vision of their gas hoods. Everson followed with Poilus. Atkins had that dashed Chatter of his, nosing its way forward on its string lead. Everson felt he was taking a chance trusting the rodent, but it was the only lead they had in finding their friends and comrades.

"Keep a look out, Sergeant. We must be almost there," Everson yelled over the staccato chunter of the Lewis gun behind him. He was vaguely aware of a thick *whoosh,* a smell of fuel oil and a light blooming and fading as Evans and Nicholls sent a spurt of cleansing flame down an adjoining passage.

Atkins HEARD A roar from Sergeant Hobson ahead of him as he fired at another mob of advancing Chatts. They seemed to exhibit no sign of fear, despite their brethren being mown down in front of them. Atkins ran forward, emptying his clip into the Chatts as he did so, but they were upon him before he could reload. One lunged with its short sword, cutting Gordon's leash. Atkins parried with his rifle before driving his bayonet through the creature's thorax and twisting the blade. His weapon caught fast on the chitinous armour. Atkins lifted his leg and stomped forwards, driving his foot against the creature's chest, freeing the blade as a second Chatt lunged at him with a spear.

Hobson fired and the Chatt fell back. Atkins brought his hobnailed boot down squarely on the creature's head, smashing its facial plate and grinding his heel into the soft pulpy tissue beneath. He fired again and took out a further two, a single bullet driving straight through both of them.

There was a loud report to his right as Lieutenant Everson finished off another Chatt with his service revolver.

As a fifth lunged with a short spear, Atkins stepped aside and swung his rifle round, catching it in the faceplate with the shoulder butt, sending it reeling against the wall. He fell against it, the length of the rifle barrel against its throat, trying to choke it. He pushed harder on the barrel and felt something crack, but the Chatt continued to struggle. Something stabbed at his abdomen. He felt the claws of the middle limbs pressing into his skin though his tunic and shirt, holding him in a vice-like grip, as the creature's mandibles scythed lethally together again and again in front of his gas-hooded face.

Then the Chatt pushed forward with its powerful limbs, slamming Atkins into the opposite wall. He collapsed heavily to the floor, gasping for breath, lights bursting in front of his eyes. His gas hood had been knocked askew in the impact and he could only see out of one eyepiece. The Chatt's mouthparts filled his small circle of vision. Atkins struggled to keep the scissoring mandibles as far away as possible, saliva dripping thickly onto his mask. He felt his strength fading. In seconds, the weight of the Chatt would bear its mandibles down towards him. He thought of the face of the German soldier he had killed in the shell hole and began to sob with desperation. He didn't want to die, he couldn't die. He had to survive; he had to get back to Flora.

Oh, God, Flora. Poor Flora.

He roared in frustration as the muscles in his arms began to burn with the effort of keeping the thrashing louse at bay, then he heard a crunch and felt the weight lifted from him. He felt a hand find his.

"Up you get, son," said Sergeant Hobson, pulling him into a sitting position. Atkins ripped the suffocating gas hood from his head and sucked in a lungful of air, his face dripping with sweat. The Chatt lay by his side, its head caved in by 'Little Bertha.'

"You were bloody lucky. By rights, that thing should have spat acid at you," said Hobson.

"It tried," he said. "But I think I broke something in its throat."

"If you get in that close again—and I don't recommend you do—go for their antennae, lad. It doesn't always stop them but it does seem to confuse 'em for a while."

"Thanks, Sarn't," Atkins rasped. Coughing, he picked up his rifle and struggled to his feet, shoving his gas hood back into its bag. It was proving more a hindrance than a help. He noticed the string hanging limply on his belt. "Blood and sand! Gordon, where are you? Gordon!"

"I have it," called Poilus, rounding the corner, holding the thing up, its belly cupped in the palm of his hand, its legs hanging limply as its nose twitched eagerly. Poilus handed him over. Relieved, Atkins held it up to his face and cooed at it. Gordon's long tongue flicked out and licked him briefly, before the creature sniffed mournfully at his chattless khaki jacket. Atkins crouched down, intending to tie Gordon's broken string leash, but the little devil struggled out of his grip.

The sergeant, back against the outside wall of the tunnel, edged forward, craning his neck in order to look as far forward as possible. "I can't see anything. They've pulled back."

"Gordon!" hissed Atkins. The sergeant looked back to see the furry rodent dash past him. He attempted to grab it, but missed. It stopped just ahead, and sat up on its hind feet, sniffing. Atkins raced towards it but Hobson stuck out an arm to stop him.

"Shh."

Atkins froze. They felt a soft draught. A faint rumble from up ahead grew louder. Atkins looked at the sergeant who raised his eyebrows, shook his head and shrugged. He obviously had no idea what it was either, but whatever it was, the noise was getting louder.

Gordon squeaked and darted back between Atkins' legs and down the slope toward the others.

"Good enough for me!" Atkins said. "Run!"

They ran back down the passage towards the rest of the party. Atkins told himself not to look back, but he couldn't help himself. He glanced over his shoulder and instantly wished he hadn't.

A large sphere of stone filled the tunnel, rolling down the incline towards them and picking up speed.

There was a sound like cellophane being scrunched up as the boulder crushed the bodies of the dead Chatts behind them.

"Shit! Come on!" grunted Gutsy as he tried to haul his sled of equipment.

"Leave it!" cried Atkins as he pounded past.

But Gutsy wouldn't. He leaned forward in his harness and cried out as he dug one foot in front of the other. The boulder was almost upon them now. Half Pint dashed forwards and gave the sled a shove from the back. The sled shot forward but Half Pint lost his footing. There was a sickening thud and the rumbling stopped.

The boulder had ground to a halt, jamming itself against the tunnel walls by the sled. Half Pint lay in front of it, screaming, his right foot under the giant stone.

Atkins reached him first and hurriedly knelt down to examine his leg. Not that he could have done anything. He had no medical training and the only medical supplies he carried were the regulation Field Bandages.

"Tell me the worst, I can take it." Half Pint said through a grimace of pain as he grabbed Atkins' forearm.

"Well, put it this way," said Atkins, "it'll really give you something to grouse about now."

Everson and Hobson trotted forward and examined the boulder.

"We're not going to be moving this any time soon," Hobson said. "Looks like this is their way to block access to the upper levels.

"The Chatts know they've got us cornered. They'll be here with reinforcements soon. We've got to clear this blockage and we can't do it with Nicholls there," said Everson. He paused briefly. "Get Blood up here."

Everson squatted beside Atkins to talk to Half Pint. "We've got to get through this boulder, Nicholls. We've got to blow it. We can't do that with you here." Nicholls looked up at him uncomprehendingly, eyes clouded with pain.

Out of the corner of his eye, Atkins could see Hobson talking quietly to Gutsy, flicking discreet glances at the trapped soldier. Gutsy sagged visibly then walked leadenly towards them.

Half Pint caught sight of him as he shucked off his pack and pulled out his cleaver, its broad blade reflecting the dull blue light of the luminescent lichen. He gripped Atkins' hand in fear, tears welling up in his eyes. "Oh God, no. Please. No. Only. No, don't let them cut my leg off. Please, Only, I'm begging you. Please!" Sobbing, Half Pint began clawing at the ground, desperately trying to drag himself free of the boulder. "Please Gutsy, don't do this."

"I'm sorry Half Pint, there's no other way," he said, avoiding his eyes.

He knelt by his comrade and tore strips from his trouser leg, making a tourniquet that he began to tighten around Half Pint's thigh.

"No, wait. Wait!" begged Half Pint.

"Sorry, mate," said Gutsy, before punching Half Pint solidly in the head. He went out like a light. "Right. Are we doing this?"

Everson nodded.

"Only, you're going to have to hold his leg steady."

Gutsy placed Atkins' hand on Half Pint's thigh. Atkins closed his eyes and heard a brief, faint whistle as the cleaver cleft the air before striking through flesh and bone and hitting the compacted earth floor beneath.

When Atkins opened them again the lieutenant was trying to apply the field bandages to the bleeding stump below the knee as blood pulsed out, soaking them as fast as he applied them.

"Ketch, Hopkiss," he called, "get up here and take Nicholls back to cover."

They jogged up, looked at Half Pint and then at Gutsy, who was cleaning his cleaver with another field bandage. He glared at them, daring them to say something. Atkins shook his head. Silently, the two men carried the unconscious Half Pint back out of sight, round the gentle curve of the tunnel.

Atkins held out a Mills bomb. "Grenades, sir?"

"Yes, I think so, Atkins," said a visibly shaken Everson, before marching smartly back around the curve himself.

Atkins approached the boulder and chose spots to wedge the grenades while trying to avoid the crushed and bloody leg that protruded from under the great ball.

Gordon had found his nerve again and was snuffling hopefully about the base of the sphere, sucking hungrily for a faint air current. Atkins scooped him up and tucked him under his arm. He licked his dry lips, pinched his lower lip between his teeth nervously and put a finger through the ring of the grenade's safety pin. He braced himself, took a deep breath, pulled the pin out and ran.

"Take cover!"

The detonation filled the corridor with clouds of dust, smoke and debris. The force of the explosion blew Atkins over one of the sleds.

Once the dust had settled Atkins followed the others as they began to make their way over the litter of rubble that was strewn across the floor of the tunnel. Gutsy shouldered his sled harnesses again and moved out, an unconscious Half Pint lying on the soft bed of fungus that covered the weapons supply. Ketch followed with his own sled. Atkins clipped a full magazine into his Enfield, fell in with Hobson on point and pushed on, Gordon nosing on ahead snuffling and sniffing, occasionally giving out little high-pitched sneezes. Then Atkins heard the familiar clatter of Chatt carapaces rubbing against each other.

"Ready, lad?" asked Hobson. "Look sharp, here come more of the verminous brood."

As the Chatts skittered toward them they opened fire, five rounds rapid, and the insects fell beneath their fusillade. Atkins and Hobson moved on, leaving any wounded to Gazette and the lieutenant.

That was when they heard the scream. A human scream.

"Sir!" yelled Hobson, running up the incline to a junction where the floor levelled out. Gordon pattered excitedly past him, his tongue flickering out of his furry proboscis as he scampered off to the left.

Atkins followed and they came to a barbed plant door. Gordon was snuffling excitedly at the bottom of it. The bodies of two Chatts lay twisted and dead against the passage wall.

Everson came up and quickly appraised the situation "Evans,

Hopkiss!" The pair came up with Evan's Flammenwerfer. "Get that door open!"

"Stand back!" cried Evans and, a few seconds later, with Hopkiss operating the valve, a spurt of flaming oil blasted the door. It shrivelled under the jet of liquid fire, spitting and popping, a sound like a human scream coming from it as it burnt. There was a crack and barbs exploded from the door, some embedding themselves in the wall opposite.

"Gordon!" cried Atkins, pushing men aside.

The little rodent lay bleeding and whimpering, impaled by one the barbs. His nose twitched as he sought comfort in the musty smell of fresh lice he would now no longer taste. He looked up at Atkins, pitifully, and was then still. Atkins sighed briefly and stood up.

Once the smoke and flame had dissipated, the chamber beyond stood revealed amid a circle of glowing cinders. The faces of about twenty men looked back at them.

There were brief cheers and backslapping as the parties were reunited.

"Where's Jeffries?" Everson said.

"He escaped, kidnapping the nurse. It turns out his real name isn't Jeffries."

Porgy pushed his way though the huddle, Lewis gun slung from his shoulder. "Edith!" he called "Edith?" He found a tearful Nellie Abbott trying to staunch the bleeding from Napoo, who was lying wounded beside her. "Where is she? What the hell's happened here?"

"He's taken her! He's going to do her in, I know he is. You have to save her!"

Atkins exchanged a glance with Everson. He'd known there was something fishy about Jeffries. Their findings in his dugout had aroused his suspicions, now the latest events had confirmed them.

"Edith said he was that murderer, Dwyer," one of the Tommies said.

"Dwyer the Diabolist?" said Everson.

"The same, sir," replied the lance corporal.

"We've got to save her, sir!" said Porgy.

"Damn!" muttered Everson. "Hobson, start moving these men out. Hopkiss go with him."

"But sir!"

"That's an order. Atkins, with me."

Hobson and Ketch began handing out weapons from the sleds and a chain quickly formed as the men passed them on. Gutsy carefully lifted a semi-conscious Half Pint so they could get to the rest. Poilus helped lift Napoo onto the empty sled.

Everson found Grantham slumped against the wall, muttering to himself.

"Sir!" he said, shaking the officer.

Grantham looked up at him blankly. "Jeffries."

"I know," said Everson. "We need to leave. Now, sir."

Grantham shook his head. "I've served my men badly, Everson. Funked it. If I go back, it's a court martial for me. At least here, I can do something useful. Give me a gun. I can buy you some time, watch your back."

Everson studied the man carefully. He didn't have the time or the inclination to talk him out of it. He was a bad officer, but if he wanted to buy himself some dignity, so be it.

"Sergeant, get the Captain a Lewis gun and magazines. Leave him some grenades and an Enfield, too."

"Thank you," Grantham whispered.

Everson caught sight of the corporal. "Ketch, follow me!"

Ketch fell in behind him and glanced at Atkins, barely managing to suppress a sneer.

"Hobson," called the lieutenant, "we'll meet you in that fungus farming chamber where we got the sleds. Maybe you can rally some of those captive Urmen to rise up, give Jellicoe a chance to exorcise his Labour urges. I think we could use a general strike after all."

Porgy grabbed Atkins' forearm as he left with the lieutenant. "Save her," he said. "And make that bastard pay!"

CHAPTER NINETEEN
"While You've a Lucifer..."

"D'you think it's true then, sir, Jeffries is that bastard Dwyer?" asked Atkins as he jogged to keep up with Everson. He'd promised Porgy he'd save Edith. But what could he do up against someone of the likes of Frederick Dwyer? He was infamous, the Most Evil Man in England according to the *Daily Sketch*. As a hate figure, he was second only to Kaiser Bill. Half the stories that were in the press you didn't know whether to believe or not, they were so far-fetched. And even though they had been thinking that maybe the Chatts had brought them here to this God-forsaken place, what if it had been Jeffries... Dwyer... whatever, all along? Could he do that? The papers had been full of sensational stories of his past, the adventure magazines doubly so. Had he really made a pact with the devil?

"Well he's as good as admitted it, by all accounts," said Everson. "Even if he isn't, he's still in a hell of a lot of trouble. If those papers are anything to go by that's fraudulent enlistment, impersonating an officer, at the very least. Not that any of that matters a jot against a death sentence. Chap was going to swing before we ever came across him."

"I can't believe it," said Ketch. "He seemed like such an upstanding bloke."

"Well, he would to you," said Atkins. "Man after your own heart by the sound of it."

"Watch your mouth, Atkins, I'm still your NCO and don't you forget it."

"How could I?" muttered Atkins. "You never bloody let me."

Behind him, Atkins heard the rattle of the Lewis gun and the confused squealing of Chatts as Captain Grantham covered their escape.

Everson halted at a junction. Ahead, the passage branched. There was an opening to their left, decorated with some kind of hieroglyphs. After the unadorned, functional nature of the rest of the edifice, this struck him as something important, at least to the Chatts.

"Damn! I think Jeffries has given us the slip."

The excited clicking of alien jaws and joints alerted them to another approaching troop of insect soldiers ahead.

"Heads up, chaps," Everson warned as he backed against the wall, pistol arm extended. Ketch stopped beside him, dropped down on one knee and raised his rifle. Atkins fell in behind him, rifle at the ready. The troops of Chatts skittered round the corner, some carrying lances, others carrying short swords and spears.

"Wait for it," said Everson. "Fire!"

Atkins and Ketch fired and cycled, fired and cycled. The Chatts went down in a hail of bullets.

"Well Jeffries obviously didn't go that way," said Everson, and looked again into the dark opening to his left.

The distant sound of Grantham's machine gun had stopped. It was replaced by several rifle shots, followed by several high-pitched squeals. There was a brief silence then a defiant shout. "Come on you bastards. I'll show you what backbone is. For the Pennines!" The tunnel echoed to the sound of a roar of rage and, following closely on its heels, a drawn out wail of anguish, pain and terror, punctuated by the explosions of Mills bombs.

"Sir?" said Corporal Ketch, looking at Everson expectantly.

"We can't help him."

A muffled pistol shot rang out from somewhere beyond the ornate doorway.

"This way!" said Everson, reloading his revolver before advancing cautiously. Behind him, the two soldiers slotted fresh magazine cartridges into their rifles.

JEFFRIES STRODE CONFIDENTLY through the dark high space of the temple, his hand tightly around Edith's wrist, dragging her along like a recalcitrant child. A large scentirrii in a silk scarlet tabard approached him with a spear. Jeffries shot it in the head. In the shadows, he saw dhuyumirrii and acolytes withdraw, melting into the shadows, clicking in agitation. He only had a few rounds left in his pistol but he only had to make it to the chamber where the Khungarrii had deposited their trench equipment. But his main priority was Chandar's little heretical collection.

"Please, stop," said Edith. "Whatever you're thinking of doing, please don't!"

"What?" he said distracted. He stormed into the library chamber of niches where he saw again the scriptural jars filled with their holophrastic scents. "Chandar!" he called, waving his pistol and swinging Edith brusquely round in front of him for a shield, like a clumsy dance partner.

The acolyte Chatts backed away. He shot a jar, taking delight in the Chatts' alarmed reaction as it shattered, leaving a sticky sour smelling unguent to drip thickly from its niche. "Chandar!" he bellowed at a cowering insect. "Chan-dar, you arthropodal cretin! Where. Is. He?"

The old, maimed Chatt appeared. "What is this? We had an agreement."

"We did," said Jefferies. "Change of plan. I'm afraid it's off. However, if you want my men they're yours. Keep them, cull them, it's all the same to me."

"This trait of disloyalty is one we know runs through Urman culture, but you took the Rite of GarSuleth. How can you do this?"

"It's called individuality. You should try it sometime," said Jeffries.

He pushed the pistol into the holster of his Sam Brown and flung Bell to the floor before picking up a jar of sacred unguent. He swirled it around and watched particles of aromatic compound dance in a thick suspension of what he surmised was some sort of oil. He pulled the stopper from it and sniffed cautiously.

"It contains a distillation of ancient proverbs," explained Chandar.

"And this?" Jeffries asked, indicating another jar.

"The commentaries of Thradagar."

"And this?"

"The Osmissals of Skarra."

"And this?"

"The Aromathia Colonia."

All Jeffries could smell was rotting plums, pine sap and a hint of motor oil. It was intensely frustrating. All this knowledge and no way to access it. He pulled out a monogrammed handkerchief from his trouser pocket and poured some of the oil onto it, soaking the cloth before stuffing the handkerchief into the neck of the bottle. From his pocket, he withdrew a battered packet of gaspers, put one in his mouth, took out a packet of Lucifer matches and struck one against the box. It flared brightly.

Chandar staggered back, awed by the sight, and watched nervously, its eyes locked on the jar.

"What are you doing?" The pungent smell of phosphor drifted around the room, which seemed to alarm and frighten the other Chatts, who backed up against the wall, all except Chandar.

Jeffries casually lit his cigarette, took a deep draw, and smiled before holding the lit Lucifer to the corner of the oil-soaked cloth. He hurled the improvised petrol bomb down a gallery where it smashed with a splash of flame, catching other containers which quickly combusted. Jeffries watched in satisfaction before making another makeshift bomb, this time ripping a strip of cloth from Bell's already torn dress to use as a wick.

"What have you done?" cried Chandar, his mouth parts slack with horror.

"I've done you a favour," said Jeffries, pulling his pistol from his belt once more. Thick heady smoke coiled against the roof of the Receptory chamber and began to sink down. He grabbed a coughing Bell and a shocked Chandar, bereft at the sudden brutal loss of its precious scent texts. He urged them at gunpoint down the interconnecting passage that led to the Chatt's alchemical work chambers, closely followed by tendrils of smoke.

The smell of the smoke had already alerted the Chatts in the Olfactory, where they worked their strange mixture of theology and alchemy. They were running hither and thither in great agitation as Jeffries shoved Bell and Chandar into the room. Jeffries casually surveyed the space and chose his target.

"No! You can not," wheezed Chandar.

"Dwyer, you're mad!" said Bell. It earned her a vicious slap across the face and she staggered back, stunned.

Taking the lit cigarette from his mouth and touching it to the oil-soaked wick, he watched the flame lick up the cloth before casting the bomb into a workshop beyond. It smashed in a spray of fire amongst the volatile distilling jars, prompting soft *whooffs* of combustion whose gentle sound belied their ferocity.

Waiting only long enough to watch the fire catch, Jeffries took a last drag and flicked the glowing Woodbine into the strengthening blaze, before pushing his hostages on.

In the chamber beyond, where the Chatts had stored the trench equipment, Jeffries reloaded his pistol and picked up a webbing belt of Mills bombs. Keeping a wary eye on Bell and Chandar he hastily emptied boxes of small arms ammunition into haversacks along with tins of Machonochies, Plum and Apple and bully beef. Using webbing, he tied them together with several rifles and, as gently but hastily as he could, lowered them out of a window opening on a length of rope. He could hear the rifles clatter against the face of the edifice below. Then the rope ran short and he had to drop his load to tumble down onto a midden heap far below. He could only hope it wasn't all damaged beyond use once he retrieved the items.

He noted the trench mortar 'Plum Puddings' and smiled to himself. They should go up nicely. There would be little danger of pursuit after that. And after his sacrilegious arson a state of such enmity should exist between the Khungarrii and the Pennines that there would be no chance of a ceasefire. They would be locked in a cycle of mutual attack and counter attack. Everson and his men would have stepped from one war only to find themselves in another, leaving him free to follow his own path unchallenged. All he needed was that map.

"Take me to your Urman artefacts," he ordered Chandar. Gripping an increasingly dishevelled Bell by the unravelling bun at the nape of her neck he dragged her along impatiently as Chandar led the way, leaving the sounds of explosions and dying Chatts in his wake.

Outside the artefact chamber he beckoned Chandar to open the plant door. Inside, Jeffries swung Bell around and flung her against the wall. She dropped to the floor, dazed by the impact. He jerked his chin and ushered Chandar over against the wall beside her. Bell felt the back of her head and examined her hand, blinking incomprehensibly at the blood she found there.

"You know, until I met you I'd begun to lose all hope," said Jeffries, addressing Chandar, as he glanced around at the priceless archaeological treasures.

He strode straight to the niche containing the map, lifting it from its bark backing where it had been pinned like some entomological specimen. He folded it along well-worn creases and thrust it into his tunic.

Jeffries wheeled about, his eyes sweeping across the niches and exhibits of Chandar's collection. He walked to the wall and swept several items into the open maw of his haversack.

"So you were aware of these things? They do have meaning?" said Chandar.

Jeffries had the feeling the Chatt was learning more about 'Urmen' now than it had done in all its studies and it didn't like what it was seeing.

"Oh yes," said Jeffries. "More than you can ever know. I will be eternally grateful to you. I'm sure you'll be eager to know that you've served your part as an instrument of Croatoan."

"You dare accuse me of heresy! This one serves only GarSuleth."

"Only at the behest of Croatoan," countered Jeffries, grabbing the wrists of the dazed nurse and ushering her out of the chamber. "And as an instrument of Croatoan, I shall spare your life, as it was you who showed me the next step on the road toward communion with Croatoan himself. But that is the only grace you have earned from me."

Once outside the chamber Jeffries pulled the pin from a Mills bomb, before tossing the grenade into the room and ushering Chandar and Edith swiftly away. No one else would have access to the secrets he now possessed. The explosion brought the earthen walls crashing down behind them. Weakened, several chambers above collapsed, leaving a gaping breach in the side of the edifice through which they could just make out the jungle beyond.

A venomous hiss was the only warning Jeffries received before Chandar launched itself at them. Jeffries swung Bell into the creature's path. She screamed as she collided with the Chatt, sending them both careening into the wall. He put the pistol against the bony chitin of Chandar's head.

"Try that again, old thing, and I'll break more than your antennae. I'll blow your bally head off, hmm?"

Chandar hissed again, but this time in impotence, its mouthparts waving in frustration.

DAZED, EDITH CAUGHT sight of the folded parchment peeking out from inside Jeffries' jacket as he bent over the insect. She was sure he would kill her but she wouldn't die quietly like Elspeth and Cissy. She had finally faced her demon—and he was just a man. And what did men want? Power. That parchment had to mean a great deal to him if he'd gone to these lengths to obtain it. So if he wanted it, she wanted it. Maybe it would give her something with which to bargain. Before she even knew what she was doing she slipped her hand into his tunic and snatched the parchment. He lashed out with a howl of fury, grabbing the hem of her torn uniform. She kicked out, ripping it away from him. He stumbled. Edith darted back into the chamber where the trench equipment was held. Perhaps there she could find something with which to defend herself.

"Come back here, you bitch!"

Edith threw herself behind one of the piles of trench equipment, her heart pounding. What was it that was so important about this parchment? Fingers trembling, she unfolded it, desperately hoping its contents might give her more leverage. It was some sort of map but she could make nothing of the symbols and writing. Shaking her head she refolded the map and continued to search for a weapon.

She heard Jeffries enter the chamber. There was a crash as he lashed out at a pile of equipment. "Give me the map, girl. Give me the bloody map."

There was a hiss and chatter. Peering out, Edith watched as Chandar attacked Jeffries again. Jeffries pistol-whipped the old Chatt and send it sprawling against the chamber wall, the last of its strength and anger dissipated. She let out an involuntary gasp. Hearing the sound, Jeffries turned. She ducked back out of sight, but too late. Jeffries strode round the pile, hauled her up by the hair, tore the map from her grasp and shoved it back into his tunic.

"I warned you," he said.

AS EVERSON FOLLOWED the trail of death and destruction through the temple, a screaming, flaming apparition ran towards them. A Chatt ablaze, sheets of fire wrapping themselves about it as it stumbled.

Startled, Atkins let off a shot. The screaming stopped and the shape tumbled to the floor.

Next they came upon the burning library and alchemical chambers. Scrolls were crisping, shrivelling and burning while jars cracked and exploded in adjoining galleries, Chatts flinging themselves on the flames in a vain attempt to extinguish them. They were so intent on saving whatever was stored there that they paid no heed to the three Tommies that hurried through their midst.

Racing down a short tunnel, the soldiers heard a scream and burst into a chamber containing large piles of trench equipment to see Edith struggling with Jeffries.

"Halt!" yelled Everson, his pistol aimed squarely at the man's head. "Give yourself up, Jeffries."

"Everson, what a surprise. I might have known it would be you. Ever the boy scout, hmm. However, I'm your commanding officer. You're only a second lieutenant. I think you'll find *I* give the orders around here."

"We both know that's not true, don't we?" said Everson. "You signed up as a private under a false name. You're no officer."

Atkins and Ketch covered Jeffries nervously as he held Nurse Bell to his chest, one arm around her throat. The injured Chatt lay crumpled against the wall, one arm seemingly broken, its antennae stumps twitching feebly.

"Let Nurse Bell go," Everson said, calmly.

"No."

"Let her go, Jeffries—or should I say, Dwyer?"

"Ah, so it's come to that has it?"

"Look, we can talk about this."

"Can we? I don't think so. Let's ask Nurse Bell, shall we?" Jeffries tightened his arm around her throat and her face began to turn purple as he applied more pressure.

"You've got nowhere to go, Jeffries."

"That's where you're wrong, though I must admit for a while there, when we first arrived here, I was worried."

Atkins, who had begun to edge along the wall, trying to flank Jeffries, found himself in Jeffries' sights as the man pointed the pistol at him.

"I think you'd better stop right there, Atkins, yes?"

"Sir?"

"Don't move, Atkins," said Everson, taking a step forward. "Jeffries, for God's sake man, give yourself up. It's a court martial. I swear you'll be dealt with fairly."

"If you know who I am then you'll know I'm facing the drop. Call that a fair trial? Besides, if you kill me you'll never get home. You're here because of me. Did you know that? I brought you here. Without me, you'll never get back. Never. It's taken the deaths of thousands of men to achieve this. I worked for years to this end; do you think I'm going to let you stop me now?"

Atkins was shaken. A way home? *Flora, oh dear God, please let it be true.* But having to deal with a rogue like Jeffries to get back? Atkins began to lower his rifle.

"Don't believe him, Atkins," snapped Everson. "The man's a congenital liar, a fantasist." He appealed to Jeffries again. "Can't we talk about this like rational men?" he asked.

"Talk about what, Everson? Your ignorance, your fear of responsibility? Do you even realise what it is I've accomplished here? Do you realise that you've been party to the greatest occult undertaking of the age?"

"You can't be serious, Jeffries. Listen to yourself. That's utter humbug!"

"Is it? Look around you, Everson. Can your small provincial mind even conceive the scope of what has happened? No, don't bother. Only a handful of people would truly understand my achievement. Magi for centuries have failed where I have succeeded. Only death on a truly industrial scale could have been sufficient to invoke Croatoan. I saw to it that those pointless deaths on the Front weren't wasted. I harnessed them. Used them to charge a pentagram set into the very landscape itself."

"You're mad!"

"That's what that hedonistic mooncalf, Crowley, said and where is he now? Skulking in America, plying his lies to Colonial toadies and lickspittles."

"It's shell-shock. Jeffries, you're not well."

"You want to go home? You want to see Blighty again?" roared Jeffries. "Well I know the way. Kill me and you're stranded forever."

Everson faltered and his pistol arm slowly lowered.

"He's bluffing, sir," said Atkins. "Isn't he?"

"He's got some sort of map," said Nurse Bell. "He's gone to a lot of trouble to get it."

A grin slid onto Jeffries' face as he arched an eyebrow. "Tick, tock, Everson. The Captain's funked it, and you're Commanding Officer now. It's your call. Your responsibility. Do daddy proud. These men that survived? Nothing more than the dregs that Croatoan rejected. I have no more use for them. I commend them into your care. It may be that their deaths can return you the way they brought me!"

"The devil take you, Jeffries!"

"The name, Everson, is Dwyer!" he spat, and with that Jeffries opened his arm, threw Nurse Bell aside and fired.

Everson grunted as the impact of the bullet into his shoulder drove him back and spun him around.

Ketch fired back. Jeffries ducked behind a pile of trench supplies and returned fire.

Behind Jeffries, Bell hoisted up her ripped skirt and swung her foot between Jeffries' legs. It connected with a satisfying thud and he doubled over.

Tears filling his eyes and distorting his vision, Jeffries fired again. Atkins ducked only to hear tiny clangs as metal struck metal. He looked around for the source and saw hissing green gas escaping from two chlorine cylinders, almost buried under a pile of trench supplies.

"Gas! Gas! Gas!" he shouted.

Jeffries grabbed hold of Bell again. "That," he said, pulling her head back with a sharp jerk, "wasn't nice. Just for that you don't get to die quickly." He released her and punched her in the solar plexus, winding her, before flinging her across the floor towards the punctured gas cylinders.

CHAPTER TWENTY
"The Caterpillar Crawl..."

JEFFRIES FLED THE way he had come, diving out past Chandar under a fusillade of bullets from Atkins. Seconds later, there was an explosion as he set a off a grenade bringing the entrance down and cutting off any pursuit. Clouds of dust and debris billowed into the room, mixing with the rising gas and blocking the doorway. The fires they passed had spread and the entrance they came in by was now ablaze and impassable. Everson and the others were trapped.

To Atkins it smelt just like the trenches again and he almost gagged. Shouldering his rifle, he dashed over to Edith who was on all fours, gasping for breath, a deadly green tide lapping about her hands and feet. Atkins pulled her to her feet before rifling through the pile of equipment. The Chatts must have taken a gas hood or two, but try as he might he couldn't find one. He turned around in a panic to see her giving him a pleading look as the gas, still pouring from the cylinders, began to rise around them. There was nothing else for it. He undid the bag around his neck, took out his own gas hood and pushed the stiffened flannel into her hands.

"Mouthpiece between your teeth. Tuck it into your collar and remember, in through the nose, out through the mouth," Atkins explained as he guided her to the wall where Lieutenant Everson lay slumped. His eyes scanned the room. The only way out was a vent hole in the wall.

The stench of chlorine began to sting his nostrils and he coughed thickly as he levered the lieutenant to his feet.

"It's all right, Atkins. He just got me in the shoulder," said Everson through a grimace, a dark stain spreading over the arm of his tunic.

"Gas, sir. You need to get your hood on," he said, unbuckling the officer's canvas bag and pulling out the contraption. Everson pulled it over his head with his good arm.

"The air shaft looks to be our only way out," said Atkins. Linking his fingers, he boosted Everson up to the hole. Once he was in, Atkins was about to do the same for Edith, when he noticed the state of her now torn and ripped uniform. Embarrassed at the sight of her stockings he averted his eyes and caught sight of a pair of part-worn khaki trousers that he had scattered from one of the piles. He picked them up and offered them to her. She took them and he turned away as she stepped into them and tore a strip from the remains of her dress to use as a belt. "I'm ready," she enunciated from inside her gas hood, tapping him on the shoulder.

He boosted her up on his hands and she disappeared into the vent.

The gas was thickening rapidly now, swirling in the rising currents of heated air from the blazing chamber next door. Atkins began to cough. Christ. This was no way to die. Something sprang into his mind from his early days in training. He pulled out his handkerchief, unbuttoned his fly and fished about inside. Thank God he was scared enough. After a brief moment when he thought he couldn't, he managed to pee on the cloth, rung it out and, blanching slightly, tied it over his nose and mouth as he went back to look for Ketch in the rapidly thickening lethal mist.

"Ketch!" he cried.

He began wafting an arm about in front of him, disturbing the gas, creating eddies that swirled sullenly apart. He spied Ketch slumped awkwardly on the floor by the chlorine cylinders, a broadening stain on his tunic, one hand clutching weakly at his throat, Atkins knelt beside him. Ketch attempted to smile when he saw him, but produced nothing more than an ugly snarl, as if it were sheer vitriol that was keeping him alive.

"Bastard's done for me," he gasped. "You could let me die here with our secret. Nobody else would know. But you can't, can you? That would mean you were really *were* a bad person. And you're desperate to prove yourself otherwise, aren't you?"

"Let me help you."

Ketch coughed again and grinned through the blood and the green foam that began to froth at the corners of his mouth. "You can't help me now, Atkins."

"I can! We can get out of here." He put his arms under Ketch's armpits and began to lift him but the corporal retched and coughed, his face beginning to blacken from exposure to the gas. "Ketch!"

The corporal clawed at his throat as the chlorine reacted with the moisture inside his lungs. His eyes widened with terror. He began to kick and thrash, reeling around the floor, gasping for a life-saving breath that would never come. It was all Atkins could do to hold him.

"Atkins..." he gurgled, "one... thing..."

"What?"

"...She's... *pregnant*..."

"Who?' he asked, before he realised. *Flora.*

"S'you in hlll..." gurgled Ketch, his back arching as he patted his tunic pocket and his last breath bubbled up out of him, leaving a satisfied sneer etched on his face.

"Ketch! Ketch!"

Coughing and spluttering now, his own eyes watering, Atkins shook the corporal's body. Unbidden he felt Flora's lips on his; insistent, soft, yielding. He could taste the salt of her tears as they lost themselves in a rising urgency that, for a moment, washed away the grief; fingers fumbling at buttons and petticoats by the light of the parlour fire. Even as he recalled the moment, he tore open Ketch's tunic and rummaged through the pockets. Inside Ketch's pay book, he found a letter, addressed to himself in Flora's own hand. It had been opened. The bastard! How long had he had it? He quickly shoved it inside his own tunic. Please God, let him not have told anyone else.

He took Ketch's gas hood from its bag and rolled it down over his head in place of the urine-sodden cloth. As he headed back to the vent, he passed the Chatt wheezing for breath in the rising chlorine. He was going to leave the disgusting thing to its fate, but overcome with grief and remorse he took pity on it, if only to prove to himself that he *was* a good person. He squatted down to lift it up. The creature attempted to scuttle back against the wall, hissing, its mouth palps fluttering briefly with the force of the exhalation. As he put it over his shoulder it protested weakly, like a drowsy wasp in the first chill of autumn.

The blaze from the adjacent room was beginning to spread now. The encroaching flames cast surreal shadows on the rising chlorine fog. Atkins hoisted the Chatt up and fed it into the vent above his head, then took several steps back and ran at the wall, leaping up towards the hole and catching its lip. He pulled himself up into the shaft and found himself looking at the Chatt.

"Why?" it asked.

"Because it's the right thing to do. Because I am a good man. We're not all like Jeffries. And because no one deserves a death like that. We have to move."

The shaft angled down steeply and Atkins could feel a strong, cold draught blowing over him as they slid down for what seemed a long way. The Chatt in front of him suddenly dropped and Atkins found himself sliding out of the vent and falling to land heavily below.

"Steady, Atkins," said Everson, helping him as he climbed to his feet. Atkins pulled off his gas hood to see Edith looking nervously at the Chatt, who cowered against the wall of the passage.

"Shouldn't you shoot it?"

"No, Bell, I don't think so," said Everson, wincing with pain from his shoulder wound.

One of her eyes was starting to puff up and bruises were blooming on her cheeks. Her hair was in complete disarray. She looked like some kind of wild woman. Atkins felt a surge of anger at what Jeffries had done to her, immediately followed by self-recrimination. Was he really any better? Oh Flora, what had he done? His whole world had been turned upside down. Again. If she was pregnant, then it wasn't going to be hard for anyone to work out it couldn't be William's child. She would have to bear the barrage of gossip, the barbed comments, the withering fire of disapproving glances and the machine gun stuttering of tutting. And she would have to bear it alone.

He was aware of Lieutenant Everson shaking his shoulder.

"Atkins, where's Corporal Ketch?"

"Gone west, sir. Gas."

There was a series of explosions high above. Rubble erupted out of the vent followed by faint wisps of chlorine gas and, from somewhere behind them, the noise of gunfire grew louder.

"Damn." Everson crouched down in front of the Chatt. "Which way to the fungus farming chamber?" he said. The Chatt looked up at him. "Do you understand me? Can you speak?"

"Yes, this one can speak Urmanii."

"Do you have a name?"

"Chandar."

"Well, Chandar, we need a way out and you're going to have to show us. On your feet."

The Chatt rose as Everson ushered it to the fore. Atkins took up the rear, making sure that Bell was in front of him as he cycled his rifle bolt. They hadn't gone a dozen yards when Atkins heard shouts and shots behind him.

"Sir," he said turning round at the sound of running feet. Sergeant Hobson, Gazette and Pot Shot came hurtling round the bend.

"Sir?" gasped Hobson. "How the hell did you get here?"

Everson nodded towards the smoking vent. "Snakes and ladders."

The burly sergeant took it in his stride. "Right you are then, sir."

There were several bursts of rapid fire from behind them as the rest of the Black Hand Gang, freed Tommies and nurses crowded along the passage, pulling the sleds with the injured Napoo and Half Pint on them, Poilus among those at the back fighting a rear-guard action.

"They're hard behind us, sir," called Hobson.

"Only!" called Porgy pushing through the throng. "Only! Where's Edith? Did you find them?" Atkins smiled as he turned aside to reveal Edith Bell stood behind him.

"Edi!" squealed Nellie Abbott, pushing past Porgy and flinging herself into Edith's arms, then stood back and looked her up and down, taking in the khaki trousers. "Edi Bell! I never took you for a suffragette."

"Times change," said Edith.

"You did good," said Porgy, clapping Atkins on the back.

Atkins didn't feel as if he had. He could hardly bring himself to look his mate in the eye. "Where is the bastard? Did you get him?" Porgy pressed.

"Jeffries? Got away," said Atkins. "But he won't get far out there, even if he makes it. He'll be something's meal by night-time, I'll bet on it. Ketch bought it, though. Gut shot and gassed."

"Hell's Bells," said Porgy. "Can't say I'm sorry, but I wouldn't wish that on a bloody Hun." Nellie and Edith broke their hug and he caught sight of Edith's face. "What's the bugger done to her?" Porgy cried, starting forward.

Atkins grabbed his shoulders. "Not now, mate. She's fine. She's a tough old girl."

Reunited, the Black Hand Gang pressed on, fighting a rear-guard action against the pursuing Chatts, the tunnel taking them inexorably downward. It soon became clear they'd missed the fungus farm chamber that marked the way to their excavated exit point. They were lost.

"Where the hell are we?" Everson asked Chandar, but the Chatt refused to answer.

"Sir," said Gazette, addressing Everson. "There are more Chatts coming the other way. We're caught between 'em."

"Not again," sighed Everson. "Atkins, I don't want to get caught between a rock and a hard place. This isn't a good place for a last stand. See if you can't blow us an exit."

Atkins placed a couple of grenades against the wall of the passage and pulled the pins. "Grenade!" he hollered, dashing back round the curve. He was beginning to hate these damned tunnels. There were several dull explosions and Atkins felt his ears crackle and pop like a dropped needle on a scratched gramophone record as the concussion wave overtook him.

A cool breeze blew through the resulting hole. Everson braced his hands on the sides and stuck his head through tentatively.

"What's through there?" he asked Chandar. "Can we get out that way?"

Chandar peered into the darkness beyond and said nothing.

"We mean no harm," said Everson. "We just want to leave with our people." Still Chandar remained obstinately silent. Everson shook his head in despair, and then addressed his men. "Right, 1 Section, secure the other side. Make it snappy. This whole thing's turning into a shambles."

The weary warriors made their way cautiously through the hole in the passage. As their eyes adjusted to the darkness beyond, they heard the scuttling and frantic clicks of hundreds of Chatt voices. Atkins' flesh crawled with revulsion at the sound. The only light came from the familiar luminescent lichens, their faint glow barely illuminating the chamber's details. Long sinuous dry channels covered the floor, converging on an entrance in the far wall. Atkins noticed the frantic activity in them about halfway across the chamber.

"This'll brighten the place up," said Mercy, brandishing his Flammenwerfer. Gutsy opened the valve for him. A fiery orange geyser of flame erupted from the nozzle, casting an infernal glow across the chamber, illuminating pale Chatt and Urmen workers dragging clusters of pearlescent white globes away from the intruders, down the channels toward tunnels in the far walls.

"Poilus, any idea what this place is?" asked Everson.

"It's their nursery," replied the Urman with mounting horror. "We are under the edifice now, underground. We shouldn't have come here."

Around them, the walls of the chamber were full of recesses. They reminded Atkins of a church crypt, only the bodies that lay in these weren't dead. Chatts and Urmen moved back and forth among them, dragging out helpless pupae. At the soldiers' end, however, the cavities had seemed empty until Pot Shot gave a startled yelp. Idly poking about in one with his bayonet, he had come across the desiccated remains of some sort of partially formed nymph Chatt.

"Scared seven shades of shit out of me, that did," said Pot Shot.

"It's dead. Mummified," said Gazette. "Been here a while, has that."

"Ugly bugger, ain't it?" said Porgy.

"You'd know," retorted Mercy.

Its head was enlarged and bulbous, three of its limbs withered and deformed, its metamorphosis gone horribly wrong. And the more they looked, the more deformed, dead Chatts they found.

They advanced slowly across the chamber. A round of rapid fire scattered the Chatts seeking to reach a dry channel filled with large fat, white wriggling larvae. Standing over the limbless grubs, Gutsy thrust his bayonet into one with a vicious satisfaction. Thick viscous fluid oozed out.

By now, the rest of the men had scrambled through into the chamber behind them.

"Light!" called Everson.

A Very flare arced up and hit the chamber roof. It fell into a channel filled with grubs, spitting out its harsh white light. The larvae began twisting and writhing in the intense heat, throwing macabre shadows on the walls as more Chatt workers, undeterred, crept forward again in an attempt to save them.

Gutsy let loose another burst of rapid fire.

"Stop!" Chandar cried.

"It's grubs, sir," said Gutsy with disgust.

"It's their young!" said Atkins in protest. "What are we now, Bosche baby-killers?"

Chandar, hissed, clicking his mandibles together in agitation. "This is the Queen's egg chamber. You have threatened Khungarrii young, there is no way out for you now. Rhengar and the scentirrii will crush you. A pity. You are like no Urmen this One has known. Jeffries promised you to us. This One would have liked to have learned more. This One senses there is much he will never know about you, but GarSuleth wills it."

"Let us go and we will leave them unharmed," said Everson.

"I have not that power."

"They're coming through!" said a private keeping watch by the bomb-blasted aperture through which they had entered the chamber.

With no choice, they moved further into the nursery. Everson and 1 Section led the way along the runways between the dry channels. "Which way out?" Everson asked Chandar.

The Chatt gave a kind of shrug, as if any answer was useless now.

Atkins noticed a glint in the shadow beyond one of the apertures, the dull sheen of lichen light on carapaces. From an opening across the chamber came the martial sound of marching.

"Stand To!" said Everson. "We'll make a stand against this wall, use the channel in front as a fire trench. Sergeant Dawson, set up the Lewis gun on our flank. Hold until they spread out and we can take down the maximum number."

The group of thirty-odd soldiers, barely even a platoon, fell into a practised routine, seeking what cover they could in the shallow channels and setting their rifles on the banks.

"Otterthwaite, see if you can't persuade them to stay back in the tunnels a little longer," ordered Everson.

"Right you are, sir." The sharpshooter looked down the barrel of his rifle towards the tunnels. He picked his target and squeezed the trigger. A squeal followed the rifle's echoing report. Otterthwaite fired repeatedly, but the march of feet and the dull clatter of armoured insectile shells grew into a din as the first of the Chatt soldiers emerged from the gloom of the tunnels.

The nurses, Padre Rand, still under the influence of his otherworldly ennui, Half Pint, Napoo and others too wounded to help were set to the rear against the chamber wall. Nurse Bell took up a rifle from one of wounded men. "They're not going to take me," she said through gritted teeth when she met Nellie Abbott's questioning look. The driver acquiesced mutely. A private with an arm in a sling offered her his bayonet. Nellie took it.

Sister Fenton stepped forward and Bell thought she was about to scold them but she, too, nodded sternly at another wounded soldier.

"Give that to me," she said, indicating his bayonet. He handed it up without protest and she gripped its handle self-consciously. The other two nurses looked at her nonplussed. "Belgium," was all she said. All of England had heard of the Bosche atrocities there in the early years of the war.

In the fire channel Atkins nervously awaited the order to shoot. Seeing the massed ranks of insects before them was unnerving, but seeing them along the rifle barrel, it became business, and a business he knew how to do. He picked his targets and waited for the order.

To his left and right Gutsy, Porgy, Gazette, Pot Shot and Mercy were doing the same. He met their eyes one by one, an unspoken conversation of wordless encouragement and silent goodbyes. If this was it, they would give as good as they got and take as many of the damn things with them as possible when they went. The anger he'd felt at himself, Atkins now turned outwards towards the Chatts.

THE FIRST WAVE of Chatt soldiers swarmed onto the floor of the nursery chamber.

Brandishing his revolver, Everson stepped forward, bringing Chandar with him. "We just want to leave," he called out across the chamber.

A Chatt stepped forward from the ranks.

"Rhengar," said Chandar. "Njurru scentirrii of the Khungarrii Shura."

"Let us go," called Everson. "Allow us safe passage out of here with our people or we will destroy your young, your nursery!" He deplored the tactic, but he felt he had no choice if he wanted to save his men. They were cornered.

Rhengar hissed. In turn, the Chatt soldiers began to hiss, some beating the flats of their short swords against their chests.

"Well, that's not good," muttered Everson, and then nodded to his platoon sergeant.

"This is it, lads," called Hobson. "Pick your targets. Fire!"

THE LEWIS GUN opened fire, raking across the lines of Chatts who fell, toppling into the partly vacated channels only to be trodden on by ranks of their fellows as their advance continued.

Covered by insects wielding electric lances, spitting Chatts charged forward spraying jets of acid from their mouths, leaving several men screaming and clutching their faces.

Any moment now, they would be upon them. Atkins readied himself for fighting at close quarters.

"We're going to need something bigger than bullets," yelled Gutsy to Gazette, hefting a grenade from his pack, from the bottom of which projected a stick. "Rifle grenade."

"Not from my rifle you don't," said Gazette. "Bugger up your own bore."

"Well there's nothing to lose now, is there?" said Gutsy inserting the shaft of the stick into the barrel of his rifle. He put the stock of the rifle butt against the ground and aimed the barrel towards an opening on the far side of the chamber, through which Chatts were swarming. He pulled the safety pin from the grenade and then pulled the trigger. The bomb arced across the chamber and exploded within the ranks of Chatts, shredding body limbs in a hail of shrapnel. Showers of dust and debris rained down from the chamber ceiling.

"Bloody hell, Gutsy, you'll bring the whole place down on top of us," said Pot Shot.

The tremors grew stronger and a deep rumble filled the chamber.

"That wasn't me," he protested.

The Chatts wavered uncertainly, their leader—Rhengar—holding them in line as the rumbling continued. To the Tommies' left, the wall began to crack and crumble before exploding out into the chamber with a tremendous roar as the great bulk of an armoured beast crashed through it.

It was the Ironclad, *Ivanhoe*, covered in the dust and dirt of shattered earthen walls as it rolled implacably forward. It came to a halt, its engines growling and filling the chamber with acrid exhaust fumes, its great six-pounder guns trained on the ranks of Chatt soldiers. Light from the breached wall behind it filtered through the settling dust, bathing the tank in an ethereal glow.

A cheer went up the from the Tommies, while the Khungarrii hissed and backed away from the terrible vision before them, sinking down on their long-limbed legs, cowering as if in obeisance to the enormous beast.

"Skarra," hissed Chandar, also sinking down.

"Skarra?" said Everson.

"God of the Underearth. Dung Beetle Brother to GarSuleth himself, who takes the dead and guides them through their last metamorphosis so that they can rise and dwell in the Sky Web of GarSuleth forever."

Another rumble filled the air. Everson looked up at the roof and, in that moment, Chandar saw its chance and scuttled back along the wall behind the line of Tommies to the hole through which they'd entered, now covered by another cohort of Chatts.

"Sir!" said Hobson, swinging his rifle round to follow the limping arthropod.

"No, let him go, Hobson," said Everson. "Best save your bullets. We might need 'em."

Safe, Chandar turned, and its eyes met Atkins', who stared back wonderingly before the scentirrii parted and the old Chatt was lost in the swarm.

"Follow the bloomin' light," yelled a face peering out from a loophole in the side of the ironclad. A hand pointed needlessly to the gaping hole behind the landship.

Everson ordered the men towards the breach, the nurses and injured going first while a burst of fire from the landship's forward machine gun kept the Chatts at bay. Everson and 1 Section kept the retreat covered, before abandoning their position and falling back to the tank. The confused Chatts, hampered by their superstition, held back.

Everson banged on the small door in the rear of the left gun sponson. It opened a crack. "You're not coming in. There ain't room!" the leather and chainmail masked crew member retorted.

"How the hell did you find us?" Everson bellowed above the growl of the engine.

"We didn't," yelled the cockney gunner. "When the explosions went off in the tower, Lieutenant Mathers ordered us forward, we hadn't got twenty yards across the clearing when the bleedin' ground collapsed beneath us. How were we to know it were riddled with tunnels and the *Ivanhoe* here a bleedin' twenty eight ton behemoth? Wah-la, as the Frogs say. We found ourselves down here."

"Well thank God you did," shouted Everson. "They think the tank is the god of their underworld, but I don't know how much time that will buy us."

"Well that's handy to know. You follow the others back to the surface. We'll keep the buggers busy." The door clanged shut again.

Everson waved 1 Section back as the tank's forward machine gun spat another hail of bullets across the chamber, keeping the Chatts at bay. They scrambled back along the tank's rubble-strewn path of destruction and into the bottom of a wide sinkhole. Ahead men were scrambling up the sides, hauling the injured up with them. Atkins and the others scrambled up the slope after them as the tank reversed back out of the nursery chamber towards them.

One of the gearsmen was looking out of a loophole at the rear of the tank, attempting to guide it. The landship lurched as it begin to climb up the side of the sinkhole; the engine labouring to propel its twenty-eight ton bulk up the steep sides, the tracks squealing in protest as they struggled to maintain purchase. At one point it looked as if wasn't going to make it but then it reared over the lip and, with a heavy crash, it slammed down onto level ground.

They emerged from the ground not thirty yards from the great earthen edifice that now towered above them, black smoke roiling up from a break in the wall high above. Further down the edifice, a familiar sickly green gas vented lazily from holes and sank down along the walls. Atkins was astounded at how much damage they had caused. And they hadn't stopped yet.

As Chatt soldiers poured out of the edifice, the air filled with the chatter of machine guns as interlocking fields of fire from the flanks mowed them down. The *Ivanhoe* fired shells at the entrances to the edifice, bringing rubble crashing down to block them, slowing any further pursuit. The hollow *plomps* of trench mortars sent shells arcing over the clearing to drop down among the remaining Chatts now trapped outside the edifice, while rifle fire and the odd grenade mopped up the rest. Plumes of smoke drifted slowly across the increasingly pock-marked clearing. It was all beginning to take on a familiar feel to the men of the Pennines. As Atkins took in the commotion, he caught a movement on the side of one of the midden piles buttressing the edifice. It was a soldier. Had they left someone behind? Atkins squinted and recognised him at once. Jeffries. The man stopped on the crest of the heap and turned to watch the carnage briefly.

"Atkins! Do you want to get yourself killed?"

Atkins looked towards the cry. Hobson was ushering the last stragglers into the undergrowth where Hepton was cranking the handle on his kine camera, filming the battle of a lifetime. Atkins dashed for the cover of the encircling woodland and the rest of the support sections. When he looked back in Jeffries' direction, he had gone.

INTERLUDE FIVE

Letter from Flora Mullins to
Private Thomas Atkins

22nd October 1916

My Dearest Tom,

I write, praying this finds you safe for I do not know what else to do. You are the only friend I have left in this world who will understand. I could not bear to lose you as well.

Although we vowed that we would never speak of the passion that overcame our prudence that night, I fear we must. I have got myself into such a mess. Oh Tom, I am with child and the child is yours. Of that, there can be no doubt.

At first I denied the possibility even to myself, but my condition has begun to show and can be hidden no longer. I cannot continue to work at the Munitions Factory for the shame of it. There was a frightful row and my father is in a terrible rage for they know the child cannot be William's. He demands to know who the father is, but I have not told them. William was always a hero in their eyes but since he has been missing, he has become a saint and they will have nothing gainsay it. They told me that to do such a deed behind my fiancé's back I must be a wicked girl and he was all for throwing me out on the street there and then, but my mother, God bless her soul, calmed him down. They are to send me to board with my Aunt Peggy in Ulverston. Tom, I am afraid they mean to take the baby from me once it is born and give it up to an orphanage. I do not know what is to become of me. Alive or dead, I fear William will never forgive us and that is anguish enough, but to lose my child, Tom, that would be more than I could bear.

Oh, Tom, I know you are a good man. You have to come home to me and make this right. I do not know what I would do if I lost you, too. I need you, Tom—we need you. I pray ardently for your safe return. Write by return of post if you are able. Each day I do not hear from you weighs heavily on me.

Your loving
Flora

CHAPTER TWENTY-ONE
"Glorious, Victorious..."

ATKINS READ FLORA'S letter several times on the long journey back to the entrenchments. The tear-stained paper in his hands left him reeling with a vertiginous sense of guilt. He was so self-absorbed he barely noticed as Gazette fell in beside him.

"Want to talk about it, mate?"

"No. Not really."

"Fair enough. Fag?" he said, offering a crushed Woodbine. Atkins shook his head.

"So, Dwyer the devil worshipper, eh?" said Gazette. "Bloody hell, that was a turn up for the books and no mistake. The most notorious man in England. Think of the reward money we'd get if we could turn him in, eh? Pity he scarpered. If there's any justice in this world he'll be a bag o' bones by now."

"I said I don't want to talk about it."

Porgy trotted up and was about to speak when Gazette shook his head, so Porgy just matched his stride with theirs and they walked along in uneasy silence.

"Wait, something's wrong," said Pot Shot behind them, holding up a hand. "Half Pint's stopped grousing."

Eyes turned to look at the curmudgeonly private being carried along on a makeshift stretcher. Behind him, Napoo was being carried on another, Poilus now constantly at his clansman's side. Around them walking wounded limped along in ones and twos or helping those blinded by Chatt acid, all of them constantly herded along by the nurses, like sheep.

"Half Pint, what's the matter?" called Gutsy, over the ever-present rumble of the tank up ahead.

"Shhh!" warned Sister Fenton. "Poilus has given him crushed berries of some sort. It seems to have numbed his pain."

"And his ability to complain, too, by the sound of it," said Pot Shot.

"No it hasn't," said Half Pint drowsily, "I just don't know where to bloody start."

"Off on the wrong foot, knowing you, probably!"

"No thanks to you, you bugger," said Half Pint, sticking up a pair of fingers in Gutsy's direction. Gutsy puffed out his cheeks with relief.

EVERSON DROVE THE men on. They had made longer marches than this in France and in worse conditions and he knew they wouldn't be safe until they reached their entrenchment. But would it still be there? That was the question that went through the mind of every man in the column, the thought that made every one of them sick at heart.

WEARY, FOOTSORE AND hungry the bedraggled column marched on, although the two day trek back was not without incident. Along the way, a small group of Chatt soldiers harried them, although they mostly kept their distance, still awed by the sight of the ironclad.

When they reached the open veldt the trail they had followed days ago was still there, cutting across the vast expanse of tube grass, but to what would it lead them?

The answer to their prayers came on the wind in the form of a faint insect drone. A dot in the sky resolved itself into the flimsy shape of Tulliver's Sopwith as it circled them. Seeing the biplane raised their spirits and sent their hearts soaring. A rousing cheer went up as it passed low overhead. They waved their rifles and hats jubilantly above their heads and were delighted to receive a waggle of the wings in return. Knowing that that the muddy field they called home had not disappeared in their absence, their mood became more ebullient. The aeroplane wheeled above them once more, then flew on ahead, leading them home.

JEFFRIES STAGGERED UP the hill, away from the crashing sounds in the forest below. Whatever it was, it had been following him for some time now.

Escaping from the edifice in the confusion, he'd managed to pick up his dropped weapons and equipment, although the barrel of one Enfield was broken beyond use and he'd had to discard it.

Panting, he reached the crown of the hill and dropped his equipment. Paled into grey by the distance he could make out the Khungarrii edifice behind him, still smoking. He took the map out of his pocket, unfolded it and smoothed it out on a rock. His eyes flicked from the parchment to the landscape and back again as he orientated himself, matching landmarks to symbols. He turned the map. Satisfied, he studied it more closely. He tapped a Croatoan sigil thoughtfully and looked out over the forest towards a line of hills some twenty miles away before folding the parchment away again. He checked his rifle, picked up his load and set off down the far side of the hill.

He was on the final road to meet his god and when he did, The Great Snake would rise again.

EVERSON HARDLY RECOGNISED the trench system when they saw it. In four days, Company Quartermaster Sergeant Slacke had begun to turn the field of Somme mud into something resembling a defensible stronghold, a corner of a foreign field that was to them, for now, all that was England. A fire trench now ran all the way around the perimeter with saps and OPs projecting out into the scorched earth cordon.

Everson went to the hospital tents, where Napoo and Half Pint were made comfortable. They were gravely ill, but stable. All they could hope for was that infection didn't set in. Padre Rand, who had been melancholic all the way back from the edifice, insisted on discharging himself from the MO's care. Everson was keen to hear about his experience.

"I don't know what to say, Lieutenant," he told Everson. "What I experienced there severely tested my faith to the point where I rejected my God, but then," he said with a self-effacing smile, "even St. Peter failed that particular test as I recall. Jeffries had me fooled. He had everyone fooled. I'm sure he had some machinations of his own. What they were I don't know, but I do know he was willing to sell us all into slavery to get what he wanted. And these Khungarrii, although they look hideous to our eyes and their culture is like none I have encountered before, would we have reacted any differently in their shoes? Even so, I have a horrible feeling that we may have started a war where none was looked for."

Everson rubbed his eyes with the heels of his palms, briefly wishing the entire world away, before dragging his hands down his face to confront it again with a sigh of resignation. "Could we have avoided it? Did we do the right thing?"

"'When I was a child I spake as a child, I understood as a child, I thought as a child,'" quoted the padre. "We're warriors, Lieutenant. We understand as warriors, we think as warriors. Was it the right thing to do? Only God can judge, although in mitigation, I must say, we *are* British."

"Well, you're back on form, then," said Everson.

The padre patted his Bible "I shall pray for us."

* * *

THAT EVENING THE elation of the men, while temporary, was a pleasant and much needed diversion. The nurses danced gamely with as many men as they could until, exhausted by the constant demand for their attention, they retired for the night.

The noises of revelry and the slurred sound of a battered, hand-cranked gramophone warbling at varying speeds drifted down the steps into Everson's dugout. *"Take me back to dear old Blighty; Put me on a train for London Town. Take me over there, drop me anywhere; Liverpool, Leeds or Birmingham, well I don't care..."*

Everson sat looking dolefully at the light of the hurricane lamp through a glass of whisky. He was now the highest-ranking officer left in the 13th. Like it or not, these men were now his responsibility and it was a heavy load to bear. It was everything he never wanted.

On the table before him, the Battalion's salvaged war diary lay open on blank pages. He didn't know how the hell he was going to write this one up. Beside it, under a now empty bottle of whisky from his father's own cellar, lay several maps and orders from Jeffries' chest. On the edge of the table sat the man's journal with its incomprehensible ciphers and sigils. Everson had spent the last hour or so examining them, looking for any clues that there might be a hint of truth in what Jeffries had said, looking for a shred of hope.

"I don't know what to think. Is he pulling the wool over our eyes? Are we chasing him up a blind alley, Hobson?"

"Not my place to say sir," said Hobson.

"This is the last of it," he said, swilling the malt around the dirty glass. "I was fully expecting to get another case when we went back into the reserves. Doesn't look like that's going to happen any time soon."

"S'not true sir. It could happen tomorrow."

"And if it doesn't, Sergeant, what then?"

"With the help of Napoo and his people we can always find more food."

"And ammunition? The only reason we survived that attack on the Khungarrii edifice was firepower. They hadn't seen anything like it. And that's another thing. I didn't see anything there that would remotely suggest they had the ability to bring us here in the first place. No great scientific or technological advances. They were little more than savages. Mind you, once our ammunition runs out, we'll be reduced to fighting on their level. And they have the superiority of numbers. They know where we are. They've come for us once. They'll do it again. That's a certainty. If nothing else, we've proved we're a threat to them now and I'm not sure that's a good thing. Slacke has done sterling work the past few days. We've got the beginning of a stronghold we can defend until we can go home, but how long will that take?"

"Can we get home, sir?"

"Jeffries—Dwyer said he had a way, a map, information."

"He could have been lying. Slippery bastard like that, you can't trust a word that comes out of that man's mouth."

"He could have been lying to save his own skin, yes, but what if he wasn't? I have to believe he's telling the truth. Who knows what information he garnered from the Khungarrii? He was willing to sell us all into bondage over it, so it must have been important. No, we have to find him, Hobson."

ATKINS FOUND HIMSELF summoned to Everson's dugout. His stomach turned. You never knew what to expect when sent for by an officer.

"Atkins!" said Everson as the private entered and snapped to attention in front of the desk. "At ease, Atkins. At ease."

Atkins relaxed his stance. "Thank you, sir."

"Your section's lost two NCOs in almost as many weeks. Sergeant Jessop was a good man. He had family, I believe."

"Yes, sir. A wife and three children. Last were born a month ago. He hadn't even seen him."

"I'd write to his wife, but—" Everson gave a dismissive wave towards the curtained doorway at the world outside and shrugged. "Even if I could I wouldn't know what to say."

"No, sir."

"Which brings me to you and your recent behaviour, Atkins. Ketch didn't have a good word to say about you, apparently."

"Sir?" said Atkins. He was not sure where this was heading, but an awful suspicion formed in his mind.

"It's all right, Atkins. Relax. I knew Ketch of old. A cantankerous old sod and one hell of a toady. Was when he was working at my father's brewery, was in France by all accounts."

"Sir."

"On the other hand, I've been impressed by your courage and actions. You've certainly proved your worth on all our recent Black Hand Gang stuff. I've spoken to Hobson, here. He tells me you're popular and a good man to have in a tight spot. Your section needs a new NCO. I can't promote you, but I need NCOs, so I'm giving you a field appointment to Lance Corporal."

"Sir, I can't. You don't want me." Atkins forgot himself and started forwards. A warning cough from Sergeant Hobson made him catch himself and stand fast.

"Nonsense, Atkins. You've earned it. If there's one thing I need, it's people I can trust. You've proved yourself worthy." Everson stood up, stepped round his makeshift desk and grasped Atkins' hand in a firm handshake he barely had the enthusiasm to return. If only Everson knew. If only his dugout mates knew his true colours.

"Is that all, sir?"

"Not yet, Lance Corporal. You and I are the only ones who have any idea what Jeffries—Dwyer—was talking about back at the edifice. I've just been looking through the papers you found in his dugout. From the bits I can make out it's quite a sordid tale."

"Sir, did he bring us here with some diabolic pact?"

"I'm sure he thinks so, but look—" Everson lifted the empty whisky bottle out of the way and turned the uppermost map around. It was an artillery map, showing British gun positions and barrage targets across the Harcourt Sector. Marked in red were five locations, two beyond the German lines, two behind the British, one in No Man's Land, all joined by pencil lines to form a perfect pentacle.

"He must have been planning this for weeks, typing up his own orders on blank order sheets, impersonating artillery officers—Tulliver thought he recognised him."

"Is that what he was saying about a geographic whatsit?" said Atkins, looking at the five-pointed star.

"I'd say so, yes. Don't believe in the mumbo jumbo lark myself. It looks like a magic circle or something, but see here..." Everson took a pencil and a piece of string. Holding one end of the string on a mark in the centre of the pentacle, he drew a circle. Atkins watched with mounting apprehension and dismay as the pencil intersected each point of the five-pointed star on the map.

"So it's true, then. He did conjure some spell and transport us here?"

"He certainly thinks so," said Everson, now planting the fingertips of his hand on the map and moving it aside, only to pull another map out from underneath. It was a similar map, only this one had a much cruder circle drawn over it encompassing the Harcourt sector, enclosing the British trenches currently held by the 13th Pennine Fusiliers. "This one was taken from observations made by Lieutenant Tulliver after we arrived here and surveyed by CQS Slacke in our absence."

"So?"

"Whatever happened, whatever brought us here, I don't think it was the result of Jeffries' occult practices. Look." He took the one map, laid it on top of the other, and held both up in front of the hurricane lamp for Atkins to see. He adjusted them slightly with his thumbs so the trench positions matched up. The two circles however, did not. Oh, there was an overlap, but they didn't cover the same ground.

"What do you think of that?" Everson said.

"They're not the same, sir,"

"No. Jeffries' circle doesn't correspond to the one we're stood in right now. It's just coincidence, d'y'see?"

"So it's got nothing to do with Jeffries. And when he said that he knew the way home?"

"That, I can't be sure about. It seems he may have learnt some things from the Khungarrii. He mentioned the name Croatoan. Poilus has mentioned it too. There's something else going on here and this Croatoan thing seems to be key, it keeps cropping up. That can't be coincidence, it means something but I don't know what. All I have are Jeffries' indecipherable notes. That damn man has caused irreparable damage. But he's left us with one thing—the *possibility* of a way home and I suppose for that we should be grateful."

LANCE CORPORAL THOMAS 'Only' Atkins stepped out of the dugout an NCO, but it was a hollow moment. He didn't deserve this. He felt he was deceiving his friends and the lieutenant. He had left chaos and calamity in his wake, as Jeffries had. He took out the letter he'd taken from Ketch, Flora's letter to him, the last post. He held it tightly in his hand as he refused to let the tears fall.

Above, the unfamiliar stars were coming out one by one; the constellation they called 'Charlie Chaplin' hung low in the heavens against the gaseous red ribbon that trailed across the alien sky. This new world, like Atkins' fortunes, continued to turn, but for good or ill, he couldn't say.

A bright point of light rose above the horizon. It was the brightest star in the sky, the star they had christened 'Blighty.' Atkins looked towards it, held the thought of Flora in his mind and made the most fervent wish he could.

THE END

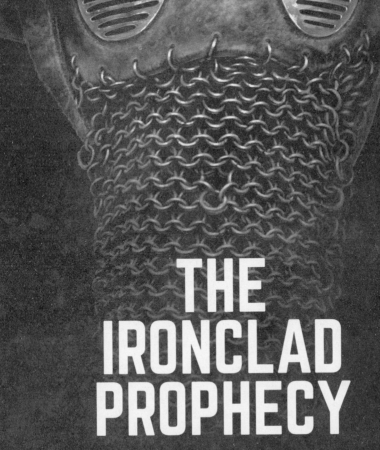

THE
IRONCLAD
PROPHECY

*"When sorrows come, they come not single spies
But in battalions."*

—*Hamlet*, Act 4, Scene 5,
William Shakespeare

ACKNOWLEDGEMENTS

I WOULD LIKE to thank Stephen Maugham and the Broughtonthwaite Historical Society for their continuing support. I am grateful to Faye Joy for her dedication in undertaking research and tracking down French newspaper reports and primary documents concerning the Harcourt Event and the subsequent Lefeuvre Find. I am also grateful to the estate of the late Arthur Cooke for continued access to his collection. I should also like to thank Ellie McDonald at the Broughtonthwaite Museum, who brought to my attention some of their more recent acquisitions concerning the Fusiliers. I am indebted to Bill Crinson at the British Library archive of British Periodicals, for his encyclopaedic knowledge on the history of British magazines of the period, invaluable help in tracking down issues of *Great War Science Stories* and for providing information on the works of Harold G. Cargill. Special thanks must go to all those people who have kindly contacted the publishers and offered me access to private family documents and photographs in my continuing research. Once more, I must thank my wife, Penny, for her continuing support and dedicated work in transcribing interviews.

Pat Kelleher

13TH BATTALION PENNINE FUSILIERS COMPANY PERSONNEL

Battalion HQ.
    CO: 2nd Lieutenant J. C. Everson
    2CO: Company Sergeant Major Ernest Nelson
    Company Quartermaster Sergeant Archibald Slacke
    Pte. Henry *'Half Pint'* Nicholls (batman)
    Royal Army Chaplain: Father Arthur Rand (CF4, 'Captain')
    War Office Kinematographer Oliver Hepton

'C' Company

No 1 Platoon
    CO: Lieutenant Morgan

No. 2 Platoon
    CO: 2nd Lieutenant Palmer
    2CO: Platoon Sergeant Herbert Gerald Hobson

1 Section
    IC: Lance Corporal Thomas *'Only'* Atkins
    Pte. Harold *'Gutsy'* Blood
    Pte. Peter *'Nobby'* Clark
    Pte. Wilfred Joseph *'Mercy'* Evans
    Pte. Bernard *'Prof'* Gates
    Pte. George *'Porgy'* Hopkiss
    Pte. Leonard *'Pot-Shot'* Jellicoe
    Pte. David Samuel *'Gazette'* Otterthwaite
    Pte. Eric *'Chalky'* White

RAMC
Regimental Aid Post
    RMO: Captain Grenville Lippett

Red Cross Nurses
    Sister Betty Fenton
    Sister Edith Bell
    Driver Nellie Abbott (First Aid Nursing Yeomanry)

Orderlies
    Pte. Edgar Stanton
    Pte. Edward Thompkins

Machine Gun Corps (Heavy Section) 'I' Company

I-5 HMLS Ivanhoe
    CO: 2nd Lieutenant Arthur Alexander Mathers
    Pte. Wally Clegg (Driver)
    Pte. Frank Nichols (Gearsman)
    Pte. Alfred Perkins (Gearsman)
    Pte. Norman Bainbridge (Gunner)
    Pte. Jack Tanner (Gunner)
    Pte. Reginald Lloyd (Loader/ Machine Gunner)
    Pte. Cecil Nesbit (Loader / Machine Gunner)

D Flight 70 Squadron: Sopwith 1 ½ Strutter
    Lieutenant James Robert Tulliver (Pilot)
    Corporal Jack Maddocks (Observer)

For Niall and Niamh

PREFACE

"It's a Long, Long Way to Tipperary..."

THE MYSTERY OF the Harcourt Crater galvanised a generation when, in 1916, nine hundred men of the 13th Battalion of the Pennine Fusiliers vanished from the Somme. Ten years afterwards, a find in a French field revealed silent film footage, letters and journals, describing the Fusiliers' existence on another planet, only for it to be declared a hoax and forgotten as time passed.

Almost a hundred years later, the publication of *No Man's World: Black Hand Gang* revived interest in the case of the missing Pennine Fusiliers. Since then, members of the public have contacted the publisher with claims of new evidence, of unseen documents and letters that have lain in ordinary boxes and in dusty attics for decades, unregarded.

This volume, continuing the account of the Pennine Fusiliers' fate, has been able to include this new information, where appropriate, with the permission of the families, in order to shed light on one of the biggest military cover-ups of the last century.

It must be remembered, however, that it was not just the 13th Battalion of the Pennine Fusiliers that vanished that day. The *HMLS Ivanhoe*, one of Britain's secret weapons, the new-fangled 'tanks,' also disappeared, along with its eight-man crew.

While the mystery of the Pennines inspired lurid pulp tales in magazines such as *Great War Science Stories*, and featured in adventures like *The Curse of the 13th Battalion; The Golem of No Man's Land; Zeppelin from Another World* and *Crater of the Somme-bies*, the *Ivanhoe* appeared in only a small number of tales published during 1928. They were written by Harold G. Cargill who, the publication's editors sensationally suggested, was an eyewitness survivor of the Fusiliers, returned from the planet.

While there was no evidence to suggest that Cargill was ever a member of the Pennine Fusiliers, his name not appearing in any official war records, nor indeed in a list of the missing, it is clear from his personal correspondence that he knew more than he was telling, or perhaps was *allowed* to tell.

The *Ivanhoe* and its crew were portrayed in those tales as cheery, jingoistic modern day knights-in-armour, riding out across a strange planet on colourful, rip-roaring quests.

The truth, however, is more inauspicious.

Military records show that the *Ivanhoe*, with five other tanks from I Company, Machine Gun Corp, Heavy Section, was ordered into battle on 1st November 1916 to support an assault on Harcourt Wood by the Pennines. Of those tanks, three broke down before they reached the front line. I4, the female tank *Igraine,* was mired in mud and abandoned. Wreckage of I3, the *Invicta*, was found at the bottom of the Harcourt Crater itself. It is assumed that it drove blindly over the edge, moments after the crater's appearance, killing all on board.

All of the major events in this account are drawn, where possible, from primary sources, including fragments of the *Ivanhoe's* tank diary. Scribbled in faded pencil and almost indecipherable in places, they were found among the papers of Arthur Cooke, author of *The Harcourt Crater: Hoax or Horror?* While incomplete, the fragments do give some clues to the apparent fate of the *Ivanhoe* and its crew, a fate that is firmly entrenched in that of the Pennine Fusiliers.

And it is uplifting to discover from these sources that while the Pennines were fighting for their existence in a place that was, most definitely, a long, long way from Tipperary, throughout the travails and terrors they had to endure their hearts did, indeed, remain right here.

Pat Kelleher
Broughtonshaw
December, 2010

PROLOGUE
"Here Comes The British Navy, Sailing On The Land..."

Elveden, Suffolk, May 1916

THE GREAT ARMOURED beast stood passively, like a great destrier waiting to be ridden into battle.

Lieutenant Arthur Mathers tried to hold his nerve in front of his men but, despite his efforts, the muscle beneath his right eye began to twitch uncontrollably. His palms began to sweat and he started to hyperventilate. He could feel his heart pounding in his chest.

To his men beside him, this thing was a magnificent brute. They crowded around it admiringly, patting its flanks and inspecting it like a prize thoroughbred.

"Bleedin' hell, it's a sight, isn't it, sir?" Wally Clegg, the small, thin-haired cockney beside Mathers, beamed with a joy the officer couldn't feel.

"Yes, Clegg. Yes it is," said Mathers, trying to temper his rising fear.

Reginald Lloyd looked over at the small man with the weary air of one given to correcting those less educated than himself. "It's not an *it*, Wally. Tanks are a *he* or a *she*." Reggie had been a butler to minor aristocracy, but had joined up to 'do his bit,' a duty he seemed to interpret as trying to instil some manners into his crewmates.

"Well, begging your pardon, Reggie, but I ain't no vet. How do you tell them apart?"

"Most of us, Wally, paid attention on the course, but for your benefit, both types have front and rear machine guns, but females have smaller sponsons either side with two Hotchkiss machine guns in each, while the males, like this one here, have bigger sponsons, each with a six-pounder gun and a Hotchkiss."

"By God, the Hun'll pay now," said Wally, with evident glee. He was a chipper bloke, Wally. A motor omnibus driver before the war, he had a wife and eight kids. Loved his family, he did, and talked about them at the drop of a hat. It was a pity that they were all dead, having died in a Zeppelin raid on the East End.

Norman Bainbridge smacked his hand on the barrel of the six-pounder. "Aye, the Hun'll be running scared all right, but only because of your driving!" Norman had been in the music hall, as he was never shy of reminding people, although often so far down the bill you needed spectacles to see his name. Life and soul he was; wherever there was a pianola, there he was leading the singing.

Frank Nichols, an electrical engineer, answered a cryptic advert placed in *The Motor Cycle* magazine by the War Office and ended up here. He walked around, inspecting the huge caterpillar tracks. "I tell you what; I certainly wouldn't like to see this bugger coming at me, Alfie."

Alfie Perkins, his fellow gearsman, was checking out the one-and-a-half-ton hydraulic steering tail, with its iron wheels, at the rear of the tank. He'd joined the Motor Machine Gun Service to be a motorcycle machine gunner, before volunteering for the new Heavy Section. "Me neither. I wouldn't want to be the Hun when we get over there."

The fearsome metal beast before him was a Mark I tank. At thirty-two feet long and eight feet high, with its distinctive rhomboid shape, the ironclad land ship weighed twenty-eight tons. This was Britain's new secret weapon. It was going to help turn the tide of the war and break the deadlock on the Somme. And put the wind up Fritz. More than that, this one, designated I5, was theirs.

The tank had been tuned, the guns cleaned, and Cecil Nesbitt had just put the finishing touches to the name, now painted on the side of the front track horn. Cecil was the youngest crewmember. An orphan and a truculent sod, he'd been signed up by his Platoon Commander, who just wanted shot of him, and he had found a real home. He looked to big Jack Tanner, who nodded with satisfaction. Jack used to be a boxer in a travelling fair until he joined up. His brother was in the Royal Navy and had been killed at the battle of Jutland. He thought joining the 'Land Navy' a fitting tribute to him.

They stood back and looked at it with pride. HMLS *Ivanhoe*.

Outside of the top-secret camp at Elveden, very few people had seen a tank, let alone knew what one was, and that was no surprise. The project was so secret that most men applied without any real idea of what they were applying for. They just knew the pay was slightly better. Three separate perimeters surrounded the camp. No one could get in or out, and it was impossible to get hold of passes for leave. Should they actually manage to see anyone from outside, there was a one hundred pound fine, or six months' imprisonment, if they disclosed anything about what went on in there. No wonder they were nicknamed the Hush Hush Crowd.

Then there were the months of training, without any hint of what it was they were training for. There was lots of drill and training on Vickers machine guns, but with no reasons why. It was months before they even saw a real tank.

And the tank before them wasn't just any tank. This was *their* tank. They were learning to drive it. It wasn't easy. It took four people just to steer it.

Today was merely battle practice, that was all, but Mathers was nervous.

He had a secret phobia of enclosed spaces, but he would master his fear. He would master this brute machine and make it his.

"Right," he said, as his crew crowded about the sponson hatch. "Top brass will be watching today. I've even heard a rumour that the King himself might be coming to watch. So, let's show them and the rest of I Company what the *Ivanhoe* can do, eh?"

His crew were in a jocular mood and gave a rowdy cheer.

"That shower in the *Igraine* reckon they can reach the 'enemy trenches' before we can," continued Mathers. "I've got five guineas in the Officer's Mess that says we'll beat them."

It may have been just a training exercise, but now there was money on it, it was serious. This meant war. They entered through the hatches at the rear of the sponsons. At barely four foot high they were a bit of a squeeze, and you had to watch your head, too.

Inside, the compartment was barely five feet high. They couldn't stand up straight without cracking their heads on the low roof. The Daimler engine almost reached the roof. With a small wooden platform behind it, it sat squarely in the middle of the white-painted compartment, taking up most of the space. Two wooden gangways, less than two feet across and eight feet long, ran down either side.

These opened out into the sponsons, the turrets projecting out either side of the tank, where the six-pounder guns sat, manoeuvred by the sheer strength of the gunner alone. Behind them were the belt-fed Hotchkiss machine guns. To the rear of each sponson was a small entrance hatch.

At the back of the engine was the large starting handle. It took four men to turn it in order to start the engine up.

Either side of that, each caterpillar track had its own gear system, each operated by a gearsman. Privates Alfie Perkins and Frank Nichols manned the independent gears, one for each track.

At the front, in a slightly raised cockpit, Private Wally Clegg, the small bantam cockney, sat in the right-hand driver's seat, and the Tank Commander, Lieutenant Mathers, in the left seat, next to him, to operate the steering brakes.

Once the hatches clanged shut, sealing the men in, Mathers felt the panic rising in him. Wally ran the engine up. Frank and Alfie stood by their track gears at the back. The *Ivanhoe* set off across the training ground.

The Tank Commander, using steering brakes for each track, could only make slight turns along with the driver, using the wheel that controlled the steering tail. Large swinging manoeuvres took four men.

The engine was too loud for verbal instructions, so Mathers had to get the attention of the gearsmen by banging a wrench on a pipe. He gave a signal with his hand to swing right. He stopped the tank and locked the differential gear. Alfie put his track gear into neutral, stopping the right hand track, while Frank pushed the left track gear into first speed, swinging the tank to the right. The tank had to stop again, while Mathers re-engaged the main gears, and Alfie took the right track out of neutral. It was a long and laborious process.

Obstacles filled the training ground: earthwork ramps, trenches, craters, barbed wire entanglements and deep ditches, all to test the prowess of the tank crews. The noise of the engines filled the training area, as six tanks of 2 Section, I Company set off over the course, the guns blazing away at targets. The *Igraine* got itself ditched in a crater. The *Illustrious* threw a track.

The *Ivanhoe* advanced on a large crater, teetering on the lip until the front track horns tilted, and the tank crashed down. The tracks caught the ground in the trough and began to haul the ironclad up the far side.

With the engine running, the temperature inside was becoming almost unbearable, and the compartment soon filled with petrol vapour and cordite fumes.

Mathers was beginning to sweat. He could feel his chest tighten and his breathing become shallower. The sooner he could finish this, the sooner he could get out. Hardly caring now, he pushed the machine to its limits.

The last obstacle of the course was a steep bank about forty yards long. The other tanks nosed cautiously over the edge, and descended gingerly.

The *Ivanhoe* raced over the top of the rise, and dashed down the slope at a terrific pace, sparks flying from its tracks. Despite having no suspension, it bounced as it crashed to the bottom of the slope.

Inside, the manoeuvre threw the crew about roughly. Cecil cracked his head on the gun breech; Norman slammed against the engine block, burning his arm. Thrown into the steering column, Wally had the wind knocked out of him. All of them were cursing, except Reggie, who managed a heartfelt, "Dash it all!" They fell out of the sponson hatches, badly shaken, coughing and retching.

Mathers staggered from the tank, gasping for breath, relieved to be in the open air again. The Company commander greeted him with enthusiasm. "Great Scott, Arthur. I was wrong about you. I've seen some devilish driving in my time, but that's the kind of gumption we need if we're going to stick it to the Hun! It's always the quiet ones, eh?"

"You know what," said Frank, catching his breath and jerking his chin towards where Mathers was talking with the other officers. "I'll tell you this for nothing. He'll either win us medals for getting to Germany first, or he'll be the bloody death of us all."

INTERLUDE ONE

Signal from the HMLS Ivanhoe,
1st November 1916*

"C" Form (Original)
MESSAGES AND SIGNALS.
Army Form C 2123

Service Instructions: *Pigeon Priority*

Handed in at .... Office 7-48 a.m. Received 8-25 a.m.

From Cpl Knott

TO: Div HQ

Day of Month 1-11-16

Tanks L-1 L-2 and L-6 broken down en route from ST. GERMAINE to starting Point tanks L-5 L-3 and L-4 proceeding on to primary objectives

FROM: Lt. Mather HMLS L-5
PLACE & TIME: Hancourt Sector 7-20 a

W.t. 1750 A.W. & Co. 40,000 Pads 8/15

*Sent by carrier pigeon, this was the last message ever received before HMLS *Ivanhoe* and the 13th Battalion of the Pennine Fusiliers vanished.

CHAPTER ONE
"Let the Great Big World Keep Turning..."

Four months later...

"Run!"

Lance Corporal Thomas Atkins of the Pennine Fusiliers could hear the terrifying rhythmic chittering noise behind him, even over the measured thud of his hobnailed boots on the crimson alien soil.

Ahead of them lay the vast expanse of the tube grass veldt and, too far away across it, the Pennines' encampment.

Atkins and the rest of 1 Section urged and cajoled the ragtag band of Urmen, the primitive humans who inhabited this planet, through the shoulder-high tube grass. Bewildered young children shrieked as desperate parents dragged them along.

Naparandwe ran up alongside him. The middle-aged native guide had been the first Urman they had encountered on this world and his help had been invaluable. The men, however, called him 'Napoo,' army slang for 'all gone,' after his initial habit of finishing everyone's food when they first met. Like most Urmen, he wore a combination of animal skins and insect shell armour. His usually cheerful face was drawn, his tanned forehead creased with concern. "Atkins, they cannot keep this pace up," he said. "They are tired, hungry, terrified."

"They don't have a choice, Napoo. Not if they want to live. We've got to keep moving." He stopped and waved past a few Urman warriors armed with short swords and spears. "Come on, come on!" They, in turn, herded and encouraged their distressed families.

"Ruined my soddin' day, this has," said Gutsy as he jogged past with a young lad on his back. Too exhausted to cry any more, the lad just clung to the brawny butcher's shoulders, his small chest heaving with dry sobs.

"Saved mine," said Mercy, the section's inveterate scrounger, with a grin. "Nobby was just about to start telling jokes. He's only got three and they're all bloody rubbish."

"Look at this, nearly took me bloody leg off!" said Pot Shot.

Mercy glanced down at the lanky soldier's charred calf-wrapping as he trotted alongside. He shook his head and grinned. "Just be thankful it's your puttee that kaput-ee, and not you, you grousing sod."

The incorrigible Porgy, and Gazette, the best sharp shooter they had, trotted along with several new replacements. Prof, Nobby and Chalky had brought the section up to strength. The other new addition, Shiner, had died three weeks earlier when, on patrol, he'd stopped to take a leak. He peed on something in the undergrowth that took exception to the act. Atkins winced whenever he thought of it.

An explosion of shrieks and feathers erupted to their right—Gazette wheeled around with his rifle to meet the threat. A flock of grubbing bird-things, startled by their passing, took to the air with raucous cries.

Atkins watched an Urman woman clutching a baby to her breast as she ran, a wild desperation in her eyes. He thought of Flora, his missing brother's fiancée, now pregnant with his own child. He had only found that out here, after discovering that Ketch, his old corporal, had spitefully withheld her letter from him. She was his Flora, now. Not William's. Not his brother's. *His* sweetheart, waiting for him on Earth. *His* child, growing up fatherless. Or it soon would be. He'd kept count. Flora would be seven months gone by now. And he was stuck here on this benighted world.

He felt more alone now than ever. More than once, he thought about confiding in Porgy, but stopped himself. That someone else would take your wife or sweetheart while you were fighting at the front was every soldier's worst nightmare. He doubted he'd find much sympathy, and he feared the friendships he'd lose.

He would do whatever it took to return home to Flora, to his child. He wouldn't rest until she was in his arms again. But to do that he had to survive the day.

To do that he had to run.

SINCE THEIR ARRIVAL on this God-forsaken planet, Padre Rand, the army chaplain, had watched the Pennine Fusiliers re-dig the parallel lines of Somme trenches into a defensible stronghold, encircling the area of Somme that had come with them, protecting all they had left of Earth.

Without the distraction of constant Hun artillery bombardment, they were able to dig deep dugouts, after the German fashion, with the time to construct them properly, dry and strong and deep.

Now linked by radial communications trenches, three concentric circles of defensive trenches ringed the ground at the centre, now home to a parade ground and assorted tents and crude wooden hutments. Lewis and Vickers machine gun emplacements strengthened the perimeter.

Above it all, in the centre of the small parade ground, the torn, tattered Union flag hung lifelessly from its makeshift flagpole.

It should be snapping in the wind, the padre thought, proud and glorious, filling the men with hope and pride. Instead, it seemed limp and forlorn, unable to instil anything in anyone. It looked the way he felt.

It had been three months since Jeffries had conducted the obscene occult ritual that had apparently condemned them all to this place. The padre had a hard time dealing with that one. That someone as evil as him could have access to such supernatural power as to bring them here while he, with his prayers and his Almighty, barely seemed to accomplish a thing. He felt insignificant in comparison. It challenged his faith in a way the war itself never had, and he felt unequal to the task now before him, caring for the souls of these castaway men.

The men had embellished the tale of their arrival, until Jeffries had glowing red eyes and magic bolts coming out of his fingers. As a result, his Church Parades were better attended now than they had been on the Somme, but it gave him little comfort.

He watched a wiring party at work beyond the front line trench. It was dangerous work, as was everything on this world. Barbed wire was in limited supply, but they had found a lethally barbed creeper they called wire weed that made a living substitute. The men, wearing old sniper's armour for protection, weren't so much laying it as cutting back the writhing vines, training it over wooden x-frame knife rests to fill gaps in the barbed wire entanglement in front of the fire trenches.

Walking over a small footbridge across the support trench, the padre wrinkled his nose. The sweaty feet, cordite and corpse stench of the Somme had long since faded, to be replaced by the acrid tang of animal dung. Gathered from the veldt, huge tarpaulin-covered heaps of it had been left to rot down. They told him it was a saltpetre experiment, an attempt to make their own gunpowder. That, however, was still some months off yet, if they succeeded at all.

The sun, that was not their sun, was just rising above the valley sides and beginning to take the chill off the morning air, and the poppies were beginning to open.

He had been surprised to see the poppies when they first appeared. They all had. Their seeds, long buried in the Somme mud, had somehow survived. In the warm climes offered by this foreign world, they had germinated and flowered, dispersing their seeds on the wind so that now a carpet of red flowed across the scorched cordon sanitaire around them and onto the alien veldt beyond in an invasion all of their own. The poppies spread out, like the red of the British Empire across the maps of the world in his old atlas. To the men, they were a cheering sight. A sign of hope. It was as if God had sent a message to say he had not abandoned them after all.

Poppies hadn't been the only things to appear. Potatoes had sprouted too: after all, before the war, before the trenches, the Somme was rich farming ground. They cleared some land beyond the encampment for agriculture. They planted the potatoes there and some native vegetables. It all went well until the alien weeds came and the new plants had literally fought each other for dominance until the entire area had to be razed.

It had put him in mind of the Old Testament story of Joseph and the Pharaoh's dream, of seven thin and shrivelled ears of wheat swallowing up the ripe ones. That unsettled him deeply, reminding him of his own vision, the terrifying hallucination brought on by the Khungarrii in a heathen ritual he had been forced to undergo, along with Jeffries. The vision itself had faded as the drugs had left his system; he had tried remembering it, but he could not. He was left with an unsettling sense of terror and despair. Recently, he had begun waking with night terrors, things that receded and vanished from memory as he awoke in a sweat. Things that made him afraid. He was terrified his vision was coming back to haunt him.

He was shaken from his thoughts by Sergeant Dixon across the parade ground, barking out instructions to a platoon of heathen Urmen. Nicknamed 'Fred Karno's Army,' after a popular song, they were dressed in skins and customised pieces of armour shaped from the chitinous shells of various creatures. They were drilling with spears instead of rifles, much to the amusement of the Tommies on work parties nearby, who had stopped to watch the entertainment.

The NCO was teaching them the rudiments of drill, forging into shape a ragtag army of Urmen refugees who, displaced by recent Khungarrii attacks, had sought sanctuary here. For the Urmen, it would give them the tools they needed to defend themselves against the Ones. It also served to bolster the numbers of the Pennines themselves.

On one side of the parade ground stood the single-storey log building that was the small hospital. Huddled around it, groups of tents served as wards and surgical theatres. A group of soldiers stood waiting to be seen by the MO.

Across the small parade ground, in isolation, was a barbed wire compound, 'the Bird Cage,' where those poor souls suffering emotional shock from the Somme, or from finding themselves here, could be kept safe. Some shook uncontrollably, and others rocked themselves incessantly, or cried or howled in torment. A few sought to hide themselves, however they could.

The padre said a silent prayer for them, trotted down into the reserve trench and headed for Lieutenant Everson's dugout.

Approaching the gas curtain, he heard a woman's voice tinged with exasperation. He knew the voice well. Only three women had the misfortune to accompany them to this place. Edith Bell had been one of those kidnapped with him and taken to the Khungarrii edifice. She, Corporal Atkins and Lieutenant Everson had confronted Jeffries, who then gutted the Khungarrii edifice and destroyed their sacred library, setting them all even more at odds with the creatures that ruled this world than they had been before.

Lieutenant Everson sounded just as frustrated. "Nurse Bell, I'm sorry, but I have over five hundred men under my command. It is becoming clearer day by day that we cannot depend on being returned by whatever forces brought us here. If we are to return, then it will have to be under our own cognisance. That map of his you saw. You said yourself he went to a lot of trouble to get it. It's obviously important. The sketch you gave us was helpful, but short on detail. Anything else you can give me, anything at all, will be most valuable."

Bell sighed heavily. "I know that, Lieutenant, and I have tried. I have wracked my brains. And I can assure you, if I remember the slightest thing you'll be the first to know."

"I'd appreciate that."

"Then give me more aid for the shell-shock patients," she asked. "Captain Lippett has no time for them. He believes they're nothing but shirkers and malingerers. They're ill. You can't keep them in the Bird Cage, like prisoners! You just can't!"

"Nurse Bell, Captain Lippett is the Medical Officer here. I don't think he'd appreciate you going over his head. Please do try and stick to the proper channels," said Everson with a sigh. "Do I have to tell Sister Fenton?"

Padre Rand coughed politely outside the rubberised canvas flap that formed the dugout's door.

"Enter!"

He stepped inside. Everson was at his desk. Scattered in front of him was Jeffries' coded occult journal and various maps and papers they had taken from his dugout. Sat opposite, Nurse Bell took the opportunity to end her interview. She stood up, brushed down her nurse's apron over her part-worn khaki trousers and bobbed a slight curtsey to Rand as she passed him. "Padre," she said curtly, pulling the canvas door aside and stepping out into the light.

Everson looked up from behind his desk, sweeping a hand across the papers and journal before him.

"No matter how many times I look at this stuff, I come up with nothing. Nothing but that damn Croatoan symbol with which Jeffries seemed to be obsessed. The rest I can't make head or tails of, even after three months."

The padre felt for him. Lieutenant Everson was a good officer, respected by the men, but where the blame for bad decisions might be passed back up the line to Battalion HQ or the General Staff, here the buck stopped with him. He was the highest-ranking infantry officer left. Whatever credit he had with the men was running out. He had turned more and more frequently to the scattered papers looking for answers, as another might turn to the bible or the bottle.

Everson gave him a weary smile. "Tea, Padre? Nichols!"

The man called Half Pint clumped into the room from an office beyond. He was twenty four, but looked twice that age. He'd lost his right leg below the knee at Khungarr. Unfit for duty, Everson had taken him on as his batman.

"What do you think, Padre?" he said with a grin, thrusting out his new peg leg. "Mercy—Private Evans, that is—carved it out of a lump of wood he found. Mind you, hurts like the blazes. Rubs something awful on me stump, it does. Me wife were the same about her new teeth when I bought her the highland clearances for a wedding present. Serves me right, I suppose. What goes around, comes around she'd say."

Everson cleared his throat.

"Sorry, sir. Tea, was it? Right away, sir," said Half Pint, hobbling off.

The padre looked down at the scattered papers littering the desk. "There's a whole world out there, Lieutenant. He could be dead by now. But somehow I doubt it. Man has the luck of the devil."

"You can say that again."

"If he's alive, a man like him won't stay hidden for long. He needs to show off. He wants people to know what he's up to, how clever he is. He only has us who would understand. We'll hear from him again, you take my word."

"I hope you're right, Padre. Sending men out to find his trail is becoming too costly. Sending the tank has become the only choice. It's practically impervious to anything this place throws at it."

"Running a risk, though, isn't it?"

"So Sergeant Hobson keeps telling me. The Khungarrii are still afraid of us. Well, of the tank, really. So they seem to be taking it out on the Urmen, stepping up reprisal raids against them. You told me they'd a mind to cull us and, after Jeffries betrayed them, it's probably no more than I'd expect. I just hope it doesn't come to that."

SPURRED ON BY the incessant rhythm behind them, Atkins ran, pushing his men on through the tube grass, harassing and chivvying the Urmen onward. The day had started out so well, too, at least for this place...

"Take your Black Hand Gang eve-ward out round the edge of the veldt," Lieutenant Everson had said. "Napoo informs me that there's an enclave of Urmen out there this time of year. Try to convince them to side with us. The more influence we have, the better our chances of dealing with the Khungarrii."

That and "keep an eye out for Jeffries," an order repeated so often that it was now becoming a standing joke amongst the men.

It had seemed simple enough. They'd left the encampment that morning on routine patrol with the new replacements. Everson had ordered that every patrol have an Urman guide, and now Napoo led the way down into a small valley through a wood of tall jelleph trees, with their smooth, bulbous trunks and broad, flat damson-coloured fronds.

Behind him, Gutsy and Porgy were talking in low voices. Every so often, a snort of laughter would burst from them only to be stifled as Atkins glanced back. Time was, as a private, when he'd be in on the joke.

Porgy ambled up to him trying to suppress a smirk. "Here, Only, I want you to meet Chalky. He's a big admirer of yours. Hey, Chalky!" he yelled.

The eager young private came running up the file, "Here, sir!" he said with a salute.

Atkins sighed. "It's just Corporal, Private. I'm not an officer."

Chalky looked at Atkins in awe.

"What?" he asked irritably.

"It's just, the stories? Are they true, Corp?"

Atkins shook his head in exasperation. The stories around his and Everson's confrontation with Jeffries had started shortly after they returned from the Khungarr raid. They spread like latrine rumours, embroidered with each retelling until men were swearing it was true, as true as the Angel of Mons.

Right now, he was up there with St. George or the Phantom Bowmen. Christ, in some quarters you'd think he'd tricked the very devil himself. But it didn't happen like that.

That was why Atkins liked it out on patrol, away from the curious stares of those who believed the stories, those who sneered at them and those who resented him, thinking he'd spread them himself for his own glory. In truth, he didn't know who had started them, but he wished they hadn't.

He scowled at Porgy and shook his head in disappointment.

Porgy beamed, having got just the reaction he wanted, and steered Chalky away. "Later, Chalky, later."

Atkins saw a faint smudge in the air ahead, above the trees.

"Gazette?"

Gazette had the sharpest eyes in the section. They narrowed. "Smoke. That'll be the Urman enclave Napoo told us about."

Through the damson-coloured foliage came a scream. At first, they hesitated. Men had gone charging off in aid of a human-like scream before only to end up gored to death. Then a second and a third pierced the leaden air.

"Stand to!" said Atkins.

The screams continued, mingled with inarticulate shouts of rage. Atkins began to trot along the forest path, keeping parallel to the valley floor. He wanted to try and see what they were up against before they went charging in. A creek roared and tumbled below them, as if to drown the screams, but the urgent notes rose above it. Great wet fronds of saltha weed slapped at them as they passed and small creatures, startled by their passing, crashed away through the undergrowth.

The strains of battle now reached them. Through gaps in the trees they caught the familiar blue flash of Khungarrii bioelectrical lances. Atkins held up his hand and the section came to a halt.

"Load," said Atkins hoarsely, fishing a fresh magazine from his webbing. He slotted the magazine home, flicked open the magazine cut-off and pulled the bolt, cycling a bullet into the chamber. From the noises around him, the rest of the section did the same, finishing the routine drill within split seconds of each other. They only had twenty rounds and one Mills bomb apiece.

Beyond that, they each had a bayonet; seventeen inches of cold British steel. Some had constructed trench clubs, brutal wooden clubs with hobnails or other protrusions. And Gutsy, Gutsy had his best butcher's cleaver, Little Bertha.

As the vegetation thinned and the camp below became visible, the source of the screams and blue flashes proved to be a circle of a dozen crude huts, several of the thatched roofs ablaze as the Khungarrii scentirrii attacked.

They were hard to miss. The arthropod soldiers were the size of a man, but thickly built and heavily armoured with a natural chitinous shell covered with sharp spines. Their face shells were broad, flat and ugly with small antler nubs, and long antennae sprouted from the tops of their facial shells. In their abdominal section, they had the two vestigial claw-like limbs common to all Chatts. They moved quickly on legs which were jointed so their knees faced backwards, giving them a powerful leap.

Twelve Urmen were under attack from three times their number. They fought back with swords and spears, putting up a valiant fight, but they were losing and the encircling scentirrii were closing in.

Atkins motioned to Gazette, who came and crouched down beside him.

"Chatt scentirrii, all right. About thirty of them. Not good odds," Gazette offered.

"Trench fighting, no. But we've got these," Atkins said, slapping the palm of his hand against his Enfield. "We'll even the odds a little first before we go down. Gazette, you stay up here with Nobby, Chalky and Prof. Cover us. Go for the head, stop 'em giving off an alarm scent. We'll make for the huts."

Gazette grunted an acknowledgement. Atkins and the others scrambled down through the trees to the rear of the huts, huddling themselves against the wattle-and-daub walls. Atkins peered round into the centre of the enclave.

It was a massacre. The crackling blue arcs of the electrical lances threw men into spasms. Chatts with curved swords and some sort of thorny halberd spat acid from their mouthparts between their mandibles. Urmen screamed as the burning liquid caught their faces or arms.

"Shit," said Atkins. "Gas masks! They've got spitters."

The men fumbled at the canvas bags on their chests and pulled their PH hoods on over their heads. They were a bugger to fight in for any length of time, but they were invaluable against the acid-spitting Chatts, as the scorch marks on several of them attested.

Atkins indicated to Gutsy that he and the others should circle around the huts to flank the Khungarrii within.

He lifted his gas hood, took a whistle out of his top pocket and blew. A rapid fusillade of bullets rang out as 1 Section poured their fire into the settlement. Cracks of sniper fire rang across the open ground as Gazette and the others picked off Chatts from the hillside.

A dozen fell before the others knew what had happened.

The Tommies let out blood-curdling, if muffled, roars and charged into the fray with bayonets glinting.

Atkins sank his bayonet blade into the thorax of the nearest scentirrii and twisted it, before stomping forward with his boot to drive it off the point.

He swung the butt of the rifle against the head of another. A dark eye burst as it went down, its mandibles opened in surprise, its small abdominal limbs twitching uselessly as it fell. Atkins stepped over the body.

The air was filled with crunching carapaces and agitated chitters as he moved on his next target, a Chatt with a clay battery pack and bioelectrical lance. Somehow, these inhuman creatures were able to store and amplify a natural electrical discharge in these devices. The lance spat out a jolt of blue fire, convulsing an Urman before he fell to the ground.

He stepped up behind the Chatt, staving in the battery pack with the shoulder stock of his Enfield rifle. As the Chatt turned, he thrust the bayonet into the soft unprotected innards of its abdomen and tore it to one side, disembowelling it, ripping delicate organs from its body. It dropped to the ground, where it clawed feebly before Atkins stamped on its head.

Napoo's attacks were as economical as they were devastating, thrusting at weak joints in the Chatts' chitinous armour.

Gutsy swung his butcher's cleaver down through the skull of another, splitting the head in half.

Mercy, stabbing and parrying with the bayonet and bludgeoning with the shoulder's stock, whirled the Enfield around through Chatt after Chatt with a dexterity that bewildered Atkins. All Mercy had ever said was that someone in the Chink Labour Battalions had owed him a favour. This, apparently, was it.

Atkins wheeled about looking for his next target and found none. Chatts lay strewn on the ground, dead or dying. He pulled off his gas hood.

"That's the last of 'em," said Porgy, jabbing his bayonet into a twitching Chatt to still it.

Atkins looked around, catching his breath. Napoo was calmly wiping his sword with a saltha leaf.

The huts were ablaze, the dry crackles of the flames mingling with the wailing of women and children as the surviving warriors sought out their families, and those who found no comforting reunion realised their loss and wailed all the louder.

As 1 Section regrouped, Napoo sought out the Clan elder. They gripped each other by the forearms in greeting and talked in low voices, all the time casting glances at the Tommies.

Wanting to secure his position, Atkins called Gutsy over. "Take Gazette and Nobby. Go for a look-see. Check downwind. Make sure nothing's picked up any alarm scent these things might have got off. I don't want any more surprises."

The three men shouldered their rifles and moved off.

Napoo and the Clan elder came over to Atkins.

"This Urman is Haradwe," said Napoo.

The Urman Clan elder grinned in hospitality, white teeth beaming out of his weathered face, but his eyes betrayed his sorrow and pain. Atkins held out his hand only for the man to reach out and clasp his forearms.

The elder shook his head. "I have heard tales of your Clan, the Tohmii; the Urmen who challenge the Ones and who have Skarra fighting by their side. Naparandwe says you will protect us."

"If you'll accompany us back to the encampment, to our enclave, and add your number to ours. Gather your people together and we'll take you now. Mercy, help them round things up, just what they can carry—and don't nick anything."

He saw Nobby running back down towards him through the trees. "Only! Corp! Gutsy told me to tell you he's found something for you."

"What is it?"

"It's a surprise, Gutsy said."

Atkins mouthed an obscenity and followed Nobby as he trotted out of the trees and up a small hillock. Gutsy and Gazette were lying just below the crest. Atkins crawled the last few yards to keep out of sight.

He was aware of an insistent thrumming. "What's that bloody noise? Sounds like something crunching with its teeth."

"I think we've got a problem, Only."

"We wouldn't be the bloody Pennines if we didn't," said Atkins bitterly.

Gutsy thrust his chin towards the summit. "See for yourself."

Enfield cradled in the crooks of his arms, Atkins crawled up the crest on his elbows, lifted his head cautiously above the lip and peered out across the open veldt.

"Fuck!"

He slid back down a few feet in shock and looked back at Gutsy, who gave him an apologetic shrug.

Atkins crawled back to the top again. Not taking his eyes from the plain in front of him, he thrust his right hand back, feeling blindly in the air until Gutsy put a pair of binoculars into it. He peered through them.

There, far across the veldt, he saw Chatts. Khungarrii. Thousands of them, column after column of a vast army on the march. Great caterpillar-like beasts writhed along in front, clearing a path through the tube grass, followed by massed ranks of Khungarrii scentirrii, their rear-most ranks lost in the dust cloud of the vanguard.

The rhythmic thrumming he heard was the marching step of the Chatts muted by the distance, as they banged swords, spears and electric lances against their thorax plates.

They were marching on the British encampment.

CHAPTER TWO
"All Our Might and Main..."

THEY RAN.

Atkins and his men half-jogged, half-walked, sure they were hidden from sight of the approaching army, but cajoling the weary and frightened Urmen on anyway. The speed of their initial flight had gained them some ground, but now the logistics of moving families slowed them down.

They briefly stopped to let the last of the stragglers catch up, an Urman urging on an old woman, and casting anxious glances behind them.

The Khungarrii were in no hurry to reach the Tommies' stronghold. Their pace was steady and persistent and their chanting and clicking relentless and pervasive.

Chalky mumbled something. Gutsy bent his ear to listen.

"Nah, don't you pay it no heed, boy. That racket there, it's meant to frit you. Don't you let it get to you. Bloody hell, Jerry's done worse than that. They're just Chatts out there. No artillery, no trench mortars. Once we're back in the trenches they can't touch you, so buck up, lad."

Atkins was reminded of the Old Contemptibles' tales of the Battle of Mons, as the BEF retreated across Belgium before an advancing German army. He'd seen photographs in the newspapers and war news magazines of fleeing Belgian peasants, on the move with nothing more than they could carry. Then, the British had turned up and made a stand. And they would here, too. But right now they still had a way to go.

Atkins scanned the sky, hoping Tulliver might be up there in his aeroplane, but he realised he hadn't heard the insistent drone of its engine all day. Tulliver would have spotted the Chatts' movements in plenty of time. These days, however, Everson didn't allow Tulliver to go up except for urgent missions. His machine may have been a marvel of modern mechanics but it was made from spit, string and paper and there were things here that would tear it out of the sky in an instant.

Nobby stumbled and fell, and Prof picked him up.

"Not now, there's a good chap," he rasped. "Be terribly inconvenient."

The clumsy private dusted himself off and mumbled an apology.

Gutsy rolled his eyes at Atkins. He shrugged his shoulders in return. Nobby suffered from a natural-born clumsiness and was the bane of many an NCO's life, which was how he ended up in Atkins' section as a replacement. Atkins wondered how he managed to fall over in the first place since he never raised his eyes from his feet.

"Going to be one hell of a scrap," said Gazette, cradling his rifle.

"Aye," admitted Atkins.

"First decent one we've had since we got here, if you don't count the trench raid on Khungarr. I hope we've not got soft and flabby. The lieutenant's a good man, but I think the troops may be getting away from him a bit."

"Aye. He needs something to bring 'em along. This may just be it," said Atkins. Inside, he felt the familiar pull in his stomach as the tide of fear sucked at his soul with its insidious undertow. "Or it may be his undoing."

"Holy Mary, Mother of God!" yelped Gutsy, snatching his foot back from a large crimson growth almost the colour of the soil. It shrank back into itself. "It moved! The damn stuff moved!"

"What the hell is it?" Atkins asked Napoo.

"Urluf, good djaja," replied the Urman with an eating mime.

Some of the Urmen quickly harvested the mass, tearing chunks off and eating it on the run, passing the lumps around young and old until it had all been consumed.

Gazette nudged Gutsy with his elbow as he jogged past. "You know that stuff the mongey wallahs have been putting in the broth to pad it out, that you thought was bully beef?"

"Uh huh."

"That's it."

Gutsy gave a dry retch. "And I thought onions in me tea was disgusting enough."

"Well the MO said it was fit to eat."

"What does he know? He'd give a number nine pill to cure the shits."

ATKINS PUSHED HIS men and their wards on as hard as he dared, driven by the awful, insistent gnashing and drumming. Ahead of them across the plain Atkins could see the hills start to rise as they ran towards the valley. From their current position, the stronghold was still out of sight, beyond the spur.

"Who's the replacement that knows iddy umpty?"

Mercy smirked. "That'll be Chalky."

Atkins hung his head. "Bloody hell."

Chalky was summoned.

"I want you to get your mirror out and send a message to the hill-top OP. Warn the dozy buggers, if they haven't already seen them, that there's an entire Chatt army headed their way. I reckon we're only an half an hour or so ahead of the bastards, if that."

"Yes, Corporal!" he said snapping a salute and turning smartly to carry out his orders.

Atkins groaned. "Blood and sand, anyone'd think I'd just gazetted him."

He felt a tug at his leg. Tearing his gaze from the ominous dust across the veldt, he looked down to see a young Urman child pulling at his trousers. He looked around for a parent. His eyes met those of a fair-haired Urman woman, who beckoned the child away from him. It was only when he looked again, as the child threw himself round her legs, that he noticed the roundness of her belly. She was with child. A desperate longing filled him, an ache he could not ease.

THE HILLS GREW larger, although much more slowly than Atkins would have liked. At last, they rounded the foothill and came to the valley mouth. He heard the faint, reassuring sound of a bugle on the wind.

Prof slapped Nobby on the back and they began marching with renewed vigour towards the mouth of the valley. "There you go, lad. Home soon."

Atkins stopped and counted his men past, along with forty-three Urmen.

"Come on! Get a move on. We haven't got all day," he urged.

The party made for the encampment at the double, while the noise behind them droned on incessantly until he wanted to stop his ears up.

They reached one of the main paths radiating out from the stronghold, trampled down by the passing of many feet. Through the tube grass, the odd blood-red poppy bloom caught his eye, until they found themselves walking through a drift of poppies populating the charred cordon sanitaire.

Atkins could see frantic activity now as, beyond the wire entanglements, platoons moved up communications trenches to man the fire trench. All along the front line, barrels of guns and tips of bayonets flashed cold in the light as the NCOs bellowed orders.

Over to his left, he heard the impatient putter of the aeroplane's motor as it ran up. At each new sight, each new sound, his optimism that they could hold the line grew.

The clashing beat of the massed Khungarrii army's approach began to echo off the valley sides, amplifying it and momentarily dousing his confidence.

He had to stop and get his bearings.

"Well, don't just stand there, Corporal!" bellowed a familiar voice. Sergeant Hobson beckoned from the trench parapet beyond the wire weed entanglement. He pointed to a section some hundred yards along to his right.

Wire weed had been trained over a small wooden tunnel to provide a temporary sally port under a ten-yard-deep stretch of entanglement. The wire weed writhed lethargically as Atkins ushered the Urmen through. They had to crawl on their hands and knees through the tunnel. For every Urman that stopped, getting clothes or skin caught on the spreading weeds, for every child that had to be bawled at and pushed through the barbed thorns, the Khungarrii came closer. At length, the last of the Urmen were through and were being escorted back to the safety of the trenches and the encampment beyond. He glanced back over his shoulder to see the Khungarrii army stretching to fill the entire valley mouth.

Without warning, the wooden tunnel collapsed, the wire weed falling to the ground on top of it. Some nervous private, whether through fear or incompetence, had yanked the shoring struts that held up the tunnel. Their way back to the trenches was blocked.

1 Section were stranded in No Man's Land, between their own front line and the approaching Khungarrii army.

BACK BEHIND THE lines, in one of the tented Casualty Clearing Stations, Nurse Edith Bell and Nellie Abbott, the FANY, prepared for the first waves of wounded to come in, setting out trays of clean field dressings commandeered from soldier's kits and bandages made from boiling old ones and cutting up the flannel shirts of the deceased.

"So how are you and Alfie the tanker getting on?" asked Edith casually.

Nellie scowled at the insinuation. "That's Mister Perkins to you. We're good pals we are, and don't you go getting other ideas," she protested, before confiding, "but he is nice, isn't he? And I do worry about him so. The *Ivanhoe* was due back yesterday. It only has a range of twenty-three miles on full tanks of petrol, and—"

"Goodness, Nellie, if only you could hear yourself. You sound like a man. It isn't feminine to talk about things like that. No one will thank you for it."

"Perkins will."

"But you can do better than that, Nellie."

"What if I don't want to?"

"Well, on your head be it."

"I ain't too worried, though. He's in the safest place, isn't he? Nothing can get to him in there. That's why Everson sends 'em out, ain't it?"

An orderly thrust his head into the tent.

"Nurse Bell, it's the shell-shock patients. They've got the wind up, well, more than usual. I can't do nuffin' with them. They'll respond to you."

Edith glanced at Nellie. They both looked over at Captain Lippett, the Medical Officer, who was deep in conversation with Sister Fenton.

"You'd better watch it, Edi. You know how Lippy feels about the poor souls."

Edith shot him a disapproving glance. "Oh, I've been well apprised of his feelings towards them on several occasions. He may not care for them, but someone has to."

Lippett was dismissive of the shell-shock victims. It was all down to low morale, as far as he was concerned. Even the Urmen gave them a wide berth, believing them possessed by malign spirits. She didn't agree. She'd been through her own traumas; the thought of Jeffries still made her shudder. She bore the mental scars and empathised with those whose minds crumpled under the weight of their experiences.

"Go," Nellie said, with a brief smile and a nod. "We can cope for the moment, but be quick. If you're not here when the wounded start coming in you'll be for the high jump. If Lippett asks I'll tell him you've gone to an Aid Post." She turned to the hovering orderly. "Stanton, get in here and help me, then."

Edith put down her tray and stepped smartly out of the tent.

The rhythmic noise of the Khungarrii chittering gave her chills and she kept her head down, not daring to look as she walked briskly across to the barbed wire compound. Nicknamed the Bird Cage, it had been constructed as a temporary solution along the same specifications as a large POW compound, but was still in use months later, much to Edith's chagrin. There always seemed to be more important things to do. Still, at least now there was a crude wooden hut at one end, rather than tents to provide shelter, and some little comfort to those that would use it. Others preferred the familiarity of the dugout at the other end.

In here, thirty-odd men had been abandoned by the meagre medical staff at the moment they needed help most, unable to cope. Some were trying to hide under blankets. Others flung themselves at the barbed wire in an attempt to escape. Others just sat weeping and howling, covering their ears, or jerking and twitching uncontrollably. Some had arrived on the planet like this, the bombardments of the Somme proving too much. Others had joined them here since, the shock of their predicament proving too much for their already fragile minds.

Lieutenant Everson had often asked her to stop them howling and wailing as it was distracting the men. It made them uncomfortable; the Bird Cage was a visible reminder of their frailties and fears, failure as men under horrific conditions. But it was not failure, not as she saw it, and it certainly wasn't cowardice.

A number of new cases had been referred to her, unable to cope with the strangeness and violence of the new world around them. One of the triggers for shell-shock had been the unrelenting artillery barrages, the sustained bombardment and the inability to do anything about it. Here, there were no minniewerfers or five-nines, but when the very landscape around you proffered a sustained barrage of unpleasant and painful experiences, when any plant or creature might try to kill you and, more often than not, succeed, to some it was much the same. Those that weathered the Hun artillery with chirpy good humour or dogged willpower could crumble here, the sight of the alien sky above them sending them into the most fearful funks.

Entrance was gained though a single gate set into the barbed wire fence. Everson had allowed the posting of a single sentry. "You!" Edith called him as she approached. "Help me get them into the hut. And be gentle."

A few allowed themselves to be herded towards the hut. Others were too physically incapable of moving by themselves, too paralysed by fear.

She dropped on her haunches by Private Miller. He was trying to claw a hole in the ground to hide, his fingers now raw and bloody as he scraped away at the hard earth, heedless of the pain and driven by a desperate desire to flee. She grasped his wrists gently.

"Shhh. It's all right. You're safe. Safe. Come with me."

He looked up at her with a vague recognition. Her window of opportunity was slim, before he slipped back into whatever nightmare he'd been trapped in. "Come on," she said, lifting him up. He acquiesced calmly, but she could feel the tremors through his arms. She led him towards the hut, distracting him every time he flinched or his eyes flicked towards the front line, muttering comforting maternal words as she led him step by step towards the relative safety of the hut, away from the clamour of the oncoming battle.

FROM THE FIRE trench, Lieutenant Everson scanned the alien army in his binoculars, chewing his lip. Every so often, the purple black of the huge slow larval beasts blotted out his view for a moment only for the advancing scentirrii to appear, as he continued his sweep, gnashing their mandibles and striking their chitinous thorax plates with their weapons.

The men called those great beasts 'battlepillars.' They were twice as high as an elephant and twenty to thirty yards long, making up the vanguard of the Chatt army. Purple and black in colour, with fearsome-looking yellow markings on their faces, their bodies were covered with chitinous sections covered with defensive spines. A rider stood behind each head in a howdah-type affair, a canopied box, reins running down to the battlepillars' head and fixed in some manner to their mandibles.

Along the beasts' lengths were slung long boat-cradles carrying yet more Khungarrii scentirrii armed with electric lances. They may not have had tanks, but these beasts weren't far off.

And speaking of the tank, where the bloody hell was it? The Khungarrii thought it was some great demon or god of the dead or something. If the tank had been here they wouldn't have dared attack. Or perhaps that was the point. Maybe they were attacking because it wasn't here. Which meant they must have been watching all this time.

Everson realised that there was the very real danger that the Chatts would try to flank and surround the encampment. He would have to hit them hard and fast to dissuade them.

He was depending on his machine guns. Normally that wouldn't have been a problem—the field of fire from their emplacements covered the entire valley mouth—but their ammunition supplies were severely limited. He'd only have one good shot at this.

Since the dwindling ammunitions reserves were rationed, and even he daren't cross Company Quartermaster Sergeant Slacke, he had taken to wearing the dress sword that his father had bought for him. Although only ever meant for ceremonial use, it was, nonetheless, a real sword. He wasn't looking forward to the day he would have to use it. He hoped it wouldn't be today.

CAUGHT IN THE poppy field, Atkins ordered his men to take up positions in front of the wire weed entanglements and find hasty cover, if they could.

The Khungarrii battlepillars began to advance, crunching their way over tube grass. Behind the great warbeasts marched the first wave of the Khungarrii assault. Thankfully, they didn't seem to possess any long-range weapons of any kind. Atkins and his section had their guns, but they'd been on patrol and in a skirmish.

"Bugger!" muttered Mercy. "I've only got a magazine left."

Gazette glanced over and smiled grimly. "Better not miss, then."

Here they were again. Same old same old. It never changed. Atkins nodded back and shifted his attention to the great battlepillars that lumbered towards them.

The wire weed behind them, he thought, was going to present as little problem to these creatures as Hun barbed wire did to their own tanks. In the pit of his stomach Atkins felt the same fear that the Huns must have felt when the tanks first came crawling out of the Somme mud towards them, crushing everything in their path.

Behind them, he could see the first ranks of Khungarrii scentirrii begin to charge, their mandibles open.

He felt his bowels churn.

"This is it, lads," he said gravely. "Pick your targets."

He could hear Nobby whimper and Prof's soothing tone trying to calm the boy. He briefly remembered Ginger. That seemed a lifetime ago. He focused on the wave of advancing Chatts marching across the poppy field towards them.

As they marched through the flowers, the closed ranks of disciplined scentirrii began stumbling about. They lost their measured step. The line broke. They began to mill about in confusion as though blinded, like chlorine gas victims.

"What's happening to them?" asked Prof.

"No idea," replied Mercy. "But it looks like they're funking it."

Gazette sneered. "That makes 'em easier to pick off."

Others had the same idea. In answer, a volley of NCOs' orders rang out along the outer front line trench. The air filled with the crackle of gunfire and the reassuring smell of cordite and the Chatts began to fall.

A jubilant cheer went up from the trenches behind them, "The Chatts are funking it. We've got 'em, lads. We've got 'em!"

Whatever was affecting the scentirrii, it didn't seem to be affecting the battlepillars. Atkins' stomach shrank to a hard knot in his belly as one of the beasts, its great mandibles scything through the tube grass, advanced implacably towards them.

EVERSON WATCHED THE centre of the Khungarrii attack collapse. On the flanks, the Chatts broke into a charge. The Lewis machine gun emplacements raked a line across the first wave and the advance faltered.

Tulliver's Sopwith 1½ Strutter roared low overhead, sweeping along the Khungarrii advance, his machine guns stuttering, enfilading the enemy.

Then, in answer to some unheard, unseen chemical scent command, what was left of the ranks of Chatt scentirrii began to withdraw, all except those in the poppy field, who still staggered round as if in a stupor, unable to obey.

Panning his binoculars across the mass of the Khungarrii army waiting in reserve, Everson caught sight of what he presumed was their general. It watched from the howdah of a large battlepillar that had reared up, its head and front legs resting atop a copse of trees, affording a better view as his mount scissored idly at the foliage with large mandibles.

And he knew he'd met this Chatt before, deep in the nurseries of Khungarr. He almost felt like saluting him, as he had once done with a German officer who appeared above the Hun parapets one morning.

That felt like an age away.

* * *

GAZETTE TOOK MEASURED shots at the electric lancers in the battlepillar's passenger cradles. Three Chatts collapsed, and one fell backwards out of the cradle to land on the ground with a crack. Its companions in the adjacent cradles now turned their attention towards Gazette. Blue streams of electric fire arced from the cradles towards the ground but fell short, incinerating the trampled tube grass.

Gutsy picked the rider off. It fell back, caught awkwardly on the howdah's side by the reins.

Atkins reached into his webbing for a Mills bomb. "Cover me!"

Porgy looked at him. "What the bloody hell are you going to do?"

Atkins grinned and patted Porgy's cap as he got up. "Something stupid."

He dashed off, running in a crouch though the poppies, zigzagging towards another oncoming battlepillar.

Crackling ribbons of blue-white fire arced down around him from the electric lancers.

He pulled the pin from the Mills bomb and threw it. It skittered to a halt in front of the battlepillar.

He didn't wait to see the great armoured larval beast, unperturbed, continue its relentless progress over it. He darted back to his section, where they laid down covering fire.

The grenade exploded beneath the beast, red-hot shrapnel shards slicing up through its vitals. It reared up, exposing a huge wet gaping wound in its soft underbelly, hot organs slopping out as it toppled over to the side. The huge beast crashed down, twitching.

Some of its riders lay crushed beneath its huge bulk. Others though, scrambled to get away from it. Gazette and the others rushed forward through the trampled poppies to mop up those Chatts still left alive.

Around the other side of the battlepillar, thrown yards from its monstrous cracked head, Atkins found the shattered howdah. The contorted body of one Chatt lay on the ground, tangled in a snapped cradle rope and reins.

The howdah's torn silken covering had come adrift from the splintered canopy. There was a rasp of movement from beneath the sheet.

Atkins nodded and he and Gutsy edged towards the cloth. An ivory chitinous arm clawed out from under the breeze-ruffled sheet. Gutsy stepped forward, ready to thrust his bayonet down though the fabric, but Atkins shook his head.

"I don't think it's scentirrii."

He inched towards it. He nodded at Gutsy who drew up his rifle to his shoulder and fixed the shape in his sights.

Atkins caught the cloth and pulled it back with the tip of his bayonet.

The Chatt tried to scuttle away on its back. It wore a white silk sash with knotted tassels and its antennae were broken, but they seemed like old injuries. Its vestigial mid-limbs at its abdomen were scissoring frantically. Atkins had been right. It was not a scentirrii, a Chatt soldier. It was smaller, its carapace a smoother, off-white colour, its head-shell smooth and ovoid. It drew in a deep breath and forced it out through its four finger-like mouth palps as if weaving the air into a crude approximation of human speech.

"This One is Dhuyumirrii. This One does not fight. This One watches, observes."

Atkins frowned, but didn't let down his guard. Something about it was familiar. Chatts all looked the same, true, but the broken antennae?

"I... know you," he said. "The edifice. Jeffries. You were there. I saved you from the gas. You called yourself..." But the name evaded his memory.

"This One is called Chandar," said the Chatt.

Gutsy turned, bayoneted and shot a charging scentirrii. "Only, this is no place for a reunion," he warned.

Chatts began to swarm around them. The section fell on the confused Khungarrii with bayonets and clubs and succeeded in driving them back.

"Better give us a hand then," said Atkins, helping Chandar up. "'Cause we've just got ourselves a prisoner."

An arc of blue fire earthed by Gutsy's feet, and he turned and fired. A Chatt fell dead.

"He'd better be bloody important," he said.

There was a sporadic ripple of jubilant cheers from the trenches behind them. The main Khungarrii force was withdrawing, but the confused Chatts stumbling around 1 Section in the poppy field still posed a threat.

He heard Sergeant Hobson's voice cut through the cheers.

"Atkins, get out of there. Make for the farmhouse!" he ordered.

Atkins looked along the length of wire entanglement behind them. Over to the right he saw the front of the old Poulet farmhouse flanked by the wire entanglements. Heavily shelled on the Somme, it was now a forward observation post. The ground floor had been converted into a machine gun emplacement, while the first floor acted as an observation platform. It might be their only chance.

One of the milling scentirrii rushed Atkins with a long, barbed spear. Confused they might be, but they still recognised an enemy. Atkins thrust Chandar back towards Gutsy, ducked under the spear thrust and brought his bayonet up, burying it deep between the Chatt's mandibles.

Running at a crouch, the section made for the farmhouse.

Behind them, he heard the soldiers in the trench open fire at the crowd of dazed, stumbling Chatts.

Atkins could see the muzzle of a Vickers machine gun poking out of the window of the farmhouse. Past it, he saw angled wooden doors leading down to the old fruit cellar.

"Lance Corporal Atkins, 1 Section 2 Platoon, C Company!" he called out to the machine gun section inside. "We've got a prisoner. We're coming in through the cellar. Cover us!"

"Stoppage!"

"Well get it cleared, man, you know the drill!"

Bloody Nora, the day just gets better, Atkins thought as he shot the bolt and flung open the cellar doors.

"In," he yelled. "Make for the sap at the rear of the house!"

Prof, Chalky, Nobby, Pot Shot, Gazette, Mercy and Porgy tumbled into the dark hole.

Gutsy pushed Chandar down into the cellar and Atkins followed.

A shadow fell over him as he hit the floor. He turned, rifle at the ready, as a scentirrii sprung through the cellar opening at him. It was dead before it fell on his bayonet, a bullet hole through its horned flat facial plate. Gazette was covering them from the cellar door across the low room.

Gutsy ushered Chandar through.

Another scentirrii appeared at the cellar opening. Crouching, spider-like, it let out a challenging hiss. Atkins pulled his trigger but his magazine was empty.

Gazette fired again, sending it spinning out of sight.

"We need to get these doors shut," Atkins said.

A third Chatt sought to clamber in. Gazette killed that, too, and a fourth crawled over the bodies of its comrades to reach them. That, too, fell. No more attempted to come through.

Atkins steeled himself, reached out and pulled the cellar doors shut, jamming them closed with the handle of a broom that he found stood in the corner.

Above, he heard the machine gun stutter start up again.

"About bloody time!" he spat. He clapped Gazette on the shoulder. "Thanks."

He staggered up the worn stone cellar steps and out of the house, following his men down the sap trench towards the front line.

Alarmed by the appearance of Chandar in the fire trench, several Tommies swung their Enfields in the Chatt's direction as 1 Section emerged from the sap.

"It's all right, he's with us," said Atkins. He looked around and saw a private with a runner's brassard. "You. Tell Lieutenant Everson that we have someone he'll want to meet."

CHAPTER THREE
"For God's Sake Don't Send Me..."

THE HEAVILY SANDBAGGED command post looked out over the lines of trenches, breastworks and earthworks now crawling with Pennine Fusiliers as they dispatched straggling and retreating Chatts. Linseed lancers of the RAMC scuttled about with stretchers, collecting the wounded and carrying them back to the aid posts and hospital, while flocks of carrion creatures were already circling and descending on the bodies. Frustrated 'hell hounds,' smelling the blood, could be heard howling across the valley.

Lieutenant Everson looked out through a loophole with his binoculars, across the wire weed entanglements and the bodies that hung on them, already being ensnared and sapped of their life by the slow-moving thorny creepers tightening around them. His gaze didn't rest there, but was drawn out across the veldt where he watched the Khungarrii retreat.

They had repulsed them, but only because of their guns, and their ammunition was rapidly running out. Of course, the Chatts didn't know that, but at some point, the Khungarrii would attack again. No doubt they could hold off several such attacks. His counterpart was exceedingly clumsy, tactically. With their short-range weapons, the alien scentirrii seemed to be much more proficient in small police actions, defending their edifice and the like, but the growing confidence evident in recent raids on Urmen enclaves showed his nemesis was a fast learner and damned if he wasn't learning it all from the Pennines.

The observation posts on the valley hilltops had reported no sign of a support column. They must have been foraging food along the way. Nor were there any signs of siege machines. So they didn't see this action lasting very long. A short brutal engagement, then, to stamp out their enemies.

However, if the Chatts were to lay siege to the stronghold and this turned into another war of attrition, then God help them. They had barely held their own against the Hun on the Somme. This time, without reinforcements, without logistical support, they couldn't hope to hold out against such a superior force. Everson gave them a fortnight at best, a month at the outside. The Pennines' own foraging parties had to range further and further to find food and wood. Even with the help of the refugee Urmen, feeding this many men was becoming a nightmare without some degree of successful agriculture. He couldn't allow a siege to happen. He needed to deliver a swift, decisive blow. Something that would have the Khungarrii give them a wide berth in future. To do that, he needed to know more about them, and he recognised that the captured Chatt represented a slim opportunity.

"Is this absolutely necessary?" asked Padre Rand nervously, from the other side of the sandbagged room. He'd asked the padre here because he'd had dealings with them in Khungarr.

"Yes, Padre, I'm afraid it is. But don't worry. You're only here to observe. It won't touch you. I've taken precautions."

The padre, though, seemed little mollified by this.

Sergeant Hobson appeared in the doorway. "The prisoner is here, sir."

Everson turned from the unsettling sight of the Chatt army regrouping out on the veldt. "Show him in, Hobson."

Atkins, accompanied by a grim Napoo, escorted the captured Chatt into the dugout. It hobbled into the room with a lopsided gait that suggested old injuries and new pains. Everson felt a cold shock of recognition. Most Chatts looked the same to him, even now after all this time, but this one, even with its featureless white facial plate, was unmistakable. Its worn stumps of antennae moved with feeble jerks like a broken clockwork toy. This was no mere Chatt soldier. This was the Chatt that Jeffries had held hostage in Khungarr. Everson remembered that the damn thing had refused to help them when they were trying to find a way out of the labyrinthine tunnels. But there was so much information it might give them, not least about Jeffries' last movements and intentions. If it would talk. But every moment it was here it could be gathering information about them; numbers, layout, weapons.

Atkins stood smartly to attention, by the prisoner. Sergeant Hobson brought up the rear of the escort party and stood, stiff and formal, behind the Chatt, his eyes never leaving it. In the far corner was Padre Rand, backed against the sandbagged wall, his hands clutching his bible to his chest as though it were a shield, his lips moving silently in prayer, his eyes following the Chatt warily as it looked around. Even captured, its curiosity seemed insatiable.

"Your herd is truly different from that of other Urmen," it said, in its breathless, monotone way. "They build their flimsy dwellings on the ground. I had heard reports from raiding scentirrii that Tohmii dwellings and burrowings imitate those of the Ones. This structure is crude, but strange and wondrous nonetheless."

Everson stepped toward the arthropod and held out a hand.

"I'm Lieutenant James Charles Everson, Acting Commanding Officer of the 13th Battalion of the Pennine Fusiliers. We've met," he added pointedly.

The Chatt finished surveying the room before answering. "Yes. This One is Chandar, gon-dhuyumirrii, olfactotum to Sirigar, liya-dhuyumirrii of the Khungarrii Shura." It appeared to swallow air and force it out, as if having to shape words with organs not meant for human speech. "In gratitude this One offers you a blessing in the name of GarSuleth," it said, opening its arms, tilting its head back and opening its mandibles.

There was a loud click as Sergeant Hobson cocked a Webley revolver and pointed it at the back of the Chatt's head.

"I've read the reports," said Everson. "Attempt to spray anything—acid, a soporific mist—and Sergeant Hobson here will shoot you. Is that understood?"

The creature lowered its head, relaxed its mouthparts and sank down on its legs in a submissive posture. "This One intended no threat."

Everson offered it a seat. The Khungarrii looked at the wooden chair incomprehensibly. He shrugged, then sat down behind his desk. "I suppose a cup of tea is out of the question, then?" He gave a nod of dismissal in the lance corporal's direction. "Thank you, Atkins."

Atkins looked at the sergeant for confirmation.

"Off you go, lad."

"Sir." Atkins saluted and snapped his heels together.

There was a strangled gasp as the Chatt abandoned its half-hearted attempt to sit, and regurgitated air. Its mouth palps seemed to knit the human words laboriously. "This Urman stays."

"I beg your pardon?" said Everson.

"The Urman stays," insisted Chandar, rearing up.

Recognising the aggressive stance, Napoo drew his short sword and took a step towards the Chatt. Everson held up a palm to stop him. Napoo relented, but remained tensed, ready to spring.

"Why?" asked Everson of the creature. "Why him?"

"That Urman saved this One from the mandibles of Skarra when your Jeffries would have me wrapped in clay and rolled into the underworld. This spinning, this same Urman spared this One again. These acts are of significance to this One. They are acts of Kurda, a basic tenet of colonyhood."

If it made the damn thing more predisposed to talk, then that was fine with him. "Very well," said Everson. He waved his hand and indicated that Atkins should stay. "At ease, Lance Corporal."

"Sir." Atkins looked uncomfortable as he stood at rest. He glanced at Hobson, who just shrugged.

Its request acceded to, Chandar relaxed its stance.

"Now, see here," Everson began. "We will not surrender to you. You will not take us prisoners to be mesmerised as slaves in your colony. We will not bow to any tyrant's yoke."

"It is too late for that," said Chandar. "Not since the days of Wuljungur has Khungarr been invaded. Now, in retribution, Sirigar has chemically decreed that you and any wild Urmen caught within our sovereign burri are to be expelled. Failing that, you are to be culled to preserve the sanctity and safety of Khungarr. Those are your choices."

There was no choice at all and Everson knew it. They could not leave this stronghold, this circle of the Somme earth that came with them. It was all they had left of Earth. It seemed they had their backs against the wall.

"We forewarned your emissary Jeffries of these eventualities," continued the Chatt.

Everson shifted forward in his chair. Atkins, too, stared at the Chatt. Only Hobson remained unperturbed.

"Jeffries?"

"He promised to deliver the Tohmii, your herd, to us. You would have been accepted into our colony, given food, shelter, purpose, treated as our own. It is Kurda."

"He had no damn right to speak on our behalf," replied Everson with measured fury. "No damn right at all. Man was a snake in our midst. He's not one of us. He's—" He searched for a word the arthropod might understand.

"Outcast," offered Napoo gruffly.

"Outcast," repeated Everson, with a degree of satisfaction at the sound of the word.

"Nonetheless, an agreement was made and breached," said Chandar.

"But at what price? What was it that Jeffries wanted from you? What was worth so much to him that he was willing to sell the rest of us into slavery?"

The Chatt's posture seemed to slump. "An old heresy thought long forgotten," it wheezed.

"Croatoan," suggested Everson.

"Yes."

He put his elbows on his desk and leant forward, hands clasped. "Tell me about this Croatoan."

The Chatt's mandible parted as it hissed, its mouth palps flapping like windsocks in the brief rush of air. "The Urman Jeffries asked the same thing before committing the most unforgivable transgression in destroying our sacred repository. Therein lay the basis of our laws, our beliefs. Ancient aromas that bottled the wisdom of generations. Tunnels can be rebuilt, chambers repaired, but the Tohmii have left us dispossessed. Robbed. The Redolence of Spiras gone forever."

The Chatt ran out of air, its human vocabulary tumbling into the incoherent chittering of its own tongue. It seemed to Everson that the thing was cursing.

"That's right. Jeffries. Not us. Jeffries tried to kill us, too. You were there in that chamber. You saw."

"Yes. The fact that this One owes its life to this Urman is one of the few mitigating circumstances in your favour."

"Yes, Kurda. You said." Everson looked to Atkins standing beside the creature. Their eyes met briefly. Atkins' face flushed and he shuffled uncomfortably. Everson felt a glimmer of almost paternal pride. He had been right about Atkins. But to think that their salvation might hinge on that single act of altruism, well, that was a very slender thread indeed.

Chandar took another hoarse breath. "There is yet another reason Sirigar wants you wiped out. Khungarr is mired in tradition. The coming of the Tohmii has ignited an old debate, long feared and unsought by some. The Unguent of Huyurarr warns against the coming of a Great Corruption. When you made your camp on our burri, the Breath of GarSuleth heralded your arrival with the stench of death and putrescence. Sirigar feared that this was the fulfilment of the long-held prophecy. We sought to discover your intentions. You resisted the will of the Ones unlike any other Urman herd we had encountered. Then by your actions you declared yourself a threat to Khungarr and your fate was sealed. Now, through your own actions, we are compelled to seek your destruction. This is regrettable."

"We won't surrender, you know. This is our land and we will defend it to the last man."

"You cannot hope to defeat the massed army of Khungarr," said Chandar.

Scraping his chair back, Everson stood now. "You're not up against savages here. You're up against a battalion of His Majesty King George's army. We've faced the worst that Kaiser Bill could throw at us and survived. And you forget," he added, "we are protected by Skarra, your god of the dead." That the Khungarrii had mistaken the appearance of His Majesty's Land Ship *Ivanhoe* as their god of the underworld was a work of providence and one he had been quite willing to take advantage of at the time, but how long could they keep up the pretence?

"Then where is he?" said Chandar looking around and gesturing to the empty air. "Why does Skarra not come to your aid? The army of Khungarr has retreated. They are waiting to see if he appears. If he does not then they will attack again and carry out the will of GarSuleth as set forth by Sirigar."

"Thank you, Chandar. You've been quite candid. Sergeant, take the prisoner to the guardhouse. Keep to the trenches. Make sure it doesn't see more than it has to."

He watched as Hobson, Atkins and Napoo marshalled the prisoner and escorted it from the dugout. He was surprised to see the padre shaking, as if the Chatt had stirred deep, unwelcome memories of his incarceration.

"Padre, go. We'll talk later."

The padre smiled thankfully with an anxious nod, not trusting himself to speak, and hurried from the post.

So it was war, then. And where *was* that bloody tank? It seemed to Everson that Chandar was not entirely convinced of their claim regarding the tank but was unwilling to question the sanctity of Skarra without further proof. If only he had it. The *Ivanhoe* should have been back days ago. He pulled out a packet of Woodbines from his pocket and was dismayed to see only two battered cigarettes left. Once they were gone, they were gone. He had no more left. He doubted the men did either, except the hoarders. Evans, his platoon's best scrounger, could probably lay his hands on some. Maybe he should ask. He pulled one out, tamped it on the desk, lit it and took a long luxurious drag before exhaling, staring absently at the haze of blue smoke, momentarily lost in thought.

Their arrival had set off ripples across this world, and those ripples were still spreading with unforeseen consequences. The Pennines, it seemed, had spent a good deal of time on this world unwittingly digging a deeper and deeper hole for themselves. Everson hoped it didn't turn out to be their grave.

AMID THE CHAOS of the Aid Post, Edith was trying to hold down and calm a wounded young soldier. He seemed about sixteen years old, barely older than her younger brother and almost certainly not old enough to join up. He lay writhing and whimpering on the mat before her. Nellie had just finished bathing and bandaging the eyes of a lad caught out by an acid spit, and Edith caught her attention. "Nellie!"

They unbuttoned his tunic and ripped open the blood-soaked shirt. The spear must have been barbed. It went in cleanly enough but ripped his guts out on the withdrawal. His belly was a mess. Nellie applied pressure to the wound with a field bandage, but he wouldn't lie still. He thrashed about in pain, sobbing openly. Blood pulsed up and soaked the field bandage; in moments it was sopping. She discarded it in a tray and pressed another to the wound.

He needed surgery, but there were several other surgical cases backed up ahead of him and it was unlikely this boy would survive long enough to make it to the table.

"Mother!" he cried, through snivelling sobs. "I don't want to die. I don't want to die."

"Shush now," said Edith, taking hold of his hand and trying to look him in the eye, but he kept throwing his head from side to side. "Look at me," she said firmly. "Look at me." He turned his face to hers but he no longer saw her.

"Charlotte, is that you?" he said with relief, spluttering through the blood.

Edith clasped his hand more firmly so that he would know someone was there.

"Yes," she said. "I'm here."

"I love you," he muttered.

"I love you, too," said Edith.

He started to smile but the life left him before he could complete it.

Edith felt the corners of her eyes begin to sting with tears. She blinked them away fiercely. It always got to her, the little white lie. The one nurses always told the dying. In her time she had been mothers, sisters, wives, sweethearts, anyone, so long as they eased the passing. Edith slipped his hand from hers and placed it across his chest. There were no words left to say. Just a job to do.

NELLIE CLEARED UP the blood-soaked bandages and left Edith to lay out the body, before summoning the orderlies to remove it to where the padre would give it the Last Rites as they cleared the space for the next poor soul. Nellie stepped outside to where a brazier burned, tipped the bloodied pads into the fire and returned to the aid tent.

Nellie was looking for her next patient when Half Pint hobbled into the hospital tent on his peg leg, clutching the thigh above it, his face ashen as he looked wildly around. His gaze latched on Nellie.

"Gawd help me, it's my leg!" he cried, limping towards her.

"Private Nicholls, you'll have to wait. There are more urgent cases," she said, only half listening as she glanced around, looking for assistance. Poilus, an Urman of Napoo's clan, was helping to bring more wounded in, some walking, others carried in on blood-soaked stretchers.

"But the pain, Nurse. Shooting pains right up me thigh. Sharp they are, like bloody red hot needles," he griped.

His forehead was beaded with sweat. He gritted his teeth and a grunt escaped his lips as his hand clutched his thigh. He lost his balance and collapsed into her.

"A little help here!" she called as she staggered under his weight.

Edi and Poilus came to her rescue. By now Half Pint's breath was coming in ragged pants and his eyelids fluttered as he struggled to keep them open, his head lolling back.

Nellie directed the pair to an empty straw mat, where they laid him down. She put a hand on his forehead and tutted. "He has a fever. The stump is probably infected. I told him not to wear that peg leg of his for more than an hour or so at a time, but he was so bloomin' proud of it. Said the pain would give him something to grouse about."

"Well let's get it off him," said Edith as she began to cut his trouser leg away to reveal the stump. She clapped a hand to her mouth. "Oh, dear Lord!"

Pale roots sprouted from the inert black wood of the carved peg leg, reaching up and entwining themselves around the pink stump before sinking into the flesh of Half Pint's thigh.

"Bloomin' hell!" said Nellie. "It's growing into him!"

"Corpsewood," said Poilus.

"What?"

"It is corpsewood. It feeds on dead or rotting flesh, but will eat living things if it can. We must get it off him. It will kill him."

Nellie knelt and, with shaking hands, unbuckled the leather straps that kept the false leg in place. Gingerly she waggled the peg leg loose, attached now only by the roots that fed deep into Half Pint's thigh.

Edith made to cut them with a scalpel in order to remove the wooden leg.

"No!" said Poilus. "We must withdraw every root cleanly, unbroken. You cannot leave any part of it in him or it will continue to grow." He pressed his thumb against the flesh of the upper leg, feeling for the roots, finding how far they had penetrated. "We are lucky. It has not grown in too far yet. We may still save him. We must ease the roots from his legs, slowly. Do not let them break."

Edith placed a strip of old leather belt in Half Pint's mouth for him to bite on and save his tongue, then leant herself across Half Pint's torso that he might not witness the operation and to hold him down should he struggle. She nodded at Poilus. He used the discarded length of puttee, wrapped it around the peg leg to avoid touching it, and took a grip. He applied a steady pressure, drawing it back. Half Pint twisted and grunted as he bit down on the leather, hard enough to leave teeth marks.

Nellie's nimble fingers eased out each of the dozen or so long thin roots in turn as Polius continued to pull. Eventually, the last thin tendril-like tips were pulled free, writhing weakly as they sought flesh to burrow into. She nodded, and Poilus took the corpsewood peg leg, dangling six inches of bloody roots, their tips writhing feebly. Like some kind of changeling child from a fairy tale, Nellie thought with a shudder. She watched as he strode outside and dropped the thing into the brazier. The flames expanded to greet it, burning a blue-green colour. The corpsewood gave off a high-pitched noise, as if it was squealing in pain.

It was only after that she thought perhaps she should have preserved the specimen for Captain Lippett, who was striving to catalogue this world's flora and fauna, but it was too late now.

Poilus returned and sank down on his haunches beside Nellie and gave the feverish Half Pint a long, appraising look. "He was lucky. It was old wood. We got it out of him in time. He should live. I will get one of our women to make up a poultice for his leg to stop the fever, though what fool thought to use it in such a manner I cannot think. Even the smallest piece can sprout roots and begin to grow again if it finds a living source. Strapping it to someone is as good as killing them." He shook his head slowly. "I wonder how you Tohmii are all still alive? You treat us as if we are the children, yet it is you who need your hands holding." He stood up, still shaking his head to himself as he left the tent.

There was another influx of walking wounded. Edith stood up and walked over to them.

Half Pint grasped Nellie's hand. "You wouldn't be a good girl and fetch me my lucky harmonica from by the typewriter, would you?" he said, his voice faint and hoarse. "And tell the Loot—tell him... I'm sorry but I think I'll be a little late with dinner tonight."

It was nearly an hour later before Nellie was able to beg a fag break from Sister Fenton and slip away to let the lieutenant know what had happened to his batman.

In the days that followed, she often wished Sister Fenton had kept her back.

SERGEANT HOBSON ENTERED the command post. Everson looked up from his desk.

"The Chatts are still just sat there, sir. They don't seem to be doing anything."

"They're waiting for a 'sign,' Sergeant, and I bloody well wish we had one to give them."

"The tank, sir?"

"As you so rightly say, Hobson, the tank." He tapped his pencil on the desk and came to a decision. "I want to see Lance Corporal Atkins. I've got a job for him and his Black Hand Gang."

"Very good, sir. I'll send him along directly." The sergeant turned sharply and left.

Everson was about to take another look at Jeffries' journal when there was a polite knock on the doorjamb.

"Come."

Nellie Abbott stepped inside, saluted and stood to attention. Unlike the Nurses, the FANYs were run along military lines.

"Yes, Miss Abbott, what can I do for you?"

"Begging your pardon, Lieutenant, it's about Half Pint—I mean Private Nicholls, sir."

"Well, if you're looking for him, I don't know where the devil he is," said Everson, vaguely frustrated.

"Sir, he's in the aid post."

Everson was a little shocked. "He's not injured, is he?"

"It's his leg, sir.

"Oh, Christ, the poor bloke. Not both now?"

"Oh. Oh, no, sir. No, the other one, the peg leg, sir. It tried to eat him."

Everson wasn't sure he heard right. "I beg your pardon?"

"It tried to eat him, it did, sir, but he's all right now. He's resting. But he won't be stomping around like Long John Silver for a while, sir. Said to tell you that dinner would be a little late and could I fetch him his lucky harmonica? Said he left it on his desk, sir."

Everson slumped back in his chair with a sigh and waved her in the direction of the small clerk's office. She gave a little curtsey and went through.

Everson ran a hand through his hair. There was another knock.

"Come."

Sergeant Hopkins and Lance Corporal Atkins entered.

"You wanted to see me, sir?" said Atkins.

"Yes, Atkins. Got a job for you. I wouldn't ask, but our backs are against the wall on this one."

"Aren't they always, sir?"

"Hmm. The fact is, Atkins, the tank is overdue. The *Ivanhoe* should have been back several days ago. And frankly if it had, we might not be in this mess with those bloody Chatts camped on our doorstep. The *Ivanhoe* has a limited speed and a limited range and, by all accounts, it should have returned yesterday. Now, either it's in trouble or it's broken down or the crew are injured or dead..."

There was an audible gasp from the back of the room. Nellie Abbott stood in the small doorframe to the next room, a harmonica in her hand. She leant against the doorframe.

"Miss Abbott, I'm sorry," said Everson. "I didn't realise you were still there."

"Injured?" she said. "Then let me go, too, sir. I can help."

"You, Abbott? No, sorry. Out of the question. If nothing else, Sister Fenton would certainly have something to say about it."

"But you said yourself they might be injured, sir," she said in earnest. "I've got first aid training. And I can drive, sir. I ain't afraid of what's out there. Sister can spare me. There's the orderlies and the vets, sir. I won't hardly be missed."

Damn the girl, but she had a point. The tank crew were the only ones who could drive the blasted thing. If they were injured... And she could drive ambulances, so she might be able to help if the crew were down. Damn it. Why did they have to be so bloody logical? "Very well," he said reluctantly. "But only if Sister Fenton agrees."

"Thank you, sir! You won't regret it."

"But, sir..." protested Atkins. "I don't want to be responsible for a woman, sir."

"Do as the lieutenant, says, son," said Hobson, leaning in with a stage whisper.

"'Only' Atkins, how dare you!" retorted Nellie. "I can do anything you can. Don't treat me like no porcelain doll, then. I'm responsible for myself. Or do you just want me to stay here and cook meals, wash uniforms and tend wounds, is that it? "

"No!" said Atkins defensively. "That's not what I meant. It's just that—"

Everson coughed. "It's done, Atkins. She goes with you. I need you to find the tank and its crew, both in one piece, and get them back here. We can hang on for a few days, a week maybe. The Chatts think it's their god of the dead; it may be the only thing that can save us. I'm relying on you."

Atkins recovered his composure while Nellie fixed him with a belligerent stare.

"If the tank can be found sir, we'll find it. Leaves a trail a blind man could follow, so we should be able to track it. And we'll bring it back if we have to push it all the way."

The tank weighed twenty-eight tons, so that was highly unlikely, but Everson appreciated the sentiment. "And take Napoo, because Christ knows what you'll find out there and I don't want to lose another patrol.

"And take that Chatt, Chandar, with you. He seems well disposed to you. We can't keep him here and we can't send him back. I have some surprises for his friends and I don't want to take the chance that he's spying."

"But sir—" began Atkins.

"It's done, Atkins. Find that bloody tank. And keep an eye out for Jeffries."

INTERLUDE TWO

Letter from Private Thomas Atkins
to Flora Mullins

17th February 1917

My Dearest Flora,
   Sometime I feel daft sitting here and writing letters that I don't know you'll ever get, but I feel like if I stop writing you'll just drift away and I'll lose you forever. Maybe it would be better not to torment myself, to lay down this burden, to forget that you and Blighty exist at all. Some blokes already have, like so many Hun souvenirs that chaps carry round with them from posting to posting until one day they just become too heavy and they chuck them.
   You may never read these, but while I write them, I feel like I'm talking to you, like I'm close to you. If I ever stop writing, then not only have I lost you but will have lost part of myself, too, so here I sit, carrying on.
   The days have settled into a routine here, although we are having a spot of bother with some of the locals. I don't think they like what we've done with the place. Mind you, if you saw it you'd hardly recognise it yourself. Lovely new trenches. Dry warm dugouts. It's like the Ritz.
   The new lads in the section seem grand. I do wish Chalky would lay off, though. Not strictly his fault. The others egg him on a bit. I don't know, you do one thing and people go on and on about it. But that's what it's like around here.
   We've got orders to go and find the tank. You can't put anything down around here without it disappearing. Most people blame Mercy when that happens. To be fair, if anything has gone missing he's usually had a hand in it. I don't think they can pin the tank on him this time, though. It's all a bit of puzzle. They should have been back yesterday. Things might have been a lot easier if they had, but there you go, C'est la guerre, as Gutsy says. Still, how hard can it be to find?

   Ever yours
   Thomas

CHAPTER FOUR
"A Wilderness of Ruin..."

Two days earlier...

THE CANYON HADN'T been carved by turbulent river waters. It was a brutal crack, a rift torn suddenly in the skin of this world by some groundquake that sundered the land in ages past. The walls rose almost vertically for hundreds of feet and only in the heat of the day did the alien sun penetrate the bottom-most depths, where great blocks of stone lay strewn where they fell.

The only scraps of vegetation to be seen were large patches of blue-green matter, scattered over the rock-face like lichen, attached to the rock and formed of small blisters of varying sizes that seemed to pulse in direct sunlight, as if breathing. The ones in shadow remained inert, as if asleep. The rocks were pockmarked with shallow circular depressions, where acid from long-vanished blooms had eaten into the surface.

An unremitting rumble filled the rock-strewn canyon, echoing off the walls like some imminent, but never delivered, avalanche as His Majesty's Land Ship *Ivanhoe* crawled along, pitilessly shattering small rocks caught under its tracks into dust. Grey smoke billowed from the roof exhaust to be snatched up by the breeze and dispersed behind it as the armoured behemoth crept and clanked through the rocky terrain as if sniffing out a trail.

Not that the crew could see much from inside, where the heat and fumes were a microcosm of hell. Progress was slow. With no suspension, the tank had reduced its speed to a crawl, not wanting to belly or throw a track.

The machine gunners, Norman and Cecil, squinted through the machine gun loopholes for threats as the rocky walls, partially obscured by dust thrown up by the tracks, rolled by with mesmerising slowness, without incident or interest apart from the blue-green pulsating growths. Cecil took a brief shot at them with the Hotchkiss to see if they'd burst. The rattle of machine gun fire reverberated through the canyon, causing

Lieutenant Mathers to turn in his seat and glare at him.

It also earned him a clip round the back of the head from Jack Tanner, the ex-prize-fighting gunner. It smacked his forehead into the handles of the gun barrel. "Quit that, you dozy mare. You're wasting ammunition," he bellowed above the engine's roar.

For the moment they were riding with hatches open to try and cool the interior. At least without the Hun firing machine guns at them there was no need to wear the stifling splash-masks and bruise helmets, and in the baking heat of the great iron oven, most of them had unbuttoned the coveralls they wore over the trousers, puttees and flannel shirts of their service dress, and undoing the shirts, too.

At the back of the compartment, by the starboard secondary gears, Alfie wiped the sweat from his forehead and tried to keep his focus on the back of the driver's chair from where, every now and again, hand signals for gear changes would come. When he wasn't doing that, he was putting grease on the gears every thirty minutes or so. He caught a glimpse of a small love heart on the engine casing in front of him, drawn by Nellie Abbot's oily finger. He smiled. That was one thing he hadn't bargained on. One of many; this bleeding planet being one of them. But Nellie, what a find she was. She was different. He remembered the first time he met her, here on this world. They had been celebrating their first fresh food and the Fusiliers' commander, Captain Grantham, God rest his soul, had given permission for a bit of a bash.

The tank crew hadn't really socialised with the Fusiliers since they found themselves on this world. They were trained to act as an independent unit and that was the way they liked it. It was part of the attraction of the Machine Gun Corps. They bivvied beside the *Ivanhoe*. It rarely left their sight. But that night he'd gone for a walk amongst the campfires. A couple of rowdy bloody infantry had tried to engage him in conversation, but on hearing his accent they began to jeer and josh him. So he'd wandered off and took a piss over a parapet into one of their trenches. Cocky northern bastards. He was on his way back to the tank when he was accosted by a young girl in a long brown skirt and jacket, who took his arm, linking hers through his, and talked as if they were old friends.

"Cor blimey, what a night. I just got the old 'eave-'o from my mate. She's over there talking to that NCO with the crutch. Well, I can tell when I'm not wanted. Mind you, she needs a bit of perkin' up, bless her heart. Then I saw you in your coveralls. And I thought aye-aye, you're from the tank, ain'tcha? I ain't never seen one up real close. Don't they look funny, like a huge great iron slug? What kind of engine has she got? I bet she's a beaut. Can I see it?"

He could tell from her accent she wasn't a northerner, but Lord Almighty, she never stopped talking, and he let her talk, because she spoke of gears and pistons and carburettors and, quite frankly, he'd never met a girl like her. He'd come all this way from one world to another and there she was, large as life and twice as brassy. Nellie bleedin' Abbott. And he'd shook his head in wonder. She'd spent time in the FANYs driving ambulances and knew how to strip an engine. Had to. No bugger else to do it for her, half the time. She'd ridden a motorcycle once or twice. They talked of the country rides they might take together if they got back, but she wouldn't have it, not in a sidecar at any rate. Oh no. Not her. She wanted a motorcycle of her own. That was when he fell in love with her. Right there. Alfie's face split into an involuntary grin at the memory.

The rest of the crew were wary of her. They were used to their secrets, their own company. They didn't welcome outsiders. They wouldn't let her in the tank. Crew only, they said. But he'd snuck her in anyway. Once he'd had to shove her out of one sponson door as Jack squeezed in the other.

The crew had been despondent at the time. It looked like their fuel would run out, and without petrol, the tank was just so much scrap. Without the tank they would be transferred into the battalion to be Poor Bloody Infantry again.

But then one of the Tommies had brewed some evil alcoholic concoction that killed one of the men daft enough to drink it. Unfit for human consumption, they said. But it gave them a new fuel. It ran a little better than the petrol they were used to, but then that was nearly all 'flogged' inferior stuff anyway. This new stuff had been distilled from what they now called petrol fruit. They were back in the game.

That was when everything changed.

They had been breathing the fumes for a week or so before they noticed. At first they felt keener, their senses seemed more acute. Colours were brighter, crisper. Sounds were clearer and smells sharper and more distinct.

"It's the clean air here," Reggie informed them. "Clears out the tubes!" he said, thumping his chest. He couldn't have been more wrong. Even Lieutenant Mathers seemed to relax now. Before, he had been a bundle of nerves in the tank, always on the verge of funking it, but now he seemed to relish driving it. Then again, they all did. Mind you, it helped when you were not being constantly shelled by Fritz artillery or hammered with machine gun fire. It was quite like the old days driving round Elveden as if it were a fairground ride. The days when they weren't in it were fraught with tension and short tempers. Even the engine, after some initial troubles, seemed to run smoother.

It was the fuel itself. They'd heard stories of how the Tommies that had drunk it saw things, hallucinated. That's why it was declared unfit for human consumption. But they weren't drinking it. They didn't have to. Fumes from the engine filled the small confined space. Ordinary petrol fumes would give them carbon monoxide poisoning. They'd end up with vicious headaches, convulsions and, in extreme cases, delirium or psychosis. They'd stagger from the tank and vomit. The petrol vapour would sting their skin and give them itching rashes and impetigo.

This new fuel had different side effects. Once they discovered the effects of petrol fruit fumes, they vowed amongst themselves to keep it quiet. It gave them a sense of euphoria, changed their vision. Under its influence they began to see the bright little whirls and eddies of indigo as the vapour swirled lazily about the cabin. The white painted iron plate surrounding them throbbed green with the vibration of the engine. Alfie soon found he could identify the state of the engine by the colour it gave off. But most of all he liked looking at Nellie. Great gaseous expanses of soft yellows billowed gently from her like silk sheets in the wind and oh, how she shone. If only he could tell her how beautiful she was. She thought herself rather plain. But he doubted anybody had ever seen her the way he had.

He hated leaving her now. Before, all he had was the crew of the *Ivanhoe*. Now, there was her.

He recalled the last time he saw Nellie, a day ago now, just before they left, but it seemed an age away when he wasn't in her company. They'd received orders to move out on another seek and find patrol. He'd spent half the night checking and tuning the engine, oiling it, having to use rendered down fats as grease. The rest of Ivanhoe's crew were full of pep and up for it, knowing they'd be able to partake of the intoxicating fumes again.

The only other person who might have an inkling of the effects was Tulliver, the RFC chap. He used the same petrol fruit liquor to fuel his aeroplane. But he wasn't confined in a dark, airless cabin with it. The wind would soon whip away any fumes he might inhale.

As the others stocked up on supplies, carefully watched by Company Quartermaster Sergeant Slacke, Alfie had wandered off to say goodbye to Nellie. He found her trying to haul a large pan of some sort of edible, well, stew, for want of a better word.

"Alfie. Can't give us a hand, can you, m'duck?"

"Sorry, Nellie. Moving out. Another one of the infantry's explore and patrol missions."

"Oh aye. And keep an eye out for—"

"—Jeffries, yes," he finished. They laughed together.

He peered into the pot. "Cor. What have the mongey wallahs come up with this time? It looks disgusting."

"Yes, well, it isn't for you. It's for them poor beggars in the Bird Cage," she said, nodding her head towards the barbed wire enclosure where the shell-shocked men were housed.

Lieutenant Mathers had climbed the steps out of the communications trench that led to the battalion HQ, his shoulders hunched and a sullen look on his gaunt, pasty face.

"Perkins. Don't dally. We've got to shove off." He sniffed the air and homed in on the cauldron. "Mmm, what's that?" He reached in and pulled out a lump of something, put it in his mouth and chewed experimentally.

"Oi!" Nellie slapped his hand. "This is for the poor shell-shock victims, not the likes of you, sir."

The rebuke caught Mathers off guard. He looked towards the enclosure at the shuffling, jerking scraps of manhood within and at least had the manners to look guilty. He coughed in embarrassment. "Yes. Right." He wagged the rest of the handful at her. "Still, not bad," he said and strode away. "Come on, Perkins. Work to do."

Alfie had shrugged an apology, "Must dash," and he'd followed his commanding officer. The last he saw of Nellie was her lugging the pan towards the Bird Cage...

BRIGHT GREEN RIPPLES burst from the floor of the compartment as the tank lurched and Alfie cracked his head on an overhead pipe.

"Watch where you're driving!" Alfie bellowed at Wally's back.

"Plenty of room up bloody top if you're not bleedin' happy with it!" Wally retorted.

"Got a real bee in his bonnet about that bounder Jeffries hasn't he, that Lieutenant Everson?" Norman was yelling above the noise of the engine. "I mean this is the fifth time he's sent us out on patrol to try and pick up his trail, and have we? Have we, billy-o. Not a sign. One of the promising directions picked out by Tulliver? Bollocks. I bet everything looks promising from a thousand feet up. Oh, and here's a map what a nurse saw. Sorry it's mostly empty, would you chaps mind filling in the blank bits as you go?"

"We could run right over Jeffries in *Ivanhoe* and not even notice," Cecil yelled back.

Norman nodded in agreement. "Wild goose chase is what it is. Waste of time."

"Not at all, dear chap," Reggie chipped in. "Travel broadens the mind, you know."

"In a place like this, Hell's back yard? Loosens the bowels, more like. Thank God I've got armour plating between me and it, is all I can say."

"Well, I'm all for these little trips of Everson's. Very nice of him. Don't care if we never find this Jeffries," said Reggie.

Frank spat on the gangway. "Jeffries, my arse."

"Frank! Please."

"Yeah, mind your language," scolded Norman. "Has Reggie taught you nothing?"

"Yeah, I holds me pinky up when I use me canteen now," Frank said, demonstrating to wild laughter. "Besides, if he ain't got a boojum like us then frankly he's probably dead meat. Why else d'you think they send us out here? 'Cause every bugger else gets eaten, that's why."

"Just makes us tinned bully beef," said Norman with a grin.

"Quite frankly I don't care if we never find the bleeder. Don't need the blighter mucking up the sweet little deal we've got going here."

"Well I don't feel too happy about that," Alfie shouted across the engine. "It doesn't seem right, somehow. Doesn't it bother the rest of you? Maybe we should discuss it again, that's all I'm saying."

Frank reached out, grabbed Alfie's coveralls and pulled him towards him under the starting handle. "And all I'm saying, Alfie, is you need to back off a little, mate. We're getting fed up with your holier-than-thou attitude. It was the Sub's idea. If our plans make you breezy, why don't you just do one and take up with your long-haired chum back with the mud sloggers?"

"Why? Because we're tankers. I'm maybe not so crazy about this idea, but I'd take a bullet for any single one of you, you know that, right?"

"Do we, Alfie? Do we? We don't even know if we can trust you." Frank thrust Alfie away from him with a snort of derision as the others looked on.

Alfie shook his head in despair. Their devotion to Mathers, who had seen them through, who had kept them supplied with the petrol fruit fuels and kept them safe and alive inside their shell of iron, was slipping into the fanatical and tinged with paranoia. Even Mathers' moods seemed to fluctuate between insanity and lucidity. Their world had shrunk and they no longer noticed nor cared. But his? His world had been expanded. He saw beyond the horizons of armoured plate and rivets. His world was illuminated by Nellie, a moon whose tidal influence was pulling him slowly from their orbit.

There was a hollow *krunng*. And another, accompanied by brilliant green migraine flashes radiating from the roof of the compartment.

"Rockfall?"

The tank lurched to a halt, and the engine died to an idle. Alfie held his breath, straining to listen above the chug of the engine. If it was a rockfall, they had no chance of getting out of there in a hurry. Their top speed was barely above walking pace.

Norman stuck his head out of the rear sponson hatch. A rock smashed into the sponson, just missing him.

"Bloody hell, we're under attack!" he yelped, ducking back in and slamming the hatch shut behind him. "It's an ambush. Place is lousy with 'em. Buggers are throwing rocks at us. Reminds me of a show at the Leeds Empire. Bloody hell, they were a hard audience that night."

The others did likewise, shutting the other hatches, their only illumination now the small electric festoon lamps.

"*Language*, Norman," warned Reggie.

There was another round of bangs as more rocks rained down on the hull.

Jack and Norman manned their six pounders and peered out of the vertical gun port slits, looking for a target. Cecil and Reggie loaded the breaches then readied their machine guns, threading fresh belts into the mechanism.

"Where are they?" said Reggie, peering through a pistol port. "I can't see anything. Where the deuce are they?"

"Above us."

"Well, we can't sit here," said Mathers. "Carry on, Clegg. They can't harm us."

"Sir."

The engine roared into life again and the *Ivanhoe* rumbled forwards for a minute before Wally raised his right fist. At the signal, Alfie threw his left track gear into neutral, disengaging his track. Frank pushed the right track gear into first speed. The tank began to swing right to avoid a large boulder the size of a terraced house before jerking to a halt. Another signal from Wally. Alfie pushed his gear into first speed too and the tank lurched straight ahead for another ten yards as it passed the boulder.

"I can't see anything. Just rocks!" said Reggie, becoming agitated, his face pressed to a loophole.

They heard a succession of softer thuds on the roof followed by a scratching clatter above them.

"They're on the roof."

Another signal from Wally and Frank slipped his track gear into neutral while Alfie pushed his into first speed. *Ivanhoe* swung sharply to the left. There was a thud on the sponson and Reggie lurched back as something chitinous blocked the light.

"It's outside!"

"Well, bloody shoot it!"

Reggie squeezed the Hotchkiss' trigger and the belt feed zipped through a few feet, firing a hail of bullets. There was an anguished squeal and light flooded in from the pistol port again.

"Damn it!" Mathers stood up and squeezed back down the port gangway past Norman and Reggie, drew his pistol and opened the manhole hatch in the roof above the rear of the engine.

There were three Yredetti on top of the tank. Ugly buggers, reminiscent of beetles, with mottled green chitinous armour. They walked upright, like Chatts, but they had better developed powerful middle limbs that they used for gripping, and were just as comfortable and fast on on all sixes. They were primitives, a race of carnivorous hunters. They had no weapons and didn't need them. Their large saw-toothed mandibles were capable of decapitating a man. One was trying to wrench off the exhaust covers. Mathers fired, and it fell over the side with a squeal. Another turned and lunged at him. He got off a second shot, which raked down the carapace and sent it spinning from the roof to bounce off the starboard sponson.

More were emerging now from behind boulders and closing in on the tank.

They charged the *Ivanhoe*. One was crushed beneath the track, and a second was cut down by Wally with a burst from the forward facing machine gun. Half out of the hatch, Mathers wrestled with the creature. A third Yrredetti was using its mandibles to slice through the ropes holding the drums of spare fuel to the rear of the tank. There was a hearting-rending *thung* and a drum fell loose and bounced off the tank's steering tail and back along the canyon, coming to rest against a couple of small rocks.

Mathers fired at the creature again. It hissed and he ducked down and grabbed the hatch, partially shutting it after him, and bellowed down into the cabin.

"Clegg, for Christ's sake stop the tank. We've lost the spare fuel!"

The tank lurched to a halt, the engine still idling. Mathers thrust himself up, slamming the opening hatch into the facial carapace of the creature, crushing a mandible. He fired point blank into the stunned creature's face and paused momentarily to watch the head explode in a myriad of colours, creating a rainbow of mist in the air. He looked back over the roof of the tank to where the fuel drum had come to rest. Several Yrredetti were gathered around it and were pounding it with stones. He boosted himself up onto the roof, ran down the rear of the track, leapt off the back and charged towards the insect-creatures, waving his pistol and bawling like a maniac.

"Bloody hell, the Sub's blood is up," said Jack as he followed the thumping footfalls over the roof and peered out of the sponson door loophole. "Better give him a hand, lads. Stick close to me, Cecil. Norman, Frank? Keep me covered. Wally, stay with *Ivanhoe*. You too, Reggie."

"Really? Don't mind if I do," said Reggie with relief. "Most kind."

Jack glanced dismissively at Alfie as he opened the sponson hatch and clambered down. It was a deliberate snub. They didn't need him. They didn't want him. Cecil followed Jack out, cocking his pistol as he went.

"Bloody hell!" Alfie muttered, clambering out and joining Cecil by the rear starboard track horn anyway.

A cry from high up on the canyon side preceded another boulder, bouncing down the rocky face, dislodging a tumble of smaller scree that chased it down the slope, like ragamuffins chasing an ice-cream cart. It bounced wide. Norman aimed his revolver and fired. The small figure of an Yrredetti tumbled forwards from its rocky perch to fall into a patch of the blue-green blisterous growths which burst under its impact.

By now Mathers had reached the drum and had shot the three Yrredetti beating it. He inspected the drum. There were several alarming dents, but it was still intact, thank God. Another group of Yrredetti shuffled warily nearby. Mathers roared at them. They scuttled back. Jack reached the drum, Cecil panting in his wake.

Jack nodded at the drum. "Better get this back on the *Ivanhoe*, sir."

"What?" said Mathers, shaking his head and looking around as if suddenly realising where he was. He glanced around the canyon walls. More Yrredetti were beginning to rear their heads from behind boulders and were crawling down the scree slope towards them.

"Hmm? Yes, you're right. Can you manage it, Tanner?"

"I can, sir."

Mathers strode back to the tank, reloading his revolver from his belt pouch as he went. Frank and Alfie crouched by the tank, using the rear track horns and the steering tail as cover, keeping an eye on the creatures that seemed to be getting bolder by the minute, or more desperate.

Mathers thought he heard whispering. He scowled at Frank. "What did you say?"

Frank looked at him, startled. "Nothing, sir. Didn't say a word."

"Hmm." Mathers held his gaze for a moment, then shook his head.

Jack rolled the drum back towards the *Ivanhoe*. Cecil, now dangerously exposed, was edging back towards the tank, revolver raised, wavering, switching targets indecisively. "I got you, Jack."

"Get it stowed, quickly," said Mathers, boarding through the port sponson hatch.

On the roof, Frank helped haul the drum into position on top of the other one while Jack, standing on the steering tail, strained as he lifted the drum above his head.

One Yrredetti flung a stone, cracking the retreating Cecil on the back of the skull. The lad stumbled and went down, clutching his head, and his revolver skittered away from him. From the cover of a nearby boulder a couple of Yrredetti darted forwards, urged on by the calls of others. A claw snapped down on Cecil's foot and dragged him back towards the shelter of the rock.

"Cecil's down!" Alfie fired his revolver. The round ricocheted off the boulder,

"Oh Jesus, help me, for Christ's sake!" screamed Cecil as he was dragged towards the boulder.

Alfie ran towards it. Time seemed to slow. Around him the air shifted in whorls of effervescent vermillion, parting as he ran and, in the periphery of his vision, orange auras blazed among the rocks indicating the position of the creatures hidden in the rocks around and above him, his fear swamped by an exhilaration.

He scrambled up the side of the large boulder even as Cecil disappeared round the back. Stood on the top, he saw three arthropods huddled behind the rock, arguing over Cecil.

A blue-green blister throbbed on a small rock, the size of a football, near Alfie's feet. He shouted. They looked up and he kicked the rock down, hitting one of them in the head, blisters bursting and drenching the creature's face, burning it. Its scream was bright orange, fading quickly to red as it reflected off the canyon walls, before dissipating as it died.

Alfie leapt down, landing on the arm that held the screaming Cecil. He felt the chitinous armour crunch beneath his boots as he fired his revolver point blank into the face of the second. The third tried to scuttle back to the safety of the scree slope, but Jack appeared, caught it by the leg and swung it against the boulder. Alfie heard its carapace crack and Jack let it fall limply to the ground, leaving a dark sticky stain on the rock.

Alfie pulled Cecil to his feet, ducked under his armpit, took his weight and helped him back to the tank. Jack stood his ground before backing towards the tank, picking up Cecil's fallen revolver and guarding their retreat. The gathering creatures hissed and clicked their mandibles, but kept their distance.

By now the fuel drum had been re-secured, and Alfie could hear Wally running up the engine in readiness to move off. He passed Cecil to Frank, who hauled him in through the sponson hatch.

"Come on, Jack," Alfie called, one foot on the starboard hatch lip as he prepared to step through. Jack danced backwards towards the tank, his eyes never leaving the rocks.

"Natives are still restless," he said, ducking as a fist-sized stone hit the tank's metal track.

"All aboard," called Reggie, banging cheerfully on a pipe with a wrench. The ironclad moved off.

Frustrated, the Yrredetti howled and a rain of rocks clattered down against the tank, setting off a rainbow of percussion inside.

"Looks like they're trying a final attempt to ditch us," said Frank, peering through his pistol port. Mathers peered through the pistol port in the side of the driver cabin. Damn things were trying to prise a boulder loose and start an avalanche.

"Put your foot down, Clegg. We don't want to get caught in this canyon." The tank lurched as it picked up what speed it could.

Several more Yrredetti were helping to lever the boulder free as the tank started to pass beneath it.

Reggie loaded a shell into the breech of the port gun. Norman took a deep breath, gritted his teeth and pushed down with all his weight, levering the gun up so that it was pointed up towards the canyon wall. He targeted the boulder as best he could in the moving tank, and fired. The boulder and the Yrredetti disappeared in a plume of fire and dirt. A cloud of dust rolled down the canyon side, enveloping the tank. A rain of clinker and debris pattered down on the hull, sending verdant ripples through the compartment.

"Yes! Got the blighters. Thank you and goodnight! That'll teach 'em to mess with old *Ivanhoe*!" whooped Norman.

Rubble rattled down the canyon sides to be crushed beneath the tracks of the *Ivanhoe* as, oblivious, it continued on its halting way towards the mouth of the canyon.

Behind it, a lone wail of frustration echoed round the walls of the canyon, before being picked up and amplified by other Yrredetti.

As the dust cloud settled, the blue-green blisters, stilled in the fleeting darkness of the cloud, began to pulse in the rays of the sun once more. On the canyon side, where the shell had exploded, something cold and metallic glinted through the shattered rock in the dust-filtered daylight.

CHAPTER FIVE
"The Outlook isn't Healthy..."

LIEUTENANT MATHERS, OPERATING the steering brake levers, peered out of the front visor at the small rectangle of world he could see before him, a world that see-sawed violently as the landship crashed up and down on the swell of ground beneath them. As they nosed up over obstacles, the bright rectangle of sky was snatched away with vertiginous speed to be replaced with lurching glimpses of soil and rock, before he was teased with a horizon line of vermillion-hued vegetation that vanished again abruptly.

Again, Mathers heard the whispering. He glanced at Clegg beside him, the bantam cockney's wiry arms tense on the driving levers.

"Blimey," the driver shouted over the noise of the engine behind them. "This place has got more pot holes than Oxford Street."

Mathers shook his head. He could barely hear Clegg speak, let alone whisper. It must be some resonant engine note he'd not noticed before.

As they left the canyon behind them, the blue-green rock blisters gave way to a cinnamon-coloured soil. Ahead of them lay a rocky plateau scored with haphazard cracks and stress marks from the same geological event that caused the canyon. Cracks and gullies splintered the landscape like crazy paving; some rocky plates tilting, some sunken, some thrust up. Some gullies were too wide for the tank to cross, even though the weight of its hydraulic steering tail was designed as a counter-balance to cross trenches of up to nine feet.

They had to find a way to safely cross the labyrinthine field. As Tank Commander, that job fell to Mathers, and quite frankly he was glad of it. He was the tallest man in the crew, a real legs eleven. Sat in the small cockpit on the hard chair being jolted and jarred had given him a stomach cramp. Even now he hated being cooped up in the tank for long periods and he found himself tensing, clenching his stomach muscles against the unexpected drops, jolts and bangs.

He had cramp. And a headache. Maybe the fresh air would help. He tapped Clegg on the shoulder.

"I'll walk on ahead, guide you through."

It was a common procedure in tanks. When going became difficult it was the commander's unenviable task to negotiate paths round shell-hole-pocked roads, and he'd done his fair share during night manoeuvres and under fire. There were times when he almost preferred that to being cooped up in an iron coffin. At least here, there was no chance of Fritz sniping at you, and that brought a great deal of relief. On the other hand, you never knew here what you were going to encounter next.

He walked ahead of the tank, checking the ground, searching for narrow enough gullies for them to cross. He could hear things moving about in the bottom of them, slithering and snuffling. He peered over the edge of one, but some form of bruised purple vegetation obscured the gully bed. In a way, he was relieved. He indicated to Clegg to swing right over a gap narrow enough for the *Ivanhoe* to bridge.

In this manner, the tank crew progressed slowly across the broken plain, having to go out of their way to find a route passable enough to be of little concern to the great metal behemoth. From then on, progress was faster and the jungle loomed ahead. A short sort of crimson brambly plant became more prevalent, its thorns scratching the leather of his calf-length boots.

One caught his ankle and sent him tumbling into a gully; he slipped to the bottom. An accompanying land slither sent dirt and soil raining down onto him. For a moment, disorientated, unable to move, the old panic rose in him again.

Mathers had been an officer in the infantry, on the front lines, until one day he found himself under heavy bombardment for days. The dugout he was in had collapsed under shellfire. There was a large bang, and then darkness. And silence. He couldn't move. He was buried, pinned under the body of an orderly, Hammond, that lay across him, staring at him with lifeless eyes for what seemed like hours, but must have been a lot less. His ears were ringing. Muffled by the dirt, the sandbags and joists, he could hear the barrage going on around him, the shriek of whizz-bangs and, in the breeze that blew gently through the collapsed dugout, a hint of gas. He could barely hear his own voice as he called for help. He knew he mustn't be seen to funk it in front of the men he could hear digging for him. He had enough gumption about him not to scream, fighting off the urge by biting his own hand while, in his head, he pleaded with a god he barely believed in to let him get out. He promised anything, everything.

When they finally dragged him from under Hammond's corpse and carried him by stretcher to the aid post, he was found to have no serious injuries. Hammond's body had cushioned him. He was lucky. But his scars couldn't be seen.

He was still shaking the next day. The tremors made it difficult to walk, so he was forced to remain in bed by stern matrons.

Commotional distress, they said. Perfectly understandable. Several weeks behind the lines helped him recover. Except that it didn't. Back at the front, it didn't take long for his nerves to fray. He noticed the tremors, the rising panic, and the tic under his eye, whenever he had to go into a dugout. He could hardly sleep. Alcohol helped, initially. Eventually they sent him back to Blighty to recuperate.

That was when he met Major Parkhurst. Damn Major Parkhurst. Man had the bloody temerity to call himself an MO. Bloody croaker, more like. The man didn't believe in neuralgia. You were either a coward or you weren't. Mathers insisted he wasn't, which was all Parkhurst wanted to hear to declare him fit for duty. The trouble was, Mathers no longer knew for sure. He had to prove it to himself one way or the other. Kill or cure, he thought.

The Machine Gun Corps' new Heavy Section was looking for officers and men. It would be a fresh start away from his old battalion. He applied, hiding the true extent of his condition. He hadn't realised what was involved until he'd arrived at Elveden. But you couldn't show fear in front of the men. You were an officer. To do so was to invite a court martial. Every time he entered the tank he could feel the pressure building inside him, like a pot that threatened to boil over, but he managed to control it, tensing his stomach and legs so that he wouldn't jump at unexpected noises or lurches. Thankfully, it seemed everyone in the tanks was ill from the fumes and the working conditions at one time or another and he found he could disguise the worse of his nervous debility. Here, on this world, however, the tank provided its own medication. The fuel fumes seemed to have a beneficial effect on him, making him less jumpy. He wondered what was in it to make him feel this way, but only briefly. Mostly he was just glad. Even that infernal tic under his left eye, that would fire uncontrollably in bursts, like a machine gun, had stopped recently.

He put it to the back of his mind and breathed deeply.

He realized he wasn't buried. The cloth of his jacket had just caught fast on the bramble. He tore his arm free, ripping the serge. He heard something in the damp shadows slithering towards him along the gully bed, under the cover of the creeping plant, and he scrambled back up the side of the gully.

As he clawed his way to the lip, he heard a sound over the noise of the tank, and he saw an apparent cluster of boulders a hundred yards away lift itself up, limbs unfolding from beneath it. He had seen one of these things before in a forest, on the way to rescue captured Tommies from Khungarr. They had only survived then by good fortune. A stone beetle, about the size of the *Ivanhoe*.

Cautiously, it stretched and unrolled itself, watching the tank warily. Clegg tried to turn the *Ivanhoe* so that it faced their foe; Mathers urged them on silently. The stone beetle was quicker and scuttled round the tank, as if looking for weaknesses. In order to turn more quickly Clegg had kept both tracks running, one in reverse. It would strip the differential if he kept that up and they'd be buggered out in the middle of nowhere with no tankodrome or machine shops. Mathers was sure Perkins would be scolding him.

The beetle crouched low on its limbs, its head down, mandibles scything, all the while watching the tank.

The tank halted, its engine growling. Mathers urged it to do something. It seemed an eternity before the tank began to lurch backwards away from the beast. The huge rock beetle advanced, keeping pace with it. It then tried scuttling round to the right as if to flank it. A burst of machine gun fire spitting across the ground soon stopped that.

Mathers watched, helpless, as the tank tried to fix the thing in its sights, but it was altogether faster and more agile than the cumbersome armoured machine. Mathers threw himself to the ground as a spray of bullets zipped over his head.

"Nesbit!" he roared, the admonition all but drowned by the noise of the tank.

The giant beetle, having abandoned its flanking manoeuvre, now sought to charge the trespasser. Head down, swaying, its great stone stag horns wove through the air. It scuttled forwards again in short, abrupt bursts, the brief spatter from the forwards facing Hotchkiss ricocheting off its carapace, merely giving it pause for thought. It was almost with reluctance that the stone beetle then backed away. It regarded the ironclad hesitantly before slinking away and slithering down into a large gully.

Mathers breathed a sigh of relief. When he picked himself off the ground, a sharp pain in his abdomen almost doubled him over. He frowned and sucked air in through gritted teeth until the sensation passed.

He felt inside his tunic, pulled out his hip flask and took a quick slug of the distilled petrol fruit. Its fumes alone weren't enough to dull the pain. More recently, he needed something stronger.

The tank slewed round blindly, trying to find its vanished foe. Mathers approached the tank and stood in front of it. He could make out Clegg's face through the driver's open visor plate, and waved him on. The tank began to clank obediently towards him as he continued to scout ahead. The crevices and gullies were becoming fewer and narrower, but he didn't want to take any chances. He hadn't gone fifty yards when he heard a pistol go off. He turned to see someone fire from one of the tank's pistol ports.

This stone beetle creature was obviously more cunning than its forest cousin was. It had used the cover of the gullies to come round behind the tank and surprise its rival.

"Swing to port!" Mathers yelled, waving his arms to his right as if he could speed up the tank's turn by the action. "For Christ's sake, swing to port!"

INSIDE THE TANK, peering out of the sponson door pistol port, Frank saw a flash of stone carapace and fired his revolver.

"Bugger's back!" he yelled. Faces peered out of the other pistol ports, searching for the creature.

"Where?"

"It's behind us," said Cecil, peering out of the pistol port in the rear door by the radiator.

"Wally, about face, ninety degrees!" yelled Alfie. He nodded to Frank and when Wally gave the signal from his driving seat, they changed gears. The tank began to turn almost on the spot.

"Where is it? I can't see it!" said Wally, peering though his visor plate. They peered out of pistol ports and gun slits, checking off their positions.

"Not here," called Jack, swinging the gun round through a hundred and twenty degrees and peering through the gun slit.

"Nor here," said Cecil.

"Can't see it," said Norman.

"Then where the bloody hell is it?"

As if in answer, there was a heavy thud accompanied by an oppressive green synesthetic flash as the creature landed on top of the tank. A noise like nails on a blackboard pierced the bass rumble of the engine as the creature's feet sought purchase. Blocked by the belly of the creature above, exhaust fumes began to belch back into the compartment, filling the space with a choking black smoke.

Alfie began coughing until spots burst before his eyes.

Reggie took the commander's seat next to Wally.

"No free rides on this 'bus!" he said, pulling on the brake lever. The *Ivanhoe* jerked to a halt. Unable to get a firm grip, the stone beetle slithered off the front.

"That'll teach it," said Wally with a self-satisfied sneer. "Go on, clear off, you great bleedin' cockroach."

It skittered off round out of his limited field of view. Back in the compartment, the crew flung themselves at the pistol ports again. It was too fast for the gunners to get a bead on it.

The back end of the tank tilted up as the creature shoved its horns beneath the steering tail and tried to lever it up. The tank crashed down again as it failed. It tried again.

"Oi!" Wally drove the tank forwards.

"Cecil, take a peek and see what the bleeder's trying to do, will you."

Cecil peered out of the rear loophole. "Lawks, it's coming after us again!"

The tank juddered once more as the back end tilted up and crashed down again.

"We can't take much more of this."

There was a brief stillness. Alfie held his breath.

Then Cecil piped up, jerking back from the pistol port in the rear door. "It's trying for the roof again."

Alfie found himself looking up at the roof, from where the noise, and jagged green spikes, of scrambling issued. Between them, Wally, Alfie and Frank tried to swing the tank and throw it off, but it clung tenaciously to the roof.

"What the hell do we do now?"

"Aaaugh. Shit!" yelled Cecil stumbling back over the differential. "It's trying to get in!" After several attempts, a thin exoskeletal tube about two feet long appeared through the pistol port. He reared back and cocked his revolver at it. He watched, open-mouthed, as the end opened and something wet and glistening, like a tentacle, protruded from the chitinous casing.

"It, it's a whatsit, a prob-sis? It's trying to suck us out!"

"I don't think so, son." Jack edged past Alfie, put a hand on Cecil's wrist and forced him to lower the weapon. "Don't shoot in here, Ces. The bullet'll ricochet."

"Fellas," said Norman, warily.

The tank began to rock as the beetle creature above them sought purchase. The rocking became more rhythmic. The tentacle, if that's what it was, began to throb.

A vile thought took hold as Alfie watched. "That's not a bloody tentacle, or a proboscis. It's a bleedin' short arm!"

Reggie blanched. "A what?"

The rocking became more urgent and the occupants of the tank were being shunted backwards and forwards with every thrust. Expressions of horror and disgust dawned on their faces as they realised what was going on.

"It's not trying to kill us. It's after a bon time," said Norman.

Only Cecil still looked blank.

"It thinks we're a lady friend?" Frank suggested.

Cecil frowned. "But this is a male tank."

Alfie braced his hands against the roof as another enthusiastic thrust rocked the tank. "I *really* don't think it cares."

"Jesus! Well don't just stand there," bellowed Wally.

Cecil looked at them. "What do we do?"

Moral indignation flooded Jack's face. "Well, I'll tell you what I'm bloody well not going to do and that's lie back and think of bloody England." He grabbed a wrench and took a swing at the now tumescent and dripping appendage. "D'you know, Ces," he said, "after this, I can see me and you is going to need a long talk about... country matters."

Frank leered. "After this, I don't think he'll need one."

MATHERS WATCHED AS the giant beetle attempted to mount the *Ivanhoe*, using its mandibles to try to bite and hold the tank's roof, its legs scrambling for leverage as it began to grind against the rear of the tank. All thought of its own safety washed away in a primal urge too strong to ignore.

The tank juddered forward, but the beetle was determined not to lose its mount and tottered forwards with it, almost comically, still attached.

Mathers felt a hint of shame that the ironclad should be misused so shamefully, as if it had been a faithful beast unwillingly put out to stud. He picked up a rock and hurled it at the creature, but it bounced off. He picked up another one and edged closer, this time aiming at its face. It bounced off a mandible. He felt light-headed, but didn't stop. Whatever he was feeling, it wasn't fear; it was... exhilaration. He picked up another rock and, yelling incoherently, he charged. He ran at the tank and, using his momentum, and the starboard gun barrel, in one swift move he scrambled onto the *Ivanhoe* and began smashing at the beetle's legs, which seemed to be the most vulnerable part. Smoke began billowing out from the smothered exhaust vents beneath the beetle. He was about to leap on its back in an attempt to stove its head in when a sheering screech ripped the sky.

A shadow flicked overhead.

Mathers looked up. A large creature like a manta ray swooped down over the rutting beetle. It had a long neck and small head, with a deceptively wide mouth and sharp teeth. The beetle, locked as it was in congress with the tank, neither knew nor cared.

The flying creature Mathers recognised; the men called it a jabberwock. They preyed on the herds of tripodgiraffes that roamed the veldt. It wheeled round and extended its hind legs and sharp talons, like a hawk's. Mathers, unperturbed, threw the rock at it, less of a defence and more of a challenge. He stood on the beetle's back as it humped and roared at the jabberwock in defiance. So close to death and he had never felt so alive.

By now, the beetle was hastily trying to dismount the tank but seemed to be having difficulty withdrawing.

The jabberwock screeched again as it dived towards the unnatural pairing. Mathers, stood atop the mating beetle, was prepared to meet the thing head on, though with what he had no idea and didn't care. The struggling stone beetle freed itself and slipped clumsily off the back of the tank, tipping Mathers from its back. He put out a hand but found no hold and fell from the creature onto the starboard tank track before tumbling heavily to the ground by the sponson. His graceless dismount saved his life, as talons tore through empty air above him.

Winded and dazed, he shuffled back on his buttocks away from the tracks, for fear the tank should start up again and crush him. Shrieking in frustration, the jabberwock banked sharply and, talons first, slammed down onto the disorientated and satiated stone beetle. Using its great manta wings to stabilise itself, the jabberwock sought gaps that its sharp curved claws could lock under, while its head sought similar weaknesses on its prey's back.

The beetle flailed pointlessly, unable to grasp anything of its attacker with its mandibles. Turning this way and that like a dog chasing its tail, desperate to dislodge its assailant from its back, it slammed into the tank, shunting it sideways. Mathers watched as the vehicle slid several feet towards him. He could only see the flapping of the great wings and hear the cries of the jabberwock, hidden from view by the tank.

His face and back began to prickle with drying sweat, he felt a wave of nausea rise up, and he vomited on the ground. What the hell did he think he was doing? His hands began to shake. Thinking of himself up on the tank beating that damn thing with a rock made him heave again. Jesus. His head began to pound.

There was a screech of triumph as the jabberwock rose from the ground, talons locked tightly onto the beetle. The stone beetle's legs thrashed weakly, defenceless. The pair rose higher and higher as Mathers scrambled to his feet. Trembling, feeling faint and clammy, he staggered towards the tank.

The jabberwock cawed loudly and released the beetle, which dropped like a dead weight. There was a wet cracking sound as the beetle slammed down onto the tank's roof. It clawed feebly. Triumphant, the jabberwock flew down and began to prise at the cracked carapace with a taloned foot. Its long neck and hooked beak began ripping at the innards, tearing its soft wet organs.

Thirty feet away, Mathers made to creep towards the sponson hatch, but the gimlet-eyed predator spotted him. For a moment, he thought it was going to attack, but it just extended its neck, screeched in his direction, warning him off, and went back to tearing at the beetle carcass.

The jabberwock kept one eye on him, jealously guarding its kill as it ripped and tore, throwing back its head to swallow lumps of offal. He needed to get the thing and its meal off the tank. Slowly, still trembling, he edged round to the front of the tank and ducked round the starboard track horn, and over the pervasive rumble of the engine shouted into the driver's cockpit.

"Clegg, the beetle thing is lying on the starboard track. If you drive forwards the track might run it off the front of the tank."

Clegg nodded his comprehension through the driver's visor. Mathers saw him turn back in the tank and yell something. Her ran up the engine and the tank jerked into life, then began, clanking track plate by track plate, to inch forwards. The beetle carcass moved. The jabberwock didn't notice at first, but when its kill was tugged away from it, it looked around for the unseen rival.

Mathers backed off and watched the progress of the dead beetle as it ground slowly forward. The jabberwock, furious that its meal was being snatched, put one clawed foot on the body to hold it. The tracks ground on inexorably, shredding the underside of the carcass and leaving viscous blue stains on the track plates. The weight of the jabberwock was holding it back.

Mathers would have to do something. Picking up a rock, he threw it at the jabberwock to draw its attention. The first one hit its body; it turned and hissed at him. The second hit its neck. It roared in his direction. A third had it rearing up over its kill and spreading its huge wings. But Mathers now felt no fear. He grinned to himself. His crew had better be ready for this.

"Come on!" he yelled at the beast, waving his arms. "Come on! You great ugly trout! Over here!" Ugly trout? Really? Was that the best he could do? Never mind. It seemed to do the trick. The jabberwock flapped its wings and took off, shrieking at him all the while. Mathers backed off even further, trying to draw the creature away from the tank. He glanced behind him. There were several boulders that might provide cover, if he could reach them.

Without the weight of the jabberwock, the beetle carcass began moving as the *Ivanhoe* advanced, and flopped limply off the front track horns, where it fell to the ground. The tank rolled over it, crushing it and staining the ground blue.

The jabberwock advanced on Mathers in short agile hops. Mathers wasn't a serious threat to it, no more than an annoyance.

Now would be a good time, thought Mathers as he backed away, facing the creature.

A burst of machine gun fire from the driver's position raked the jabberwock, perforating a bloody line across its wingspan. The jabberwock turned on the new threat. The landship lumbered towards it. There was another burst of machine gun fire and the jabberwock's head vanished in an explosion of bloody vapour. The body staggered on another few yards under its own momentum before collapsing, also to be crushed under the tracks of the advancing *Ivanhoe*.

Mathers collapsed against the boulder, his breath coming in great heaving pants, sweat trickling down his back. He could feel his heart banging in his chest and waited for it to settle down.

The tank halted and Clegg called out through the driver's visor. "Lieutenant, are you all right?" Mathers nodded and waved his hand to brush off his driver's concern, his mouth too dry to speak.

From the back of the tank, he could hear the sponson hatches clang open and the crew staggering out into the fresh air, a tangle of voices, to survey the bodies.

Perkins ignored the dead creature, turning his attention to the tank. Mathers watched him. He walked along its length checking the tracks and track plates, tapping rivets. Eventually he was satisfied.

"Damage?" asked Mathers, remembering his position, straightening himself up, and striding purposefully towards Perkins.

"We were lucky, a couple of buckled plates, but they should be all right. The track tension will need adjusting soon, but we're all tickety-boo, sir."

"Good man," he said, patting him on the shoulder and walking off towards the tank.

"Sir?" asked Perkins.

Mathers turned. "What is it, Perkins?"

"I was just wondering, sir, shouldn't we be heading back to camp? We've come far enough. We've found no sign of Jeffries so far and we're reaching the limits of our range. Our fuel *is* limited, we should think about returning. I mean, they'll be expecting us back, sir."

"But we're all right for now?"

"Yes, sir, but—"

Mathers stepped closer and fixed Perkins with a stare, aware that his eye had started to twitch again. "Any complaints?"

If Perkins noticed it, he didn't say anything. "Complaints, sir? No sir."

"Then we'll carry on. As you were, Perkins."

THE *IVANHOE* HEADED off, leaving the corpses behind to be picked over by whatever scavengers found them. They made for the forest a couple of miles off.

Mathers was still walking in front of the tank, only now he carried a large suitably gnarled wooden staff tied to the top of which was a PH gas hood, looking like some desiccated head. He wore his 'turtle shell' helmet and splash mask, even though he was outside. It afforded him some meagre protection at least. But more than that, right now it served to accompany his rain cape, daubed as it was with hand prints and strange arcane symbols, or at least what the crew had decided passed for magical signs: spirals, stars, lightning flashes and unblinking eyes. Mathers fancied himself the subject of some fantastical Arthur Rackham illustration. He looked for all the world like a tribal shaman leading some great, tamed antediluvian beast.

Which was exactly how it was supposed to look.

Behind him, the *Ivanhoe* squeaked, clanked and growled its way closer to the jungle, its periscopes up, looking like eye-stalks or antennae.

Mathers could hear the whispering again. This time it was more insistent. This time he thought he could detect words in the tinny susurration. It was coming from behind him, from the *Ivanhoe*. It *was* the *Ivanhoe*. No, not the *Ivanhoe*. It was Skarra.

Mathers walked on. And listened.

THEY HALTED AT the jungle edge. When Mathers *looked* there was nothing, but he knew they were there. The fumes from the tank allowed him to *see* their breathing; slight yellow eddies in the air around the undergrowth.

Through the protective eye slits of his splash mask, he caught a movement from the tree line. A group of Urmen stepped out from under cover. One came forwards hesitantly.

Mathers braced himself. You could never be quite sure of the reaction, but he heard the great six pounders coming to bear behind him, and Clegg running up the engine so it sounded like a throaty growl. That usually did the trick. Behind his chainmail mask, Mathers smiled. He enjoyed this next bit.

The warrior stopped, his eyes wide with fear and, while still a full twenty yards away from the ironclad, gave a great cry, threw up his arms and dropped to his knees, genuflecting until his forehead touched the ground. Behind him, his fellows did the same, hardly daring to look upon them.

Then from his position of supplication, he spoke. "We have been expecting you. Your coming has been foretold."

Mathers hadn't expected that.

CHAPTER SIX
"Here Comes the Bogey Man..."

THEY WERE RUNNING with hatches and pistol ports shut now. Inside the tank, it was stifling, with only the four small festoon lights illuminating the compartment. The stench of sweating bodies, engine oil and rendered animal fats filled the small space, along with the ever-present hallucinogenic fumes from the engine. The men breathed deeply of it, oblivious to all but the petrol fruit fumes; each lost, momentarily, in their own little internal worlds. They might have been in an opium den but for the noise and the infernal juddering as the tank lumbered along the uneven ground. With his visor shut, Clegg had to use his look-stick in order to drive.

"What's going on? Have the natives bought it?" asked Norman.

"Yeah," he said. "Now pipe down 'til the Sub gives us the signal."

Norman winked. "Looks like we've got another performance coming up, boys."

"Good, we haven't had any decent scran for ages. I wasn't going to eat that fungus muck they was dishing out before we left. God, what I wouldn't give for a nice bit o' mutton."

"Speak for yourself," barked Reggie. "Give me a nice fillet steak any day."

At the back, by the starboard gear levers, Alfie watched small close-knit ripples of red emanating from the vibrating engine and saw each man glowing with a faint aura. He shook his head to disperse the sight as he had tried many times before. The coloured patterns remained drifting in his vision like the stubborn after-images of a star shell. He didn't like much about this stunt. Everything in his gut told him they shouldn't be doing this, but do it they did, each time more brazenly and more confidently than the last.

On their first encounter with an Urmen enclave the natives, thinking the tank was Skarra, this world's god of the underworld, prostrated themselves before it and treated the crew as holy men. The crew went along with it in a bemused manner, because it suited their purpose. They rather liked the idea. Too much, it seemed. After months of subsisting on half rations and whatever vile local stew the mongey wallahs came up with, it was a relief to be feted for a change.

Reinforced by the euphoria and confidence imparted by the constant inhalation of the fumes, they were soon exaggerating and expanding the act until it was like a carnival sideshow. Norman, the ex-music hall actor, painted their rain capes with magic symbols and did a few conjuring tricks. At first it was just a jolly, but as the weeks went on their attitudes were tempered by the fumes, and as their side effects took hold, they began to half-believe the act themselves.

Alfie felt a sharp rap on his turtle shell. Jack was staring at him. He looked around to find Frank, Cecil and Norman staring across the engine at him.

Norman stepped up to him and put his mouth close to his ear in order to yell over the sound of the engine.

"I'll say this once. We've got a chance to be something here, to be someone. Don't you dare muck this up for us." He poked Alfie in the shoulder to emphasise his point.

Alfie was a little taken aback. He glanced at each of his crewmates in turn. They looked at him with expectation. They wanted his compliance. Alfie, disappointed in his mates but more so in himself, gave a reluctant nod.

Norman held his gaze a little longer, pointed to his own eyes and then at Alfie, "I'm watching you," before turning back to his gun.

OUTSIDE, MATHERS TURNED around and, with an expansive gesture, held his staff aloft, like Moses before the burning bush, and bowed low before the tank. The ironclad wavered gently in his vision, an effect of the fuel fumes, although it seemed to him that the tank was breathing, its sides expanding and contracting, a fact he now accepted as quite natural.

He wheeled smartly to face the front, his rain cape whipping around him as he turned. He had them in the palm of his hand. He raised his staff like a regimental sergeant major on a parade ground and nodded at the Urman. "Lead on. Skarra, god of the underworld, will follow."

The Urman backed slowly away on his knees before getting to his feet and walking back into the jungle with his companions, casting fearful glances behind them. The warriors before him slipped into the undergrowth and vanished from sight, only to re-emerge tens of yards further on.

* * *

BEHIND HIS MASK, Mathers took a deep breath and began to march imperiously behind them, ushering the way for his god. Behind him, the armoured juggernaut kept up a stately pace as they entered the jungle.

The undergrowth closed in about them, the shrubbery and saplings groaned and snapped, giving way under the rolling plates of the *Ivanhoe*. Mathers was aware of shapes in the undergrowth surrounding them. Quick, fleeting, almost insubstantial. More Urmen. He pretended not to notice, keeping his steady pace.

The noise of the oncoming tank quelled the chatters and whoops of unseen beasts and the high boughs shook as creatures, startled by the unworldly noise beneath, took flight through the canopy.

The tank took no heed. An air of death, of lifelessness, surrounded it, striking trees and ploughing over stricken trunks as if gorging itself on the life that fell before it. That life should flee it or be crushed beneath it seemed only right and something the Urmen expected from a god of the underworld. No wonder they melted into the undergrowth, reappearing only to offer a brief benediction and a direction, unwilling to approach for fear of their very lives being sucked from them.

All the time as he walked, Mathers could hear the tank muttering to him in its mechanical growl, whispering encouragements and dark truths, pattering out half-perceived homilies, making promises, soothing with words of power. It filled his head with such concepts that it began to pound, luring him with talk of other spaces, other realms. Ideas so profound that he couldn't hold them in his mind and they slipped from his consciousness, leaving only a vague sense of loss and shame as though he had somehow disappointed it.

So rapt was he by this communication that he scarcely noticed the slavering creature with matted fur and great long limbs, all angles and joints, as it swung screeching down towards him, teeth bared. He felt nothing. No fear, no anger, just a complete disinterest. Then his god, Skarra, the god of the underworld, spoke, its words a brief staccato chant of death. The gangly beast, its momentum stilled in mid-air by the abrupt invocation, dropped to the jungle floor, dead.

His primitive escorts froze as the machine gun burst ripped through the air, but seeing the beast die they bowed and bobbed towards the *Ivanhoe* before moving off, emboldened by the protection now offered by the crawling god.

Mathers looked down at the body, its long limbs twisted and snapped beneath it. He cricked his neck, cleared his throat, gathered himself and walked on for what seemed like hours, but he had no way of telling. Time seemed to expand and contract. The only constants he had were the jungle and the iron murmurs of Skarra.

An excited muttering rippled between their Urmen escorts. Mathers saw the reason for it. A totem. The mouldering body of an Urman lashed to a carved post by liana vines, his chest split open, its soft tissues eaten long ago, leaving only a mummified husk. Echoing the hollow-eyed stare of the PH helmet on the top of his staff, its eye sockets were empty but for shadows and its jaw hung slackly as if in an eternal scream. Was it a sacrifice, a warning, a boundary marker or all three? It didn't funk the Urmen. If anything, they seemed relieved to pass it. It no doubt marked the edge of their territory.

Transfixed by it, Mathers watched as darkness seemed to seep from the skull's sockets with a malicious intent, threatening to drown him in the rising shadows. Yet he could not take his eyes from it.

A voice reached out to him and he used it to pull his attention away from the deepening shadows about him.

"A sacrifice."

"I'm sorry, what?"

"A sacrifice," said his Urman guide. "He was *jundurru*. Now he's a warning to other bad spirits that come to tempt or trick the Gilderra Clan. They will face the same fate. Jarak's magic is strong. You will see."

Mathers swallowed dryly, his tongue rasping against the roof of his mouth. He caught the tortured thing out of the corner of his eyes as he walked past it. If there was a chance to turn back, this was it. But now he felt no fear, no guilt. After all, he thought, why should he? Was he not under the aegis of the god of the underworld? Urged on by its whisperings in his mind, he took the first defiant step beyond the grisly totem. That broke the spell, and from thereon his fate was sealed.

The *Ivanhoe* rumbled past it, oblivious to its petty magics. The ground shuddered under its passing and the totem trembled in the wake of its iron tread.

As THE TREES thinned, Mathers saw the Urmen escort waiting expectantly on their edge. Beyond, a great wall of living bark rose up before them. Great thick sheets of it spanned the spaces between rising tree trunks, forming a stockade. They were not cut and hewn by crude tools, but grafted by some esoteric form of arboriculture from the very trees themselves, shaping and training the living wood so that planes of thick rough bark, some twenty or thirty feet high, grew from one tree to the next to form a natural living barricade, supported and strengthened by pleached boughs. Roots thrust out from the base of the living bark wall like natural buttresses. In spite of himself, and anything he expected to find on this world, Mathers was impressed. This was obviously a much older enclave than they had visited before. Established, less nomadic than those of their previous encounters. The gnarled and cracked bark fortification told of decades of growth, if not a century or more. This looked promising.

The jungle had been cleared from around the stockade and overhanging boughs cut back, right up to the canopy, which spanned out high above to become a natural vault.

Their Urman escort called out with a yodelling cry towards the bark-walled enclave. A single great crack echoed around the clearing, followed by a succession of dry creaks. Two large gates of bark opened, revealing the compound within. Stood in the open gateway was a small party of Urmen, who moved aside out of deference and fear as Mathers entered the clearing, the tank waiting in the jungle shadows behind him.

Cerulean trees, their trunks ten or twenty feet in diameter, rose high above into the vaulted canopy overhead, many stripped of their bark to a height of some fifty or sixty feet. Mathers soon saw why. The dwellings clustered below within the stockade were themselves made of great curved sheets of bark. Crepuscular fingers of light sliced down through the canopy, illuminating the clearing with an almost ethereal glow. There, he found nearly a hundred Urmen women and children, watching him in silence.

He threw out his arms and, almost as one, the Urmen dropped to their knees.

"I offer you a blessing in the name of Skarra!"

Behind him, the tank came to a halt, cresting a mammoth tree root where it squatted like some monstrous toad. There was a muttered response from the gathered enclave, who looked afraid and uncertain.

Mathers strode forwards towards the small central group, where a man wore a headdress made from an Yrredetti facial plate. He was dressed in a mottled fur cloak over a chest plate assembled from the carapace of some dead creature, scraped clean and now inscribed with symbols.

Next to him stood a smaller, wiry man, patterns of ritual scarification obvious on his face even under the ceremonial daubings of white clay smeared across his skin. Mostly naked, he wore only a loin cloth and bands of chitinous exoskeleton, harvested from some arthropod's limbs, decorating his wrists, upper arms and ankles. The man regarded him with a sullen stare. This must be Jarak.

A group of tense and jumpy warriors stood behind them.

"I am Dranethwe of the Gilderra," said the headdress wearer. When he spoke it was with the same inflections but a more heavily accented English than any other Urman Mathers had heard before. It *was* recognisable, however, if a little hard to follow at first. "My clan is honoured by your presence," the Urmen went on. "We are grateful that the gods have heard us and that our offerings did not go unheeded."

"Skarra hears all," replied Mathers. Really, it was no more difficult communicating with them than with any other foreign subject of the British Empire. Learning a few words of their lingo always helped, but above all, keep it short and keep it simple. That way there would be no misunderstandings. Failing that, they always had the *Ivanhoe*. He turned back towards the tank. With great pomp, he anointed each track horn with the tip of his staff, while hissing out a command to Clegg.

"It's showtime."

ALFIE WATCHED AS the others grinned and struggled to put on their rain capes, helmets and splash masks in the confines of the tank, with all the eagerness of actors in the wings. Alfie wanted to speak out, to take one last chance to persuade them, but now wasn't the time. That time had long since passed, he realised. They were committed to a course of action, and he felt very uneasy about it.

Handing out the 'turtle shell' bruise helmets, Norman thrust Alfie's into the mechanic's chest and held it there. He leaned in close, his mouth close to Alfie's ear.

"Don't funk it. If you mess this up for us, I'll have you."

Alfie felt his face smart as if he'd been struck. As if he would. As if he'd put his crewmates in jeopardy. How could he even question that? He said nothing, but met his gaze with a sullen silence. Then, with Norman still watching, he put on his splash mask and helmet. Norman nodded, apparently satisfied, before popping something into his mouth and putting on his own splash mask.

Wally cut the engine and the tank's growling died in its throat as if pleased by the enclave's submission to its will. He lit the hurricane lamps and hung them before the driver's visors then opened the front visor hatches. The light from the lanterns flooded out as Skarra's piercing gaze lit the clearing. As quietly as possible, the crew bundled out of the hatches in the rear of the sponsons, hidden by the bulk of the *Ivanhoe*. At the rear of the tank Cecil and Reggie lit torches with a Lucifer. They fell into Indian file.

Glumly Alfie fell in with the others behind Mathers as they began intoning their version of a mock liturgical chant, but he couldn't muster any enthusiasm for it. Like Mathers', their rain capes were daubed with symbols, only less ornate. Wally and Frank were in front carrying rifles, bayonets fixed, in the *present* position, like crucifixes. Behind them came Cecil and Reggie, bearing the flaming torches. Alfie and Norman brought up the rear of the procession. Alfie knew it was so that Norman could keep an eye on him, and he resented the fact. Jack stayed in the tank, ready with a loaded gun, should the Urmen require the ultimate demonstration. Alfie felt nauseous. The padre would be spitting feathers if he could see them now.

The first thing they did was to put the local shaman in his place with a display of superior 'magic.' After that, the others usually fell over themselves to worship them.

Behind him, under his rain cape, Norman was preparing his trick.

"I love this bit," said Cecil, the glee evident in his voice under his mask and cape. "Especially when Norman does his Great Stromboli bit. I wish he'd show me how it's done."

Reggie nudged him. "Ces, be quiet."

"I feel sorry for the poor old fool that's got to go up against us this time," hissed Norman from underneath his mask. "This is going to be my best performance yet."

"Well, I still feel dashed ridiculous."

"Should be right at home then, Reggie."

"Keep your bloody voices down and do it just as we've done before," warned Frank.

Within the whispers and flutters of the torch flames Mathers heard the voice of Skarra. He cocked his head and listened. He halted the procession before the Urman chief and his medicine man. Dranethwe glanced sidelong at his white-faced shaman, who sized up the masked commander, smacking his lips, unimpressed.

"Behold the Warrior Priests of Boojum," said Mathers, indicating his crew. "We serve Skarra when he is in this world and we speak for him."

The white clay smeared shaman stepped forward, proud and defiant.

We're on his turf, thought Alfie, and he don't like it one little bit. And I can't say as I blame him, either.

"He looks like a slippery little bugger," hissed Frank.

"Oh, aye, he looks proper carny, he does. We ought to keep an eye on this one," said Wally.

Mathers thumped his staff end down on the ground, affronted. "You think you have the power to summon Skarra? Your magics are not strong enough for that. Skarra came because he wished it. As for us, you may question our power. But you may not like the answer."

"Bloody hell, the Sub's piling it on a bit thick isn't he, what's he up to?" muttered Cecil. Alfie kicked him, warning him to be quiet.

The shaman approached Mathers and performed a series of practised moves of some magical significance, flicking his tongue in and out. Was this some sort of ceremonial greeting, or was the wily old codger sizing up the opposition? Perhaps it was more of a challenge. I'll show you my juju, you show me yours. Mathers had seen the same thing in the Officer's Mess, when the new blood, cocksure of themselves, goaded the old guard, feeling threatened and having something to prove. This man's ability had been called into question and they had appeared to challenge it. Best sort this now. Let this shower know who was in charge.

The shaman prised open a small leather bag hung from his waist, reached in and dug out a handful of white ashes. He began to dance around them, chanting, before throwing the ashes into the air above them. He sank down on his haunches and, with great intent, watched the ashes caught like swirling motes above them, drifting down over the crew in the shafts of sunlight, as if their motions divined some truth or intent.

"What on earth's the geezer doing now?"

"Not Dulgur," Jarak said finally.

"Is that the best he's got? We're well in here."

Mathers thumped his staff on the ground twice and the file of tank crew behind him opened out into a well-drilled rank, sticking the torches into the ground either side of the *Ivanhoe*'s track horns.

The tank squatted like a great iron idol for him, its track horns open and welcoming like beneficent arms, lit by the torches planted either side. Alfie did have to admit it looked damned impressive.

Norman slipped something into his mouth under the chainmail that draped down over the lower half of his face. He stepped forwards and smoke and sparks began to billow through the chainmail curtain in front of his mouth.

The few simple conjuring tricks from his time on the boards had served him well at concert parties or for charming French peasant girls in the estaminets. Now, he made objects disappear and reappear and the Urmen shuffled back uneasily with groans of fear. He tore up a large leaf, burnt it by breathing fire on it and brought it back, whole, to life again. To end the performance on a spectacular note, Jack fired the flare pistol from a pistol port and a bright white light arced into the vaulted forest space above.

"TRULY, YOUR MAGIC is great," declared Dranethwe for all the assembled clan to hear. He glanced at Jarak, who glared back. Defeated, the shaman slunk away to lick his wounds, which were deep. He had lost face in front of his chief and his clan. The rest of the enclave fell to their knees, lowering their foreheads to the ground before Skarra.

"Up, up," boomed Mathers. "Skarra accepts your genuflection and while Skarra may not feel the trials of life, his acolytes do. Bring food and water. Bring tribute for Skarra and his benevolence. Hurry. Do not anger him."

The clan scrambled to their feet. Dranethwe clapped his hands and the throng burst into activity, mothers snatched children into large bark dwellings, afraid the god of the underworld would take their children before their time.

Dranethwe clapped his hands again and villagers brought forth platters of fruit and meats and laid them before the masked crew. Sat between the track horns of the *Ivanhoe,* the crew fell on the food, tearing at sticky wet pulps, spitting pips and stones and ripping greasy meat from carcasses.

"Oi, manners!" said Reggie.

Frank belched loudly, provoking raucous laughter from the crew.

"At least have the decency to say Grace. We are British. We are not savages. Have you forgotten everything I've taught you?"

"Sorry, Mother," Frank said, with mock contrition.

One by one they put their food down and clasped their hands half-heartedly as Reggie said Grace, the sound of 'Amen' starting a race for the food again.

Reggie sighed. "Savages."

Mathers, still wearing his splash mask, sat with them but ate little, watching his men with a sense of beneficence.

"Sir?" said Clegg, offering a platter of meats to Mathers. "Aren't you eating?"

"Hmm? Shh. I'm listening to Skarra."

"Skarra, sir? You mean *Ivanhoe*?"

"Hmm. Yes, I suppose I do. Don't you hear it?"

"Hear what, sir? The engine is off."

"You don't hear it? No. No, of course you don't. I'm blessed, aren't I?" Mathers said, fingering his jacket collar through the neck hole of his rain cape.

Clegg looked at the two lieutenant pips winking in the firelight. "Yes, sir. I guess you are."

Sated, they sat back, picked their teeth, and wiped their mouths on their sleeves. Round the fire before *Ivanhoe,* the crew spoke in low voices.

"This isn't right," muttered Alfie.

"It's an offering. It's their way. If we didn't take it, they would be offended and what's more, they'd know we wasn't big juju men. Besides," Frank added with a grin, "the women will come along later. They always do."

"We used to be a tight-knit crew. What happened?" asked Alfie.

Frank glared at him. "*We* are. What happened to *you,* Alfie?"

"Got himself a long-haired chum is what happened."

"Leave Nellie out of this. She's got nothing to do with it. Can't you see? What we're doing, it's wrong."

Norman rolled his eyes. "Oh, listen to Uncle Joe, here."

Wally leaned forward. "Look, we could live like these fellows, grubbing an existence, of course we could. But that's no better than living in the trenches, is it? There's nothing for us back there. Here we've got a chance, a real chance to be something better."

Jack sat, whittling, not saying a word. Cecil kept glancing at him, watching him for cues, eager to jump whatever way Jack did, but Jack for the moment kept his own counsel.

NORMAN SPOKE THROUGH a mouthful of meat. "Look, we've extended our travel range a little by bringing extra petrol fruit fuel with us, but if we got each of these enclaves to distil the petrol fruit as, say, an offering to the great Skarra, then what have we got?"

Cecil looked at him blankly, stuck out his lower lip and shook his head.

Alfie could see which way this was going.

Norman waved the meat bone about. "We've got ourselves a supply line, Reggie, haven't we? Fuel dumps. We'd no longer be dependent on the camp. We'd have our own followers, our own army. We could push on and conquer more. We don't need the poor bloody infantry. They need us more than we need them."

Cecil nodded eagerly. "That's right."

Mathers, who had been silent until now, and content to listen, spoke up. "Why be soldiers, when we can be kings? Why be kings, when we can be gods?"

"Exactly, sir."

Frank warmed to the theme. "And with an army of Urmen we could enslave the Chatts. They love digging, can't get enough of it. But we can channel them, enslave them, and get them to dig for what we want them to dig for. This world is virgin territory, from what I've seen. Untapped wealth. We can get them to mine for gold, for silver, for rubies. Anything we want. We'd be rich."

They sat back and each contemplated, for a moment, their own private fantasy.

Dranethwe made a sign of reverence, approached and cleared his throat. "Jarak, our shaman, he was once strong. He had the sight, but I fear he no longer has the strength to lead us in these matters. We made offerings and sought to invoke the gods. We are truly glad such strong magic has come to our aid. You have come to rid us of this torment."

The crew exchanged wary glances. This was a new one. No one had asked anything of them before. They looked to Mathers for guidance.

"You sought... aid?" he asked.

"For many radii we have been plagued by an evil. A spirit taunts our enclave and snatches our people, takes our strongest and boldest with impunity. Jarak has cast wards and spoken charms but he cannot stop it. His attempts at banishment prove fruitless. The spirit's magic is strong. You are the answer to our prayers." He cast a submissive glance toward the tank.

"This spirit you speak of, how many has it snatched?" asked Mathers.

The tank crew's gaze switched, as one, to Dranethwe.

"A dozen over the last three radii. Only the bravest of my warriors hunt now, but they cannot bring in enough game. The spirit takes from our hunting grounds, too. We are without the food we need."

Mathers sat silently, contemplating the information.

The tank crew held their breath.

"The Warrior Priests of Boojum have heard you, and will intercede with Skarra on your behalf."

Satisfied, Dranethwe backed away, bowing.

Mathers looked at his quizzical crew. "We have a tank. How hard can it be?"

They nodded and muttered in agreement.

Mathers sucked in air through his teeth and his brow furrowed briefly. The cramp in his stomach had returned, sharper and deeper than before. He suppressed a groan and eased himself up. "I'm just going into the tank. I don't want to be disturbed."

He walked unsteadily along the ironclad, one hand clutching his gut; he used the other to support himself against the tank's side as he worked his way round the port sponson, wincing as he ducked under the gun. He clambered into the tank by the hatch at the rear of the sponson and pulled it shut behind him.

Making his way forwards to the driver's cockpit, he pulled off his helmet and splash mask, took the hip flask from inside his tunic and took a quick slug of the liquid.

He sighed with relief. It was as if a great pressure had been released. It stopped his head from banging and eased the cramps in his stomach. He rested his head back against the shell rack at the front of the sponson and took another slug.

Outside, a long, unearthly shriek cut through the night.

CHAPTER SEVEN
"We're Not Downhearted Yet..."

HIGH ABOVE THE encampment, Atkins and 1 Section, accompanied by Napoo, Chandar and Nellie Abbott, proceeded to make their way in Indian file up the valley side above the tree line. They'd make quicker time up here, and it was less dangerous skirting the forest below than going through it. They could easily pick up the tank's trail at the valley head. It wasn't going to be hard to find.

As the party climbed the trail across the face of the hillside towards the valley head, slowed by the fact that they were wearing marching order packs, Atkins paused to look back down across the encampment and at the arthropod army beyond. From this distance, they really did look like insects. It seemed hard to believe that he couldn't just crush them under his foot.

He felt disconcerted, leaving his comrades behind to face the foe. It felt like they had cut and run, leaving the battalion to their fate, but orders were orders. The Chatts would run scared when they returned with the tank.

"I just hope we find it in time," said Pot Shot.

"I just hope we find it in one piece," replied Mercy.

"Better hope the crew is in one piece as well," muttered Gazette, "because I don't know how to drive one of them things."

"Shh!" said Prof. "That FANY back there is sweet on one of them."

If Nellie Abbott was sensitive about the issue, she didn't show it. "He'd better bloomin' well be alive," she called forward. "'Cause I'm going to kill 'im if he ain't."

Atkins had assigned Gutsy to be Chandar's guard, especially during this early part of the trip. They had been uneasy about having one of the Khungarrii along, so they tied the Chatt's long three fingered hands in front of its body and placed a gas hood over its head to prevent it sending any scent signals to those out on the veldt.

"The thing makes my skin crawl, Only."

"Gutsy, this whole place makes my skin crawl."

Frankly, Atkins thought, he'd rather be facing the Khungarrii than whatever lay out beyond the confines of their valley. At least here, you knew who the enemy was. Out there, it was everything. It took a toll on a man's nerves, did that.

He wished he hadn't looked back, though. He felt the familiar lurch in his stomach as his heart skipped a beat. It wasn't wistfulness that did that. It was cold, gnawing fear. That small circle of Somme mud with its drifting splash of bright red poppies looked so small and insignificant from this height. What if that small circle should vanish now, going back home and leaving them behind? Feeling sick, he forced himself to turn away and carry on walking up the hillside.

Chandar had stopped to look back, too, and hissed beneath its hood. Atkins' lip curled. It seemed excited at the sight of its army below. "Do you not see it?" Chandar said in a muffled croak through the gas hood.

"See what?"

"There. Do you not see it?" Chandar touched the heels of its hands to its head beneath the mask and thorax as a sign of reverence.

Atkins squinted and stared at the Khungarrii army, frowned and shook his head irritably.

"No. What? Where?"

"There!" said Chandar. It pointed at the valley below them. "The Sky Web of GarSuleth." At the name of its god, it made the reverent sign again.

It took Atkins a moment more before he saw it. Not the Khungarrii. Chandar had been looking at the encampment. The circular trenches and the radiating communications trenches did indeed resemble a spider's web, after a fashion. Out beyond the wire weed entanglement, long paths extended out into the landscape, like anchor lines.

"So it looks like a web, what of it? Why's that so bloody important?" he snapped.

"It is a sign," said Chandar, fingering the scent-laden knots from its shoulder cloth.

"Of what, your certain victory?" asked Atkins with a sneer.

"Maybe. Yes," said Chandar. "But not here, not now." It said nothing more but its vestigial middle limbs clicked together rapidly. Like a dog wagging its tail, thought Atkins.

Gutsy pushed the Chatt on up the path ahead of him. The aerial sight of the encampment had excited Chandar and beneath the gas hood, it went on chittering in its own tongue as it walked.

"Move it, y'bug-eyed Bosche," said Gutsy gruffly.

"Where are you taking this One?" it asked.

"On a pilgrimage, to meet Skarra, and if you don't behave you'll see him a lot sooner than we will."

* * *

THE RUSH OF injured and wounded had slowed to a trickle now, and in the aid post, the orderlies were preparing for the next flood of casualties.

Edith Bell stepped from the tent for a breath of fresh air. She put her hands to the small of her back and arched it to relieve the ache. God, what she wouldn't give for a nice cup of tea.

Beyond the trenches, in the aftermath of the attack, the bodies of several large battlepillars lay sprawled across the great wire weed entanglements, and might have provided bridgeheads for the besieging army if the wire weed wasn't already beginning to grow tight about their elephantine carcasses. Nearer, she could make out the occasional flashes of bayonets above the paradoses as men moved about otherwise unseen in the trenches before her, preparing for another assault.

The massed Khungarrii army had retreated perhaps half a mile or so to regroup, and sunlight glinted off a myriad iridescent carapaces until it seemed that the veldt sparkled in a dazzling rainbow display. It's almost pretty, she thought. But she'd seen them up close and knew them for what they were. She shuddered. The memory of her imprisonment in their nest was still fresh in her memory. She looked back up along the valley in the direction that her friend had left and felt a pang of emptiness. She had grown to depend on Nellie's common sense and companionship and she hoped she would see her again.

Edith only had a short rest break and hurried over to check on the shell-shocked in the Bird Cage, unsure as to what she would find. The sounds of the fighting had agitated them, and she feared many of them might not have coped at all well.

She found Oliver Hepton, the kinematographer, smoking a cigarette, staring at them through the barbed wire in a contemplative manner. From his demeanour, he might have been on a promenade looking out to sea.

"They've calmed down remarkably," he said, without looking at her. "Don't they usually, you know..." he mimed a neck spasm and twitch.

She regarded him coldly. "They can't help it."

He pulled out a partially crushed Woodbine packet from his top pocket and offered it to her. There were three battered but serviceable cigarettes left in the carton. With supplies running low she recognised the generosity of the gesture. Her father never approved of women smoking, especially in public, but that didn't stop her aunt from introducing her to the habit and, truth be told, she rather enjoyed the illicit thrill of drawing on the odd cigarette. However, his derision of the patients irked her.

"No, thank you. I don't."

He shrugged and put the packet away and Edith immediately regretted refusing.

"I hear when the battle began some ran screaming into their dugout, and some just curled up crying." The thought seemed to amuse him. He took another drag from his gasper.

The man's attitude irritated her. "Don't you have something to film?"

"I already have some battle footage, but I've only got two canisters of unexposed film left. I want to save it."

He turned to look at her.

"Those trousers don't do anything for you, you know. I can imagine you were quite pretty once."

Edith felt her hackles rise. She wasn't a suffragette, and the trousers weren't a political statement. She left that kind of thing to Nellie, who seemed to have more of a taste for it. However, if Mr Hepton found it distasteful, then right now it was a flag worth sailing under.

"They're practical, Mr Hepton, as your sex will doubtless admit. Which is more than can be said for you at this particular moment. You obviously have nothing better to do but amuse yourself by watching these poor souls."

"Oh, I dare say they'll have me running ammunition or messages or some such if the Chatts charge again," he said, with an insouciant air. "Still, they do seem remarkably quiet."

Edith looked through the barbed wire fence. Almost all of the shell-shock victims had emerged from the hut or the dugout now. She had to admit, Hepton was right. They all seemed quite calm. Unusually calm, considering the state they were in earlier.

Private Jones was one of the shell-shocked in whose plight Edith had taken a special interest. He suffered from almost uncontrollable spasms, to such an extent that he found it hard to walk, eat or do anything for himself. Yet there he was, sat on an old ammunition box, as still as anything.

Her brow creased into a frown. She strode towards the gate where a soldier stood hastily to attention. She stopped and waited by the gate until he unslid the crude bolt.

She walked through, looking at the lethargic men in the compound around her as she made a beeline toward Jones, a practised smile easing onto her face. The young man looked up with eyes much older than his years.

"Hello, Private. How do you feel?"

"It's stopped," he said, holding out a hand, palm down. "See, steady as a rock."

"So I see. Can you stand for me?" She held out her arm.

He stood up in one smooth motion without taking it.

She turned the young man's head this way and that, gently, forewarning him of everything she was doing so he wouldn't become alarmed.

"It feels like such a relief."

"I can imagine," she said, holding his wrist and taking his pulse. It was slow and steady.

She felt his forehead with the back of her hand. It was slightly clammy. "A bit of a fever."

"I have a bad belly too, Nurse," he said, cradling his gut. "It's started churning ever so bad."

"Have you been sick?"

He shook his head.

"What about your... bowel movements?"

"Fine," he mumbled.

Food poisoning of one form or another was a common enough hazard here, but she was puzzled. It didn't seem to be that.

Jones looked past her at the cigarette in Hepton's mouth. "Have you got a spare fag, even a nicky would do right now?" he said. "I haven't been able to hold one for ages."

Hepton shrugged. "Last one," he lied. He took a last suck at the fag as it shrivelled rapidly toward his lips, dropped the smouldering dimp to the ground and crushed it into the dirt with his boot.

"Well, as you're here, Mr Hepton, if you want to help, you can fetch Captain Lippett and Sister Fenton."

He clicked his feet together, gave her a mocking salute and turned on his heel with a wry smile.

Edith went around the compound checking other patients at random. All had a restful pulse rate. All complained of some gut pain. Most exhibited some swellings or other.

She spoke to Private Miller, his hands now bandaged.

"How do you feel?"

"Unafraid," he answered, with a smile. "For the first time in ages. How about you?"

The question caught Edith off guard. "I beg your pardon?"

Miller jerked his head towards the gate. Hepton was returning with the agitated MO and Sister Fenton bringing up the rear. "It looks like you're in trouble, Nurse Bell."

From the look on Lippett's face as he entered the compound, Miller was probably right. She knew she should have followed proper procedure and referred this to Sister Fenton first, before sending for Lippett, and knew Fenton would haul her over the coals for the breach of hospital protocol, but had thought this too urgent.

The MO looked from Edith to the shell-shock victims and back again with a bad-tempered glower. "Is this important? I haven't time for your malingerers and skrimshankers, Bell. I have other things that require my attention. What seems to be the matter?"

Edith bobbed a little curtsey, which looked odd in her part-worn serge trousers. "I don't know, sir. I wondered if you'd take a look? They don't seem to be themselves. As you can see, the hysterical tremors seem to have stopped. They all seem calm, although some are developing swellings and all are complaining of stomach pains."

"Is this what you brought me out here for, a bit of indigestion? Although if something they've eaten has eased their 'symptoms,' then we can send them back to the front line, can't we? Lieutenant Everson could use every available man right now, wouldn't you agree?"

Sister Fenton stepped up with a fierce glance of disapproval at Edith, warning of an imminent telling off. Nevertheless she covered for her nurse. "With respect, Doctor, if that is the case then we should wait and see. We wouldn't want them becoming hysterical in the trenches again. Bad for morale. And it would reflect badly on you as Medical Officer."

Lippett considered this for a moment. "Quite right, Sister." He turned to Edith. "Nurse, as you seem to have worked miracles here, do you think you could do the same with the bed pans? They need emptying."

Edith's face flushed. She had expected him to listen to her, at least. "Yes, Doctor."

She hurried away, humiliated, taking a last glance at the calm, listless men behind her.

Something didn't feel right.

THE NEXT DAY, 1 Section arrived at the canyon.

"Perfect for an ambush," said Gazette after a brief recce. "But the tank definitely came this way." He looked down at the trail left by the vehicle. The wind had begun to obscure it, but there was no mistaking the parallel tracks.

"Right. This place is just one bloody big trench, so trench clearance duties. If there are any surprises in there, I want it to be us. And conserve your ammunition. Don't fire unless you have to. We may need it even more later."

Chandar was reluctant to proceed. They had taken the gas hood off it now, but its hands remain tied. Gutsy tried prodding it with his bayonet. It hunkered down defensively and hissed angrily.

Gutsy pointed his rifle at the Chatt. "Don't you dare spit. Don't you dare, or I'll shoot you right here."

Chandar cocked its head to one side and gulped another mouthful of air. "No further. This is not Khungarr burri. It belongs to other Ones, the Zohtakarrii. Ones do not enter the burri of other Ones."

"Well, you were all for pushing everyone else off your territory into someone else's, so it's a little late to worry about them now," Atkins gave it a shove on the back. "Gutsy, watch it," he said. "Make sure it doesn't bolt."

"Oh, I'll make sure all right," said Gutsy. He took the length of rope around Chandar's long three fingered hands and yanked it until the arthropod began to move reluctantly.

Atkins turned to Nellie. "Miss?"

"Nellie, please," urged the FANY.

"Miss," insisted Atkins. "I want you to stay close to Porgy."

Atkins took the lead with Napoo as they entered the canyon. Mercy and Gazette came next, then Prof and Nobby. Gutsy and Chandar followed, and behind them Porgy escorted Nellie, while Chalky and Pot Shot brought up the rear.

Out of the sunlight, the early morning chill in the canyon was noticeable. The Tommies' banter had stopped now. The men were intent on their surroundings.

The walls rose straight up on either side of them. After several hundred yards, the canyon curved to the left and opened out. The shadow that encompassed the canyon walls was beginning to retreat before the sun's climbing advance on the right. High up on their sides, clusters of large blue-green blisters began to pulse in the sunlight. As they moved cautiously along the canyon floor, the shadows continued to shorten.

Napoo put a hand on Atkins' wrist, pointed along the canyon and sank down on his haunches. Atkins turned and indicated the rest of the section to do the same. Silently they sank towards the floor.

"Yrredetti," said Napoo.

Several arthropod bodies lay scattered about, which was odd. Yrredetti were lone hunters, blessed with a natural camouflage that helped them blend into their surroundings. It was one of the reasons the section had avoided the forest. These ones, though, with their mottled green carapaces, stuck out like a sore thumb against the rocks.

Atkins looked down at one of the Yrredetti bodies. Stitched across its thorax was a neat line of holes, the *Ivanhoe's* work.

"These are forest Yrredetti. Not stone. See their markings?" said Napoo, squatting and examining one with the point of his short sword. Atkins nodded. They were certainly out of place in this vegetation-free landscape, where the only growing things seemed to be the large patches of blue-green blisters that populated the walls and the rocks. "The Khungarrii attacks have driven not only the Urmen from their hunting grounds, but the Yrredetti, too. They are solitary creatures but here they are working in packs to hunt. Such co-operation is almost unheard of. "

"You mean there could be more of them?" asked Nellie, hefting the unfamiliar weight of the revolver in her hand and glancing up at the scree slopes around them.

The rest of the section were eyeing the boulders and rocky clefts warily, too. A wind gusted between the rocks stirring little dust devils as it passed.

"There could be, and we're a lot more vulnerable here than a bloody tank. We'd better move on," said Atkins.

They proceeded cautiously along the canyon following the faint tank tracks. There was no sign of any living Yrredetti, forest or stone. Around another crook in the rock, the canyon widened again. Large boulders sat patiently on the scree slopes, perfect hiding places.

A landslide had slipped down to the canyon floor in a fan of scree and rocky debris, blocking their path. The tank tracks led right up to it. Atkins' stomach plummeted. The tank wasn't under there, was it?

Nobby scrambled clumsily up the landslide and stood triumphantly at the top.

"I can see tracks on the other side," he said with a grin.

"So they're not buried, then. That's something," said Chalky.

"Nobby, get down before you fall," said Prof.

"I'm the king of the castle!" yelled Nobby, spinning round, arms out, his voice full of boyish glee. "Whoooo-hoooo!" his voice echoed off the canyon walls.

"Nobby," barked Prof. "I'm not going to tell you again. Down. Now."

Nobby stopped and gave him a sullen stare. "I was only havin' a bit o' fun. There ain't no harm in that."

"There is if you bring a ton of shit down on our heads, you dozy git," said Porgy.

"Porgy! He didn't mean no harm by it," Nellie protested.

"He didn't have to."

Sulking, Nobby came clambering down. He trod awkwardly on a rock, then slipped and fell, his rifle clattering down the rocks.

"I told you..." Prof began to say.

Nobby tumbled face first into a large blue-green blister, which burst under his impact. He didn't even have time to scream. His fists beat the rock and his feet kicked feebly for a second but subsided and stopped before anyone could reach him.

"Nobby!" cried Prof.

Nobby didn't answer.

"Careful!" warned Mercy.

They turned him over to a collective gasp of horror. Atkins turned his face away.

"Jesus!"

"Poor sod!"

Nellie gasped and buried her head in Porgy's webbing. Atkins had seen many things on the Front and worse here, but this had them beat.

The front of Nobby's head and chest—his uniform, flesh, muscle, fat, cartilage, down to his sternum—had gone. It had been eaten off where he'd fallen into the thing. There was nothing but fizzing bone. Through his ribs, his internal organs continued to dissolve into a slop from the inside out where he'd breathed the stuff in.

"Nobby!"

Pot Shot held Prof back.

"He's gone, Prof," said Pot Shot. "He's gone."

"No!" Prof slumped in his arms. "I warned him. I told him a thousand times to be careful, the soft bugger." Prof's voice trailed off. He looked lost. He'd taken it upon himself to shepherd the hapless Nobby through the war. He'd got all the way through the Somme, and three months of this place and the clumsy sod trips over his own feet and dies.

With nothing else to do, they buried Nobby under stones from the scree slope. There wasn't even an identity disc to collect. The acid had seen to that. Useless, clumsy Nobby. Nobody deserved a death like that.

As THEY SAID a prayer over Nobby's grave, a flash of light caused them to shield their eyes.

"What the hell?" Atkins squinted up to find the source.

There, on the canyon wall, where the scree slope met the rock face, a large expanse of metal had been exposed by the rock fall and was catching the sunlight. It was a flat, featureless wall of dull silver metal, hidden behind the rock until it had been blasted away.

Atkins looked to Napoo, who just shrugged. Chandar let out a long wet hiss that set its mouth palps flapping.

"Holy Mary Mother of God, will y'look at that."

"Blood and sand!"

"What is it?"

"I have no idea," said Porgy. "It has to be the result of some sort of manufactory, though. I mean, look at it. There is no way that's natural. Maybe whatever brought us here is inside. I'll bet this is exactly the sort of thing the lieutenant wants us to keep a look out for."

Atkins pushed back the cap on his head and puffed out his cheeks. Hopes suddenly welled up, unbidden. It was true. There was no way this could be natural. It was artificial, made, constructed. And if that was the case, somebody must have built it. They may even still be in there. Could this be it? Could the reason they found themselves here be found in there? Maybe even a way home? Home to Flora. The thought overwhelmed almost all else. He had to know.

"Gutsy, you and the others take cover on the far side of this rock fall while me and Porgy go up and investigate. Gazette? Keep us covered. If anything goes wrong, you should be able to make it out of the canyon."

"If anything goes wrong? What the bloody hell are you planning to do, Only? We've got orders. We've got to find the tank."

"Shh!" snapped Atkins, flicking his eyes toward Chandar.

"Sorry," said Porgy sarcastically. "Skarra."

"Look, Porgy. This is the first thing we've found here that isn't built out of dirt or sticks; no offence, Napoo. Don't you want to know?"

Atkins and Porgy scrambled up the scree slope towards the metal wall. Rocks and stones slipped away beneath their feet and skittered down to the canyon floor as they clawed their way up the spoil. "Look for a door, a hatch, anything," Atkins said. "There must be a way in."

Prof turned towards him. "And what do we do if we find one? Nothing else has been too friendly lately."

"We'll cross that bridge when we come to it, eh?"

As they drew closer, he could see that the metal wall had been hidden behind a crust of rock three or four feet deep. The surface wasn't polished, but brushed; their reflections were misty shapeless hazes of khaki, like a fogged funfair mirror.

A cursory examination, however, revealed no seams or rivets, no joins of any kind. Porgy rapped on the metal with his knuckles. It was solid. Atkins unshouldered his rifle and slammed the butt into the metal, half expecting—half hoping—to hear a hollow ring. All he got was a dull, solid thud. He tried scratching it with his bayonet but the blade slid impotently across the surface patina without leaving a mark. He smacked it with the palms of his hands. "Hello! Hello? Is anyone there? Can anyone hear me? Open up!" Nothing.

He put his ear to the metal, expecting it to be cold, only to find it warm. He looked at Porgy and put a finger to his lips hoping to hear signs of life within. He heard nothing; no gentle electrical hums, no machinery and no great thrum of turbines, nothing, except the rocks shifting and clattering beneath his feet as he tried to maintain his balance. Not that that meant anything in itself. The wall could be so thick as to prevent him hearing anything. Anger and frustration welled up. Were there beings in there now, observing them, judging them?

He was contemplating his next move when there was a shout from the canyon floor. The dull crack of a rifle shot echoed briefly round the canyon walls. Atkins glanced along the scree. The Yrredetti were emerging from behind large fallen blocks of stone, and were scuttling across the slope towards the two men. They seemed to have found their nerve. That, or they were desperate.

"All right, Porgy, time to get out of here."

"No argument from me."

Porgy turned and started scrambling clumsily down the scree, half running, half trying to keep his balance, riding a small wave of rock fall as the spoil slipped from beneath his feet.

Several more shots rang out from below. Atkins took aim at an Yrredetti that was hunkered low along the scree line and fired. The creature's head exploded and the body tumbled several yards down the slope before coming to a halt. Atkins grimaced as several other Yrredetti turned their attention to it instead, and began tearing at it and cracking its carapace with rocks to get at the still warm meat within.

Porgy had almost reached the base of the scree and hands were reaching out to grab him.

Atkins was about to follow when he hesitated. "Ah, what the hell. It's worth a shot."

He pulled a Mills bomb from a pouch on his webbing and hastily set it against the base of the metal face, jamming it between two rocks. Maybe he could blast a hole in it. He took a deep breath, pulled the pin and leapt down the scree slope. He landed heavily, skidded, stumbled, and lost his footing. The world became a disorientating whirl and tumble as he careened head over heels down the slope.

Seconds later the concussion wave of the grenade blast caught him, propelling him further and showering him with dust and dirt. Small pieces of rubble rained down about him.

He felt hands pick him up and set him right, dust him off and thrust his rifle back into his grip, even as he blinked tears from his eyes and coughed out dust. Words gradually resolved from the ringing in his ears.

"Well, Only, you scared them Yrredetti off, good and proper," Gutsy was saying. "Scuttled back under their rocks like spiders in a privy. You should have seen 'em."

Atkins doubled over and coughed again, a deep chesty cough that made his diaphragm ache, before hawking out a gobbet of dusty spit. "Good. What about the wall?"

Gutsy shrugged.

"What?" Atkins looked up. Another rock fall completely buried the metal face. He had hoped to blast a hole in the metal wall, but the bomb seemed to have had the opposite effect. "Bugger!" His shoulders slumped. Nellie came up to inspect his injuries, but he brushed her off. She had her webbing and pack all stuffed with field dressings and whatever medical supplies she could beg or steal. Atkins suspected she was almost as good a scrounger as Mercy.

"Porgy, mark it on the map. Lieutenant Everson can send another party along to investigate it."

"If we don't push on and find that tank, there might not be anybody else left to investigate it," Gazette reminded him.

Atkins was in low spirits. After Nobby's death they all were, especially Prof. For a brief moment, Atkins had hoped the mysterious metal wall hinted at a way back to Blighty. All these months, thoughts of Flora had driven him on. Now he felt he had lost her again. He lashed out and kicked a stone.

Gutsy stepped forward to comfort his mate, but Porgy shook his head.

As they headed for the mouth of the canyon, Atkins thought his spirits couldn't get any lower.

He was wrong.

CHAPTER EIGHT
"The Chances..."

DESPONDENT, 1 SECTION left the canyon and picked their way over a fan of debris down on to a great fractured plain with deep cracks and fissures crazing the landscape.

Mercy pushed his battle bowler back on his head. "Bloody hell, just when you think things might get easier."

"My wife says the same thing about our marriage," said Gutsy, slapping him on the back.

An escarpment behind them, through which the canyon ran, rose several hundred feet and stretched away on both sides into the distance. With no compass reading worth spit on this world, landmarks like this scarp were invaluable. Atkins scratched another '13/PF,' their battalion abbreviation, on a boulder by the canyon mouth to mark their trail before they moved off across the plain.

It was hard going for all, so Atkins cut Chandar's wrist bonds to help it to deal with the uneven terrain. It now scurried about, to Atkins' mind, like the insect it was.

Unable to follow the tank tracks directly across the wider gullies, they had to pick their own way. They scrambled and slid down the sides of great rocky protrusions like giant's steps, before they reached level ground. There, the gullies narrowed and the rocky terrain between levelled out.

It took them longer than anticipated to cross the plain and pick up the tank's tracks again. It was coming to mid-afternoon when they found the bodies of the jabberwock and the stone beetle on the fractured plain beyond the canyon. They could smell them on the wind before they even saw them. Nellie clapped a handkerchief over her mouth and blinked away tears.

When they came across the carcasses, they couldn't see them at first. A moving carpet of flat, woodlouse-like scavengers the size of

Labradors were burrowing inside the rotting carcasses. As the section approached they slipped into the surrounding cracks and fissures with their prizes. The sight caused the party to avoid the cracks wherever possible.

The tank tracks headed towards the belt of vermillion and damson vegetation in the distance.

"Not more bloody forest. I hate forests," said Porgy. "You know, I didn't see a lick o' nature until I joined the Army. Gimme brick an' cobbles any day."

"See them tank tracks?" said Atkins conspiratorially.

"Yeah?"

"Where do they go?"

Porgy knew where this was headed. "Into the forest, Lance Corporal."

"So that is where we're bloody well going. I don't like it any more than you do, Porgy."

They followed the tracks into the jungle as it closed in about them completely. Atkins hated this. He hated what these places did to him. Every noise was a potential threat, every pair of eyes, every screeching call, a potential predator. The unrelenting tension was exhausting. Trying to breathe lightly so as to hear better only to have the rush of blood in your ears drown out the advantage. Starting at every crack and rustle around them. Napoo's presence helped little in negating that. A man's sudden death might be the only warning the rest of them got and none of them wanted it to be them. Still, thought Atkins in an all-too-brief flash of optimism, if they kept to the tracks they didn't have to worry about things like sting-a-lings, the spring-loaded barbed plants that had killed two of their section when they first arrived.

His body ached from the fall down the scree. It was a bed of bruises that had begun to bloom purple, blue and yellow. Small lacerations itched and stung beneath his heavy serge uniform. A bruise on his face swelled and stretched his skin uncomfortably, but he forced himself to ignore it.

"What are the chances we'll find the tank crew alive eh, Only?"

"Well, as I heard it told, Chalky, ain't no more than five things that can happen to a soldier: nowt, wounded—bad or cushy—prisoner, killed or doolally."

Napoo disappeared up ahead and every so often came jogging back into sight. Scouting. "Footprints. Urman footprints."

"After us?"

"No, too old. With tank. With *Ivanhoe*. Their footprints cross the beast's tracks."

"It's not a beast, Napoo."

Napoo shrugged. "I know what I know."

Atkins could never be sure whether the man was simple or mischievous. He suspected Napoo knew a great deal more than he let on.

"These tracks?"

"They were with it. Urmen were accompanying it."

"Stalking it or escorting it?"

"I cannot say."

Urmen had generally been friendly towards the Pennines, so that was good. There must be an enclave nearby. They could restock with supplies, maybe rest up. Sleeping out in the wild here was not easy, it was nigh on impossible. If the Urmen had been following the tank, they might know its whereabouts, or at least which way it went. After all, it was hard to miss.

So was the totem they came across with the body of the Urman lashed to it.

Gazette regarded it nonplussed, "Well, if this was them, they don't seem too friendly, like. Talk about your crucified Canadian. Fritz has got nothin' on these fellers. Jesus."

"You don't think this is what they do to captives, do you?" asked Mercy.

Chandar let forth a sound that could have been a sigh. It wandered up to the body and stretched out a chitinous arm, its long slender fingers reaching out to touch it.

Napoo stepped forward and grabbed it by the wrist.

"No."

Chandar flicked its gaze to Napoo, then back to the gutted corpse, enraptured. "This is wonderful," the Chatt rasped, its fingers fidgeting, eager to touch it, but it restrained itself. "Wild Urmen. I have never seen such a thing. What is its function? What is it for?"

Gutsy's lip curled in disgust as he watched the Chatt enthuse over the poor sod.

"Can't we cut him down?" asked Nellie.

Napoo glanced around, examining the area around the totem without touching it. "No. It's a warning. A totem to ward off *jundurru*—bad magic. Its power is strong."

"To-tem," repeated Chandar, its fleshy mouth palps moving thoughtfully, as if committing the word to memory.

"At least somebody's happy," muttered Mercy.

They walked past it, each man intent on following the tank tracks at their feet, avoiding the hollow-eyed gaze of the totem sacrifice.

THEY HAD NOT got far beyond it when the section found themselves surrounded by Urmen with spears and bark shields. Long blowpipes were aimed at them. The Tommies raised their bayonets to the guard position.

The agitated Urmen were restrained only by a strong voice that barked out of the shadows. The Enfields came up and bolts cycled. It was a stand off.

Napoo stepped forwards, fingers splayed, patting the air, as he passed the Tommies. "Lower your firesticks."

The Tommies looked at Atkins. He nodded and the bayonets were lowered. He hoped their Urman guide could persuade his kin of their honest intentions and at least find out if they had any information before things went to hell. Atkins glowered and shook his head. An Urman with a white-painted face stepped from the shadows. Napoo bowed. "I am Napoo, chief of the Horuk Clan. This Urman is Onli of the Tohmii."

"Those aren't our real names," muttered Atkins.

"This man is a shaman," Napoo told him. "They believe given names have power. I spoke our taken names, which have less power."

"You give your name too freely, stranger." The shaman rolled his eyes upwards, scanning the canopy. "Here in the Thalpa groves, the spirits may take them. If they haven't already."

"The Tohmii are strong," replied Napoo. "Our names are still our own. We seek kin of theirs, keepers of a great beast. We have followed its spore here." He pointed at the twin tracks on the ground.

Several of the Urmen muttered amongst themselves before one suddenly let out a tongue-trilling alarm. It had spotted Chandar.

"You walk with the Ones," the shaman said, his lip curled in loathing. "You are not true Urmen. You are their chattel!" He gave a signal.

Atkins felt a sting and clapped his hands to his neck to find a feathered dart protruding from his skin above his collar. He plucked it out and looked at it in a quizzical way as it swam out of focus. "Bollocks," he muttered, through a suddenly drying mouth as his sense of balance went and he fell over. The skull-like visage of the shaman appeared in his tunnelling vision before all faded into blackness.

TIRED AND ACHING, *he found himself walking down a cobbled street of familiar terraced houses, the numbers on the front doors counting down as he walked. The sky above was grey, leaden, and laced with the promise of rain. The smell of hops from the brewery hung heavily in the air and he breathed the familiar aroma deeply. With every step he took, he felt the exhilaration of a soldier on leave, nearing the end of his journey. He sensed lace curtains twitching. He could feel the weight of his pack on his back. An old woman shaking a tablecloth into the breeze tutted as he passed and shut the door on him.*

A man in a flat cap and shabby jacket passed him on the street. "You're no better than you ought to be," he said with venom.

Still the numbers counted down as he walked, and there it was. Number 12. Flora's parents' house. Flora Mullins. The girl he had loved all his life. He dropped the pack from his back and began running. As he approached, the door opened and Flora stepped out. She was wearing a white blouse and long skirt, a shawl across her shoulder, no, not a shawl, something cradled on her shoulder in a shawl. A baby. He came to a stop yards from her, his heart wanting to burst with joy and pride. He smiled at her. She smiled back, and he took a step towards her. Someone else stepped from the door behind her, a man in shirtsleeves and braces, a man he knew well, better than any other. His brother William, declared missing on the Somme.

"William! You're alive. Thank God."

His brother stepped towards him. The smile vanished from William's face as he did, contorting into a black scowl of anger and resentment, his hand clenching into a fist.

"Alive? More than I can say for you, you little shit, you bastard, I'll kill you! I hope you rot in whatever hell you find yourself in!"

He heard Flora scream as William swung at him. The fist connected with his jaw and he went down, the world spinning into blackness, the scream still ringing in his ears.

THE SCREAM WENT on and pain flooded his consciousness. He opened his eyes. He was lying on his side. He tried to move and couldn't; his hands were tied behind his back. He strained his neck to find the source of the screams. It was Nellie. She was lashing out at their captors with her legs, the accuracy of her kicks hampered only by her calf-length khaki skirt, until they kept their distance, regarding her warily, and she had to settle for glaring at them. Atkins' eyes met those of Mercy. "Bastards ambushed us with blow-pipes," said the private.

Rough hands hauled Atkins to his feet. There were groans of protest around him as the others were pulled up, too. He counted all his men, Napoo, Nellie and Chandar. Their guns and equipment were piled up across the clearing, where some Urmen were rifling through their haversacks.

He took in their surroundings. They were in an open space bordered on three sides by forest. On the fourth side, the land came to a stop and dropped away steeply. A gnarled narrow platform, grown out from the tree roots around it, extended out over the precipice.

Stood before the platform was the Urman with the white-painted face. The shaman. His warriors stood solemnly around the clearing behind the bound soldiers.

"My name is Jarak," the shaman said. "I had a clan. I had an enclave. I had honour. Now all that has been stolen from me. I have nothing left but my power. Our chief was weak, desperate, and he found my magic wanting. Your kin came to our land with their spirit, Skarra, saying that their magic can banish the devil that has been taking our people. But why need it take my people when it can take you instead? If you are as strong as you say, then you will make worthy sacrifices to the spirits. Maybe then they will deliver us from the dulgur."

He nodded and two of the warriors started herding Porgy towards the platform, his feet digging into the tree spoil as he struggled.

"Porgy!" Atkins started forward, but two warriors restrained him.

Porgy cast him an empty glance as he passed. He'd seen the same look in men's eyes before they went over the top; the look of men without hope.

"Wait," said Atkins, standing as erect as his bonds and aching body would allow him. His dream was still fresh in his mind, and the self-loathing it provoked still stirred within him. "My given name is Atkins, Thomas, 19644, C Company, 13th Battalion, Pennine Fusiliers."

The shaman regarded him with interest. "You are not afraid to reveal your given name?"

"No."

The shaman's eyes narrowed. He nodded at his warriors who shoved Porgy back with the others, knocking them over like skittles.

"Only, don't!"

"It's done," he said. "Make the most of it. Get out of here alive."

Atkins walked out onto the platform under his own steam, a little unsteadily, but his resolve seemed to impress the shaman. He was the NCO in charge. It was the right thing to do. It might not pay for all the wrong he'd done, but this was all he had. It would have to do. If this could buy his section time to free themselves, then all to the good. Right now, his brother's words were still fresh in his mind; never mind that they were a dream, they only served to remind him of his own thoughts. He deserved whatever fate had in store for him.

The shaman anointed Atkins' forehead with some greasy, rank smelling unguent. Atkins flinched involuntarily. He looked straight ahead at the horizon, framed on either side by the entwined and fused branches and roots that formed the living wood platform. Beyond it, the jungle tumbled headlong over the precipice, falling in a tangle of branches, roots and liana as the ground plunged away, where, hundreds of feet below, the jungle continued almost uninterrupted by the drop.

The shaman called out in his own tongue, his arms thrown wide in invocation. Warriors with spears urged Atkins to the edge of the platform out over the precipice. Around him, the boughs and roots of the platform groaned and squeaked. The wood beneath his feet had been worn smooth. How many other sacrifices had it taken over the years? How many had plunged to their deaths here? He looked straight ahead, the sense of vertigo making him stagger, but the root rails prevented him from falling. Far out across the jungle below he saw another escarpment rising on the far side. A discolouration of the jungle canopy below, marking out a long, wide, straight line, caught his eye. It didn't seem natural, but he had other things on his mind.

As the shaman continued his liturgy, Atkins' world shrank, the pleached boughs either side of him becoming revetments. He was back in the trenches, waiting for the whistle, listening to the artillery barrage and the sound of machine gun bullets zipping through the air over his head, like invisible insects. He smiled bitterly as he remembered his own personal good luck ritual; if he could still smell the perfume on Flora's last letter he would survive. His hands were tied behind his back. The letter was in the inside pocket of his tunic in his paybook. He guessed that was that, then. Time to go over the bags. He heard the shouts of the men and the loud boom and wail of an artillery shell. A second later, a plume of fire and dirt and shredded wood exploded up from the jungle below.

The Urmen warriors wailed. The shaman turned, a look of puzzlement on his face. A look that transformed into one of fury as the crushing of trees and the clank and whine of heavy armour filled the clearing. The *Ivanhoe* rumbled out of the jungle and the machine guns spoke, sewing a line of dirt that vanished off over the precipice.

A band of Urmen accompanying the tank spilled into the ceremonial clearing, seizing some of the shaman's warriors as others fled into the trees.

The men of 1 Section let out a rousing cheer at the sight of the landship. Chandar let out a hissing cry and sank down in supplication, fingering its silken tassels and hiding its face at the appearance of one of its gods.

"Keldoth spoke the truth," the chief bellowed across the clearing. "I had him follow you and your shaman's party, Jarak, and glad I am that I did."

The shaman, petulant and defiant, screamed incoherent obscenities at the disturbance of his sacred ritual. "How dare you defile this sacred place? These strangers would have gone straight to the spirits as an offering to rid us of the dulgur."

"They are under the protection of Skarra," the chief said. "His priests have ordained it. I am chief. You no longer speak for the clan in these matters. Accept that or be banished." His voice softened. "You know the law, old friend."

The shaman shifted warily on the platform. "I know the law, but you have shamed me in front of these outsiders. I have known and nurtured the ways of our clan all my life. My sacrifices to the spirits have kept the dulgur at bay."

"Until now. It takes more and more. Your magic cannot stop it. Skarra's magic can. The spirits do not listen to you anymore. I must do what is best for the enclave. "

"And I have lost face. I have lost everything to these strangers but, as shaman, I tell you now, you will have no cause to thank them!"

He ran up the suspension boughs that supported the platform, vanished into the foliage above, and was gone.

Atkins slumped against the rail of roots and watched as the new Urmen freed the section from their bonds. Porgy came running up, bayonet in hand, and cut his friend loose.

"It's all right, mate. You're safe. And so, thank God, are the tank crew."

Atkins cast a sullen glance over at the *Ivanhoe*. "Until I get my bloody hands on them..."

NELLIE RAN TO the tank, calling Alfie's name. Alfie, still wearing his symbol-daubed rain cape and his splash mask, stumbled out of the *Ivanhoe's* sponson hatch and caught his breath, a clean fresh breath that sluiced away the intoxicating fumes of the compartment.

"Alfie?"

He turned at the sound of his name.

"Nellie?"

He looked at her in astonishment, and then he took her by the wrist and pulled her behind the *Ivanhoe*, out of sight of the others, and took his helmet off. They embraced each other for a moment, completely uninhibited, before decorum got the better of them, and they stepped back and shuffled uncomfortably at the ease of their intimacy. She shoved him away, a business-like scowl appearing on her face.

"Where the bloomin' hell have you *been?*"

"Alfie! Quit your bloody spooning and get back in here. We can't leave without you!" barked Frank from inside.

Alfie smiled weakly and shrugged. "Better go."

ATKINS PICKED UP his equipment from the pile where the shaman and his men had dumped it, walked up to the tank and banged on the front with his rifle butt. "Lieutenant Mathers? Lieutenant Mathers, sir?"

"He ain't here," said a cockney voice from within.

"What do you mean, he isn't here? He's the Tank Commander. I have orders for him."

"Oh, he won't like that."

"What do you mean?"

"Orders. He won't like 'em. Doesn't do orders now." And the visor slammed shut.

Atkins stood looking at the tank, dumbfounded.

"Mathas is at the enclave. We will take you there now," said the chief.

1 Section walked behind the familiar backside and raised steering tail of the ironclad as it grumbled and slithered its way back along its own path.

Chandar hadn't said a word since the tank turned up. At first, it averted its eyes from its god, as if hardly daring to accept its presence, but as the journey progressed Atkins caught it sneaking glances at the tank. He wondered how much longer they could maintain the illusion.

Atkins didn't know whether to be mad at the tank crew or thankful for the rescue. There was something going on here and he didn't like it. He was sure he'd like it even less once he knew what it was. And why were they so cagey about Mathers?

"What's their game, then?" Gutsy pondered.

"I don't know, but I can guess," said Atkins, darkly. "I just hope I'm wrong."

When Atkins had caught his first glimpse of the enclave, he still felt frustrated at being unable to breach that metal wall they found. That, at least, had offered the hope of some advanced civilisation. This, as strange and magnificent as it was, with its huge living bark walls, seemed like a step back, a complete lowering of expectations. His heart sank, the way it did when he first spotted the Khungarrii edifice, three months ago. There seemed little hope of finding a way back to Flora here.

They were escorted into the compound by the Urmen warriors. Even Napoo seemed impressed by the scale and age of the place.

"I want to speak with Lieutenant Mathers," demanded Atkins. "Tell him I have an urgent message from Lieutenant Everson."

The chieftain smiled. "If he sees fit to grant you an audience."

Porgy leaned over. "An audience? Who the hell does he think he is?"

"A bloody officer," muttered Atkins.

The chieftain walked over to a semi-cylindrical bark hut on the far side of the compound. Smoke gently coiled up from a hole in the hut roof. It was more ornate that the other huts around the perimeter. Outside, it had torch posts decorated with some kind of animal skins. It had two small lean-tos, one on either side, constructed of thick branches and covered with overlapping leaves, in which mounds of fruits had been stored under one and meats under the other. Atkins watched as a young girl, wide-eyed and awe-struck, hurried up nervously with slices of a large red fruit and laid them under the lean-to with the other fruits. It was like a small shrine or chapel for offerings, then, thought Atkins. Great flat leaves were laid in bands on either side of the hut's length. There was something familiar—

"It's a bloody tank," said Atkins. "They're trying to copy the tank. A lean-to either side, like sponsons? The lengths of leaves, like tracks? They've turned the hut into a mock tank."

"It's a form of sympathetic magic," said Prof. "They think they can capture the power of the tank within their enclave, make themselves strong again by doing what the tank does."

"Napoo, what do you make of this?"

The Urman nodded in approval. "Strong magic. Not yet, but it will be."

"So you approve?"

"They do what is necessary for the survival of the clan."

The Chieftain appeared at the door of the hut and beckoned Atkins. "'Ullo, you've been summonsed," said Gutsy.

Atkins strode over towards the hut. As he passed between the burning posts, he took off his cap and ran a hand over his hair.

"Mathas, high priest of Boojum, grants you audience," said the chieftain with a bright, welcoming smile.

Oh, does he indeed, thought Atkins. He ducked his head and stepped into the dark cloying space beyond. It was like stepping into a dugout. It took his eyes a moment or two to adjust to the gloom, the interior lit only by a small fire beneath a large shallow plate that held a liquid slowly vaporising with the heat. The fumes caught in the back of Atkins' throat and he coughed. He recognised the taste. Petrol fruit.

"Lieutenant Mathers, sir?"

In the dark, he heard the sound of laboured breathing. As his eyes grew used to the light, he could make out the figure of a man slumped back on a pile of furs and skins, as if on a throne. The chain links of the splash mask he wore caught the light from the flame and glittered. The guttering flame also highlighted one or two of the runes painted on the man's rain cape. Either side of him sat an attentive Urman woman, but in the dim light, he could make out no more than that.

The apparition on the fur throne spoke. "What do you want?" The voice was slow, each word carefully enunciated, as if speech was an effort.

Atkins snapped a salute. "Lance Corporal Atkins. 1 Section, 2 Platoon, C Company—"

The man waved the introduction away. "Yes, yes, I know where you're from."

Atkins fished about in his jacket, pulled out a slip of folded paper, and stepped forward.

"Lieutenant Everson asked me to give you this if we found you, sir."

Mathers sighed and gestured to one of the waiting women, who leant forwards and took it from Atkins' hand. She handed it to Mathers. He opened it and held it by the incense burner. "Leave us!" he told them. The women nodded and silently left the hut.

Once they had gone, Mathers took off his leather 'turtle shell' helmet and removed his mask. "Can't see a damned thing in that." He held the paper towards the flame and squinted at the writing, drew his head back and tried to focus on it.

"Can't read it. You'll have to do the honours." He handed the paper back. As he did so, Atkins saw his face.

"Blood and sand!"

"Corporal?"

"Your eyes!"

Mathers' eyes were as black as coal with refracted iridescent rainbow swirls constantly drifting, moving lazily over their surfaces to some unknown imperative, like oil on water. Atkins was reminded of his own hallucinogenic episode shortly after they'd first arrived here. Mercy had built an illegal still and used some alien fruit to make alcohol.

"Can you see?"

Mathers learned forward, sharing a confidence. "More than you know. More than you'd want to know."

"It's the fuel isn't it, sir? The petrol fruit?"

Mathers sank back languorously into the furs. "Yes. The way it heightens one's senses. It's marvellous."

"Marvellous? It killed one poor bastard. Bloody near did for me."

Mathers sat forwards keenly. "That was you?"

"Yes, and I was bloody lucky."

"Then you'll know? You have some inkling of what I can see? The enormity of it."

"Oh, aye, and I'll tell you another thing. I never want to see it again. It's enough to send a man mad."

"Only if you can't comprehend it. But it's beginning to make sense to me." Mathers took a slug from a hip flask. A small sigh of relief escaped his lips.

"What, you're *drinking* it now?"

"It's the only way to numb the pain."

"Pain? What pain?"

"In my guts. They seem to churn more frequently now, and I long to feel the wind upon my face. In the tank, I can see the noise. I can see your words tumbling from your mouth, warm and soft and inviting but tinged with sharp reds and treacherous oranges. And your khaki uniform sounds shrill and discordant. It does not fit here."

"Sir," said Atkins, holding out the orders again. "Lieutenant Everson orders you and the *Ivanhoe* back to the encampment, effective immediately."

"No."

"Sir?"

"Holding on to your paltry trenches, the last few square yards of Earth. You're clinging to the rock as the tide comes in. Do you really think you'll ever get home? You're deluding yourself. Look to the future. This is it. Here. We were promised our reward not in this world but in the next world. This is the Next World. Can't you see? There is so much more here. What were you? Before the war, I mean?"

"Shop assistant, sir, but—"

"Shop assistant. We can be so much more here. Join me. You can be a lord, Corporal; a baron, if you wish. You've seen these people, these Urmen. They can be ruled. They *want* to be ruled—by us. And those Chatts. We can defeat them; enslave them as they have enslaved mankind here. They're good at digging, at building. They're insects. Ants. They can mine for us. Gold, diamonds, silver, rubies. We can stake our claims. We can all be rich as Croesus here, every last one of us. There is enough world for us all. Imagine. A British colony among the stars. A new British Empire where we can all be kings. Think of it, man."

Atkins listened to Mathers. All the riches of this world were as bitter ashes in his mouth if he couldn't be with Flora. That was all that mattered.

But the fumes began to pervade his senses, warping them gently, slowly. He had to get out of there. He shook his head, as much to clear it as to signify his rejection of the proposal before the drug seduced him.

"So you're disobeying a direct order, sir?" he asked as bluntly as he could.

"Order? I don't recognise Everson's authority here, Corporal. As Commander of the HMLS *Ivanhoe*, when we've gone dis from Battalion I have the authority to act as I see fit."

"But, sir, without the tank the battalion can only hold out for so long."

Mathers waved him away, no longer interested.

"Sir, you if you think about it, you don't have a choice."

"Is that a threat, Corporal?"

"No sir, but you will have to return to refuel. You're at the limit of your range now. Your current supply will just get you home, otherwise you're stranded."

Mathers took another swig from his flask and nodded to show he'd heard. "I will think on it overnight, but now I need to... rest. My head hurts."

Atkins' couldn't hide the disappointment and bitterness in his voice. "Sir." The word dripped with resentment. He turned on his heel and stepped out from the claustrophobic confines of the hut.

INTERLUDE THREE
Letter from Private Thomas Atkins
to Flora Mullins

19th March 1917

My Dearest Flora,

We've found the tank. The good news is that it's in one piece. I'm sure Lieutenant Everson will be pleased about that. The bad news is that the crew seem to have gone native and, as Porgy said, if you've seen the natives, that's not a good thing!

On the positive side, we've had our first proper food after a couple of days existing on emergency iron rations.

I know I didn't want Nellie Abbott to accompany us, but she really is a good sort. She's kept up with the marching and hasn't complained once, even when Gutsy got his feet out for a foot inspection. Talk about plates of meat! If those are a sample of his wares, I'll not be shopping at his shop when I get back. She packed out a haversack and webbing full of first aid stuff. I've no idea where she managed to get it all from, but I'd say Mercy has a rival in the scrounging stakes.

I think you'd like her, Flora. She has a good heart and a strong spirit.

I'm scared, though. For days now, the perfume on your last letter has been fading. I dread the day I can no longer smell it, for on that day you will have drifted just a little bit further from me and Lord knows you're far enough away already.

Tomorrow it seems we're going hunting, but given the size of some of the game here, I'm never sure that's too wise.

I hope you are well. I think of you and our baby often. Will it be a boy or a girl, do you think?

Ever yours
Thomas

CHAPTER NINE
"Tuppence All the Way..."

As A NEW DAY dawned, the second Khungarrii attack advanced steadily on the trenches, but the Pennines were ready. The outer ring of fire trenches facing the enemy was fully manned. In the centre were the two full companies of Fusiliers fit enough for duty. Either side of them, 'Fred Karno's Army,' the companies of partially drilled and trained Urmen platoons, stood armed with spears, swords, slings and longbows. They only had about a hundred longbows; still, it was enough to assess their potential. If they didn't get home first, the Pennines would have to get used to fighting with weapons like this once their ammunition ran out.

Salvaged Leach trench catapults, with a range of two hundred yards, and originally used for hurling grenades, were loaded with stones.

Over on the left flank, a copse of tall saplings had hastily been commissioned as rudimentary catapults. Bent back, ropes held the supple trunks under tension. They had been stripped of boughs, and large woven slings had been attached to their upper ends and the cups loaded with large hard-shelled segmented pods, shrapnel fruit or 'shrapples' as some of the men called them. They'd lost several men to the shard-like seeds as they exploded out from their pods. It had been Poilus's idea. In nature, if you could ever call this place natural, the parent tree would fling these rugby ball-sized seed pods away from itself and the things would burst on impact, flinging seeds and shell in a wide circle with explosive velocity in order to propagate the plant. It was crude and difficult to aim, but they didn't have to worry about accuracy. Unused to open warfare on such a scale, the Chatts charged bunched up, with little cover.

Everson scanned the oncoming army through his field glasses. Assuming the Chatts didn't change tactics, his plan should hold together. If it didn't he had a few surprises up his sleeves, but they were far from inexhaustible.

There had been days on the Somme when Everson had cursed having to stick to a battle plan devised days or weeks before; plans that only worked if conditions were perfect and the enemy did exactly what was expected of them, which they very rarely did. Nevertheless, the plan could not be deviated from and must be followed to the letter. Stilted thinking like that needlessly cost thousands of lives. Here, there was no immutable battle plan to which they had to stick. No pig-headed red tabs ready to march men into a maelstrom of machine gun fire, simply because that was what the original plan had said they must do, no matter what the changes of circumstance on the battlefield. He was free to respond as he saw fit, to adapt his tactics. God help him, there was a kind of exhilaration in that, especially as he watched the Chatts marching towards them.

On the other hand, everything now rested on his shoulders and his shoulders alone.

It was a stroke of good fortune that, somehow, the poppies seemed to disrupt their chemical communication and scent orders, confusing the Chatt soldiers, and Everson had no hesitation in taking advantage of it. He would look into whys and wherefores later.

The plan involved something akin to a box barrage, boxing the enemy in, forcing them to attack the centre. That was their cone of fire. The heavy Vickers guns on the flanks would drive the Chatts into the centre, where the poppy field spread out across the alien veldt. There, disorientated, unable to attack or regroup, the Chatts would be in the Lewis guns' cone of fire, with the Vickers guns then able to enfilade the Chatts from their flanks. It was risky, but less of a risk than letting them flank and surround the encampment.

On the right flank, soft hollow *whumps* signalled the beginning of the defence as plum puddings soared smokily into the air from trench mortar positions, exploding amid the Chatt ranks, throwing whole bodies and limbs into the air.

THE FUSILIERS MANNED the fire steps, bayonets fixed.

Sergeant Hobson patrolled the fire bays, holding the line. "Look to your front. Hold your fire," he bellowed. "Look to your front. Hold your fire."

The men of Everson's old 2 Platoon stood nervously on fire steps. Behind them in the trench, Sergeant Hobson marshalled them, dispensing fatherly advice, bolstering a crumbling private here, sharing a joke to keep the spirits up there. "Make sure you keep your gas helmets handy, lads. You know what them buggers are like for spitting acid. Woodward, you keep 'em in your sights, son. Skelton, put that magazine cut-off back to its shut position. Did I give you permission to open it?"

"No, Sarn't. I just thought—"

"You don't have to think, lad. Thinking gets you into trouble."

Hobson knew they couldn't afford any nervous shooters. Every bullet that fell short or went wide was wasted and they couldn't afford to squander a single round. Soon they would have to take the enemy on hand-to-hand, he had no doubt about that. The fighting would be hard and bloody and, for some, it would be short.

"Wait 'til you see the whites of their—Well, wait 'til you can see their eyes, you can't bloody miss 'em, isn't that that right, Benton?"

"Yes Sarn't!"

THIS TIME, THE scentirrii general, Rhengar, held back its battlepillars. As the ranks of scentirrii came into range, sappers cut the lines holding the saplings and the trunks whipped up, flinging their rope slings into the air. Shrapnel fruit arced out across the wire weed entanglements. The seed segments exploded with a velocity that tore through carapaces, decapitating and shredding the Chatts around the impact sites.

The first wave of Chatts used the corpses of the already slain battlepillars as bridgeheads and springboards to leap across the wire weed. Slings, arrows and bullets picked them off and they fell into the waiting thickets, where the barbed tendrils pulled them down into a deadly embrace.

Once over the wire weed, they would again be in the poppy field.

"Watch your heads, lads. Fix staves!" ordered Sergeant Hobson.

Gas gongs were beaten. "Gas! Gas! Gas!"

Men fumbled at the gas bags on their chests and pulled on their gas hoods that would protect them not from gas, but the acid spit of the Chatt scentirrii.

One man in every bay dropped from the fire step to fix sharpened, vertical twelve-foot staves into the sump of the trenches behind them. They had seen the scentirrii leap over their defences and into their trenches before. This time they would be ready.

Above, the aeroplane roared across the trenches and out over the Chatts, its machine gun fire herding stray Chatts in towards the centre and the field of poppies.

Driven into the blood-red flowers, their meticulous advance began to waver and break. Chatts stumbled blindly, trance-like, jostling each other chaotically. The rear ranks ploughed into the muddled vanguard until they, too, became bewildered and the entire advance disintegrated.

Everson's fist hammered a parapet sandbag triumphantly. "Yes!" Now it was Lieutenant Baxter's job.

The machine guns began their deadly harvest.

*　*　*

A FEW ADVANCING Chatts escaped the machine gun fire and leapt into the air, like grasshoppers, dropping down into the trenches from above, spitting atomised mists of acid into the defenders' faces. Some scentirrii were impaled on the waiting staves. Others shot arcs of electric fire that jumped and earthed around the trench, or through unlucky men. Others plummeted into the fire bays, their barbed spears lancing soldiers.

The Tommies' bayonets thrust up even as the Chatts plummeted down. Now the fighting became dirty and vicious. Sergeant Hobson swung his trench club again and again, stoving in Khungarrii heads like clay jars.

The sounds of electrical fire whipped down the trenches, mingling with screams of Tommy and Chatt as the mopping up began.

Everson watched Tulliver and his Sopwith harry the retreating Chatts as it swooped down, strafing them, dropping grenades and flechettes. Several Chatts had the presence of mind to turn their electric lances on the flying machine. Most of the blue arcs shot harmlessly into the sky, forking and fizzling into insignificance. One, though, hit its target, scorching a hole in the fuselage. Everson watched as the aeroplane veered off, his observer attempting to pat the flames out with a gloved hand. He vaguely wondered who was up there with Tulliver; he *had* been told. Maddocks? Maddocks, that was it.

Now Everson had repelled the first attack, he had to figure out his next move. He hadn't many more left.

SISTER FENTON DEALT with the influx of wounded to the Aid Post quickly and efficiently, deciding who needed immediate treatment and who could wait.

After the confrontation with Captain Lippett, Sister Fenton had shared strong words with Edith. Afterwards she put her to work sorting field dressings and bandages. She wasn't too worried about the nurse's absence in the aid post. The girl had to be taught her place. Besides, the Urmen had long ago proved their worth with their native salves that calmed burns, and pastes made from crushed leaves that protected wounds from infection. On the Somme, you could survive the wound but die from infection and gangrene from the smallest cut. Here, their native poultices made all the difference.

EDITH WAS FOLDING fresh bandages when Orderly Stanton popped his head into the tent.

"Edith. You ought to come and see your lot."

"They aren't 'my lot,' and I'm already in Sister's bad books."

"No, but summat strange is going on," he insisted.

Curiosity got the better of her and she scurried over to the Bird Cage. The shell-shocked patients stood about calmly. Edith went from one to the other. On each man, she saw the same blank trance-like face, each possessing a serenity that had managed to elude him in previous months.

"Townsend, Townsend, can you hear me?" She waved a hand in front of his face. There was no response. His eyes remained fixed ahead. She brought her hands up and clapped them together. Not even an involuntary blink. She took him by the shoulders and shook him, then wheeled around and strode over to another. "Hello?" She snapped her fingers in front of his nose. Nothing. It was as if they were all in a trance.

She went back to Townsend and this time took his hand in hers. He offered no resistance. She tightened her grip, squeezed and relaxed. Townsend's hand lay limply in her own. She lifted it to take his pulse. It was then that she noticed the swelling on his forearm; the skin stretched taut and hard over it, hard and round like a cyst or a ganglion, firm and resistant to her touch. She pushed his sleeve up and found another in the crook of his elbow. There was another on the back of his neck at the base of the skull. She unbuttoned his shirt and found a further eleven on Townsend's torso alone. All the others had them too, to a greater or lesser extent.

Captain Lippett would have to listen to her now. This could be contagious, some sort of disease. At least they were quarantined, she thought. She glanced back at them as she stepped through the compound gate.

She hadn't realised before, but they all stood facing the same direction. They were facing into the wind...

That alone sent a shiver down her spine.

ALL NIGHT, SKARRA had whispered to Mathers and he knew now what he must do. As the sun rose to penetrate the canopy above, he summoned Atkins to the hut.

"We will go with you on one condition," he said.

"There are no conditions, sir. It's an order," said Atkins.

Mathers regarded the belligerent corporal. "One condition."

Atkins considered for a moment, then, seeing he had no option, sighed. "Which is what, sir?"

"We have promised the Gilderra to rid them of this 'spirit' that is snatching their villagers. Doubtless, it is some wild animal, but we have given our word."

"What? Sir, we haven't got time for this. We need to get back to the encampment."

"Then the quicker we get this done, the sooner we can return. The help of you and your men will speed up the hunt."

Atkins turned and paced and turned again, caged by duty and military obedience. "I have your word, sir? Once this beast is killed we return to the encampment?"

"As an officer and a gentleman, Corporal."

MATHERS STAGGERED UNSTEADILY from the hut, his splash-mask and helmet in place, his gas-mask-topped staff in his hand. Atkins stood awkwardly by his side.

The chief, dressed in his ceremonial finery, the warriors and their families had assembled before the hut.

Mathers raised his staff; silence fell, and he addressed them. "Skarra has heard your pleas and will rid you of the evil spirit that has been plaguing your clan. The Warrior Priests of Boojum and their brethren, the Tohmii, will accompany him on his quest. But we shall return. As a sign of our bond, we leave you the Totem hut of Skarra."

Across the compound by the great bark gates, Atkins' section was waiting, webbing and backpacks on, eyeing the tank crew in their painted rain capes and splash masks with suspicion. The tension was palpable and Atkins was keen to get them separated as soon as possible. Nellie stepped forward and kissed Alfie on the cheek, which earned her a glare from Frank and Wally.

The chief accompanied them to the bark gates.

An old Urman woman appeared and stood beside him. She looked at Atkins and Mathers with pitiless eyes. "Skarra will take the dulgur to his realm. I have seen it. But you, Mathas, shall not accompany it." She fixed Atkins with her gimlet-eyed gaze. "Your companion here will know such grief that might only be assuaged in the underworld. But he will have a hard choice to make."

Atkins frowned. He'd had enough grief so far. Being ripped halfway across the universe from Flora, the woman he loved, was grief enough for anyone's lifetime, but a grief so deep, so all consuming that he would kill himself over it? He didn't see it. It was the ramblings of a native woman. Superstition. He shrugged it off.

However, it seemed that Mathers took her words to heart and walked a little taller, a little more soberly.

"You see, Atkins? Mother Dreamer has told me I won't die. I won't die."

Atkins shook his head in exasperation.

The chief spoke. "The spirit haunts the thalpa groves evewards," he told them, pointing towards the direction in which the sun set.

Atkins stood close behind Mathers. Now that he had found the tank crew well and the tank operational, his anger at being dragged out on a wild goose chase needlessly festered and bordered on insolence. "All right, that's enough, sir," he hissed. "Let's go and get this thing done."

A breeze blew across the compound, rustling the huge leaves above. Mathers stood still and turned to face into the wind with a heartfelt sigh.

Frank turned to Reggie. "Give us a hand with the Sub. He'll be as right as rain once we get him into the tank."

The clan watched as the tank crew escorted Mathers to the waiting *Ivanhoe*. A great ululation rose up from a small group of young women as the tank's engine roared into life. The tank lurched off in the direction indicated by the chief and 1 Section fell in behind it.

"Why the hell are we going along with this devil hunt of theirs, Only? It's not our fight," asked Pot Shot.

"Well, it is now. For better or worse, the tankers have won these Urmen over. If they don't deliver, it's our reputation on the line as well. If the story gets out that we don't protect our own, or keep our word, then the Urmen will desert us; and we need allies here, so Lieutenant Everson tells me. But I'm still not sure if I bloody trust them."

AFTER SEVERAL HOURS of slow progress through the jungle they had seen nothing but trees, and the trees, to Atkins' mind, were the colour of old blood on army issue shirts, their barks blackened and rough like scabbing, but the men of 1 Section were getting tense and jumpy and eyed the armoured leviathan in front of them enviously.

Atkins, aware of Everson's order to press the Chatt for information, dropped back to where Gutsy was walking along with Chandar and Napoo. Chandar's feeler stumps were waggling furiously as if trying to detect something despite its disability.

"Is something wrong?" Atkins asked it. "You seem nervous."

The Chatt gulped in a mouthful of air and indicated the jungle around them. "Zohtakarii burri. You should not be here. Khungarrii should not be here. Our scents will carry. Ones do not enter the burri of other Ones."

Napoo grunted in agreement. "It is true. If Chandar is found in Zohtakarii burri, it will be killed. As will we."

"This just gets better," said Atkins with a sigh. "We're being attacked by the Khungarrii. These Zohtakarii will kill us if they find us and we're off hunting something that's probably stalking us, with a tank crew that would sooner we just dropped dead." He shook his head. "The Pennines up to their necks again. So, this thing. Any ideas what we're up against, Napoo?"

"The Gilderra clan says dulgur, a bad spirit."

"Load of codswallop," Pot Shot said. "If it's taking people then it ain't no ghost, which, as I'm sure Gazette will tell you, means it can be killed."

Gazette clicked his tongue, winked, and patted the stock of his Enfield. "Maybe Bantar," admitted the Urman.

"A bantar?"

"A four armed, fur covered Urman-like creature that dwells in the trees, but perhaps twice our size."

Chandar chattered, as if it disagreed.

"This One does not know, but this One fears what this dulgur might be." Chandar struggled to gulp a mouthful of air again but, as it tried to speak, nothing came out from its mouthparts but an empty belch. It tried again in its own tongue, a long sibilant sound combined with glottal stops and mandible clicks that meant nothing to Atkins but clearly meant a great deal to Chandar. The Chatt seemed to shrink down on its legs into a submissive posture before swallowing more air. It regurgitated it and hastened to form words with its mouth palps. "This One means that perhaps this One was mistaken. Maybe Sirigar's prophecy of the Great Corruption was not so wrong after all," it said, looking round at the Tommies.

"What, that we're some great evil come to blight your land? Look mate, we don't even want to be here," challenged Atkins.

"Jeffries did. Jeffries was searching for something dark and forbidden. He sought knowledge of an ancient heresy. I think perhaps he may have found it."

"Found what?"

"Croatoan," it hissed.

ALFIE WIPED HIS brow. The engine shifted into the blues, and the noise tasted of tart rhubarb as he shifted his gear lever in response to Wally's hand signal.

He felt the wary, sullen gaze of young Cecil on him. The lad was staring at him with undisguised distrust. Cecil always had an unswerving loyalty to the *Ivanhoe* and its crew and had more than once got into a fight defending it against some imagined slur or slight. Alfie always knew the lad was trouble. Until they'd come here it looked like Jack had calmed him down after taking him under his wing, but maybe leopards couldn't change their spots.

"If you've got anything to say, say it!" said Alfie.

"I saw you talking with them Tommies. They want us to go back to the camp. They'll put us on a charge for mutiny. You're supposed to be one of us but that bint has turned your head. You don't know where your loyalties lie anymore!"

He launched himself at Alfie, who had nowhere to go, crammed as he was in the corner of the compartment by the shell racks. He fell back and cracked his head on the bulkhead. Cecil was on him, saliva frothing at the corners of his mouth as he screamed obscenities over the engine noise, hands at Alfie's throat, trying to choke him.

Several things happened at once.

Jack Tanner grabbed Cecil under the armpits and pulled him off. "But you all say it," protested Cecil. "You all say it about him behind his back. None of you trust him." Still snarling at Alfie, he lashed out with his foot. His boot caught Alfie on the cheek, sending his head into a shell base. Alfie slumped on the gangway planking, heaving in gulps of air down his raw, crushed throat.

Wally Clegg signalled for a right turn from the driver's cabin.

Alfie was still struggling to get up and reach the starboard track gear lever when a shuddering vibration, and a loud grating noise from under the tank, filled the compartment. It was a noise Alfie knew. The bottom of the tank had risen off the ground over some obstacle and the tracks could no longer gain traction. They had bellied. The tracks clacked and rattled impotently.

Mathers turned round in his seat. "What the hell is going on back there?"

There was a banging on the sponson door. "Hey, you're stuck. Looks like the British Land Navy has run aground. Is everything all right in there?"

Mathers looked at his crew. He fixed each of them with a stare, reserving the last and longest for Alfie. He spoke in a low, measured voice, quavering with suppressed anger. "Later. Not in front of them. Perkins, clean yourself up." Then, to make it clear that there was to be no further discussion, he called through the visor to the accompanying infantry in a cheery voice. "Spot of bother! We'll need a hand."

THE SPONSON DOOR swung open and the crew clambered out. The little bantam driver, Clegg, crouched down between the front track horns looking underneath the tank.

Atkins joined him. "What is it?"

The little man pointed under the tank. Atkins got down to have a look. An outcrop of rock had caught the low-rising tank floor and lifted the tracks from the ground.

"Is it serious?" Atkins asked, barely trying to hide his annoyance.

"Well, that depends," said the driver, standing up and rubbing the back of his neck. "We need some logs to put under the tracks."

"Well, we're in a jungle aren't we? That shouldn't be too hard," said Atkins curtly.

Alfie Perkins stumbled out of the tank.

Atkins noticed the other members of the tank crew cast him black looks. They didn't even try to disguise it.

"What's all that about?" Gutsy asked Jack.

"His fault," said Jack flatly.

Atkins accepted the explanation, figuring it wasn't any of his business. "1 Section to me," he said. "We need to find some logs to get this thing moving again, but I don't want anyone going off alone. I'll take Chandar. The rest of you, pair off. Gutsy and Porgy. Gazette and Pot Shot. Mercy and Prof. Napoo, Chalky, you stay here with Miss Abbott." He stepped in towards Chalky and added in a low voice, "And keep an eye on that lot. I don't trust 'em."

"Oi, excuse me, don't I get a say in all this?" said Nellie. "I'm quite capable of looking for logs. If you think I'm going to sit around here like a helpless gel then you got another think coming. You ought to know better than that by now. Shame on you, Only Atkins, shame on you."

Gutsy grinned at him. Atkins shot him a glance.

"Don't look at me," said Gutsy, with a look of guileless innocence. "My missus has a voice like that. If you want my advice, you'll let her have her own way. It'll be less painful in the long run."

"Fine!" agreed Atkins irritably. "Go with Napoo and Chalky. Meet back here in ten minutes. Watch out for the wire weed."

"And Jeffries," said Mercy with a grin.

"I should bloody well think so, too. Come on, Chalky!" Nellie growled as she stalked off. Flustered, Chalky ran to catch up, the jeers and catcalls of his mates ringing in his ears.

The question was, where to find logs? True, this was a jungle, but the trees were like no trees Atkins had seen before. Now that the ironclad's engine had stopped, he could hear low clicks and creaks permeating their surroundings. More than that, he could feel something reverberating through his chest, like the deep bass notes of the organ at church; felt, rather than heard. Was it an animal, or the trees themselves?

Atkins pushed on warily through groves of scab trees. Chandar kept pace with him, looking around with quick bird-like movements. It was impossible to read any expression on its chitinous white facial plate, but its chitterings had become more profuse. As the resonant note continued, he became aware of a rising nausea and, while he didn't feel sick enough to vomit, he was left feeling distinctly queasy. If the noise bothered the Chatt, it was hard to tell.

"So, you really think this dulgur is this Croatoan, that's taking the Urmen?" he asked, as they searched for logs big enough to suit the tank crews' purpose.

The Chatt regarded him for some moments before replying. "It is a possibility," it said. "You Urmen and Croatoan are inextricably linked in the lore of the Ones."

Atkins resented the remark. "Look, don't try and tar us with the same brush. We're not Urmen. We're nothing like them. We don't even come from here. We don't belong here."

"No," agreed Chandar. "You migrate from burri to burri scavenging off the land granted by GarSuleth to the Ones."

Atkins shook his head in disagreement. "No, really. You don't understand. We're not like them. We're not Urmen at all. We come from somewhere else."

Atkins pushed his bayonet into some coiled plants.

Chandar's middle limbs opened. "But where else is there?"

Atkins wheeled on him, annoyed by the Chatt's questions. He leant in towards its face. "Up there!" he said, pointing at the sky through the forest canopy. "We came from up there. From the stars!"

The Chatt craned its head for a moment, looking up at the firmament above it. Then looked at him. It stepped back on its chitinous legs, as a man might, staggered by the news. "That is the Sky Web of GarSuleth," it hissed, rising up on its legs in the threatening manner of the Chatts and striking a defensive pose. "It is not possible. It is heresy."

Atkins was unprepared for the strength of Chandar's reaction. His goaded, off the cuff remark seemed to have struck a nerve at the very heart of its beliefs. He brought his bayonet into the guard position, ready to run the Chatt through should it attack.

He had no further time to ponder the consequences of his remark as, from out of the scabrous boughs with their scaly leaves, half a dozen hissing arthropods leapt down around them, while others in red silken robes stepped from hiding, their mandibles open, spraying an atomised mist into the air about them.

CHAPTER TEN
"To Hunt for Vermin..."

ATKINS GOT A shot off with his rifle as he sank down to the ground. Holding his breath, he struggled for the gas hood in the bag at his chest. When the atomised mist didn't burn, he knew it wasn't acid. It was the mild euphoric spray that Chatts used for control, which didn't make it any less dangerous.

One of the Chatt scentirrii stepped towards him, a hiss rippling its mouth parts, and swung its staff at him. He blocked it with the butt of his rifle and countered by lunging forwards with the bayonet, but as he did so, another Chatt drove the end of its staff into his solar plexus, winding him. Involuntarily he gasped for air, realising too late what he'd done.

However, once he'd caught his breath, Atkins felt relieved. He relaxed and looked up at the creatures. There were nine of them. They looked like Khungarrii. From the knobs of bone on their facial plate and the dark iridescent chitinous armour, they were obviously scentirrii; so, a war party, then.

But then, what were those other ones doing there, tall and regal ivory white with a featureless facial plate, and the metal bands around their heads, the ones that had breathed on him? The burden of worries that he had carried with him lifted. Still cradling his bruised stomach, he sat back on his haunches and looked up at the creatures that surrounded him and Chandar. He smiled at them. He felt quite content to let them take over the situation. Whatever they wanted, that was fine by him.

They urged him to his feet with clicks and hisses and he obliged, not wishing to put his hosts out. The regal ones with the silken cloaks seemed to be having some sort of angry exchange with Chandar. He turned to scold Chandar for being rude towards the tall ones. After all, weren't they Chandar's people? He didn't exactly like them, but he was no longer afraid of them. In fact, for the first time in a long time he felt happy. As they ushered him along, he was able to look at the trees and plants around him and appreciate them for possibly the first time, without expecting something to leap out and kill him. It reminded him of his gun. He checked his shoulder. It wasn't there. Never mind. He didn't need his gun anymore anyway. They would protect him.

IN THE END, Alfie and the others found a fallen log large enough for the job and laid it into place just under the front track horns. Mathers stood watching, still wearing his splash mask. Alfie saw him slip an arm under his rain cape and clutch his stomach.

"Are you all right, sir?" he asked.

"Of course! Mind your own damned business," snapped the lieutenant. "Just do your job and get the tank unditched. Hurry up." He turned away from the crew and thumped his free fist against the side of the hull.

Wally and Frank hauled clanking lengths of chains out from under the gangway floor boarding. They wound them round the log and, struggling with spanners and bolts, attached the chain to track plates. When the tank started forwards again, the log would be dragged under the tank by the movement of the tracks, lifting the tank's belly free of the obstruction. At least, that was the idea.

Alfie started at the sound of the gunshot. "Nellie!" He stood to run off after it.

Frank put a firm hand on his upper arm and pinned him with a hard stare. "Where d'you think you're going?"

Alfie shrugged his hand off. "She could be in trouble."

"Guess we know where his loyalties lie now, don't we?" said Norman brusquely.

"They're here because of us," yelled Alfie as he ran off. "If some great devil thing has got 'em, it'll be our fault!"

Wally just shrugged.

Sod 'em, thought Alfie, sweeping the undergrowth aside as he ran. They're not in danger. Nellie might be. Although the way Lieutenant Mathers had been acting this trip, maybe they all were. He was becoming unpredictable. The petrol fruit fumes seemed to be affecting him more than the others. And the way he walked round wearing that medicine man rain cape, splash mask and helmet, as if that was now more his uniform than the officer's garb beneath it, where did *his* true loyalties lie? Alfie wondered. And what was wrong with him? He didn't look well. He'd have a word with Nellie. Maybe she could give him the once over. If she wasn't—

Alfie almost collided with two Fusiliers. The tall one and his mate, Pot Shot and Gazette? They heard the others pounding in from all directions, snapping through the undergrowth, also drawn by the sound of the gunshot. As they arrived, it became clear who was missing.

Nellie came running up with Chalky and Napoo. She and Alfie exchanged looks of relief, but they didn't last long.

"We heard gunfire," she said. "What happened? Where's Only?"

"And where's the bloody Chatt? You don't suppose it turned on him, do you?" suggested Mercy.

Gutsy spat. "Wouldn't put it past the sneaky bastard. Never did trust it."

Mercy found Atkins' rifle lying on the ground, He bellowed into the trees. "Only! Only! Where the hell are you? Only?" He spat on the ground in frustration. "You don't think it was that evil spirit, do you?" he asked Prof.

"I don't know. Three months ago and I'd have said it was superstitious nonsense, but here?" He shook his head. "I'm not so sure."

Alfie shuffled uncomfortably as some of the Fusiliers shot him black looks.

"What the hell are you doing here? Shouldn't you be with your mates?" sniped Porgy.

He shrugged. "I heard the rifle shot."

Mercy held them back and waited expectantly while their Urman, Napoo, studied the ground. "No sign of struggle." He pointed to several sets of scattered impressions. "Ones." His fingers gently traced the shallow pad marks. "Scentirrii—heavy, others not so. These sets are deeper," he said, describing an arc with his arm. He looked up into the boughs and the broken branches overhead. "They ambushed them from above."

Nellie sniffed the air, her nose wrinkled. "I know that smell from when we were captured and taken to the Khungarrii edifice—" She sniffed again. "They breathed out something that drugged us."

Napoo tipped his head back and inhaled slowly, his nostrils dilating. He looked at Nellie and nodded in agreement. "Dhuyumirrii," he said.

"Do what?" asked Gutsy.

"Priests," explained Napoo as he softly followed the tracks for a short distance.

Gazette's eyes narrowed. "A Khungarrii rescue party?"

Napoo returned to the group. "No. This is Zohtakarrii burri. It is Zohtakarrii patrol. No Khungarrii here."

Gazette seemed relieved that they hadn't been followed. Alfie suspected he would have taken it as a personal slight if they had been pursued without his knowledge.

"What will happen to them?" asked Nellie.

Napoo's features darkened. "They will be interrogated and then killed. But the presence of the Dhuyumirrii puzzles me. They do not usually accompany normal patrols. There is something else going on here."

"Oh, great," said Pot Shot, throwing his hands in the air, "as if we didn't have enough on our hands." He glared at Alfie. "It's this bloody Hush Hush bunch that has led us to this."

Gazette patted the lanky private on the shoulder. "Yeah, but they'll bloody well help us out of it." He walked over to Alfie and poked him in the chest with a finger. "Won't you?"

Alfie clenched his fists, but restrained himself, as he caught Nellie out of the corner of his eye giving him a slight but emphatic shake of her head.

"Later, chum," said Gazette with a sneer. "We've got to find Only first."

Alfie led the way back to the bellied tank. As they approached the *Ivanhoe*, the Fusiliers crowded together, like a pack.

The tank crew abandoned their task to face them. Norman slapped the spanner head against the palm of his hand.

Alfie rubbed his sweaty palms on the thighs of his coveralls and stepped forwards to defuse the situation. "One of the Fusiliers and the Chatt. They've been taken."

"What, by the spirit?" blurted out Cecil, his eyes almost popping out of his head.

"No, another colony of Chatts, by all accounts," Alfie informed them.

"And you lot are going to help find them," said Gutsy, daring them to contradict him.

Alfie turned to appease the soldier. "Of course we will. That goes without saying."

"No, it doesn't." Mathers appeared from round the back of the tank. "I'm in command here, Perkins. Not you."

At the sound of Mathers' voice, the Tommies squared off bullishly. Gutsy stepped forward, Mercy and Gazette either side of him, backing him up. The tank crew fell in behind their commander as he strode towards the belligerent infantrymen.

Mathers studied them. "We'll find your man," he said eventually. "Just as soon as we get the tank unditched. Now let us do our job."

"If you'd been doing your job in the first place this wouldn't have happened," said Mercy under his breath.

Mathers wheeled round. "I beg your pardon, Private?"

Mercy stood to attention. "I said, these things happen, sir."

Mathers continued to stare at Mercy before turning on his heel with a dismissive grunt. The two groups broke away from each other, the immediate tension dissipated. Whatever grudges they had with each other, they could wait.

Nellie reached for Alfie's hand. "You did good, I know that wasn't easy for you, siding against your pals," said Nellie.

Alfie raised his eyebrows and shook his head. "I'm not sure they are my pals. Sometimes lately, I don't even know who they are."

* * *

INSIDE THE TANK, Alfie, Cecil, Frank and Reggie turned the large starting handle that ran between the motor and the gearbox at the back of the compartment until the engine caught. The tank jolted as the ditching log rolled underneath it with the tracks, lifting it free of the outcrop. Wally stopped the tank before the log could damage the steering tail. Once they unchained the log, the party was able to proceed. Napoo led the way, following the trail left by Atkins' captors.

With the engine spewing out its mind-altering fumes into the compartment once more, the crew calmed down, the familiar smells and routines settling the men's fractious nerves. The news of yet more Chatts seemed to galvanise them. Wally especially. In the absence of Huns, he hoped to face more Chatts. He was regretting not being back at the encampment now.

The tank rumbled on through the jungle, Wally running up the engine as he ran over small trees, sending the rest of the crew grasping for hand holds to save themselves from falling against the hot engine.

"For Christ's sake, Wally, watch it, you've already ditched her once!" chided Norman.

But Wally, it seemed, was on a mission, and Mathers was inclined to give him his head.

Cecil and Reggie manned the machine guns, aware that they were heading into trouble. The aft storage slots that held the tins of ammunition were nearly two thirds empty now, a conscious reminder to be careful with the remainder.

With a callous chuckle, Cecil mimed shooting the infantrymen that walked alongside. Alfie contemplated saying something, but his position within the crew was precarious enough. Fortunately, Jack clipped the lad round the back of the head and Cecil stopped.

The jungle landscape outside passed as every landscape did, whether picturesque French countryside or shell-pocked hell, in a series of bumps, jolts, lurches and shocks, sending kaleidoscopic patterns of colour through the compartment. In the gloom of the tank, the only beautiful landscapes were the ones that passed by smoothly, without hindrance.

Alfie longed for a road. He began to feel faint from the mounting heat. The engine was running hot, hot enough to fry bacon. The sweat began to trickle off his forehead, making his eyebrows itch, before trickling into his eyes, which began to sting. He pulled a knuckle across each of his eyelids to wipe them clean.

The compartment of the tank was beginning to waver, and seemed to expand and contract as though he were looking at it in a funfair mirror. Feeling a familiar cold flush, he flung open the sponson hatch beside him and vomited. One of the Fusiliers walking behind the tank stepped neatly to one side as he came to the splatter of puke. He looked up and grinned at Alfie, who was too intent on his own body to care. He took advantage of the open hatch to take in some untainted air before wiping his mouth on the sleeve of his coveralls and pulling the door shut, entombing himself in the iron hull again.

STILL UNDER THE influence of the euphoric mist with which they had sprayed him, Atkins felt quite content walking along beside his captors, as if he were on a Sunday afternoon walk, even though the pace was more akin to a forced march. His new companions were silent as they marched along beside him. He wasn't chained or tied, but felt no desire to dive headlong into the undergrowth either side of him and escape. He was in more danger out there than he was here. He was more than happy to let the Chatts lead him wherever it was they were going. He was beginning to feel hungry, however. He hoped there would be food soon.

"Where are you taking us?" he asked, politely.

He received no answer. He heard nothing but the deep bass groan and clicks of the jungle about them and the soft rhythmic rubbing click of chitinous armour as his captors walked on. But that was all right; they probably didn't speak English. The scentirrii he'd encountered barely knew enough to communicate to Urmen in anything but the most brutal of ways. The two Chatts leading the procession, though, were taller, less bulky and more regal, similar to the Chatt Atkins once saw carried in a litter in Khungarr. Like Chandar, each wore a length of silk, worn thrown over the shoulder and tied around their abdomens, allowing their vestigial mid limbs to poke through, though hung with many more tassles. These were their priest class, he assumed. They looked similar to Chandar, but it was a poor broken specimen, a reject, a factory second compared to them. They carried themselves with a sense of entitlement. Their carapaces were smoother and a weathered ivory in colour, like something that crawled under rocks and stones in the dark and damp and hadn't seen the light in a long time. Atkins experienced a mild shudder of revulsion, but it passed as quickly as it came.

Atkins lost track of time as the Chatts drove them on, down small tracks, switching this way and that, whether along their own or fortuitous animal tracks, he didn't know, but there was a sense of purpose to the journey. He watched their antennae moving. They were following a scent trail.

There was a crack and an agitated chittering from behind, as one of the scentirrii guards hit Chandar on the back in order to speed it up. The crippled Khungarrii was having difficulty keeping up with the speed of the group. It was cowed and walked in a submissive stoop, trying not to antagonise them.

The effects of the euphoric mist began wearing off and Atkins' thoughts slowly started to gain speed. "Where are they taking us?" he asked Chandar.

"Back to Zohtakarr? This One does not know. But this One fears," the Chatt replied, through gulps and belches of air. It looked at the two red-clad Chatts leading them, the priest Chatts with their headbands of metal. "If those Ones are what this One thinks they are, then this One fears we have strayed too far. We should not be here. We should not be here at all."

"Why, where are we?"

Chandar looked at their guards and clicked its mandibles. "This One cannot say. This One must not say. It is Dhuyumirrii knowledge. Not for Urmen."

Atkins knew that there was only one thing Chandar was afraid of talking about, an idea that petrified it. But it was also a lodestone that would swing and point to Jeffries. Croatoan.

"I've told you, we're not Urmen."

Chandar hissed, its mouth palps caught in the brief spurt of air like tiny windsocks. "So you say. It does not help your case. This One would advise you not to repeat it. Scentirrii might not speak urmanii, but Dhuyumirrii may. Say no more."

Atkins couldn't let it go. "Why shouldn't we be here? What is it that we aren't allowed to know?"

"If this One's suspicions are correct, they are guarding something that does not exist. We should not have come here. No One is permitted. No Urman is permitted."

"Why?"

Chandar didn't answer.

"Chandar?"

But the Chatt had sunk back into silence and wouldn't be drawn.

The trail they were following broke into a glade. There, among the scab trees, the Chatts broke their march. Two of the scentirrii circled the glade, their antennae waving in a frenzied manner, as if they were looking for something. Another trail? Atkins didn't know, but they seemed lost.

The Zohtakarrii Chatts hissed and chattered in their own tongue and they sank down on their legs, not in submission, but tensed, ready, as if expecting an attack, gathering the three Dhuyumirrii behind them.

Atkins noticed again the loud bass sound that resounded through his chest cavity. It felt as if someone was thumping his chest—from the inside. It was very unsettling. Had this just started or had he not known or cared before now, thanks to the mist of the Chatts?

Fine, white diaphanous shrouds hung from the surrounding scab trees like mouldering bridal veils. They moved and billowed in the slightest air movement. At first, Atkins thought them ghosts or spirits. Maybe even the evil spirit for which they had been searching. Passing close by one, they seemed to be only a collection of fine white filaments, like a fungus.

Beyond, the vegetation began to move and shake as though something large was lumbering through the undergrowth.

A scentirrii with a clay bioelectrical pack on its back and electric lance in its hands hissed and leapt, springing into the engulfing shadows beyond to challenge whatever lay there.

It was then, through the clearing fog of euphoria, that Atkins recalled the 'devil' of the Urmen that the tank crew had been seeking, and wondered if the lurking menace ahead was the thing they sought.

Without warning, the scaly leaves of the scab trees were silhouetted against a brilliant blue-white electrical flash that died just as quickly as the high-pitched Chatt squeal that pierced the leaden air.

Shreds of roiling, greasy black smoke slipped through the low bushes, easing across the ground. A Chatt fired its electrical lance at it to no effect. They all fell back before the stygian cloud's advance.

The fog lapped around the legs of several scentirrii and from within it things coiled around their feet. On gaining a grip on its prey, they recoiled rapidly into the jungle, like taut rubber suddenly released, dragging their victims away with them at tremendous speed, cracking them carelessly against tree trunks as they retreated.

Atkins staggered back drunkenly as the sooty smog rolled towards him, pulling Chandar with him. There were still secrets this Chatt was withholding and he didn't mean to lose it now. As they staggered back, they brushed past the ethereal shrouds, like cobwebs, tearing them before tripping over a tree root and falling to the ground. Chandar fell heavily on top of him.

The sooty cloud drifted towards them blindly. Somehow the gossamer shrouds and the greasy black smoke were connected, that much was clear. He knew enough from the past few seconds not to let it, or the things within it, touch him, but how to stop them?

Another scentirrii was snatched into the jungle with squeals and cracks as its carapace collided with trees and fallen trunks.

Atkins felt in his webbing. He still had some Mills bombs. The Chatts hadn't known enough to take them from him. He dragged Chandar over a fallen scab tree.

A scentirrii grabbed at Chandar and caught it by the leg, even as another thing coiled round its limbs from within the oily black smog.

Holding onto Chandar with one hand, Atkins pulled the bomb's safety pin with his teeth and threw it into the middle of the smoky black cloud filling the glade.

The grenade exploded, blasting the cloud apart and shredding the thing within it, even as others thrashed and retreated into the jungle in alarm.

The concussion wave sent him crashing back into the undergrowth, even as it dispersed the ebony vapours and disintegrated the ghostly white veils that hung about them.

The deep bass rumble resonated through the jungle like a cry that made the very trees shudder.

Atkins, dazed and concussed, saw Chandar lying unconscious several yards away before he too sank into blackness.

IN HIS TANK, enveloped in the eternal mutterings of Skarra, Mathers felt safe. Outside of its iron embrace, he felt naked and mortal, like a hermit crab out of its shell.

It had become his cloak, his home, his bed, his temple. A cocoon, perhaps. He felt he was changing. But into what? Gone was the old Mathers, the Mathers that had stared at the tank in that Norfolk field and felt it haul up the fears and horrors from the bottom of his soul. That man had been asphyxiated with every breath of the petrol fruit fumes that had ultimately freed him. Even now, its vapours numbed the pains he felt in his abdomen, the pains that fogged his mind. In here, he could think more clearly.

Sat at his right hand, Clegg hunched forwards over the steering wheel as he peered out of the driver's open visor. Mathers watched him, single-mindedly engaged in his task, and allowed himself a beatific smile. His crew were loyal, unquestioning. Had they not all shared in the Sacrament of the Fumes, their perceptions of the world around them transformed by its Grace, the truth revealed to them all on that Pentecostal fuel day? But one of the Ironclad Temple had lost his way, lost his faith, and been seduced by life outside these armoured cloisters. The disharmony among his disciples was troublesome. He didn't need a Judas. Mathers wondered how best to deal with him. Of course, he must be given a chance to regain his faith, to repent his actions and reject the life outside. Being a member of this crew was a gift, albeit a gift that demanded sacrifice, and the others felt that Perkins wasn't sacrificing enough. Yes, Perkins should have a chance to recant and do penance. But if he didn't, Skarra told Mathers what he had to do.

He stared out of the visor of the driver's cabin. As the ruddy vegetation rolled past, he lost himself in the cacophony of the tank. The engine sang psalms, like a host of mechanical angels, each noise producing colour, shapes and smells that blended and combined in arcane forms that seemed to him to be on the verge of unveiling meaning and knowledge.

He was jolted out of it by a bright flash. There it was again. Bright blue, with an aftertaste of sour limes. He pulled on the *Ivanhoe's* brake levers and ordered Clegg to let the engine idle in neutral. He peered out through his visor in the direction the flash had come from.

It appeared the infantry had seen it too. They all held their rifles at the ready, straining to hear over the tank's chuntering.

"What's going on?" Mathers demanded.

"Flashes—looked like the Chatts' electrical lances—and an explosion, possibly a Mills bomb."

There was a crashing and snapping as if something large and bulky were moving through the jungle with little regard for it, or little impedance from its vegetation. In another place, a world away, it might have been another tank crashing blinkered and uncaring through the undergrowth.

A deep, booming howl ripped the air, overlapped by a high-pitched squeal, the flavour of sarsparilla and carbolic. One of the infantrymen winced.

"That was a Chatt, I've heard enough of 'em die to know it," said the tall Fusilier.

The older, bullish one with the large hands gave orders. "Mercy, Porgy, Napoo, scout forwards. See what's going on. Don't engage. Come back here and report."

Mathers watched them and their Urman guide vanish into the undergrowth.

The sound of something flailing in the jungle continued for a short time. Several more high-pitched squeals punctuated the thrashing, before the sounds were lost in an explosion and diminished until the stutter of the *Ivanhoe*'s engine drowned it out.

ATKINS HEARD HIS name called faintly and from far away, but he wasn't bothered. He was warm and safe. He wanted to stay here in the peaceful dark but then he remembered Flora. For a brief moment, he was content to bask in memories of her—her eyes, her smile—and then he remembered what he'd done. Shame flooded in, washing away the contentment, and he began to hurt. He deserved to be punished. He deserved pain. The more he listened to the voice and the nearer he drew to it, the more he hurt. The next time he heard his name called from afar he struck out for it, struggling for the surface, and with each wave of pain he thought only one thing: Flora.

Atkins opened his eyes and saw a female face staring down at him, lined with concern.

"Flora?"

"No. It's Nellie. Remember?" The FANY turned and looked at Gutsy, who was peering over her shoulder. "He's suffering from commotional shock."

"Things came out of the trees," Atkins croaked through dry lips, struggling to get up. "A black, oily smoke."

"Well you seem to have done a bang up job of taking care of them," said Gutsy.

"*One* of them," Atkins pointed out. "The rest took the Chatts."

Gutsy shrugged. "Then I don't think they'll be back. I reckon we'll be safe here for a while."

Atkins looked around. A thin greasy black film, like an oil vapour, covered the part of the glade obscured by the smoke. "In that case, we'll make camp here for the night. Porgy, Chalky, Pot Shot. You're first on sentry duty."

Atkins looked around and saw Chandar, who was squatting close by, chittering to itself. Evidently, its carapace had protected it from the worst of the blast.

Across the way, he saw the tank, half hidden by the undergrowth like a stalking beast. The tank crew were huddled together, muttering among themselves, Mathers in his rain cape and mask, sitting in-between the front track horns, holding court. Every now and again, one or another of them would flash an acrimonious glance at the Tommies.

As they settled down to sleep, another deep bass rumble made the ground beneath them vibrate and an ululating howl, that made them all shiver and huddle closer to their fires, cut the twilight.

Above them, half glimpsed through the canopy of leaves, the alien stars came out and the Sky Web of GarSuleth began to sparkle in the dark.

INTERLUDE FOUR
Letter from Private Thomas Atkins
to Flora Mullins

20ᵗʰ March 1917

My Dearest Flora,
    We went for a bit of a nature ramble today with the tank lads. It didn't go so well. The tank got stuck and I was attacked by insects.
    Still and all, I had a happy time wandering through the woods, thinking how wonderful it would have been if you were here. Would a nature ramble agree with you in your condition, do you think? I don't expect your Aunt lets you out of the house much.
    Of course, all good things must come to an end and I came to a bad one right enough, banging my noggin. Out cold, I was, but I dreamt of you, so that was a bonus. It was just a pity that I had to wake from it so soon.
    I write this now by fire light as we are camping out in the wilds. Not that Gutsy notices, he can sleep anywhere. I hope that tomorrow we can return to the comfort of our dugout. There's a thing you thought you'd never hear me say. And here's another, what I wouldn't give for a pair of me mam's knitted socks. I can't darn to save me life and my last pair has got more holes than I've got toes.

    Ever yours
    Thomas

CHAPTER ELEVEN
"That Wind Blowing..."

CHILL DAWN JUST tinted the pallid sky with vermillion smudges, like roughly smeared lipstick on a "lady typist's" damask cheek. A thick, low fog had settled in the early hours, sinking down into the trenches, drifting sinuously through the valley and blanketing the veldt.

Everson chewed his bottom lip and felt the old familiar mixture of thrill and fear, as he walked along the duckboards from bay to bay along the fire trench, giving encouragement to weary soldiers who had withstood two days of attack and stood it with courage and fortitude. Even though losses had been lighter than he'd expected, here and there he noticed gaps beginning to open in the front line. Another day of assaults and he might not have the men left to close them.

His thoughts turned to Lance Corporal Atkins and his mission. There was no way of knowing how they were faring. No matter how much he wanted to, he could not depend on them now. He was resigned to fighting with what he had and determined to hold out here as long as possible.

After all, there was nowhere else to go.

Every man was Stood To on the fire steps, looking over the parapets and down their rifles towards the enemy, in expectation of a dawn attack.

High above, on the hill-top on the valley side, a lone light twinkled its iddy umpty message from the observation post to the HQ below.

A runner darted through the communications trenches, calling out in a low voice, "Lieutenant Everson?" and was passed along from bay to bay by weary, hungry soldiers.

Everson heard his name. "Over here, Barnes. What is it?"

The private handed over a scruffy stub of folded paper. "Message, sir."

Everson unfolded the grubby sheet, read and reread the hastily scribbled note, and shook his head in disbelief. "It's not possible."

*   *   *

THE PAST COUPLE of days had meant little sleep for anyone, least of all the medical staff. Captain Lippett had worked long hours in the surgical tent ceaselessly cutting, sawing and sewing, and Sister Fenton, organising the orderlies and the Urmen volunteers, seemed indomitable and tireless. Edith Bell *was* tired. The demands of the wounded were constant, from the small, frequent and easily answered requests for water or a smoke to the anguished pain-spurred appeals that only God could now fulfil. All she wanted to do was fall on her little bed and sleep, but not yet. She strode briskly through the fog, over to the compound, to check on her coterie of shell-shocked men.

"How have they been?" she asked the sagging sentry, who shivered in the dawn chill.

"Quiet as the grave, ma'am. Not a peep."

"Nothing? Nothing at all?" A hint of suspicion tinged her voice.

"Not so as I heard," he said, as he unbolted the gate to let her pass.

There were those amongst the men who couldn't tolerate any kind of confined space, not the hut or the dugout, who slept in the open as best they could with their tremors and nightmares for company. Letting a soft smile spread across her face, she went to the first pile of bedding to check on the patient. The crude mattress was unoccupied, its blanket thrown aside as if in haste. At this discovery, she merely raised a quizzical eyebrow.

As she went from one to another, she found the bedding heaps of straw-filled mattresses were all empty. That in itself was unusual. Now she was becoming perturbed. Where were their occupants? Her heart racing, she scanned the compound once more, as if to be sure of her eyes, before heading across to the hut with a rising sense of urgency. She pushed the door open. As the pale light from the doorway cut through the interior gloom, the silence that met her only increased her sense of alarm. The self-absorbed muttering, the yelps of alarm, the constant scuffling and thrashing that usually greeted her were absent. Blankets lay abandoned on the floor. The hut, like the compound, was empty.

Her mind racing, she turned and made for the dugout where some of the men huddled for comfort. In her haste, her feet slipped on the crudely constructed wooden steps and she slithered to the bottom, almost losing her balance. She recovered herself and fished in her trouser pockets for a box of Lucifers. Regretting the use, she struck one. The sulphur-bright flame flared and flickered, chasing away the chill gloom. The acrid smell of sulphur hung in the still air about her, clinging to her hair and stinging her nostrils. She held the dwindling match aloft. The dugout was as empty as Christ's tomb on Easter Sunday.

The guttering glow could shed no light on the mystery, but a shrivelled knot of fear formed in her stomach. She shuddered, dropping the match as she rushed up the steps, trying to quell the irrational panic that rose within her.

"They've gone!" she cried. "They've all gone!"

EVERSON HEADED ALONG the fire trench to the bay where Sergeant Hobson was stationed. By the time he found his old platoon sergeant, the rumours were already beginning to spread. Being a good platoon sergeant, he'd already heard them.

"Is it true, sir?" Hobson asked. Everson had known him since training and the man was a fount of practical knowledge and experience, and had been his right hand man on the Somme through the bloody summer of 1916, but he doubted if even Hobson had seen anything like this.

"Apparently. The message from Hill OP is that the Khungarrii have vanished overnight. Just melted away. Their whole army. At least, that's what it looks like."

The sergeant coughed and looked uneasy.

Everson knew the sound well enough. "Out with it, Sergeant."

"I don't like to say it sir, but isn't that exactly what happened to us? There one minute, gone the next?"

"I had the same thought, Sergeant. But it can't be that, can it?"

"The way our luck's been running recently, I wouldn't like the thought of them Chatts running round the bloody Somme on our return ticket. If I allowed myself to think of that, I'd fair bloody weep with the injustice of it, sir. But one thing you can be sure of, if we've thought of it the men will have, too."

"Yes. Best keep them Stood To, Sergeant, until we can find out exactly what's happened. The last thing we need is a damned mutiny. Maybe there's some other reason, some Khungarrii high day or holy day, perhaps."

"Then again, maybe the buggers have got a trick up their sleeves, sir?"

"There is that. Either way, I don't like it, Sergeant. I'll send Tulliver up for a look-see when the light's better, but for now I need to know what's going on out there. I want you to take a patrol out, see what you can find. Take Poilus with you."

The sergeant grunted an acknowledgement, glad to be doing something, and went along the first five bays, picking one man from each.

"Wilson, Draper, Cox, Monroe, Carter. With me."

The men fell in behind him and they worked their way to a spare bay. They pulled up lengths of duck boarding fixed with rope handles for just this eventuality. Leaning a ladder up against the revetment, Sergeant Hobson led the party out over the parapet, four of the privates carrying the duckboards. They made their way over the churned battleground towards the wire weed, hidden by the drifting mists.

Hobson stepped over the twisted, broken bodies of fallen Chatts, blackened crusty ichor drying on their cracked carapaces.

The once-bright field of poppies lay trampled and crushed. Here and there, one or two had escaped the melee and still stood erect, their crimson petals unfolding defiantly like bloodied flags in the early morning sun.

The wire weed had begun moving sluggishly in the thin light, its tendrils drawn by the fallen bodies nearby. The party lay lengths of duckboard across the writhing thickets and crossed hurriedly, not wanting the grasping vines to catch them.

Even as they tottered unsteadily over it, they could make out the shapes of bodies, both Chatt and human, drawn down and enveloped deep within the entanglement where the weed punctured them with its thorns to leech the nutrients from the corpses.

Beyond the wire weed, Hobson led the party past the partly-charred body of a battlepillar rising from the fog like a beached whale. Thrown catastrophically from their mount, the bodies of its riders lay broken and scattered around it. A blackened hole gaped in the side of its scorched armour, from which drifted the rank smell of partly cooked offal. Shrieking flocks of najib birds squabbled and tore at the flesh, dispersing resentfully as one of the soldiers threw a stone at them.

Hobson set off at a stooped run, using the low mist banks as cover, followed in short order by Poilus, Monroe, Carter, Draper, Cox and Wilson. They were some twenty yards beyond the wire now. He held out an arm and gestured for the men to drop down.

Where Hobson expected the tube grass to obscure their view, they found it trampled and flattened by the huge army that had occupied the veldt a day previously. Through the mist, he saw the shadows of hastily dug earthworks that the Khungarrii had been working on the day before, great heaps of spoil thrown up like breastworks. It looked as if they might have been settling in for a siege and digging their own system of trenches, or else a mine. But why abandon it, if indeed they had done? Hobson wouldn't put it past the buggers to be hiding underground ready to swarm out over them, just as the bloody Bosche did.

Carter squinted into the mist beside him. "Bloody hell, it looks like they really have done a bunk."

"You don't think they've really been whisked off to Earth, do you?" asked Monroe.

Draper shook his head. "Don't see how. It was Jeffries with his black magic got us here in the first place. Known fact, that is. Why would that bastard conjure 'em back and not us?"

"Spite? Fun? Who knows? Necromancing bastard like that. Just because he can, probably. What do you think, Sarn't?"

"I don't, son. I'm just paid to follow orders and so are you."

"Well, I haven't been paid for over three months—" Cox chirped up.

"Don't worry, lad. If I hear you grouse about pay again, I'll give you a thick lip on account," said Hobson. "That Jeffries is a blackguard of the first order, but I don't think he's responsible for this. Our job is to find out what is. How many bombs have you got?"

The men consolidated their Mills bombs. They had eight. It wasn't a lot, but they needed to check out what lay beyond the earthworks.

"Monroe, Wilson: bombers. The rest of you on mop up. Hand them your bombs. Ready?"

There was an exchange of determined glances and curt nods. Cautiously they walked across the No Man's Land to where the Chatts had been encamped. They sank down on their bellies and crawled towards the long line of crimson spoil, using the thinning fog as cover.

When they got to within thirty feet of it, Hobson tapped Monroe and nodded. The party rushed to the earth wall and hunkered below its lip. It was about four feet high and ran for thirty or forty yards. Hobson nodded again and Monroe threw a grenade over the lip. The explosion came seconds later and they felt the wall shudder as dirt showered down on them. Nothing else happened.

With a well-honed howl of fear and rage, they leapt over the earthworks to confront whatever faced them.

They found several hastily delved round-mouthed tunnels sunk into the earth at an angle, the source of the spoil. Monroe flung in a grenade down one to clear it, should Chatts be hiding down there. When the smoke, sand and debris cleared, they discovered it to be deserted.

Monroe, Draper and Cox checked out other tunnels. Some went five or ten yards before petering out, each of them empty, as if the work had been abandoned.

Scanning the misty veldt before them, they could see similar lines, the result of other delving and burrowings, all in various states of construction, but their purpose was unknown.

They found weapons lying on the ground, dropped and abandoned, among them swords and barbed spears as well as a number of the clay backpacks that charged the electric lances. Hobson made a mental note to salvage some later. They might prove useful.

Here and there, they found large crude balls of earth, six or so feet across, stacked in pyramids twenty odd foot high. Made from the spoil from the delving, Hobson had seen these things before.

"It's an important part of their burial ritual," Poilus explained. "Bodies of dead Chatts are encased in clay balls to be rolled into the underworld by Skarra, their god of the dead. They have left them here for him. In the underworld they will undergo their final change into their spirit form and rise to join GarSuleth in his Sky Web."

Hobson's face gave away nothing, but Monroe shuddered. "So these are like mausoleums?"

"But there are still dead Chatts lying about," Carter pointed out. "How come they didn't finish the job?"

"That is strange," said Poilus. "Never have we known the Ones come in such numbers. Had it not been for the Tohmii, we would have fled and never seen such a sight as this. That may have been the wisest thing to do."

They almost missed the Chatt in the fog, standing as still as it was, tiny beads of condensation forming over its carapace in the chill morning air. The scentirrii was unarmed, but that didn't make it any less dangerous. Even unarmed, its ability to spray acid was reason enough to stay away from it.

Hobson was actually relieved. A very small part of him really had wondered if the Chatts had been sucked back through the aether to Earth.

The Chatt didn't move as they circled it. It should have smelled them, but it gave no indication that it had.

Carter challenged it. "Oi, Chatt! *Hände hoch*!"

"It's not a bloody Hun," said Wilson, expecting the worst at any moment.

Carter shrugged. "Sorry, force of habit."

Even when they surrounded it and thrust their bayonet points towards it, the arthropod showed no recognition of the peril of its situation.

"What's it doing?"

"What do you think it's doing?"

"I don't bleedin' know. If I knew, I wouldn't ask."

"Fuck!" Cox fell back a step. Nictating eyelids flickered across the Chatt's eyes. It was the only sign of movement, or indeed life, about the creature. "Did you see that?"

Poilus backed away. "Dulgur," he hissed. "An evil spirit. They are possessed. We should not be here."

Hobson was about to press Poilus further when there was a shout from Cox. "There's more over there, Sarn't."

Scattered through the thinning fog like stone angels in an unkempt smoggy cemetery, they found hundreds more of the disorientated Chatts spread out over the trampled ground. All of them were standing aimlessly. Their passivity emboldened the soldiers who began to prod them with bayonet points. No amount of cajoling or shoving could induce a reaction.

"All right. A joke's a joke. I've 'ad enough now," said Private Wilson.

If it had been just the Chatts, that would have been disturbing enough, but then they spotted Tommies stood in among them in a trance. All of them, human and alien alike, just standing. In union. Like statues. Not moving. For no apparent reason at all.

By their armbands, these were the men suffering from shell-shock.

"What the hell are they all doing?" Carter asked no one in particular.

"I don't know, but it's giving me the screaming abdabs," confided Cox, as they trod warily between the mesmerised individuals.

Private Draper recognised one of the men, an old mucking-in pal. They'd shared a dugout on the Somme. The bugger always had the cheek to complain about *his* snoring. "Townsend? Townie?"

Townsend offered no response. Draper put a hand on his shoulder and pulled him round, only to be met with a vacant stare. "Townie?" Not a flicker of recognition. As soon as he let go Townsend returned to face the direction he had been facing. Draper shuddered when he noticed a large swelling at the base of Townsend's skull.

"Let me try," said Cox, "you need to know how to treat these types." He slapped Townsend across the face. There was not a flicker of anything; not pain, not surprise, not anger, just a small trickle of blood from the mouth that the man also ignored.

"There was no need for that!"

"I was trying to snap him out of it!" said Cox.

"What are they *doing* out here?"

Draper was spooked. "You heard the Urman. Evil spirits. Possession. It's Jeffries' doing. 'E's using the 'fluence, I tell you. He's coming for the rest of us!"

"Draper, shut your cake 'ole before I shuts it for you!" barked Hobson.

"They're all the shell-shocked blokes, Sarn't."

"Aye. Dixon. It seems Little Bo Peep has lost her sheep," said Hobson. "Nurse Bell won't be happy having her patients wandering about out here. She won't know where to find 'em. Carter, Cox. Go back to camp. Fetch some men to help round 'em up and take 'em back home."

"Waggin' their tails behind 'em!" said Monroe with a grin.

"Very droll, lad," said Hobson. "Very droll."

Private Wilson pushed his soft cap back on his head and rubbed his forehead, perplexed. "Here, Sarn't. How come they're all facing the same direction?"

"What's that, Wilson?"

Wilson pointed it out. "The same direction, Sarn't. Tommie. Chatt. They're all facing the same way. It's fair giving me the creeps seeing 'em doin' it all together like that. Like a drill parade."

Now Hobson could see it himself, he could feel the hair on the back of his neck bristle. He had to admit it was damned odd. None of them made a sound. They just stood there. Chatt and man, together.

"That, Private, is a bloody good question and one I feel is for better heads than mine."

Private Monroe yelped with alarm. In the distance, something large rose out of a fog-enshrouded copse. It was one of the great armoured battlepillars. Ignoring them, it reared up to start languorously stripping the disc-like leaves from the treetops.

The party came across two more further on, their great mandibles crunching their way through the tube grass unperturbed by the carnage around them.

Hobson put a hand on their rifle barrels and pushed them down. "Enough. They could be right useful to us, beasts like that."

"It's all very well saying that, Sarn't, but how do we get 'em back?"

Hobson puffed out his chest, played with the end of his moustache, and pointed up at the great larva-like beast. "See that box on its back, just behind its head? That there's called a howdah. They have them in India when ridin' helephants. Same principle."

"And how do we get up there? Magic rope trick, I expect?"

"I've got me penny whistle if it helps," suggested Draper.

Hobson's eyes narrowed. "If I thought you two was taking the mick I'd have your names so fast me pencil would leave skid marks."

"Us, Sarn't? No, Sarn't. Perish the thought, Sarn't."

"Right, then. Wilson, go back and report to Lieutenant Everson. Tell him we'll need some more men out here, jildi."

HALF AN HOUR later, the sun was burning off the fog, revealing the strange, new landscape before them with its scattered pyramids of clay coffin balls, earthen banks and trampled tube grass.

Everson watched as a battlepillar lumbered towards the stronghold with a couple of Tommies sat in the howdah behind its head. The other two larval beasts fell into line and followed on behind.

The parties that went out afterwards rounded up the dazed shell-shocked Tommies, carefully avoiding the mesmerised Chatts.

Other than them, the veldt was empty. It was true. The Khungarrii army had decamped, although exactly why still remained a mystery.

SERGEANT HOBSON STOOD at ease as Lieutenant Everson digested his report. Outside, he could hear ragged and muted cheers as the men celebrated their apparent victory.

"They've gone. Just like that," said Everson, shaking his head in disbelief.

"They seem to have left in a hurry, sir. Weapons have been left scattered around. There are pyramids of the dead, after their fashion and, as you can see, we have captured several abandoned battlepillars and a good many of their electric lance packs. They have been digging sir, but I couldn't say for what purpose, exactly. Mines, perhaps, to dig under our positions. And then there were the mesmerised scentirrii, sir. Sent shivers down my spine, they did. Especially when we found a number of our mob amongst them, dazed like. Like they'd been sleepwalking. None of 'em seemed to realise where they were or how they got there. Poilus claims they're possessed."

"And you, Sergeant? What's your opinion?"

"Couldn't say, sir."

"Hmm."

The report left Everson with more questions than answers. "It doesn't make sense," he muttered. "They had us. Why did they leave? And why abandon their soldiers like that?"

EDITH COUNTED THE shell-shocked patients back into the compound. She bridled when she saw them strung together with rope looped around their waists, and accosted the private escorting them.

"Is that absolutely necessary?"

"It were the only way we could get 'em, back, miss. It were like herding cats. They kept trying to wander off. But once we got 'em like this, they came quiet like," he said, somewhat abashed.

"Yes, well, they're not wandering loose now. Take the ropes off, please."

The private obliged and untied each one as they went quietly and compliantly into the compound.

"Thank you," said Edith with a curt nod, and turned to follow them in.

"Nurse Bell, a moment please!"

Sister Fenton came striding towards the compound from the hospital tents. Edith sighed with frustration. What was it this time? She turned and waited diffidently as the senior nurse approached.

"Yes, Sister?"

"These men were in your charge. How on earth did they get out?"

Edith felt her face flushing. "There was a gap in the wire, Sister. It's been dealt with."

Sister Fenton seemed to find that acceptable. "I know Captain Lippett's attitude to these men is a little harsh—"

"A little harsh?" retorted Edith.

Sister Fenton did little more than arch her eyebrow. Edith knew she'd just stepped over a line and lowered her eyes. "Sorry, Sister."

"As I said," Sister Fenton reiterated for emphasis, her features softening. "I know Captain Lippett's attitude is a little harsh, but he does have a greater responsibility here. If you had concerns, you should have brought them to me. I appreciate that you have managed to care for these men in your own time and now that the fighting seems to be over, at least for the moment, I came to see if there was anything you needed for them."

Sister Fenton's show of concern caught Edith off guard. She was so used to seeing her as some dried-up old dragon, even though she could scarcely be more than ten years older than herself. Sister rarely, if ever, let that mask slip, but Edith realised that the woman was in an unenviable position. She was alone. At least Edith had got Nellie to befriend, to talk to and confide in, but Sister Fenton's station as a senior nurse, and a spinster at that, left her somewhat out on a social limb. They didn't often spare any thought for her or her plight at all. Lord knows it was hard enough for them on this world, amongst all these men, but for her? Was this her reaching out for female companionship?

"Oh. Well, I was just about to examine them. It seems they've been out all night and an extra pair of hands would be welcome, Sister."

Fenton smiled. It was a disconcerting sight. "Right, well, let's get on, shall we?" she said, rolling her sleeves up and stepping past Edith into the compound, her businesslike mask hardening into place once again.

The soldiers were meandering around aimlessly, some were whimpering quietly, some fidgeting, but it was a restless movement, not the involuntary spasms and jerks of shell-shock.

"I thought you told us that their hysterical symptoms had abated. Do they seem agitated to you?" said Sister Fenton as they walked slowly through the Bird Cage, running appraising gazes over their charges.

"Yes," Edith agreed, a frown creasing her forehead. "Yes, they do."

She found Townsend.

"Townsend. What happened? How did you get out there?"

He looked at her blankly at first, recognition only coming a few seconds later. "Nurse?"

"You were found wandering out there," she indicated the veldt.

"I don't remember," he said. "I remember wandering around out there, but I don't remember how I got there..." He looked at her in entreaty.

She didn't know how either. Avoiding his eyes, she began checking his hands and arms. There were lacerations, but from what? Barbed wire? Wire weed? She couldn't tell.

She opened his shirt. The swellings on his body had grown in number over the course of no more than a day. The growth at the back of his head had enlarged. She would have asked one of the Urmen who helped out in the hospital tents if the swelling was anything they had come across, but they wouldn't come near the compound, claiming it was full of 'bad magic.'

She was distracted for a moment as a breeze picked up and blew stray stands of hair across her face. She pursed her lips to blow it away before impatiently sweeping and tucking the offending locks away behind her ear.

"Bell!" called Fenton with a note of urgency. "Bell, look!"

She looked up. The men were all turning in unison, as if performing some parade ground manoeuvre. They turned into the wind. Was it her imagination, or was there an almost audible sigh of relief, when they felt the wind on their faces as it blew in across the veldt, ruffling hair and billowing shirts?

Fenton strode from one to another. "They've all responded in the same manner. Must be some sort of mass hysteria." She shook her head. "I've never seen the like. It appears they're responding to some atmospheric change," she observed. "What might it be? Air pressure? Temperature? Humidity?" She looked at Bell, who was just as perplexed by their behaviour. "Maybe your concerns were valid after all, Bell. I think Captain Lippett should see this."

Edith stepped in front of Townsend, who now faced the oncoming wind, and waved her hand in front of his unseeing eyes. "Townsend?" There was no reaction.

She shook another man. "Miller? Miller, what are you doing?"

Miller said nothing. She tried tugging on his arm, but he stood immobile, transfixed by the wind. They seemed oddly at peace. "Miller!" She turned and faced Sister Fenton, a look of consternation on her face. "I don't understand, Sister. What's happening?"

"I don't know, Bell, but the wind seems to calm them."

Edith looked in the same direction as the men, following their gaze, out across the trenches and the wire weed, out across the veldt with its flattened tube grass, where the last shreds of mist were dispersing; where, among walls of dirt and pyramids of earthen balls, the abandoned Khungarrii also turned to face the oncoming wind.

She looked up into the blue sky, where carrion creatures shrieked and wheeled, awaiting the first warm updrafts of the day, before dropping her gaze to the horizon, towards the great grey line of clouds that hunkered there. They were moving fast, rolling across the sky towards them. Another few hours and it would be upon them.

She shivered. "The weather is turning. Looks like there's a storm on the way."

CHAPTER TWELVE
"Hallo, Hallo! Here We Are Again..."

ATKINS CURLED UP against the bole of a tree, his pack by his side and his rifle clasped to his chest. He was weary to the bone, aching and stiff, but too tired to sleep.

He was acutely aware of Mathers. It was hard not to be. He sat cross-legged atop the tank on the driver's cabin, surrounded by lighted candle stubs, still wearing his rain cape, splash mask and turtle helmet, which he never seemed to take off at all these days. He muttered to himself while the rest of his men slept fitfully below.

It was disconcerting, because he couldn't make any sense of what Mathers was saying. Sat there in the candle glow, with the small night creatures buzzing and whining around him and crawling all over him, he just looked damn unnerving.

MATHERS IGNORED THE pain. The unsettled feeling in his stomach was getting worse. The fumes from the engine seemed to be a balm for it, but the engine was off. He had already taken several slugs of distilled petrol fruit from his flask and that seemed to calm it. The problem was he was having to drink more and more of the stuff. Just inhaling the fumes was no longer enough. Now, as he sat here, small creatures of the night attracted to the flame swarmed around him. He let them crawl on him. Any one of them might have a bite that would kill him, but this was a test of faith. He could hear the voice of his god, Skarra, in their incessant buzzing. His god would protect him. All he had to do was give himself over to Skarra completely, without fear. He felt none. Even though he felt a myriad of scuttling legs, fluttering wings, stings and bites, he didn't even flinch.

AMONG THE MEN, the fragile truce between the two groups of Tommies was barely holding, each group giving the other distrustful looks, as if just waiting for an excuse.

Atkins hated being stuck on a wild goose chase with an officer whose orders he couldn't countermand. They should have been heading back to the encampment. God alone knew if it was still even there. He sat there, imagining a bloody slaughter as the Chatts overran the trenches, and all because he hadn't returned with the tank in time.

He glanced over at the tank crew, bivouacked beneath a tarpaulin strung out from the starboard sponson. Alfie Perkins was in the middle of them. He was lying down, his head propped on his hand, looking across the clearing to where Nellie Abbott slept, near Napoo. After a while, one of his crewmates poked him roughly and reluctantly he lowered his head.

Chandar lay curled up on its side, almost in a ball, like a woodlouse, a length of rope tying its ankle to a tree root, a formality to mollify the others. There had been several opportunities when Chandar could have escaped but had chosen not to do so. As harmless as the old Khungarrii duffer seemed to be, it was definitely hiding something, part of which involved him, and Atkins very much wanted to know what it was.

Porgy, Chalky and Pot Shot sat on watch by the fire, and Gazette, Gutsy and Prof lay sprawled out. Gutsy was snoring loudly enough to wake the dead.

Atkins watched as Porgy got out his deck of cards. It was no ordinary deck. Each card was a small photograph of a girl he claimed he had stepped out with, which was odd because there were at least two of the music hall sensation, Marie Lloyd, in there. When quizzed, Porgy just winked and called them 'his jokers.' He started showing them to Prof, trying to engage the depressed man's interest, reeling off the stories of spooning attached to each one. Atkins grinned as Porgy slapped Prof's hand away as he tried to have a closer look at a particular card. Porgy's ambition was to collect enough to create a full deck of cards from them. Poor Porgy. He wondered how his mate would ever complete the set now.

Gazette turned over. "What's up, Only, can't sleep?"

"No, Gutsy's farted."

"Yeah, at least it'll keep the beasts at bay."

They watched the large Tommy roll over in his sleep smacking his lips contentedly, like a dog in front of a fire.

Goaded gently by the others, across the campfire, Chalky was in full flow. "The way I heard it, right," he was saying in a low voice. Pot Shot leaned forwards conspiratorially and smiled encouragingly as he continued, "Only, Everson and Ketch had cornered Jeffries, right, and he was only in the Chatts' own temple planning to use it for his own black art. He had Nurse Bell tied to an altar and he was poised with a big knife, about to sacrifice her to the devil and it should have been a shoe-in 'cause Jeffries had no other weapons. So Lieutenant Everson tells Jeffries that the game's up and that he was to give himself up and come with them, his silver dagger poised above Nurse Bell's heart. But he laughs at them as he raises his hand, right? Like he was going to plunge the knife down, so the lieutenant fires, right, and he shoots it right out of Jeffries' hand. And he curses, but not in English like you or I—"

"Or an NCO," said Porgy, winking at Gazette.

But Chalky was lost in his story now, conjuring his own retelling before the fire. "Aye, or a bloody NCO," he acknowledged before plunging on. "He curses in a foul and ancient language what no one honest and God-fearing would understand, the language of devils, and he raises his arms like he was surrendering, like, but then there were this evil red glare in his eyes and he began chanting, and suddenly bolts of green lightning blasted out of his finger tips. The first blast got Corporal Ketch and he were, like, burnt to a crisp in an instant."

Porgy nudged Prof. "Sends shivers down your spine don't it? It's like he was there."

"Oh aye, and what happened next?"

"Well, then Only—that is, Corporal Atkins—takes a shot at Jeffries, but the mad magician just waves his hand and flings the bullets back at them through the air and one gives the lieutenant a Blighty one, right in the shoulder. An' then Jeffries starts saying as how if he can't send Nurse Bell to hell then he'll summon up summat to fetch her there. Then he starts to conjure a demon to kill them while he makes his escape and there's a horrid green glow and a smell of sulphur as something from the inner circles of Hell begins to take shape..."

"Inner circles of Hell, I like that," said Porgy, nodding with approval.

"...and Nurse Bell screams. And Only realises he has moments to act before the demon becomes as solid as you or I. So Corporal Atkins, not having no holy water or the padre's bible, decides he has to save the lieutenant the only way he can. That's when he notices the magic circle Jeffries is stood in is made from salt, and he scuffs away the circle breaking the spell, like, before it's complete. Enraged, the demon brings down the chamber before vanishing back into the Pit he came from. Then, with the Chatts' temple collapsing about him, the corporal rescues Nurse Bell and the lieutenant and pushes them down a shaft to safety. Then, he turns to Jeffries who is not best pleased at his evil plans being thwarted and all. The corporal charges him with his bayonet but then Jeffries vanishes in a cloud of black smoke and a demonic laugh and Only—Corporal Atkins—vows: *By blood and sand, we'll find you and when we do we'll make, you send us home you diabolical fiend!*"

"It's true," said Porgy, wide-eyed and impressed. "He said them very words."

"Blood and sand," muttered Atkins. He hadn't caught all of it, but he'd overheard enough. "Stop encouraging him, Porgy, that's not how it happened and you know it," he growled, turning his back to them and pulling his army blanket about him. Bloody hell, every time he overhead that story it got bigger with the retelling. He was pretty sure that soon his bloody bayonet would be Excalibur itself in disguise. If Chalky knew what kind of man his corporal really was he'd be severely disappointed.

SOFTLY, ALMOST IMPERCEPTIBLY, the nocturnal noises of the jungle segued into a dawn chorus as shrieks and cries and deep bass clicks gave way to bleary hoots, whistles, trilling and whoops, alerting the men to the slow, incremental creep of daylight.

Atkins woke, stiff and aching, to see Napoo squatting on his haunches over the fire. It appeared that the Urman had already been up and caught breakfast, as he was cooking several small animals on skewers over the fire.

"Right, just off for me morning ablutions," announced Gutsy, stepping into the undergrowth with his rifle.

"Keep an eye out for Jeffries!" came the usual riposte.

Atkins looked over at Mathers, still sat on top of the tank. He must have slept sitting up all night, his head lolling. Mathers' head snapped up and turned to look at him through the eye slits.

Disconcerted, Atkins started like a guilty schoolboy and averted his gaze.

Chandar was silent. It hadn't said much since their kidnapping. It was watching the tank crew pour the last of their petrol fruit fuel from the drums into the *Ivanhoe's* petrol tanks in the two front track horns. Atkins wondered if Chandar was beginning to suss them out.

"It's... an offering," he suggested.

Chandar looked at him briefly then returned its gaze to the tank. It chittered to itself, and fingered the tassels on its shoulder robe, like the padre told his rosaries. It seemed to Atkins that the old Chatt's beliefs were being tested, though he couldn't tell how. It seemed uneasy, and that made him nervous. If it were human, Atkins would have thought it windy. Even before their attempted abduction by the Zohtakarrii, something had agitated the Chatt, something it was reluctant to share. Combine that with Mathers' attitude, and Atkins felt this entire stunt was going to Hell in a handcart.

*   *   *

ATKINS PERFORMED HIS usual morning ritual. Every man on the Front Line had his little good luck ritual. Gutsy had his rabbit foot; Porgy had his deck of cards. Atkins had his letter. If he could still smell Flora's perfume on her last letter, then he would be safe. However, for some days now, a week perhaps, the scent had been fading almost beyond his ability to sense it. Today he couldn't smell it at all. He felt a rising panic before remembering that, back in the Urmen's 'tank' hut, Mathers had been drinking the petrol fruit, and claimed it heightened his senses; maybe he could sense any faint, lingering scent. As much as he loathed humbling himself before the Tank Commander, the appeal might go some way to appeasing him and smooth over the rift between them. It was worth a try. Besides, he *had* to know.

He ambled over to where the officer was inspecting his tank. The words almost stuck in his craw. "Sir, I—may I ask you a favour?"

The Tank Commander cocked his head to one side, intrigued, and invited Atkins to continue.

"I've got a letter from my sweetheart. I—I can't smell her perfume anymore. I was wondering if you could tell me if there's any trace of it left."

"Hrm." The masked subaltern seemed to consider the request. From the tone in his voice, the idea seemed to amuse him. "Let me see it."

Reluctantly, Atkins took out the worn envelope from his tunic pocket and eased the sharply creased writing paper from it. Mathers snatched the folded note with more haste and less care than Atkins would have liked, and held it up to his chainmail and leather mask. He noticed the welts and insects bites on Mathers' hands as he held the letter. Atkins heard a quick audible sniff from beneath the chainmail. Mathers' head lolled back in a languorous manner, as he inhaled again, this time more slowly, deeper, relishing what he found there.

"Hey!" Atkins snatched the letter from his hands, scowling at the officer as if he'd just insulted the lady.

"Merely making sure, Corporal," said Mathers, his head moving as though sucking up the last faint dregs of scent, his chainmail rattling faintly.

Atkins reverently slipped the letter back into its envelope and returned it to his pocket. "Is there anything left, sir?"

Mathers appeared to be lost in a reverie.

"Sir?"

Mathers looked at him. "Yes. I can still smell it." He turned on his heel and went back to inspecting the tank.

Atkins sighed with relief. He hadn't even been aware of holding his breath. He closed his eyes, tipped back his head to the heavens and offered a muttered, but heartfelt, thank-you. He would see the day out and that, at least, gave him some little comfort.

He returned to 1 Section, who were packing their gear and getting ready to move off, and approached Nellie Abbott.

"I'm worried about Lieutenant Mathers," said Atkins. "Can you give him the once over? The last thing we need is a windy ruddy officer." Nellie looked uncomfortable with the idea. Atkins pressed the point. "Look, Alfie's life depends on this man. Do you really want that if he's funked it?"

"That's not fair, Corporal."

"Maybe not, Miss Abbott, but it's true. Will you do it? If not for me, for Alfie?"

There was a stony silence and he felt himself wither under Nellie's glare. Yet another thing of which he wasn't proud. As she turned on her heel, he grabbed her earnestly by the wrist. "He's been badly bitten by insects," he confided. She looked down at the importunate hand on her wrist, arching an eyebrow, and he released her. With a dismissive huff, she strode over to Lieutenant Mathers, who was still inspecting the tank.

"Lieutenant?"

"Yes, Nurse?"

"I hear you were bitten a lot last night, I was wondering if you'd just let me look and make sure that you're all right?"

He waved her away. "There's no need."

"Mr Mathers, it's my job. It'll only take 'alf a mo'. An' if it's serious, then maybe I've got something that'll help, and if not, I'm sure Napoo could whip up one of his poultices."

"This isn't necessary."

She reached up to lift his chainmail curtain and he slapped her hand away.

"I said it isn't necessary. I'm perfectly fine."

"Mr Mathers," she said with wounded dignity. "I'll be the judge of that. Now let me help you."

Mathers turned to go, but Nellie, surprised by her own audacity, caught hold of the chainmail curtain in his mask and ripped it upwards and back, knocking off his toughened leather turtle helmet in the process. It clattered to the ground as he wheeled round and turned on the small FANY, who now held his mask in her hand.

She gasped as she saw his face. It wasn't the usual impetigo and rashes from petrol fumes that she normally saw on tank crews. Large raised red plaques covered his skin and there were swellings at his throat, but his eyes—his eyes were completely black, upon which a shifting rainbow film swirled continually, like petrol on water.

He turned those eyes upon her now. "How dare you!" he snarled, before crumpling with a groan and clutching his stomach.

"Are you all right?" asked Nellie, putting her hand on his shoulder and noticing the growth at the base of his skull. "Let me help you."

Mathers forced himself upright. "You've done enough. The fuel fumes help me all I need. They stop it spreading." He snatched back his mask from Nellie's hand and, stooping to pick up his fallen helmet, he stormed off to the tank.

"Wait, stops what spreading? Stops what, Lieutenant?"

The chunter of the tank's engine filled the clearing, drowning out the possibility of any further conversation as Clegg ran the engine up.

"Did you see?" said Nellie, still shocked.

"Yes. Yes, I did," said Atkins, thoughtfully.

"But his eyes!"

"The petrol fruit."

"Alfie doesn't have that, none of them have."

Atkins shook his head. "No, they haven't been drinking the stuff. Mathers has."

"He has some kind of infection, too. Those plaques on his face and the swellings on his neck, I've never seen anything like them."

Atkins hadn't either, but then this world was full of particularly unpleasant surprises. "I think he's drinking the petrol fruit to relieve the pain of it, but it makes him see things. Believe me, I know. I think he's mad, Miss Abbott, but he has a great influence over his men. They're fiercely loyal. If we move against him, they'll do everything they can to protect him, which will get us nowhere, and we need that tank. Lieutenant Everson needs that tank."

Napoo had a different opinion on Mathers and had no qualms about telling the rest of the section. "Someone has cursed him, and he has been possessed by an evil spirit. Who might have the power to do such a thing?"

"Jeffries," exclaimed Chalky. "Jeffries could do it, couldn't he, Only?"

Mercy clipped him round the back of his head. "Prat!" Some people just saw Jeffries everywhere.

Jeffries had sprung to Atkins' mind, too, but he dismissed the idea. Despite all the claims and the stories, his own encounter with Jeffries suggested that he was nothing more than a man. "Can you help him?"

Napoo shook his head sadly. "Those possessed by dulgur are cast out of the clan for fear of the harm or bad fortune they bring. I do not understand why the Tohmii keep theirs around."

Atkins frowned. It took him a moment to realise that he was talking about the shell-shocked. No wonder the Urmen gave the Bird Cage a wide berth.

"So," said Atkins, none the wiser. "Mathers is either possessed, or mad."

"Well, that's nothing new, he's an officer," said Mercy.

* * *

1 SECTION MOVED out behind the tank as it rolled forwards, crushing a path through the undergrowth as they set off in the direction in which the smoke creatures had dragged the Zohtakarrii. The Chatts had been hauled through the jungle at speed, even without the thin oily residue that coated the trees and undergrowth, the trail of snapped branches, gouged ground, and occasional Chatt limb wasn't hard to follow.

Atkins dropped back and matched his stride with that of Chandar's. The Chatt was silent, fidgeting with the tassels of its shoulder cloth, watching the tank closely as if still debating with itself on the matter of its divinity.

"You say the Tohmii came from the Sky Web?" it asked, unexpectedly.

"From the stars, yes."

Chandar hissed and chittered to itself and came to a decision. "Among the Khungarrii Shura there is a secret olfaction of Ones who believe, as this One does, that Urmen have a greater part to play in our Osmology. Sirigar holds the old-established view; that Urmen, casteless and queenless as they are, were put here by GarSuleth merely to service the needs of the Ones as they see fit. Sirigar's interpretation of the prophecy, that the Tohmii are the Great Corruption, is flawed and self-serving. That One seeks to unite wavering olfactions of the Shura behind it and consolidate its position with the defeat of the Great Corruption—the Tohmii."

"So there are some Chatts that believe we are not this 'Great Corruption' then? That's heartening to know," Atkins said sardonically.

"It is an ancient prophecy, its interpretation an old debate, going back generations. The arrival of the Tohmii is but the latest. This One, however, believes the prophecy refers not to an external threat but rather an internal one; the warping and narrowing of our own beliefs to serve a baser purpose."

"Sirigar."

The Chatt concentrated as it gulped down air to speak. "Yes. The only way to challenge that One is through the Supplication of Scents before the Shura. If our argument proves persuasive only the Queen can issue the necessary chemical decree, acknowledging our interpretation as the correct one, to be accepted by all." Chandar paused for another breath and bowed its head. "Our only hopes of distilling the essence of our argument lay in the Aromatic Archives of the Fragrant Libraries destroyed by Jeffries. There, too, were held the records of one of the Divine Disciplines, the recreation of the Celestial Scent, an attempt to understand its totality by alchemically capturing the Sacred Odour of GarSuleth itself. There are those, like this One, who believe that some note of the Urman scent is inherent to this endeavour. Both of these sacred undertakings were dashed by Jeffries' sacrilege and the Tohmii's actions. We are diminished because of it."

"That wasn't our fault," said Atkins. "We simply wanted our people back."

"Nevertheless, the atrocity was committed," said Chandar.

Atkins was shocked. Was it really all their fault? Had they brought all this on themselves? "Why are you telling me this?"

"Your act of Kurda, saving this One, was unforeseen, unprecedented. It has cast a new anchor line into the world, a silver thread of possibilities. A web of potential not yet woven. This One would know what may be spun from it."

"You're talking in riddles."

"To you, maybe, but to this One these are signs, portents. Upon these rest the fate of your herd, make no mistake."

It was almost too much for Atkins. Internal divisions within the Khungarrii, one of which might be sympathetic to the Pennines, now powerless because of the Pennines' own actions. In one of his blacker moods, he could almost believe that God was having some cruel capricious joke at his expense. All he'd tried to do was the right thing. Almost fearing to broach the subject, he pressed on. "You said some things, yesterday. Was that smoke creature Croatoan?"

"This One does not know."

Atkins felt himself beginning to lose his temper. "Look, Chatt, I'm leading my men into God knows what here. If you have any information about what we're heading into, then tell me. You once said that we had some sort of connection."

"Kurda."

"Right. Kurda, because I saved your life. Now it's your turn. Save mine. What's going on here? What is it you're not telling me?"

Chandar fell silent, but glanced occasionally at Atkins as they walked. Perhaps, Atkins thought, the Chatt was struggling with its conscience, if it had one. God help them if it didn't.

THEY HAD BEEN walking for about half an hour when Chalky stopped to relieve himself by the trackside. He screamed and stepped back, still voiding his bladder. Losing his footing, he turned round to maintain his balance, flinging out an arc of yellow drops as he went.

Mercy stepped back to avoid the spray. "Hey look out, Chalky. Bleeding hell, ladies present."

"Ruddy hell, lad! Did Shiner coming a cropper teach you nothing?" bawled Gutsy.

"There!" Chalky cried, trying to tuck himself away. "There!"

"All right, lad. Leave this to us," said Mercy, stepping past him as he, Gazette and Pot Shot approached the side of the tank's path.

Pot Shot looked down into the scrub and found he was peering into the piss-filled eye socket of a skull staring up at him through the reddish bracken.

Living on the Somme had hardened most of them to such sights. You couldn't walk ten yards without coming across a body in some state of decomposition. One trench they held had a Frenchie's arm sticking out of the trench wall. Their old sergeant, Jessop, used to hang his equipment from it.

Atkins hollered forward for Gutsy to stop the tank.

It jolted to a halt, its engine idling, splutters of black smoke coughing from the exhaust on the roof. The port sponson door opened and one of the crew, Frank, poked his sweaty face out. "What's the bloody hold up?"

"Bodies," Atkins snapped back. "Urmen."

They used entrenching tools to pull away at the tangle of bracken to expose what was left of several skeletons after the scavengers of this world had done their work. Red lichen partially covered the bones. Whatever clothing they might have once worn had completely disintegrated. There was no way of telling how they died, but this planet had a hundred and one different ways to kill you, none of them pleasant.

Mercy's clearance also uncovered the remains of some kind of wagon. There wasn't enough wood left to tell much more. It was rotten and crumbled at the touch.

These were no recent deaths. The bones had lain here for years, decades, maybe even longer.

Nellie shook her head sadly. "Poor people."

Intrigued, Chandar came over to look, its stunted claw-like mid-limbs fidgeting as it clasped its hands together. "This One never thought to witness such a sight. At Khungarr, all this One had were the artefacts scentirrii patrols brought back. To see them like this is marvellous."

Looking at the remains, Atkins thought of the old Urman woman's prediction concerning his own mortality. He shuddered. All of a sudden, he felt very vulnerable to the capricious whims of this planet.

They dug a small pit and buried what they could find of the bones, the sight of which unsettled Prof, already withdrawn since Nobby's death, even further. Nevertheless, he managed to say a prayer over them before they moved on.

THE TANK LURCHED to a halt. Before them, looming out of the thinning jungle, Atkins recognised a familiar structure: a Chatt edifice, or rather what was left of one. It was an overgrown and crumbling ruin, swathed in vegetation, like an old dowager decked out in the family jewels. Vines overhung the main entrance into the edifice. The top half of the structure had collapsed long ago, and creeping foliage smothered the rubble and debris strewn about the clearing. The tide of alien nature, no longer kept at bay, had flooded in to reclaim the area once more.

The Section wandered cautiously towards the once great structure. Even in its heyday, it would not have been as big as Khungarr. Nevertheless, these places were feats of engineering on a par with medieval cathedrals. They stood over many generations of constant habitation, each generation repairing and expanding the ancestral edifice to house the growing colony. What catastrophic event could have overtaken this place to leave it abandoned and in ruins? Atkins couldn't speculate.

"I have never seen such a sight," said Napoo. The spectacle of the edifice, a symbol of the Urman's oppressors' might and skill, lying shattered and dashed to the ground, must have been a profound sight; an intimation of his oppressor's mortality, of their fallibility.

Pot Shot stood beside him and nodded, seeing in it the symbols of his own political beliefs. "And so shall tumble the ivory towers of all tyrants," he muttered.

There was an abrupt silence as the tank engine cut out. The silence immediately struck Atkins. The trees and the undergrowth were still and quiet. There were calls and whoops, but only far off, in the distance, as if even the jungle creatures avoided this place.

Gazette sized up the ruined edifice. "Well, if I were a man-eating evil spirit, that's where I'd set up shop, all right."

Chandar clicked and chattered and, making its sign of deference, began to back away. It seemed to know, or at least suspect something.

Gutsy clapped a heavy hand on its shoulder. "Oh, no, you don't."

Atkins rounded on it. "What is this place?"

For a moment, Chandar gabbled in its own language, its mandibles and mouth palps moving rapidly in a torrent of clicks and tuts before it remembered, caught its breath, and translated the words into something they could understand.

"It is forbidden!"

A loud clang shattered the silence as a hatch swung open on the tank and the crew emerged, blinking and disorientated in the light, coughing and wheezing.

Nellie, looking for Alfie, saw Mathers stumble out and clutch his stomach. She pointed it out to Atkins with a nudge. They watched as Mathers pulled his hip flask from under his rain cape, lifted the splash mask chainmail aside and took a slug. He straightened up. A breeze blew across the clearing and he turned into the wind for a moment, as if wistfully looking for something, half-remembered.

"Ah, here come our land navy privateers," said Prof, nudging Chalky.

"What did you say?" said Cecil, his blotchy face clouding over as he rounded on the Fusilier. "Nobody calls the crew of the *Ivanhoe* mutineers, least of all mud-sucking infantry!"

"No, what I said was—"

Prof staggered back under the lad's tackle, trying to block Cecil's furious punches.

"Oi!" shouted Jack, striding towards the pair and pulling them apart. He grabbed Cecil and yanked him back by the collar of his coveralls. "This isn't the time or place."

"But he was bad-mouthing our mob!" insisted Cecil.

1 Section gathered protectively round a stunned and shaken Prof and the two groups regarded each other with animosity.

"That's enough!" yelled Atkins. "Christ knows there are enough things out here that want to kill us without bloody doing it ourselves!"

THE ALTERCATION BARELY registered with Mathers as he strode between the two groups, scarcely acknowledging the Fusiliers. "Nesbit, that's enough. We haven't time. They are inconsequential," he said. He had other, higher matters to attend to, matters that did not require their presence. This was Hush Hush business. "Our evil spirit dwells within. So let's make it quick. I don't like being outside the tank any longer than necessary. The pain is worse out here. Grab your revolvers and weapons and follow me."

With derisive mutters and black glances at the Fusiliers, the tank crew fell in behind their commander as he strode towards the ruined edifice. He didn't need to look back at the *Ivanhoe* for reassurance, for Skarra was with him. He could hear the god's insistent ever-present whispers in his mind, directing him, encouraging him.

A SUDDEN FLUSH of fear washed over Alfie. He turned and looked back at Nellie, taking comfort in the calming, yellow glow she gave off. By comparison, the rest of the tank crew around him radiated ugly, bruised hues of suspicion and paranoia. He knew which he preferred.

Frank gave him a shove. "What are you going to do, run after your long-haired chum or stay with us?"

"Nellie can look after herself," Alfie said.

"The right choice, Alfie boy," said Frank, leaning in close. "Maybe there's hope for you yet."

MATHERS' SUDDEN DEPARTURE caught Atkins off guard. Why the hell should he have expected anything less from a madman? "Lieutenant, wait! Where the hell are you going? Come back, sir!"

Driven on by his own rationale, Mathers didn't even break his stride, but continued towards the ruins. "You forget, Corporal, I have a spirit to kill and when I do so, I shall become even greater than I am now. I shall add its power to my own. Skarra has promised me!"

At the mention of Skarra, Chandar hissed gently and made a sign of reverence towards the tank. Could it be that Mad Mathers was actually convincing Chandar of their deception, Atkins wondered? After all, if Mathers had started to believe it...

The Tank Commander had reached the overgrown, cavernous entrance and led his men into the ruined edifice.

A low, continuous moan issued from its depths.

Atkins hoped it was just the wind through the tunnels.

CHAPTER THIRTEEN
"Across the Untroubled Blue..."

OUT ON THE veldt, the ominous low rumble that accompanied the line of leaden grey clouds in the distance continued long past the point where it should have died away.

Everson made his way from the fire trench, along the sap. The disappearance of the Khungarrii was weighing heavily on his mind. What the hell were they up to? He didn't know and he didn't like it. This damn planet was full of unknowns. He seemed to spend too much time just reacting to things and trying to keep their heads above water. So far, he'd been lucky. This latest manoeuvre by the Khungarrii, vanishing like that, had unsettled him. All he could do was keep the men stood to in expectation of—of God knew what, frankly. However, they could only do that for so long and they were reaching the end of their tether already. He felt himself floundering, not knowing what to expect next.

The sap came out by the old Poulet farmhouse. Lieutenant Baxter and his machine gun section occupied the ground floor. They had set the Lewis machine gun up in a window bay, the walls reinforced by sandbags.

Baxter took him aside and, in a low voice, proceeded to question him. "Everson, any idea what the hell is going on out there? Where have the damned Chatts gone to?"

"I don't know, Baxter. They seem to have abandoned the field, but whether it's a feint or not, I just don't know. Keep your eyes peeled. I've only come here for a look-see myself. The Hill OP will keep us informed. As soon as I know anything, you will, Bernard."

He patted the officer on the shoulder and, with a shrug and apologetic smile, started up the stairs to the observation platform.

The whole of the upper level had been roughly refloored with wooden boards, and the old roof, which had been in danger of collapsing, had been removed. Most of the upper walls had been saved. Loose bricks had tumbled down and the rubble still lay scattered around the farmhouse walls. It was open to the elements but for a large tarpaulin that flapped and snapped over his head in the strengthening breeze. He stopped and sniffed. There was a pungent odour on the wind. Damp. Acrid. Rank. Animal.

"Sir!" The corporal and two privates on watch snapped to attention as Everson arrived up the stairs. Everson found the RFC lieutenant, Tulliver, there too, checking the weather. A makeshift windsock billowed in the breeze.

"Anything to report?" asked Everson, walking up to the empty window frame and looking out over the now desolate veldt. The heavy grey clouds sailed towards them with the threat of rain. Beyond, the rumbling persisted. "What the hell *is* that?" he muttered, half to himself.

"Sir!" snapped the corporal, calling his attention to flashes coming from the OP up on the hillside. Everson watched them for a moment, spat out an oath, pulled out his field glasses and raised them to his eyes.

A dust cloud rolled along the veldt. Was it the Khungarrii again, hoping to catch them with their guard down? He quickly scanned the field deserted by the alien army. He spotted the immobile Chatts facing the oncoming storm with an almost preternatural patience. He focused on the dust cloud. It seemed to stretch right across his field of vision, obscured only by the foothills of the valley.

"Hell and damnation! It's a bloody stampede."

"Stampede, sir?"

"Animals, Corporal, thousands of bloody animals headed this way, driven before the storm. When they pass the head of the valley I want you to fire a flare. Understood?"

"Flare. Understood, sir."

"Tulliver, get your machine off the ground, do it now before the thing gets trampled! I don't want to lose it."

"You're not the only one!" He didn't have to be told twice. He sprang down the stairs in several leaps and pelted off to the cleared take-off strip.

Everson trotted down the stairs and rushed out of the farmhouse, past the machine gun section. "Bernard," he yelled. "Bloody stampede. Best hole up there and stay under cover. They'll be here soon. Let's hope they decide to go round instead of through, eh?"

"Maybe we can help 'em decide?"

"Be obliged to you!"

Everson jumped down into the sap and ran along the jinked trench back to the outer fire trench ring. At least down in the trenches the men should be safe; well, safer. Any animals that got beyond the wire weed should just jump right over them.

At the junction with the fire trench ring, he turned right. Privates turned and looked at the sight of an officer running as he darted past, body swerving round the sandbag traverses, looking for the first NCO he could find. It was Sergeant Hobson.

"Sergeant, there's a stampede headed this way. Keep the men stood to. And for God's sake, preserve your ammunition. Don't fire unless you have to. Send runners and pass the message on. Everyone else to the dugouts. We can't guarantee their safety if they're in the open."

"Sir."

Everson ran on through several more bays and took a sharp left down Pall Mall, the first communications trench he came to. Scarcely slowing his speed for the tight confines of the trench, he wove down the zigzags, careening off revetments and almost colliding with a ration party bringing up hot soup.

"Gangway!"

"Christ, watch it you silly—"

Everson didn't wait for their mortified apologies. The soldiers in the trenches and dugouts might well weather the stampede in relative safety, but there were the tents and huts in the middle of the encampment that would be vulnerable, most of those housing the sick and the wounded and several small clans of Urmen. He had to evacuate them into dugouts. He didn't want to think about the consequences if he didn't.

He collided heavily with someone running the other way, winding himself. He looked up to see the kinematographer straightening his wire-framed glasses.

"God damn it, Hepton!"

"You're in an awful hurry, Lieutenant."

"That's because there's a bloody stampede headed this way."

He caught the eager glint in Hepton's eye as he pushed past.

"Alien animal stampede? I say, that's excellent!" he heard him call back, from beyond another jink in the communications trench, as he put distance between them.

Everson shook his head as he ran on past the crossroads that connected with the support trench. The damn man was all about the sensational. Well, let him have his stampede. If he got trampled underfoot for his film, it was no skin off his nose.

He took a left turn into the support trench, the inner ring. Traffic here was heavier and he had to slow down.

"Private!"

"Sir?"

Everson jerked his head in the direction of the parados. "Give me a leg up."

"Sir?"

"Now!"

The private, nonplussed but knowing better than to ask, linked his fingers together, palms up. Everson stepped into the cradle and the private boosted him up, over the parados sandbags, to the open ground in the centre of the ring of trenches. He made his way to the hospital tent with its shabby fading red cross. He strode in, sweeping the flaps aside.

"Lippett? Where's Captain Lippett?" he demanded of the white-coated orderly.

Lippett stepped out from behind a hung blanket cordoning off a section of tent for private use—his office.

"Yes, Lieutenant, what can I do for you?"

"There's a stampede headed this way. You need to get your patients down into the dugouts."

"Stampede? But some of them can't be moved."

He had no time for this. "Now, Doctor!"

The doctor spluttered at the impudence. Again, Everson didn't wait for a retort and heard Lippett giving orders to the orderlies and 'light duty' injured.

Most of his men were disciplined enough to follow orders, but the new Urmen platoons, Fred Karno's Army, didn't seem to grasp the idea. Everson caught sight of several NCOs barking furiously at Urmen, who weren't obeying. They should have been going down into the trenches. Instead, they were gathering portable possessions.

"Do I have to do every blasted thing myself," he muttered, as he made his way over to them. "Corporal, what the hell is going on here? Get those Urmen into the trenches."

"They won't go, sir. They keep shouting something and pointing at the veldt, sir."

Everson turned on the nearest Urman and threw his arms up in frustration. "What? What is it?"

The Urman, now Everson looked at him, had a haunted look in his eyes, a look of barely suppressed panic restrained only by their awe of the Tohmii. He kept casting anxious glances at the horizon.

"What is it, what's out there?"

"Dapamji!" It was an Urman word for death. As if the very word absolved him of any loyalty to the Tommies, he herded his family away back towards the valley, pausing only to shout the warning again. "Dapamji!"

"Sir?"

"Let them go, Corporal. It's out of our hands. Get down into the trenches."

Across the encampment, he saw Tulliver's aeroplane take to the air. That was one less thing to worry about.

A flare arced into the darkening sky with a whoosh and burst in a bright white bloom.

Everson could feel the ground begin to reverberate beneath his feet. The rumble of hooves and the snorts, whinnies and screams of animals in terror, filled the air and grew louder. There was little time left.

Sister Fenton, Nurse Bell and a couple of sentries were herding reluctant shell-shocked patients down to the dugout in the Bird Cage. Nurse Bell was attempting to round up several of the patients, but one man had other ideas. With a single-minded determination, he scrambled out through the barbed wire fencing that surrounded them, oblivious to cuts and scratches, and was now making for the front line. Nurse Bell made for the compound gate and gave chase.

"Jones! Private Jones, come back!"

Everson looked around the encampment. Most soldiers were too busy saving themselves, or their own, to notice or care about one shell-shocked straggler heading *towards* the wire.

Above, caught by a gust of the steadily rising wind, the Union flag snapped and furled, briefly catching his attention. It embodied all the things he had been taught were right; King, Country, Duty. However, there were some things that he never needed to be taught. Some things were innate, tacit.

"Oh, for heaven's sake!" he said, racing after Nurse Bell and towards the oncoming stampede.

He leapt over a communication trench like a steeple chaser, almost losing his footing on the parapet, sending sandbags tumbling down into it. He pounded over a trench bridge. With his lungs burning in his chest, he headed for the barbed wire entanglements. The shell-shocked man had found the gap in it and was wading through it like a rising tide, heedless of the barbs that snatched and tore at him.

Bell clung desperately onto his arm, her weight on her front foot as she tried to use her meagre frame to halt his dogged advance.

Drawing his revolver Everson raced towards her. He could see the approaching herds now, their stench heavy on the wind. They flowed round the mausoleum mounds of the Khungarrii like a river as they met the first of the mesmerised Chatts. The arthropods fell beneath them without resistance and they trampled them under foot.

He reached Bell and grabbed her arm. "Come on. We have to go. Now!"

"No, we have to save him."

"We can't. You've done enough!"

But she wouldn't give up her patient.

Everson levelled his revolver at the unwary man, who was still trying to advance despite their added weight. "God damn it, woman, if you don't let go, I'll shoot him."

"You wouldn't!"

"Watch me!" He cocked the Webley with his thumb. "It's technically desertion anyway!"

"No!" Bell let go of the man's arm, only to grab Everson's revolver and push it towards the ground.

She watched, all hope lost, as the man, suddenly free of the dead weight, surged forwards towards the wire and rushed out to meet the oncoming wall of flesh and fur.

"Jones!"

"He'll have to take his chances, though why he chose now to show some bloody gumption, I'll never know!" Everson, still gripping her wrist, began dragging her towards the trench. He leapt down on to the fire step, almost knocking a soldier off, and dragged Bell in after him. He lost his balance and ended up on his back, Bell sprawled across him and struggling to free her wrist from his grip. He relented and let her go, only for her to repay him with a sharp slap to the cheek. He guessed he deserved that. Edith scrambled to her feet, trying to recover her dignity. She stepped onto the fire step, with every intention of going out after her patients again, raised her head above the parapet, and gasped.

Everson glanced around the fire bay and, spotting a funk hole in the side of the revetment, yanked out the equipment and pulled Edith over.

"What are you doing?"

"Keeping you safe, since you seem incapable of doing it for yourself." He indicated the shallow hole, as if he were opening a door for a lady. "In."

She looked for a moment as if she might object, and knowing Bell, as he had come to over the past few months, she probably would. He shoved her into the vacant hole anyway. She looked up at him, half-annoyed and half-thankful.

"Stay there."

The rumble of hooves and feet now seemed to encompass their whole world. He returned to the fire step, risking a quick glance over the parapet. He had faced waves of charging Huns before, but nothing prepared him for the sight that met him now.

All he could see was a bow wave of dust and chaff as the solid wall of fear-driven herds bore down on what now seemed flimsy defences against such an unstoppable force. The lines of Tennyson's poem rang in Everson's head. *"Half a league, half a league, half a league onward, all in the valley of death..."*

SERGEANT HOBSON STOOD in a fire bay beside Monroe, Carter and Cox, rifles loaded.

"Here they come, lads!" Hobson bellowed, taking aim. He fired five rounds rapid, bringing three beasts down short of the fire trench, but it was like Canute trying to hold back the tide.

"Bugger this!" he said, ducking. "It's like trying to swat minnies with me battle bowler. Take cover, lads. We've done all we can. Let's just try and ride this out."

They hunkered down in the trench to sit out the beastly barrage.

A GREAT WAVE of fur and bone, of blood and sinews, claws and horns, of hide and carapace rushed pell-mell towards them across the veldt. The spur of the foothills served to part the wave, funnelling stampeding animals into the adjacent valleys. It also channelled a good proportion of what was left of the panicked herds down the valley towards them.

Everson watched as the first wave of the stampede reached the wire shores of their island home, the greater parts flowing around the great circular encampment and past it, on up the valley.

Still, unrelenting waves of animals crashed and broke against the wall of wire and weed, driven headlong by some uncontrollable fear. Those behind pressed those in front ever onwards in a surge of bodies, advancing over those caught in the tightening bonds. Within moments, the tide of dead and dying had clogged the entanglements, providing purchase and passage over the wire.

The animals surged towards the front line. Everson was depending on the support and reserve trenches to take out as many animals as possible before the fire trench was overwhelmed, trying to slow or derail the stampede, to spare the centre of the camp the worst of it.

Some enterprising soldier threw a grenade into the marauding mass. It exploded in a ball of shrapnel, meat and bloody vapour, anguished animal screams piercing the heavy bass thunder.

Those animals near it tried to veer away from it, momentarily sparing the fire bay directly in front, channelling them instead towards adjacent bays. Men there, in turn, threw their grenades to avoid the onslaught. It seemed to have the desired effect, lessening the strength of the initial frontal assault, but it only worked for the first wave. It wasn't actually stopping it. They didn't have enough bombs to sustain the tactic, and the great press of creatures continued unabated, bellowing, snoring and roaring towards the trenches.

Everson could do nothing but bear witness. The sandbags shook and, through the revetment, he felt the ground tremble against his chest. The noise and the stench of musk and fear were overwhelming. He feared even the tank would not have fared well against such an onslaught of flesh.

Predators and prey ran together, their natural enmities temporarily forgotten in their headlong flight. Creatures he recognised, others he didn't, tore towards him in an unheeding rush, snapping, biting and rearing at those that got in their way. From his worm's-eye view over the parapet, Everson felt more vulnerable than ever.

Great three-legged tripodgiraffes tried to maintain their balance as they tottered headlong, striding above the packs below. Two-legged pelths, twice the size of ostriches, with sharp, hooked beaks, wove in and out of their legs, threatening to trip them, or be trampled. One tripodgiraffe did fall, its great long neck flailing as it crashed to the ground like a felled tree, to be lost, trampled under hooves.

Hell hounds bounded, snapping and snarling at each other in fear.

Large, heavy, prehensile-lipped gurduin, herbivores with great bone head-ridges, and mottled hides riddled with wart-like protrusions, thundered headlong, their brutish looks belying their usual passivity, distorted by foam-flecked mouths and white eyes rolling with terror.

"Look out," called Everson, to the men around him. "Here they come. Keep down!"

One of the gurduin stumbled, its forelegs folding beneath it. Trying to get to its feet, it was pummelled back into the ground. Others, too slow to react, and too hemmed in to manoeuvre around, barrelled into it. Some attempted to leap over, but their short legs and cumbersome bodies weren't meant for such athletic moves, and they caught their legs and tumbled over, losing their balance, to join it in the same fate, and the pile up began.

One beast, leaping the fallen, clipped the bodies beneath. The beast's scream cut through the thunderous thrumming of the hooves around it as it tripped and fell forwards, breaking its foreleg. It crashed headlong through the sandbag parapet, its momentum and weight carrying it slithering over the edge into the narrow trough of the trench.

The soldier barely had time to scream before its huge bulk threw him off the fire step. It drove him into the duckboards, snapping planks and bones, where the beast struggled, screaming and kicking, trying to right itself, grinding the Tommy's body beneath it and smashing the revetments with its hooves. A wild kick splintered another soldier's thigh, the jagged shards of femur ripping though his khaki serge as it quickly began to stain with blood.

His mates dragged him clear of the bellowing animal, yelling for a stretcher bearer. Quickly, three bayonets were plunged into the creature, briefly increasing the thrashing and squealing. Barely had Everson stepped up and shot it in the forehead, than Bell was out of her funk hole, taking charge of the casualties, as along the front line other panicked animals leapt over the trenches, losing their footing and tumbling madly into the man-made ditches.

Choking dust sifted down from the hurtling herds above as they leapt over the trenches. The men knew enough now to keep their heads down, and huddled at the bottom, their hands over their heads, to sit it out. Some sat back against the parados revetment, their feet braced against the opposite wall, their rifles and bayonets pointed up against the prospect of a clumsy beast. Others lit up what fags they had left and smoked nonchalantly as the beasts thundered and pounded by, feet above their heads, showering them with dirt, dust, and the occasional fear-voided droppings, much to the amusement of their fellows.

Several chanced their heads and took pot-shots at the rampaging creatures from the fire steps. Caught by a stray hoof, one careless man's neck snapped back, breaking in an instant. He crumpled to the duck boards like an empty sack.

With the thunderous pounding surrounding them, dirt raining down on them, it began to feel like an old-fashioned Bosche artillery barrage of minniewerfers and five-nines. It seemed to last forever. Everson almost laughed at the thought. Who would have thought he'd miss the good old days?

THEN, AS IT seemed the stampeding rumble would go on forever, it was over. The thunder of hooves receded, leaving only the odd squealing animal chasing after the rest.

The men waited, fearing more. It didn't come and they began to relax, laugh and chatter with the exhilaration of survival. Hobson sniffed, straightened his waxed moustache, picked up his rifle and stood up, intending to peer over the parapet, but shouts of alarm over to his right distracted him. The screams grew louder, moving along the trench towards them. Several fire bays away, he heard shots fired.

A maddened hell hound careered round the traverse, confused and panic-stricken, cornered like a boar in a run. Men leapt onto fire steps and scrambled up the parapets out of its way. Several Tommies skidded to a halt behind it in the traverse and levelled their rifles. It slewed to a halt, snarling and snapping, cornered between the traverse and Sergeant Hobson.

Hobson aimed his bayoneted rifle and pulled the trigger. The rifle jammed. Stoppage. He cursed silently but didn't back down. He gripped his rifle more firmly and dropped it into a low defensive guard. The bayonet was his weapon now.

Its way blocked, the hell hound attempted to turn in the tight space, but couldn't. Frustrated and enraged, it snapped at a man's legs on the fire step, sinking its teeth into his calf and dragging him down off the step, as the man clawed at the revetment, stretching hands that reached down, but not far enough.

It tossed its head, shaking him. Even over the man's scream, Hobson heard the man's leg snap.

Hobson let out a roar, and the beast turned its head to look at him. It opened its jaws and let the man drop. Hobson lunged forward with his fixed bayonet; the hell hound shook its head in challenge and sprung forwards to meet him. With a blood-curdling cry, Hobson thrust his rifle, plunging the bayonet deep into the creature's chest. The hell hound's attack faltered. Stuck on the bayonet, it snapped at Hobson, who held it at bay with the length of the rifle.

He glanced up at the scared men on the parapets, who looked unsure of what to do. "Well don't just bloody stand there taking bets. Fire, damn you or I'll have your names!"

Shaken from their fear, the men took aim and a fusillade of bullets slammed into the creature. Amid the cordite smoke, Hobson felt the rifle take the full weight of the hell hound as it died, and withdrew his bayonet.

Hobson looked at the firing squad on the parapet, glaring up at them from under the lip of his steel helmet. "If I find out any of you bet against me," he said. "I'll have your bloody guts for garters."

EVERSON TENTATIVELY RAISED a look-stick over the collapsing parapet and squinted through the aperture. The dust was still settling, caught as it was by wind eddies.

The bodies of beasts littered the ground: the sick, the old, the young, the unlucky, lay twisted and broken, dead or injured. The living squealed and whinnied in pain.

Satisfied that the stampede had run its course, he climbed out of the trench to survey the encampment. Around the fire trench, others climbed out, too, pushing back their helmets in bewilderment and disbelief at the devastation wreaked by the stampede.

Everson's heart sank as he turned around. Animal bodies hung from the wire entanglements, trenches had collapsed, tents had been trampled, and hutments razed. It might as well have been a bloody Hun artillery barrage.

Hobson walked up and joined him.

"All that work and we're back where we started," said Everson with a sigh.

Hobson stuck out his chest and rocked on his feet. "It'll give the men something to do, sir."

"We're going to have to strengthen the trenches, relay the entanglements, repitch the tents, rebuild the hutments..."

"Still," said Hobson, brightly. "Plenty of dung for the gunpowder experiments now, I'd say."

Everson sighed. "Thank you, Sergeant, I hadn't realised there was such a silver lining."

Hobson glanced down modestly, and shrugged. "You just have to look for it. Or in your case, sir, tread in it."

*　　*　　*

THE STAMPEDE OVER, the gas gong sounded the all-clear. Edith and Sister Fenton climbed out of the dugout. Together the nurses looked out towards the approaching storm.

Edith didn't relish the prospect of the quagmire the trenches would become under a torrential rain, and she suspected the men wouldn't either. They had grown used to the comfort of dry trenches and dugouts.

As she watched the storm shadows slide across the veldt towards them, she squinted at the voluminous roiling grey mass in the distance and shivered.

TULLIVER CIRCLED THE trenches in his Sopwith, looking for somewhere to land. The hooves of thousands of bloody animals had churned up his carefully kept strip. They'd trampled the whole landscape to buggery. There had to be somewhere to land.

His attention turned to the oncoming weather, to the great grey-blue mass rolling towards them, blotting out the achingly blue sky as it came.

Only they weren't clouds. From up here, that much was clear now. Tulliver could see what those on the ground couldn't. The danger wasn't yet over because the stampede was never the threat. It was what *caused* it that was the real threat.

CHAPTER FOURTEEN

"Into Your Dugout and Say Your Prayers..."

EVERSON FOCUSED HIS binoculars on the storm front and felt a hoarfrost of fear creep down his spine. He adjusted the focus and blurred shadows sharpened into a moment of confusing detail. He lowered the field glasses to get context and quickly raised them again, panning across the rapidly advancing cloud front. He passed the glasses to Hobson, soliciting the platoon sergeant's opinion. "What do you make of it?"

With no other hint, Hobson took the glasses. "Bloody hell!" he spat, adding a hasty, "sir."

It could have been a great armada of blimps, dirigibles of enormous size, driven along by the wind. There seemed to be no source of motive power. Was this the cause of the stampede? Some kind of air force? If it was a fleet, it threatened to fill the sky.

"What are they, some kind of Zeppelins? Some sort of foreign airship?"

"Maybe, sir. No, wait, they're..."

"They are the Kreothe," said a voice, filled with horror and realisation. It was Poilus. "The great drifting sky shoals of Kreothe. Huge airborne creatures that live on the winds, never coming to earth."

"Thank God," said Everson with relief. "You had me worried there for a minute."

"And so you should be," said Poilus, looking at the approaching things in wonder. "The Kreothe may live in the air, but they feed on the ground. They come, blown by the winds, by the breath of GarSuleth. They have not passed this way in generations. I have only known them exist in tales the elders tell of older times. The last time they passed this way, our clan were still Khungarrii Urmen, safe in Khungarr."

"Sir?" Hobson knocked Everson on the upper arm with the back of his hand as he held out the binoculars. "I think he's right. It's not over yet. You'd better take another look..."

Everson did.

What they had mistaken for a cloud front or a zeppelin fleet was, in fact, thousands of individual creatures, of varying sizes, floating from gas sacs, hundreds of feet in the air. Their progress was calm and measured, and above all silent. It was impossible not to be impressed by the things as they crowded the wide sky in their slow stately progress above the veldt. Air sac followed air sac in a mass of varying sizes; from huge towering majestic creatures that appeared, to Everson's imagination, like the old bulls of the shoal, to skittish flimsy little things, like younglings.

Great long thick tendrils, hundreds of feet long, hung from the creatures, dragging along the veldt, dredging for food.

Everson watched, almost spellbound, as tentacles caught animals up, lifting their catches into the air, before handing them over to the shorter fronds that clustered around the bodies protruding below the great air sacs. These, it seemed, were great prehensile tongues, that seemed to taste the creature's food before it ingested it. Everson knew many creatures on this planet were inedible or, perhaps, had defences against such predation. This was obviously the Kreothe way of countering that, testing it perhaps, before drawing it up into pulsing mouth tubes and into the belly of yet another swelling.

Everson watched, in horrified fascination, the great bull Kreothe at the head of the shoal grazing languidly, as they drifted inexorably towards the encampment. He was reminded of seeing an elephant at feeding time or, perhaps, a Portuguese Man-o'-war, as he once did as a young boy, preserved for display in a newly opened museum wing donated by his father.

He had seen enough. "So this is why the Khungarrii vanished. They didn't want to be caught out in the open under these things." He looked at Hobson. "How long have we got, do you reckon?"

Hobson pursed his lips and squinted. "Judging by the wind speed, maybe ten to fifteen minutes?"

"Here we go again," muttered Everson as he started to give orders.

There was a roar as Tulliver flew low over the trenches, waggling his wings to attract their attention. Everson looked up and saw Maddocks, the observer, pointing back towards the approaching Kreothe. A warning.

The plane circled. Everson waved to show he understood. Tulliver pointed to his machine gun, and then at the Kreothe, and headed out to meet them.

Everson grunted an acknowledgement as he turned his attention to the various runners who were now appearing, ordering all but a small defensive force into the deep dugouts. "We can't fight these things. I've no idea how. All we can do is try and warn them off. Keep any more damage to a minimum."

The translucent gas sacs of the oncoming Kreothe cast a peculiar light as the sunlight filtered through them, and the sky began to darken.

IN THE BIRD Cage, Townsend, Miller and the other shell-shock victims stumbled out of the dugout, determined, like Jones before them, to escape their confinement again at any cost. Everson said he couldn't spare extra men to guard them. Nurse Bell, Sister Fenton and Padre Rand found themselves unequal to the task.

"What's got into them, Sister?" asked the padre, his arms wide, trying to block one man from reaching the fence, as if he were playing British Bulldogs.

"I don't know, Padre," said Sister Fenton, as she struggled to keep hold of one man. "They seemed docile and compliant until the wind changed and now, I don't know, they seem *compelled* to escape their confinement. Oh!" Flailing about, the man smacked the sister across the face with the back of his hand, barely aware that he had done so. She recoiled in shock and he broke free and joined the surge for the fence.

The padre watched those escaping patients, already out of the compound, dash over the trench bridges towards a section of trampled barbed wire entanglement beyond.

Townsend and the others stumbled out past the mangled bodies of tripodgiraffes and gurduin.

Edith darted back past the padre after the straying men.

"Nurse, no!" he yelled.

"Nurse Bell!" cried Sister Fenton.

"They don't know what they're doing!" she called back. "Somebody has to help them!"

QUICKLY REALISING THAT she was right, Padre Rand let out a brief growl of frustration. He could not, should not, leave them while there was still a chance. The parable of the shepherd and the lost sheep and all that.

For years, he'd told that allegory from his cold pulpit in St Chad's. They were words meant to mollify and soothe, one of many platitudes he issued daily to his congregation. The words lulled him as well, and there, in his parish, he slept. There were no great hardships for him to face, no great tests of faith. The shepherd slept as his flock wandered blithely into a new century and towards the precipice.

It was the Great War that awoke him, to find his flock in jeopardy, physically and morally, and awoke him to the meaning of the words. The true meaning. Having to live by those words he had stood by for so many years, to put himself to the test. Armed with only the small black leather-bound bible that enshrined those words, and the conviction in his heart that they must be true, he set out to steer his flock through the valley of darkness.

There, in the dark fastness of that valley, he came across evil. And there the words failed him. And he had been afraid. In Khungarr, with Jeffries, the Khungarrii put him through a ritual. It had felt like a personal test: his faith, and that of Jeffries' obscene beliefs, versus theirs. His God against theirs, and his had proved wanting. No, not his God, his faith. His faith, for one brief instance, had failed him and he was almost lost. There, he had suffered tormenting visions that challenged and tested him and found him wanting, while Jeffries had shrugged it off. Memory of the visions faded, like a bad dream he could not recall. He struggled to put it behind him, convincing himself that it was nothing more than a drug-induced delirium. Recently, the visions had tried to surface again, haunting his nights and clawing at his mind, like an itch he couldn't scratch. Every day became a battle to keep it at bay because he didn't have the courage to face it.

However, here and now, on this damned and God-forsaken world, he would screw his courage to the sticking place. Here and now, he would place his faith in his God, as Abraham had done.

He ran after Nurse Bell.

BEYOND THE FRONT trench, past the few remaining poppies that had survived the stampede, the shell-shocked now clambered over the bodies of trampled beasts, and the barbed wire, to the cat calls and jeers of the soldiers in the trenches.

Edith ran after them.

"Wait! Townsend, Miller!"

The men, neither helping one another nor hindering, each hell-bent on some personal goal, pushed forwards, free of the defences now, out into the veldt.

Edith followed, scrambling over the burst and blood-slicked carcasses of the beasts bridging the wire.

The veldt before her was a scene of ruin and devastation. The ground had been churned beneath thousands of hooves, pock-marking the surface.

The stacked pyramids of Khungarrii dead lay tumbled, and the funeral balls crushed, exposing chitinous limbs and vacant alien faces embedded in the shattered clay.

The earthworks had been toppled and yet more animals lay dead in some of the Khungarrii excavated holes.

If one squinted, it could almost be the Somme.

Here and there, a few of the mesmerised Khungarrii still survived. Most were injured, but several, that Edith could see, were remarkably unscathed. They stood motionless and patient in their enigmatic vigil.

Padre Rand caught up with her, a couple of orderlies and Sister Fenton hot on his heels.

Once clear of the entrenchments, on open ground, the shell-shocked men simply stopped, joining the surviving Khungarrii. They stood waiting as one might expect a commuter to wait, in expectation of an imminent train or motor omnibus, and with as little concern.

By now, the wind was carrying the slow stately procession of Kreothe towards them. No sound issued from the great creatures, at least any sound that she could hear. They were silent, like clouds. She heard only the abruptly terminated screams of the beasts plundered from the plain, as the huge tendrils plucked the animals into the sky. Padre Rand saw in them the false gods of this world, cold, unheeding, and uncommunicative.

There were twenty-seven men who, for whatever reason, stood waiting patiently, motivated by some unfathomable compulsion to be there. Only five people had ventured out to help them.

As the great air-shoal of the Kreothe drifted closer, the curtain of tendrils hanging below worked industriously, plucking the veldt clean, and lifting the creatures to taste them, before depositing them into their tubular maws, from where they were sucked into their huge digestive nodules. Every now and again, they rejected some creatures and let them drop the hundreds of feet to the ground, where they impacted with dull thuds and explosions of fluids and offal. It sounded, to Padre Rand, like those first big, fat, wet drops of a summer shower.

Bell, almost hysterical with desperation now, yanked at Townsend's tunic with unprofessional urgency. "Townsend!" she screamed, looking up at the great creatures gliding towards them. Their sheer size was apparent now. Getting no reaction, she slapped him across the face. For a brief moment, she thought she noticed a reaction before it faded, replaced by the emotionless mask once more. "Townsend!" she slapped him again.

His eyes flicked towards her ever so briefly.

"Help me," he said, a frail whisper barely escaping his lips. Then he was lost again, leaving only a tear sliding haltingly down his face.

She put a hand to his cheek and wiped it way with her thumb, then gave a startled yelp. A shadow moved on the back of his neck beneath his collarless shirt. The swelling pulsed briefly and she thought she saw a dark shadow, as if something moved under the taut blister of skin. She blinked. The swelling looked much as it had done over the last two days. Maybe she had imagined it.

The Kreothe were close now, almost overhead. She had to crane her neck to look up at them.

"We can't stay here!" said Stanton the orderly. "We have to go!"

"But the men!"

"We can't do anything for them."

"We can. We must!"

She took hold of Townsend's arm and pulled at him. Reluctantly he began to move with her, like a recalcitrant child.

"Stanton, take another one. Padre, help us!"

The padre ran forwards and grabbed the nearest man.

"Come with me, my son." He met with no resistance, but no help either.

Stanton threw his man over his shoulder and staggered back towards the trenches. He got into trouble trying to negotiate the bridge of dead animals over the barbed wire. One or two men came out of the trenches and sprinted towards him to help him with his patient.

Edith ducked under Townsend's arm to take his weight. As she stood up and braced herself, she glanced back over her shoulder and regretted it.

Above them, like huge towering cumulonimbus clouds, the gas-bloated Kreothe drifted with a sedate grace while underneath the tendrils groped, picked and plucked rapaciously.

They plucked the first of the shell-shocked, a tendril wrapping around him and lifting him into the air. Edith watched with mounting horror. By some method she could not discern, the man's body proceeded to unfold like the petals of a flower, bright and wet and red, like the poppies that populated the ground below, exposing his innards as the poppy petals unfurled to expose their stamen. It was as if he were being peeled or flayed as he ascended into the sky in some otherworldly sacrament.

Others were being plucked now, like matured fruit, ascending to waiting tongue tendrils where flocks of carrion things snatched and tore at them before they were directed into the soft wet waiting maws of the mouth tubes.

Stumbling under Townsend's dead weight, Edith realised, with a sickening lurch, that they weren't going to make it.

"BELL! BELL!"

Edith looked about at the sound of her name. She saw Sister Fenton calling to her from the opening of one of the Khungarrii delvings.

"Get in quick," said Sister Fenton, holding out her hand to take Townsend. Edith pushed him down the hole and, with only a brief glance over her shoulder, followed. The delving was about twenty feet deep and sloped down at a gentle angle. The padre was down there with two other shell-shocked soldiers, Miller and Jones. The group huddled as far down the sloping tunnel as they could.

"Keep still," said Fenton in a low voice, as if afraid they might be heard.

One tendril dragged across the opening, throwing the burrow into darkness. Its tip probed the entrance, sending loose clods of earth and slips of soil slithering down into the hole. It began feeling its way down. Then it was gone, drawn away by the ever drifting air sacs above.

"I can't look," said Sister Fenton, turning her face from the hole. But a terrible fascination drew Edith's gaze back to the circle of sky before her, striated now by passing tendrils.

Overcome by an unquenchable desire, Townsend struggled and jerked a little and Bell tried to calm him, but he worked free of Edith's grasp, scrambling desperately for the light, and stood momentarily at the entrance, offering himself.

"Townsend!" Edith started after him.

"No!" Sister Fenton held her, and firmly forbade her from going after him. All she could do was watch as a dredging tendril found him, and after a tentative caress, caught him up and drew him into the air.

"He's gone, Nurse, but we still have two more we might save," said Fenton. Edith swallowed her grief and her anger, set her face for the practicalities of her craft, and nodded. Their job was to assist the living.

"Yes, Sister."

In bleak resignation, Edith sat huddled with the others, waiting for the ordeal to be over, the tunnel lit by stroboscopic flickers of light and shadow as the moving forest of tendrils coasted past. There, more than in the dugout, she knew something of the fear these men must have felt under constant barrages that numbed the mind and pummelled the senses, until there was nowhere a man might take refuge from the shattering conditions outside, or from himself within.

As she weakened, Padre Rand seemed to draw strength from the trial and began muttering prayers; not meek prayers, begging to be spared from this tortuous test, but rather of strength, asking for the fortitude to bear it. It seemed to Edith as if his faith was an old, much loved, but discarded coat that he had newly rediscovered and was trying on again for size, and found it still fitted.

LIEUTENANT TULLIVER NEEDED to get his Sopwith 1½ Strutter above the shoal of Kreothe drifting implacably towards them and, given the rapidity with which they were approaching, he needed to gain height fast.

They were flying at a thousand feet, but still hadn't cleared the height of the great voluminous air sacs that kept the creatures aloft. The sun had disappeared, blocked out by the Kreothe that now filled the sky above them, and it filtered through their translucent bodies, casting a weird green twilight on everything below. It was like flying in the vaulted nave of some obscene flesh-built cathedral, the tentacles dropping down like clusters of gargantuan columns. There was nothing to do but fly through them until they could find a way up.

Several smaller Kreothe drifted by beneath them. Tulliver glanced down past his fuselage as they slipped by a hundred feet below. They looked for all the world like misshapen kite balloons, and he could deal with balloons.

First, he had to avoid the death-dealing tentacles as they found themselves weaving through a forest of the things.

Tulliver glanced up through the transparent pane in the upper wing above him. Overhead he could see the underside of the mammoth air sacs of a great Kreothe. It bulged with several huge fleshy globules and growths. One cyst-like swelling resembled a large udder from which extruded three slick, wet lipless mouths. A circle of long tongue-like members surrounded each one of them, one of which was feeding a flayed lump of raw wet flesh into an open maw. Tulliver noticed scraps of khaki serge uniform hanging from it as a flock of dark green winged creatures gathered round it, squawking and tearing at the offal, like gulls in a trawler's wake.

Filled with disgust and fury, Tulliver worked rudder and stick, threading the machine between the tentacle roots, up towards the swollen cupola above, before letting loose a prolonged burst of machine gun fire, wishing he still had burning tracer bullets left.

The winged creatures turned their attention to the Sopwith as it banked away, swooping down as one, towards the machine, with raucous harridan shrieks.

Maddocks turned the rear machine gun on them as they flew past the tumorous mouth bag.

Tulliver felt a downdraft of warm, foul-smelling air that briefly buffeted the machine as they passed beneath the maws and their writhing tonguedrils.

He had to get away from the damn things before they tore the aeroplane apart. The winged creatures seemed to keep away from the great harvesting tentacles, flocking instead around the mouth things. Perhaps they weren't immune to the juices with which those things dripped.

"Hang on," he bellowed over his shoulder at Maddocks.

Putting the machine into a spin, he went corkscrewing down around a tentacle. Maddocks peered back, to see the scavengers dropping away and returning to easier prey, and once more resuming their mouth-tube squabbles.

Tulliver levelled out, seeing a patch of bright blue sky between the huge sacs above, and put the aeroplane into a steep climb, racing to rise above a monstrous Kreothe, whose size dwarfed the tiny fragile machine.

At it passed from the green twilit world of the Kreothe's underside into the bright glare of the sun, the Strutter's shadow crossed the taut skin of the giant air sac, like a bott fly among a herd of horses—and he was going to bite. Tulliver continued climbing to gain the height he'd need for the attack. Below him now, the tops of the Kreothe were spread out in a landscape of bulbous towering sacs.

Tulliver pushed the Sopwith into a steep dive towards the Kreothe he'd targeted. He loosed a quick burst from his forward facing machine gun. The stream of bullets raked the huge billowing field of skin stretched out below them. Parts of it seemed to deflate, crumpling slowly under the withering fire of the Lewis gun, but the whole did not collapse, suggesting chambers of buoyancy.

He pulled out of his dive and flew along the Kreothe. There was nothing else they could do. They weren't going to bring one of those things down, so, instead, he pulled back on the stick and climbed, just for the sheer exhilaration of it.

The shoal of Kreothe shrank below them, the blue sky expanded to meet them and, briefly, Lieutenant Tulliver felt at home.

IN THE FIRE trench, Sergeant Hobson craned his neck and looked up at the huge translucent fleshy canopies as they passed overhead, went to the storage box and brought out a Very pistol.

"What are you going to do, Sarn't?"

"What am I going to do, Draper? I'm going to give one of those things a *very* nasty surprise."

He fired the flare pistol. The flare arced up into the sky, bursting brightly against the soft moist nodule attached to the under side of a Kreothe air sac.

An involuntary shudder ran through the tentacles that hung below it, and the nodule itself seemed to shrink and contract from the burning white light that seared through the skin.

The men watched from the trench, mesmerised.

"It's shrivelling like your balls on a wiring party, Coxy!"

"Fuck off, Draper."

The great air sac that carried the creature aloft began to burn and wither and, with its buoyancy lost, the Kreothe began to sink slowly, its now limp tentacles dragged along the ground like anchor chains, weighting it down. It descended slowly, like a holed titanic ocean liner, sinking down to its final resting place further up the valley, beyond the trenches.

The other Kreothe, if they knew or cared about the fate of their shoal member, did not react. They drifted by overhead, oblivious to the ruin they left behind, feeding off stragglers from the fleeing herds further up the valley.

* * *

THE KREOTHE HAVING drifted on, Edith, Sister Fenton and Padre Rand staggered into camp with the two soldiers, Jones and Miller, that they had managed to save. The pair were now practically comatose.

"Stretcher bearers! Stretcher bearers!" called the padre.

Stretchers were rapidly found and the party ushered across what was left of the encampment, to the Aid Post down in the support trench.

"What have we here?" asked Captain Lippett, his concentration on a man's gashed scalp before him as he threaded a needle through the skin.

"The only two surviving neurasthenia patients, Mr Lippett. They all just walked out in the veldt and waited, waited... to be eaten by those... things," Sister Fenton informed him.

"And these two weren't, eh?"

"We dragged them into a Chatt ditch."

"Quick thinking, Sister."

"It was the padre's idea."

"Good show, Padre."

"Just looking after my flock, Doctor."

Lippett looked up at Edith. "I thought that was your job, Nurse Bell. You know the men call you Little Bo Peep, do you?"

He obviously knew she didn't. The remark rankled with Edith. She had got used to being belittled and bullied and she had borne it. She knew her position. But she didn't have to like it. It was funny, but before she came to this world, she would have just taken it meekly and perhaps had a cry to herself later. Now, she felt incensed. She had tried to tell him there was something wrong with them, but he didn't listen, he wasn't interested, not in malingerers, not in cowards. She clenched her fists and felt the nails bite into her palms. She stepped forwards. Doctor or no doctor—

"Nurse!" It was Miller. He was looking in horror at Jones, who had begun fitting on his stretcher, his spine arching, his hips bucking.

"Right, get him into the aid post, we'll have to try and relieve the pressure in those cysts," said Lippett, all airs and graces vanishing in an instant. "Stanton, prepare the equipment, come on, man."

As Lippett set about his operation, Sister Fenton gave Edith a look. "A word, Nurse." She led Edith away from the Aid Post.

"Two!" said Edith through gritted teeth, doing her best to contain her anger. "Two out of twenty seven. We could have saved them if Mr Lippett had listened to me in the first place, if he had the slightest—"

"You can't know that."

"He didn't even try."

Sister Fenton fixed her with a hard stare, one that said she would brook no nonsense. "Nurse Bell. I will deal with this. I'm sure I don't have to tell you this isn't a hospital. We don't have the facilities of a hospital. We don't even have the supplies of a Casualty Clearing

Station or an Ambulance train. God knows, those would seem like luxuries here. The drugs, the surgical procedures, the medicines. We are all doing the best we can. This place brings illnesses, infections, things we've never seen before, and without the benefits that modern medicine has to offer. What more could we have done?"

"But Sister," Edith protested.

"Nurse Bell!"

But Edith could no more keep quiet now than a whizz bang, or she felt she would explode. "I will not let a man like that dismiss—"

Sister Fenton interrupted. "You're letting Driver Abbott's suffrage go to your head. Mr Lippett is a qualified doctor. You're a VAD. You've had, what, six months' basic medical training? It wasn't all that long ago you were just emptying bedpans and changing dressings. By all means, note and report your observations of your patients to me, and I will do what I can, but do not suppose to tell him what to do. Do I make myself clear?"

Edith could barely trust herself to speak. "Yes, Sister," she managed to mutter.

SOMETIME LATER, DRAINED and blood stained, Captain Lippett came out of the tent and approached the nurses. He shook his head. "He's dead, I'm afraid. Died on the table."

Edith struggled to restrain her emotions and choked back a sob. Sister Fenton remained impassive.

"If it's any comfort, the other one you brought in, Miller, is still alive." Lippett finished wiping his hands. "Though it appears you were right, Nurse Bell. They were more than just neurasthenic," he added with a trace of resentment. "Come and see." He ushered them into the tent. Edith entered, wary of what she might find. Jones' body was still on the table, covered by a bloody sheet. "They were host to some sort of parasitic infection," Lippett continued. "Fascinating things. I managed to remove some of them from the intestines."

He showed them a steel surgical tray. A thing, smaller than Edith's little finger, lay in a pool of blood. At first glance, its small delicate-looking grey body seemed ribbed, but on closer inspection, Edith realised it was corkscrewed. It looked gruesome enough as it was, but to imagine it *inside*? She suppressed a shudder. Her real horror, however, was reserved for the small head. The body tapered toward it. It was eyeless. Needle sharp hooks, as fine as fish bones, surrounded an oral sucker. As she tore her attention away from the thing she realised Lippett was still talking.

"...it's an intriguing pathology. Although most of them remained in the gut, I found a cluster of them curled round the brain stem, from where it seems they can affect the nervous system of the host," he was saying.

"Making them do things against their will?" asked Edith, her face crumpled with disgust.

"It appears so. The hosts acting against their own best interest for the parasites' benefit. It would certainly explain the patients' uncharacteristic behaviour. From the reports, I believe a number of Chatts were affected, too," said Lippett, getting to grip with his subject. "I suspect that they might be the parasite's natural hosts. As hive insects, they probably have weaker individual minds. As for the neurasthenics, perhaps their weakened mental state made them more susceptible to the parasites' control. From what you've witnessed, I'd hazard a guess that the parasite's life cycle required it to be eaten by those Kreothe creatures,"

"Like tapeworms?" enquired Sister Fenton.

"Quite," said Lippett with enthusiasm. "Of course, this is only an *initial* theory. I shall continue to study the creatures—and we still have Miller."

Edith opened her mouth to say something, but was silenced by a stern glance from Sister Fenton.

"For now, our first course of action is to trace the infection back to its source," said Lippett, looking at the nurses expectantly.

"We've had no reports of strange behaviour from any of the other men," said Sister Fenton. "It must have been something specific to the neurasthenics."

Lippett nodded in agreement. "Perhaps something the men ate in the past week. It would have contained the eggs which the patients would have ingested. Once in the digestive tract, they hatched and grew into their juvenile forms. Some would have bored into the bloodstream and travelled round the body until they reached the brainstem."

Edith's face burned with shock. "Oh," she said. She was going to say more, but Sister had only just berated her for presuming too much with Doctor Lippett.

Sister Fenton raised an eyebrow as Edith turned to look at her. "Yes, Nurse Bell?"

"The stew," Edith explained.

"I beg your pardon?" said Lippett.

"The stew, Doctor. I didn't know. Honestly."

"It seems none of us did, Nurse. Did anybody else eat any of it? Did you?"

Edith shook her head emphatically. "No, it was specifically for the patients. Although..."

"Yes, Nurse?"

Edith put her hand to her mouth. "Lieutenant Mathers. I remember Nellie saying he had some, a small amount I'm sure."

"Mathers?" queried Lippett.

"The Tank Commander," said Sister Fenton.

"Well, I'm sure he's in little danger. I mean it's not as if he's one of Nurse Bell's little lost sheep, is he?"

THE TWILIGHT OF the Kreothe passed and, in dribs and drabs, the soldiers climbed once more out from their dark holes into the alien sun.

Everson sighed. He stood looking at the flagpole, which was now leaning at a precarious angle, knocked by a careless Kreothe tentacle. The Union flag flapped and fluttered weakly, like an ailing dog, still wagging its tail at its master's approach.

It put Everson in mind of the leaning Madonna and Child at Albert, in France. It had stood atop the basilica there until it had been bombed. The statue survived, but leaning at an angle. It was thought that if it fell, the war would end. If only things were that simple.

Several small nearby copses had been uprooted, but in the shelter of another, the three captured battlepillars survived unharmed. Maybe, thought Everson, because the Kreothe found them unpalatable. Still, the Kreothe's loss might be their gain.

"Ever have one of those days, sir?" asked Hobson.

"Nothing but, Sergeant. Nothing bloody but."

"So, what do we do now, sir?"

"Now, Hobson?" he said, looking around at the carnage and sighing heavily. "We start again." And not for the first time, Everson's mind turned to Atkins and his black hand gang and to that damned tank. Where were they?

CHAPTER FIFTEEN
"The Better 'Ole..."

"HELL!" GROWLED ATKINS in frustration. "We'll have to go in after them."

"But they're not even our mob," objected Porgy.

Atkins looked at him. "Yes. Yes, they are. They're British Army, like us. We're all we have. We're in a hole, Porgy. If we don't stick together, if we don't look out for each other, we'll end up like those poor old sods we found back there, unknown, unmourned and forgotten, without even a decent grave. That's not a fate I intend to suffer. I intend to survive and get back home, Gutsy. I made that promise on the Somme and I'm making that promise here and, by God, I'm going to keep it. If Lieutenant Everson says we need that tank, then we need the tank—and that means we need its bloody crew, too. God knows what kind of trouble they'll get into in there, led by that madman..."

Gutsy nodded his head. "We're with you, Only." He turned round to the rest of the section. "You heard the corporal, lads. Battle order."

The rest of 1 Section took off their packs, leaving themselves only their webbing with ammo and grenade pouches, and gas mask bags at their chest. They checked their rifle magazines and cycled the bolts so there was one in the spout, ready.

"What about me?" asked Nellie, planting herself obstinately in front of Atkins. "They might get hurt, so I'm not staying here."

Atkins had learned his lesson where Nellie Abbott was concerned. "No, I didn't think you would," he said, with a trace of a smile. He nodded towards the Section's Urman guide, who was cutting lengths of branches with his curved sword and wrapping them with some dried mossy substance to use as torches. "Stick with Napoo."

Prof and Chalky had started to make their own torches, cutting at a little grove of saplings. Saplings with a black bark with silver-grey veins. Nellie frowned. They were familiar...

"No!" she yelled, lifting her skirt and running towards them as they hacked away at the slender trunks. "No, stop. That's corpsewood. It'll kill you!"

Hearing the name, Napoo whirled round and raced across the glade, knocking the cut wood from the Tommies' hands. "She speaks true. It will drain you of your life to keep its own."

The men backed away from the saplings as if they'd been bitten—which they very nearly had.

"Ruddy hell, Chalky," joshed Mercy. "I can't turn me back on you for five minutes without you getting into some trouble or other."

Chalky shrugged sheepishly, and smiled gratefully at Nellie.

Prof shuddered. "Corpsewood?" He backed away in horror and stood in the clearing, looking round, like a spooked horse, not daring to move as if everything around might be the death of him.

"Hey, it's all right, Prof," said Nellie. "You're safe now. You scared me, is all. I'd just seen it before, what it can do."

"I don't think you're helping," said Gazette, looking up from checking his rifle one more time.

"You aren't, neither," retorted Nellie. "If I want your opinion, I'll ask the corporal."

The rest of the section laughed and jeered. Nellie ignored them and turned her attention back to Prof. She knew that haunted look. She'd seen it in soldiers' eyes before.

"Corpsewood," Prof kept muttering to himself, shaking his head, "corpsewood."

A GENTLE DRAUGHT blew from the cavernous opening as they approached the main entrance of the edifice. Roots and boughs were woven round and embedded in the wall of the doorway until they formed a jamb, roots thrusting buttress-like into the ground, but the great bark-like doors, that would have sealed the edifice, had long since dried and shrivelled as the door plant itself had died, leaving the cavernous entrance open. Other vegetation had taken advantage of the fact, clinging to the walls and invading the fallow spaces beyond. Great hanging carpets of plum-coloured shrubbery tumbled down from cracks in the edifice wall.

As they stood on the threshold, Atkins paired the men up; one man with their rifle and bayonet at the ready, accompanied by one holding a torch. Gazette walked with Pot Shot, Porgy with Chalky, Mercy with Prof. Gutsy, gun shouldered, held Little Bertha, his meat cleaver, in his hand, the flames of the torches reflecting off its polished surface. Napoo and Nellie Abbott brought up the rear. Atkins kept an eye on Chandar.

The Chatt sank down on its legs and moved reluctantly. Atkins had half expected it to make a break for it and run. It could have fled, but something kept it with them; against its better judgement, as far as he could tell.

"So, what is this place," he asked. "It's an edifice, right? Made by your people?"

Chandar craned its neck, looked up at the outer wall of the ruined edifice towering above them and hissed. "It is a colony of lost Ones."

Atkins' eyes narrowed. "You knew about this place?"

"Not exactly," rasped Chandar. "Of places like this."

"So, what is it, some mythical missing colony?"

"No, you misunderstand. It happens that once every so often a new queen hatches, while one still rules. It is a time of great regret. Usually the colony's current queen and her nursery entourage kill them, but some survive to attract followers from among the Dhuyumirrii, scentirrii and Djamirrii. We have had such divisions at Khungarr, though many generations ago. If they are strong enough they can replace the old queen, but more often than not, they are killed or driven from the colony and must attempt to start a new one if they are to survive. The difficulty lies in where they can do this, for the ancient scent texts tell us that GarSuleth divided the world between all his children. The world is spoken for. Judging from the size of this edifice it was a small one and could not sustain itself. It also sits within the Zohtakarrii burri."

"The Chatts that attacked us?"

"Yes. Because of this One's injuries, they thought that this One was outcast from Khungarr. This One let them think that. If they had known that this One was not, then we would have been killed. They seemed to show very great interest in you."

"As I recall, so did you lot."

"Agreed."

"How *did* you get your injuries?" asked Atkins, his curiosity piqued.

"This One once tried to challenge Sirigar in open ceremonial debate and paid for it, as you can see." Chandar opened its arms, inviting Atkins to study its body.

Atkins looked at the Chatt with its hobbled gait and broken antennae. "Sirigar did this to you?"

"Sirigar's followers did, before this One had a chance to challenge Sirigar, no doubt under that One's instructions."

Atkins let the matter drop, he had more pressing problems right now. "So this place is nothing special."

"No, it is merely a failed colony."

Atkins regarded Chandar with suspicion. "So, if this place doesn't worry you, what does? You mentioned these Zohtakarrii guarding something that isn't there. It obviously isn't this because it's quite clearly here. I can see it. What is it you're not telling me, Chandar? Do you know what that thing is in there, this evil spirit? Is it Croatoan?"

Chandar hissed at the mention of the name. "No, by GarSuleth's Breath, this One does not know. This One merely feared what it *might* be."

This was getting him nowhere. Atkins waved the others on, and they walked into the cool cavernous gloom of the derelict, rubble-strewn antechamber.

"Here would have been the work area," Chandar said. "Here the djamirrii, the workers, would have brought and sorted their harvest before taking it to storage chambers or the fungus farms." The Chatt looked around at the desolate place it had become. "All colony life was here."

Their feet stirred the dust and debris that had fallen from the chamber roof. The once smooth walls were now home to invasive creepers that poured in round the opening. A shaft of sunlight falling inside the main door cast a suffuse reflective glow across the rest of the chamber. Here and there, they saw the brittle, dried up husks of long dead Chatt bodies, their outlines softened by decades of drifting dust, as if overcome by some long-forgotten catastrophe.

Atkins pushed on into the gloom beyond the penumbra of sunlight, at least knowing that the end of this mission was in sight. All they had to do was kill the creature that had gone to ground here and they could return to the encampment. They had rifles, Mills bombs; they even had a couple of flares. If that lot failed, they had the tank. They could blow this entire ruin sky high if they had to. Either way, it ended today. After that, Mathers was Lieutenant Everson's problem.

There were several tunnels leading off the antechamber. Napoo knelt and examined the dust on the floor, while Nellie held the torch for him. It was easy to spot the footprints left by the tank crew. "This way," he said, leading them across the dusty floor. The party fell in behind him, bayonets at the ready. Atkins looked back at the bright entrance, the hard outlines softened by translucent hanging fronds and back-lit by the sun, and turned back to face the dark. He shuddered. He hated these places.

The tunnel they entered sloped up perceptibly. Roots and creepers had slithered on in advance of them long ago, affixing themselves to the floor and walls, and they had to watch their footing. Eventually the tunnel began to level out. Their torch flames guttered in a soft breeze.

In places, the luminescent lichen, that Chandar told them used to sit in niches lighting the passages, had grown wild and unkempt, giving an opalescent glow to the tunnels.

Here though, the trail was lost. Something had swept along these tunnels so frequently there was no dust trail left to follow. It must be the creature, Atkins realised. There was a hardened black sheen to the walls here, as if the oily residue it left behind had dried. There was no way of telling which of the branching passages the tank crew had taken.

They moved cautiously along a passage. The further they went without incident, the more anxious Atkins became.

Openings yawned in the passage walls. They all had to be checked out. Some were adjoining tunnels, others chambers, empty and bare.

Porgy thrust his torch into another room as they passed, while Chalky lunged forwards in an "on guard" stance with his bayonet. Holding the torch high, lighting the gloom with a flickering orange glow, Porgy cast a glance around the small chamber. There was another passage exiting on the far side. He edged across the room and along the short passage beyond, holding out his torch to illuminate a second chamber.

"Jesus, Mary and Joseph! Only, you'd better come and take a look at this!"

THE TANK CREW had no idea where they were, but they followed Mathers, who seemed to know which way he was going. They didn't need torches. They could see well enough, thanks to the synesthetic petrol fruit fumes that now flooded their bloodstreams. Their footsteps produced colours and flavours that rippled down the Chatt-made circular tunnels.

Mathers led them deeper into the labyrinthine tunnels of the ruin, taking switches and junctions without a second's pause until, deep in the ruined edifice, they came to an empty chamber. Alfie could not see anything remarkable about the chamber, there was nothing to indicate why they might have stopped here.

"This will do," said Mathers. "We don't want any interruptions."

The crew turned to Alfie. Their looks were not pleasant.

Alfie edged back towards the chamber entrance, but the others surrounded him. "What's all this in aid of?" he croaked. "I thought we were going to kill this evil spirit, this devil."

"We are, but first we have some business to attend to," said Mathers. "You."

"Me, sir?"

Alfie felt a surge of fear drive into his limbs, ready for flight. Too late. Frank and Norman seized him by the arms and held them out at his sides, as if he were being crucified. He struggled but they held him fast.

"Sorry, old bean," said Reggie, with a weak, apologetic smile. "It's for the best."

"I don't understand, sir. What have I done? What have I done to any of you? I've followed your orders, sir. I've helped keep the tank running. I've kept your secrets."

Mathers shook his head in disappointment. His voice was calm. "True. You are with us, as you have been since Elveden. Your mind, however, is... elsewhere."

Without effort, Alfie's thoughts turned to Nellie. Was that it? Was that what all this was about?

Mathers stepped towards him. Bruise-coloured auras rose from his mates on the convection currents of their own body heat, and collected gently in the dome of the chamber above their heads.

He looked up at Mathers, who now stood over him in his rain cape, the leather and chainmail mask inscrutable. "Sir, what're you doing?"

Mathers nodded. Frank and Norman forced Alfie to his knees, still holding his arms out straight at his sides. "I'm offering you a chance to recant, Perkins, a chance to rejoin the fold, as it were."

"But I never left, sir."

"You're forgetting, Perkins. I can *see* you. You're confused, afraid. You have to let go."

Mathers nodded at Wally.

The cockney stood behind Alfie and pulled his head back with a hand on his forehead.

Alfie continue to struggle, but to no avail. "No! Whatever you're doing, sir... don't!"

Mathers reached under his rain cape and retrieved his hip flask. He took the top off. Alfie felt Wally's calloused fingers on his nose and briefly smelled the cigarette-stained tips before they pinched his nostrils shut. Alfie struggled, refusing to open his mouth. Mathers stood and waited patiently. The moment Alfie opened his mouth to gasp for air he poured the petrol fruit down his throat.

"Receive the Sacrament of Skarra," he said, in reverent tones.

Alfie coughed and spluttered, but Wally clamped his hand over his mouth until he swallowed. He felt the spirit burn down the back of his throat, bringing tears to his eyes.

Then his world exploded.

Frank and Norman let go of Alfie, and the gearsman slumped back on his heels. Briefly, the world was afire, all his senses screaming. The chamber was a shifting kaleidoscope of unnameable colours, bringing vertigo and nausea. Unfathomable shapes of sound danced at the periphery of his vision. He paused, dry-retching. He took deep breaths, one hand braced against the floor, until the vertigo passed. Like a newly struck Lucifer, the initial flare of sensation died down and the world settled, more or less, but brighter and keener than before, as the undiluted petrol fruit coursed through his system.

"You *see* the world the way I do," he heard Mathers say, or was that smell? "Transubstantiated by the grace of Skarra."

He looked towards the taste of Mathers' voice as he stood over him holding out a hand. Alfie reached out, took it, and found himself hauled to his feet through a dizzying wave of vertigo. It took a moment for his new world to reorient itself.

Alfie looked round and *saw* Mathers. And he saw the things *within* Mathers. The lieutenant put a finger to his chainmail, where his lips were. The meaning was clear. *Shhh.*

WITHOUT A TORCH, Atkins edged cautiously down the dark passage, towards Porgy's light, emerging into another, larger chamber.

He drew an involuntary gasp at the tableau he found there. Around the chamber were four mummified human corpses; dry, taut skin stretched thinly over bone, brittle hair still attached to the skulls, perfectly preserved in the arid atmosphere of the edifice. It was clear from their sizes that they might be a family. Two small bodies, children, lay in a crude moss-stuffed mattress on the floor, clinging to each other, as if in their sleep. One was a boy, dressed in a nightshirt, the other, a girl, in a dress. The body of a man, sat on a rough chair, slumped over a makeshift table constructed of rough-hewn planks. He was dressed in a shirt and trousers, with braces. The remains of a once full and bushy beard now straggled wispily from his chin. On the table was an oil lamp. The body of a woman lay sprawled on the floor, as if trying to drag herself towards the children. Her hair was tied in a bun at the back of her scalp and she wore an ankle-length skirt and a blouse. The skirt and dirty white underskirt had ridden up to expose the shrunken and desiccated legs and feet still laced in worn leather boots.

A dark and terrifying thought began to uncoil in Atkins' mind. His mouth went dry, and he suddenly found it hard to breathe, as if all the air in the chamber had been sucked away. It felt as if he were standing on the edge of a vertiginous black chasm.

Porgy came back from a brief exploration of further chambers beyond that one. "There are three more chambers like this one. Bodies in each of 'em."

"Like these?" Atkins said in a hoarse croak, his mouth dry with fear.

"Yes, poor buggers."

He felt his stomach screwed into a knot, as tight as that he felt when about to go over the top. A cold sweat broke out all over his body, chilling him. He shivered as he numbly followed Porgy into the next chamber; he could hear the pulse of blood in his ears, and his heart beat loudly in his chest, straining to burst out of his ribcage.

Beyond them, in the next chamber, Mercy held the torch high so he could see. Here was another group of people. On one side of the chamber were two bodies laid out and covered with sacking sheets. They had obviously died before the others and been laid out with the respect due to the dead. The other body had not. It belonged to a woman wearing a small white cap on her head, wisps of ginger hair escaping from underneath it over her brown, parchment-like skin. The body was sat slumped against a wall on another mattress, a tartan blanket covering her legs. Shadows cast by the torch danced in her sockets and her lips were drawn back, exposing rotten teeth. Her skeletal fingers were covered with a translucent film of skin, and they lay over a black object that sat on the blanket in her lap.

Atkins squatted down, his hands trembling, as he gently tried to pull the object from her hands. He winced as a finger snapped off, but retrieved the object. Covered in black leather, it was a book; embossed in gold on the front were the words *Holy Bible*. He opened it up. There was writing on the fly page in a neat copperplate hand: *This gift is of Ichabod Wallace to his beloved daughter Eliza on the occasion of her marriage to James Edwin Bleeker, April 1832.*

These were no Urmen. These were humans, from Earth.

Atkins staggered back to the first chamber in a daze. Unlike him, the others hadn't quite grasped the significance yet.

"The poor little things," Nellie said, as she draped a blanket over their small frames.

"Blimey, even you couldn't get much meat off this lot, Gutsy," Gazette said.

"Maybe not," he replied, "But my wife would damn well try and sell 'em if she could. Don't let a scrap go to waste, she don't."

Gazette took in the butcher's ample frame. "So, every little bit gets used, does it?" he asked, with a wink, indicating Gutsy's trousers.

"Get away!" said Mercy. "You know what they say about butchers' wives, only the best cuts for them, am I right, Gutsy?"

Gutsy replied with a lecherous grin and a wink, "Oh, aye, lad."

Nellie gave a discreet, lady-like cough. It had more power than a dozen barking NCOs and resulted in a muttered chorus of embarrassed apologies.

Chandar was in its element. To the Chatt, this was a treasure trove of Urmen artefacts. It hardly knew where to start. It had learnt, though, not to touch the bodies, however much it might desire to.

"Here," said Porgy sombrely. "This was on the table."

It was a journal. Atkins leafed through the diary, taking in snatches of information like a hungry man tearing at bread.

They were a party of pioneers from Oak Springs, Illinois in the United States, emigrants under the captaincy of Edwin Bleeker, travelling west on the California Trail looking for a new life in California. It seemed that they, like the British Empire, felt they had a 'manifest destiny.' There were eighty-six people in the party and fifty-four wagons pulled by oxen and horses. They had made it to the frontier and Independence, Missouri, where, in March 1846, they started the two thousand mile trek that would take them north towards the Great Salt Lake along the California Trail.

Atkins didn't understand the geography, but at some point, there had been an argument as to which way the overlanders should proceed. Oh, there were names he recognised from old *Western Adventure* story magazines—Chimney Rock, Fort Laramie—but the rest meant nothing. Having made it to the Rock Independence in late June 1846, where the travellers had carved their names, they set off again. More names: Fort Bridger, Sheep Rock, Devil's Gate, Salt Lake.

A guide they had picked along the way, one Barnaby Witger, advocated a short cut, the Campbell Cut-off through the Wasatch Mountains, and across the Great Salt desert towards the Humbolt River.

From the earliest diary entries, it was clear it wasn't an easy journey, between exhausted oxen, broken axels, and deaths from cholera.

Right now, though, the events on Earth were of little importance to him. His hands shook as he looked for entries telling of their arrival here, in this place, on this world.

He flicked forwards until he found it. August 14th 1846. He skimmed through from there.

August 14th. Today a fog descended as we made our way. We lit lamps but we could barely see the wagon in front of us. It was decided we would stop and wait for the fog to lift before we continued, but we were afflicted with a violent nausea and many of our party began bleeding from ears, nose and mouth...

A violent vertigo drove our oxen to their knees...

Louisa May Franklin fell from the wagon and under the wheels...

Lukas Bergen's compass no longer works. We cannot tell North from South.

...when the fog did clear the sight that met our eyes was not one we expected. Some say we must have taken a wrong turning and that we should turn back and retrace our steps, but we can find no landmarks.

...the night sky is passing strange and affords no familiarity...

He read on...

August 16th. Foul demonic beasts descended on our wagons, mauling and killing most of our oxen, dragging them away. They overturned the Marchants' wagon, breaking William Marchant's leg...

August 17th. This place is a hell. Hourly we cursed Campbell and Witger's names. The Campbell Cut-off has cost us dearly. Today we lost three dear children, stolen away by winged creatures...

August 24th. William Marchant died today of an ungodly infection to his leg. We made a coffin and buried him.

September 3rd. We have found shelter, an abandoned ruin in the woods. It is better than the wagons, which we had to abandon. We could not get them through the trees...

September 9th. Isaiah Walker led a party of twelve to find help.

Dear God, the people lasted barely three months in this place. He turned the page and turned back again. There were pages missing, torn out; over an entire month, gone. He turned to the last entries, a panic rising in his chest.

October 13th. We ate the last of our surviving oxen today...

November 19th. Last night, my dear George passed away of a terrible fever. He was delirious and did not know me. The Hollands died yesterday in fearful agony. I fear that if Isaiah Walker does not return soon he will come too late. May the Almighty preserve us and see our souls safely to Paradise.

Atkins closed the book. Feeling light-headed, he shoved the diary at Mercy and staggered from the chamber. Mercy said something, but he didn't hear it. The world had shrunk, pressing in on him, constricting him. He shoved his way past the damn Chatt, which was clicking at him. He needed air. He stumbled out into the dark of the passage and felt some small relief from the cool breeze that blew along it.

The Pennines were not the first humans to find themselves here. But after what they had just found, the thought brought little or no comfort to Atkins now. Those people had *died* here. They died *here*. There was no way home. It was a one-way trip. Everything he had clung to had been washed away. He felt bereft, adrift.

Gutsy called out from back up the passage, "Only, are you okay? It's just that Mercy said you seemed a bit windy."

"A bit windy?" said Atkins, with a sardonic laugh. "Ha, that's a good one." He wiped away the tears with the coarse serge sleeve of his tunic. He welcomed the rasping pain on his eyelids and cheeks. "I bloody well funked it, Gutsy. I funked it."

"It happens to the best, Only, you know that," said Gutsy, walking towards him. "What matters is you pick yourself up, get yourself back on the fire step."

"Yes, because that worked so bloody well for Ginger, didn't it?"

"Ginger had mates. So do you."

"There's no point, no bloody point. There's no way home, Gutsy. I promised I'd look after Flora, but you saw yourself, there *is* no way home."

"Flora? Your brother's fiancée? Very noble sentiment, is that. You're to be commended."

"No, you don't understand."

"Oh, for God's sake, Only. You're not the only person to have lost people! We all have family and loved ones back in Blighty. Do you think you're the only one who doesn't feel sick looking up at the stars? Do you think you're the only one who doesn't wake with a start in the middle of the night with their name on your lips? Do you? D'you think you're the only one whose heart breaks with every dawn we see here? We're all in the same hole here, Only. If you know of a better one, go to it!" Gutsy sighed, shook his head sympathetically and softened his tone. "Look, whatever's going on in your head, you need to sort it. Box it up, put it away. If your head's not here, you're going to get yourself killed. You're going to get *us* killed. And I'm not going to die because *you've* got a broken heart."

Atkins looked at him and nodded. There was nothing more to be said. Together, they walked back to the chambers.

When they got there, Mercy had the diary open in his hands. Atkins could tell from the stunned, downcast faces of the men around him that they had all heard the contents of the journal. Even Chandar seemed aware that something had happened, even if it wasn't sure what. Atkins looked at each of the men in turn. "We can tell no one of this. We must keep this secret. Can you imagine what would happen to morale if the rest of the battalion find out? It would tear it apart."

The rest of the section shuffled uncomfortably. They knew, right enough.

"No," said Atkins decisively. "We keep this a secret between ourselves for now." He looked at Nellie. "Not even the tank crew are to know. We tell Lieutenant Everson and no one else, and he can decide what to do with this information. Is that understood?"

There was a muttered agreement.

"Good. Now let's do right by these folk."

Salvaging only the family bible and the journal, they used a grenade and blew the entrance to seal the chamber, burying the families within and burying, in their own hearts, a little of the hopes each of them had nurtured of getting home again.

INTERLUDE FIVE

Letter from Private Thomas Atkins
to Flora Mullins

21st March 1917

Dearest Flora,

Today has been a black day. Today I fear I have lost you for good. I will never see you again, never hold you in my arms, and never hear your laughter again. The scent on your last letter has faded now and is lost to me forever. Perhaps it was an omen.

For all the months I have been here, I have held onto the fact that one day, one day soon, I will return to you. If I can't do that, I

PENNINE FUSILIERS

CHAPTER SIXTEEN
"All the Sunshine Turns to Gloom..."

As THE MEN of 1 Section continued their search for the tank crew, the mood that seized them was a sombre one, akin to those moments before the whistle blew and they went over the top. Under the burden of the new secret they carried, each man was momentarily adrift, alone on a sea of his own thoughts. If they had lucky charms they sought them out now in the privacy of the semi-dark catacombs.

"Oh, Christ, we're really stuck here. We're never going to get home," moaned Chalky.

"And we're stuck here with you, but you don't hear us moan about it," said Porgy.

Prof, who could usually be counted on to chivvy Chalky along, had sunk into a morose silence.

Nellie tried to cheer the young lad up. For all that these men were soldiers, some were little more than boys. "Shhh. Don't say that. You don't know that."

Atkins chalked another wall to mark their way and turned to the sweating butcher by his side. "Chalky's right, Gutsy."

"Maybe he is and maybe he isn't, but there's no need to say it. How many times has a man thought that in the trenches? And what good has it ever done him?"

"Aye, but there, home was only a Blighty one away, Gutsy. Now..." he left the sentence hanging.

How did Lieutenant Everson do it, wondered Atkins? How did he marshal his own fears, which must have been the same as any man's, and yet be able to go down the line and dispense encouragement and fortitude?

Atkins felt he had nothing left to give. He was empty. Empty of zeal, empty of heart. Empty of hope. Yet again, this world had ripped the wind from his sails. He was completely sapped. It was like wading though a quagmire of Somme mud, when concentrating on putting one foot in front of the other was almost too much, and some men allowed themselves to be sucked under and drowned, rather than fight against it to take another step.

Maybe he deserved this. What if this was his punishment? Had his indiscretion with Flora finally reached the ears of God? For a moment, self-loathing rose up within him. This place was now his Purgatory, and on some level he welcomed it, embraced it. Whatever it threw at him he would endure, the penitent Fusilier.

They moved on through a honeycomb of passages, threading their way through tunnels, traversing chambers and inclines where ancient, inhuman passages branched and branched again, leading to dead ends and roof falls. Piles of rubble and debris made some corridors impassable; thick infestations of plants, weeds and roots choked others. There was, however, still no sign of either the tank men, or whatever haunted these earthen halls. Only the odd, discordant piping notes from the few air vents not choked with weeds broke the silence.

"Mathers!" Atkins called at intervals, hoping for a reply. "Mathers!" The place was a labyrinth. Even supposing they heard him, they might never find him.

Chandar wandered alongside, ostensibly as a guide, but scent-blind as it was, it seemed just as lost and disorientated as the men and just as unwilling to be there. Atkins regarded the Chatt with repugnance. Its featureless ivory white face plate and rasping monotone voice revealed nothing of its own feelings. It toyed with the tasselled knots of its shoulder throw, its stunted middle limbs clicking together lightly. Nerves? Impatience? Who knew? Atkins pressed on, deliberately trying to ignore it. He hated the fact that this creature was somehow drawn to him, that this Kurda thing had somehow bound them together in its eyes. Well, not this soldier, no sir. He wasn't beholden to this creature.

The incline levelled out and they came upon a small rubble-strewn concourse that once might have been a major thoroughfare. Various passages and chambers ran off it. Haphazard shafts of sunlight punctured the gloom from collapsed roof sections above, the holes draped lazily with questing vines and roots.

Atkins spotted a doorway, ornately inscribed with Chatt hieroglyphs round the entrance. He'd seen one like it in Khungarr.

"The chambers of their Anointed Ones," Chandar said, making its deferential gesture, touching the tips of its long fingers to its forehead and thorax.

It was their temple. He nodded to Gutsy, who ordered the section to cover the other entrances to the concourse. Gazette, Pot Shot and Prof took up positions using what rubble there was as cover. They didn't want to be caught out by whatever haunted this place.

"Hold this position, Gutsy. I'll check this out. Porgy, Chalky, Mercy, with me. The rest of you stay here. Napoo, stay out here with Miss Abbott."

Atkins and Porgy entered first, Chalky just behind, holding the torch high above his head. The great domed chamber was twenty yards across, but in comparison to the great one at Khungarr, this was a country chapel. Several openings led off the main chamber and Porgy and Chalky covered them with their rifles as Atkins and Mercy slowly circled the room, checking each of them in turn.

The first went several yards before a roof fall blocked it. The second curved round the outer wall of the chamber, at a steep incline, before debris blocked it, too.

"Well, Mathers didn't come this way," said Mercy.

They retraced their steps back down to the sacred chamber. Chalky held up his torch. Above, on the domed ceiling, Atkins caught sight of a broken pattern of lines and dots, the remains of a painted fresco, the rest of which had crumbled from the ceiling. From the patches left, it looked like a night-time sky marked with constellations.

"The Sky Web of GarSuleth," hissed Chandar. The Chatt grabbed Atkins' arm and pulled him back. Chunks of the ceiling had fallen down. They lay on the floor under a sifting of dust that crunched under his feet. "Watch where you walk," it chattered, after its asthmatic fashion. "The representation of the Sky Web is still sacred, whether on the ceiling or in pieces on the floor. Stepping on it is blasphemy."

Around the walls of the circular chamber, there were niches that looked as if they might have held statues. Each was empty but for hieroglyphs that covered the surfaces in whorls and spirals, some separate, some interlinked.

The Chatt hobbled eagerly over to the alcoves, avoiding the fallen chunks of fresco. Stepping into one and facing the wall, its long fingers traced the inscriptions with light, rapid touches, before moving to the next.

"Well?" asked Atkins with impatience.

"If it's anything like our trenches it'll be rude jibes about the last mob," observed Porgy.

"The niches contain sacred texts for contemplation and prayer. The glyphs on the wall between seem to be a history of this colony. They called themselves the Nazarii. This One was aware of such splinter colonies, but never thought to see one. They did not act in Kurda. If a false queen and her retinue escaped, all mention of them would be expunged from the colony's records. It would be as if they had never existed. They were outcast. Even among Khungarr's aromatic annals there were but the vaguest references to such dishonourable incidents and then only in far gone spira."

"He's actually happy about this," Gutsy commented.

"Well, he's about the only bleedin' one," said Mercy. "The place fair gives me the willies, it does."

It was true. The incessant piping tone from the air vents soon began to grate on their nerves, like the whistling of whizz bangs.

Chandar moved to a section of wall between niches. "At first, all went well, but the Queen fell prey to a grave sickness. Large numbers of eggs were laid to become workers but they were born malformed." It paused and clicked its mandibles. "Such a sickness also affects the Queens of Khungarr."

"Tell me about it. We saw some of those things in the Khungarr nursery. Ugly buggers. Haunted my dreams for bloody weeks, those things did," said Mercy, with an affected shudder.

"This One thought Khungarr alone in suffering such a curse," hissed Chandar, moving to the next section. "The Nazarrii began to fail within the first few generations. There were not enough healthy workers hatched to sustain the colony's growth and expansion."

"So the place was doomed?"

"Without workers, it could not succeed."

"I thought your mob used Urmen slaves."

"It is true. GarSuleth provided."

"Well, that's one way of looking at it," said Porgy.

"But it seemed that it was GarSuleth's will that this colony fail." Chandar bowed his head towards the wall, and its antennae stumps waved in a wistful fashion. "Here, the script ends. The colony was failing, that is beyond doubt. Even the Nazarrii recognised the fact." It turned to face Atkins. "But something else happened here."

"What?" asked Atkins uneasily.

"The glyphs do not say. Some catastrophe befell the edifice, causing them to abandon the place."

"Or be killed."

"Perhaps the coming of the evil spirit that now dwells here?" Chalky offered.

"Perhaps, yes. There may be so much more here, but so much more information that is lost to this One." Chandar lifted a finger to touch its antennae stumps. "Why would any Ones abandon their edifice? This One does not know. This One cannot read the scent text."

"I can," said a voice from the gloom.

THE MEN OF the section wheeled round, their rifles raised and bolts ratcheted, training their weapons on the opening even as the clipped voice reverberated around the chamber.

Mathers stepped from the shadows, with his crew behind him grinning like jackals.

"Lower your weapons," said Atkins, with a scowl.

"I can read your scent texts," repeated Mathers.

"You, sir?" asked Atkins, barely trying to suppress his sarcasm.

"Yes, Corporal. I am open to so many things, now." He gestured expansively at the darkened vault above them. "I see things. The air here is full of them. My senses are flooded."

"Well, he's flooded with something all right," muttered one of the Fusiliers. "I wouldn't bloody trust him if I were you."

Mathers beckoned. "Perkins will agree with me, won't you, Perkins?"

Alfie Perkins stepped unsteadily out of the gloom, held upright by the big boxer, Tanner, and Atkins saw his eyes; black like oil slicks.

Atkins shook his head. "Not, you, too?" He turned to Mathers. "What have you done?"

The bantam driver sneered. "Oh, he's with us, now, good an' proper."

Reggie smiled apologetically. "Well, he always was. He just didn't know it. Our own doubting Thomas, if you will, until the Sub granted him his own personal Pentecost."

Mathers stepped past Atkins to the wall Chandar had been examining. Atkins gripped the officer's upper arm. "Why should we trust you, sir?"

Mathers looked down at Atkins' hand, his contemptuous look lost behind his splash mask. His voice was cold and measured. "Let go, *Lance* Corporal. Or I'll have you for striking an officer."

Atkins held his grip long enough for it to border on insubordination and for the pair of them to know it. "How do we know you can do what you say?"

Beneath his mask, Mathers smiled. "Lily of the Valley," he whispered.

Atkins frowned. "What?"

"That was your sweetheart's perfume, wasn't it? On the letter? Lily of the Valley. How else could I know?" He let that sink in for a moment. "Do you trust me now, Corporal?"

Dumbfounded, Atkins released his arm.

"Hm," Mathers added with a satisfied grunt, tugging his tunic sleeve straight as he stepped past Atkins.

He looked at Chandar, the Chatt's visage as blank as his own masked features. "You say there are scents here? That's the way you things communicate, isn't it?"

"It is so," said Chandar, watching him carefully, "but Urmen cannot read them."

Mathers paused, fished out his hip flask, took a slug, and emptied it. Damn. He upended it and shook the last drops from the rim, through the chainmail into his mouth, then proceeded to do what the Chatt thought impossible.

He turned his attention to the wall. He could see the glyphs and the blank, unfilled space. He stood before it and concentrated. He inhaled, slowly and deeply. As he did, faint colours began to permeate the surface of the vacant space, like an after image. There was something here; a scent message impregnated into the wall. With each purposeful breath, the colours grew stronger, and began to take on form in the space between him and the wall, hovering before his eyes, taking a shape he had come to recognise, a base note, on which the whole composition was built, pungent and overwhelming, one of the first words he had learnt in his synesthetic vocabulary.

"Fear," croaked Mathers. "Something is coming." He reeled back as the next aromatic note almost overwhelmed him. "Here!" he gasped. Another stringent note subsumed and washed this one away; a lingering top note that persisted after the others had faded. "Fear. Flee."

"What the hell is that, some kind of warning?" asked Atkins.

Chandar stepped forwards, its mandibles ticking together as it forced the Urman words out through its mouth palps. "No, you misunderstand. It is merely history, a few scraps of scent from the past." It turned to Mathers, its clawed middle limbs open, its antennae stumps jerking. "How is this possible? Urmen are scent-blind. How is it that you can decipher the chemical commentaries of the Ones? This is unforeseen, this is beyond wonder."

Mathers threw his arms wide. "It is a gift from Skarra, the gift of tongues."

Chandar let out a long low hiss, but its eyes fell on the empty hip flask in Mathers' hand and it fell silent, lost in thought.

Mathers felt the overwhelming scent of fear from the message rousing him to panic. He felt the urge to flee, and might well have done had not a spasm in his stomach sent him doubling over as ripples of pain washed though him. He rode each agonising wave until they subsided and, with them, the feeling of fear.

"Something, I don't know what, was coming. It arrived. They fled," he said, still panting though the pain.

"That's it?" said Atkins, unimpressed.

Mathers stood, steadying himself against the wall as he pulled himself to his full height. "Can you do better, Corporal?"

"No sir. But we already know about the dulgur."

"*If* that is what they were talking about, Corporal."

A SHOT ECHOED around the chamber. It came from the concourse. "Gutsy, Mercy, stay here. Keep an eye on that lot."

Atkins ran to the opening and peered round, ready for anything. Anything but what he found.

He was greeted by Pot Shot with an anguished looked on his face. "It's Prof."

Prof? Atkins couldn't see with the others gathered around but, as he approached, they parted. Between them he could see a large pile of rubble, and protruding from behind it he could make out a bare right foot. That was all he needed to see.

"Oh, Prof," Atkins groaned. "You stupid sod."

Prof lay slumped against a pile of debris. He had discarded his puttee, boot and sock to one side, his bayonet to the other. The top half of his skull had been blown away and his brains splattered over the rubble behind him. His rifle lay along his chest. Nellie knelt by him, but there was nothing she could do.

"He was sobbing quietly for a while. I thought it best to leave him, then I heard him say 'sorry,'" said Pot Shot. "I never thought—"

Suicide. Not always easy for a soldier. Some just stuck their heads above the parapet and waited for a German sniper. Others, well... The barrel of the Enfield was too long. You couldn't just stick the muzzle in your mouth and use your finger to pull the trigger. You had to take your boot and sock off, then use your big toe instead.

For some of the Tommies, the only thing that kept them going was the fact that they might find a way home. There had been a flurry of suicides when they'd first arrived, and every so often they found another poor bugger who'd found he couldn't take it anymore, in a trench or a dugout. With the discovery of the Bleeker Party came the realisation that that there was no way home, that they were stranded on this hell world. It was just too much.

"You know the routine, Porgy," said Atkins quietly. "Paybook and disc. Redistribute his bombs, rations and ammunition."

Nellie shook her head slowly in disbelief. "Why would he do that?"

Gutsy put a big fatherly arm round her and steered her away from the sight. "He'd just had enough, love. He hasn't been quite the same since Nobby died. I think perhaps finding them emigrants was the last straw. It takes something like that, when you're a long way from home."

Although there was no love lost between them, the tank crew hung back, and gave 1 Section the space to briefly mourn their dead comrade.

It was then Nellie caught sight of Alfie. Her mouth formed a silent 'o' of shock when she saw his eyes, but he shook his head to dissuade her from any action. She relented, reluctantly, and only for the moment.

They piled blocks of rubble and debris over the body, burying Prof where he lay. Chalky muttered a hurried prayer before they moved on.

Atkins was angry now. If it hadn't been for Mathers and his blasted quest, Prof might still be alive. But he had his orders. If they were going to get Mathers and the tank back, they had to kill this blasted creature. He turned to the masked Tank Commander. "Right, let's get this done. Which way, Lieutenant?"

Mathers paused for a moment, considering the options, then pointed to one of the passages leading off the concourse. "That way."

* * *

ATKINS AND 1 Section fell in behind him. Mathers nodded, and the tank crew brought up the rear as they began to descend into the edifice's subterranean levels.

Nellie fell back, snatching a chance to talk to Alfie.

"What have they done to you?" she hissed angrily.

"Not here," he begged her. In the dark, his fingers found hers. He squeezed her hand to placate her. "It's all right, it will pass."

She glanced at him with suspicion.

"It'll pass," he reassured her.

Frank gave Alfie a shove from behind. "No fraternising with the enemy."

He let go of her hand, taking comfort in her soft golden glow, as she returned to Napoo's side. She glanced back, searching for reassurance. He offered a smile for her sake.

Small galleries and chambers led off the curved passage at regular intervals. They searched each set. Atkins barely noticed. None of it mattered. It was all dry as dust, and dead, just as they would be. All he could think about was Flora, how he would never see her again. Never smell her perfume again, or see their child growing up. His child. He imagined the life he had lost, married, with the child, little William. He could feel his weight in his arms and smell its hair. See his smile as he recognised him. Gone, all gone.

Atkins became aware that someone was talking to him.

"Only," Gazette was saying. "Chalky's found something. I think you ought to see it."

Atkins looked at Chalky. "Show me."

Emboldened, Chalky took the lead and showed him a tunnel running off the main passage. Chandar accompanied him. Chalky pointed to the far wall of the chamber. "It were down here. I was just checking and saw it glinting in the torch light. There."

Atkins saw the glint on the floor by the wall. He walked over, sank down on his haunches, and picked it up.

"What is it?" asked Chandar.

Attached to a small scrap of bloodstained khaki cloth was a brass button. Atkins examined it, rubbing it clean with the pad of his thumb. There upon the button, in relief, was a bomb, fuse aflame, with crossed rifles and a crown, all cradled in a wreath. It was the crest of the Pennine Fusiliers.

He blinked and looked up at Gazette. "Check your uniform buttons," he said, his voice imbued with a sense of urgency.

After a little fumbling, it became clear that they all had the requisite number.

"It's not from any of us," reported Gutsy.

Atkins hardly dared think it. There was only one man who might have made it this far. One man.

Gutsy stared at him. "Christ, you don't think—"

Atkins nodded. "Jeffries. Who the hell else could it be?"

SKARRA CONTINUED TO mutter in Mathers' head. In the confines of the edifice, his heightened awareness was flooded with new sensory details. The information was pressing in on him and he was powerless to stop it.

"I can see him," said Mathers, taking the bloodstained scrap and staring fixedly at it.

"Who?" asked Atkins.

Mathers waved the button at him. "Jeffries."

The corporal stared at him. "What do you mean?"

"I can *see* him, his scent on it. I should be able to track his scent trail if there is any left to follow."

"You can do that?"

Mathers looked at the Chatt. "Skarra tells me I can."

He was aware of the Chatt watching him intently as he concentrated on the scrap of cloth. Using the shapes, sounds and textures that danced around it, Mathers was able, with some effort, to draw Jeffries' scent out of the surrounding kaleidoscopic mists. He watched as vaporous tones of purples and reds coalesced and evaporated rapidly around each other, trying to confuse and deceive. They shifted and changed, into blues and yellows, like a snake shedding skin after skin, as it sought to slip beyond even his heightened perception, but he held it fast in his attention. Under the haze of stale, sour human aromas, he had his base note now; that part of a man that was immutable, unchangeable, distinctive. It resolved itself into a thin green thread of scent that he could follow.

He had no doubt that others in his crew, Clegg or Perkins even, who had received such a concentrated dose of petrol fruit juice recently, might see something of what he saw, but they lacked the education, the intuition, to make the connections he was now experiencing.

Fascinated, he began to walk haltingly, following the fragile drifting airborne trail, constantly checking it with the control scent of the khaki scrap. The others followed at a distance. Slowly, he became attuned to it, to the dancing particles of scent, sweat and blood. At first, it was nothing more than a scent echo, a faint trail hanging in the air, then it began to take on a phantasmagorical shape. Indistinct at first, it coalesced into the faint, ethereal figure of an infantry officer. Hardly daring to breathe, he followed the redolent wraith as it continued its journey. It entered a series of chambers. He watched as it crossed to a wall and crouched down, inspecting something there.

Mathers stepped closer to see.

As if sensing him, the wraith turned. Mathers recognised it as Jeffries. It looked directly at him. A disdainful smile spread across its face as it stepped towards him. With the guilty start of an eavesdropper caught red-handed, Mathers cried out and lurched back, out of reach of the apparition as it advanced on him, and lost his concentration.

In that moment, it seemed to him that Jeffries gesticulated and, upon that gesticulation, proceeded to evaporate until there was nothing left of his incorporeal form but a faint drifting trail suspended in the air.

Mathers reeled from the chamber. "He was here. He was reading... something on the wall."

A wave of pain rippled out from his abdomen, through his torso, up his spine and down through his limbs, causing him to double over. He'd been away from the tank for too long. He fumbled for his hip flask. He'd forgotten it was empty. He grunted with frustration and pain, pulling his splash mask and helmet from his head, and sucking in great lungfuls of air. The plaques on his face were now red and livid and his eyes, iridescent swirls on black, seemed unfocused and inhuman.

"Easy sir, I've got you," said Jack Tanner.

Following her instincts, the FANY approached the group, her eyes catching Alfie's as she passed. "Let me help," she said.

Cecil stood up, held out his arm, and refused to let her pass. "It's all right, miss," he said belligerently. "We've got him. He don't need nobody else."

"She can help, sir," Alfie insisted.

Mathers turned his head and looked at him through the slits of his splash mask.

"No, Perkins, you know she can't."

LEAVING MATHERS TO the care of his crew, Atkins took a torch and pushed past them with impatience into the chamber. Holding it high, he could see the markings on the wall. They were not like the Chatt glyphs. With a swell of frustration, he realised they weren't in a language he could read either. He couldn't make any sense of it. But it *was* familiar. He brushed his hand briefly over the scratched graffiti with curiosity. It looked like the coded script he had seen in Jeffries' journal, the one Lieutenant Everson pored over obsessively. Then he saw something he did recognise. His brow furrowed. He fished in his top pocket and pulled out a folded piece of tattered paper. The leader of every patrol had one, Everson insisted upon it. He unfolded it to reveal a carefully copied symbol. He compared the two now. There was no doubt.

It was the Sigil of Croatoan from Jeffries' journal.

Atkins' mind was a flurry of thoughts, like a shaken snow globe. He found an ember of hope in the ashes of his world.

Jeffries had been here. It couldn't have been by chance. He had a map. Had he expected to find this place? What was its significance? What information did the coded writing contain? What did it all *mean*?

He had no answers. One thing he did know was that Jeffries was his only lifeline, and his mind seized on it and wouldn't let go. If Jeffries wanted the information, so did he. Somehow, Jeffries was the key. Maybe his boast back in Khungarr, that he was their only way back, wasn't just a desperate tactic to buy himself time to escape. One way or another, Atkins wanted to know the truth. Taking a pencil stub from his pocket, he laboriously copied the symbols on the back of the piece of paper.

With his mind consumed with thoughts of Jeffries, he exited the chamber. He turned to the Tank Commander, who had recovered his composure and replaced his mask and helmet, once again hiding the ravaged face and the unnerving eyes that, Atkins now knew, saw things beyond the reach of normal human senses.

"Sir, you said you could follow Jeffries' scent trail. Lieutenant Everson expressly ordered that any leads on Jefferies' whereabouts be reported. I need to know which way he went from here. Can you do that much?"

Mathers looked up at him. Around him, his crew glared at Atkins with undisguised suspicion. The young lad, Cecil, watched Atkins like a hawk, his fists balled by his sides. Mathers put a hand on the boy's shoulder and he relaxed slightly.

"Once I have killed this spirit and taken its power, and not before."

AS THE PARTY readied to move off again, Atkins led the way, eager to pick up whatever kind of trail Jeffries had left, clambering over a low mound of rubble partially blocking the passage. As he held out the torch into the stygian space beyond, an arm reached out of the darkness and pulled him off balance. A hard, calloused hand, that smelled of dirt and sweat, clamped over his mouth and Atkins felt a blade bite into his throat, under his Adam's apple, as he struggled to catch his breath...

CHAPTER SEVENTEEN
"The Far Gone Dead..."

THE TORCH FELL from Atkins' hand as he grabbed the wrist holding the blade to his neck.

"Be still," said an insistent voice at his ear, "or you will die here."

He recognised it. It was Jarak, the ousted shaman from the Urmen's forest enclave.

The shaman swung him around as a shield between himself and the soldiers. Atkins saw his mates bring their rifles up. The tunnel, however, was too narrow for them to flank or get a bead on his assailant without hitting him, too.

The shaman adjusted his grip, dropping his free arm across Atkins' chest to grab his webbing, the knife still at his throat.

"Go on, kill me," Atkins growled at him. "But the moment I drop, they'll shoot."

Jarak ignored him. "Where is your shaman?" he barked at the soldiers.

Mathers stepped forwards.

"You shamed me before my people," the shaman said, the fury in his voice barely under control. "You took my place."

"You could have stayed and served me," said Mathers.

Napoo shook his head. "No, he could not. He has but two paths to regaining his place with the clan now. Banishing the dulgur, or killing his usurper."

Jarak sneered at Napoo and jerked his chin towards Chandar, half hidden behind the soldiers, and snarled. "You consort with the Ones, yet do not wear their mark. What trickery is this?"

"No trickery. The One is our prisoner. The Tohmii are free Urmen, like you, like me. They are a powerful clan. They have fought the Ones and triumphed."

"Now I know you lie."

"You have seen their power for yourself."

"The Urman speaks the truth," Chandar chittered.

Napoo turned his attention to the shaman. "And where is the rest of your party?"

"The shaman's party is dead," said Jarak bitterly. "The dulgur took them; the dancers, the dreamers, the warriors. What use is a shaman without his party, without his apprentices? Who will safeguard the clan now? You?" he snapped at Mathers. "Your crawling god is mighty, but I have seen you. You are in thrall to it and it will drag you with it into the underworld. You are not long for this place, and what will the clan do then?"

Atkins might have felt for the shaman; he, too, had lost everything. He, too, was between a rock and hard place, no thanks to Mad Mathers, but the pressure of the blade on his throat cancelled out any sympathy he might have had.

"And you," he growled into Atkins' ear. "Your sacrifice at the precipice would have saved my enclave then. Perhaps it might do as much now. If you are such a powerful clan, then maybe your sacrifice may be acceptable to the dulgur, and it will leave my enclave alone, and I shall regain my place among my people. I will return to them in glory having banished the spirit by my own deeds, or else revenged upon my usurper."

The blade rocked against Atkins' throat as the Urman shifted his weight and began to drag him back down the passage.

"Stop!" shouted Mercy, but Jarak wasn't listening.

Atkins missed his footing and the blade bit into his skin as he struggled to keep his balance. He glanced down and saw the passage was coated with a thin layer of black deposit.

There was a warm, foetid breeze from the depths of the passage behind Atkins, as if something large and fast were pushing the air before it, causing the flames from the torches to gutter wildly in the dark.

"GarSuleth preserve this One!" hissed Chandar, sinking as low as it could.

The rasp rapidly became a slick sucking sound, and the shadows around Atkins grew darker as an oily cloud billowed round their feet. He scrambled to maintain a footing on the slick residue.

The sound stopped. For a heartbeat there was silence.

The shaman screamed as he was ripped away from Atkins, his knife raking across Atkins' neck. As the great black tide retreated into the darkness, the shaman was dragged with it and his cries were swiftly smothered, like those of a drowning man.

Atkins dropped to the floor, his hand clasping his throat. Above him a hail of gunfire roared out, muzzle flashes bursting in the darkness, one or two bullets whining off the tunnel walls.

As the fusillade died away, Nellie burst from the pack, pushed past Mathers and dropped down by Atkins.

He coughed and spluttered, gasping for breath, and she gently, but firmly, prised his hand away from his neck. It came away slick and hot. She worked to wipe away the blood and sighed with relief. "You're lucky, Corporal. It's not as bad as it looks. This will sting," she said, as she applied an Urman poultice to the wound from a pouch at her waist.

Atkins sucked in air through his teeth against the pain. "Funny, I don't feel bloody lucky."

She took off Atkins' tunic, removed his braces and undid his shirt. She pulled a field bandage pack from the bag at her hip and tore open the paper wrapping, all with a practised ease. "Hold that," she said, placing his hand on it. Nellie wrapped and rewrapped a length of bandage round his chest and shoulder to keep the neck dressing in place. "What the hell was that thing?"

"The dulgur," said a grim-faced Napoo.

Mathers wandered past them, staring down the sloping passage into the dark, looking at something nobody else could see.

"Curious. That creature doesn't belong here," he said, to nobody in particular. "I *see* it. It is not of this place. It should not exist here. It was brought forth from... elsewhere."

Chandar clicked its mandibles together rapidly. "It is true. It is an abomination."

Chalky crossed himself. "Jesus, Mary and Joseph, I knew it. It's a demon from the depths of Hell, isn't it? Summoned by Jeffries to do his bidding. Oh, Lord and his saints preserve us."

"Don't talk daft. A demon? How is that even possible?" asked Gazette.

Porgy intervened. "*We're* here. How is *that* possible?"

"Man has a point," admitted Pot Shot.

With the attack of the creature, the place had gone from labyrinth to lair.

Atkins got to his feet. "We need to get out of here. That thing, whatever it is, knows we're here now, and I don't want to get caught in these tunnels again."

Mathers cocked his head. "What?" he said.

"I said we need to get out of here, sir."

"Quiet, Corporal. I wasn't talking to you," Mathers snapped, listening to whatever phantom voices were enticing him. "Yes, of course," he answered.

He turned back to Atkins. "We're headed this way, Corporal." He began walking down the tunnel in the direction the thing had taken.

"Sir?" queried Atkins, but he received no reply. He pressed the point. "Sir, you're not well. It's not safe," but the officer ignored him.

The tank crew shoved through the Fusiliers, to fall in behind their commander, with an insolence that made the Fusiliers bristle.

As he passed Nellie, Alfie didn't dare look at her. He didn't need to. Her shining aura was all he needed to see. Nevertheless, he contrived to walk by her and his fingers found hers briefly.

"Mad Mathers is going to get us all killed," Porgy objected in a low voice.

"Quite possibly," said Atkins, his voice laced with resentment. "But he is an officer and, as our orders are to bring the tank back, we can't very well leave here without him, can we?"

Chalky broke his step to try to stay alongside Atkins for moment. "It's all right, Only. I'm not afraid. I know you can kill the demon."

Atkins rolled his eyes and swore under his breath.

"Boy sees you as role model," said Gutsy, wrily.

"Oh, believe me, I'm nobody's bloody role model." The thought of Flora burned brightly in his mind.

"Maybe not, but apparently you have a reputation. Poor Chalky's probably expecting you to magic up Saint George himself right about now."

"Well, you'd know about that."

"Eh?"

"Saint George. You're the one married to the bloody dragon by all accounts."

"Now *that's* the Only I know and love," said Gutsy, with a guffaw, slapping him on the shoulder. "Good to have you back."

MATHERS PUSHED FORWARD, trusting to his new abilities. He could see the scent trail of the creature, the spirit, now—a thin, tenuous vapour trail, so delicate that any movement tore it and it dissipated on the air current. "This way," he declared, indicating the right hand fork without a second's hesitation. The bantam driver, Wally, was at his right hand, as ever. Frank and Norman were flanking the stupefied Alfie, while Cecil, Jack and Reggie trailed in their wake. Atkins and 1 Section followed on behind as rearguard.

ATKINS HEARD A sound in the tunnel behind him, like a tide sucking on shingle, as something rushed along the tunnel walls towards them. "Run!" he yelled.

Ahead of him, after a moment's confusion, the tank crew took him at his word, herding Mathers before them.

Atkins turned and knelt and, with Gutsy, held the tunnel as the rest of the section raced swiftly past. They felt the wash of foetid air, and in the darkness something moved, bearing down on them like a train. Gutsy pulled off his bayonet, slipped it back into its sheath at his waist, and fitted the wooden baton of a rifle grenade into his Enfield barrel. He pulled the trigger and the pair ran up the tunnel to where Mercy and Porgy were holding the second line.

The grenade exploded, the shock wave almost blowing Atkins off his feet as he raced past Mercy. Porgy fired three rounds rapid into the dying fireball and the pair joined Atkins and Gutsy in the retreat. They reached a gallery at the junction of five tunnels, where the others had taken shelter from the funnelled blasts.

No sooner had the noise of the grenade died than they heard a low rumbling howl, not from behind them where the creature had taken the brunt of the attack, but from below, the dread sound funnelled up from the depths via the surrounding tunnels.

"Bloody Nora, don't say there's more of them!" groaned Mercy.

Atkins jerked his head at the tunnel openings. "Pot Shot, Gazette, find one that goes back up to the surface." His gaze met Mathers' inscrutable mask, almost daring the officer to countermand his orders, but he didn't. He was clutching his stomach and holding onto the small driver.

"This way, Only!" called Gazette, at the mouth of a tunnel. The section and tank crew retreated into it, alert, their rifles sweeping the tunnel mouths around them.

Not taking his eyes from the direction they had come, Atkins ordered Gazette and Mercy to scout the tunnel. "And hurry!" he said, hearing the tidal rush of things moving up through the adjoining tunnels towards them from the darkness below.

"I want two volunteers," yelled Atkins.

"I'll stay," said Mercy.

"Me too," said Chalky, although he seemed less certain than Mercy.

Atkins shook his head. "Go up with the rest, Chalky."

Chalky stuck his chin out, like a stubborn child, and clasped his rifle until the whites of his knuckles showed, as if he expected Atkins to take it off him. "No. I'm staying. I know you'll protect us, Only, the way you did Lieutenant Everson."

Atkins nodded and waved the others off.

With Mathers' indomitable will crumbling, as he lost his fight with whatever was ailing him, the tank crew took it upon themselves to protect their precious bloody commander. They took off up the tunnel, Wally and Alfie supporting Mathers between them, the rest of 1 Section herding them along. Napoo grasped Nellie's hand and raced up the tunnel with her, even as she drew her revolver.

Atkins, Mercy and Chalky held the tunnel mouth at the gallery. A foul breeze blew around it, and the dust on the floor began to swirl in eddies, as things rushed up from the depths towards them.

Chalky began muttering the Lord's Prayer.

"Cover me," Atkins said, as he raced around the gallery, tossing a grenade down into each of the four tunnels. He heard them land, rattling off into the darkness, and he dived back for cover between Mercy and Chalky. They crouched down as the grenades went off one after the other, like a barrage, bringing down the tunnels. Dust and debris billowed into the gallery, filling it with a gritty, choking cloud.

From deep below came a low awful sound, that reverberated in his chest and made his very bones ache. He could hear rubble and debris clinking as something with weight and speed rammed against the tunnel collapse, attempting to drive its way through.

"Go!" he cried.

Mercy needed no telling. Chalky hesitated until Mercy grabbed his arm. "Run, you daft bugger!"

ALFIE FOUND HIMSELF leaving the gallery behind and herded up the passage, under the insistent barking of the Fusiliers. The initial barrage of hallucinations from his 'baptism' were wearing off. If that was the world Mathers wanted him so badly to inhabit, then he could keep it. It was as if Mathers needed him for his own shaman's party. The others may have bought into it, but Alfie wouldn't. He struggled against the horrifying new world invading his senses. The comparatively gentle side effect of the fuel fumes he could put up with, but this enforced ingestion was a brutal assault on the senses. It terrified him, but what terrified him more was the fact that Lieutenant Mathers wasn't scared at all.

Alfie fought against it, as hard as it was to cling to the mundane when your world was ablaze with wonders and horrors. Nellie's presence helped. Without her, he feared he would be as lost as the others.

"The lieutenant needs to rest," panted Clegg, under the subaltern's weight. "He can't carry on."

To their right the tunnel wall had partially crumbled away to reveal a void beyond.

"This'll have to do," said Jack, stamping his boot into it several times. The edges of the hole collapsed, creating an opening big enough to enter. He thrust a torch through to reveal an empty space, which would provide some protection against the concussions. "Get in, hurry!" He directed the tank crew and Fusiliers into the space beyond.

They found themselves in another round chamber. One of the Fusiliers held a torch high to illuminate the place.

"Jesus!" exclaimed Alfie.

The bodies of several Chatts lay on the floor of the chamber: Scentirrii, judging by the heavy carapace casings. They were covered with fine dust or ash, which had hardened over them, softening their outlines. With them were the bodies of two more Chatts, priests. Alfie knew them by their featureless faces and the mouldering tasselled silk sashes. They lay on the ground under a covering of calcified dust, as though they had died peacefully, resigned to their fate. They had seen others like them, but not this far down.

Across the chamber, as though unfit to die with them, were the bodies of three worker Chatts. These, however, had died violent deaths, their carapaces broken open.

Chandar stepped reverently around them, chittering to itself softly, its stunted middle limb restless. But it wasn't the bodies that agitated the Chatt. It was what had been entombed with them; a motley collection of jars, amphorae, and pots of varying sizes, hastily gathered and stacked on shelves in niches and on the floor.

Smirking, Norman picked up a sealed stone jar. "Here, lads. SRD rum rations, and about bloody time!" He made to smash the neck against the wall. Chandar rounded on him, reared up on its legs and advanced towards him, its mandibles open as it hissed.

ATKINS GAVE MERCY and Chalky five seconds. He slung his rifle over his shoulder, then took two grenades in one hand and pulled the pins. He dropped the grenades into the middle of the gallery, on the floor at the mouth of the tunnel, and sprinted up the incline. Five second fuses. How far could he get in five seconds?

Four thousand. He heard something ploughing through the rubble below him.

Three thousand. He felt his stomach churn as another low howl reverberated through his body.

Two thousand. An arm reached out of an opening to his left, grabbed his webbing, and yanked him into a passing niche.

One thousand. The bomb went off. A blast of dirt roared past the opening.

Coughing, Atkins looked up to see Mercy and Chalky grinning at him.

They waited for almost a minute, but heard no further sounds of pursuit from below. They allowed themselves to breathe again. The three dust-covered men grinned at each other with the elation of survival.

"I could murder a bloody fag," said Mercy, patting his pockets. "But I'm right out."

"Blood and sand," said Atkins. "If *you're* all out, things are a lot worse than I thought."

* * *

THE LIGHT OF a torch, filtered by the still settling dust, bobbed back down the passage towards Atkins, Mercy and Chalky. "Only!" It was Pot Shot, speaking in a low, urgent hiss. "Only? The Chatt's turning nasty. You'd better come and sort it out or Gutsy says he might have to kill it."

"Bloody hell!" Atkins' jubilation melted away and his face set again as he, Chalky and Mercy followed the lanky private up the gently rising passage until they could hear Chandar hissing and spitting.

By the time Atkins arrived, the unsealed chamber was the scene of a tense stand-off. Mathers had slumped to the ground, a couple of his crew clustered around him. The big one, Jack, was holding back Norman, who looked as if he wanted to bash the Chatt's brains out. The others were squaring off against Chandar. 1 Section had leapt to the Chatt's defence. Napoo had stepped in front of Nellie, his sword drawn, watching the proceedings warily.

Atkins was stunned. He turned his back for five minutes and they were at each others' throats! "What the hell's going on? There's a thing—things—out there that are trying to kill us and you lot want to do this? Now?"

"That's your problem!" Frank said with a snarl, jabbing his revolver towards Chandar. "Bleedin' Chatt freak. Norman picked up one o' them old jars and it got all cut up about it."

Porgy butted in. "Lieutenant Mathers was looking a bit ropey so we ducked in here to rest. We saw these Chatt bodies and jars and stuff, and Chandar gets all excited until that tanker starts clowning around with 'em."

Chandar raised itself up on its legs, in Norman's direction, and hissed, slicing its mandibles. Cowed, Norman slunk back.

Atkins stepped between the Hush Hush crowd and the Chatt, his bayoneted rifle pointed at it. "What's going on, Chandar?"

The Chatt turned to him, but did not relax its defensive stance. "These receptacles, they contain many sacred texts. To treat them like that is disrespectful."

Atkins glanced at the shattered vessels. "All right. He won't do it again. Now calm down. What's so important about them anyway?"

"There are copies of scentopedia, holy books, here, that were destroyed in Khungarr by Jeffries. There are aromatomes, even older. This one"—it indicated a jar—"this one was declared heretical in Khungarr many spira ago. Some of these are older than Khungarr itself. Do you not realise? This is a find of incalculable importance. The Ones here sealed themselves in with them in order to protect them from whatever befell the edifice. They gave their lives to guard them. There are scent texts here of great significance and antiquity, and that Urman almost destroyed one—on a whim."

"I don't understand, why didn't they dig themselves out?"

"Because these Ones were commanded not to, or commanded to await rescue when it was safe. This one cannot say. But with these, Khungarr can begin to replace the scent scriptures we lost, that you cost us. Some may even provide the scriptural proof we need to finally move against Sirigar and his olfaction. But if these ignorant Urmen proceed to destroy them, then this One will never know and the Tomhii Clan may yet be doomed. They must be salvaged and taken back to Khungarr. You must aid this One. It is Kurda. If this One had not accompanied you to this place, then these would have been lost or destroyed forever. Their discovery is the will of GarSuleth, and so is their retrieval."

"What, so we're working for Chatts now?" said Mercy, with disdain.

Atkins knew from Chandar's interrogation by Everson, and his own conversations with the thing, that there were bigger matters at stake here. He didn't quite understand, but he knew this scent library was important. They had the tank. They could transport all these things back. It wasn't going to be a popular decision, but it was the right thing to do.

"It's not good enough they've got Urmen slaves to do their dirty work for them, now you want us to help them?"

"It's not that simple." Atkins lowered his voice briefly so the tank crew couldn't hear. "You saw those American pioneers. They're dead. They couldn't survive on this world by themselves. Besides, *we* have Urmen flocking to *us* for help, and protection, too. Tell them, Napoo."

The wily old guide nodded. "The Tohmii are powerful, like the Ones."

"But the Chatts use chemicals to keep the Urmen docile!" said Nellie. "I've experienced it."

"I said it's not that simple," said Atkins, remembering his recent experience with the Zohtakarrii. "Those Urmen work for them in return for food, shelter and protection. How is that different from you, Gazette, at the mill, or you, Mercy, at the Brewery, or your uncle down the pits, Pot Shot?"

Pot Shot shrugged, as if pained to admit it. "The man's right, we may not use chemical decrees to keep our workers in place but we use money to the same ends. It's not that much different. Still, doesn't make it right, though."

"But the Chatts are attacking our trenches right now and you want us to help them?"

"Chandar's part of a movement that can stop that, and these jars can help. We have orders to return to the encampment with the tank anyway, so we might as well take these back with us."

Gazette spoke up. "Only has a point. Whatever way you look at it these jars are valuable. It gives us an advantage. We have something they want. We can hold them to ransom." He looked round the chamber, meeting everyone's eyes with a challenging glare.

There was a murmur of agreement, even among the tank crew.

Chandar began pointing out the most important jars to salvage. Atkins' section took off their packs and began filling them.

Reggie and Norman slipped off their coveralls from over their service dress, tied knots in the arms and legs to create makeshift bags and began to load them up under Chandar's direction.

In their haste, one of the tank crew, Reggie, let an amphora slip from his fingers.

"Dash it!"

It shattered against the earthen floor, its thick oily contents permeating the chamber as its contents splashed into the dirt. A pungent odour rose from the spreading pool.

"Be careful!"

There was a loud clicking from Chandar as it picked over the shards of stoneware jar. It hissed and clicked rapidly as it turned one over, marked with Chatt glyphs.

"What is it?" Atkins asked, recognising the sounds of agitation.

"A heretical unguent, prepared from the living bodies of Ones. Used to aid prophecy. The prophecies that arise from it are said to be dire and inescapable. No One has dared use it for spira, beyond counting. Perhaps it is just as well it is gone." Chandar sank down on its legs.

Gutsy tapped Atkins on the shoulder. "Then again, maybe it hasn't." He nodded towards Mathers, who had begun to clutch his stomach in pain and pushed off his splash mask and helmet.

MATHERS JERKED, HIS back arching as though he were having a fit. He took a deep gasping breath, inhaling the vapours that coiled and entwined as they rose from the smashed jar.

In the air around him, expanding with the vapours, an alien world of shape, sound and colour, translated from the scent, began to take shape, drowning out all else.

The soldiers and crew around him faded like ghosts, as he railed against the synesthetic visions that overwhelmed his mind. The pain in his stomach dulled to a vague throb.

A spot burned on his retina. It grew larger, and Mathers realised he was witnessing events long ago.

The world was as it should be. GarSuleth watched over its children from its great Sky Web, beads of dew glistening on it in the night sky. The Nazarrii, already failing, pleaded for GarSuleth's intercession to save them.

The spot burned in the sky, bringing with it fear. The horror mounted, as its cursed name spread on the Breath of GarSuleth, from colony to colony. Mathers could taste the acrid tang of the sky usurper's name on his tongue. It tasted of blood and iron and bile. Croatoan.

The light grew brighter and brighter, outshining all the other dew-bedecked spots that shimmered and shone in the great Sky Web. It grew brighter still, seeking to outshine GarSuleth itself and tear the web asunder.

A mighty struggle ensued and burned across the vault of sky for days and nights, as GarSuleth fought the interloper before making the fatal bite, defeating the usurper and casting it from the Sky Web.

It took days for the defeated deity to fall. The false god tumbled from the sky web that spanned the heavens. It fell in fire, and as the usurper fell, the Nazarrii took this as a sign from GarSuleth and forsook the edifice, but too late. The sky giant fell not far from ill-fated Nazarr.

The world shook with its impact. The edifice felt the full wrath of the usurper's death throes as its final breath tore across the land, blasting all that stood in its path, and fire followed fast on its heels.

It was bound and imprisoned by GarSuleth's brother, Skarra, god of the dead, god of the underworld, to dwell in eternal punishment.

The middle notes told how some were selected to entomb themselves, to protect their most sacred scents against the death throes of the usurper.

As those middle notes died away the full horror of the top note became apparent. Buried alive, the priest Chatts, abandoned by their god, harvested and prepared the unguents necessary to make one final horrific prophecy from the very bodies of the worker Chatts that remained sealed in with them. And now that cannibalised chrism flooded Mathers' mind.

He gasped for breath. His voice became a hoarse whisper as he began to prophesy. *"As the breath of GarSuleth leaves us, so do these Ones leave this scent of prophecy. Our trail has led to this place at this time. Heed, then, the final inescapable prophecy of the Nazarrii that yours may not. In the spira when the Breath of GarSuleth grows foul, the false dhuyumirrii shall follow its own scent along a trail not travelled, to a place that does not exist. Other Ones will travel with the Breath of GarSuleth, the Kreothe, made, not tamed. Then shall Skarra, with open mandibles, welcome the dark scentirrii. There shall emerge a colony without precedent. The children of GarSuleth will fall. They shall not forsake the Sky Web. The anchor line breaks."*

The final notes of the scent, hastily distilled from the dead Chatt workers, died away, leaving Mathers' mind entombed with them in the dark. A dark he knew. And feared.

He screamed.

CHAPTER EIGHTEEN
"The Lonesome Dark..."

MATHERS COLLAPSED AS his mind returned to this world. As he did so, the men about him solidified and the pain in his stomach returned.

Atkins stared at him. "What the hell was all that about?"

"It is a prophecy," said Napoo, in awe.

Mercy dismissed the idea. "Mumbo jumbo more like. It don't mean anything. The man funked it a long time back."

"Oi!" snarled Norman.

Mercy flashed a sheepish smile, and held up his hands apologetically, before turning back to his mates and tapping his temple.

Chandar chattered as the prophecy-inducing liquid soaked into the dry earthen-packed floor where it could do no more harm. "This does not augur well. It would have been better if this liquid had been destroyed than used to make a heretical prophecy. But it is too late, the words have been spoken. The deed is done."

"You can't believe that stuff?" said Atkins.

"Things will be as GarSuleth wills them."

Nellie sank down beside Mathers. "Let me see him?" With reluctance, the tank crew let Nellie minister to their commander, who sat slumped against the chamber wall, saliva dribbling from his mouth, his face an ugly patchwork of livid red lesions. She unbuttoned his collar to find the swellings at his neck had now spread down over his torso. She felt for the pulse at his wrist. It was racing.

She looked up at Reggie. "His condition is worse. I don't know what to do about it. I certainly can't do anything here."

Reggie nodded in agreement. "We got to get him back to the *Ivanhoe*. It always goes better for him when he's in it, Miss."

Nellie frowned. "The fumes, yes. Well, first things first, we must get him out of here."

Atkins could hear the sound of something below repeatedly ramming roof falls. One of the creatures was attempting to clear its way through the rubble of the collapsed tunnels. "Then, Miss Abbott, you go with them. Hurry."

"Are you sure, Corporal?"

"Yes. Keep an eye on Lieutenant Mathers. Napoo, go with her." The Urman was reluctant to accompany one he considered possessed, but Atkins had gambled that his loyalty to them would extend to Nellie. The Urman nodded.

Atkins resented the fact that they had come all the way for the tankers, and now had to put their lives on the line for them again. However, when he spoke, the tone was matter-of-fact. "We'll buy you time. Keep going up. If we're not out in an hour, use the tank to bring this place down and kill these things, then get back to the encampment, toot suite. Go."

The big boxer, Jack, nodded his thanks and, supporting the semi-conscious Mathers between them, Jack and Frank led off up the passage. Alfie followed, cocked revolver in one hand, torch in the other. Nellie and Napoo fell in behind them. Reggie and Norman carried their makeshift coverall bags, with Cecil and Wally, which tapped and clinked as they walked.

Atkins watched them go as the light from their torches receded up the slope and the tunnel faded into blackness again.

Below them, the sounds became more urgent, as the repeated clinker and clatter of tumbling debris told them that the creature was breaking through.

"Stand to!" Atkins ordered. He knelt with Chalky and Pot Shot in the tunnel. In a rank behind him stood Gutsy, Gazette, Porgy and Mercy, their packs and webbing bulging with stone jars. Despite the number that the men were carrying, Chandar looked despondently at the containers they had to leave behind. "So many, so much... knowledge..."

The intermittent smash of rubble became constant as the creature found enough momentum to push through the barricade, ploughing a wave of rubble as it raced up the tunnel incline towards them.

"Fire!" ordered Atkins.

A fusillade blasted into the darkness. The onrushing wave of rubble didn't slow.

"Fall back!" yelled Atkins. "Fall back!"

THE SOUND OF gunfire behind them spurred Nellie, Napoo and the tank crew on, passing through several galleries, taking any upward tunnel, the jars clanking together as they tried to pick up their pace without breaking any.

"We'd get out of here faster if we didn't have to carry these bloody things," Wally groused. "Why can't we just dump 'em?"

"Because, like the infantryman said, these things can hit the Chatts where it hurts, wherever the hell that is. And I'm all for that," said Norman.

"Just imagine you're on ration party and quit griping," said Reggie.

Mathers stirred. "Sir. Are you all right?" asked Jack.

He shook off his crewmen's help. "Never better, Tanner, never better," he said, breathing deeply. The pain in his stomach was fading fast. Mathers felt calmer than he had done in days. It was as if whatever fever he had been suffering from had broken.

He felt an insistent need to feel the wind on his face. He stopped, confused. There, a faint cooling air current from a branching tunnel to the left. He turned towards it, not a doubt in his mind. The draft in his face drew him on and he gave in to the impulse.

Behind him, his crew called after him, perplexed, "Sir! Sir!"

"Stay there!" he commanded. He did not need them now. He walked on down the tunnel, and the breeze grew stronger. He luxuriated in the feel of it upon his skin. He heard the sound of something rushing up the tunnel towards him, but he wasn't afraid. He smiled to himself, content. He saw a slick, black bulk that filled the tunnel bearing down on him, and he stopped and welcomed it with open arms.

ATKINS AND THE others, meanwhile, raced up the tunnel and took a fork, which led to another gallery. Passages and chambers led off in several directions, up and down. The discordant whistling from the choked ventilation system seemed amplified here, making the men, tense and edgy already, feel even more windy. Chalky had started to fret and whimper.

In the centre of the gallery, they found recently dead Chatt bodies. Atkins recognised the scentirrii and the priests. "Zohtakarrii," he said, as he passed them. Something had deposited them here. The Section spread out and scouted the gallery.

Gutsy pointed at another pile. "Urmen. Must be that shaman's bunch."

"The Chatts were killed outside. Why have they been left here?" wondered Atkins.

A hard translucent substance plugged several adjoining chamber entrances, sealing them. Atkins cupped his hands to one and tried to peer through. For a moment, he couldn't make anything out. Something moved, slapping against the translucent barrier, something with the texture of tripe. The pressure from within grew. The whole of the barrier began to click and snap under the pressure. Cracks raced across the surface. The plug began to splinter.

"I think that's why!" said Atkins as he stumbled back with the others, retreating to the centre of the gallery, as the seals on the other chambers began to creak under the strain from within.

Chandar sank down on its legs and hissed.

Chalky whimpered, a wet stain spreading down his khaki trousers. Poor sod. Atkins reckoned it was as much from the unsettling sound of the whistling, that reverberated unpleasantly in the bowels, as from fear.

"Stick with me," he said, patting the lad on the shoulder. Chalky looked at him through the tears he was trying to fight back. "I'll see you, right, lad."

"I don't think it's a good time to be here," said Mercy.

The seal shattered and something began uncoiling from within. Two shapeless black creatures, the size of motor cars, slopped out of their foetal chambers on a tide of thick fluid that sluiced across the gallery floor, washing up against the piles of bodies and depositing the creatures on the chamber floor. The glistening creatures lay like great excised viscera. They seemed totally without skeletal support, with no discernable head, limbs or features of any sort. Then after a moment their shapeless bodies began to contract and flow, drawing themselves in; whether as a defensive reflex or like the first awkward attempts at movement by a newborn calf struggling to stand, it was hard to say. At the same time, orifices formed, gaping black lipless holes that began to suckle blindly at the air.

Gazette nudged Pot Shot. "Better hope it goes for the dead ones first."

"Would you go for Machonochies when there's steak?" asked Gutsy.

"Fair point."

The heaving black bulks extruded tendrils, which quested blindly towards the waiting bodies and, finding them, began to drawn them towards their open maws.

A third creature was expelled from its chamber like afterbirth and, unable to reach the food thanks to its birthmates, it sent tendrils out after the Tommies.

"And for my next trick," Gazette announced, "pick a tunnel, any tunnel."

Atkins picked one and they ran, the stone pots and jars chinking and clattering as they did.

THE TANK CREW, abandoned in the passage by Mathers, began to turn on themselves.

"We'd better go after him," said Frank.

Norman shook his head. "He told us to stay here."

Reggie stepped forwards. "He's ill, even if he won't admit it himself."

Norman glared at him. "Well, there's no point us all going. Send him." He jerked his thumb at Alfie. "*If* he's got the balls. I want to see him put himself on the line for the Sub."

"No!" Nellie protested.

"It's all right, Nellie," said Alfie. "I'll fetch him. I'm not afraid."

"Alfie, don't!"

Alfie smiled shyly and gave her a wink that exuded more confidence than he felt. "I won't be long. Back in two shakes of a lamb's tail. The lieutenant can't have gone far."

"And why the hell should we trust you?" snarled Cecil, stepping into his path. "You've never understood the lieutenant's plans. He's a genius, he's got it all sorted out, up here," he said, tapping his forehead. "He's a man of vision. He has plans for this world and he's taking us with him. But oh, no, you don't want to go. You know better. You'd rather be with your bint, here."

"'Ere, you watch your lip!" snapped Nellie.

"Or what," Cecil jeered, "your beau will swing for me?"

Nellie's eyes narrowed, full of focused fury. "He won't bloody have to, I'll do it myself."

Alfie sighed. He didn't want to do this. Not here, not now. "You can't see it, can you? Any of you! It's the fumes talking, all of this. This isn't the crew I knew back in Norfolk. You lot have been riding my back about my loyalty. I've done as much to keep the *Ivanhoe* going as any of you, and we're standing here arguing about it while the lieutenant could be in danger. He's not himself." Cecil didn't back down. "Fine. In return, I'm trusting you. With her!" he pointed at Nellie, knowing that he didn't have to trust them. The Urman, Napoo, would keep her safe, and she had her revolver.

"Seems like a fair deal," conceded Reggie, arching an eyebrow. "Cecil?"

The sullen loader muttered under his breath, but let Alfie pass.

"Look after her," called Alfie, holding up his torch, "and if we're not back in five, get the hell out of here."

"Alfie!"

It was hard leaving her, but he had to do this. He had to regain their trust. Mad or not, Mathers was still the Tank Commander and, despite what the others may think, he wasn't himself. He was the only other one who knew about the things inside Mathers, the things Mathers had been fighting. Holding the torch high, he turned and gave Nellie a bright smile and an airy wave and, with a deep breath, plunged into the waiting dark.

DRIVEN ON BY hunger, the black mass of the freshly hatched creature propelled itself after the Tommies. Atkins and the others raced along the tunnel, desperate to stay ahead of it. Chandar bounded alongside them, its legs showing a power and spring it had kept well hidden. Around a slight curve in the tunnel came a faint glow of light.

"Lads, daylight! We've made it!" yelled Porgy.

Atkins grabbed the flagging Chalky by his webbing and dragged him on. They pelted up the curving inclined passage as it led upwards for several hundred yards. The light grew brighter until, used to the gloom of the labyrinth, their eyes ached. They could see a round opening now, draped with foliage.

The low susurrating sound of pursuit still harried them, closer now.

"Run!" shouted Atkins. He gave Chalky another shove and felt one of the Chatt pots in the lad's pack break. A green sticky stain spread over the canvas. He hoped it wasn't anything important.

Mercy and Gazette came to an abrupt halt at the mouth of the opening. Gutsy barrelled into them, almost sending Porgy sprawling, but Mercy caught his webbing. Chalky came staggering up.

Atkins glanced over his shoulder. The creature was gaining. "Get out, get out!" he bellowed, closing the last few yards between him and the rest of the section.

"Not this way, we can't," said Mercy, sounding grim.

"What do you mean?" said Atkins, pushing through them to where the foliage draped across the opening. He parted it with an impatient sweep of his arm.

The ground fell away. The tunnel opened onto empty space. A hundred or so feet below, he saw the canopy of the jungle spread out before him.

"Eh, up!" said Mercy, grabbing Atkins' webbing as he flailed to keep his balance.

The tunnel came out on the side of the precipice. Only it wasn't just a precipice. Looking out across the top of a jungle canopy below, he could make out the far side of the valley with its rising cliff face, the one he'd seen before, when Jarak tried to sacrifice him. He saw now that it wasn't a rift valley as he previously thought. From here, he could see that the cliffs curved round and met, the sides of a vast crater hundreds of feet deep and filled with jungle. Over to his right he could see the mysterious discoloured line of vegetation in the crater that he'd noticed before.

None of which helped them now. They were trapped, and the creature was rushing towards them.

ALFIE SHUFFLED CAUTIOUSLY down the passage, holding the torch high, and peered into the gloom. From somewhere up ahead he could hear a constant muttering.

"Sir?" he called. "Lieutenant Mathers, sir!"

At the very edge of the torch glow, he caught sight of the scarecrow figure of the Tank Commander in his shamanistic rain cape.

"Perkins? Don't move. Stay there."

Beyond Mathers, something filled the tunnel space, writhing. Alfie held his breath. The creature waited, small tendrils waving tentatively in the air around Mathers, apparently mollified by the lieutenant's muttering. The tentacles retreated into the body of the creature, and Alfie watched it withdraw back down the tunnel with a sucking sound, the way it came.

Alfie edged forwards, uncertain as to whether the thing had truly gone. "How?" he began.

"I wondered that myself," said Mathers, unperturbed. "But you've seen them."

"What, sir?"

"These things inside me. I think it could sense them. I don't think it likes them."

Alfie remembered the glimpse he got after being forced to drink the petrol fruit. He didn't like them either.

Mathers turned to the Gearsman. "I need to get back to the tank, Perkins. I can't fight them any longer. I was ready to give myself to them just then. I can feel them interfering with my mind. They want me, *need* me to die, for some reason. The fumes seem to subdue them somehow, but I can't hold them back by myself for much longer."

"We'll get you back, sir."

"Don't tell them, Perkins. Don't tell them about the things inside me. They don't need to know."

Alfie thought they did. He didn't want to be a confidant. He didn't want to be burdened with secrets, but he bit his tongue. "My lips are sealed, sir," he said, guiding the weakened officer along. Mathers offered no resistance.

Alfie saw the bloom of torchlight ahead. "We're here," he called. The light moved along the passage towards him, highlighting Jack and Frank below it, as they approached.

Mathers had lapsed from lucidity again and, vacant-eyed, muttered to himself.

"We need to get him back to the *Ivanhoe*," said Alfie, as Frank and Jack took Mathers from him.

"Alfie!" Nellie rushed forwards to hug him but stopped herself, the fleeting moment of impropriety before the others embarrassing her. Alfie was amused to find the tank men averting their gaze and shuffling awkwardly.

"We must carry on," Napoo reminded them.

The crew picked up their jar-stuffed coveralls and let the Urman take the lead, thinking to blame him if they remained lost. They pushed on, the tunnel spiralling upwards at a gentle gradient.

Mathers was delirious. He revived briefly when they felt the fresh air blowing down the tunnel. The tank crew stumbled towards it, finding a breach in the wall. They pushed through the tangled mass of creepers and vines obscuring their view, and caught sight of the tank across the clearing.

"Yes!" A weary cheer went up. Even Alfie was relieved to see the great iron beast again. It was like coming home. Inside that, they would be safe.

MATHERS ROUSED SLIGHTLY, his brow furrowed as he listened intently. He couldn't hear it anymore, the constant whisper of Skarra. It had gone and he didn't know if it would ever return. He felt an unassailable grief so profound he wanted to howl. Then he felt the wind on his face. For a fleeting moment, he caught sight of the faint scent spectre of Jeffries, a supercilious smile on his face, as he turned and waved before walking away from the edifice and dispersing on the breeze.

As the breeze blew, all his cares blew away on it. He forgot Jeffries. He remembered a vague feeling of sorrow, but not why. A moment later, he no longer even remembered that. All he knew was the wind. He turned to face it and waited.

THE COLUMN OF air pushed ahead of the creature and ruffled the curtain of foliage behind them.

Chalky was whimpering with fear. Gutsy muttered to him in calm tones.

"We've got bombs. We can kill it," suggested Pot Shot.

"If we don't bring the tunnel down with it, it's still going to block our way back," said Atkins. "No, we're going to have to lure it out of the opening." He peered out of the gaping hole at the surrounding rock. Above, there was a large overhang, that looked impassable. The top of the cliff was seventy or eighty feet above them, but seemed too sheer to climb. Around the opening, however, were small trees with spreading root systems, holding them to the cliff face, that might hold a man? There was only one thing for it.

Atkins swung back in. "There's a small ledge to the right, and creepers that should hold our weight."

"Should?"

"Best I can do."

Gazette shook his head. "I'm not bloody going out there."

"Well, that creature is headed this way whether we like it or not. Jump or be pushed."

"Let's do it," said Gutsy, reaching out and grabbing a root. The plant creaked, but held, as he stretched out for another further along. "Well, if it'll hold me... You follow me, lad," he called to Chalky, "and just follow the advice of me missus when she's getting undressed—don't look down. Many's the time I wished I'd followed her advice, son, believe me. Brr." He shook his head vigorously until his jowls wobbled.

Gazette edged out. "I hate heights."

Pot Shot, Porgy and Mercy scrambled out over the other side.

"You too," Atkins told Chandar.

"But what about you?" the Chatt asked.

"Oh, I'll be joining you shortly, don't you worry."

The Chatt scuttled out with a cockroach-like speed that startled Atkins as he watched it use the invading roots to scurry up the passage wall and out of the tunnel mouth. He shuddered, then checked that his men were out of the way.

He ran back down the passage a short distance, intending to bait the creature. He fired a couple of rounds, not imagining that he'd stop it, but just to goad it. The bullets buried themselves in the oncoming flesh with sucking *thwups*. "Come on, then, you ugly bugger. Come and get me."

He turned and ran. The great glossy wet bulk, spraying its lubricating oily mist to ease its way, barrelled towards him. He could see the opening ahead. It wasn't far, but it was further than he wanted it to be. He had grossly underestimated the speed of the thing, and its blind, instinctive need for food. It began to put forth thin tendrils that flailed blindly, closing the distance between them.

As he raced towards the end of the tunnel, he saw Mercy's face and arm silhouetted against the light. "Run!" he yelled.

How the hell did he think that was going to help? Of course he was bloody running.

As he pounded the last few yards, Atkins felt a tendril wrap round his puttee. No! He was so damn close. A couple of yards shy of the tunnel mouth, he took a deep breath and bellowed his rage and fear, putting everything he had into one last, desperate lunge. He leapt through the curtain of foliage.

For less than the space of a heartbeat, he hung in the air. He saw the blue sky ahead and glimpsed the awful fall to the jungle below, before strong hands grabbed his webbing and swung him aside.

Another heartbeat. He crashed into the cliff wall with a force that winded him; one of Chandar's precious amphorae shattered in its pouch. He saw Mercy's sweaty, grinning face and grabbed instinctively for the roots in front of him.

A heartbeat later the newly birthed creature, oiling the tunnel as it came with its greasy black vapour, shot out, arcing into space, glands on its body spraying Atkins with the disgusting stuff as it passed.

The limbless thing tumbled down through the air to the jungle canopy below, losing the slug-like shape forced upon it by the constraints of the passage. Freshly extruded tendrils writhed helplessly in mid-air.

Atkins breathed a sigh of relief. "Blood and sand, that was too close by—"

He felt a tug on his leg, and then a wrench that almost pulled him from the cliff. The creature still had a tendril wrapped round his leg as it fell, threatening to drag him down with it. He could feel the root he held tear from its anchorage. Wide with horror, his eyes met those of Mercy.

Mercy made a desperate grab for Atkins' wrist, but his hand was as sweaty as Atkins' own. Atkins slithered from his grasp.

"Only!" roared Gutsy, fumbling to free Little Bertha.

He could feel his wet clammy fingers slipping from the root. His eyes still locked on Mercy's as he shook his head, absolving him of any blame. There was nothing more to be done.

The coarse texture of the root began to slip away under his fingertips.

With a rapidity of movement none had seen from it before today, Chandar scuttled, face-down, over Atkins' back. The Chatt's mandibles scythed through the tendril holding his ankle, and the creature crashed down through the canopy below and was lost from sight. Atkins felt Chandar's vestigial claws bite deep into his tunic, gripping him long enough for hands to reach down and haul him back up.

They clambered back into the tunnel and the shocked party caught their breath.

Gutsy looked at Chandar and shook his head in wonder. "Jesus, Mary and Joseph, I didn't know they could do that. Did you know they could do that?"

Slumped against the tunnel wall, Atkins looked up at his saviour. "Thank you."

The Chatt sucked in a chestful of air. "It was Kurda," it lisped.

Atkins nodded, still catching his breath. He regarded the Chatt for a moment. "What is that place?" he asked, waving a hand at the crater beyond the tunnel mouth.

Chandar hissed and sank down on its legs. "Forbidden. That place does not exist."

"Well, it clearly bloody does exist. It damn near killed me!"

"It is forbidden to the Ones."

"I like the sound of that," said Gutsy. "Anywhere the Chatts can't go has got to be good."

Mercy snorted. "I wouldn't be too sure. This world would kill you at every turn. If you ask me, there's probably a bloody good reason why they don't want to go there."

Atkins got up and stepped towards the Chatt. "You've been windy since we came across the Gilderra enclave. When the Zohtakarrii captured us, you knew then where we were, didn't you? You knew about that place down there, that crater."

"It is forbidden, forbidden to speak about. It does not exist for us. Other Ones, like the Zohtakarrii, whose territory borders it, patrol to make sure no One goes in and nothing comes out. It has been that way for spira upon spira."

Atkins stared hard at the Chatt, but its facial plate gave nothing away. It had no expression to read. He had no choice but to take what it said at face value. For now.

"Let's get moving before another of those things decides to corner us here again."

In the birthing gallery, two creatures were cracking the dead Chatts' chitinous shells. Another freshly-birthed horror had fallen upon the Urmen bodies, gripping them with extruded tendrils, and sucking the meat from them, leaving nothing but ichor-covered skin and bone, like discarded greasy chicken carcasses. Such was their voracious appetite that they paid no attention to the Tommies.

Atkins tapped the air with a finger, pointing towards a passage on the opposite side that seemed to run upwards. They skirted the repulsive, shapeless things and, once the section was safely in the tunnel mouth, Atkins ordered Pot Shot and Mercy to throw a brace of Mills bombs into the centre. The creatures exploded in balls of flame and silent thrashing tendrils that shrivelled in the heat.

They followed the passage as it curved upwards, until Atkins felt sure they had climbed more than the hundred or so feet that would bring them back to ground level. Light blossomed in the distance, filtered through hanging foliage. With the point of his bayonet, Atkins parted the curtain of leaves and vines. "Blood and sand, not again!"

Wherever the passage may once have led, it now looked down on a large overgrown amphitheatre formed by the collapse of the entire central core of the edifice, the once raw and jagged violence of the edifice's destruction now softened by alien nature's reclamation, overgrown with tangles of creepers, fighting for dominance. Tree-like things clung to the shattered walls. Around them, on the now exposed and weathered walls, they could see other tunnels and runs, at various levels and angles, opening just as abruptly out into the central space.

It reminded Atkins again of when he and his brother William dug up woodland ants' nests as boys, breaking open the mound to reveal the network of tunnels within, Flora protesting as the disturbed ants swarmed around their feet.

Looking down into the ruined bowl beneath them, it became clear that the great creatures that had pursued them through the Chatt-built tunnels, that had come out to the jungle to search for prey, were not many creatures at all, but a single many-tentacled one. The small ones they killed were merely hatching young.

In the basin of ruined tunnels and collapsed chambers, something huge and shapeless heaved and pulsed. They could see no eyes or mouth, in fact no organs or limbs of any kind other than the tendrils that fed into open tunnels like roots.

Atkins had no doubt that Jeffries could well have summoned what he saw from some demonic circle of Hell. Its existence stirred a deep revulsion, not just in him, but the whole section, and this from men who had seen bloated corpses move and writhe obscenely in the Somme mud, infested by feeding corpse rats burrowed into their putrefying innards.

This was the evil spirit that had been stealing Urmen. This was what they had come to kill.

CHAPTER NINETEEN
"You Have Only Once To Die..."

THE THING SQUATTED in a large ruined central chamber. The roof had collapsed around it, leaving its back, if that's what it was, half-exposed to the elements. It was a great black mass larger than several zeppelins. The black, feathered tripe-like flesh bore a cross-hatching of scars, old and new. It had tentacles sunk into lower tunnels, like roots. Others were constantly dipping into seemingly random passage openings around it, even as others withdrew. It seemed rooted to the spot. That would explain the absence of animals around the edifice. It had exhausted its local food supply. Forced to stretch its tentacles further to find food, it had encroached on the enclave's hunting grounds to snatch Urmen.

The thing throbbed as it withdrew a tentacle from a tunnel below where the Tommies stood. It was wrapped delicately around the remains of one of its young. Following some primitive instinct, it dangled the sloppy, burnt, shapeless mess before it, shaking it gently, trying to revive it. It created other, more delicate, tendrils to prod and probe it. After a cursory examination, they retreated into the mass. Then it drew the tendril, holding the dead creature, back into its body, and its offspring along with it.

"It doesn't look happy," said Mercy.

Gutsy peered down. "You wouldn't be, either, if someone had killed your baby."

"It just *ate* its dead baby, so I hardly think it's that bothered," Porgy declared.

"What the hell is it?" Atkins asked Chandar.

"This One does not know," it wheezed, forcing out the words. "It—it is not mentioned in any aromapedias. It is not GarSuleth-made."

"Whatever it is, I think we're going to need the damn tank to take it out," said Gazette, unfazed, his mind never straying from the job.

"Hell, no!" Porgy slapped Atkins on the back. "Only here can do it single-handed, can't you, Only?" He grinned at his mate. "Come on, Chalky's told us all the tales."

"Aye," said Mercy with a grin. "Seven at one blow!"

Atkins curled his lip. "Piss off. How many bombs do we have left?"

Gazette did a quick tally. "Six."

Atkins leant forward to get a better look at the thing, doubting that they would be enough. He stepped back sharply as the edge of the lip crumbled away beneath his feet. Several large chunks skittered down the exposed walls before hitting an outcrop, and bouncing off over the lower slopes, where some were ensnared by thickets of creepers. The rest bounded down in ever increasing arcs, before landing on the creature's back in a shower of thuds.

A stream of tendrils exploded upwards towards them from around the fallen rubble.

"No, it's definitely not happy," said Mercy.

"Back!" ordered Atkins, but the section was one step ahead of him. Chandar, though, hesitated, mesmerised by the sight, until Atkins put a hand on its carapace and pulled it away.

He took a last look over his shoulder as thin black tendrils appeared over the lip of the truncated tunnel. Some had already begun searching the gaping hole where they had stood. As they explored the tunnel further, they began to entwine and merge into one, growing in bulk, thickening and expanding until one single tentacle filled the space, blocking out the light.

Rushing down the tunnel, it expanded further until the walls began to crack and shudder under the pressure of its passing.

Atkins ran for his life.

THE GREAT IRON hulk of the *Ivanhoe* sat where they had left it, hunkered in the clearing, waiting patiently like a faithful beast.

Exhausted, the tank crew staggered towards the waiting behemoth.

Norman, Reggie, Cecil and Wally set down their coverall loads of Chatt jars and stretched. In the daylight, Mathers' swollen face looked much worse than they had imagined.

"And I thought impetigo from petrol fumes was bad," Norman remarked.

"How comes he's the only one that's got it, though?" asked Cecil.

"Officer in't 'e? They've got more sensitive skin than us lot. Known fact, is that."

"The sooner I'm back in the *Ivanhoe*, the better I'll feel," said Wally.

"Best get the tank started up, then, I reckon," said Jack.

Nellie patted Napoo on the forearm. "Thank you."

With a faint smile, the Urman gave a grunt of acknowledgement and nodded as she left his side.

He squatted down on his haunches, looking decidedly uncomfortable. He was wary of the lieutenant, but just as cautious about the tank. Although aware that men operated it, he was convinced that there was sorcery involved. Alfie approached the Urman, "Thanks for looking out for Nellie—I mean, Miss Abbott."

Napoo looked up at him. "She is a good woman." It was a threat as much as a statement of fact.

"Yes. Yes, she is," replied Alfie, sensing that he had outstayed his welcome. He made for the tank. His path took him past Nellie, who was splashing water from her canteen on the back of her neck. She was relieved to see that Alfie's eyes had almost returned to normal. He wanted to tell her about the thing inside Mathers, but changed his mind. "Will you check the lieutenant out, again? He doesn't look too clever."

"Do I tell you how to tune your precious engine?" she remarked.

"Yes, actually."

She beamed as she made her way over to check on Mathers, who seemed to be enjoying the soothing wind on his face. "Then I'm much too good for you, Mr Perkins."

Norman saw her examining the lieutenant. "We just need to get the engine started up, is all, Miss. Once the Sub can take a drag on the fumes he'll be top o' the bill again," he insisted.

"Top o' the bill?" said Nellie. "He's had so many turns he's a regular Marie Lloyd. It's not those blessed fumes he needs, it's rest and proper medical attention."

Frank intercepted Alfie on the way to the tank. "Where do you think you're going?"

"To start the engine, if three of you lazy buggers'll lend a hand."

Frank shook his head. "I don't think so, Alfie." He leaned in. "You may have won the lieutenant over, but he's not quite himself at the moment. Me and the lads? We ain't decided on you yet, you and your sweetheart. You see, we was all cushy 'til she and them Tommies showed up. The Sub's scheme has all gone to pot since then. You was never for it, was you? I reckon you've been sabotaging us all along. You stay there, with your lady friend."

"What the hell's got into you, Frank?"

Frank crossed to the tank and noticed an oily stain on the grass under the sponson. "Bloody hell. Perkins. I knew it. Look like something has been leaking here!" He went to open the sponson hatch. His forehead creased with disbelief as he tugged at the handle. "It's stuck." He pulled at the handle again.

"Put some oomph into it!" jeered Cecil.

The door resisted, then came free with a sticky, sucking sound. He toppled backwards onto his arse, causing a ripple of belly laughs across the clearing.

Frank's brow buckled under the weight of incomprehension as he sat staring up at the open hatchway.

Something slick and black filled the tank compartment. Something with the texture of tripe.

Tendrils whipped out from the mass, wrapped around Frank's head, and yanked him into the tank. He didn't even have time to scream.

1 SECTION RAN hell-for-leather down the narrow sloping tunnel, almost stumbling down the incline. Cracks and rumbles accompanied the sound of tide-sucked shingle behind them, as the creature's extruded limb ploughed after them, shattering the walls as it went. All the while, the passages resounded to the ultra-low keening rumble that made Atkins want to loose his bowels.

Ahead, the tunnel wall exploded in a choking cloud of debris and dust, as a second tendril smashed through the wall at right angles, cutting off their escape, before punching out through the opposite wall. With the thing approaching from behind, they were cornered.

The men collided to a halt as the tentacle passed in front of them.

Atkins pointed behind them. "Gazette, Gutsy. Watch our backs."

Porgy groaned. "Jesus, what're you going to do now?"

"Quit your griping. What's the worst that can happen?"

"You'll get us all killed?"

"You're not afraid of that, are you, Porgy?" said Mercy.

"What? Of course I bloody am, I don't want to die—when you die they stop your pay."

Atkins grinned and snatched a Mills bomb from Chalky's webbing pouch. If he set it off here, the tunnel would channel the explosion. They had no cover. At this distance, the concussion wave would render them senseless. The shrapnel blast would shred them. Standing inches from the passing tentacle, he pulled the pin with his teeth and held down the safety lever.

"Chalky, stab the damn thing with your bayonet," he yelled.

Chalky hesitated.

"Chalky, for fuck's sake—*now*!"

The lad's training took over. He charged the still passing tentacle in front of them, as if the sergeant major was standing right behind him, and let out a battle roar before thrusting his bayonet deep into the dark, otherworldly flesh. As the tentacle moved past, the blade opened up a slit along its surface. Thick black ichor sprayed out.

Like gutting a fish, Atkins thought. He took a deep breath and, hoping to God this worked, thrust the grenade into the gash as it raced by, flinching away from the stabbing bayonet, taking the bomb with it.

"Down!"

Every man in the section dropped to the ground and covered their head, smashing another couple of amphorae in the process. Gutsy pulled Chandar to the floor and pressed its head to the ground. Somewhere beyond the tunnel wall, the grenade exploded, precipitating more showers of dust and rubble.

The tentacle before them reared back sharply from the pain in a reflex action, withdrawing back across the tunnel; a ragged, torn stump leaking a trail of thick, black liquor. Within seconds, it was gone.

"You did it! You banished Jeffries' demon!" Chalky cried in jubilation. "Thank the Lord. I knew the Corp would kill the fiend. Didn't I say? Didn't I?"

Mercy reached out, patting him on the shoulder. "Steady on, lad. We don't want it going to his head."

Gutsy rolled his eyes and grinned. "Hear that, Only? Everson won't know whether to mention you in his dispatches or his prayers, now."

Behind them came the rumble of a roof fall. The tentacle thrashed about as the creature reacted in shock to its injury, bringing the tunnel crashing down. A great cloud of dirt and dust billowed towards them, overtook them and left them gagging and coughing.

"Go!" ordered Atkins, picking himself up.

The Tommies scrambled to their feet and rushed on. All but one torch had been extinguished. It was enough to light the way, but not bright enough to give them much warning of anything else in the deep dark of the tunnels.

They passed an earlier scrawled *13/PF* chalk mark with some relief, and took a broader, descending passage.

As they ran, they could hear muffled thuds and thumps from all around, some too far away to be of concern, some too close for comfort.

It put Atkins in mind of the interminable Hun artillery barrages they suffered when the minniewerfers and five-nines would pummel the front lines for hours or days. The nerve-shredding pounding continued around them, accompanied more and more often by the long, slow rush of tunnel collapses.

"What's going on?" cried Chalky, flinching at every crash.

The demon creature was thrashing about, trying to find them, Atkins guessed. It was no longer content to use the Chatt-built tunnels and passages to hunt them, but was tearing down galleries and punching through chambers, searching for the bugs that were tormenting it.

"I think the damn thing's reading its shirt, looking for us."

"You mean it's chatting us?" Porgy came back.

"You could say that, aye."

"Bloody cheek!" said Porgy, affronted. "No offence," he added, nodding an apology at Chandar as it raced alongside with its hopping gait.

They wound their way down through tunnels and galleries, threading their way back through the labyrinth as best they could, avoiding the many tentacles now ploughing through the tunnels in search of them.

The passage roof in front of them bowed and buckled, as cracks appeared. Slivers of silver daylight drove down into the dark confined space, slicing through the dust motes before the roof caved in. A tentacle punched down through the tunnel, and on through the floor, with a force that almost threw them off their feet. They darted to the right, down a smaller tunnel. Further down, daylight streamed in from some kind of window or breach. They were against an exterior wall. Atkins wondered how far they were above ground.

"FRANK!"

Frank did not respond.

Jack darted towards the tank in the vain hope of rescuing him.

The tank came alive. Black tentacles burst from the drivers' visors, from the pistol ports around the tank, and from the hatches, all thrashing wildly.

Jack ducked and danced, as light on his feet now as he had been in the carnival boxing ring before the war. He edged towards the open sponson through which Frank had been pulled, but was driven back as the tendrils lashed out at him.

Napoo drew his sword and pulled Nellie behind him. "Alfie, stay back!" she screamed, as he joined the others, trying to find a way past the pseudopodia as they whipped through the air.

They took pot shots with their revolvers, aiming for the pistol ports or at the portion of the writhing black mass that presented itself through the sponson hatch. Alfie shouted at them to stop. "You might damage the *Ivanhoe*!"

Nellie peered round Napoo in horror. "What on earth is it?"

Distracted, Mathers looked towards the tank. He seemed clear and lucid, for the moment. "It is the spawn of the thing that inhabits the ruins. It is not of this place," he declaimed.

Reggie started towards him, concern etched on his face. "Sir?"

Mathers turned to him and spoke as if he might have been discussing the finer points of cricket over cucumber sandwiches on a summer's evening. "Didn't you realise?" He gestured vaguely towards the ruined edifice. "It has no protection of its own against the predations of this world. Its sire found its way inside the ruins for shelter. This one found its way inside the tank. Don't you see? It's using it as a shell, as a hermit crab does, to armour itself."

"But Frank. What about Frank, sir?"

"Frank?" Mathers stared blankly at the tank, unconcerned. "Frank's gone."

Norman tried to follow the lieutenant's logic. "So you're saying all we have to do is winkle it out? Then we're going to need a bloody big pin, if you don't mind my saying so, sir."

"A bayonet!" suggested Cecil.

"Going to need something bigger than a pig sticker, son," said Jack.

Nellie frowned. "I know just what we need to lance this boil." She ran over to the undergrowth, to the little copse of black-barked, silver-veined saplings she had spotted when they arrived at the edifice. "Napoo, help me."

Napoo joined her. He arched an eyebrow as he realised what she was looking at. "Corpsewood?"

"Will it work, do you think?"

"What is it?" asked Alfie.

"It's a scavenger plant. It usually feeds on dead or rotting flesh, but eats living things if it can, hence the name, so be careful."

"It... might work," said Napoo, with caution. "But it must be handled with great care. We have never used it in such a way."

Alfie was insistent. "We need the tank back. If this is the only way, then let's do it."

Since the creature in the ruins had frightened off anything that the corpsewood might feed on, pickings were thin. The wood had grown up around the bodies of small creatures, their bones embedded it its trunk and protruding from the black bark.

The tank crew watched, fascinated, from a safe distance, distracted occasionally by the creature within the tank as its tentacles whipped and thrashed hungrily.

Wrapping his hands in bandages from Nellie's webbing pouches, Napoo set to work, cutting down the stand of black corpsewood saplings. Thin and reedy specimens, eager for sustenance, the silver vein-like creeper stems around them unwound and inclined towards Napoo's hands, like a plant following the sun. He threw them aside too quickly for them to latch on. With deft strokes of his sword, he stripped them of their spiny branches and fashioned their tips into sharp points. He bound part of the shafts with a lengths of split vine to give some protection against the corpsewood for the wielder. Within fifteen minutes, Napoo had a brace of crude corpsewood spears.

Alfie watched in awe as Napoo threw the makeshift spears with confidence. Lashing tentacles knocked some aside to clatter harmlessly off the iron plating, but he targeted the open sponson hatch, and the corpsewood spear buried itself in the exposed black flesh. It puckered and shrivelled around the wound as the silver grey creepers wormed their way slowly into the creature. It was enough to prove that the idea worked, but not enough to rid them of the thing.

"We can't get close enough," said Norman, as he and the others tried to target the creature while avoiding its tendrils.

Mathers walked up and hefted one of the corpsewood spears experimentally. "I can," he said, exchanging a look with Alfie. He picked up a bunch of the spears and walked towards the tank. Reggie and Norman tried to stop him, but he waved them back.

The tendrils whipped and lashed wildly, but he pressed on, showing no fear, for he had none left to show. The things inside him saw to that, he was sure of it. He was within the reach of the flailing tendrils, but they wavered uncertainly, and then retreated before his advance, as if loath to touch him. Its sire could sense the things within him, and so, too, could its spawn. He was anathema to them. By the time he was in striking distance of the tank, the creature had completely retreated inside it.

He thrust the corpsewood spears through the drivers' visors, the pistol ports, and through the view slits in the gun shield. Trapped inside the ironclad, the creature recoiled from the pain as the corpsewood sought to burrow into it.

Mathers climbed onto the top of the tank, threw open the manhole in the roof and thrust another spear down into the compartment, driving the creature down. In desperation, the thing began to squeeze itself out of the port sponson hatch. He dropped down into the tank to push his advantage, herding the shapeless creature back out of the tank with his last spear.

The heaving bulk flopped gracelessly from the ironclad and it grew tendrils to help drag itself away. However, the creature's back half was dead, atrophying beneath the corpsewood. Starved for so long, the many spears had sent their vein-like silver creepers deep into the creature's body, and had begun to leech its life from it. Weakening, the creature's tentacles could no longer keep the men at bay.

Once they realised it was dying, the tank crew fell on it in a fury, using sticks, wrenches and chains to take out their fear and anger.

"That's for Frank!"

"Do that to our *Ivanhoe*, will you?" bellowed Cecil, stamping on a weakly twitching tendril.

Wally, incoherent with rage, thrashed his chain down, over and over again. His face turned red, and spittle flew from his lips, as he took out the frustrations he realised he could no longer take out on the Hun.

Alfie held back, fretting. "Stop!" he cried, "stop!" But they weren't listening. Alfie grabbed Norman's arm as he raised it to land another blow. "Stop it! Look," he said. "Look!"

Amid the now beaten, shapeless bulk, its wounds running with thick viscous fluid, they could make out a shadow in the depths of the creature that looked vaguely human in shape. Because it had been.

"Oh Jesus. Frank!"

Norman dropped the wrench, drained. The others too, sobered up, their chests heaving.

Mathers clambered unsteadily from the sponson, a tin of grease in his hand. He tipped it over the creature as the roots of the corpsewood spread further into it. He lit a Lucifer and dropped it on the thick lubricant. It ignited with a bright indigo flame. The tentacles writhed feebly in the flames before shrivelling. As the grease melted with the heat, it ran, spreading out, coating the rest of the creature, basting it. The flames followed, consuming it, the corpsewood, and Frank.

Jack pulled Cecil back from the monstrous pyre. Reggie made the sign of the cross and muttered a prayer.

"Get the tank started," Mathers ordered, quietly.

Alfie, Cecil, Reggie and Norman squeezed in through the small sponson hatches, one after the other. Wally followed. Mathers paused in the sponson hatchway. He heard the grind of the giant starting handle. The engine caught and the *Ivanhoe* awoke from its slumber with a growl.

A breeze caught the burning creature, fanning the flames, causing the corpsewood embers to burn brighter, and the flesh to char and crackle in the heat.

Mathers turned into the wind, a hand on his belly as if it pained him. He felt weary, too weary to worry, too tired to care, and too exhausted to fight it anymore.

"Now it comes," he said, almost with relief, before climbing into the tank.

THE TOMMIES RACED down the sloping tunnel and burst out into the giant space of the ancient antechamber. It echoed with the continual pounding of the creature around them, unseen.

Exhilaration mixed with fear as, across the open, rubble-strewn space, they caught sight of the withered bark gates that once guarded the main entrance to the edifice.

The ground shuddered beneath their feet as something pummelled away beneath them, making it hard to keep their balance. Great chunks of hardened earth, compacted to rock-like density, plummeted from the domed ceiling high above, like a barrage, exploding around them in rocky shrapnel.

It was just like going over the top into No Man's Land, Atkins thought, as they sheltered in the mouth of the tunnel, only here there

was no officer's whistle to set them off. It was down to him. Another
time, another place, they had done this before. Atkins checked his rifle.
"Mercy, Gutsy, you're with me. The rest of you, wait for my signal.
Leapfrog us. We'll hold the middle ground while you make for the
door. Cover us from there."

His section returned almost imperceptible nods. He took a deep
breath and darted out in the domed space, amid the pounding and
crashing rubble, Mercy and Gutsy at his heels.

They made a stooped run to the middle of the chamber, weaving
between the crashing debris. They threw themselves down by a large
chunk of rubble, sweeping the other openings for pursuing tentacles,
as the pounding continued around them, reverberating through the
chamber. "Come on!" hollered Atkins, beckoning the others.

Gazette, Chalky, Pot Shot, Porgy and Chandar raced across the open
space, dodging masses of falling masonry that sent showers of dirt and
rocky shrapnel into the air.

"Bleedin' hell, it's just like old times!" yelled Porgy, flinching as chips
and shards of rock whistled past them.

"Yeah, what price your soft caps now, eh?" said a cocky Pot Shot,
patting the steel battle bowler on his head.

A huge chunk of masonry plunged to the floor and shattered close
by. A lump sheered off, smashing the lanky Fusilier in the back of the
head. He dropped to the floor like a bag of bones.

Gazette had gone a few paces before he realised his mate wasn't by
his side. He turned and saw the gangly figure lying on the ground like
a broken marionette. "Pot Shot!"

Gazette ran back to him. He knelt, gathered in the lanky man's limp
limbs, and turned him over. He lifted Pot Shot's head. His hand came
away covered with blood.

Mercy crouched at his side. "Come on, mate, let's get him out of
here." He gathered up Pot Shot's rifle, and slung it over his shoulder,
and together the pair of them dragged their fallen comrade to the
shelter of the rubble.

The walls shuddered under the continual impacts. From around
them, in the ruins of the edifice, came the sound of collapsing tunnels,
crumbling passageways and the awful *thud, thud, thud* of pounding
tentacles. The whole place was coming down.

Atkins ducked as a piece of roof, the size of a gun limber, smashed
down a dozen feet away. They couldn't stay here. Atkins gave the
order. "Make for the door!"

Gazette and Porgy carried Pot Shot, staggering under his weight
and the juddering impacts from under the floor. Chalky stuck with
Chandar as they weaved drunkenly towards the opening.

Cracks crazed across the walls, racing them to the entrance. The mouth of one of the tunnels began to flake and crumble. A tentacle burst from it, flailing blindly.

Porgy opened fire, five rounds rapid, driving it back.

"Did you see the size of that?" he grinned.

The floor bucked beneath their feet. Great blocks of floor split and lifted. The broken slabs tilted violently. Another pounding sent them spinning up into the air.

"That?" said Gutsy. "Pff. That was a tiddler. Now that," he said, as a huge tentacle erupted through the floor, "is something worth worrying about."

"Don't like the look of yours much!" Atkins yelled to Gutsy, as they ran, stumbling over the debris towards the door.

Lumps of roof rained down around them, exploding into dust, adding to the clouds of dirt that already hung in the air.

Smaller tentacles sprouted violently from the weakened floor about them. They swerved to avoid them, Gutsy taking a swipe at one with Little Bertha.

Reaching the entrance with Chandar, Chalky gave covering fire, sniping at the tentacles until his ammunition ran out.

Mercy and Gazette, with Pot Shot between them, stumbled into the sunlight cutting into the chamber. Atkins, Gutsy and Mercy followed close on their heels.

"Good shooting, Chalky," said Atkins, patting the lad on the shoulder. Chalky beamed with pride.

Under cover of the dust cloud that billowed from the edifice, an oily black mist drifted out of the entrance and something caught Chalky's ankle. It yanked his feet out from under him. Chandar hissed in alarm.

"Atkins! Dear God, Only, save me!" Chalky shrieked, his fingers scrabbling at the dirt, leaving brief, bloodied gouges in the earth, as he was dragged feet first back into the waiting darkness.

Porgy grabbed his wrist, but found himself dragged along too, until his shoulder crashed into a boulder. He screamed and let go.

Gazette fired three rounds rapid at the tentacle before his magazine emptied, but it wouldn't release Chalky.

As the tentacle pulled Chalky into the edifice, he looked pleadingly at Atkins to save him one way or another.

Gazette spoke urgently. "Only, he's being dragged into Hell. You can save him from that at least."

Atkins blinked away the stinging tear in his eye, raised his Enfield, gritted his teeth and fired. Chalky went limp as his now lifeless body was reeled back into the collapsing edifice.

* * *

1 SECTION WAS racing from the shadow of the crumbling building and running towards the tank, shouting. Mathers, peering out of the sponson, couldn't make out what they were saying over the sound of *Ivanhoe's* engine, the ground trembling under a relentless pounding, and the roaring of rubble slides, as parts of the ruined edifice toppled and collapsed.

Gauging from their urgent waving, however, it meant trouble. Best to be safe. He clambered into the tank, the fug of petrol fruit fumes embracing him as he entered. The engine ran up. The tank made a jerky turn to face the edifice, then lurched towards the retreating soldiers, black smoke belching from its back.

Tentacles writhed out of the edifice now.

The soldiers ran past, carrying one of theirs between them, the Chatt scurrying alongside. The tank clattered and clanked towards the edifice to face the large writhing tentacles of the creature. This was no job for infantry now. This was a job for the Machine Gun Corps Heavy Section.

Cecil was loading a shell into the breech of Jack's starboard six pounder when a huge tentacle unfurled from the disintegrating ruins. It seized the *Ivanhoe* and began to drag it, slowly, inexorably, towards the edifice.

PENNINE FUSILIERS

CHAPTER TWENTY
"There's a Silver Lining in the Sky-ee..."

EXHAUST FUMES BELCHING from its back, its engine growling, the *Ivanhoe* clawed doggedly at the ground as it hauled against the tentacle clutching it, like a determined hound worrying a rope. It made some ground, its track plates pawing at the earth, pulling away from the tentacle until it began to lose its grip on the tank, but the creature was unwilling to let its prey go. More tentacles whipped out, lashing themselves around the ironclad, drawing it back again, foot by foot towards the collapsing ruins.

In a tug of war for its life, the tank fought back valiantly. Bursts of machine gun fire tore through the tentacles. The port gun spoke, demolishing a section of the edifice, bringing it down on yet more tentacles.

The *Ivanhoe's* engine began to whine under the strain. The tracks slipped, losing traction against the slow, insistent pull of the tentacles. Gradually, but certainly, it was being drawn into the edifice. The tank's tracks scored great long furrows in the ground as the tentacles dragged it towards the gaping entrance.

Inside the *Ivanhoe,* the compartment began to fill with black smoke from burning oil and grease. The track wheels clanked and whined, trying to keep purchase on the iron track plates as they slipped.

"Oh hell, don't let us throw a track now, please God," said Reggie, crossing himself as he passed Norman a shell for the port gun. Before returning to his gear station, he let off a short burst from the belt-fed Hotchkiss machine gun, the bullets chewing through another tentacle.

"It's no use, I can't get a shot!" Norman bellowed over the engine noise.

From his seat at the front, Mathers indicated that Reggie and Alfie should use the track gears to try to swing the tank to starboard and get him a better shot.

Reggie put his track into second as Alfie, cursing under his breath, shifted his into neutral. The tank began to swing round to the right. Alfie could feel the gears beginning to judder through the gear lever.

*   *   *

As THE IRONCLAD occupied the creature's attention, Atkins, Mercy, Gutsy and the others dragged Pot Shot to safety across the clearing. A little distance away, a foul smelling fire was still burning itself out.

Lying discarded on the ground nearby were the two tank crew coveralls, stuffed with stone jars and sacred scents. Chandar chattered and insisted they carry them to safety, too. They picked them up as they passed, dragging them along.

"Over here!" Nellie waved from the edge of the clearing. "Where's Chalky?"

Mercy shook his head.

"Oh."

As soon as they laid Pot Shot down, Nellie, thankful for the opportunity to do something other than watch the tank struggle with the creature, fell to her knees and set to work examining him.

"Is he going to be all right?" Gazette asked, fearful of the answer.

With as much care as a battlefield would allow, she gently slipped Pot Shot's steel helmet off. In some cases she'd seen, that had been all that was holding the skull together, or the brains in.

Delicately Nellie felt his skull, feeling for fractures or breaks.

"Is he—?"

She let out a small sigh. "No. Thank God. It's only a scalp wound. He's suffering from concussion. His helmet probably saved him. He'll live."

Atkins turned his attention to the tank. All he had to do was bring the tank back. One simple order. One simple *bloody* order. It should have been a piece of cake. His heart sank as he saw it losing its struggle against the creature. The engine whined and the tracks churned up the ground. Despite its weight and power, it seemed to be fighting a losing battle, but at least it was still fighting. "Let's see if we can't convince that thing to let go!" Atkins said.

They moved as close as they dared, took up position and fired at the sinuous tentacles gripping the ironclad. Bullets tore through flesh; others struck the iron hide, sparking as they did so.

Inside the *Ivanhoe*, splashes of molten metal, caused by the impact of the bullets, flew around the compartment.

Cecil shrieked as one hit his cheek, "Jesus, now our own side are trying to kill us too! Why the hell are they shooting at us? Oh, God. Frank said Mathers would get us killed, he did!"

Jack turned and with a warning glance at Mathers' back in the driving seat, bellowed into Cecil's ear. "Button your lip!" Not that Mathers could have heard him over the noise of the engine.

Across the clearing, Gutsy pulled out a rifle grenade. "Last one," he said. He dropped it into the barrel of his rifle, braced the shoulder stock on the ground, and fired. The grenade arced through the air, landing near the entrance. It exploded, shredding a tentacle and releasing the tank, even as others sought to take its place.

The *Ivanhoe* lurched backwards as its tracks, running in reverse against the pull of the edifice creature, engaged with the ground. Once it had ripped free of the smaller tentacles, Mathers slammed on the brakes. "There's your shot," he yelled over the engine.

"Thank you, sir!" shouted Norman ecstatically as he manhandled the portside gun round. He fired. Through the gunner's vertical viewing slit in the gun shield, he saw the shell explode and a section of huge, black tentacle vaporise in a plume of atomised flesh and ichor. "Yes!"

Seconds later, Jack fired the starboard gun. That, too, hit home. The creature thrashed in pain, its tentacles demolishing the edifice, sending rubble crashing down on the *Ivanhoe*. The tank jerked into motion, reversing clear of the tumbling debris.

The *Ivanhoe's* guns fired again, bringing down more of the decaying structure. The tentacles wavered uncertainly, and then, by degrees, retreated into the ruins with a long, low rumble of pain.

WATCHING THE ROUT of the creature, as the shelling of the ironclad drove it back underground, the Fusiliers cheered in jubilation. It was short lived.

Cutting through the rumble of the edifice and growl of the tank, came the crashing sound of trees creaking and falling and the high-pitched jabbers and squeals of animal fear.

Atkins' eyes narrowed. Where the hell had they come from? The dulgur had hunted the area clean of game, hadn't it? He noticed the queer cast of light across the clearing, a strange kind of pre-storm twilight. It was as if the sun were being filtered through dirty glass.

"What now?" He looked up, irritated.

An immense bank of drifting clouds was obscuring the sky. No, not clouds; creatures, with vast snake-like members hundreds of feet long, hanging beneath them, tearing up trees, lifting them into the sky, plucking animals from the canopy as though they were grazing.

The ruined edifice and the clearing around it fell under a twilight shadow as they drifted across the sky, eclipsing the sun overhead.

Atkins watched in horror as the animals were flayed, as they rose to where yet more tendrils grasped the things and fed them into great wet mouth tubes. Underneath the tubes, swarms of black things danced like flies around dung.

Mercy gaped up at the sight. "Holy Mary, Mother of God!"

"Get under cover!" yelled Akins. Not that anyone needed telling. They ran for the shelter of the trees. They all saw what was happening to beasts snatched up by the shoal of airborne leviathans overhead. None of them wanted to be next.

The great sky-borne creatures filling the sky drifted over, oblivious to their presence. The light strained through the massive translucent gas sacs that kept them aloft, like huge living zeppelins.

"What the hell are they?" Atkins yelled above the cacophony.

Chandar chittered and shrunk down on it legs, almost as if it were trying to curl itself into a ball. "GarSuleth protect us!"

"Kreothe!" said Napoo, craning his neck and watching them in fear.

"That's bad, then, is it?" Mercy remarked as he looked up to watch the stately procession of creatures across the sky. Most had their long limbs curled up under their gas sacs. Only a few of the bigger ones fed as they drifted lazily over the jungle, dragging their long snake-like limbs, dredging the ground for food.

There was a terrible sound, a long low bass cry from the edifice, accompanied by the sound of collapsing walls crushing vegetation as they fell.

A huge Kreothe floated sedately over it, its long harvesting tendrils draped below it, into the ruins. Although the creature was hidden by the ruins, Atkins could see its black tentacles lashing and wrestling with the trailing tendrils of the Kreothe, wrapping themselves around them, trying to pull the sky leviathan down.

The two great beasts grappled tentacle-to-tendril, appendages slipping and sliding through and round and over as they each tried to gain an advantage.

The Kreothe's vast gas sacs inflated and it rose up, accompanied by the sound of crashing as walls collapsed. There was a terrible cry, a deep bass groan that shook the ground around them and a deep sickening tearing as the Kreothe ripped the creature from its setting amid the ruins, uprooting it, and drawing it up into the air.

As the Kreothe drifted over the section, it worked to haul in its slippery catch. Long harvesting tendrils firmly gripped the black, shapeless creature. Where they gripped it, great wounds opened, as if it were being flayed. Now seen whole, the creature looked to Atkins like a shellfish plucked from its shell, slick, wet and raw.

In retaliation, the creature threw up tentacles around the Kreothe's feeding tendrils, while lashing down at the spindly scab trees below, trying to anchor itself, but they, too, were torn from the ground.

The black shapeless mass writhed and shifted, extruding new tentacles to thrash against the gas sacs of the Kreothe. Locked in a life or death struggle, the two creatures each fought to dominate and subdue the other, tentacles wrapping, enfolding, and choking.

The flock of scavenger things began to swarm about the shapeless creature, pecking and tearing.

The creature had now gained a purchase on the sky beast's gas sac and pulled itself up, allowing its form to change and flow, trying to engulf and swallow its opponent.

They drifted off over the crater, the slow silent battle shifting first one way and then the other. It seemed that the epic sky duel would continue until one lost out to sheer exhaustion.

"Only!"

Atkins' attention returned to the ground. A smaller Kreothe had latched onto the tank and was trying to haul the *Ivanhoe* up, but the sheer weight of the ironclad resisted its efforts. It lowered several more harvesting tendrils in an effort to increase its grasp on the vehicle.

It proved too heavy for the Kreothe to lift, yet it was unwilling to let go of its prize and, as the wind drove the enormous creature on, it dragged the *Ivanhoe* backwards with it across the clearing, almost, but not quite, lifting it clear of the ground.

The tank couldn't get enough traction on the ground to drive in the opposite direction and break free. Occasionally, the tracks would bite into the earth and it would make some small, defiant gain of ground, only to be lifted off again. Atkins could see its guns trying to target the Kreothe above, but they couldn't get enough elevation.

"Damn! Come on!" said Atkins. "Napoo, stay there with Nellie and Pot Shot, don't let anything happen to them."

The section moved off quickly, staying in the shelter of the trees to take cover from the great dredging sky limbs. Chandar lagged behind, hesitant.

"Oh, no, you don't," said Gutsy, dropping back and waving the Chatt on with his rifle. "We're not losing you as well."

Chandar snapped his mandibles together aggressively, but complied with great reluctance.

The Kreothe was slowed down by having to drag its dead twenty-eight ton weight through trees. The section raced ahead of it. The thinning jungle gave way to hardy shrub for several hundred of yards. Beyond that yawned the great crater, the land that, according to Chandar, did not exist.

Already, those Kreothe at the head of the shoal were drifting majestically out over it.

INSIDE THE TANK, the crew were thrown about as the *Ivanhoe* was dragged, crashing through a small grove of scab trees. Much to Reggie's disapproval, they were shouting and cursing, peering through pistol ports to see what the hell was going on.

All except Mathers. The officer was calm almost to the point of indolence, and seemed heedless to the danger, just when his crew needed him the most.

For all Alfie's efforts, the engine was beginning to show the strain. His petrol fruit-filtered vision was returning to full strength now as the engine fumes flooded his body. He could see from the deep blues and indigos emanating from the engine that it was at the limits of its capacity. The track gears were engaged in second forward speed but it wasn't making a blind bit of difference. They were still being dragged backwards.

Cecil opened the sponson door, hung out looking up at the underside of the Kreothe, with its tongue tendrils and mouth tubes, and fired his revolver up at it. They didn't have any effect. "Bleedin' 'ell!" you ought to see the size of this bugger! It's bigger than any bloody Zeppelin."

"Get back in, you daft sod!" yelled Jack.

Cecil ducked back in. "Like a giant bleedin' jellyfish it is!" He reached out to close the sponson door and stared in horror. "Fuck! There's a cliff coming up!" he yelled.

The petrol fruit fumes building inside the iron hull worked on Mathers, helping him break free of the ennui exerted over him by the things he carried inside him.

Jack heaved on the shoulder stock of the gun and howled in frustration. "I can't get enough elevation on the gun to hit it, sir, if I could hit it, we'd have a chance."

"Get out," said Mathers. "Abandon the tank."

"We won't leave you, sir."

"You don't have a choice, I'm ordering you out. If the *Ivanhoe's* done for, then there's no point in you all dying."

"But, sir..."

"That's an order, Clegg. And... Wally? Some good has to come out of all this. Tell the corporal, tell... Atkins, I've seen it, Jeffries' trail. It leads to the crater. It leads there for a reason. It's the blank on the map the Chatts fear, the place that doesn't exist. The name they will not admit to. Make sure he knows that. It's more than Chatt myth. I suspect it'll be of some importance to him."

"Sir." Wally slipped from his driver's seat and joined Jack in the starboard gangway.

Cecil opened the hatch again. He could see the precipice approaching fast. Above, he saw the great long tendrils reaching up towards the underside of the Kreothe as it dragged the *Ivanhoe* along.

"Time to go, lad," Jack said. He pushed Cecil out of the sponson hatch before the lad could object, and then followed him.

Wally braced himself on the hatch jamb, looked across at Alfie, still at his gear station, and nodded before launching himself from the tank, rolling clear of the tracks.

Over on the other side, Reggie and Norman jumped from the port sponson hatch. "And you, sir?" called Alfie.

Mathers turned and looked at him. "We've both seen these things in me. I'm dead already, Perkins."

"But not yet, sir. And neither is the *Ivanhoe*. I'm not leaving, sir."

Neither knew if the Kreothe could bear the weight of the tank without the ground to support it. If the Kreothe could carry its weight then it would sail out hundreds of feet over the crater, where it still might drop to destruction. On the other hand, its weight might just drag the thing right out of the air.

The tank, in one last effort to avoid its fate, roared its defiance as its metal tracks grated and clawed at the ground, raising a cloud of dust that momentarily obscured it, until updrafts from the crater snatched it away.

For a moment, the *Ivanhoe* held its own against the great sky creature, anchoring it as others drifted on past. The Kreothe's long harvesting tendrils stretched taut, like an anchor chain against the pull of the tide.

Snorting like an obdurate old bull, the *Ivanhoe* inched forwards away from the precipice. The men cheered the ironclad on. It seemed beyond all belief that the intrepid machine could take on the weight of the vast creature above. Slowly, however, its little gain was lost and it lurched back towards the edge of the crater, its back end sliding perilously close to the rim. Then, with a lurch, the rear steering tail toppled over the edge.

The track wheels clanked and squealed, trying to gain traction, but as they churned, they ate away at the very ground supporting the ironclad. Its nose rising up off the ground, the tank began to tilt over the edge.

Mathers smiled though the pain. "You've made your choice after all, Perkins. You could have left with the others, been reunited with your sweetheart."

Alfie ignored him. "We've got one chance, sir. We're tipping. We just need a few more degrees to get the gun elevation we need to hit that thing. I need you to be ready."

The tank lurched, tilting sharply. The sponson door swung open, banging against the bulkhead. Alfie reached out to grab it, catching a vertiginous glimpse of a steep rocky cliff below them, bevelling out to a shrub-covered slope descending into a canopy of thick jungle below.

A spanner skittered down the gangplank, hit the rim of the hatch with a clang and pinwheeled out into the void.

Blanching, he reached out, pulled the hatch shut, and secured it. He didn't want to lose his balance and topple out.

"This is it, sir!" He lurched unsteadily towards the loaded gun. Grunting with effort, he gripped the shoulder stock under his armpit and heaved the gun barrel up as far as it would go and fired.

The *Ivanhoe's* gun pounded. Above it, the shell exploded against the Kreothe. The concussion wave sent ripples round the gas sac, before tearing out of the upper side. The blast shrivelled the smaller tendrils beneath it and, with raucous shrieks of alarm, the flock of scavengers that swarmed beneath it scattered. The harvesting tendrils holding the tank whipped back up, like cords cut under tension, and the *Ivanhoe's* front track horns crashed back down onto solid ground.

FROM THE SHELTER of the trees, Jack and Cecil burst out in a jubilant chorus and Reggie, Norman and Wally joined in.

"The Sub did it! He bloody did it!"

"The Sub *and* Alfie," Jack reminded them.

Atkins puffed out his cheeks and exhaled. Jesus, that was close. A slow, burning anger overwhelmed his relief. From now on, he was bloody well in charge. He had orders to get the tank back to camp and, now, that was exactly what he was going to do. It helped matters that the tank would have to return with them to refuel. All of a sudden, he was eager to start back.

INSIDE THE *IVANHOE*, Alfie, dazed, picked himself up from the gangway and saw Mathers slumped in the commander's seat. The visor plates had slammed shut with the impact and nothing but a flickering festoon light lit his plaque-ridden face. Alfie clambered forwards into the driver's seat to check on him.

Mathers' chin rested on his chest. Alfie gently lifted the officer's head to check for injuries. His eyes snapped open. "I can feel it, Perkins, a pressure inside my head, in my belly."

"We need to get out, sir."

"No."

"Sir, we're on the edge of the cliff."

"You go, Perkins."

"Come with me, sir."

"If I go out now, I'll die. Whatever's inside me, they're making me want to go out there. They need me to go out there. They want me to offer myself to those *things*. But I won't. I refuse. *I absolutely bloody well refuse.* I am clothed in iron and armed with cordite. I will not go like this!"

Alfie's eyes met Mathers', but the iridescent swirls that looped and whorled within them disconcerted him. "Then just drive forward, sir. Away from the cliff edge."

Mathers shook his head. "The track gears are jammed."

Jammed? Perkins frowned and glanced back down the compartment, over the top of the engine. "Then I'll go back and see if I can free them. You hang on, sir." The gearsman stepped down onto the gangway and edged his way to the back of the compartment.

Mathers continued talking, raising his voice over the engine. "It's a bloody good machine, Perkins. How you've kept it running these past few months is beyond me. A bloody miracle. I was... wrong about you."

Alfie shrugged it off. Now wasn't the time for recriminations, least of all against an officer. "You weren't yourself, sir."

"Did you know I had shell-shock, Perkins, before I joined the Heavy Section?"

Alfie didn't know what to say, but felt that the moment called for honesty. "There... there were rumours, sir," he called back.

The tank groaned and creaked under him as he edged his way past the gun and Hotchkiss towards the starboard gear panel.

"I was buried in a dugout for four hours, couldn't move a muscle. Dead man lying of top of me. Bugger probably saved my life. Funny how fate catches up with you." He waved his hand, indicating the interior of the tank. "Here I am, entombed again. No matter how far you run, there you are. It's a rum old world."

Something in the tone of Mathers' voice made Alfie glance back. Mathers was raising his revolver to his temple. "I wonder if Skarra will be waiting..."

Alfie lunged up the gangway. "Sir, no!"

There was a grinding crunch and sudden lurch. The tank tilted, slipping backwards, sending Alfie reeling back down against his gear station. The weight of the hydraulic steering tail, ironically designed to be used as a counterbalance when crossing wide trenches, was now having the opposite effect and was dragging them over the edge to destruction. He felt the tank pitch steeply as it slipped backwards.

Alfie could almost imagine the scene outside, as if he were back at Elveden, watching one of the tank trials. In his mind's eye, he saw the rim of the crater, weakened by the grinding of the tracks and the weight of the ironclad, begin to splinter and crumble. Boulders tumbled away, drawing with them steady streams of soil.

He tried to reach for the manhole above him, but lost his footing as the *Ivanhoe* tilted further and he fell back against the gear station.

The ground beneath the tank slipped away like sand through an hourglass, crumbling under its weight in a gentle but inevitable landslide of rock, soil and roots. The *Ivanhoe's* front track horns reared into the air, like a startled stallion, its angle becoming more unstable until, like a sinking ship, it slipped from sight.

A gunshot reverberated loudly inside the iron hull.

Stores broke free and tools tumbled loose, ammo boxes crashed out of their slots. A Pyrene fire extinguisher slipped from its fixings and span toward Alfie. He screamed.

The ironclad went over the edge.

SHOCKED, THE FUSILIERS and surviving tank crew watched as the tank toppled over the rim. From the crater came the sound of tortured metal and rock. Seconds later, there was a loud crashing, an eruption of animal calls and flocks of green-skinned bird-like raptors took to the air in panic from the crater jungle below.

Atkins ran to the edge, Gutsy, Mercy and Porgy hard on his heels. Nellie came running up, in time to see the tank go over the edge. She screamed. Gazette wrapped his arms around her, not so much for comfort as restraint.

Atkins stopped, feet from the lip, and cautiously stuck his head out over the edge. A few loose rocks broke away and tumbled down. "Oh, bloody Nora!"

"Jesus!"

"Buggerin' hell!"

The drop wasn't sheer but it was a very steep camber. They could see the twin furrows gouged down the escarpment as if the *Ivanhoe* had been dragged down into hell, fighting all the way. It was possible to track its path down the crater-side, where it had torn trees and plants from their roots before it crashed down through the canopy hundreds of feet below, to be swallowed by the jungle beneath.

Atkins felt sick and lighted-headed. His whole body sagged.

The tank was gone.

Above, the last of the Kreothe drifted sedately over the crater, and the sun began to peer out from behind them, a gleam of sunlight reflecting off the edge of its translucent gas sac.

INTERLUDE SIX
Letter from Private Thomas Atkins
to Flora Mullins

21st March 1917

Dearest Flora,

For a while today, I thought I had lost you forever, but the great big world keeps turning and showed me there is always hope. Sometimes in our darkest moments, that is hard to remember. It's funny how the smallest and most insignificant of things can give you hope. Today I found it in a lost button.

And for the rest of the day, we tried to winkle something from its shell, had our fortunes told and were stung by some jellyfish. It sounds like a day at the seaside and I wish it had been. I bet I'd look pretty dapper in a blazer, straw boater and you on my arm as we stroll along the pier.

Having said we'd found the tank, we lost it again. I don't think Lieutenant Everson is going to be very pleased. Nothing to do now but go and face the music, if there's any music left to face.

I don't even know what I'll find when I get back to camp. I have never been so far from it. The thought that it might have vanished and left me here tortures me.

All of us live in daily fear of that, whether we speak about it or not. But then, I suppose that's selfish. Folks back home live in fear of their worlds vanishing, too. In many cases, theirs have. Too many good men have not returned from the trenches. I vow to you now, Flora, I will not be one of them.

Ever yours,
Thomas

CHAPTER TWENTY-ONE
"Each Night, After a Fight..."

ATKINS FELT NUMB.

He stared down into the crater, not sure what to do next, hardly able to believe that the tank had gone at all. Cecil, Norman and Nellie all tried calling out, for Mathers, for Alfie, hoping for some reply, some sign of life. They shouted until their voices were hoarse. There was no reply but the sound of the jungle.

The tank crew had an urgent whispered discussion, and finally pushed a reticent Reggie towards the Fusiliers. He straightened himself up, cleared his throat and marched over to Atkins. "We've had a talk and we've agreed, we have to get down there," he informed him.

"How?" said Atkins, with a shrug. "We have little rope, certainly not enough to reach the bottom. And even if you do get to the bottom, what are you going to do? You can't get the tank back up here again. There nothing we can do."

Nellie strode up to him. "It's not just a tank, there are people down there who might be alive, or had you forgotten?"

"No. Have you forgotten we've lost three of our mates for this bloody mob? Have you? Because I haven't."

Her face clouded over. "But you *know* yours are dead, Corporal. You saw them. We haven't. Have you any idea what it's like to have someone listed as 'missing'?"

Her rebuke stung. Atkins thought of his brother, William, lost since the Big Push back in June. He thought of his mam and Flora and how they felt and his cheeks briefly flushed for shame. He tried again, in a more conciliatory tone. "I'm sorry, but it doesn't change anything. We were sent to bring the tank back for a reason. I have my orders. I have to report back to Lieutenant Everson, if he's still there to report to." He cast a meaningful glance at Chandar, who hung well back from the crater's edge, chittering to itself, and fiddling with its damn tassels.

"Oh well, orders!" Nellie gave up, threw her arms up in disgust and walked away.

Reggie coughed. "We're staying here. There must be some way to help the Sub and Alfie. We were wrong about him. Stayed trying to save the Sub and the tank. More than any of us did."

Atkins placed a hand on Reggie's upper arm, an awkward gesture of comfort. "We'll return with help. We'll bring teams of sappers. If we can salvage the *Ivanhoe*, we will."

"Then I'm staying here, too." said Nellie belligerently. "Alfie could still be alive. They could be injured."

Atkins was torn. He would do the same if it were his pals. Still, he had to get back to the trenches if he were to return with help. "Napoo, stay here with her. We'll go back to the encampment, if it's still there, and get what help we can. We can leave you a couple of rifles and a little ammo. Don't do anything stupid while we're gone."

Hesitantly, Jack came over to Atkins. "Before you go, the Sub asked me to give you a message."

Atkins looked at him blankly. "Message?"

"He saw Jeffries' trail. Said it led to the crater. Said something about a place that doesn't exist, that Chatts is feared of? It didn't make much sense to me, but he said you'd know what he meant."

Atkins looked at the Chatt again. This whole journey the damn thing had been talking in riddles. He went over to Chandar. "What is that place?" he demanded, waving an arm airily in the direction of the crater.

Chandar looked at him, its mouth parts knitting the words. "It is forbidden. It does not exist."

He rounded on the Chatt. "Yes, so you keep bloody saying, but *why* do you keep saying it? What is it you're not telling me? Why is it forbidden? Answer me!"

Chandar hissed, torn between postures of threat and submission. "It... it is Nazhkadarr, the Scentless Place. The place that should not be. The Burri of the Fallen..."

Atkins shook his head slowly, his anger now a slow burning fuse. "Talk sense! For God's sake, talk sense, just for once!" The discussion was attracting attention now; Gutsy moved in.

"It is the Crater of... Croatoan," it hissed quietly. "That is why. That is why it is forbidden to us. It is heresy, a blasphemous stain on the world GarSuleth wove for his children. It should not exist."

"Why the hell didn't you tell us?"

Chandar reared up on its legs, its mandibles scissoring. "Because the last time an Urmen of the Tohmii asked about the fallen one, half of Khungarr was laid waste." It noticed Gazette pointing his rifle at it and sank back down again. "Your capture of me was no accident. I was sent to seek out the intentions of the Tohmii." Stung by the revelation,

Atkins listened as Chandar carried on. "Your acts of Kurda have cast an anchor line of fate. Between this One and you something is being woven. The question remains, what?"

Atkins looked out across the vast jungle-choked depression. "The Croatoan Crater?" No wonder Jeffries had come this way. "What's down there?"

Chandar became meek and evasive again. "Nothing must enter the crater, nothing must leave. That is the will of GarSuleth."

Atkins could feel the short fuse of his anger burning down. He balled his fists. "Gutsy, get this... thing away from me until it decides to talk some bloody sense!"

Chandar turned as Gutsy escorted it away. "Nothing must enter, nothing must leave!"

"Yes, well it's a bit bloody late for that!" snapped Atkins as he looked at the crumbled lip and the track marks left by the tank.

Mercy steered Atkins away. "We're all a little tense, mate. I think we should just go. The sooner we leave, the sooner we can come back with help."

Atkins' eyes never left the Chatt while Mercy spoke, but he nodded in agreement.

1 SECTION WAS ready to depart. They had made a litter and were carrying all the jars and amphorae of sacred scents they had managed to salvage from Nazarr before its collapse. There were more than they thought and less than Chandar would have liked. He fussed over them, adding torn crushed leaves to the roughly woven wattle frame that Napoo had constructed, as packing to prevent them from breaking on the long journey back. Atkins, still angry, avoided Chandar, although the Chatt was coming back with them. Everson ought to hear what it had to say.

Atkins went over to where Jack and the other tank crew, Reggie, Cecil, Norman and Wally, waited with Napoo and Nellie. Atkins held out his hand. Jack took it. "We'll be back as soon as we can. Napoo's a good man. Look after Nellie."

Jack nodded. "We'll be here."

He stepped over to Nellie. "Look, I'm sorry. But we have to do this. We'll be back in four or five days."

Nellie nodded. "Tell Edith I'm fine."

Atkins and the remains of his section set off. Pot Shot, his head swathed in bandages under his now-lucky battle bowler, insisted on making the journey with them, even though Nellie was just as adamant he should stay and rest. "I'm hard-headed," he said, tapping his bandaged skull. "My place is with these reprobates. You don't know the trouble they'd get into without me."

They followed the paths through the jungle, bypassing the Gilderra enclave.

"Shouldn't think they'd be too pleased to see us," said Mercy.

"We got rid of the evil spirit, didn't we?" said Porgy.

"And the tankers cost 'em one shaman and got their replacement killed. I expect Napoo would have something to say about that," Pot Shot informed them.

"Oh, aye," said Porgy. "No doubt."

Atkins had plenty of time to mull over all that had happened in the past few days, and figure out how he was going to tell Lieutenant Everson.

He worried about the awful truth behind the Bleeker Party. It was a terrible secret he was asking his men to keep and he wondered what kind of price it would exact, not just on 1 Section, but also on the rest of the Battalion. That burden would soon belong to Lieutenant Everson.

But there was hope, too. Well, hope of a kind. He felt the button in his pocket, rubbed his thumb over the raised casting. Atkins had to believe there was a way back to Flora—and his child. He had to put that right, even though it might cost him everything else.

Right now, though, the fear of not knowing what he'd find back at camp drove Atkins on, and he kept the pace up. They had done forced marches before and nobody complained this time. They all wanted to get back, even though none of them knew what was waiting for them.

EDITH BELL WAS in the Bird Cage with Stanton, the orderly. They were gathering up the personal possessions of all those killed by the parasitic infection, the patients she had nursed for the past three months. The place was vacant, depressing and forlorn now. Blankets and discarded mess kits littered the ground. The emptiness was heartbreaking.

She saw Captain Lippett making his way across the parade ground towards the compound. He was the last person she wanted to see right now. She put another blanket on the pile and pretended not to notice him.

He approached and looked at her in that brusque surgeon's matter-of-fact manner. "I thought you ought to know, Nurse, Miller died less than an hour ago."

Edith replied in a similarly sterile manner. "Thank you, Doctor." Edith had steeled herself for the news since she had brought him in, but you always hoped. Thinking that was it, she returned to her task.

However, Lippett had more to say. "I couldn't have operated without killing him. We have no anaesthetic. I'm reduced to the level of a Crimean butcher here, which is a wholly unsatisfactory state of affairs, as I'm sure you'll admit. And even if I could have removed those parasites from his bowels, I doubt whether I could have done the same to those attached to his nervous system without inflicting great damage and pain."

"I understand that, Doctor."

Lippett opened his arms. "I'm not an ogre, Nurse. Being stranded here, trying to be everything to everyone... I wanted to be a surgeon, not an army butcher. I can't do everything and I realise I need staff who can think for themselves, who see things I can't. Fenton tells me I have such a woman in you, should I but care to listen."

His openness took Edith aback. Her reaction must have shown on her face.

He coughed to cover his discomfort. "This is a new situation for all of us, Nurse Bell, and something we're going to have to learn to cope with."

She wasn't sure whether he was talking about their general circumstances, here on the planet, or more specifically, his having to listen to a nurse for once. Either way, she gracefully accepted the compliment.

"On another note, Nurse, if you're right, and this neurasthenia is the result of emotional shock, then we shall doubtless have more of these cases as men fail to cope. The war may no longer affect them, but this hell of a world may, and we can't send them down the line for convalescence so there is no relief from it. If you want more responsibility, I'd like you to set up a special ward for them. None of this barbed wire, eh? At least that way they won't come back to you more injured than when they left if they escape." Lippett smiled stiffly. He was clearly uncomfortable with the situation. "Now if you'll excuse me, I must go and report my findings to Lieutenant Everson."

Edith curtseyed. "Yes, Doctor."

Despite her grief, she walked away taller and straighter, with a renewed vitality she hadn't felt in a long time. She took a deep breath and smiled. She already had ideas.

WALKING ACROSS THE fractured plain, back towards the canyon, Atkins and 1 Section saw the unmistakable shape of Tulliver's aeroplane above, no doubt searching for them. Atkins frowned. Everson must be anxious if he allowed Tulliver up in the air. The pilot waggled his wings in response to their frantic hat waving and headed home. It was a cheering sight. If nothing else, it meant the encampment was still there. It hadn't vanished back to Earth without them.

On the other hand, it dismayed Atkins. Everson would know now that they didn't have the tank with them and that failure ate away at him.

Atkins and the others were shocked when they came over the valley head and looked down into the encampment. He had to be honest, he wasn't quite sure what to expect, but to see the churned and trampled ground below them was quite a blow. Even Chandar let out long low hiss at the sight of the devastated trenches.

At first, Atkins thought it was the result of the battle with the Khungarrii, and then he saw the burning pyres of animal corpses and the body of the dead Kreothe, splayed along the valley like a washed up jellyfish at low tide. The veldt beyond, what they could see of it, had fared little better. However, there was no sign of the Chatt army that had occupied it scant days ago. He shook his head in disbelief. Myriad questions tumbled through his mind and he was eager for answers.

As they made their way down the hillside and along the valley towards the encampment, Atkins saw fatigue parties at work, repairing trenches and wire.

"Eh, up. It's King Arthur returned from his latest quest," jeered one working party NCO. "Found the Holy Grail then, have you lad?"

"One of your admirers?" asked Porgy.

SERGEANT HOBSON MET Atkins and escorted him straight to Battalion HQ. "Good to have you back, lad."

"Glad to be back, Sarn't. What happened here?"

"What hasn't happened, more like. I'm sure the lieutenant will tell you all about it. He's anxious to hear your report."

Atkins avoided Hobson's eyes. "I expect Tulliver has told him."

"Maybe, but he's waiting to hear it from you."

Atkins knocked on the doorjamb to the battalion HQ dugout.

"Come!"

He stepped inside and stood to attention before the lieutenant's desk. Everson was writing in the Battalion War Journal; he'd have a lot more to write once Atkins had given his report. "At ease, Corporal." He finished writing, and then looked up. "Where's my tank, Atkins?" Everson could tell from the corporal's face that it wasn't good news. He sighed. "You'd better tell me everything."

Atkins did. He told him about the canyon and the mysterious metal wall. He explained about the Gilderra enclave and the evil spirit, but kept back Mathers' worst excesses.

Everson nodded and waved them away. "It's all right. I can't say I'm surprised. Mathers always struck me as a bit windy. Hid it well, though."

Atkins frowned. "Sir?"

"We had an infection here. Some sort of parasite, the MO says. It affected the shell-shocked; their weakened minds were apparently more suggestible to the parasites. The infected act as if they're possessed. I suppose they were. They're all dead, now, the shell-shocked. Seems this parasite needs its hosts to be eaten by the those Kreothe things in order to 'continue its life cycle' or some such." Everson paused and let out a sigh. "Lippett thinks the parasites' main host is probably the Chatts and *they* wouldn't have been infected if they hadn't marched here to fight us, foraging for food on the way.

Atkins felt he was in some bizarre estaminet bad news contest. He told Everson about the ruined edifice of the Nazarii and the tentacled creature, and their Kreothe. They both assumed it must have been the same shoal. Everson countered with the stampede.

Then Atkins produced the Bleeker Party's bible and the journal from his haversack. Everson flicked through them with a wonder that transmuted to fear as the ramifications set in.

"Dear God," he said. "We weren't the first?"

"It doesn't look like it, sir."

"And they all died here?"

"As far as I can tell, yes, sir. They didn't find a way back."

Everson looked at him in alarm. "You've told your men to keep this a secret?"

"Yes, sir. And Miss Abbott. I thought you'd best know what to do with the information, sir."

Everson ran his fingers across the battered journal, as if to make sure it was real. He was silent for a while, and then he looked up. "You did the right thing, Atkins. Leave this with me. At the moment, things round here are a powder keg. I'm not sure how the men might take the news. I'd prefer to have something positive to say to them. Anything positive, really."

Finally, Atkins told him about the *Ivanhoe*.

"So it's lost, then," said Everson.

"No, sir. We know exactly where it is, we just can't reach it. I believe the technical word is ditched, sir."

"And where is it?" asked Everson. "Exactly."

Atkins took a deep breath and dealt his trump card. "The Croatoan Crater, sir."

Everson felt as if he had physically had the wind knocked from him. He sat back in his chair. "The *Croatoan* Crater?" He hardly dared voice his next thought. In the end, he didn't have to.

Atkins fished about in his tunic top pocket and pulled out a bloodstained scrap of khaki. He tossed it onto the desk. Everson looked down at the button attached to it, and then up at Atkins, for an explanation. "We believe it belonged to Jeffries, sir. I believe he was at the Nazarii edifice on his way to the crater. For what reason, we can only guess. But to my mind the name is a big clue. Along with this." He produced the tattered paper with the Croatoan symbol and placed it face down, revealing the hastily copied symbols from the edifice.

"I've seen this before, or something like it," said Everson, leafing through Jeffries' coded journal. "Aha." He stabbed a finger on a page and placed the book down next to the paper. The arrangement of symbols was identical.

"What do they mean?" asked Atkins.

Everson's shoulders sagged. "I have no idea." He looked up at Atkins in earnest. "But the Chatt, Corporal, this Chandar. Did you find out anything more from *that*?"

Atkins exhaled heavily. Where to start? "Half truths, prophecies and riddles, sir, but it seems there are factions who don't agree with Sirigar's Urman culling policy, Chandar among them. Factions that might look on us favourably, especially since we've come back with some holy scent texts from Nazarr. Chandar seems very keen to return with them to Khungarr. Thinks they might start a revolution, sir."

"In the meantime they're ours, are they?"

"Yes, sir."

"Right, well, let's get them somewhere safe; keep them under guard until I find out what best to do with them." Everson got up from his chair and began to escort Atkins to the dugout door. "Thank you, Atkins. It can't have been easy, especially losing the tank. It wasn't your fault."

"About the tank, sir. We've left the tank crew, Miss Abbott and Napoo out there, trying to do what they can."

"We'll organise a salvage party and, while we're at it, we'll take a patrol to check out this mystery wall."

"But how are we going to raise the tank, sir, even it is in one piece?"

Everson smiled. "Don't worry about that, Atkins. We've got something that'll do the job, believe me. Now go and get yourself some food and a rest. You and your men have earned it."

Everson sat back in his chair, feeling strangely pleased with their new situation. Since they'd been here, they had done nothing but react to things. Now he had enough information to act, to do something here. The question was, what?

IN THE JUNGLE of the Croatoan Crater, half-buried by the torn and shredded undergrowth that caught and halted its headlong rush to destruction, the great ironclad ticked and creaked, like a wounded beast gone to ground, its monstrous roar, for the moment, silenced.

THE END

THE
ALLEYMAN

"When ants unite, they can skin a lion."

—Iranian proverb

ACKNOWLEDGEMENTS

I WOULD LIKE to thank all those people who have helped bring the true story of 'The Broughtonthwaite Mates' to light. As ever, I am indebted to the members of the Broughtonthwaite Historical Society for their tireless efforts in collating the new information that has come to light since the publication of the first book. I would also like to thank Robert Scotton of the Media Museum North, for an insight into the work and career of the kinematographer Oliver Hepton, including his early pre-World War One erotica. I am grateful to Elizabeth Thompson of the National Archives for helping to trace the RFC service record of Lieutenant James Tulliver. I must also thank Jon, Jenni, David, Ben, Simon and Michael at Abaddon Books. Without their enthusiasm and unstinting support for this project, it wouldn't have happened. Once again, I must thank my wife, Penny, for her continuing love and support. Finally, I would like to thank all those descendents of the men of the 13th Battalion of the Pennine Fusiliers who spoke to me, still hoping that the truth about the fate of their loved ones will come to light.

Pat Kelleher

13TH BATTALION PENNINE FUSILIERS COMPANY PERSONNEL

Battalion HQ.
   CO: 2nd Lieutenant John. C. Everson
   2CO: Sergeant Herbert Gerald Hobson
   Company Quartermaster Sergeant Archibald Slacke
   Pte. Henry *'Half Pint'* Nicholls (batman)
   Royal Army Chaplain: Father Arthur Rand (CF4, 'Captain')
   War Office Kinematographer Oliver Hepton

Signals
   Corporal Arthur Riley
   Pte. Peter Buckley
   Pte. Richard Tonkins

'C' Company

No 1 Platoon
   CO: Lieutenant Morgan

No. 2 Platoon
   CO: 2nd Lieutenant Palmer

1 Section
   IC: Lance Corporal Thomas *'Only'* Atkins
   Pte. Harold *'Gutsy'* Blood
   Pte. Wilfred Joseph *'Mercy'* Evans
   Pte. George *'Porgy'* Hopkiss
   Pte. Leonard *'Pot-Shot'* Jellicoe
   Pte. David Samuel *'Gazette'* Otterthwaite

RAMC
Regimental Aid Post
    RMO: Captain Grenville Lippett

Red Cross Nurses
    Sister Betty Fenton
    Sister Edith Bell
    Driver Nellie Abbott (First Aid Nursing Yeomanry)

Orderlies
    Pte. Edgar Stanton
    Pte. Edward Thompkins

Stretcher Bearer
    Pte. Jenkins

Machine Gun Corps (Heavy Section) 'I' Company

I-5 HMLS *Ivanhoe*
    CO: 2nd Lieutenant Arthur Alexander Mathers
    Pte. Wally Clegg (Driver)
    Pte. Alfred Perkins (Gearsman)
    Pte. Norman Bainbridge (Gunner)
    Pte. Jack Tanner (Gunner)
    Pte. Reginald Lloyd (Loader/ Machine Gunner)
    Pte. Cecil Nesbit (Loader / Machine Gunner)

D Flight 70 Squadron: Sopwith 1 ½ Strutter
    Lieutenant James Robert Tulliver (pilot)
    Corporal Jack Maddox (observer)

For Elliott and Miles

PREFACE
"Keep the Home Fires Burning..."

THE BRITISH OFFICIAL History of the Great War, *Military Operations: France and Belgium, 1916 Volume II (1938)* simply states that on the 1st November 1916, the nine hundred men of 13th Battalion of the Pennine Fusiliers went over the top at dawn to attack a German position in Harcourt Wood on the Somme. They advanced into a gas cloud and vanished, leaving a crater nearly half a mile wide and eighty feet deep. The official explanation was a mass explosion of German mines dug under the British positions using an experimental high explosive. This is still the official position.

And it would have remained that way, had not a chance find in a French field by a farmer, ten years later, sparked a controversy that exists to this day and led to the one of the greatest mysteries of the First World War.

Known as the Lefeuvre Find, it contained several rusted film canisters of undeveloped silver nitrate film, along with, amongst other things, journals, letters, keepsakes, notes and what purported to be the Battalion War Diary. When developed, the black and white silent film—believed to have been shot by Oliver Hepton, a War Office kinematographer who had been assigned to film the attack—showed the Pennines apparently alive and well and on an alien world.

The film was dismissed by the Government as a hoax, playing on the hopes of the relatives and loved ones of those missing. However, there were those who believed its provenance and campaigned for the truth. Some of their descendants still do.

It became clear from the items recovered in the Lefeuvre Find that there were other casualties of the Harcourt Event, and that the phenomenon even extended up into the atmosphere. The Hepton footage (HF232) shows a member of the Royal Flying Corps, who has since been identified as Lieutenant James Tulliver, who was presumed to have been shot down and killed and whose body and plane wreckage were never found.

The First World War was one of the first truly technological wars, where industrialisation changed the nature of warfare. Manned flight was barely ten years old at the outbreak of the war, and within months, it was being used to kill. The war in the air developed into an arms race, with technological advances rendering machines and engine designs obsolete within months, as the push for advantages in speed, height and manoeuvrability drove huge leaps in innovation.

To those at home, the war in the air was a romantic notion that the RFC fostered. It seemed like an echo of a previous age, of chivalrous knights duelling in single combat. The mixture of romance, adventure and technology caught the public imagination, and many adventure story magazines of the time featured tales of derring-do in the air. None more so than *Great War Science Stories,* which featured a series of highly colourful pulp tales about *Tulliver, Ace of the Alien Skies* as he battled everything from flying dinosaurs to robotic sky pirates until the magazine ceased publication in 1932.

This third volume of the *No Man's World* series continues the account of the Pennine Fusiliers' true fate. It is based on the accounts of those who were there, where possible, although some events are inferred. All major events have been drawn from primary sources, including the papers of Arthur Cooke, author of *The Harcourt Crater: Hoax or Horror,* personal letters, and entries from the Battalion War Diary, as well as from the Flight Log of Lieutenant James Tulliver. This is now in the hands of a private collector in Australia, who wishes to remain anonymous but for the truth to be known.

1st November 2016 will see the one-hundredth anniversary of the disappearance of the Pennines. Renewed interest in the fate of the Broughtonthwaite Mates is constantly bringing new evidence and facts to light and so, while their hometown of Broughtonthwaite prepares to commemorate the centenary of the Heroes of Harcourt, we may yet finally discover the true fate of the Pennine Fusiliers.

Pat Kelleher
Broughtonshaw
Easter, 2012

PROLOGUE

"They Told Me He Had Gone That Way..."

THE GREAT BATRACHIAN ironclad tumbled into the crater, its tracks gouging broad ruts as it slid down the steep slope towards the tangle of alien jungle below. Poisonous barbed vines lashed its ironbound hide as the *Ivanhoe* ploughed through them, ripping them out at the roots and dragging them along with it.

Trills, howls, roars and whoops of alarm reached a crescendo as the intruder blundered through the undergrowth.

The great steering tail broke free and tumbled through the jungle on its own lazy trajectory, spewing hydraulic fluid as it spun.

The *Ivanhoe* plunged on, every impact slowing its momentum, the ironclad only coming to a halt as it collided with the buttress root of a huge trunk with a thunderous, hollow *thud*.

Overhead, the canopy thrashed as startled creatures bolted in terror and a tense silence descended. The jungle seemed to pause.

No predatory growl rose from the intruder to challenge them.

Half hidden by the dappled shade and torn foliage, the intruder clicked and groaned. Large leafy fronds sprouted from its tracks, caught in the track wheels. Shredded leaves and broken boughs lay strewn over its hull. The drivers' visors hung shut and the ironclad's great guns lay listless and bowed.

It was just another dead thing. Nothing to fear.

The sounds of the jungle began to trickle back into the silence, timid at first, but slowly gaining in confidence. Soon, the raucous chorus resumed.

Emboldened, scavengers loped through the undergrowth towards the ditched ironclad, perhaps sensing easy prey.

Inside the belly of the tank, Alfie Perkins opened his eyes.

Although the festoon lights had died, shafts of light punched their way in through pistol ports, boring down through the smoky haze that filled the compartment, criss-crossing the dark space like searchlights seeking out a Zeppelin.

He coughed as he breathed in the smoke. It smelled of burnt grease. He dragged himself into a sitting position, so his back was against the sponson door. The spasm of coughing set off a chain reaction of other pains, which only subsided when he stopped hacking. He was slumped in the gangway. He looked up to see the starboard six-pounder gun and Hotchkiss machine gun, its spent cartridge casings rolling around him with a tinkle of brass as he moved.

To his right, filling the centre of the compartment, the huge Daimler engine ticked to itself as it cooled.

His hand was covered in blood that had collected in a sticky pool on the gangway planks. In a surge of panic, he checked his body. His forehead felt tender, swollen. He shifted his weight and sharp pain flooded his right leg. His hand groped down the leg of his coveralls. Another jangle of pain. Broken, probably. At least he'd still got his leg. For the moment. He felt something warm and sticky below his knee. It was blood, but not enough to cause the sticky pool around him.

The blood that lay thick and pooled about him on the gangway wasn't his.

He saw a crumpled shape further up the gangway.

"Lieutenant?"

There was no answer. He waited a moment for his nerves to stop screaming, and for his eyes to adjust. Lieutenant Mathers, the Tank Commander, was crumpled on the starboard gangway, having fallen from the commander's seat at the front, his leg twisted and caught awkwardly under the bucket seat.

"Sir?"

There was no answer. Alfie struggled to recall what had happened. It would be easier if the pain in his head would stop. The last thing he remembered was the fire extinguisher flying towards him.

Frozen pictures, like shell-flash afterimages, burst in his mind. The *Ivanhoe* toppling over the edge of the crater. Falling. Mathers. A gunshot. The pyrene fire extinguisher. Blackness.

He looked at the slumped body in the gangway. He saw the glint of the Webley revolver and the sheen on the blood as it spread from Mathers' head. Alfie remembered now. Possessed by some alien parasite, in a moment of lucidity, the lieutenant had shot himself.

Alfie tried moving again, but couldn't find the strength. He searched around, his hand groping among the scattered ammo boxes and tools within reach. It closed around a wrench. Steeling himself for a moment, he banged on the side of the sponson with what strength he had and yelled with as much gusto as he could muster.

"Help! In here! Anybody?"

Panting, he waited for a reply. None came.

He tried again and again, each time weaker and with less conviction that there was anyone outside to hear. Eventually he lost his balance and his broken leg twisted. He screamed, and when the pain had passed, he closed his eyes.

His voice low now, almost like a prayer: "Anybody."

He woke up. Minutes later? Hours? He didn't know. The only thing he knew was that he didn't want the *Ivanhoe* to become his tomb, as Mathers had known it would become his.

Alfie breathed deeply of what faint traces of petrol fruit fumes were left to dull the pain, and then hauled himself to his feet. He waited for the nausea to pass. He pulled the handle on the sponson hatch and pushed. The hatch gave a little, but didn't open. He put his shoulder to it and shoved. It gave a little more, but recoiled back. There was something against it outside, preventing it from opening.

Feeling his strength ebb, he kept his weight on his good foot and shoved again. This time light briefly flooded the compartment, and he could see a mass of russet leaves.

Gathering his strength, he shoved the hatch again, roaring. This time it gave, swinging open. Alfie lost his balance, tripped over the lip of the hatch and fell out, screaming as he caught his broken leg.

His fall was cushioned by the tangle of shrubbery in which the tank had come to rest. He shook his head, trying to clear the fug of pain that threatened to smother him.

A deep, mucus-addled panting filled the air. Alfie felt waves of warm, foetid breath wash over him.

He twisted his body to see, barely twelve feet away, a huge mouth, lips pulled back in a snarl, long serrated incisors dripping with drool. From deep within its thick matted pelt, two dark eyes regarded him with seeming contempt as it crouched on its six legs, pondering.

A growl began building in the back of its throat.

Never taking its eyes off Alfie, the creature let out a roar and pounced.

CHAPTER ONE
"At Some Disputed Barricade..."

THE SMALL, FLIMSY flying machine puttered across bright blue space, defying possibility; the persistent putter of its tiny engine echoed through the vast vault of the alien sky, belying its small size, like a skylark rising to sing.

In the forward cockpit, Lieutenant James Tulliver wiped the speckled build-up of oil from his goggles and revelled in the cold air. Fresh and sharp, it made him feel more alive than he ever did on the ground. Beneath the scarf wrapped round the lower part of his face, a broad grin spread until it almost ached. This was why he'd joined the Royal Flying Corps. At a thousand feet, the two-seater Sopwith 1½ Strutter had the alien sky all to itself, while winged creatures wheeled and soared on unseen currents below.

Lieutenant Everson had sent him up on a recce flight out to Croatoan Crater to check on the stranded tank crew. It was a simple flight. It had to be; compasses didn't work on this Godforsaken world. He had to fly by sight, from landmark to landmark, and that meant keeping below the cloud cover as flocks of cumulus drifted along overhead. While Everson rightly valued the aeroplane, he was as a needy child with a cock linnet in a cage who never let it spread it wings. Tulliver resented that. What the hell use was a grounded pilot? Granted, the alien sky wasn't without its dangers. There were jabberwocks, mountain-dwelling wing predators, and the huge atmospheric jellyfish-like Kreothe and a dozen other vicious air raptors, any one of which could reduce his bus to kindling and rags. But then, dodging airbursts of Archie on the Western Front hadn't exactly been a joyride either.

On top of that, for the last several days, dud weather had kept him grounded. Still, he was up now. He felt a tap on his shoulder. It was Maddocks, his observer-come-gunner, seconded from Lieutenant Baxter's Machine Gun Section. It always paid to have two pairs of eyes up here, although his own were keener than most; things seemed brighter, sharper, as though he had just got spectacles after being myopic for years.

It was all thanks to the petrol fruit fuel the bus now ran on. Some hapless Tommy had distilled it in secret. The resulting alcoholic concoction proved to have undesirable side effects, and the commanders had declared it unfit for human consumption, although it did solve their dwindling petrol supply problem. It was another bone of contention between Everson and himself. Ever since they had discovered that the crew of the ironclad tank *HMLS Ivanhoe* had suffered from the psychoactive effects of its fumes, Everson had been more than a little suspicious of Tulliver, and had him up before Captain Lippett, the Medical Officer. Tulliver had explained at great length that the confinement of the crew within the tank for long periods had increased their exposure to the fuel vapours and heightened its psychotropic effects. He, meanwhile, was in the open air and travelling at almost one hundred miles an hour. Whatever vapours were expelled from the engine were whipped away by the aerial winds. The MO's examination seemed to bear out this hypothesis, and reluctantly Everson had let the matter drop.

Tulliver decided to keep his new acuity to himself. He didn't want to be grounded, and besides, what harm could it do?

Maddocks was pointing down. A couple of hundred feet below them, a pair of jabberwocks were engaged in territorial aerial combat, luckily too busy to notice the Sopwith.

Ahead, Tulliver could make out the depressed green circle of the jungle-filled Croatoan Crater. Almost a mile across and over two hundred yards deep, it was darker than the surrounding jungle, its bowl-like depression obvious and ominous. The strange strip of faded, discoloured foliage that cut across it was quite marked from this perspective. It didn't seem quite natural to Tulliver's eyes.

They came in low over the jungle surrounding the great depression. Without warning, the air came alive with cracks and bangs, like gunshots. Tulliver pulled back on the stick, gaining height.

Across the jungle canopy, huge vine-like things—whipperwills, Maddocks called them, anywhere from twenty to nearly a hundred feet long, sensitive to a combination of air movement and shadow— cracked above the trees, like whips. The fast-moving shadow of the Sopwith set them snapping ravenously behind them, like a living wake.

The treetop field of whipperwills gave way to the ruins of the Nazarii edifice, which had belonged to a long-dead colony of Chatts, the race of intelligent arthropods that dominated this planet. It now lay completely destroyed after the Fusiliers' encounter with the Dulgur that inhabited it, and which had cost them the tank. The ironclad *Ivanhoe* now lay scuppered somewhere down in the crater. The crew had refused to abandon it and the two members that had gone over with it.

Tulliver banked the plane and circled over the brush leading to the lip of the crater. With his eyesight heightened by the petrol fruit fumes, they were easy to spot. He waggled his wings. Six small people waved back. A seventh Tulliver took to be the Urman guide, Napoo. He seemed to be intent on some kind of work, squatting on the ground, ignoring the plane. Tulliver turned and nodded to Maddocks, who leant over the side and dropped the tin. As it fell, he saw the tank crew run towards it and then lost sight of them as he pulled out of the bank and set a course back to camp, following the line of the Strip that fortuitously pointed back to the trenches.

"Hold onto your lunch!" he bellowed out over his shoulder.

Tulliver performed a few rolls, simply for the joy of it, and then pulled the stick back, climbing up to meet a small flock of clouds. The bus soared over the bright white fairy-tale landscape. Up here, above the clouds, Tulliver could almost believe he was back on Earth again...

Barely five months ago, on the first of November, 1916, at six twenty ack emma, he and his observer, Hodgeson, had taken off with the flight from the aerodrome at Fine Villas, along with Captain Parkhurst and Biffer, with orders to take down a German observation kite balloon behind the lines near Harcourt Wood.

Thousands of feet below, flashes of artillery fire glittered like fallen sequins as they bombarded the already pitted and pocked German positions.

As they closed in on the observation balloon, the Hun observer in the basket beneath spotted them, and his ground crew began winching the tethered sausage balloon down.

Then Tulliver saw the two Hun Albatros D2s protecting it.

Parkhurst, red flight-commander's streamers trailing from his outer wing spars, gestured that they should break and try to gain the higher ground.

Tulliver pulled back on the stick and indicated to Hodgeson to keep his eyes peeled. Hodgeson, as well as being the observer, also had a Lewis gun attached to the rear of his cockpit, mounted on a ring that allowed him freedom of fire, unlike Tulliver's forward-facing gun.

Tulliver raced after an Albatros as it tried to escape them when suddenly, from round the huge mountain of cloud high above them, swooped a third.

A burst of machine gun fire from the new machine raked across Parkhurst's Strutter. Tulliver saw smoke streak from its engine before an urgent thump on his back from Hodgeson alerted him to the fact that there was another Hun on their tail. While the 1½ Strutter outgunned the Albatros, the Hun machine was quicker and more manoeuvrable.

Tulliver banked hard to avoid a stream of tracer bullets and caught a glimpse of the Hun in his rear-view mirror. Hodgeson let out short bursts from the Lewis gun as the Albatros dived, trying to get below the Sopwith.

He felt the thud of bullets sewing themselves along the fuselage. Behind him, the rattle of Hodgeson's machine gun ceased. He risked a glance over his shoulder to see Hodgeson slumped in the rear cockpit, his head lolling back.

"Hodge!" he yelled. "Hodge, old man?" There was no answer.

Above, Biffer was trying to shake off another Hun. Tulliver went after it. He came up below the Albatros and, without pity, strafed the machine. Gone were the days of playing the game, of chivalric aerial jousts. These days it was kill or be killed.

It went down, threading a smoky trail across the sky.

There was just the glory hound to worry about now. He liked to hang high and dive. Tulliver searched up and around for it, but everything seemed wrong, even the clouds. His compass began spinning wildly. The engine sputtered, misfiring. Try as he might, he could no longer find the horizon. He found himself suspended in a featureless grey miasma that billowed sluggishly around the bus. All sense of movement, direction and speed ceased.

A deep bass rumble filled the air about him.

Turbulent currents buffeted the machine, threatening to snap off its planes.

As he fought with the spade-handled stick to regain control over the Strutter, Tulliver felt a sticky warmth in his ears and tasted the metallic tang of blood trickling from his nose and down the back of his throat. His breathing became rapid and shallow. His eyes flickered shut and lights burst against his eyelids.

The noise died and the buffeting ceased abruptly. From above, a bright, diffuse light illuminated the encompassing haze. He breathed a sigh of relief. He was in cloud, that was all. He eased the stick forward and dropped. He could get his bearing and fly back along the front line until he came to a landmark he knew.

He wasn't prepared for what he saw. Spread out below was an unfamiliar landscape: a blaze of green plain and glistening rivers with mountains in the distance. Beneath him, set in a valley that existed on no maps or aerial photographs he had ever seen, he spotted the only remnant of the world he knew: an ugly circular scab of land, pock-marked with shell holes and raked by crenellated fire trenches. A pitiful, pulverised corner of Earth on a world that was not the one from which he'd taken off...

All that was in the past now, and the alien world was momentarily hidden by the undulant white landscape around them. Vast billowing mountains rose about him and he flew his bus through their wraith-like canyons and gorges; the cloudy cartography of an insubstantial world. At play in the fields of the Lord, as his old flying instructor used to say. He chased their contours until the rigging wires sang and he let out a whoop of exhilaration that the wind snatched from his lips the moment he uttered it.

He caught sight of something out of the corner of his eye. A fleeting shadow rippled across the face of the cumulus mesa above them. Was there something else up here? A predator? He turned to Maddocks and jabbed a finger in its direction. Maddocks nodded and swung the Lewis machine gun round on its Scarff ring. Tulliver pulled on the stick and banked the bus to look for its source, his head constantly moving as he held up a hand to shield his eyes from the uninterrupted glare of the alien sun.

The shadow flitted into a narrow chasm between two great cumulus tors as he raced up the vertiginous slopes after it, scanning the shifting vista as mountains roiled up and melted together.

High above, a haze of cloud moved across the sun and the shadow vanished along with whatever cast it.

Perhaps it was just as well, Tulliver thought. Nothing up here was ever friendly. The thought that there was a fast and predatory creature existing at this altitude, sliding through cloud like a shark through water, filled him with trepidation. He'd hate to give Everson cause to curtail his flights even more.

Sooner or later, he would have to find this creature and kill it. He knew that. It might be that it was a rendezvous with death, but it was one he would not fail.

He throttled back, dropped below the drifting clouds and found himself over the Fractured Plain. It was a barren expanse of uneven cracked and tilted slabs of sand-covered bedrock that looked as if someone had smashed the landscape with a giant hammer.

He pulled out of the dive and followed the great rift face along the edge of the sunken plain until he saw the gorge that pointed the way back, its mysterious metal wall flaring in the sunlight.

As they neared the valley that the marooned Tommies now called home, Tulliver felt his mood sink with every foot of altitude he lost.

LIEUTENANT EVERSON, ACTING CO of the 13th Battalion of the Pennine Fusiliers, heard the droning approach of aeroplane.

"Back in one piece. Thank God for that!" he muttered, before returning his attention to the ongoing repair work. The circular rings of defensive fire, support and reserve trenches that now protected the precious circle of Somme soil had been pulverised in recent weeks; not by a German barrage, but by an animal stampede precipitated by a storm front of Kreothe, giant aerial creatures that drifted in herds on the wind. The decomposing corpse of one of the jellyfish-like creatures lay up the valley, not half a mile beyond the trenches, like some tentacled, demonic leviathan washed up from the depths. The men had already become accustomed to its stench, having lived in a charnel field of rotting corpses on the Somme.

Hobson, a barrel-chested platoon sergeant whose most prominent feature was an immaculately groomed handlebar moustache, followed behind him, catching anything the lieutenant missed, snatching words with other ranks about undone buttons and the other hundred and one petty breaches of Regulations that blighted the life of a private, even here.

Everson felt the weight of his responsibility keenly. He had gone to Oxford with the intention of escaping the weight of his father's expectations. With the outbreak of war, in the summer of 1914, he joined the patriotic throng of other young men in front of Broughtonthwaite Town Hall and signed on as one of Kitchener's volunteers. When his father found out, he was furious. Over his son's objections, he used his considerable influence to buy him a commission, as a Platoon Commander, in the local regiment. In seeking to avoid responsibility, Everson had found himself saddled with it. He hated his father for that.

The longer they remained here, the harder it was to maintain the men's morale. He felt the respect they held him in being eroded week by week. They wanted leadership, and all he could offer was survival. It wasn't enough. A slow drip of deserters sloped off to take their chances in the alien wilderness, whittling their numbers and further undermining the men's confidence in him.

Now, though, they had a solid lead on Lieutenant Jeffries. There was a deeply held belief among some of the ranks that Jeffries was responsible for their transportation to this hellish place, one Everson tentatively shared. Jeffries was a self-styled diabolist and rival of Aleister Crowley. He was also a con man and a wanted murderer. It was Jeffries' boast that they were here on this planet as the direct result of some obscene ritual he had conducted, powered by the staggering scale of human sacrifice on the Somme. Before he vanished, leaving them at war with the Chatts, Jeffries declared that only he knew how to get them back.

For over three months, they had searched for him and now, at last, they had a lead—the Croatoan Crater. Not only that, they also had the Chatt prisoner, Chandar, and a collection of ancient sacred scent texts unearthed at the Nazarii edifice. They could give him leverage with the Khungarrii, the local colony, on whose territory they had materialised and under whose attacks they had suffered in recent months.

With these, Everson felt he could finally *act*, rather than react. He could galvanise the men, give them a purpose other than survival. He only hoped it wouldn't be too late. First, though, he must arrange a salvage party to recover the tank if at all possible.

Following the jinking traverses of the radial communications trench, they turned left and clockwise into the support trench ring. Soldiers saluted as they passed. Some looked him in the eye with defiance. Others averted their gaze. Everson smiled briefly and nodded to all in acknowledgement.

He noticed an awkward figure, his right leg missing below the knee, hobbling on crutches round the traverse ahead of them. It was a hard figure to mistake.

"Nicholls?" The man had been in his own platoon. Half Pint, the rest called him, on account of his constant grousing. He'd lost his right leg below the knee in a battle with the Khungarrii. Anywhere else but here it would have been a Blighty wound, poor sod. Since then, Nicholls had served as his batman, at least until his new peg leg had tried to kill him. Now he was just a Category Man, unfit for active service.

"Sir?" Nicholls attempted to turn but got one of his crutches stuck in the duckboards that ran along the bottom of the trench. "Damn thing!"

"Sergeant, give him a hand."

"It's all right. I've got it, sir," said Nicholls from between gritted teeth as he gave the crutch a vicious tug. It came free. He let out a strangled cry and lurched backward against the revetment. The crutch clattered to the ground.

Everson stooped, picked it up and handed it back to him. Nicholls took it, reluctantly, avoiding his gaze.

Everson's brow furrowed with concern. "Everything all right, Nicholls?"

"Fine, sir," said the Fusilier. "Never better. Everything's tickety-boo."

Hobson leaned forward and pinned the man to the revetment with a gimlet eye, a note of threat in his voice. "Any complaints?"

Nicholls shook his head. "No, none at all, Sarn't."

"Very glad to hear it. Hop along now."

HALF PINT ROUNDED the traverse and shot a furtive glance over his shoulder, to check if he was being followed, but he'd left Lieutenant Everson and Hobson behind.

He stood at the top of a set of the dugout steps and called hoarsely down into the gloom. "It's me, Half Pint. Someone give us a bloody hand, then!"

There were footsteps and a Tommy, his tunic undone, emerged into the light at the top of the steps. "About bloody time too," he said. "Where've you been? Bains is waiting."

Ungraciously, Half Pint allowed himself to be manoeuvred down into the gloomy dugout lit by a single hurricane lamp, where he was dropped unceremoniously onto an empty bunk. Sat and stood around him were a collection of discontented Fusiliers, brought here like himself by word of mouth. He wasn't surprised to see Hepton here, either. Officially a War Office kinematographer, he always had a nose for trouble, or a "story," as he preferred to put it. His rankless officer's uniform covered by an Army Warm, he smiled affably and nodded at Half Pint as he entered. Half Pint ignored him.

"It's not easy getting round on one leg," he said, kicking out his stump to illustrate the point. "You should try it sometime."

"If I thought it was a Blighty one, then perhaps I would," said Wilson. "But it ain't any more, is it? And that's the bleedin' point, i'n't it?"

Across the way, Rutherford groaned. "Oh, don't start, Wilson."

"Look, I signed up for the duration," Wilson retorted. "I did me duty. I volunteered to defend my country. But look around you. Is this la belle France? No, it bloody isn't. As far as I'm concerned, my war is over. And so's yours, and yours," he said, jerking his chin round the dugout at the gathered Fusiliers.

"You don't know that. The lieutenant will get us back somehow," protested Carter, but there was little conviction in his voice.

"Look, if your officer bloke don't know the way home," said Rutherford, addressing Half Pint, "then I do think he should tell us. If there isn't one, if this is it, then fine. Let us make a new start, I say. Out there." He gestured vaguely at the dugout roof.

"Well, you would say that," said Hepton with a leer. "A little birdie tells me that you've got yourself a piece of Urman skirt."

"Her name's Duuma," Rutherford insisted. "And her enclave has got this place sussed. I'd rather be out there with them than stuck in these trenches, or back in a crumbling terrace, any day. Not that I could go back anyway, not after what I've seen. I wouldn't fit in there no more."

Wilson snorted with derision. "So what do you think, Bains?" he asked the silent figure in the corner.

The shadows hid Bains' features, his face only visible in the red glow of his burning gasper whenever he took a drag. Blue smoke drifted up to the roof, snaking its way through the hanging knapsacks. Sitting on an upturned ammo box, he leaned out of the shadows, his elbows resting on his knees. He was an unremarkable man with large ears and untamed eyebrows. His cheeks were speckled with flecks of dried blood, nicks from a blunt razor. He had a chevron-shaped patch on his sleeve, slightly cleaner than the khaki serge around it, where once had been a lance corporal's stripe. It was faint, but it was there if you knew where to look, and everybody in the dugout did. He took a final drag on his cigarette before dropping it on the dugout floor and grinding it into the dirt.

"We've been here nigh on five months now," he growled. "I think Everson has had his chance. He doesn't know anymore than the rest of us, I reckon. Like it or not, we're here for good, I'd say, and I've had a bellyful of doing what the Army tells me. All I want is a fair chance to make summat for myself, and I'm prepared to take it if I have to."

Monroe piped up. "But blokes have been doing that; desertin', I mean. And patrols have come back saying they've found their bodies barely miles from here."

"All right," said Bains. "But how's that any different from getting blown up by a Minnie, eh?" He looked round the gloomy dugout of malcontents and grousers. "Or ripped apart by shrapnel, or dying of a gut wound in a shell hole? We're sitting ducks if we stay here."

"But this place is all that we have left of Earth," said Cox.

"And you're really going to miss all that, are you?" said Bains. "People say the world will change after the War, if it ever ends, but I doubt it. Them as has money will still have it and them as hasn't still won't. I'm going to be no worse off here. But at least I can be me own master. And so can you. Starting right here, right now."

"Why, Bains, you're beginning to sound like a Bolshevik," said Hepton with an oily grin.

"So what do we do?" asked Cox.

"It's already being done. Word has gone out. Some of our brethren will be on sentry duty. They'll let us pass. All I ask is that if you don't join us, stand aside and let us take our demands to Everson. We just want a say in how things is run from now on, and we'll man the barricades to get it if we have to."

Half Pint heard Bains' speech with despair. Grousing was one thing, but this was another kettle of fish altogether. It had started out innocently enough—they had genuine grievances, after all—but now it seemed to be gathering a momentum all its own. Bains spoke with passion, though it wasn't altruism that was forcing his hand. He was letting his ambitions get the better of him. He hadn't lost his stripe for nothing. Bains wanted power and over the past few days he had been giving the same speech to many small discontented gatherings like this. Half Pint, his glass by nature being half empty, expected the whole thing to blow up in their faces.

"And what on earth makes you think Everson's going to listen?" needled Hepton.

Bains grinned. "He won't have a choice."

* * *

AT THE APPOINTED time, gangs of men, many with their faces covered, took advantage of the chaos caused by the mutineers, and rampaged through the trenches, and across the open ground between, in a spirit of mischief, revelling in the irresponsible respite from daily military routine.

Other men had darker motives.

Padre Rand, the army chaplain, knew the men felt lost, far from home as they were, and far from the sight of God. He knew because that was how he felt himself. However, he had his faith, or at least had rediscovered it out here. And with the largesse of the shepherd he knew he must use it to protect his flock from straying.

So it was that he found himself stood on a firestep, pleading with a mob of unruly men who sought to pass by. He raised his arms in the air, appealing for calm, but his uniform wasn't helping. Although they held no army rank, chaplains wore an officer's uniform with a dog collar and black bib.

"Let us past, Padre," a voice from the masked crowd called out. "We just want to talk to Lieutenant Everson."

The padre, middle-aged and sandy-haired, looked down at them more in sorrow than in anger. "Then why cover your faces and go armed with clubs?" he asked, attempting to look them in the eyes. "Go back to your dugouts. This isn't the way."

A large bruiser of a soldier pushed his way brusquely to the front and stood before him. "Don't be a martyr, Padre. This isn't your fight. Step down."

The padre smiled sadly and shook his head. "I'm very much afraid, my son, that it is. You're going down the wrong path. I am, for better or worse, stood at the fork in the road. You would do well to listen to me."

"Then you can't say I didn't warn you." The man pulled back his arm, drawing a gasp from the surrounding mob crowding the fire bay.

A man surged forward, ripping the kerchief away from his face as he did so, to restrain his arm. "Wilson, have you gone mad? You'll lose your name."

Wilson turned and snarled. "Take your hands off me, Rutherford."

The padre watched, startled, as the two men struggled. The soldiers around them tried to move back, away from the grappling pair, but in the cramped confines of the fire bay it wasn't possible. An arm flailed out and caught the padre on the jaw; he lost his footing and slipped, cracking his head against a revetment post.

An accusing cry went up from Wilson. "Rutherford, what have you done?"

Rutherford stood, looking shocked.

As the padre went down, the mob fled in panic, and Rutherford with them.

Beyond the trenches, the first shots rang out.

The world faded and the padre found himself sinking into darkness. There, the nightmare vision he fought to keep at bay, the one he experienced in a heathen Khungarrii ritual, waited for him...

TULLIVER TRUDGED ALONG the trenches to his dugout, lost in a moment of maudlin introspection. He still felt bitter. The RFC had fought for two years to be taken seriously by Brass who couldn't see how to use them. And now Everson was making the same mistake.

A group of rowdy Tommies filed along the kinked communication trench, singing and shouting, and jostled him from his thoughts. Some wore gas hoods, others covered their faces with scarves or kerchiefs. From all about came raucous shouts and yells. This was far from boisterous high spirits.

One man, a balaclava and scarf round his face, seized Tulliver roughly by the arm.

A mate, catching sight of his double-breasted RFC tunic, quickly dissuaded him. "Leave him, Spokey. He's Flying Corps, not even a proper soldier."

The fellow let him go with a grunt and moved on.

"What's going on?" Tulliver called after the mob.

"The proletariat are rising up!" said another jubilant Tommy, shoving past, rifle in hand. "Some of the boys are off to tell Everson what they think of him. We've got no argument against you, sir. You keep out of our way and we'll keep out of yours." He ran after his comrades.

Tulliver understood their resentment, even shared it to a degree. The camp had been on edge since the Khungarrii siege and the animal stampede. But he hadn't expected this.

From up beyond the trench, there were angry shouts and barked orders, answered by jeers as disorderly soldiers rampaged recklessly across the camp, dismissive of the NCOs' calls to order.

"Damn!" Tulliver shook his head and drew his revolver.

He raced along a comm trench, swerving round the traverses, in an attempt to get to the command post.

The points of several bayonets brought him up short.

He slipped to a stop on the wet duckboards, inches from the glinting steel as a small section of men, led by a lance corporal, glared at him.

"Just what the hell's going on here?" Tulliver demanded.

"Mutiny, sir."

CHAPTER TWO
"Hold Your Hand Out..."

TULLIVER POINTED HIS revolver at the lance corporal's head.

Lance Corporal 'Only' Atkins didn't flinch, confident in the clatter of several rifles he heard behind him as they were raised and pointed at Tulliver.

The RFC officer cleared his throat, but didn't lower the pistol. "We're not the mutineers, sir," said Atkins. He glanced over his shoulder at the men behind him. "Lower your weapons, lads."

"You sure, Only?" asked the tall, lanky one.

"Uh huh."

The men behind him lowered their Enfields, albeit reluctantly.

Warily, Tulliver lowered his gun too, but kept them pinned with a sullen stare.

"What's your name, Corporal?"

"Atkins, sir."

"Atkins? Everson's Black Hand Gang Atkins?"

"That's one way of putting it, I guess," he said with truculence. "Though we prefer 1 Section, 2 Platoon."

"Oh. Right you are," Tulliver said cheerfully.

Tulliver studied the soldiers in their worn, ill-fitting uniforms; the tall lanky one must be Pot Shot, no mistaking him. The one who never took his eyes off him, that must be Gazette, the sniper. The other with the roguish good looks must be Porgy. He'd heard the stories that had circulated around camp about them, and the ones about Atkins in particular. He knew Everson trusted him and his section implicitly, and decided to do the same.

Tulliver raised an eyebrow. He held out a hand. "Tulliver, Royal Flying Corps." Atkins took it warily, and Tulliver gripped his hand firmly. "So you're Atkins, eh? Glad to meet you."

His eye caught the telegraph pole overhead, the cable now hanging limp in the mud.

"Damn them. They've cut the telephone wires. Signals won't be happy. You and your men come with me. We'll have to report the situation in person."

EVERSON SAT WRITING up the Pennines' recent fantastical experiences on this foreign world in the Battalion War Journal. They were totally at odds with the dry reports of troop movements, battles and trench raids of earlier pages. Sometimes he wondered if he wasn't mad, and if all this wasn't the product of a febrile shell-shocked imagination. He even thought that might be preferable.

The sound of faint jeers and gunfire leached through the gas blanket.

His forehead creased with annoyance and he looked up as Atkins and Tulliver clattered down the steps into the command post, closely followed by Sergeant Hobson. "What the devil is going on out there?"

"The men are running amok," said Tulliver in a tone of incredulity, as he paced around, gesturing wildly towards the door.

By comparison, Hobson and Atkins stood smartly to attention.

"Seems to be a bit of a riot, sir," said Hobson, delivering his assessment with wry understatement.

"Seems?" Everson turned and cocked his head, listening to the gunfire and sporadic shouts. "There doesn't seem to be any 'seems' about it, Sergeant."

Atkins chipped in. "No, sir. But the majority of the men are staying out of it. Mostly it's a few malcontents stirring up trouble, but we should nip it in the bud, sir."

Everson paused to listen to the chaotic sounds a moment longer. "Do we know what they're mutinying about?"

"You name it, they're grousing about it, sir," replied Hobson.

Everson shot a questioning glance at Atkins, who gave a near-imperceptible shake of the head. That was something, at least.

He struggled to subdue a rising feeling of guilt. If the men had known what he and Atkins knew, then they would have cause to riot. For they both knew that the Pennine Fusiliers weren't the first or only people displaced here from Earth. There had been others. Atkins and his section had found the remains of a party of American emigrants in the Nazarii edifice. The Bleeker party had been travelling west on the California Trail in 1846 when they suddenly found themselves here, much as the Pennines had. If there was a way back, they didn't find it and they died here. They survived barely three months. Everson had ordered Corporal Atkins' Black Hand Gang to secrecy. He needed it kept secret; he believed the only thing holding the battalion together was the hope that they still *might* be able to get home.

Today, though, it looked like even that might not be enough.

He slammed a fist on his desk in frustration. Just as he was getting on top of things, he could feel them slipping away. But this was the Army and, like it or not, he needed to quell the potential mutiny and reassert his authority, if they were to survive at all.

"God damn it. I hoped it would never get to this." He looked up at Hobson, his face set, determined, his voice as hard as stone. "Sergeant, read them the Army Act. They get one chance. One."

"Leave it with me, sir," said Hobson, saluting smartly and making for the doorway.

"Thank you, Hobson."

Everson turned his attention to the flying officer, who was still pacing about in an agitated manner. "The gall of the fellows!" he said, still stung by their impudence.

"Tulliver! I'd be obliged if you'd fly over the camp; see if you can't help break up some of the larger groups."

"What? Oh, now you want me to fly," said Tulliver, archly.

Everson wasn't in the mood. "Just do it," he said wearily, "or you may find that once this lot get hold of it, you'll have no flying machine left at all!"

Tulliver stood for a moment, about to say something, then thought better of it, turned on his heel, and left.

"And me, sir?" asked Atkins, standing at ease.

"You're about the only man I can trust right now, Corporal. I want you and your men to mount a piquet outside. Are they all with you?"

"All apart from Evans and Blood, sir. They're guarding Chandar, sir."

"Oh, God, the Chatt!"

"Don't worry. They'll keep it safe, sir."

"I hope so. Like it or not, Atkins, we need it."

Everson took his Webley out of his holster and, with a deep sigh of regret, began to load it.

MERCY AND GUTSY, of 1 Section, stood on guard duty either side of the gas curtain to the dugout where Everson held the Chatt, for its own safety. For theirs, they tucked their gas hoods in knapsacks on their chest, for ease of access. They were supposed to wear them all the time when on guard duty with the Chatt. But they were hot and foul smelling, and neither wanted to be mistaken for a rioter.

Mercy, as wiry as a terrier and an inveterate scrounger, was listening in sanguine mood to the drone of the aeroplane and wash of rioting and looting that ebbed and flowed around them.

"Thought you'd want to be out nicking a few things yourself," said Gutsy, a stocky man with large, meaty hands, a ruddy complexion and a balding pate beneath his battle bowler.

"Nah. All the bon stuff's long gone, mate."

"Really?" asked Gutsy. "Where to?"

Mercy just smirked and tapped his nose.

The wave of noise grew louder as a rabble of men approached round the traverse.

"Eh up." Mercy nodded and he and Gutsy turned to face the direction of the noise, bayonets fixed. Mercy's short, sharp bark brought them up short.

"Halt."

The leader, a scarf wrapped round his lower face, didn't seem concerned. His confidence bolstered by the men behind him, he stepped up to Mercy's bayonet point.

Mercy could see the length of rope in the man's fist. This wasn't a rabble, this was a lynch mob. "You've not really thought this through, have you?" Mercy said.

"We were passing and thought we'd pay the thing a little visit. Those things killed my mates. So are you siding with one of them murderous insects against your own kind? Have you got no shame?" he snarled.

"No," said Gutsy. "We've got orders."

At that, the men surged forward. Unwilling to use bullets or bayonet their own men, Mercy and Gutsy swung the shoulder stocks of their rifles into the first wave. Men fell to the duckboards, winded, or careened off wattle revetments before sliding down into the mud.

"Bloody 'ell!" said Mercy, ducking under the swing of a trench club to land a hard punch in a soft belly.

From behind the gas curtain came a thin skittering sound that made Mercy's skin crawl. A prolonged hiss followed.

The fight broke off as everyone's attention turned toward the rubberised cloth covering the dugout entrance.

Something tore the curtain aside. In a swift, inhuman motion, a pale, chitinous creature leapt out of the dugout and onto the trench parapet before scuttling back down the revetment behind the mob, who now found themselves trapped between the guards and the Chatt.

It stood like a man, had the height of a man, but that was all the humanity one could ascribe to it. The Chatt reared up on its backward-bending legs to its full height, a posture of threat. It spread its chitinous arms wide, exposing the small vestigial limbs at its abdomen. Then it splayed its mandibles and hissed again, spraying an atomised mist into the air, enveloping the men.

Within moments, the lynch mob's expressions softened, changing from fear and anger to contentment. Their unifying purpose forgotten, they began to wander off individually, in a daze.

The Chatt sank back down and advanced toward Mercy and Gutsy, who turned their rifles upon it.

"This One has merely blessed them," it said. "By GarSuleth's Will they are at peace. They will not harm us now."

Mercy and Gutsy looked at each other, wide-eyed with amazement, as the Chatt returned to the dugout of its own volition, the stake and rope that had kept it imprisoned still tied to its ankle.

"Well, bless me!" said Mercy rubbing the back of his head and exchanging bemused looks with Gutsy.

Gutsy watched the mob staggering off like happy inebriates. "Best not," he said, reaching into his knapsack for his gas hood. "Not on duty."

NURSE EDITH BELL looked over the beds, filled with recently blinded patients newly under her charge, all of them victims of Chatt scentirrii acid spit. She still berated herself for the loss of the shell-shocked men, led to their deaths by alien parasites and flayed alive by the huge airborne grazing Kreothe. However, she had experienced the death of patients before and, as Sister Fenton reminded her, the dead weren't her purview, the living were.

Sister Fenton interrupted her thoughts now.

"No time for shilly-shallying," she said, nodding towards the end of the tented ward. "Warton needs a bed pan."

"Nurse!"

There was a desperate tinge to the voice. As the matron left, she bobbed in an almost imperceptible curtsy, her nurse's apron sitting oddly over her part-worn khaki serge trousers. "Yes, Sister."

She walked along between the two rows. She reached the end bed and searched underneath for the hollowed-out gourd that now served as a bedpan.

"Can you manage?" Edith asked.

"Yes, I'm sure I can, Nurse," said Warton in a strained tone. Bandages made from an old army issue shirt covered his eyes, but didn't hide the extent of the livid acid-etched flesh.

The gourd vanished beneath the blanket. Warton's features softened with relief.

Edith turned her back. She heard a fast stream splash against the inside of the gourd and subside into a rising gurgle. The trickle died. She turned round as Warton carefully manoeuvred the gourd out from under the army grey blanket and handed it back to her.

"Here you go, Nurse. Sorry, Nurse."

"Nonsense," she said softly.

The gourd was heavy and warm, and sloshed. She put it under the bed for collection later. The urine wasn't wasted. The experiment with gunpowder was still ongoing. That was one good thing to come out of the animal stampede. There was a surplus of dung. They added urine to the dung, in the hope of making saltpetre, apparently. With ammunition running low, even crude gunpowder would be welcome.

She became aware of a rowdy jeering outside. It wasn't unusual for the men to become boisterous and rowdy, but that was usually in the evenings.

"What's going on?" asked Warton, cocking his head toward the sound. Edith pursed her lips. "I don't know."

Several men burst into the tent, throwing back the flaps.

Edith bustled towards them, arms out, preparing to herd them from the tent, out of concern for her patients.

The men stood in the entrance, leering as they looked about. Their tunics were undone. One wore a kerchief over his lower face; another wore his PH gas hood.

"Privates, what's the meaning of this? This is a casualty ward. Please leave," she insisted in a stage whisper.

Several other men attempted to enter behind them, and the masked men staggered forward. Gas Hood stumbled into Edith's arms and clung to her. His mates cheered him on.

"What about some fun, Nurse, eh? How about a dance?" The mask muffled the voice. "If you were the only girl in the world, and I were the only boy!" he bellowed in a rough baritone. She found herself staring at her reflection in the mica eyepieces. She looked startled and afraid, and she hated herself for that. She braced her hand against the man's shoulders and pushed him back.

"Get your hands off me."

The blinded patients, confused by the noise, called out in alarm from their beds.

"What's going on?"

"Leave her alone."

His grip tightened around her waist. His head leaned in for a kiss, the gas hood's red rubber non-return valve poking out obscenely. Repulsed, she twisted her face away and took a swing with her foot. Her boot connected with his shin. The private bellowed in pain and let her go, her hair askew and tumbling down from her hair pins, her chest heaving with adrenalin.

"Ooh, quite the wild woman, eh?" The others began to circle her.

"I haven't had a woman in months," said one.

Warton groped his way out of his makeshift bed. "You men ought to be ashamed of yourselves." Rising to his feet, he thrust his hand out, feeling blindly for obstructions. He found a tunic. He gripped it and pulled the man toward him. "Who the hell are you, eh? Not a man, that's for sure. I'll have your number for this," he snarled.

A large hand planted itself in his bandaged face and shoved him to the ground, to the accompaniment of mocking laughter.

Someone shunted Edith. She lost her balance, tripped over Warton and landed on her back, on the vacated bed.

A cheer went up. Kerchief loomed over her. "Them trousers won't protect you, darlin'. I'm a dab hand with trousers," and to illustrate the point he flung off his tunic, flicked his braces off his shoulders and began to unbutton his flies. Edith, alarmed, tried to rise from the bed, but found herself pushed back down.

Her hand searched blindly down by the side of the bed for a weapon, something, anything. All she felt was hard, dry soil. Her fingers clawed at it, trying to get a handful of dirt, but it was too compacted. Her hands met something hard and warm.

He loomed over her, khaki trousers down round his knees exposing pale hairy thighs. She lashed out with a foot between his legs. His eyes bulged and he grunted into his kerchief. Edith swung her arm upwards, the hollowed gourd in her hand, and flung the contents in his face. There was no mistaking the smell of urine.

Edith scrambled from the bed and, panting, faced her attackers. Before, she had been scared; now, she was angry. That same righteous fire that once urged her to denounce Jeffries burned within her now.

A howl of derision went up, the men enjoying the turn of events even more.

A gunshot silenced the laughter.

Half Pint stood in the tent entrance, leaning on a crutch with one hand, his other crutch cast to the floor, the better to hold the revolver.

Sister Fenton arrived on his heels to see the aftermath.

"What the hell are you doing?" yelled Half Pint. "Get out! You've got no argument here! Your grouse is with the officers. The next one who makes a wrong move gets plugged. And you can bet your arse it won't be a cushy one, so just remember who's going to have to patch you up. Now move."

The rowdy mood deflated almost instantly, leaving the shame-faced men to shuffle out, their consciences pricking.

Kerchief, his eyes red rimmed, his hair plastered to his head by warm piss, struggled to pull up his trousers.

"Not you," said Sister Fenton and belted him round the head with the fallen crutch.

Edith watched, her mouth a perfect 'o' of surprise. He crumpled to the floor. Fenton handed the crutch back to a bemused Half Pint.

HOBSON STOOD BENEATH the flagpole on which the battle-tattered Union flag fluttered with little enthusiasm, as though infected by the general malaise affecting the men.

Backed up by 4 Section 3 Platoon, he confronted the disorganised mob heading towards him. They stopped, more out of amusement and curiosity than discipline. Many were wearing gas hoods or kerchiefs over their faces to hide their identities.

"Just what the bloody hell do you think you're doing?" Hobson roared. "Get back to your duties."

The mob stood around insolently, interspersing the resulting sullen silence with the occasional boos, jeers and catcalls, like a rough music-hall crowd.

Hobson was disgusted. He'd helped train these men. He'd wiped their arses, patted them on the shoulders and listened to them when they cried for their mothers.

He took a piece of paper from his tunic pocket to a rising sarcastic "Oooooh," from a crowd that grew bigger as other rioters drew closer.

Hobson unfolded it to more mock amazement.

"Hey up, lads, he's going to read us a monologue!"

Hobson's lip curled as he glared at the ill-disciplined rabble in front of him. He cleared his throat. "I have been ordered by Lieutenant Everson, Acting Commanding Officer of the 13th Battalion of the Pennine Fusiliers to read from the Army Act of Nineteen Hundred and Thirteen."

"Give us a song!"

Hobson ignored the lout and began his recitation. "Every person subject to military law who causes or conspires to cause any mutiny or sedition in any forces belonging to His Majesty; or endeavours to seduce any person in His Majesty's forces from allegiance to His Majesty, or to persuade any person in His Majesty's regular forces to join in any mutiny or sedition; or joins in, or being present, does not use his utmost endeavours to suppress any mutiny or sedition; or coming to the knowledge of any actual or intended mutiny or sedition in any forces belonging to His Majesty, does not without delay inform his commanding officer of the same, shall on conviction by court-martial be liable to suffer death."

Every word was as bitter as bile to him. He never once believed he would be reduced to reading these words. He stood and stared down the insolent glares not obscured by gorblimey cap peaks, gas masks, scarves or kerchiefs. Some, at least, looked shame-faced and cast their faces down.

"Sod this for a game of soldiers," someone yelled from the crowd. The throng began to scatter, dodging the clumsy-footed soldiers who had no heart to engage them. Some sprinted straight past Hobson, whose face flushed with rage as he bellowed. "You men! Come back here!"

Before him, the remnants of the mob, perhaps two thirds of their number, shuffled uncomfortably.

Hobson, looked at them, disappointment etched on his face. "I don't want to see your faces. Get back to your dugouts and remain there unless otherwise ordered."

The men, their mood subdued, removed their hoods and kerchiefs once their backs were turned. They began to disperse, although not quick enough for Hobson. "At the bloody double!" he yelled.

He felt the weight of his trench club in the frog at his hip. Right now, he could really do with breaking a few heads.

THE STRUTTER FLEW over the field of red poppies that had sprung from the Somme mud, before it dived low across the camp, causing men to duck, or to dash for cover.

There was a time when Tulliver loved doing this. He and Biffer had often flown down French roads buzzing staff motor cars, sending bloated red tabs scrambling for the car floor or columns of soldiers diving into ditches. All jolly good fun. Here, though, the sport palled.

He chased and harried, breaking up large mobs, herding them back from the open ground and into the trenches, watching men sprawl in the dirt as his landing wheels roared inches above their heads.

"Christ, what am I doing?" he muttered.

All the rage at being grounded, at the loss of his squadron mates, at the lack of understanding; he balled it up and screamed at the unearthly world in frustration.

The indifferent roar of the engine drowned it out.

AS THE RIOTOUS din rose and fell about them, Atkins and the rest of 1 Section stood to arms in the trench outside Battalion HQ. Thin columns of smoke rose into the air from indiscriminate arson.

"You can't blame them for rioting," said Pot Shot, remonstrating. "We've had no rest or pay for five months. We haven't suddenly found ourselves back on Earth, and it doesn't look like we're going to, either, does it?" The lanky Fusilier shot a sullen glance at Atkins. "Don't you think the rest of those poor buggers deserve to know, too?" He was talking about the Bleeker party, and Atkins knew it. They all did.

He wanted to do the right thing, and of course, he had sympathy with those rioting, all of which made his choice to stand here right now all the harder.

He shook his head. "That's not our problem. Lieutenant Everson ordered us to keep it secret, remember? And for good reason."

"Doesn't mean I have to like it," countered Pot Shot. "Even so, if there isn't a way back, then we're not exactly anybody's army anymore are we? Maybe we should all have a vote," he suggested.

"What, the women, too?" said Porgy, never usually given to deep political thought.

Gazette poked him in the shoulder. "You're only worried that if they get to vote on everything, they'll never let you walk out with them again," said the taciturn sniper.

Atkins watched the mob approach the Battalion HQ, hands bristling with trench clubs, sticks and rifles. Porgy, Gazette and Pot Shot stood beside him, blocking the way.

"Go back," he warned them.

Bains stepped to the fore, the shaft of an entrenching tool in his hand and a greasy smile on his face. "Well that's the whole point isn't it? We haven't gone back, have we? We're still here. All we want is a chance to make a new life for ourselves."

Impatient, the men behind Bains began to jostle, bracing for a fight.

Atkins raised his voice and addressed the rabble. "Is that what you all say?"

Bains took a step forward, daring Atkins to react. "They're not going to listen, Atkins," he said, "not even to you. You don't have any believers here. In fact, most of these men think you're a bit of a sham. Those campfire tales of you fighting Jeffries, magic bolts of lightning, demons, all that?" He wrinkled his nose in contempt. "Don't believe 'em. You're no better than I am. You're just a jumped-up lance jack who wants a bit of glory. Well, they don't give out medals for bullshit." He paused and shrugged. "Unless you're on the General Staff, of course."

"You ain't half pushing it, Bains," said Porgy.

"On the contrary. It's Everson that's been pushing it for far too long, and it ends here. Where's Everson?" He looked around and began singing. "'If you want to find the CO, I know where he is, he's down in the deep dug—'"

A gas gong rang out. Everson stood on the trench bridge above them, the artillery shell casing hanging at the end of the bridge still swinging where he'd struck it with the butt of his Webley.

"You men! Stand down. That's an order. I've asked once. That's more than generous, given the circumstances. I won't ask again."

"We don't take orders anymore," yelled Bains. "We've done our duty, but there are no Huns left to kill, no King to tell us what to do, no country to fight for."

"It doesn't excuse mutiny," said Everson, looking down at him.

"It does if you don't recognise military law anymore."

"Your uniform says different. Now disperse and go back to your dugouts," Everson ordered.

From around the camp, indiscriminate rifle fire popped and crackled.

"You hear that?" he said. "Every bullet you and your fellow mutineers squander means one less creature we can kill, one less horror we can dispatch. So each round you waste only hastens your own deaths."

"Or yours," countered Bains with a sneer. "At 'em, lads!"

The mob rushed the Tommies in the trench.

Porgy grabbed a sandbag from the parapet and swung it round. It smacked a mutineer on the side of the head with a thick, wet thud, slamming him into the trench wall.

Atkins hooked the shoulder stock of his Enfield behind a mutineer's knee, snatching the man's leg out from under him. A shunt of his shoulder sent him over.

Striding forward, he drove the shoulder stock of his rifle into a stomach of another and brought it up, cracking the gas-masked man on the chin as he doubled over, then swung it down on the back of his head, driving him onto the duckboards.

He never thought he'd be fighting his own. But he fought with a desperation born of fear, knowing that everything he held dear depended on Everson staying in command. Every man jack of these mutineers was an obstacle to a goal that was his guilt and his disgrace. He knew that they were stuck here. He knew with more certainty than these poor bastards did. He chose not to believe it. He chose to hold on to a possibility so slim it could be said to be barely there at all. It was the one Everson had pinned his hopes on, too. Every moment he was stuck here in camp was a moment lost, a moment when he could be pursuing Jeffries, the only man who might conceivably know of a way back. Back home to Flora, his missing brother's fiancée and, to his eternal shame and joy, the mother-to-be of his own child.

Bains grabbed Atkins' rifle.

"What makes you better than me, eh? What really happened in Khungarr between you and Everson and Jeffries?" he grunted.

"Really?" snapped Atkins, snatching the rifle from his grip. "I saved a Chatt's life."

A shadow crossed his face and he flinched instinctively. Bains took advantage of the distraction and melted into the mob.

Atkins glanced up at the parapet to see Sergeant Hobson leaping over the sandbags, using the firestep below as a springboard as he leapt into the fray, swinging his trench club. Atkins didn't envy the mutineers now. He'd seen Hobson in trench raids and he fought with a brutal efficiency.

Atkins' brow furrowed with mock concern. "I was worried you wouldn't get here in time, Sarn't!"

"Thanks for saving me a few, lad," said Hobson, raising his trench club, and as he waded into the skirmish, skulls cracked and punched faces flung bloody mucus into the air.

* * *

BAINS, SEEING THE tide turn, scrambled up the side of the trench and made for the makeshift bridge that spanned it, where Everson stood. All pretence at negotiation was gone now. This was a bloody coup.

Everson caught the dull yellow shine of a brass knuckle-duster and a glimpse of a short blade. A dirty little weapon, he thought, as Bains charged him; a Hun souvenir.

He moved off the footbridge to meet Bains, blocked the first punch thrust and grabbed Bains' wrist. He stepped past and brought the handle of his revolver down on the back of Bains' head. Bains' momentum carried him across the bridge into the gas gong. It *clonged* as he slipped, lost his footing and tumbled over the edge into the trench.

His unconscious body lay awkwardly on the duckboards below, a red stain spreading over the wet wood of the duckboards and bleeding into the muddy sump below.

Standing on the footbridge, Everson combed his hair back off his forehead with one hand, establishing order and decorum in his own mind once again. He looked around for his cap, picked it up by the peak and placed it on his head, just so, with a nod of satisfaction.

"Mop this lot up, Atkins," he said.

INTERLUDE ONE

Letter from Lance Corporal Thomas Atkins to Flora Mullins

29th March 1917

My Dearest Flora,

We've been back in camp for a while now. Don't worry. It was still here when we returned, despite my fears. At least we have fresh rations now, if you can call what the mongey wallahs cook up fresh.

I thought coming back to camp, I'd find some peace, but it seems there's none to be had anywhere here, least of all here. Some of the lads are unhappy with the situation and want to be somewhere else, but 'C'est la Guerre' as they say. Lieutenant Everson is trying to do his best, and believes it's for our own good, but there's always some barrack-room lawyer who thinks they know best.

I've been thinking about what happened between us. Sometimes, I think of nothing else. I don't regret it for one moment, but I feel so helpless stuck here so far from home, so far from you. I know some say that what we did was wrong, but that night I didn't believe it, I still don't, and I hope you feel the same.

It's human nature, I suppose. You'd think with everything else out there against us, that we could show some common sense. Sometimes we can be our own worst enemy.

Ever yours
Thomas

CHAPTER THREE
"I Was Their Officer..."

EVERSON WALKED DOWN the hutment ward towards the padre's bed. Captain Lippett, the MO, had assured him that the chaplain's injury wasn't serious, although it had resulted in a mild concussion.

Hearing of the padre's assault had a profound effect on Everson, perhaps more so than the riot itself. How was it that the morale of the soldiers under his command had slipped so low? A chaplain, of all people. He was glad that the man who did this was under guard and would face retribution under court-martial.

The padre looked wan and older than his years. A bandage was wrapped around his head. An odd, almost comic tuft of sandy hair stuck up from the middle of it, like a tonsure in reverse. He sat in bed reading the black-leather-covered Bible that rarely left his side. It was, as he had said many times, his only weapon. As he saw Everson approaching, he put the Bible down and smiled for him, but it was a weary smile that took effort.

A chair had been put out for him. Everson took off his cap and sat down.

"You look tired," said Everson.

The padre waved a hand. "I haven't been sleeping well. A few... nightmares."

"Night terrors, Sister Fenton said. You wake up screaming."

The padre shrugged off his concern. "So do many here," he said, gesturing around the small ward. "You forget, Lieutenant. There are no reserve trenches here. You can't take them out of the line. There is little relief for them, even here."

"Or you, Padre. You seem... troubled," said Everson.

The padre ignored him and continued to press his point. "The men have a legitimate grievance," he continued gently. "They have homes and families far away, with no knowledge of if they will ever see them again. They've endured more than they ever should. They have done

534

far more than you expected of them. But even they have their limits, John."

He was more forgiving than Everson. But then, Everson reminded himself, that was his job.

Everson bowed his head. "They're not men," he corrected. "They don't have that luxury right now. They're soldiers. They have to be. It's the only way they'll—we'll—survive. We have to maintain discipline. Unless we stay together, unless we remain as a battalion, we're going to get picked off, one by one. Each man that dies or deserts lessens our collective chances of survival."

The padre looked into his eyes and clasped Everson's hand in both of his. "Then you have to find a way of keeping them together. You need to give them hope."

WHAT FEW OFFICERS there were, along with the NCOs and compliant soldiers, managed to re-establish order and calm within the camp quite quickly, suggesting perhaps that ill-feeling didn't run as deep as the ringleaders had hoped. It took less than a day to round them up. Everson surveyed the camp in the aftermath. In truth, the rioters had caused less damage than they might have, but that wasn't the point. They could be dealt with swiftly, but it would take much longer to deal with the consequences of their actions. In the wake of the Khungarrii attacks, the Pennines had sought to ally themselves with local nomadic Urmen enclaves, offering them protection from Chatt attacks. Now, thanks to the riot, and the behaviour of some of the men, those alliances were in jeopardy as some enclaves prepared to move out.

Most of the men, their immediate frustrations spent, returned reluctantly to the routines that had structured their lives these past few months. Most of the men complied because it was all they knew. Ultimately, they sought comfort in the companionship of their comrades.

Everson didn't fool himself into thinking that this was an end to his problems. For months he had held the battalion together. He had been relying on their respect for him, but that currency had diminished rapidly. He had been given a warning. How he dealt with the mutineers would send a warning back.

The courts-martial ran for two days. The court dealt with most minor charges by forfeiture of pay or field punishment. It heard the more serious charges toward the end. They were the cases that Everson dreaded.

The bell tent requisitioned for the courts-martial was humid and smelled of damp tube grass, sweat and fear. Army justice was often brutal and uncompromising.

Everson sat at the centre of the table, with Lieutenant Baxter, of the Machine Gun Section, to his left and Lieutenant Tulliver to his right, as they dealt with one case after another.

The padre's assailant was one Everson took a particular interest in. He sat impassively as Second Lieutenant Haslam, prosecuting, read out the charge sheet. "The accused, number 9658798, Fusilier Francis Rutherford of the Pennine Fusiliers, as soldier in the regular force, is charged with striking a superior officer, being in the execution of his duty. The maximum punishment is death. How do you plead?"

The prisoner Rutherford, who stood to attention in front of his escort, looked visibly shocked. "Not guilty, sir."

Despite the plea, the case itself was straightforward. Rutherford had taken part in the riots by his own admission.

"I was trying to stop Private Wilson, sir," he protested. "There was a struggle. During the incident, I may have struck the padre by accident."

"By accident," said Haslam, unconvinced. He waved a sheaf of papers. "There are eight witnesses—eight, including Private Wilson— who testified that you struck the padre deliberately, in an act of malice and insubordination."

"What? But that's not true, sir," Rutherford protested. "Ask the padre!"

"Unfortunately the padre isn't fit to give evidence at these proceedings. And may I remind you that you have already admitted to taking part in the mutiny. Do you wish to further address the court?"

Rutherford, when faced with these facts, merely hung his head, realising the futility of any further protest. "No, sir."

To his dismay, Everson felt no satisfaction in pronouncing sentence.

Wilson got away with field punishment.

Private Nicholls' intervention on behalf of the nurses had seen him acquitted as he had done all possible to prevent the actions.

The ringleaders, though, were of a different cloth and were court-martialled jointly. They stood together surly and resolute: Bains, Swindell and Compton.

Bains stood to attention, his face swollen and bruised with a dark red hatching of scabs on his left cheek. He refused to make eye contact with anyone in court, a look of undisguised insolence on his face.

The charge against him and his fellow conspirators was mutiny.

He offered no plea, just a sullen, defiant silence.

"Bains," said Everson wearily before he passed sentence. He waved a fragile piece of paper in Bains' direction. "You drafted these demands, I believe."

Bains looked straight ahead, refusing to be drawn.

"Damn it, Bains. We're all trying to work together here. You don't think we all want to get home?"

Everson saw Hobson behind the prisoner lean forward and whisper something he didn't catch. Bains' eyes flicked to the side before staring straight ahead again.

"This is your chance, Bains. Your only chance," Everson said. He read from the scrap. "Your demands here: one, to recognise the fact that we are no longer at war and that our duty to King and Country is done. Two, to allow those that wish to do so to leave and seek their own fortune. Three, that those men who wish to stay be allowed to do so on equal footing, that a council should be elected and voted on by all.

"Laudable sentiments, Bains. But I'm afraid I can't allow it. You signed up for the duration of the war. And, if you haven't noticed, we are still at war—with this entire world. Our lives and safety depend on well-ordered military discipline. It represents our best chance of survival.

"The court sentences the accused to suffer death by being shot. However, the court recommends the accused mercy on the ground that they have been present in the line without relief for over four months and this may have gone some way to contributing to their behaviour."

Bains' Adam's apple bobbed as he swallowed. He didn't meet Everson's gaze, but he nodded.

"May God have mercy on your souls," said Everson heavily.

EVERSON ORDERED ALL men fit for duty on parade at dawn the next day. This was not something he wanted to do, but punishment had to be seen to be done.

The prisoners were marched out, under guard, past the Union flag, out across the rings of defensive trenches and between the waiting ranks; the two full companies that were all that was left of the battalion, a couple of orphan platoons from the remaining two and several loyal Karno platoons. The men were escorted to the old bombed-out Poulet farmhouse, which now served as a gatehouse and watchtower to the camp.

Everson stood stiffly to attention as he addressed the condemned men, his voice hard and cold. "If I carried out the sentence as required it would, frankly, be a waste of what bullets we have left, and mercy has been recommended by the court. Privates Bains, Swindell, Compton and Rutherford, I hereby exile you from the camp. You will be sent forth with such provisions as we can spare and forbidden to return on pain of death. Is that understood?"

Company Quartermaster Sergeant Slacke handed the men two days' provisions, water and one magazine of ammunition of ten rounds for their Enfields, which he felt was more than they deserved given the circumstances.

Everson wasn't entirely sure how merciful the commuted sentence was. It was in effect still a death sentence, expecting them to survive out there for any length of time. At least they had a chance. Rutherford had a 'wife' among the nomadic Urmen. Everson knew that her Urmen enclave was planning to move out, unsettled by the riots. It brought him some comfort. If the men survived long enough to meet up with them, then they might improve their chances.

They walked past the poppies that spread out across the scorched cordon sanitaire and strode out into the veldt of tube grass. Only Rutherford turned to glance back. It was a look of hurt, betrayal and sorrow, and it shook Everson to the core.

Standing up on the observation platform on the remains of the ruined first floor, Everson felt duty-bound to remain long after the other ranks had been dismissed, not to make sure they actually left, but out of a sense of guilt.

"It had to be done, John," said Lieutenant Baxter, coming up and standing at his shoulder. He watched with him as the dwindling figures were finally swallowed by the veldt. Although a couple of months younger than Everson himself, Baxter, with his full moustache and easy smile, exuded the air of a favourite school master. Everson found his company comforting.

From behind, within the wireweed-bounded camp, the barks of NCOs urged work parties on, a little harder than necessary in revenge for the rioting.

He looked out across the camp. "I've lost them, Bernard."

"They'll come round, John. They need you, more than they think."

THE OFFICERS GATHERED in the Command Post. Their mood was sombre and subdued. All of them looked shaken. Their world of entitlement and privilege had come close to being toppled. Next time, they might not be so lucky.

There were seven of them left, a smaller and more exclusive club than they were happy with: Baxter, Palmer, Tulliver, Lippett, Haslam and Seward. They sat on old salvaged chairs or ammo boxes, each lost in their own thoughts or, perhaps, wondering whether to give voice to them.

From his desk, Everson looked around the room. The mutineers' stupid little act had almost cost him his men. He didn't want it to cost him his officers, too.

"Right. First things first. If anyone has anything to say about my leadership of the battalion since Captain Grantham's death, best get it off your chest now. I don't want another coup on my hands."

Palmer let out an awkward cough. "Everson, old stick, no one thinks anything of the sort." He looked around at his fellow subalterns. "Do they?"

There was a chorus of *nos* and *of course nots*. The position of battalion commander seemed to be a poisoned chalice. No one else wanted to oversee the decimation of a once-proud battalion.

"Have I lost them?" he asked.

"Just got to keep them busy, old man, that's the thing."

"How about an inter-company football tournament?"

Lippett sat polishing his glasses, breathing on the lens, watching them fog and rubbing them between a thumb and forefinger with a scrap of cloth before hooking the wire arms back over his ears again. The MO was considerably older than the young officers around him, and his rank of Captain purely honorary. Eager young bucks once, now cautious and fatigued. Old men before their time, their bright, once-flushed faces now drawn and pasty.

Lippett considered his words. "You're losing them," he said, "but you've not lost them yet. They need something concrete to focus on. Vague hopes of being spirited back home are no longer enough."

Baxter stroked his moustache, arched an eyebrow at Everson, and nodded with encouragement.

Everson stood up and braced his palms on the table. "You're right," he said with resolve. "We must move forward from this, carry the men with us. Our first priority is to relieve the tank crew and salvage the tank, if we can. That operation has been delayed far too long."

"Exactly! The ironclad is a great boost to morale. It scares the dickens out of the Chatts. With that back in our midst, morale should soar."

Tulliver spoke up. "Well, the tank crew were still alive and camped by the crater as of my last patrol three days ago."

"But I thought the tank was at the bottom of the crater. How are we going to get the bally thing up?"

Everson smiled for the first time in days. "That's the easiest part," he said. "We'll use the captured Khungarrii battlepillars."

The battlepillars were great larval beasts of burden, giant armoured caterpillars larger than an elephant and up to thirty yards long.

"There are secondary objectives too," said Everson, his confidence growing with every moment. It was a relief to be putting a plan into action again. "On the way, I intend to leave a party of sappers at the gorge to investigate this mysterious metal wall that Corporal Atkins found."

Haslam, his curiosity piqued, leant forward. "Yes, what the hell is it?"

"That's what I intend we find out. Atkins reports that it's a machined face of metal in the gorge wall, perfectly flat, with no visible doors or windows. Indicative of some civilisation, perhaps. We won't know until we take a closer look at it.

"In addition, once we reach the Croatoan Crater, we can pick up Jeffries' trail. This is the closest we have come to him, gentlemen."

"But how do you know he was there?" asked Seward.

Everson fished in his tunic pocket and tossed onto the table a scrap of bloodstained khaki cloth with a button attached.

"This was found at the Nazarii edifice by the crater. The button bears the Pennines' crest. Since Atkins and his men were the first Fusiliers to reach that place, this can only have belonged to Jeffries. He was there. I'd stake my life on it."

"You may well have to," warned Haslam.

"In the meantime, what of the Chatts?" asked Seward. "Without the tank, we're still vulnerable to another attack."

"We've made progress there, too," said Everson. "I think we may be able to broker some kind of deal with the Khungarrii."

"How? We have one Chatt prisoner and not an impressive specimen at that," said Seward, looking round the room to nods of amused agreement.

"It turns out that it's more important than we thought. It's one of their priest caste."

"Well let's hope we've got an ace up our sleeve, because we bally well need one."

Everson smiled. "Oh, we do, gentlemen. We do."

EVERSON MADE HIS way to the dugout where they held the Chatt prisoner. Atkins and Evans stood to attention as he approached.

"I need to talk to Chandar," he said.

"Best take this, then, sir." Atkins handed the officer a PH hood. "Just a precaution after what it did to the rioters."

Everson nodded, took the proffered gas hood and pulled it on. He ducked his head and descended the steep steps. He never got used to the idea that the creature was not of Earth. There was no precedent in religion or science to explain it, yet here it was—or rather, here *they* were, for this, he forced himself to remember, was their world.

At the bottom of the steps was a bolted door with a small judas hole in it. They had erected it after the attempted mutiny, for the Chatt's protection as much as that of the soldiers. He unholstered his revolver, and peered into the gloom beyond.

Chandar was one of the priest caste from the Khungarr colony of an arthropod race that called themselves the Ones, or the Children of GarSuleth, their insect deity.

Its only clothing was a woven silk garment made of a single, seamless piece of cloth that went over the left shoulder of its chitinous chest plate and wrapped around its segmented abdomen. Tassels hung from it, the knots scented with scriptural scent texts, like a prayer book or a rosary. Once white, like its carapace, the cloth was now stained and soiled.

Everson coughed. Chandar turned its head toward the door. Wet clicks issued from the mucus-slick maw between its mandibles. The smooth ivory white carapace of its facial plates caught the light of the hurricane lamp hanging from the roof beam. Its visage gave nothing away. Everson couldn't tell whether it was afraid, indifferent, or angry at its incarceration. On top of its cranial carapace, the remaining stumps of its antennae twitched and jerked, as if phantom feelers were still scenting the air.

Everson regarded it thoughtfully for a moment. "We need to talk," he said.

He heard an asthmatic intake of breath forced out over organs unsuited for human speech.

"If GarSuleth wills it."

"Stand back," he ordered as he slid the bolt and pulled open the door. It caught against the uneven earthen floor, and he had to jerk it several times to get it open.

The Chatt waited patiently, and when Everson entered, sank down slightly on its legs. The vestigial middle limbs, little more than chitinous claws, splayed from its abdomen. It regarded the reflection of itself in the mica eyepieces of Everson's gas hood, as he looked back at himself reflected in its large, featureless black eyes.

Another intake of breath and its finger-like mouth palps moved within the arc of its mandibles like a loom, almost as if it were weaving the words out of its breath. "Ev-er-son?" it asked.

Everson pulled his gas mask off. It was a token of trust, but only a small one. The guards outside would kill it if it tried to escape.

A sharp acrid smell assailed his nostrils. His nose wrinkled. He almost wanted to put the mask back on. He looked around and saw a damp patch in the corner of the room. The thing didn't even know enough to use the bloody bucket.

"This One offers you a blessing in the name of GarSuleth," it said, refraining from the benediction spray that was the gift of all Dhuyumirrii, the Chatt priest class.

Everson got straight to the point. "I need to know if the Khungarrii will attack again."

The Chatt allowed its stunted middle limbs to fold inward against its segmented abdomen again. Its answer sailed on the top of a wheeze, the clicking of its mandibles punctuating the words. "Unless this One returns to Khungarr, it is a certainty." The tone was flat, emotionless. There was no emphasis. It was hard to tell whether this was a threat or merely a statement.

"That's what I'm here to discuss," said Everson, stepping into the small dugout, leaving the door open, as much to help ventilate the place as to suggest trust.

"This One wishes Atkins' presence," it said, shuffling back.

"No," said Everson calmly. "You will talk to me." He didn't wish his authority undermined by one of his own men. Not right now. This was something he had to do for himself.

The Chatt blinked, but otherwise didn't move. Stalemate.

"God damn it," Everson wheeled round, the dirt scrunching under his heels as he pivoted. He called up the steps. "Atkins, get down here!"

It was as if the thing found some comfort in the corporal's presence. If it made it talk then he'd have to put up with it.

Atkins thudded his way down the steps. "Sir?"

"Seems Chandar won't talk unless you're here," said Everson sourly.

Atkins' face flushed. "It's this Kurda thing, sir, some Chatt sense of honour, as far as I can make out. Since I saved its life, it thinks we have a connection."

Chandar looked from one to the other. "This One wishes to know what you have done with the collection of sacred salves recovered from Nazarr."

Everson turned back to the Chatt. "They're safe for now. That's all you need to know. You are in no place to make demands."

Nictitating membranes flicked over the black orbs of its eyes. "That is where you are wrong," it said, its mouth palps quivering as it spoke. "It appears that this One is in exactly the right place."

Everson indicated the earthen walls surrounding them. "You're in a prison cell."

The Chatt's vestigial limbs opened and closed in what might have been a shrug. "This One is exactly where GarSuleth wants this One to be."

"Why are they so important to you? What do they contain, exactly?"

"Quite possibly, your salvation and this One's substantiation," the wheezing Chatt said. "There has long been a debate in Khungarr that has consumed every generation, concerning the nature of what the aromatic scriptures refer to as the Great Corruption. At present, Sirigar, Liya Dhuyumirrii of Khungarr, seeks to join the disparate olfactions of the Shura in order to consolidate its position. That One's interpretation of the perfumed prophecy holds you Tohmii to be the embodiment of the ancient scriptural evil. Your actions in attacking Khungarr have only strengthened that interpretation, along with Sirigar's standing within the Shura. With the defeat of the Great Corruption, that One's power will be assured. Thus has Sirigar ordered your herd to be culled."

"You mean it's using us as a unifying threat?"

"Yes. However, there are those in the Shura that believe that Sirigar's interpretation is false and merely a political expediency. Those Ones believe that references to the Great Corruption refer not to an external physical threat, but warn against a theological dilemma that would see our own beliefs diluted to serve a baser purpose. We believe it refers to Sirigar's debasement of the Scents of GarSuleth.

"The only way to challenge and defeat Sirigar is in ritual debate before the Shura, the Supplication of Scents, but we must have arguments and commentaries to back up our claims. We had been diligently searching the Aromatic Archive of the Fragrant Libraries for such truths when Jeffries destroyed them. Irreplaceable scents that have been Khungarr's guide and strength for generations are gone forever. And with them this One's chance to defeat Sirigar."

"And you think this collection of lost scents will provide those answers?"

"Yes. It is this One's fervent hope that the scent texts discovered in Nazarr with Atkins will provide the scriptural proof this One's olfaction has been seeking. They could hold the scriptural arguments necessary to absolve the Tohmii of their apocalyptic role."

Everson paced back and forth, absorbing the information. "So you're saying our only hope of survival is to aid you in your religious insurrection to unseat Sirigar?"

"It is."

Having just put down a mutiny of his own, the irony was not lost on him. At least now he knew just how valuable the collection of stone jars was. That was worth knowing, and the jars themselves worth holding to ransom.

"Right. And how likely is this to happen?"

"That would depend on the contents of the scriptures."

"Don't you know what they are?"

It indicated its antennae stumps. "This one is unable to read the scents texts since Sirigar had this one's antennae broken."

Of course. With no feelers, it was crippled and scent-blind, effectively an invalid in their culture.

Everson exchanged looks with Atkins, who shook his head and shrugged. He hadn't really expected the NCO to have any answers. After all, this was his call. Everson returned his attention to the Chatt. "You're not making this easy for me, are you? You want me to let you walk out of here, taking all those jars with you. Even supposing they provide whatever it is you need, there is no assurance that you can even dispose of this Sirigar."

"This is true."

He stopped pacing and turned to face Chandar. "Yet you expect me to trust you?"

"If GarSuleth wills it."

Everson considered the implications, and then shook his head. "No. While it is clear that these jars are of great importance, I'm not willing to let them out of my possession. Not without knowing what they contain. Not without guarantees. Quite honestly, your continued presence here is problematic."

Chandar cocked its head to one side. "So is yours, if this One does not succeed."

The thing was wily. It might act helpless, but its immobile features hid a cunning intelligence. It had the perfect poker face. Everson paced the small cell while the arthropod watched impassively. The thing had him over a barrel, but he wasn't going to let it know that. It had dealt its hand and it was a strong one.

His own hand was not so strong, but far from useless. He didn't trust it. To that end he had put plans in place, a fallback position, but for now he would let it return to Khungarr, although he'd be damned if he gave up the one advantage they appeared to have.

He approached the Chatt, staring straight into its black eyes. "Very well," he said with deliberation. "I'll let you return to your colony."

Chandar became quite animated, clicking its middle limbs together. "GarSuleth wills it," it said. "In sending the sanctified odours of GarSuleth you will have demonstrated that you Urmen are part of GarSuleth's will, that you possess a fraction of his essence, a fact Sirigar denies."

"That's not my problem. You say your olfaction means us no harm. Well, we want proof. Until there is some sort of deal struck between the Khungarrii and the Pennines, the scents will remain in our possession. You can take one. One jar, as a sample. The rest remain here."

Everson ushered Atkins from the dugout and made to follow.

"But this One cannot read the scent texts," said Chandar.

Everson turned and regarded it coolly. "Then you had better choose carefully."

CHAPTER FOUR
"The Clays of a Cold Star..."

"CORPORAL ATKINS TOLD us to wait here," Norman snapped at Nellie Abbott.

Nellie arched an eyebrow and stared him down, arms folded. The FANY, dressed in her calf-length brown skirt and brown jacket, stood her ground, short curly hair framing a plain face. Some of the men assumed her hair was cut short in support of women's suffrage. The truth was she simply found it more practical.

"I don't care what Corporal Atkins said. And, frankly, I'm surprised you do. You never did before," she retorted. "They should have been back here days ago. That's what Lieutenant Tulliver's message said. Something must have happened. We've waited long enough. We'll have to go down without them. The *Ivanhoe's* down there. Alfie and Lieutenant Mathers are down there, too, in case you'd forgotten!"

It had been a week since they watched, horror-struck, as the tank tipped over the edge of the Croatoan Crater, the Sub and Alfie inside, to be lost in the jungle-filled depression below. There had been no sign of fire, no billowing smoke and no string of explosions from the dozens of shells the tank carried, so there was every hope that it was still in one piece.

Since then the remaining tank crew had been without the tank's addictive petrol fruit fuel, whose vapours had heightened their senses, and they had begun to exhibit withdrawal symptoms. Some had suffered more than others had, although they all felt sorry for themselves. Tempers grew short, then the cramps came, and the cold sweats, then the shaking, and finally a fever took hold.

Jack, the brawny gunner, trembled but never groused, never uttered a sound, though his pain showed in his eyes.

Cecil, the youngest, whimpered and called out in his delirium. Although he was the one who had taken most against Nellie, it was him who sought her out for comfort now, glad, as he said in the midst of his fever, that they now had a lady to take care of them.

Norman rolled, groaned and complained, as if playing out the most prolonged and dramatic death scene of his far from distinguished stage career.

Reggie, polite as ever, apologised profusely throughout his withdrawal for every cross word and whimper and every request for succour.

Wally, the bantam driver, took himself off away from the others and suffered stoically, his pain private.

Through it all, Nellie dutifully took charge of them, bathed their brows, gave them water, hushed them and soothed them. She wondered if, down there, Alfie was going through the same terrors. The mechanic was not quite the beau that Edith took him to be, but she had to admit, to herself at least, he had potential. He had an easy smile, a shared enthusiasm for motorbikes and engines and a willingness to accept her for who she was. Although Edith thought she could do better, Nellie found that she did not want to. Now Alfie was down in the crater, and she didn't know whether he was alive or dead. She would move heaven and earth, or at the very least a truculent tank crew, to find out.

They would have to go down there. To that end, she conceived a plan while the others were ill and set about putting it into practice. It would give them something to focus on while trying to deal with their petrol fruit addiction.

Atkins had charged Napoo, the Pennines' Urman guide, with her wellbeing. He was a grizzled, weather-beaten man, his skin criss-crossed with scars. The clothing he wore was of animals' skins and he was partially armoured with plates of hard-won Chatt carapace. He was older than any of them, and that spoke of a certain tenacity and wisdom, especially on this world where nothing seemed to survive for long.

He hunted and kept them fed, a task made easier by the destruction of the Nazarrii edifice not too far away. The collapse of its subterranean levels had disturbed the warrens of some burrowing animals Cecil called snarks. Napoo took great delight in catching them by the dozen.

He took a great many to the nearby Gilderra clan as gifts, as Nellie determined they would need their help. The Gilderra saw this as a turn in their fortunes, for which the *Ivanhoe* and its crew were responsible. The crew had killed the Dulgur for them that haunted the Nazarrii ruins, and now animal life returned to the area. However, so, too, had the patrols of Zohtakarrii Chatts, in whose territory the tank crew found themselves. Although the patrols did not venture too close to the crater, or the ruins of the Nazarrii edifice, Napoo had no doubt that the Chatts had scented them on the wind and knew they were there.

During their recovery, the tankers had meekly allowed Nellie to take charge while their senses returned to normal, only to find that, having been under her care, they now found themselves susceptible to her natural authority as a nurse. All except Norman. In his withdrawal, she had seen him exposed and vulnerable. She had seen beneath the actor's mask that he chose to show the world. It embarrassed him, and he resented her for it.

"Why should we listen to you?" Norman asked petulantly. The tanker glared at her, his lip curled with bitterness, his hands shoved deep in the pockets of the dark blue coveralls the tank crew wore over their regulation khaki uniforms.

"Because she looked after us," said Cecil. "Because those are our mates down there. And the *Ivanhoe*."

"*Oh, Nellie, lady, be our mother!*" Norman retorted in a sing-song tone.

"Leave the lad alone, Norman," said Jack.

"Cecil's right," said Nellie. "We've been sat up here for nearly a week. We're not going to give up on them, or the *Ivanhoe*."

"Says you, but how are we supposed to get down there?" said Norman.

Nellie sighed. "The Gilderra have vine rope. We have been trading snarks for rope while you have been... recovering."

Realisation dawned. Wally stepped forward to hug Nellie, but caught sight of the look in her eye and thought better of it.

"We can really do this?" asked Cecil.

"Yes, we can," said Nellie, with relief.

Napoo scowled his disapproval. His only words on the subject were the last warning Chandar gave them regarding the Croatoan Crater. "Nothing must enter, nothing must leave."

THE NEXT MORNING Nellie looked out across the wide expanse of the crater. The morning sun was just beginning to light the lip of the far side. The alien sun steadily devoured the crater's shadow, raising a curtain of vapour that swept towards them, like a creeping barrage of mist.

It took three of the crew to drag the thick vine rope to a sturdy tree. They hauled it round the trunk and struggled to tie it securely.

Jack braced his foot on the trunk and gave the rope several violent jerks. The knot tightened and held. He gave a satisfied grunt and followed the rope back to the coiled mound by the crater's edge.

Despite his misgivings, Napoo had been charged with Nellie's safety and had made rough sacks to carry food supplies, amongst which were dried snark meat, fruit and a little edible fungus. There were also several gourds of water. Napoo had his knife, Jack, Wally and Norman had their revolvers and Cecil and Reggie carried a couple of Enfields left by Atkins and his men.

"So," said Reggie, looking round at the others. "This is it. Do or die."

Wally took a deep breath. "Well, I wouldn't have put it quite like that."

Napoo's hand clasped Nellie's shoulder. "You should not do this."

"Napoo. Our friends are down there. And there are supplies in the tank, guns and food that we can use."

She took hold of the vine rope, heaved a loop of it from its coiled bulk and dropped it over the edge. The rope unspooled under its own weight with a speed she didn't expect. Seconds later, it snapped taut from the tree.

"Well, I was expecting to say a few words before we launched it," said Norman with a sour face.

Nellie sighed with relief and brushed her hands against each other. "Well, it's done now. I'm sorry."

"No need to stand on ceremony, then," said Jack brightly. "At least you saved us that. Norman's speech would have turned into an oratory anyway."

Norman gave him a petulant sneer.

"Well, I ain't going first," said Cecil.

"Manners dictate ladies first," said Reggie, "but in this case I don't think it wise."

Jack stepped forward. He had been a boxer and was by far the heaviest of the crew, his brawny frame filling his coveralls. "I'll go first," he volunteered. "If it takes my weight, the rest of you'll have no excuse."

"At least we'll have a soft landing if it doesn't," said Wally with a grin.

They clustered at the edge; Nellie looked along the crater lip to the place where the tank tracks ended and then dismissed them, focusing her eyes on the rope, almost aa thick as her wrist, that hung over the edge.

Jack took the rope in both hands and stood with his back to the lip.

"Cecil, you next; then Norman, Wally, then Reggie."

"Why does Reggie get to go last?" asked Cecil.

"Because he's got manners," said Jack.

"Manners?"

"Yes. He's a gentleman. He won't look."

"Look where?"

"Up."

"Up?" Cecil looked at Nellie. "Oh!" Jack clipped him round the back of the head before the growing leer could smear itself across his face.

Nellie, although quite used to the company of men, blushed and averted her eyes. So used to being treated with filial affection, she often forgot her feminine aspects. It was sometimes a shock to be reminded of them, and her brothers had the bruised arms to show for it.

"Nellie, you next and Napoo can come down last. We'll secure a position below," Jack told her.

He walked backwards, feeding the rope through his hands until he got to the edge. He leaned out slowly and began to walk down the steep camber of the rock face.

"It's like Jack and the beanstalk, ain't it?" said Cecil.

Nellie watched with dread. All of a sudden, she wasn't sure she could do this. But she had committed them to this course of action. She couldn't back out now, could she? For a brief moment, she thought of falling back on her womanhood for an excuse, and instantly despised herself for it. Of course she could do this. She could do anything they could do. And what's more, she bloody well would.

One by one, the men disappeared over the edge. She fixed her eyes on the rope. It jerked spasmodically as if it had a life of its own.

Nellie wiped sweaty palms on her skirt.

"Do not look down," Napoo said gravely.

She turned her back to the edge and grasped the rope as she had seen the others do. One foot after the other, she took hesitant steps backwards until the ground gave way beneath her heel.

From below, she heard Norman yell out "Rock" as something careened down the crater side, impacted with the scree slope and skittered down into the jungle.

Her face creasing into a frown, she stepped backwards. Her breath came in short, sharp pants. Inside she was screaming. She bit the inside of her mouth hard, to stop it from escaping.

Planting one foot below the other, she slowly fed the rope though her hands as she stared at the crimson rock in front of her. She could hear Napoo climbing onto the rope above her.

As she descended the near-vertical wall, the panic and terror within transmuted into exhilaration. She was doing it. Carried away with the audacity of her actions, she glanced down, and immediately wished she hadn't. The ground seemed so very far away.

When she couldn't move, she started to panic, only to realise that her skirt had caught on some thorny shrub clinging to the crater side. With every inch she descended, her skirt rode up. She tugged at it in an attempt to free it, and the thorns held it fast. She tugged it again. The skirt ripped, and the momentum sent her twirling round in a vertigo-inducing spin, holding onto the rope by one hand. She managed to find the cliff face and braced her feet against the rock again to stop the spin and steady herself. It took a moment to recover her composure and, holding the rope tightly in both sweat-slicked hands, she continued her slow walk down the rock face. She had read of mountaineers doing this for fun. She couldn't think why.

After what seemed like an age, she reached the top of the scree slope. There, she could take more of her weight on her legs; she realised how much her arms hurt, muscles burning with effort.

It wasn't until she made her way down the slope, still holding the rope for balance, and found the others staring at her that she realised the extent of the torn skirt. It had ripped right up above the knee. Exposed as it left her, it did seem to allow her a good degree more movement.

"Lads," said Reggie. "Lads! Turn your backs. We're not brigands, you know."

They turned round, some faster than others, earning Cecil another clip round the ear from Jack as his gaze lingered longer than it ought to.

Reggie climbed out of his coveralls, leaving him in his greyback shirtsleeves, regulation khaki trousers and puttees as he held them out behind him towards Nellie.

She reached out and took them with gratitude. "Thank you, Reggie, that's very decent of you."

By now, Napoo had reached them. "Napoo, could you?" Nellie indicated that she needed a screen from the men. The Urman grunted and stood in front of her, glaring at the backs of the tank crew.

Nellie quickly slipped off her ruined skirt, stepped into the coveralls and buttoned them up. The sleeves and legs were too long, but she just rolled them up.

"There," she said, arms spread as she modelled her blue coveralls. "What do you think?"

Cecil whistled, and—sensing Jack behind him—flinched involuntarily. Jack laughed. "You'll do."

As THEY DESCENDED the scree slope, the cries of unseen creatures echoed through the canopy rising before them, underscored by arboreal creaks and groans in the undergrowth ahead.

It wasn't hard to follow the tank's trail. Churned earth, shattered rocks, broken boughs and the exploded smears of creatures not quick enough to escape from its headlong rush marked its path. Following the ironclad's furrowing, they headed into the jungle, where everything seemed draped with large pallid creepers.

"Lieutenant!"

"Alfie!"

They called out at regular intervals, but there was no reply.

Norman spotted the first piece of wreckage, tossed aside in the undergrowth like abandoned farm equipment.

Nellie let out a gasp.

"Don't worry, said Reggie kindly. "It's just the—"

"Steering tail. I know," said Nellie. "I just wasn't prepared."

Attached to the rear of the tank, the steering tail had broken loose. Its great quarter-ton iron wheels lay on their sides, embedded in the ground. The boxes and packets of supplies it carried lay strewn back along its path, some lying pawed and torn open by curious scavengers. The steering tail's hydraulic fluid had long since leaked from it, pooled, and sunk into the ground.

Norman inspected the wreckage. He shook his head. "No way can we save this. Always thought the thing was a waste of space. Only ever worked on solid ground. It's good riddance, if you ask me."

With all the caution that this world had taught them, they advanced slowly along the *Ivanhoe*'s path, feeling naked and vulnerable without the ironclad shell that they had taken so much for granted.

Nellie's every step along the way was an agony of emotional turmoil; wanting to press on, but fearing what they might find.

"There!" cried Cecil.

In the arborous gloom of the forest floor, the huge bulk of His Majesty's Land Ship *Ivanhoe* squatted half-hidden in the undergrowth, at the edge of a clearing of its own making. It had come to rest surrounded by the tangled vegetation it had dragged along with it. Facing the tank crew, its drivers' visors down, it looked like some antediluvian beast asleep in its den.

Nellie felt a flood of relief. She wanted to rush towards it, but Napoo put out an arm to stop her.

Instead, Jack took a tentative step forward. "Lieutenant?" he called out. "Alfie!"

There was no answer.

Nellie found herself praying under her breath. "Oh, please, oh, please..."

A lingering aroma of petrol fruit vapour hung about the ditched ironclad. Nellie was quick to notice that Jack inhaled deeply once he recognised it.

"Is that the fuel?" she asked, her nostrils flaring as she sniffed the air. Jack gave a guilty start and avoided her gaze.

With a wave of his arm, he gestured for Norman, Reggie and Wally to circle round to the starboard side. Nellie, Jack, Cecil and Napoo edged around the port side.

The tank's two six-pounder guns hung, dejected but intact. Miraculously, the tracks were still in place, although they were gummed up with torn and shredded foliage. It seemed that the jungle undergrowth had absorbed most of the impact of its crash.

From round the far side, Nellie could hear the soothing tones as Wally tutted and talked to the iron behemoth. "What have they done to you, eh?"

At the front of the port sponson, Jack peered in through the vertical slit of the gunner's sight alongside the lifeless gun.

"Well?" asked Nellie.

Jack shrugged. "Can't see a thing."

They edged along the sponson, past the machine gun toward the rear. Jack held up his hand. They stopped as he peered round the back of the sponson to the entrance hatch, before swinging round out of sight, his revolver raised. A heartbeat later, his head reappeared back round the sponson and jerked them on.

There was a squeal from above. Startled, the soldiers glanced up, guns at the ready. Something small and furry fell out of the trees above, hitting branches as it fell, to crash limply into a small grove of black saplings at the edge of the clearing, where it lay still.

Distracted by the poor dead creature, fallen from some nest, it was a moment before Nellie recognised the saplings themselves. "Corpsewood! Be careful."

They knew the plant well enough, having used it to kill the Dulgur's young that ate Frank, their other gunner. It generally fed on dead animal matter, but would feed on the living where it could. They made sure to give it a wide berth.

Nellie heard a despairing groan from inside the tank. Up in the driver's cab, Wally had found Mathers' body slumped in the starboard gangway. The lieutenant's revolver was still in his hand. There was a small entry wound in his right temple, but its exit had blown away half his skull. Blood, bone and brain matter splattered the white-painted interior and blood had pooled below him and dried on the wooden planking.

The lieutenant's death shocked the crew; not so much the fact of it as the manner. They hadn't expected suicide.

They lifted Mathers' body from the tank with as much dignity as they could, given the cramped space, strapping the Subaltern's turtle-shell helmet to his head to keep what was left of his skull intact. Suicide or not, he was their commander, and as such he deserved their respect. Not wanting to leave his body to predators and scavengers, they used the entrenching tools from the *Ivanhoe* to dig a shallow grave at the edge of the clearing.

Wally collected the lieutenant's paybook, a couple of letters from his inside pocket and the metal identity disc from around his neck.

They laid the body in the grave and Norman said a simple, improvised prayer. They stood for a moment round the fresh grave, lost in their own thoughts. Then they buried him, enclosing him in the clays of a cold alien world. At the head of the mound of fresh dirt, they marked his resting place with hastily-cut boughs lashed into the form of a cross and hung Mathers' splash mask from it.

Despondent, the tankers mourned the loss of their commander, but Nellie could not mourn. All she could do was hope.

"Where's Alfie? Where is he?" she asked each of them in turn, trying to hide her rising panic. They shook their heads and would not meet her eyes. "He could be out there, injured," she insisted. She wanted it to be true, although she knew there were other, more likely possibilities on this world, possibilities about which she didn't want to think. "He could be out there. We have to find him, Napoo," she said, desperation seeping into her voice.

Napoo regarded her solemnly. "I cannot give you that hope. On this world, the likelihood of an injured man not falling prey to a predator is small." He bowed his head and turned from her.

Unwanted tears pooling in her eyes, Nellie watched horrified as pale tendrils unfurled from the stems of ebony corpsewood and felt their way towards the body of the small fallen animal before burrowing into its flesh, almost as if to illustrate Napoo's point.

It wasn't the only thing attracted by the small, broken carcass. From a puckered fruiting body, a fibrous white fungus spread slowly, weaving a cobweb of filaments across the soil as fine white mycelia quested through the humus towards it. The fungus wasn't fast enough. The corpsewood was already desiccating the carcass.

Nellie turned her head away, unable to watch.

Around the tank, the creaking continued, punctuated every now and again by sharp reports that they initially took for gunfire.

Moving so slowly she wouldn't have noticed had she not been still, it was possible to see the large pallid creepers that draped everything, gradually entwining themselves round the trees, seeking to choke and leach the life from them.

As she watched, it became clear to Nellie that there was a battle going on here, a battle she and the others were ill-equipped for. Two sets of competing flora were in a struggle for dominance: the forest and something else. Down here, the trees were engaged in a slow war and they seemed to be losing. Nellie felt uneasy being caught in the middle of it.

A SHOUT FROM Napoo roused her from her maudlin thoughts. He had found footprints.

They were human-like, but they weren't the distinctive hobnailed bootprint of the Tommy. These were smooth, less defined and deeper.

"Someone else has been here," he explained. "They arrived here. See? Lighter." He pointed out the shallow footprints across the clearing. "They left carrying something heavy."

Nellie stared at them. "Alfie?"

A continuous cracking sounded through the clearing. This wasn't the slow vegetable conflict she had begun to realise was all about them. This was something altogether faster and heavier. Something that was crashing through the undergrowth towards them, and gathering pace.

"Into the tank. Look lively!" cried Jack.

Without waiting to see what was coming, they scrambled through the sponson hatches, Nellie and Napoo with them, the Urman more than a little unwillingly. Once inside, they slammed the hatches shut and sat panting in the dark.

The crashing stopped. There followed loud low snorts and several heavy thudding footfalls. A low wet sniffing proceeded around them. The tank juddered as something large butted it.

The tank's crew glanced at each other in the semi-dark, came to a silent consensus, then loaded the guns and machine guns and flung themselves to the pistol ports, peering out, looking for their assailant.

"We can't drive this, there aren't enough of us," said Wally, scrambling into the driver's seat, trying to ignore the dried viscera that once belonged in Mathers' head.

"Yes, there are," said Nellie.

"But you're a woman," said Norman.

Nellie raised her eyebrows. "Yes. And this is the starboard track gear. This is the first speed. This is neutral," she said, showing him the gear levers.

Across the starting handle, Reggie grinned.

"Do you want me to tell you how the differential works?" she asked defiantly.

"I can see why Alfie likes you," said Reggie.

"All right!" said Wally. "Start the engine. Norman, get up here. I need you to operate the driving brakes."

It took four of them to turn the giant starting handle between the Daimler engine in the middle of the cramped compartment and the differential in the rear. The engine coughed unwillingly once or twice until it caught and roared into life, and the electric festoon lights flickered on.

Nellie couldn't stop the broad grin from spreading across her face as she took hold of the gear lever and waited for Wally's command. The thrill was muted when she saw the love heart hastily drawn in the grime of the engine casing. The heart she had once drawn for Alfie. She tried to ignore the dried blood at her feet. Was it Mathers' or Alfie's?

Napoo sat by her feet, hunched by the sponson door, his hands over his ears. She wanted to comfort him the way he had her, but she had a job to do.

She heard the two bangs from the wrench Wally wielded to communicate above the engine's roar and put the lever into neutral. The tank began to turn clockwise, presenting a broadside to the creature.

Cecil struggled to bring the six-pounder on the port side to bear on the thing as it paced round the tank. He squeezed the trigger. The loud report filled the compartment, contained and echoing off the metal walls.

Nellie gasped at the noise, loud even over the roar of the engine directly in front of her. It was beginning to get hot in there. She could feel the perspiration prickling her hairline. And that smell. Was that the petrol fruit fumes? She wondered what effect it would have on her.

The tank rocked again under the beast's charge.

To Nellie's left, Cecil let loose a burst of machine gun fire, the cartridge shells clattering to the floor and rolling out through a slot in the gangway.

The engine spluttered.

Jack leapt forwards and began working the manual pump for the starboard petrol tank by the commander's seat. Reggie did the same on the other side. The engine coughed a couple of times and died for good.

"We're out of fuel," he said in disbelief, his voice loud in the sudden silence.

Outside, they heard a thrashing in the undergrowth and a howl of frustration and pain that receded into the distance.

"It's gone," said Wally.

Nellie breathed a sigh of relief, her ears ringing. "Is this—is this what it's like all the time?" she asked Reggie, not sure whether she was drunk on the exhilaration of battle or the fumes.

"Mostly?" asked Reggie.

"Mm-hmm."

Reggie shook his head. "It's worse."

They clambered out of the dead tank. The ground was churned where the ironclad had turned. Black ichor dripped down the side of the sponson. It looked like Cecil had hit the creature. Jack grinned and rubbed his finger knuckles across Cecil's head as the lad beamed with pride.

They had used the last of *Ivanhoe's* fuel to fend off the attack. It had survived the fall into the crater, but without fuel the *Ivanhoe* was twenty-eight tons of scrap.

"So what do we do now?" asked Reggie.

"We find Alfie," said Nellie decisively. She looked around at the crew, an iron determination in her gaze, almost daring them to challenge her. None did. Even Norman, if he had anything to say, kept it to himself.

Taking what supplies they thought useful from the tank, they took a last look at the *Ivanhoe* and set off into the crater to find Alfie.

IN THE SHADE of the abandoned ironclad, the pale feeding tendrils of the ebony corpsewood saplings inched towards Mathers' freshly dug grave.

The fungus, too, stretched out a fine filigree of threads towards it and this time reached the prize first, its mycelia spreading out over the mound, like a hoarfrost blanket, as they began probing down through the newly turned soil for the freshly buried remains...

PENNINE FUSILIERS

CHAPTER FIVE
"One Grim Shadow..."

"It wants what?" said Everson in disbelief as he looked up from the daily reports.

Sergeant Hobson stood before the desk and winced in apology. "Petrol fruit fuel, sir. The Chatt asked for it quite specific, it did, sir."

"Did it now?" Everson sighed heavily and strode impatiently along the familiar trench route to the Chatt's dugout cell. He was trying to impose his authority after the mutiny and he resented the fact that he was here on terms other than his own. He saluted the guards, descended the dugout steps and peered into the makeshift cell. Chandar stood in the middle, facing the door, as if it expected him.

"Petrol fruit?" demanded Everson.

"This One had been thinking," said Chandar.

"Evidently." Everson slid the bolt on the door and dragged it open. "So enlighten me."

"The Urman called Mathers, he ingested the liquid. He was able to see what no Urman ever could. He was able to read the odorglyphics, divine the sacred scents. He sensed the prophecy of the last of the Nazarrii."

"So I believe."

"You said this One had to choose which scent to take. It is this One's belief that this liquid could help restore this One's ability to read the scents. This One could divine which would be most useful to this One's interpretation, one that will be of benefit to us both mutually, Khungarrii and Tohmii alike."

Everson considered the proposal before shaking his head. It was a big risk. "I don't know. It's made our men mad, killed others. We have no idea what effect it would have on... one of your kind."

Chandar hissed. It stepped forward, arms out, its two long fingers on each hand flexing, pleading. It swallowed a great gulp of air and regurgitated it into words: "For too long the Odours of GarSuleth have

556

been denied this One. This One will take the chance. Would you not do as much for your clan, for the Tohmii?"

Everson pursed his lips. He had to admit it could be a solution to their stalemate, and he couldn't see any other way forward. He just wasn't very happy about it. "Very well," he said. "But only under medical supervision. I don't want anything happening to you."

As THE CHATT watched from across the cell, Captain Lippett poured a measure of petrol fruit fuel into a small canteen sat on a small Tommy cooker, under which he had set a short candle stub.

"I'm not going to let you drink it," he told the thing. "This stuff has killed people. If you must persist in this madness, then breathe slowly and deeply as it vaporises."

He turned to Everson. "I don't know what help I can be if anything happens. Dissecting them is one thing, keeping them alive is another."

"Well, I hope it won't come to that, Doctor."

Atkins arrived with a selection of stone amphorae and clay vials rescued from the ruined edifice.

Chandar studied the sealed containers. "This one. This. That one."

Having made its choice, Atkins placed the selected jars on the floor.

"I want everybody out before I light this," said Lippett by the Tommy cooker.

Everson and Atkins withdrew from the cell.

Nurse Bell stood by with a tray of medical supplies Lippett thought they might need if the worse came to the worst. Her lips curled in disgust. "What's it doing?" she asked.

Atkins shrugged. "It seems to think that the petrol fruit fuel will restore its ability to smell."

Edith's eyes narrowed. "Is that possible?"

"With them? Hard to say. Killed a man, though, and damn near killed me; drove Mathers mad and made his crew paranoid."

Despite her revulsion, she forced herself to watch, lost in thought, as Lippett lit the candle with a Lucifer and stepped sharply from the cell.

Everson pushed the door shut. He watched through the judas hole for a moment as Chandar arranged the jars in front of him. The small candle flame guttered under the bowl of liquid, casting high shadows and imparting an almost demonic quality to the Chatt.

Chandar began fingering the knotted tassels on its silk wrap as if it had never seen them before. It lifted another tassel, looking at it. Then another.

It breathed deeply of the vapours rising from the bowl and reached out for one of the amphorae. With its two fingers and thumb, it drew the stopper from the jar and swilled the contents. It tilted its head back, its gaze following the imperceptible whorls and eddies of the rising vapours, as if watching the emergence of an invisible genie from the bottle. Occasionally it swirled the contents of the bottle to refresh its perception. It stoppered that bottle and repeated the same performance with the other two.

Slowly, it rose up to its full height, its mandibles clicking as its mouth parts smacked rapidly in its own speech. It seemed excited. It turned to face Everson, almost belching out the words "It is GarSuleth's Will," before staggering sideways and collapsing against the wall.

Everson yanked the cell door open and Lippett was first in. He blew out the candle and handed the bowl to Atkins. "Dispose of this," he said, "out in the open."

Nurse Bell hung back, unable to bring herself to enter.

"Nurse, we have a patient," Lippett chided.

Hesitantly, she entered the dugout cell. Everson pushed in past her.

Chandar stretched out an arm towards Everson. "This One has been blessed. GarSuleth speaks to it once more." In its excitement, its speech dissolved into the harsh smacking and clickings of its native language.

"It was a success, then?" Everson said.

Chandar cast its arms open, its vestigial limbs following suit. "It was... different, strange. This One saw nuances and connections it had never noticed before. It will take practice, but in time this One could once more sense the text as this One has always done. Perhaps better." It picked up a jar. "This," it said. "This One will take this scent back to Khungarr. It contains the Commentaries of Chitaragar. Khungarr has not possessed this essence for generations. The original has long since evaporated. Only fleeting notes of it exist in other distillations."

It reached out to Everson, grasping his sleeves with its long fingers. Everson fought against the reflex to pull away.

"This One shall return to Khungarr," it said. "It is GarSuleth's Will."

The Chatt had put the ball back in his court. He couldn't allow the threat of the Khungarrii to loom over them for much longer.

Everson knew he had to keep his word and let the Chatt go, but he didn't trust it, not completely.

"Then I want someone to go with you to make sure you stick to your side of the bargain," he said.

"Very well," it said.

Now all Everson had to do was find a volunteer.

PADRE RAND HAD already forgiven the man who hit him. However, since the assault, the visions he suffered had begun to plague him with greater frequency, fraying the edges of his faith. They were shades of the vision he had experienced in Khungarr, when along with Jeffries, the Chatts forced him to undergo a cleansing ritual. Since then they haunted him, just beyond the edges of his perception. He would wake up in a cold sweat, the visions receding faster than he could recall them, leaving only the memory of terror.

A pulse of pain built and flared, hot and sharp in his skull. He touched his bandaged head as his vision darkened and the world tilted. He reached out to balance himself against the wall of the trench; in the momentary blackness that swallowed him, he felt something waiting for him, in the heart of the pain. Then, just as suddenly as it had appeared, the pain faded and his sight returned to normal.

He looked around as he recovered his composure, to see if anyone had noticed, but there was no one else in that stretch of trench. He was distressed to find the vision plaguing him even during his waking hours. Was there to be no relief from it?

He prayed to the light for guidance, but he knew what he had to face was hidden in the dark.

"I BELIEVE YOU need someone to accompany the Chatt to Khungarr," the padre told Everson.

"How did you know about that?" Everson asked.

The padre was in an aid post, sat on a barrel, having his wound redressed by Nurse Bell. The bruising on his still swollen temple was now turning a dull green. It throbbed.

"Secrets of the confessional," said the padre, glancing absently at Nurse Bell. "Never mind how I know, John. Is it true?"

"Yes. If there is a possibility of some armistice with these creatures, then it's a chance I have to take. I need someone who can be diplomatic, who can advocate for us. I can't pretend it won't be risky. I can't assure the safety of anyone who goes."

From the moment he heard of Everson's dilemma, the padre knew with certainty what he had to do. He had been looking for a sign. Surely, this was Divine Providence at work. A return to Khungarr. There, where it all began, he might uncover what dark revelations his vision harboured. He drew himself up, grimacing as his head pounded.

"Then I will go," he said. "As commanding officer you can't go yourself; you can't send a soldier, you can't spare the officers. I'm the logical choice. They might hold you responsible for the damage caused to their edifice, but a priest? I might be more acceptable as an observer."

"I'll go with him," said Edith, taking a step forward before she knew she was saying it.

The men stared at her.

"What, might I not know my own mind?" she countered. "I'm

concerned about the padre's injury. He's not yet fully recovered. At least if I am with him, I can take care of it."

"It's not necessary, Nurse," the padre protested.

"Nurse Bell—" Everson began.

"What?" Nurse Bell glowered. "You let Nellie go off to find the *Ivanhoe*. I've faced many fears since we arrived here, Lieutenant," she said, "and become the stronger for it. And both the padre and I have been to Khungarr before."

"As prisoners," Everson reminded her gently.

"Then let me go back of my own free will, face my fears, and do my job!"

Everson raised his eyebrows in appeal to the padre for support, but the chaplain seemed just as taken aback by the strength of the young woman's conviction.

Everson sighed with exasperation. "Nurse Bell, if you're convinced the padre needs medical supervision, then yes, I agree."

"I beg your pardon," said the padre.

"You're letting me go?" she asked with disbelief.

"Yes, although any more outbursts like that and I might change my mind."

Nurse Bell's face flushed.

Everson clasped the padre's hands. "There's not a lot I trust on this world, but I trust you, Padre. I need you fit and well."

The padre smiled faintly. "I tend to put my trust in the Lord, John, but I'm sure He won't take it personally."

EVERSON COULDN'T SPARE the men to escort them across the veldt, but then he didn't need to. They had the captured battlepillars. It would be much quicker and safer to cross the veldt on one of those.

In the aid tent, Edith hid the small jar containing the Commentaries of Chitaragar in her haversack of medical supplies. They hoped that the scents and aromas of the various medicines and unguents would disguise any tell-tale signs of the potential heresy they were effectively smuggling into Khungarr. Everson also provided her with a bottle of distilled petrol fruit fuel, for Chandar's personal use.

Atkins and his section escorted the Chatt to the old Poulet farmhouse where the battlepillar was waiting, a sapper sat in the howdah at the great beast's head.

Everson shook the padre's hand. "Good luck, Padre. And thank you."

The padre nodded towards the camp. "Don't forget, John: they're not soldiers, they're men."

Everson nodded, then turned to Nurse Bell. "Look after him. And yourself. I don't want another Edith Cavell on my hands."

"I will, Lieutenant. Thank you," she said.

The padre and Nurse Bell climbed a ladder to a large cradle slung along the side of the beast.

"I don't want them to come to any harm," Everson warned Chandar as the Chatt clambered aboard the cradle.

"They will be safe under this One's protection."

EVERSON STOOD ON the OP platform of the Poulet Farmhouse and watched the small party as even the huge battlepillar was gradually swallowed by the immensity of the veldt before them.

Hobson appeared beside him and watched in silence for a moment.

"Do you trust 'em, sir? The Chatts, I mean."

"Chandar? Maybe. The rest? Not as far as I can throw them, Sergeant," Everson said.

"Glad to hear it, sir," said Hobson, walking along behind him as they strode down the communication trench and up the crude earthen steps onto the ground towards the hospital tents.

"This is why I want insurance."

Everson entered the Aid tent, and Stanton the medical orderly stood to attention. He returned the salute crisply and got down to business. "I'm given to understand you used to work in a cotton mill in the chemical labs before the war, Stanton."

"Sir."

"Then I have a job for you. I need your expertise, not as a medical orderly but as a chemist."

"Sir?"

"You remember the Khungarrii attack on the trenches?"

"Of course, sir."

"The poppies out beyond the front line disorientated the Chatts somehow, threw them into confusion. Maybe it was something in their scent."

"Excuse me, sir, but poppies don't smell."

"Maybe not to us, Stanton. But one cannot doubt their effect on the Chatts. We all saw it and were able to take advantage of it. Maybe there is something in the poppies against which they have no natural defence, because it's alien to this world. There has to be a way we can harness that effect deliberately; enhance it, strengthen it, turn it into something we can use against them."

"Like a gas, sir?"

Everson nodded his head with approval. "Yes. Something that we can use to de-louse on a large scale. Do you want to have a crack at it?"

Stanton's eyes widened and he stood straighter, taller. He pushed out his chest. "Me, sir? Just give me a chance, sir."

"Then you've got it, Stanton," said Everson, handing him a scrap of paper. "The men on this list have chemical or horticultural experience that might help. See what you can come up with."

Stanton took the paper and saluted. "Yes, sir."

"The padre was right," Everson confided in Hobson as they left the tent. "I'd forgotten that they were men before the war. Appealing to their sense of duty wasn't enough. I have to appeal to the man."

"Very wise, sir," said Hobson.

Several electric blue flashes crackled and bloomed briefly above the trenches within the support ring, accompanied by too brief a scream.

"What the hell?"

Everson had seen the phenomenon before in the presence of Khungarrii electric lances. Was it a raiding party? And if it was, how the hell did they get past the sentries? Shouts of alarm went up from various quarters. Everson drew his Webley and weaved his way through the trenches towards the disturbance.

Everson and Hobson met near the fire bay with several other soldiers also converging on the scene.

Hobson nodded at them.

"Trench clearance formation," he hissed.

After the mutiny, only those on sentry duty had magazines and loaded rifles. The others had to make do with their bayonets.

Hobson peered round the sandbag traverse. "Clear," he hissed back.

The clearance party slipped into the unoccupied fire bay as Everson moved to enter the next.

He peered cautiously round the separating traverse, his revolver cocked.

A soldier lay splayed on the floor of the bay, his body wracked in spasms. He kicked and thrashed spastically, his boots scraping against the duckboards. Wisps of smoke rose from the soles. A corporal was knelt beside him, trying to place an old strip of leather belt between his teeth. "Bite down on this, now, Tonkers. Bite down, that's it."

There was no sign of any Chatts, although shards of a Chatt's clay backpack lay strewn about the bay and an electric lance lay against the firestep. Everson jerked his head and Hobson sent a couple of men peering over the revetments.

"All clear, Sarn't," they reported.

Everson stepped into the fire bay.

"What happened here?" asked Everson urgently.

He noticed the Signals brassard on his arm. The NCO looked up. It was Corporal Riley.

"Sorry, sir," said the NCO with a disarming shrug. "Didn't mean to alarm you. Just an accident, sir. Tonkins here'll be all right," he said. The signaller's fit seemed to be passing. The corporal held him, all the while talking to him in a low voice. "You'll be all right, lad."

"Stretcher bearer!" Everson hollered.

"No, it's all right, sir. He'll be right as ninepence shortly. It's not the first time."

Everson looked at Hobson, who dismissed the soldiers back to their posts. He turned his attention to the fusilier on the ground. His tone softened a touch. "What do you mean, it's not the first time? What's wrong with him?"

"One moment, sir." The corporal called out. "Buckley!"

A soldier swept back the gas curtain, stepped smartly out and saluted the lieutenant. The sandy-haired lad had shiny red cheeks that looked as if they'd been polished, like an apple. "Sorry, sir. Didn't see you there."

"It's all right, Buckley," said the corporal. "Give me a hand with Tonkers here."

Buckley helped the corporal get Tonkins to his feet and the pair half-dragged, half-carried the dead weight of the still twitching Fusilier into the dugout.

Corporal Riley reappeared, holding the gas curtain aside. "If you wouldn't mind, sir?"

Everson and Hobson entered the dugout. It was crammed with crates and boxes of stores. The place served as office, workshop and storeroom for the few signallers that had been stranded with them. The three men from Signals kept the telephone and heliograph communications working with the observation posts. Three more were up on the Hill OP.

Large reels of copper wire lay against the walls, like huge cotton bobbins. There were lengths of cable, batteries, boxes of signal flares and several heliograph machines on closed tripods. In the corner lay a collection of semaphore flags. On a bench, several wooden-boxed field telephones sat in various states of disassembly, and an assortment of salvaged Morse code keys lay amidst scattered screwdrivers, wire cutters, wire strippers and other tools. However, what caught Everson's eye was the untidy heap of the Chatt clay backpacks and electric lances. Some were broken, some merely cracked, and quite a few were intact, although they were in marked contrast to the ones that stood neatly against the opposite dirt wall.

Tonkins lay on a rude bed in an adjoining room. He seemed more peaceful now. The spasms and twitches had stopped.

"Corporal Riley, just what the hell is going on? What just happened to Tonkins?"

Riley cleared his throat. "What do you know about telephony, sir?"

"That it's a damned nuisance when the wires get shelled or cut."

Riley's cheeks reddened. "Tell me about it, sir. We're the ones who have to go out and fix it. Only just finished repairing the lines after that damned mutiny. 'Scuse my French, sir."

"Riley," said Everson, beginning to lose patience. "What have telephones got to do with that Chatt electric lance out there?"

"Well as far as we know, the electric lances are charged by the Chatts themselves, kind of like an electric eel. They generate their own charge. The clay pack is kind of like a battery, storing and amplifying this charge, which they release through the lance."

"And the field telephones?"

Riley picked up a wooden box and sat it on the bench with a thump. "A field telephone, sir. Type C Mark II, using two cells, electric, dry, charged by a magneto via the crank handle.

"We managed to recover a lot of these here backpacks after the Chatt siege, and Tonkins there said, 'Well if all they need is a charge, why can't we just fit 'em with a magneto?' He's been tinkering all week, and we think we've got it licked."

"Licked?" Hobson nodded toward Tonkins. "You call that licked?"

"Oh, aye, we're learning all the time."

"And what exactly have you learnt this time?" asked Everson.

"This time?" Riley rubbed the back of his neck as he gave it some thought. "Not to connect a wire straight into the conductive slime, for one. And if you do, wear gum boots, feet, for the use of."

Riley picked up one of the smooth crimson clay backpacks. It had a number '5' scratched onto it. Everson glanced around. He couldn't see numbers one to four; although he had a suspicion that number four lay outside in pieces. The clay container was curved in the inner surface to sit flush with a scentirrii carapace, but Riley had rigged it with some 1908 Pattern leather webbing and empty sandbags for padding, for a more human fit. Near the top of the clay container, inserted in a carved round hole, was a crank handle Everson recognised as coming from a field telephone.

"Buckley, come here, I need you," said Riley.

Buckley shot a nervous glance at the prostrate Tonkins.

"Never mind him, lad. Probably picked up a cracked one. You'll be all right if you wear gum boots for the test."

"Will he?" asked Everson confidentially.

"Probably," said Riley with a shrug. "Anything has to be better than earthing through bleedin' Army-issue hobnailed boots."

"Hmm."

A sour-faced Buckley picked up a pair of trench waders and pulled them on before lifting up and shouldering the backpack. They had reconnected the electric lance to it with a length of rubber-insulated cable in a braided hessian sheath.

Riley picked it up and handed it to him, then bent forward, inspected the backpack and tugged on the webbing. "You'll do," he said finally, giving him a shove through the gas curtain.

"After you, sir," he said with a sweep of his arm. Everson ducked his head and stepped out into the trench. Buckley waited, holding the lance awkwardly. Hobson joined them and Riley brought up the rear smartly, stepping over to Buckley and standing behind him.

"If you wouldn't mind, gentlemen?" he said, indicating that the officer should take cover. Everson and Hobson stepped back by the sandbagged traverse.

"Well, on guard, lad, on guard!" said Riley, noting Buckley's less than enthusiastic posture.

Buckley took a step forward, taking a stance as if the lance were a rifle and bayonet. Riley tapped Buckley once on the shoulder and began to wind the magneto's crank handle that now protruded from the clay pack. A quiet whirr built as the spindle inside the magneto revolved faster and faster. For a moment, it seemed as if nothing would happen. A nervous Buckley fidgeted as he gripped the lance.

Everson and Hobson exchanged concerned glances.

Riley gritted his teeth and wound the handle furiously a while longer. Then he let go and tapped Buckley on the shoulder. Twice. This time, a brilliant blue-white arc of energy blasted out across the fire bay, exploding against the far sandbag traverse. The sandbags erupted. Scorched, shredded hessian and dirt showered down on them.

When the dust settled, Buckley was still standing and the Chatt device was still in one piece.

Riley turned and grinned. "Well, that went better than expected, eh?"

WHEN THE BATTLEPILLAR reached the edge of the forest, the driver would go no further. The padre, Nurse Bell and Chandar dismounted and, under the Chatt's guidance, proceeded on foot. From here on in, they were on their own.

They walked for several hours through the forest until Chandar directed them to stop by a grove of trees. There they waited.

Several hours later, a patrol of Chatt soldiers, scentirrii, led by none other than Rhengar, the Khungarrii general, appeared. Its antennae waved, sensing something.

Chandar stepped forward and greeted them, its arms open wide as it breathed its benediction over its fellow Chatts.

"Where have you been?" wheezed Rhengar. "Was your undertaking a success? This One has waited here every spinning at the appointed time. This One had given up hopes of your return, Chandar."

"GarSuleth has willed it, Rhengar."

Rhengar and Chandar fell to speaking rapidly in their own language, with many glances toward the chaplain and the nurse. The padre got the feeling that Rhengar didn't approve of their presence. Eventually the two Chatts reached some agreement and the party headed on into the forest, the scentirrii, their antennae twitching, escorting Padre Rand and Nurse Bell along a path only they could detect.

In a way, Padre Rand felt that he too followed such an invisible path, guided by a Divine hand; from his comfortable parish of St Chad's in Broughtonthwaite, to the trenches of France, where he lost the trail, like a path petering out on featureless moors. It was only once he found himself here, on this world, that he found his path again. Here, where he thought himself lost from God's sight, that still, small voice could be heard if he but listened, for the men of the Pennines were themselves God's creations, even if nothing else in this world was. A spark of the Divine existed in each one of them, so even out here, in the shadow of death, there was a light to mark the way. He drew comfort and strength from that. Like Daniel in the lion's den, he felt a calmness, as though he was at the centre of a storm. He walked erect and with a feeling of peace he hadn't known for a long time. But he knew this was only a moment of clarity, for even Our Lord had His Gethsemane.

Nurse Bell walked close beside him, but whether out of fear or concern he couldn't say. Maybe both. It wasn't surprising. He had surprised himself by volunteering for this, just as she had surprised him by offering to accompany him. Her Christian charity touched and partly shamed him. In coming here, he had an ulterior motive. Bell could have none, other than his welfare at heart. He did wonder briefly whether that made her the better person.

Nevertheless, he offered up a silent prayer of thanks for her presence. At least now, he would be forced to go through with his plan. Alone, he might not have had the strength. His resolve might have failed as it had before. His faith was gaining the fervour he once held, but it still felt fragile.

"You are one of the Tohmii's dhuyumirrii?" wheezed Rhengar, waving its mouth palps behind its mandibles.

"A priest, yes," said the padre.

"You do not worship GarSuleth." There was no intonation in its voice. There never was with Chatts. It took them enough effort to form the words in the first place. He wasn't even sure if they had emotions as he experienced them.

"No. I do not."

Rhengar fell silent, clicking its mandibles together in a thoughtful manner as it walked.

The padre wondered whether he had gone too far, spoken out of turn and offended them.

Chandar caught up with them and limped alongside. "They are scentirrii," it explained. "They are not bred to question."

"Stop," said Rhengar, coming to a sudden halt.

The group of scentirrii stopped with him. Rhengar turned towards the padre and Nurse Bell. "You go no further," it told them.

Nurse Bell stepped forward, affronted. "But you said—"

"You will be killed." It signalled to the scentirrii guards. They turned and advanced towards them.

The padre wheeled on Chandar in disbelief. "You told the lieutenant that we would be safe."

There was no time for the crippled Chatt to reply. The scentirrii closed in about them. The padre gathered Nurse Bell to him, putting his arms around her. She looked up into his eyes, and then turned to face the Chatts with defiance as the padre rattled out a hasty orison under his breath.

The gathered scentirrii opened their mandibles and hissed as one...

INTERLUDE TWO

Letter from Lance Corporal Thomas Atkins
to Flora Mullins

1st April 1917

My Dearest Flora,

Off to get the Boojum back tomorrow. Don't worry, I know where we left it. Not only that, we get a ride there, too. Should be a cushy number, which would be a first for this place. Just a case of 'there and back to see how far it is,' as Dad says. Porgy's happy and you know how workshy he is, so that bodes well. Pot Shot says it's going to be like riding elephants from the Raj. Not sure what I think about that. I know Mam will worry about me getting airs and graces what with riding round like a maharajah, though. Perhaps I should get Pot Shot to send her one of his pamphlets about how all workers deserved to be treated like that! Not that I'm complaining. I may even get used to it. Gutsy's not happy though. He's never been a good traveller, unless it's by Shanks's pony.

The padre is going to visit the locals, with whom we've been having a little difficulty. You could say it's raised a bit of a stink. I thought the French could be a bit off, but this lot take the biscuit. Still, with a little bit of luck it might all be sorted out by the time we get back, and we'll all come up smelling of roses.

Ever yours
Thomas

CHAPTER SIX
"I Knew That Sullen Hall..."

EVERSON CALLED THE officers together for a briefing in the Command Post. They had to be ready for whatever might happen next and he was trying to prepare them as best as possible. Unfortunately, most of them were like Palmer, good solid officers who could take orders, but not the initiative. Tulliver, on the other hand, he felt had too much initiative.

"So you've let the Chatt go?" said Palmer.

Everson shook his head. "Not exactly. We've come to an agreement. Right now, we have something they want. We're holding the sacred scent texts we found to ransom until we get the deal we need."

"Which is?"

"Basically? They leave us alone, we leave them alone. If Chandar can convince its colony that we are not this Great Corruption their high priest speaks of, then there's a good chance that can happen. From there, we'll have to have further negotiations."

"But to send the chaplain and a nurse back with it!"

"Chandar wanted someone to speak our case to the Khungarrii council, the Shura. Padre Rand volunteered. He felt they might listen more to a priest than a soldier. I think he may be right."

"And the nurse? Good God, man."

"The padre sustained a head injury during the mutiny. Nurse Bell feels he may still need medical care."

"I can confirm that," said Lippett. "It does mean that I'm short of two nurses thanks to your plans, Everson. Damn fine nurses, too."

"I thought you didn't approve of women on the front line, Doc."

Lippett shifted in his chair. "I didn't, but since those three arrived, they've done their damnedest to make themselves indispensable, blast them. You make sure that Abbott and Bell get back, John, or it won't be me you have to answer to, it'll be Sister Fenton; and I, for one, wouldn't want to be in your shoes then."

"Point taken."

Seward still wasn't convinced. "If this gambit of yours fails, Everson, the padre and the nurse will be killed," he protested.

"And many of us shortly after," said Everson. "They knew the risks, Seward, and if the padre can tip the scale with a few impassioned words rather than bullets, then that suits me."

"And if he doesn't, the Chatts will come for us again?" asked Haslam.

"Without doubt," Everson told them candidly. "But we'll be ready for them. We already have battlepillars. We have several platoons of Urmen that Sergeant Dixon has trained. In addition, Corporal Riley in Signals has had a breakthrough with the electric lances. We are adapting, gentlemen."

"And what about the gunpowder experiment?" asked Seward.

The huge tarpaulin-covered heaps of manure were a source of contention for the sanitation parties.

There, Everson had to admit defeat. "The dung and the charcoal are no problem and, with the men, there is no shortage of urine for saltpetre, but we're still looking for a source of sulphur. We've had a production line of jam tin grenades being made and when we run out of Ticklers' tins, Houlton of 'A' Company has found a substitute casing in some sort of fruit gourd."

"Hand 'gourd'-nades, eh?" said Palmer with a chuckle.

Everson's shoulders dropped with relief as a ripple of light laughter washed round the dugout. He knew these officers well. Once they'd found the humour in a subject, it spoke of a certain acceptance. He had won them round. All he had to do now was to rescue the tank, to bring their defences up to full strength.

"Palmer, I'll leave you in charge of defences. Keep a tight rein on the NCOs. I don't want them using my absence for personal reprisals. The ringleaders, and those caught for offences, have been punished. That's an end to it. And for God's sake, see what you can do with that Kreothe carcass up the valley. It's beginning to rot and the stench is frankly appalling. It'll bring every scavenger for miles down here."

"Actually, they don't seem to care for it," said Palmer. "It seems to be doing a damn fine job of keeping them away."

Lippett coughed. "Actually, I wouldn't mind studying this aerozoan Kreothe before you do anything. Portions of its body seem to be decaying into some sort of gelatinous matter. Some of the men are calling it 'star jelly.' They've reported a sulphurous smell associated with its decomposition and, if that's the case, it might solve our gunpowder problem."

"Are you sure?" asked Everson, intrigued.

Lippett shrugged. "No, but it bears further investigation, don't you think?"

"Very well, I'll leave that in your capable hands. Communications. Tulliver, you're going to have to be our line of communication to camp. You'll be our lifeline and our eyes, so yes, you'll get to fly."

Tulliver needed to hear no more. He rocked his chair onto its back legs and beamed at the rest of them, like a man who had just got a two-week pass.

"I'll be leading the salvage party out to the Croatoan Crater to recover the tank. On the way I'll leave a party to take a look at this mysterious 'wall' that Atkins found. I must admit, I'm eager to see it myself."

"Maybe take some men from Signals, see if they can pick up anything with their Iddy Umpty gear, hear anything inside," suggested Baxter.

"My thoughts exactly," said Everson. "We'll also take a couple of Riley's jerry-rigged electric lances, too. Give them a proper field trial." Everson looked round the room. "That's all, gentlemen. You have your orders." He gathered up his papers to indicate that the meeting was over. "Dismissed," he added lightly.

As they left, Everson fingered the khaki scrap and button in his pocket. The metal wall and the tank were certainly priorities, but he had one more objective for this trip, and that was to find Jeffries' trail.

TULLIVER STRODE ACROSS the parade ground from the briefing with a spring in his step and a grin smeared across his face. He was walking on air. He felt he barely needed his bus to fly, but fly it he would.

He felt no need to stick to the trenches, even though they felt familiar and comforting to most of the men. Those of a nervous disposition didn't have to face the alien landscape about them, and it helped hold their nerve. It felt like home.

Not to Tulliver, though. Up there, that was his home and that was where he was going. That new predator up there would have to watch out; next time, he'd be ready for it.

AT DAWN THE next day, the tank salvage party—a platoon of Fusiliers and a platoon of Fred Karno's Army, drilled and trained Urmen outfitted in an odd combination of part-worns, carapace chest plates and steel helmets—fell in around the two captured battlepillars that Everson hoped would be able to haul the tank to safety.

The Fusiliers had outfitted the captured Khungarrii larval beasts of burden for their own use. Several people-carrying panniers had been slung along the sides of the beasts, Chatt-style. Unlike the Chatts, the Fusiliers had modified them to ride at varying heights, allowing for a wider field of fire by the pannier occupants, fore and aft, without their neighbours obstructing their view or aim. They had also constructed a less ornate, more functional howdah for the 'drivers.' One had been a drayman before the war, so it stood to reason in the minds of most that his be the unenviable task of controlling the brutes.

The private saluted as Everson passed. "Woolridge, isn't it?" asked Everson.

"Yes, sir."

Everson's face softened. "Your father was an Everson's drayman, wasn't he?"

"That were my uncle, sir."

"Ah. Right."

Everson looked up at one of the beasts. "What do you think to them?"

"Big Bertha and Big Willie, sir? They seem docile enough, sir. They're easy to command now we've got the reins figured out."

"I certainly hope so." Everson nodded his approval. "Carry on, Private."

It was more than a mere battlepillar omnibus, however. Lieutenant Baxter and his Machine Gun Section had mounted a Lewis machine gun tripod to a small chariot-like basket just forward of the driver's howdah. They had also turned the section of the fuselage salvaged from a downed 1½ Strutter from Tulliver's squadron, with the observer's seat and the Scarff-ring-mounted Lewis machine gun, into a tail-end machine gun emplacement down the creature's armoured back.

Everson saw Hepton, pushing through the milling soldiers assigned to the salvage operation as they checked their gear and bartered for final supplies from mates, but ignored him. Everson couldn't bring himself to like the man. He had been foisted on them to record the battle for Harcourt Wood for the folks back in Blighty. He was only supposed to be with them for a day or two. In the end, he had got rather more than he bargained for, and so had Everson. Hepton had been a constant irritant ever since. He turned his attention to the supply manifest that Sergeant Hobson had handed him.

Hepton spotted him. "Lieutenant, you weren't thinking of going without me, were you?"

Everson looked up from his clipboard. "As a matter of fact, yes, I was."

Hepton pulled a face of mock hurt and put a hand to his heart. "You wound me, Lieutenant. It's my job. I'm authorised by the War Office to make you look good for the folks back home. You want to look good, don't you? All I'm looking for is a little excitement, a little action."

"Exactly the things I was hoping to avoid," said Everson.

Hepton smiled his greasy smile and shrugged. "In that case, I'll settle for a spectacular otherworldly landscape. Can't say fairer than that, eh?" he said with a wink, rubbing his hands together.

Hobson tapped Everson on the arm and drew him aside. Hepton, hands behind his back, proceeded to rock back and forth on his heels, pretending to inspect the battlepillar in whose shadow they were standing.

"It might be better to keep him where we can see him, sir," said Hobson in a low voice. "He's a troublemaker, by all accounts. If we leave him here—well, the devil makes work, sir," he said in a low voice.

"Is that your considered opinion, Sergeant?"

"It is, sir. The chap's a malcontent, a real four-letter man, sir."

Everson *hmphed* his agreement.

"Hepton?"

The kinematographer turned at the sound of his name.

"Very well. We move out in ten minutes. You have five to get your equipment together."

A straight razor grin sliced open Hepton's face. "You won't regret it, Lieutenant, you won't regret it." He turned and began to wade back through the crowd, waving and calling over the men as he went, "Jenkins, Jenkins, bring my things. Over here, man. Hurry."

Everson blinked. "Did you give him permission to use one of my privates as a batman?" he asked Hobson.

Affronted by the question, the NCO frowned. "Certainly not, sir."

"Damn the man."

THE NCOs BARKED their orders and the men began to embark the battlepillars. They climbed the ladders, one section to a pannier. Six panniers each side, the rear two panniers filled with supplies and equipment. They also carried drums of spare petrol fruit fuel for the tank strapped to the back of Big Willie, and two of the experimental magneto-powered electric lance backpacks and various sets of telephonic equipment.

"Careful, don't drop anything, lad," cautioned Corporal Riley as Buckley hauled the gear up into the pannier with Tonkins' help.

The battlepillars moved out up the hillside towards the head of the valley. The Khungarrii reprisals against the Pennines had also displaced clans of nomadic Urmen in the process, some of whom sought the shelter and protection of the British Tommies. NCOs had drilled and trained their men into platoons to replace those of the 13th Pennines who were wounded, missing or dead. The training had worked, mostly. Many of them stood their ground when the Khungarrii laid siege to the trenches, and the jeering from the Fusiliers that assaulted them during their training had turned to respect in most cases. However, many would not board the battlepillars, preferring to run alongside or scout ahead. Everson watched them with an odd feeling of nostalgia. Seeing the Urmen in their mixture of native and British equipment brought a Colonial air to the whole endeavour.

1 Section was in the first of Big Bertha's starboard panniers. Gutsy was leant over the side of the basket. The undulating movement of the battlepillar didn't agree with him.

"He was like this on the boat over from Blighty," said Porgy cheerfully. "As green as the meat he sells."

Gutsy straightened up and whirled round with a raised finger to contest the slur, but he clamped his lips tight as his cheeks bellowed out. He leant over the side of the pannier and threw up again.

"And that," said Porgy to the section replacements who had edged to the far end of the pannier, "is why he's called Gutsy."

THE CANYON WAS less than a day's travel by battlepillar. It was a lot quicker than walking and, by comparison, quicker than the tank or a Hom Forty. The battlepillars' size also deterred the more opportunistic scavengers and predators, and they reached the canyon by late afternoon without incident, much to Hepton's disgust.

As eager as he was to see the mysterious wall, Everson erred on the side of caution. The canyon was a good place for an ambush.

"We'll make camp here for the night," he ordered. "We'll go down into the canyon in full light."

Knotted ropes were thrown over the sides of the panniers and the men shimmied down, thankful for the solid ground—Gutsy most of all, although it took him a few minutes to find his land legs, much to the amusement of the others.

NCOs began barking orders and the men fell to their appointed tasks. Woolridge saw to the battlepillars. They seemed content to spend the night tethered side by side, nose to tail, like horses. Two sections established a secure perimeter and others unloaded supplies while the men set up their bivouacs.

Gazette set about starting a cooking fire for their section. Porgy, however, slunk off before someone volunteered him to collect firewood.

Half an hour later, he crept back to the fire, a grin on his face and patting a couple of webbing pouches.

"I'd stay clear of 4 Section, if I were you," he said slumping down on his bedroll. "They're in a bad mood. And it'll be even worse tomorrow morning."

"Oh, bloody hell, Porgy. What've you done now?" asked Pot Shot with a sigh.

"Just relieved them of their last gaspers in a game of 'Housey,'" he said pulling a battered cigarette packet from his webbing. "Fag, anyone?"

* * *

THE NEXT MORNING, the battlepillars descended out of the early morning sunlight into the cold shadow of the canyon, past the still-inert deadly blister-like blue-green hemispherical growths scattered over the surface of the canyon walls.

Atkins and his men had found to their cost that these bloated alien lichen contained reservoirs of some acidic substance. They ate away at the rock itself, absorbing the minerals and leaving the shallow circular pockmarks that scarred the rock all around them.

The battlepillars moved down into the canyon as it twisted and jinked down through the rock strata. Round a bend and high up on the cliff face, at the top of the scree slope, Everson caught his first sight of the mysterious metal wall.

The wall was embedded in the rock, as though the rock face had crumbled away to expose it. A glimmer of dawn light caught the face of the brushed silver metal, suffusing it with a warm crimson glow.

The working party began to disembark with their equipment. By the time they returned this way, he hoped the working party might have some answers, but Everson couldn't resist seeing the thing for himself. He summoned Atkins to accompany him up the scree slope, eager to inspect this mysterious wall up close.

Everson laid a hand on the sheer metal with a sense of wonder. It was flat, smooth, and warm to the touch, despite the chill of the morning air. "Intriguing," he said as he considered the conundrum in front of them. It seemed so much at odds with what they had experienced of this world so far. When they first arrived, there had initially been hopes of civilisations with gleaming citadels. Their first encounter with the Chatts and their earthen edifices disabused them of that romantic notion. This, however; this was different. "You're right. This isn't natural," he said as Atkins scrambled up the last few feet of scree to meet him. "So the questions are; what is it, who built it and why?"

"I don't know, sir. We came across it tracking the tank. We couldn't dent it, or scratch it, not even with a grenade, and as you can see, no markings, no doors, no windows, no features of any kind. Nothing. It might as well be solid for all the good it did us."

Everson took off his cap, smoothed his hair back and, slipping the cap under his arm, pressed a cautious ear to the metal.

"And no sound from within?"

"None we could hear, sir."

He stood back and replaced his cap. "I'm hoping the Signals chaps can pick up something we can't," he said, considering the wall.

He was silent for a moment, then let out a sigh. "But right now we have more important objectives to achieve."

"The *Ivanhoe*, sir?"

"Yes, I want to get it back to the camp as soon as possible. If Chandar's scheme fails, we're going to need it." He paused, considering the wall a moment longer, then clapped his hands. "Right," he said and began to pick his way down the scree slope, sending rocks skittering down as he picked up speed and momentum.

Atkins followed unsteadily, and more carefully, so as not to dislodge rocks onto his superior.

"Sergeant Dixon, you and your work party see if you can't clear some of this scree by the time we get back, so we can get a proper look at this thing."

"Right you are, sir."

"Riley!" Everson called as he reached the bottom. The Signals corporal turned from overseeing the unloading of gear from one of the panniers on Big Willie.

"Sir?"

"See what your man makes of that by the time we get back," invited Everson, gesturing towards the wall.

Riley turned to Buckley and put his arm around his shoulders. "Buckley, I'm leaving you here with this sorry bunch of reprobates and a Moritz station. See what you can pick up. And don't get into trouble while I'm gone."

"No, Corp."

"Good lad."

Everson wasn't unduly concerned about leaving the two sections of working party at the canyon. They had Urmen Karnos to guard them, and Tulliver would be flying over three times a day. The party could signal the aeroplane if there were any problems or important developments.

With a last look at the wall, Everson ordered the battlepillars to move out, and they set off for the Croatoan Crater.

ALFIE AWOKE WITH a start to find himself lying in darkness. "Lieutenant?" he croaked. His lips were dry and cracked, his mouth parched.

He felt around with his hand and was startled to find warm, damp earth under his hand, not iron plate. He wasn't in the tank, then. He lay still for a moment, trying to collect his thoughts. All around him, with his petrol-fruit-muddled senses, he could *see* the faint ambient sounds of animals' noises bursting and fading like Very lights. He felt a vague craving for the fuel. He didn't usually feel that unless he'd been away from the tank for some time. How long had he been here? Where was he?

He could make out a soft, low horizontal glow of light, as if from under a door. He raised himself up on his elbows to get a better look. His head began to pound and his right leg jangled with pain. He let out an involuntary cry.

The hide draped across the doorway as protection against the elements swept open, and the shock of radiance caused Alfie to cry out again, throwing up an arm to block the light.

The silhouette of a man resolved itself against the flare. It spoke. It took a moment for Alfie to make out the words, as his fuel-addled brain interpreted them as the bittersweet flavour of marmalade and the childhood feeling of the tassel ties on his mother's front parlour curtains against his skin.

"...name is Ranaman, shaman of the Ruanach clan."

In the light, Alfie could see he was no longer wearing his coveralls. His right leg had been crudely splinted. Lengths of wood had been strapped against it, and they had unwound and used his puttee to bind it.

He tried to move, thinking about escape, but his leg was bound tight; and if that didn't stop him, the pain surely would.

The man, clearly an Urman, knelt before Alfie and bowed until his forehead touched the earth. The youth who entered behind him did the same.

God, not again, thought Alfie. They revered him. The crew of the HMLS *Ivanhoe* had met such reactions before. Lieutenant Mathers had decided in the past to take advantage of it and of the Urmen they met. It started out as a scam, growing into a mad scheme to build a colony of the British Empire here on this world. Urmen had bowed before them, thinking them gods, or the heralds of gods. Some, like the Khungarrii, thought the tank to be Skarra, the Chatt god of the underworld. The crew didn't disabuse them of it; it had got them food and women. Alfie's opposition to this madness had almost cost him his friendships. He had never agreed with Mathers' scheme, but now it might save his life.

"Where am I?" he asked.

"Croatoan's Barrow," said Ranaman, hardly daring to look up. "After his battle with GarSuleth, defeated and cast down, here fell Croatoan. To be thus conquered broke his heart in twain, and he was dragged into the underworld to be punished by GarSuleth's brother, Skarra. And here the Ruanach stand vigil, as our ancestors did before us, keeping watch over his heart, awaiting his return and eventual triumph over GarSuleth."

The crater, thought Alfie. They must mean the crater.

"Where are my friends?" he asked in a deep imperious tone, one that he'd heard Norman adopt on occasions like these.

Ranaman cocked his head to one side and frowned. "Friends?"

"Others. Like me."

The youth shook his head, puzzled. "There were no others. There was only you. You were alone. You appeared before Tarak on his vision quest to become a man, a warrior."

The words spilled from the youth's mouth in a torrent of nervous energy...

TARAK WAS NOT yet a man but no longer a boy. He was in the process of becoming. Or dying. That was always a possibility. It was his time, and he had undergone the rite. He had ingested the venom of the hurreg and had then been ceremonially cast out of the enclave. Now he must circle the Barrow and seek out his vision. If he survived, he would return to the enclave a warrior.

His skin burned, his eyes itched from the poison, his palm felt slick around the handle of his knife and otherworldly visions came and went. He heard a tortured screech that made him wince, followed by a roar so terrible that it silenced the jungle. There followed an impact he felt through the soles of his feet.

Fearful, he headed towards the sound. He stumbled through the undergrowth until he saw it, resting where it had fallen, as Croatoan had once fallen from the sky.

He watched as if in a dream as an opening appeared in the sky rock and an Urman like himself—no, not like himself—stepped out and fell to the ground. Tarak watched, trying to decipher the vision.

There was a deep growl and something dropped from a low bough and landed on all sixes, ready to leap on the sky-being.

Though the hurreg poison seared his joints, Tarak leapt on the creature's back with his knife firmly in his fist. He felt the warm pelt beneath his flesh, smelled the damp fur and thrust the blade in. The creature bucked and writhed, trying to throw him off, but he pressed his thighs against its flanks, tightened his hold on the shaggy fur with his other hand and drove the knife in again. And again. Its legs crumpled beneath it. Tarak pulled back on the horns, exposing its throat, and slipped his knife across it. The creature shuddered beneath him, blood pulsed out of the ragged slit. He held it until it had stopped, then let the head fall. Ordinarily he would have taken it back to the enclave as a gift from Croatoan and returned a hunter. But he had something more important to bear.

He looked at the sky-being.

He stood up and circled the great iron rock from which he'd appeared. Never had anyone in his clan had a sign like this, though many had sought it. This was his omen, given to him, but he had no idea what it meant. Ranaman would know.

He hoisted the sky-being over his shoulders and began his triumphal return to his enclave, not as a boy but as a man. As a warrior...

* * *

"TARAK IS TO be envied," announced Ranaman proudly as the young man finished his tale. "But his fortune is the clan's fortune. Your arrival when the Torment of Croatoan is nigh, when the earth erupts with his pain, is a great omen!"

"And if the boy's vision proves false?" Alfie's voice quavered, looking at Tarak.

"Then he will be cast out as punishment for bringing a Dulgur, an evil spirit, amongst us. He will die and his spirit will not join the ancestors in the Village of the Dead. His body will be left to ward off other Dulgur."

Tarak looked alarmed and glanced at Alfie for confirmation that he had done the right thing.

God damn it. He couldn't risk harm to the lad who'd saved him.

Very well, he would play his part. As much as it stuck in his craw, he would have to play the game for which he'd held Mathers in such contempt. He needed to buy time. He had to stay alive until the crew of the *Ivanhoe* could find him. He couldn't be sure that they would look, but he had faith in Nellie.

"The man Tarak has acted truly," intoned Alfie, cringing inside as he spoke.

Ranaman nodded in approval. He bowed before Alfie. "The one who was sent before has gone to prepare the way."

"The one who was sent before?" asked Alfie, confused.

"He, too was garbed as you are."

Alfie looked down at his khaki uniform. Another soldier? There was only one man he knew who had been as far as this. Jeffries. If the rumours were true, the man could beat Mathers at his own game.

"Where is he, this other one?"

Ranaman looked at him blankly, as if Alfie should have known. "He communed with the ancestors and joined them in the underworld."

Jeffries was dead?

"Soon you must do the same to make possible Croatoan's return. The ritual must not fail."

A chill froze halfway down Alfie's spine. Dear God. He'd always known Mathers' deception had been a fool's game, and now it was going to kill him.

He was going to be a human sacrifice.

CHAPTER SEVEN
"They Were Only Playing Leapfrog..."

THE PADRE BLINKED and looked up. They were alive. Around him, the gathered scentirrii stepped back and parted.

"I thought they were going to kill us," said Edith in a low tremulous voice, checking her hands and face for acid burns.

Trembling with fear and relief, the padre turned to Chandar for an explanation.

It spread its vestigial middle limbs. "They cannot hurt you," it said. "They have received this One's blessing. They have merely scented you. If you are not scented, you will be killed. Now you will smell Khungarrii. You will be safe."

The precaution proved well founded. As they journeyed, they met more scentirrii patrols and parties of worker Chatts in the forest. They noted their approach with a cautious waving of antennae, and then ignored them.

Ahead, dominating the large managed clearing, was the mound-like Khungarrii edifice, rising hundreds of feet from the cinnamon earth, like a cathedral tower. The last time the padre had seen the edifice, a large section had been destroyed by Jeffries, blowing up a stolen dump of grenades, mortars and other weapons. It had since been repaired and once again stood pristine and whole above the forest. Unadorned and functional, the structure bore no ornate inscriptions or decorations, no carvings, but was speckled with a thousand points of light as the sunlight caught flecks of mica bound into the dirt walls.

Scattered around the perimeter of the edifice were the peculiar funerary mounds of large clay balls, each sphere containing the body of a dead Chatt, waiting to be rolled into the underworld by Skarra, the dung-beetle god of the dead. There were a good many of them—no doubt due in part, the padre realised, to the actions of the Pennines.

Ahead of them, columns of worker Chatts, djamirrii, and Khungarrii Urmen, carrying the day's harvest in baskets or on litters, streamed into the edifice through great open bark doors some fifty or sixty feet in height, bound into the edifice itself by root-like hinges and framed by great earthen buttresses.

The padre noticed that the shantytowns that had once clung to the midden heaps against the edifice had been swept away. The free Urmen who had dwelt there under sufferance, scraping a subsistence from the scrap heaps of Khungarrii society, were gone; the first victims of the reprisals after the Pennines' attack to rescue the padre and some twenty-odd Fusiliers and the three nurses captured by a scentirrii raiding party.

He felt Edith's small hand slip into his, giving reassurance and seeking comfort in equal measure. His hand closed about hers and together they walked toward the cavernous entrance of the edifice.

INSIDE, THE GREAT cathedral-like entrance hall bustled with activity. Chatt workers and djamirrii assessed and sorted the continual influx of the day's harvest; battlepillars berthed against earthen jetties to be unloaded. The place seemed half port, half market.

Edith could remember arriving at Calais on the boat from Dover to scenes such as these. She had been a very different woman back then. The sharp formic smell of the place, of the Chatts, made her want to flee. She had to force herself to walk on.

The scentirrii led them up inclined passages lit by niches of bioluminescent lichen to the higher reaches of the edifice, to the network of sacred chambers where the dhuyumirrii conducted their ritualised business.

The scentirrii left them by a circular portal, a door grown from a tough fibrous living plant. Chandar breathed a mist at it, and the plant matter recoiled from it, dilating open. Rhengar ushered them through into an ancillary chamber. They had barely arrived when the circular door shrivelled open again. Two scentirrii stepped through, followed by a tall, regal dhuyumirrii wearing a similar over-the-shoulder arrangement of many-tasselled silken cloth to the one that Chandar wore, with the addition of a light, finely spun cloak. They had both seen this creature before.

"This One is Sirigar, Liya-Dhuyumirrii, High Anointed One of the Khungarrii Shura," it said, surveying the chamber. It had chosen to speak in English, something it was not wont to do. It was making a point.

Chandar bent its legs, sinking into the Chatt submissive posture.

Sirigar looked down on it. "So you have returned, Chandar?"

"This One went to observe the battle at the direction of the Shura and was captured. This you know," said Chandar.

"And they let you go?"

"They wish to bargain."

"The time for bargaining is long past," said Sirigar. "And these creatures?" it said, indicating the padre and Nurse Bell. "What are they doing here? This One could smell their stench the moment they entered Khungarr. Your fascination for them is unbecoming, Chandar, maybe even heretical."

"The Shura has not declared it so, yet," said Chandar.

Sirigar hissed and turned to inspect Edith, who shuddered in spite of herself. Sirigar's mandibles opened wide, as if to suggest that it could take her head within them and crush it. Warm breath washed over her as moist labial folds opened, exposing its glistening mouth palps. Its long segmented antennae waved above her head.

She held its gaze, defiance and terror wrestling within her, conscious of the contents of her haversack. In moments like this, she thought of Edith Cavell and found a well of courage within her which, while not inexhaustible, saw her through the moment.

Sirigar hissed and withdrew, immediately losing interest in her.

"They... they are emissaries. They cannot harm us. They have been anointed with the blessing of GarSuleth," Chandar gestured toward the padre. "That one took the Kirrijandat, the rite of purification—"

"So did their Jeffries," said Sirigar, loading every word. "And look at the ruination that he visited on Khungarr. They are the Great Corruption. Their presence here sickens this One. Yet again you have exceeded your bounds, Chandar."

The padre saw his chance. He had expected to persuade them, but to have the opportunity presented to him like this seemed heaven-sent.

"Jeffries was not one of us. You cannot judge us all by him. We are not answerable for his sins. I will take the rite again!" he declared.

Edith stepped forward. "Padre, no. Remember what it did to you the last time."

The padre remembered very well. The rite was one that new immigrants to Khungarr were required to undergo as a test of loyalty and faith. It was seen as a symbolic washing away of old lives and old beliefs. He would be lying to himself if he said he wasn't afraid, but he was more fearful of the shadow it had cast over his life since he first experienced it, of the night terrors that hid in the dark corners of his mind during the day. This was why he had returned.

He clasped Bell's hand in his own and flashed a beatific smile. "I survived last time, I will do so again," he reassured her.

Sirigar regarded the padre, its large dark eyes unblinking. "Very well, undergo the Kirrijandat. It will not save you. When the Shura stands behind this One and decrees your herd to be the Great Corruption the perfumed prophecies speak of, you will be the first of the Tohmii to die. You and your djamirrii."

Sirigar turned and directed its ire at Chandar. "Despite knowing what they are, you dare bring them here, when the Great Corruption has already tainted Khungarr and may even now threaten the very future of the colony itself—"

Sirigar glanced at the padre and lapsed into its own tongue; a guttural stream of harsh smacks, clicks and snips. Chandar countered him, both creatures swaying and moving with each exchange, until Sirigar, rearing up on its legs, let out an aggressive hiss. It swept from the chamber, its scentirrii following. The plant door contracted shut behind it.

Both Padre Rand and Edith held their breaths for a heartbeat before exhaling with relief. They were still alive, and the seditious scents they had smuggled in had not been detected.

Chandar turned to the pair. "This One has bought some time, but precious little. Your submission to the Kirrijandat has bought more. But unless this One succeeds before the Shura then it will have been to no avail. Sirigar will consolidate the Shura behind it and your herd will be culled."

The padre and Nurse Bell exchanged anxious glances. This was becoming more dangerous than either of them had realised.

"You can't leave Nurse Bell here while I undergo the rite," said the padre. "Not now Sirigar knows where she is. Not when you know what she carries."

"This One agrees," said Chandar. "This One will make sure that your djamirrii is kept out of the way and hidden from Sirigar's spies."

Chandar addressed Nurse Bell. "Rhengar will escort you."

"Where to?" she asked.

"The safest place in Khungarr."

CHANDAR ESCORTED PADRE Rand through the high, domed cathedral-like Chamber of the Anointed Ones. Set in the walls of the great circular hall were large alcoves, decorated with hieroglyphs impregnated with sacred scents. Chatt dhuyumirrii occupied many of the alcoves, facing the walls, their antennae waving over the glyphs. The susurration of Chatts at prayer filled the space, their clicking mandibles sounding, to the padre's mind, like a women's knitting circle making socks for soldiers.

They continued down a passage, past the alchemical chambers where the Chatt apothecaries distilled and stored the sacred scents. Here had been the Scentorum, the repository of all their knowledge. Jeffries had destroyed it; thousands of years of accumulated scent scriptures and commentaries boiled, burned and vaporised in the conflagration, generations of knowledge gone. It had been an act of desecration akin to the burning of the library at Alexandria. The chambers had since been rebuilt, but many ancient scent texts had been lost forever.

The padre was here to rectify that, if his mind survived the rite.

They left the Scentorum behind and proceeded to a string of small chambers barely big enough to stand erect in. They reminded him of confessionals.

Two acolyte dhuyumirrii nymphs approached, guiding them towards the ritual chamber. The padre paused for a second. If he was going to back out, now was the time. God knows he wanted to. But this wasn't just about him anymore.

"You will be safe in here. No One will harm you while you are undergoing the rite," Chandar told him. "Not even Sirigar."

With a deep breath, he ducked his head and entered the small chamber. A large clay oil burner moulded up from the floor dominated it. The padre sat as the acolyte poured viscous oil into the burner, then lit it with a taper before retiring from the chamber.

"GarSuleth guide you," said Chandar as the plant door expanded to close off the chamber.

As he breathed in the fumes, the padre began to pray. "Our Father, who art in heaven, hallowed be thy name—"

Under the influence of the alien fumes, the prayer became a mantra, the words warping, shifting, slurring, as the alien vapour enfolded his mind.

"Our Father, give us this day our hallowed Earth which art our English heaven, forgive us our daily trespass and deliver us from this evil kingdom. Forgive us our sins and lead us not into the earth. Lead us not into temptation, but into glory. Thine is the power to grant this. Amen."

He began to feel hot and faint. His fingers reached for the dog collar around his neck and pulled it free. "No, let this cup pass from me," he gasped. He struggled to get up, but his limbs wouldn't obey. He slid to the floor, staring into the guttering flame of the oil burner.

The vision came and he was powerless to stop it...

CHATTS MADE EDITH'S skin crawl. It was a base, primal revulsion, something she had no control over, no matter how much she tried to rationalise it. She wished that Chandar had blessed her again; frankly, the Chatts' ability to affect your mind like that revolted her, too, but the mild euphoria had helped last time. However, both she and the padre needed their wits about them here. So why, she wondered, did the padre feel the need to undergo that rite again? What was it he was trying to prove?

She didn't know, but she couldn't wait to be out of here. She'd thought she could face it and conquer her fear of Chatts, but it was proving harder than she'd expected. When she first signed up to be a VAD she had little knowledge of what it might entail. Oh, she had some romantic girlish notions about mopping the brows of wounded heroes. Experience disabused her of that: maggots in wounds, the telltale smell of gas gangrene, suppurating sores; all these she had faced and conquered, until now she was able to deal with them as a matter of routine. But the Chatts still made her squirm.

Rhengar led her down through narrower utilitarian tunnels. Here, the lichen light became less frequent. Despite promises of safety, Edith began to feel uneasy.

"Where are we going?" she asked.

"You are a nurse," it replied.

"Yes," she said cautiously.

They arrived at a small, unremarkable plant door at the end of a passage.

"Do you have a patient you want me to see? Are they in here?" she asked.

"Here, yes," said Rhengar.

Edith suddenly became afraid. She wanted to turn and flee, but where was there to flee to in this nest of insects, when every denizen could be turned upon her in an instant with an insubstantial chemical alarm?

She gripped her haversack tighter and tensed as Rhengar breathed on the door. It opened, and Edith found herself pushed through.

"No, wait," she pleaded, but Rhengar was already striding back up the passage and the plant door was blooming shut.

Oh, how she wished Nellie were here.

Edith found herself confronted by a small Chatt, its carapace a smooth pale white. It wore no silk garment like Chandar and its caste, or like the scentirrii. It stepped forward as its antennae investigated her. It seemed satisfied that all the required scents and aromas were in order and scuttled off down a ramp, stopping only to see if she was following.

Very well, she thought. She straightened her back, lifted her chin and turned to face her fate with a very English decorum.

As she descended, the passage opened out. The gloom beyond was filled with the scuttling and clicks of hundreds of Chatts. As her eyes grew used to the low light, she was able to make sense of the space. She realised with a shiver of revulsion that she had been here before. It was the Khungarrii nursery.

No wonder Rhengar thought she would be safe here. It would be the last place Sirigar would think to look. It was also the last place she wanted to be.

She looked around and saw no signs of the battle that had raged there months before as a platoon of Pennine Fusiliers fought their way out of the edifice. The great hole in the wall, where the *Ivanhoe* had smashed through, had long since been repaired, as if they had never been there.

Around the walls of the chamber were recesses where the grubs pupated into nymphs. Only a quarter of the cells were sealed and occupied. The rest lay open and empty. Running across the floor of the chamber were long sinuous channels where Urmen women and nursery Chatts fed blind, wriggling grubs.

She noticed precious few eggs about the nursery. Surely, these things should be like factories. But there was no time to contemplate the problem, as her guide walked on down a large side passage. It curved and Edith could make out something huge and worm-like at the end, to which Chatts were attending.

As she came closer, she realised that it was only part of some larger creature; the rest lay in a chamber beyond. Edging alongside the worm-like protuberance, she entered the chamber. Her mouth went dry and she could feel her heart pound in her chest. Occupying almost the entire space, as though they had built the chamber around it, was what she guessed to be the Khungarrii Queen. Its abdomen was a pulsating sac, twenty or thirty feet high, and grossly distended, to the point where the taut, glistening pale skin verged on translucency. Whatever limbs the Queen once possessed had withered or been swallowed by its vast bulk. Atop of that, dwarfed by its body, its head and thorax were of normal Chatt size, making it all the more grotesque. It was incapable of moving, grooming or feeding itself.

To that end, the chamber wall ran with a spiralling gallery, and slung across the huge corpulent form were bridges and gantries, so that its attendants could groom every inch of its body. Even now, Chatts scurried across it, licking up sweat. While others laboured in trenches dug beneath the vast bulk, removing excreta, a continual procession wound up the spiral gallery to a gantry level with the Queen's thorax and head. There, attendants supplied the Queen with an endless supply of bowls of some sort of substance which they first masticated and then fed to it, like some sort of royal jelly.

However, this obese creature was more than just an egg-laying machine. It controlled the state of the colony through unspoken chemical decrees. Above the Queen, in the roof of the royal chamber, were a cluster of vents that drew the royal scent commands up into the edifice, where they were circulated on the air.

Edith stared up in horror at the creature.

The whole machinery of attendance ground on around her, with Chatts ignoring her, until one touched her on the shoulder, making her yelp in alarm. It directed her back to the tunnel where the appendage from the distended belly ran.

She realised what was wrong. There should have been a steady stream of nursery attendants carrying eggs from the ovipositor, the egg-laying tube, to the nursery chamber, but there were none to be seen. Was that what Sirigar had been referring to when it was talking about the future of Khungarr?

A Chatt spoke, struggling with the language, its exalted position not needing much interaction with Urmen.

"Queen. Ill. Sickness. No eggs."

Whatever was wrong, it was beyond their abilities to heal, and they were desperate. That was why she was here.

That changed things. With a patient, Edith was able to focus. Slowly, the terror she felt being surrounded by these creatures receded. She had a job to do. This was why Chandar hadn't blessed her. In a euphoric state, she would have been in no position to help.

"Light. I need light," said Edith, sharply.

The Chatt chittered a command, and within moments, a blue-white light bobbed toward them. It made Edith think briefly of Tinkerbell. Her aunt had taken her to see a performance of *Peter Pan and Wendy* many years earlier with her young cousins. And she'd clapped; how she'd clapped to save poor Tink. If only saving the Queen were as easy, she thought.

Edith rolled up her sleeves as a dozen or so more Chatt attendants arrived clutching bunches of luminous lichen, their light bathing the tunnel.

She set about examining the appendage. The tube was inflamed and swollen, with several large sores, two of which were open and suppurating. The translucence she'd found so awful also proved to be a great aid, almost like an x-ray. She could see that the tube was swollen and not allowing the eggs to pass. They were backing up, impacting on the side of the canal. Somehow, they would have to be released.

She knelt before the opening of the ovipositor and gently inserted her hand, feeling her way up the inside of the lubricated tube. Her shoulder was almost touching the ovipositor sheath by the time she felt the constriction. The swelling had all but closed off the canal. Slowly, she withdrew her arm to find it coated with mucus. She tried to hide her disgust as she flicked creamy opaque strings of it at the tunnel wall before hurriedly wiping her arm down with a length of silken cloth provided by the Chatts.

After her internal exam, she returned her attention to the infected wounds. If the infection had got into the bloodstream, then there was no hope of saving the creature.

"Water!" she demanded. "And bandages." They brought water and more fresh silk almost immediately. She sluiced out the sores as best she could.

The open wounds needed debriding, the dead infected matter cutting away, but she had no knife, no scalpel, no way to do it. She looked around and met the inquiring eyes of the Chatt. She looked at its mandibles. They would have to do.

"Here!" she said pointing at a wound. "Here!" she mimed snipping mandibles. The Chatt understood, and under her direction, it chewed away at the dead matter.

When she was satisfied that the wounds were clean, Edith opened her haversack, sorted guiltily past the sacred scent and petrol fruit juice, to retrieve two precious ampoules of iodine. She broke one into each wound.

Next, she pulled out sealed bags of dried moss. It had been a method she had learned in London, before she came out to France, where they used sphagnum moss as an absorbent surgical dressing for wounds in war hospitals. Here on this world, it proved a Godsend, once they had located a suitable source.

She packed the wounds with the moss and bandaged them using lengths of silk that the Chatts provided. She hoped that it would bring the ovipositor swelling down enough to allow the passing of eggs. The dressings would have to be changed every couple of hours. That, for now, was all she could do.

Tired, she found a nook out of the way of the constant scuttling, crawled into it and hugged her bag to her. The ability to sleep anywhere, at any time, was a skill the Fusiliers had long since mastered, and one she had soon acquired. Despite her unfamiliar surrounding and the constant, unsettling chittering, she fell quickly and deeply asleep.

SHE WOKE SEVERAL times throughout the night; or at least, she assumed it was still night. Down here, in the bowels of the edifice, it was hard to tell. She changed the dressings on the wounds and found that, whatever the hour of day or night, the level of attendance to the Queen did not drop.

The Chatt who had conducted her attended her closely. It watched her, intently, so she taught it as she went along, seeing it not as a repulsive Chatt, but another creature wanting to care for others. On the other hand, it would probably kill her if it looked as if she was harming the Queen in any way. They probably all would. She tried to push that thought to the back of her mind.

The dressings seem to have done their work. The wounds were less inflamed and the tube was looking less swollen. As to what had caused the wounds, she couldn't say, but she did wonder how such injuries were possible in a place where the Queen was cosseted and cared for every hour of the day. If Sirigar did not cause this, it had certainly gained great capital from it, seeking to blame the illness and possible reproductive crisis on the 'Great Corruption.' If the Queen had not responded to Edith's treatment, the chances of the Pennines' survival would be very bleak indeed.

She turned her attention back to the task in hand. Had she done enough to ease the egg blockage?

Parting the fleshy sheath, once again Edith eased her hand into the ovipositor canal. Gently but firmly, she pushed her arm up inside. There had been some improvement. She could pass her hand beyond the swelling now. At full stretch, she could feel an egg with the tips of her fingers, pressing against the wall of the canal. She struggled and flexed, trying to get another inch or so of reach. After a minute or two of frustration, her fingers finally curled round the far edge of the egg and she managed to retrieve it, scooping it slowly down the canal. Almost immediately, another slid down. Matters would improve as the swelling reduced.

When she delivered the pearlescent egg to the waiting Chatt, a wave of excited chittering passed round the chamber. It almost sounded like soft, polite applause.

Edith glanced up along the ovipositor, over the vast, throbbing, translucent abdomen to the small thorax and head high above her, and saw the Queen staring back down at her over its vast bulk.

As soon as Edith delivered them, the Chatts took the eggs to the nursery chamber, each one carried away with awe and reverence.

It might be days before the infection was gone, but she showed the Chatt what to do. Its slender arm and longer fingers might be better suited to retrieving the eggs than hers.

In response to some unspoken command, Edith found herself manhandled, despite her mild protestations, from one Chatt to another and guided swiftly up the incline of the spiral gallery until she reached the audience gantry. There, ushered by the arthropod attendants, she stepped out to come face to face with the Queen itself; with the greater part of its obscene bulk hidden below like an iceberg, the portion Edith faced looked natural, or as natural as these creatures ever could.

With feeble arms, it beckoned Edith closer. She took a faltering step toward it. The Queen leaned forward, waving its long antennae at her as an attendant tried to feed it from a bowl. The Queen chittered at it. It froze, not comprehending its instructions. The Queen spoke again, more forcefully this time. With reluctance, the attendant turned and proffered the bowl to Edith. Unsure as to the etiquette of the situation, Edith pointed to herself.

"Me? You want me to eat?"

The Chatt offered the bowl again. There was no mistaking the gesture. Those Chatts nearby halted briefly in their tasks to watch.

"It is an honour no Urman has ever been given," said the Chatt, watching her.

Edith looked at the grey, glutinous and masticated jelly in the bowl. It didn't look at all appetising. She could feel her stomach rebelling just looking at it. Seeing no way to decline politely, she smiled weakly at the Queen, cupped her hand and slipped her fingers into the warm gelatinous mess.

The Queen watched expectantly.

Edith took a deep breath and spooned her fingers into her mouth. She gagged a little at the thick and slimy texture, and had to force herself to swallow it. It was curiously filling, and it was a struggle to finish the bowl. She could feel it rising back up her throat and she swallowed hard, determined to keep it down.

The Queen watched in approval, unblinking.

Unsure what to do next, Edith gave a little curtsy. Another attendant ushered her away along the gantry as others resumed the chores of feeding and cleaning their Queen. Her royal audience was over.

Edith reached the other side of the royal chamber and looked back. They had forgotten her presence already. Down below, Chatts once more resumed the collection of eggs.

A Chatt led her down another passage to another circular plant door. The Chatt breathed on it and the circular plant portal shrivelled open to reveal Rhengar.

"Come," it said before stopping. It looked at her, tilting its head to one side like a curious dog, its long antennae waving in an agitated manner. Then it did something Edith had not expected. It knelt before her, touching its head and thorax in reverence.

CHAPTER EIGHT
"Shall They Return..."

PADRE RAND VACILLATED all night. It had just been a dream, a hallucination, nothing more. How could it be anything else? Then he looked around at the small chamber, here in an edifice of arthropods on an alien world. The comfortable boundaries of what was and was not had shifted. Anything seemed possible. Here, so far from Earth, God had spoken to him, as He had to His people of old. He had asked something of him and the padre wondered if he would find himself wanting.

He hadn't truly understood the function of the rite last time. The Khungarrii called it the Kirrijandat, the cleansing, a ritual ordeal meant to be a symbolic pupation for Urmen, a casting off of old ways, a rededication. If he wanted to, he could see it as a re-Baptism, a Confirmation. But for God to ask this of him? Now he comprehended the night terrors. But if it was the Lord's will, then so be it.

The plant door dilated open and Chandar waited outside the small chamber.

The padre got to his feet with a groan as he felt pins and needles prickle his feet and calves.

He nodded to the Chatt. "It's done," he said.

"This One has spent the night meeting with members of the Shura. They are willing to consider a supplication of the scents," said Chandar as the padre joined him. "Sirigar now knows that this One has something of importance to say, but does not yet know what. Many of the Shura are convinced by Sirigar's words, that the Queen's illness is the taint of the Great Corruption spread by the Tohmii. Singar will call for the scentirrii to march once more and eradicate your clan for good."

"Where's Nurse Bell?" the padre asked.

"Your djamirrii is safe. Do not forget she carries hidden about her the sacred salve that will be your salvation and the liquor that might be this One's. This One has sent for her."

Chandar led the way along an inclined passage, taking them up into the further reaches of the edifice. Streams of Chatts went about on unknown business: scentirrii and dhuyumirrii, mostly, with the odd workers and Urmen. Two tassel-robed dhuyumirrii approached from the other direction. One bumped into the padre, and a small vial dropped to the floor in the collision. It shattered and oozed oil.

"I'm terribly sorry," the padre said, almost as a reflex. "Here, let me—"

He looked around, but they had slipped away.

Chandar let out a long, low, wet hiss.

The padre, wheeled round to see several worker Chatts step out of the passage shadows, blocking their way. "What's going on?"

"Sirigar is trying to prevent our appearance before the Shura," wheezed Chandar.

"I thought I was marked with Khungarr scent, I thought you said they couldn't harm me."

"Normally, no," said Chandar, eyeing the workers. "But the scent can be masked. A stronger chemical decree can negate it."

The shattered vial. One smell being used to hide another, thought the padre.

The workers began to circle, their long mandibles snapping together rhythmically.

"It is how this One became crippled, when Sirigar once before thought this One a threat to its plans," said Chandar as they watched the worker Chatts advance.

Chandar hissed, expelling its euphoric benediction in the hope of stalling the workers. It failed.

Several workers leapt upon it, barrelling it into the ground. The padre thought he heard a carapace crack.

Another lunged at him. He had done a little boxing in his youth, and now he put up his fists for the first time in years. He swung a right uppercut under the guard of its open mandibles, connecting with the soft mouthparts. They mashed satisfactorily under his knuckles. The Chatt stumbled backwards, its mandibles slicing empty air.

"Hah!" cried the padre.

His initial spark of triumph was soon doused as another Chatt sprang at him. The padre was thrown off balance and the pair crashed to the ground. It crouched over him, its splayed long-fingered hands pressing down on his chest.

"Dear God in Heaven preserve me!"

Its smooth facial plate was vacant of any expression. Mucus dripped from its mouthparts onto his face as it opened its mandibles and placed them either side of his head. As the pressure on his temples began to increase, the padre screwed his eyes shut and prayed.

Without warning, the crushing pressure eased and the weight from his chest lifted. It was a moment before he dared open his eyes. His attacker was crouched motionless before him. The others likewise had abandoned their attack and were sunk low in submission, their mandibles open, their antennae waving gently, rhythmically, in unison.

The padre heard a woman's cry.

Nurse Bell. Dear God, no. They'll take her as well. He wouldn't let that happen.

"Padre!"

"Bell, run!" he called out. "Run! Run!"

He scrambled back away from the now-motionless Chatts until he was against the wall of the chamber.

Chandar lay against the other side, its head slumped on its chest plate, its mouth palps hanging limply, bubbles frothing through them as it breathed. A thick bluish fluid oozed from wounds in its soft abdomen, where one of its vestigial limbs had been ripped off. Its claw lay discarded on the floor nearby.

The padre and Chandar exchanged weary, pained glances, each alive, but neither knowing how.

Rhengar entered the chamber, and several spear-carrying Scentirrii filed out either side of it.

"You. So it's come to this, has it?" said the padre with bitter recrimination. "Assassination?"

Rhengar regarded him blankly. "Yes."

Breathing heavily, the padre braced himself, glaring at the Chatts' general with outright defiance. He'd given these creatures the benefit of the doubt. But now he realised he'd let his Christian nature be swayed by these soulless things—for how could they be anything else on this world?

"Come to finish the job, have you?" he said brusquely. "Then do it, but spare Bell. She's just a nurse. You know 'nurse'?"

Rhengar crouched by the shard of vial on the floor, waving his antennae over the fading evaporated spill.

"The musk of the Sanfradar, a predator. It breaks into edifices to devour the young. The workers reacted instinctively. They thought you were a danger. They would have torn you to pieces."

Dazed, the padre leant against the chamber wall until the place stopped spinning, the Chatt workers' confusion now his. "Then why didn't they? What stopped them?"

"I did, apparently," said Nurse Bell, stepping from the safety of the passage shadows into the chamber, a shy smile of embarrassment on her face.

"You did? But how?"

She strode over to him. "Padre, you're hurt."

He obliged by bowing his head and smiled apologetically. "I think I banged my head again. I'm all right."

"I'll be the judge of that," she said, gently examining his head. "Nothing's got through your skull yet." She looked him in the eyes. "Has it?"

The padre met her gaze. "I'm fine," he said.

Rhengar gave orders to the remaining four scentirrii, who stood guard round the chamber while Nurse Bell went over and knelt to examine the injured Chatt.

"Is it safe?" it asked, the words coming in pained gasps as it struggled to regurgitate enough air for speech.

She continued to examine his abdomen. "It's safe," she said. "But you're not." She turned to Rhengar. "We must get Chandar somewhere I can treat its wounds."

Rhengar stooped to pick up the wounded Chatt and directed them down a maze of side passages that eventually led to a chamber. It left two of the scentirrii outside as guards; the others it dismissed. It set Chandar down and looked at Nurse Bell.

"Chandar must speak before the Shura soon, if you wish to save your clan."

She wasn't going to be bullied. She didn't even look up from her examination of Chandar's abdominal wounds as she spoke. "I'll do what I can. I'm not promising any more."

She bound Chandar's wound where his vestigial limb had been, winding the silk bandage around his abdomen. She was able to disguise most of the bandage with Chandar's own ceremonial silk shoulder throw, as she wrapped its excess around its abdomen.

"There," she said, sitting back on her heels.

"It is done?" asked Chandar.

"Yes, for the moment, so long as you don't exert yourself."

The padre, who had been watching her work, finally spoke. "You said it was you that saved us."

"I'm rather afraid it might have been," she said with an apologetic shrug as she got to her feet. "The Khungarrii Queen gifted me with some sort of royal jelly, anointing me with her own scent. From what I gather, it's rather like getting the keys to the city."

"An anointed Urman," said Rhengar. "This One cannot recall such a thing. However, the royal odour is unmistakable. Every Khungarrii knows it. But we must keep it secret a while longer."

"Why?"

"It strengthens this One's position, but only if this One can successfully couple it with this One's argument," croaked Chandar as it struggled to its feet. It held out an expectant hand towards Bell. "Do you have it?"

She nodded and fished in her haversack, bringing out the small stone amphora holding the sacred scent she had brought with her from the camp. Chandar took it with reverence. Edith pulled out another small jar. "Lieutenant Everson told me to give you this when it was time. I think it is. It's petrol fruit liquor."

Chandar took the bottle and uncorked it. Tilting its head back, it opened its mandibles and poured the liquor through its mouth parts.

"What is this?" asked Rhengar.

"It revives this One's ability to scent."

"How is that possible?"

"It is GarSuleth's Will," replied Chandar. "And yet more proof, if it were needed, that our olfaction is right."

It tucked the amphora of sacred scent into the abdominal wrap of its garment, hobbled over to a small opaque roundel of plant matter, and breathed on it. Much like the door, it contracted open, revealing a view looking down on the Shura chamber.

"You may watch from here until summoned. Whatever happens, do not leave this chamber until you are sent for," warned Chandar as it turned and limped for the door, escorted by Rhengar.

THE PADRE LOOKED down into the chamber. It was a sunken amphitheatre. At one end, a raised dais was dominated by a shallow ceremonial bowl about six feet across, a low flame burning underneath its centre. High above it, around the walls of the chamber, were window apertures that funnelled light onto the empty space at the centre of the chamber. Around it rose earthen tiers, which were steadily filling as Chatts filed into the chamber. The space buzzed with the low burr of ticking and scissoring mandibles. Judging from the tasselled silk they wore, the padre assumed they were all dhuyumirrii, like Chandar.

From an opening between two stands of tiers, Sirigar entered, wearing a light silken cloak that billowed out as it walked, its deep hood covering its head and antennae. Two acolyte nymphs followed, swinging burning censers.

The assembly fell silent as it strode to the centre and cast its gaze across the serried ranks of dhuyumirrii, almost as if challenging them to question its authority.

Chandar entered the amphitheatre, hobbling towards the imperious figure of Sirigar, whose presence dominated the chamber. Chandar cut a poor comparison, with its limp and its broken antennae; if the padre had been a betting man, he'd put his money on the thoroughbred, not the nag.

Chandar had explained the nature of the debate. It would have to openly challenge Sirigar's stance and Sirigar in turn would defend it.

But debate among the Khungarrii could go on for hours, if not days, requiring not just mental but physical stamina. Statements were accompanied by stylised movements, punctuating argument and proposition, counter-argument and denial. When they were last here, the padre heard a disparaging Jeffries compare them to dancing bees. No blows were landed, though in the far distant past perhaps it had been a more bloody affair that had become ritualised over time.

The padre hadn't quite appreciated what Chandar had meant until he saw it.

"Are—are they fighting?" asked Nurse Bell, dismayed.

"After a fashion," said the padre.

As challenger, it was Chandar's place to begin by proposing the statement to be debated. It stepped forward in a low lunge, pushing its arm out, as if physically delivering the challenge, its blow not striking, but the proximity of the blow to the defender no doubt signalling the strength of feeling on the subject. The heel of its hand stopped inches from Sirigar's facial plate. It seemed more oriental martial art than debate.

Shifting its centre of gravity, Sirigar stepped back gracefully, then responded, symbolically brushing aside Chandar's opening statement with a sweep of its arm and a rapid statement of its own.

As the ritual debate progressed, there seemed to be an element of chess to it; forms of statement and response with which both debaters were practised, perhaps restating old arguments or theological positions, familiar forms of attack and response. The padre noted that one tactic was to lure your opponent into a physically and maybe philosophically weak position while you considered your next point. Sirigar, once it discovered Chandar had been weakened by injury, forced it to maintain a stressful position. Chandar began to lose its concentration and its theological points were blocked, struck down or conceded, one after another.

Nurse Bell watched in frustration. "What is Chandar waiting for? Why doesn't it produce the amphorae?"

"It seems to be more complicated than that. There's a ritual formality to the proceedings. I think it has to bring the argument round to it. Sirigar seems to be countering and blocking that line of enquiry. Chandar has to find new ways to introduce the point."

"I didn't realise it would be like this. It shouldn't be doing this with its injury. I thought it would just be talking."

Sirigar was well versed in the arguments that kept it in power, and practised in deflecting challenges, but it had grown too confident. In a devastating series of attacks, it forced Chandar to recant and concede. However, it was a feint, drawing Sirigar onto ground where it was less certain in order that Chandar might bring in its new evidence. Chandar, it seemed, was more cunning than the padre had given it credit for. Chandar was rallying, building a convincing argument-attack, batting away Sirigar's increasingly feeble and desperate counterpoints.

From the reaction of the watching Khungarrii Shura, the padre and Nurse Bell could see a change in fortunes as Chandar went on the attack. Sirigar fell back, apparently unable to defend his position.

"Yes!"

"What's happening?"

"I think Chandar is about to make its point."

Weakened by its exertions, Chandar stumbled up the steps to the ceremonial bowl, the flame guttering beneath it. It grabbed the edge of the bowl and felt inside the robe for the amphora, the Commentaries of Chitaragar, ignoring the spreading blue stain soaking through its bandage.

Sirigar, unwilling to admit defeat, cried out harshly and several scentirrii with spears stepped into the amphitheatre. Even as the scentirrii moved forward to stop it, under the caws of protest from the ranks of the Shura, Chandar poured the sacred scent text into the bowl. The scentirrii rushed the steps, seized it by the arms and dragged it to its feet.

The oil ran slowly down the curve of the bowl toward the heated centre.

Chandar was taken down the steps towards a crowing Sirigar, its arms thrown open as it gnashed its mandibles together, addressing the assembled Chatts.

Unseen, the oil pooled and bubbled in the bottom of the ceremonial crucible, boiling and evaporating into the air, carrying its message up on warm currents to the domed roof, where it cooled and sank down over the gathered dhuyumirrii.

The Shura fell silent as antennae twitched, absorbing the delicate notes of the ancient aroma, as shifting layers of subtext from the long-lost scent scripture revealed themselves. The Great Corruption so feared by the Khungarrii was not the Pennines. They had been used unscrupulously by Sirigar to further its power. The danger the Commentaries forewarned against was the corruption of their own faith by those who would use it for their own ends. The tide turned against Sirigar. Here was the proof that it had tried to deny, incontrovertible and damning.

Sirigar whirled round in confusion as his support fell away, until it too sensed the top notes of the ancient commentary, warning against false dhuyumirrii, and let out a harsh venomous hiss of frustration.

"By God, I think Chandar's done it!" said the padre, turning round to Nurse Bell, but she was fleeing from the room. The scentirrii stood aside for her, but stopped the padre from following.

*   *   *

EDITH COULD THINK only of her patient. She raced along the passages and before she realised it she had entered the amphitheatre. She barely noticed the reaction of the Shura about her as she rushed to Chandar's side.

"Let me see," she said to Chandar, examining the sodden bandaging.

Chandar brushed her hand aside. "Not yet." It raised its head, looking past her. "Look," it wheezed.

Edith looked. Around her the entire Shura was sunk on their legs, looking down at them, at her. The Queen's scent, she realised. She had been Chandar's final proof.

"You are blessed. Untouchable. Even Sirigar dare not move against you while you exude the Queen's scent."

Chandar steadied itself and addressed the Shura.

"The Shura has seen how they have been misled, and if further proof were needed that these Urmen were not the Great Corruption we long feared, behold, this Urman djamirrii, anointed by the Queen herself. How is that possible if they were ever such a threat? The true threat has been amongst us all this time. The Shura's attention had been falsely turned outwards, when the real threat was within." And it pointed at Sirigar.

Sirigar sank into a crouch. The evidence of its treachery was inescapable, permeating the very air around it.

Rhengar stepped from the shadows, and at some chemical command, the scentirrii seized Sirigar and led it away.

It was only once Chandar had the Shura's assent and had been instated as liya-dhuyumirri, the position held by Sirigar, that it allowed Edith to escort it back to the chamber to treat its wounds once again.

"What will happen now?" she asked.

"Now? The Tohmii will uphold their end of the bargain. They have been absolved. A chemical decree has already been disseminated throughout Khungarr. This view will become the established view. This will always have been the view."

THE THREE KHUNGARRII battlepillars had been decorated with lengths of coloured, scented silk and bore a multitude of silk pennants. There was an air of pilgrimage about the procession as it headed to the Pennines' camp, accompanied by grating dhuyumirrii chants and the beating of chest carapaces.

The swaying of the battlepillar's howdah unsettled Edith's stomach and she grasped the sides to steady herself as it rocked from side to side. Despite the little fluttering of girlish glee, Edith had to keep reminding herself that none of this was for her benefit, favoured by the Khungarrii Queen as she might be. No, this was in celebration of the long-lost ancient texts in the Pennines' possession, which would now be returned to the care of the Ones. It was part of the agreement made with Everson, in return for some kind of Treaty between the Pennines and the Khungarrii. She looked out happily across the veldt. She hadn't felt this relaxed since they had come to the planet. For once, the alien sun was shining and all seemed right with this world.

THE PADRE DIDN'T feel quite so ebullient. Thoughts of his vision churned away at his guts like three-day-old army stew. Like the men, he knew that being out of the line was temporary. At some point, courage or not, they would march back up the line towards the mud, shelling and shooting. He, too, knew that the terrors of his vision, and the choice he would have to make, were still waiting for him out there somewhere. But now, for Nurse Bell's sake, he smiled and allowed himself to be distracted.

TULLIVER'S SOPWITH SWOOPED low over them several times in their progress across the veldt, adding to the carnival atmosphere with its rolls and loops.

Delighted, Edith leaned out of the howdah and waved joyfully at the flying machine as it performed its daring aerobatics.

Beside her, Chandar watched the aeroplane with keen interest...

LIEUTENANT PALMER STOOD on the observation platform of the old Poulet farmhouse. He handed the binoculars to Sergeant Hobson, who stood beside him. "What do you make of it, Sergeant?"

Hobson peered through the glasses at the approaching procession. "A white flag of truce. I can't tell if the padre or Nurse Bell are there."

The battlepillars didn't present a huge threat. The Machine Gun Section could cut them down before the Chatts came within the range of their own electric lances.

Still, their appearance sent a ripple of unease along the line, men shuffling nervously on the firesteps. But this was a delicate time; Palmer didn't need nervous or trigger-happy troops. Those not on sentry duty were confined to the support and reserve trenches. Nobody wanted an incident.

The battlepillars stopped several hundred yards beyond the wireweed, along the line of the old Khungarrii siege, and upwind of the poppies that spread like a bloodstain across the scorched cordon sanitaire.

"Learnt their lesson, then?" said Hobson. "Bloody good job, too."

"Quite," said Palmer.

The white pennant flapped and snapped above the lead battlepillar as it chewed the tube grass.

Lieutenant Palmer, Sergeant Hobson and a small party walked out to meet them under a white flag of their own. Nervous, Palmer glanced back at the lines, like an unconfident swimmer too far from shore.

A faraway muffled cry rang out from the trenches and a shot cracked across the veldt, echoing off the hillsides.

There were angry chitterings and hissings from the Chatts.

Several arcs of blue-white lightning leapt from electric lances towards the Fusilier party.

Palmer threw himself down on the ground and drew his Webley. Hobson hit the dirt beside him.

"What the hell's going on, Sergeant?" he yelled, picking himself up. "The men had strict orders!"

There was a deep, wet roar and a woman's scream. More shots. Roars. The keening cry of injured scentirrii. The brief buzzing crackle of electric lances.

Palmer froze as several hundred pounds of fur, muscle, fangs and claws leapt out of the tube grass at him.

A bright, white-blue, erratic bolt of lightning arced through the air, blasting the animal, earthing through it as it crashed gracelessly to the ground with a dull thud and a snapping of bone. The smell of charred meat, burnt fur and voided bowels filled Palmer's nostrils.

Hell hounds. They must have been stalking the battlepillars.

Rolling away from the smouldering corpse, Palmer got to his feet, seeking another target. He turned and emptied his revolver into another hell hound as it slunk through the tube grass toward the Chatt party.

By the time the gunshots and electric bolts had died out, the ground was littered with hell hound dead.

Life had been difficult for the veldt predators since the arrival of the Pennines. The Fusiliers had decimated them, driving their packs further and further out into the veldt, and the recent harvesting of their natural prey by the airborne Kreothe had forced the packs into desperate actions to survive. The battlepillars were much too large to be brought down, but their passengers were a different matter.

Miraculously, there were no casualties on either side. Between them, the Fusiliers and Chatts had made short work of the hell hounds. Perhaps this was the first sign of an entente cordiale?

PALMER AND HOBSON approached the battlepillars. The scentirrii watched them intently, waving their long segmented feelers in their direction and tracking them with their electric lances and spears.

Nurse Bell climbed down a rope ladder from the battlepillar's howdah and graciously accepted the padre's hand as support as she stepped down onto the ground. The Chatts around her all sank down and bowed low, their feelers almost touching the ground.

Palmer glanced at Sergeant Hobson, who just shook his head. The sergeant had ceased trying to figure this world out, and just got on with it.

"That's quite an effect you have on the Chatts there," said Palmer, intrigued.

Nurse Bell blushed. "Long story."

He stuck out his hand and shook the chaplain's. "Padre."

"It's done," the padre said. "Chandar has carried out its side of the bargain." He nodded toward the encircled system of trenches and Somme soil. "We're still on their territory, so there are things to be worked out, but generally a state of truce now exists between us."

"It is as your dhuyumirrii says," agreed Chandar. "Now you must keep Everson's side of the bargain. The sacred scents must be returned home to the Ones."

Palmer nodded to Hobson. The sergeant sent a runner back to the lines.

Bearers brought out several ammunition crates carried on long poles thrust through their rope handles. They carted them over with less respect than they deserved, but more than the Army Service Corps usually mustered for items in its care.

Palmer opened the crates to show the repository of sacred knowledge, the ancient amphorae and jars packed with dried grasses. Chandar and the others touched their heads and thoraxes in signs of reverence. Chanting in veneration, the dhuyumirrii took up the crates and bore them like tabernacles before loading them into the battlepillars' panniers for the journey back to Khungarr.

"So THAT'S THAT, then," said Palmer with relief as they watched the procession depart, banging their carapaces and chittering like a tiding of magpies.

"Oh, I doubt it, sir," said Hobson.

"What do you mean, Sergeant? There's an understanding between us. We're at peace with them now."

"With respect, sir, we've *made* peace, yes. Now we have to *keep* it. We've still got to live with them, and I don't think that's going to be as easy as it sounds."

EDITH STRODE INTO the hospital tent to find Captain Lippett. She had debated with herself all the way back from Khungarr whether to bring this up, but while there was a possibility of helping those under her care, she decided she would try. She took a deep breath.

"Doctor Lippett," she said. "I'd like your permission to start medical trials of petrol fruit liquor on the blinded men."

Lippett arched his eyebrows. "You do know that Lieutenant Everson has specifically passed an order forbidding its use for human consumption, Nurse?"

The words tumbled out before he could silence her again. "But Doctor, consider the anecdotal evidence of the tank crew and the efficacious effects of the liquor on the Chatt. I think it could help those poor men blinded by Chatt acid. It may not return their sight as they were used to it, but in time, might they not learn to see again in a different way?"

Lippett's stern gaze held her like pins splaying open a dissection specimen. She knew it, she'd gone too far. Perhaps it was a pity after all that her newfound status didn't extend beyond the Chatts.

Lippet smiled faintly. "I must admit, Nurse Bell, the same thought had crossed my mind, too. Perhaps we should see about setting something up."

Humming gaily to herself, Edith sauntered into her tent with the lightness of soul of one who had just crept in late from a jolly good evening out.

She didn't care that the entire Khungarrii colony would now fall at her feet when she passed. Her exalted position didn't matter a jot. She had been away too long and had work to do.

SERGEANT DIXON LOOKED up at the canyon wall and sized up the pile of scree at its base. The metal wall stood bright and impervious above him in the rock. A challenge.

He turned back to his men. "Lambert. Bring me the guncotton and a number eight detonator."

Dixon and his men scrambled to the top of the scree slope where it met the metal wall and, several yards below, they packed the guncotton into the rocks as deep as they could, running a cable along the top of the slope to a large boulder that would shield them from the blast.

Sergeant Dixon blew his whistle.

Below, everyone moved back round the turn in the canyon, where they would be sheltered from blast. Two whistles indicated everyone was in position. There was one long whistle, and then Lambert pushed the plunger on the detonator. It sank with a ratcheted whirr. There followed the briefest of delays. The explosion echoed off the canyon walls, filling it with smoke, dirt and falling debris.

Then they waited for the raining clinker of rocks to stop and for the dust to clear...

CHAPTER NINE
"And There His Foot-Marks Led..."

EVERSON STOOD BY the lip of the Croatoan Crater. Across the far side, over a mile away, waterfalls half hidden by diaphanous mists plunged silently into the sunken world below. Nazhkadarr, the Scentless Place. The place that should not be, Chandar had called it.

He leaned forward and peered over the edge. To his right, the forest around them tumbled pell-mell into the crater. To his left, he could see the crumbled lip where the tank had gone over. He saw the gouged ruts it had made as it slid down the steep crater wall toward the dark hole in the jungle canopy.

Of Nellie Abbot, Napoo and the tank crew there was no sign. When the Fusiliers' battlepillars reached the crater, he had expected to find them waiting. His first thought had been some sort of attack, but their camp had not been disturbed. Then they found the vine rope slung over the crater side.

Again he found his plans frustrated. Why did they have to fight for every bloody inch on this planet? This was supposed to be a simple operation; salvage the tank and pick up Jeffries' trail. Now, even if they found the tank and managed to salvage it, there was no one to man the bloody thing. He'd gambled everything on this.

"God damn it!"

He kicked out in frustration. His boot clipped a small stone, and it skimmed over the ground, bounced once and skittered over the edge of the crater.

"I thought you said you'd ordered them to wait for the salvage party?" Everson snapped at Atkins, regretting it instantly. He watched the lance corporal shuffle uncomfortably.

"I did, sir, but Nellie, that is Driver Abbott, seemed very concerned about Lieutenant Mathers and Private Perkins, sir. We should have been here days ago. If it wasn't for—"

"The mutiny, yes, I know. So they've gone down there?"

Atkins sighed. "Knowing Nellie, sir? Yes."

Nellie Abbott. She had a stubborn attitude forged in suffrage. Which might have been fine if you were chaining yourself to the Town Hall railings. She might have had a point and he might have agreed with her, but out here? Couldn't the damn woman just do as she was told for once?

Even Nurse Bell, who wouldn't say boo to a goose the first time he met her, had become headstrong. What was it about this place and women?

The Urmen treated their women as equals, sharing the work and the danger. Was that what happened when society started fraying at the edges? Wild Women?

Only Sister Fenton seemed to maintain a sense of propriety and decorum. Her exterior was stern, proper and unassailable. They had a saying in the hospital: 'Laugh and the nurse laughs with you, if Sister enters you laugh alone.' She could keep the girls in check, if she wished, but she seemed inclined to give them their head. Frankly, she was just an enigma.

"Bugger," said Everson on reflection.

Atkins peered down into the crater. "As you quite rightly say, sir, bugger."

"OH, THIS IS marvellous," crowed Hepton, framing the sunken lost world of the crater, with thumbs and forefingers. "Jenkins, bring my equipment over here at once. We've got to get this before the light goes. Jenkins, where the bloody hell are you man?"

Private Jenkins staggered up, carrying not only his own battle order kit but the tripod for Hepton's camera and several canisters of film. Shining with sweat, he dropped them on the ground, gasping.

"Careful with them, lad! Bloody expensive things, they are. I'll have your guts for garters if you break 'em."

Hepton panned his imaginary camera across the scene again to find Corporal Riley and Tonkins having a pissing contest over the lip. The awe-inspiring sight was clearly lost on the two soldiers.

"Philistines!" Hepton muttered.

MERCY WAS SAT on the lip of the crater, feet hanging over the edge, oblivious to the height and happily tossing small stones into the jungle canopy below.

Porgy watched Hepton set up his camera. He took his cap off and preened his hair. "Think I'll try my luck, see if he wants a grin and a wave for the folks back home."

"What?" said Porgy, at their sceptical looks. "It's a chance to be famous, innit? When his film gets shown in all the picture houses, yours truly is going to be a matinee idol. The shop girls are all going to want my autograph."

Pot Shot shook his head. "I've seen the size of your 'autograph,' it's nothing to write home about."

Atkins made his way over to his section.

"What did the lieutenant say?" Gutsy asked.

"Might have to send people down there after them."

"By 'people,' you mean us?"

"Probably," said Atkins. "That's the way our luck runs. In the meantime he wants us to set up a rear guard by the ruins, against any Zohtakarrii patrols, so look sharp."

USING THE VINE rope that had been left there by the tank crew, 3 Section, led by Corporal Talbot, descended into the crater to salvage the tank, Walker, Hardiman and Fletcher, going down first to secure the ground and cover the rest of the party. Hume, Owen, Banks, Preston, Cooper, Mitchell and Jackson climbed down after them and waited on the scree as the others advanced into the jungle.

The trail left by the tank was obvious. Not even Hardiman could miss it.

"Keep your eyes peeled," said Talbot as they edged down the verdant tunnel the ironclad had left in its wake, wary of every crack and rustle. If the tank crew had been here, they weren't here now. Anything might have happened. Wise to the ways of this world, Preston and Mitchell kept their rifles pointing up, scanning the canopy overhead. The whoops, squeals and shaking branches set them on edge.

They found the tank in a crushed bank of tangled foliage, broken saplings and trampled shrubbery. Anything that stayed still here was soon strangled by the ever-present pale creepers, and the tank was no exception as the thick, pallid creepers spread their grip over the ironclad.

"We've got it!" Corporal Talbot hollered back to Walker at the jungle's edge, who relayed the news back up to the crater rim.

"Below!" came the reply as several hundredweight of rope and chains tumbled down over the edge, snapping and unspooling as they crashed down the crater side.

"Jesus!" yelped Fletcher as the chain whipped down past them in a flurry of dust and gravel. "Nearly took my bleedin' head off!"

While half the rest of the section set to work with their entrenching tools, hacking the tank free of the creepers' unwanted embrace, Talbot, Hardiman and Walker set about hauling the heavy lengths of rope and chain towards the tank and securing them.

The all-clear was relayed up to the top. The drums of petrol fruit fuel had been unloaded from the battlepillars and stacked by the crater ready to refuel the tank, and the ropes had been connected to the battlepillars' jerry-rigged harnesses.

From his howdah, Woolridge urged Big Bertha and Big Willie to take the strain. The great ropes thrummed taut as the huge larval beasts edged forward towards the prospect of food at the forest's edge.

In the crater, the chains clinked as the slack was taken up and took the weight of the tank. The remaining creepers, unwilling to give up their prize, clung desperately to it, like a mother at a railway station whose son was setting off to war. But in this case, as with that, the army's pull was relentless. It ripped the tank from the creepers' grip, and those that didn't release their hold were wrenched from the ground by their roots as the ironclad machine was dragged inch by inch from the crushed and broken tanglewood that had saved it.

"Whooooo!" Owen waved his battle bowler as the *Ivanhoe* advanced foot by foot through the pulverised bower, back along its own track towards the jungle's edge.

When, with agonising slowness, the tank began to crawl up the scree slope, Talbot pushed his steel helmet back on his head. "You know, I never reckoned this would work, but they're only bloody doing it."

Fletcher clapped him on the shoulder and grinned. "That'll be a tanner you owe me, then."

ATKINS AND 1 Section took up position in the ruins of Nazarr to defend the approach to the Croatoan Crater, along with the men of 2 Section. The ruins had collapsed inwards on the subterranean tunnels, leaving obstinate pinnacles of wall standing here and there. Had it not been for the exotic vegetation already reclaiming the barren ground, it could have been any small Belgian village bombed to buggery by German shells.

"We're so close I can feel it," said Atkins as they kept watch on the jungle beyond the ruins. "We should be down there, going after Jeffries."

"You're certain Jeffries knows a way home, then," asked Gutsy.

"Not certain, but he claimed to have brought us here. I just want to get back to Blighty, and if there's the slightest chance he knows how, then I think we have to take it."

"I thought you said he was just a bloke," said Gazette. "Are you telling me you believe all that magic stuff now? You're not starting to believe your own press, are you, Only?"

"Blood and sand, of course not!" protested Atkins. "You know what happened. I told you. I didn't start those bloody rumours about me battling black magic. In case you forgot, it was believing those tales that got Chalky killed. Whether that diabolist gubbins has any truth to it, who knows? All I know is I didn't see any."

"You have to admit, that mumbo jumbo stuff does seem to follow you around though," Porgy chipped in. "There's that thing with the Chatt, Chandar, too—all that Kurda stuff about how you two were connected by some web of fate or something."

Atkins rolled his eyes. "Give me a break. Look, I'd just like my soddin' life back, all right? My life, to do with as I please, not have all these people with expectations, telling me what I should be, and what I should be doing."

"Shouldn't have joined the army, then," said Mercy with a smirk.

"So you don't put much store in Mathers' mad prophecy, last time we were here, then," asked Pot Shot, mischievously. "*In the spira when the Breath of GarSuleth grows foul,*" he intoned portentously, "*the false dhuyumirrii shall follow its own scent along a trail not travelled, to a place that does not exist. Other Ones will travel with the Breath of GarSuleth, the Kreothe, made, not tamed. Then shall Skarra, with open mandibles, welcome the dark scentirrii. There shall emerge a colony without precedent. The children of GarSuleth will fall. They shall not forsake the Sky Web. The anchor line breaks.*"

The rest of the section just looked at him as if he'd gone doolally.

"I memorised it," said Pot Shot warily.

Atkins raised his eyebrows with disbelief. "You memorised it."

"I thought it might be important."

"And is it?"

"I couldn't say," Pot Shot admitted with a lop-sided grin and shrug. "I don't know what any of it means."

His mood lightened, Atkins shook his head softly, smiled, and cuffed the lanky Fusilier around the head with his soft cap. "Daft ha'p'orth."

A thing the size of a man's forearm, like a corpse rat crossed with a spider, skittered out of the undergrowth.

Almost preternaturally fast, Gazette swung his rifle round, following the movement, before dismissing it.

"What the fuck?" Another ran through Porgy's legs.

Then a gaggle of the critters scuttled out of the undergrowth.

Atkins' eyes narrowed as he stared into the gloom of the forest surrounding them. Something had made those things funk it. Another gesture and the rest of the section sought hasty cover behind the lip of the old Nazarrii edifice, scrambling at their chests for their gas hoods.

Hood in hand, Atkins called out. "Don't fire unless you have to. We may have to repel more than one attack until they can haul the *Ivanhoe* up."

"And then they'll be in for a surprise," said Porgy, his voice muffled by the layers of chemically impregnated flannel.

Atkins removed his soft cap and tugged the hood over his head, tucking it into his collar. The world yellowed and cracked, filtered by the mica eyepieces. He could feel his forehead begin to prickle with sweat under the thick cloth.

For a moment there was only silence and tension. Sweaty palms gripped barrels. Eyes scanned the wall of forest from behind dirty lenses of the gas hoods.

Zohtakarrii scentirrii swarmed out of the forest like cockroaches, leaping from the cover of the trees with angry, rattling hisses. Those with swords and spears bounded like grasshoppers, covering the space between the forest and the ruins in seconds.

One launched itself over the shattered wall. Atkins, braced against a large block of rubble, thrust up with his bayonet, slipping the seventeen-inch blade up into the soft abdomen, and used the Chatt's momentum to swing his rifle like a pitchfork. He threw the Chatt over his head, pulling the trigger as he did so. The Chatt flailed through the air and fell against the rubble blocks, where its carapace cracked and a thick dark ichor seeped out of its broken body.

Gazette settled down into cover and picked off charging Chatts with mechanical precision, flanked by Pot Shot and Porgy.

The ruins, though, were in danger of being overrun. Further afield, Atkins heard the sound of shooting. The Chatts were flanking them and attacking the main rescue party. And he and his section were about to be cut off from the rest of them.

"2 Section! Fall back and give covering fire!" yelled Atkins.

They didn't have to be told twice. The section retreated to the rear of the ruins to give covering fire to Atkins and his Black Hand Gang.

On hearing the first shots, Everson barked orders. "Stand to. Fix bayonets. Gas, gas, gas!"

There was no gas, of course, but the hoods protected against the Chatts' acid spit and the command had been drilled into the men. Everson saw no point in changing it.

Everson turned to the Fusilier astride the battlepillar as it and its partner continued their obstinate plod forward, each footfall hauling the tank nearer. If they could get the tank to the top, then it could turn the tide for them. They might not be able to drive it, but its machine guns and six-pounders would bring much needed support. They had to cover Woolridge and his battlepillars for as long as possible.

He called up. "Woolridge, whatever happens, keep pulling. We need that tank. We'll buy you as much time as we can."

Woolridge waved his acknowledgement from Big Bertha's howdah. Ferris and Carlton manned the battlepillar's forward machine gun. Merrick and Bailey took the rear.

Woolridge saw Atkins and the two rearguard sections retreating towards the main party across the no man's land of scrub, with the lines of Chatts advancing behind them.

"Covering fire!" he yelled.

Ferris and Carlton opened fire, their elevated position giving a good beaten zone. The Lewis gun chuddered out in short bursts, shattering carapaces and felling advancing Chatts.

The rest of the platoon, having taken cover, yelled encouragement as Atkins' men pelted towards them, some helping injured or blinded comrades.

They reached the safety of the firing line, hurdling over the crouched soldiers.

BIG BERTHA AND Big Willie were now advancing beyond the front line towards the Chatts, as they continued to haul their ironclad load from the crater. For Woolridge to do his job, Everson couldn't afford to lose ground to the enemy.

There was nothing for it; they would have to attack and defend every yard they could. Their only problem was lack of ammunition. Whatever they faced today, even if they were to repel it, they would still need to conserve ammunition for whatever happened afterwards. To be out here this far from the trenches without ammunition would leave them effectively defenceless.

Everson summoned the nearest private. "Ellis! Tell the NCOs. On my order, we're going to advance towards the enemy. Single-round fire."

"Sir." The Fusilier dashed along the line as the first wave of Chatts sprang towards them.

Everson blew his whistle and the sections stepped out from behind cover.

The skirmish line advanced: the bombers, flanked by riflemen, took advantage of the close bunching of Chatts as Mills bombs arced through the air to explode in balls of fire and red-hot shrapnel, throwing limbs and razor-sharp shards of carapace whirling though the air.

"It's pig-sticking time, lads!" howled a corporal, and the air was filled with cries and roars honed on English training grounds under the eyes of disdainful NCOs.

The Tommies charged with bayonets and crashed against Chatt carapaces in close quarters fighting, too close for electric lances to be effective, fighting to hold the line. Everson slashed and parried with his sword, taking out his frustrations with every cut and thrust.

Atkins swung his rifle and bayonet, countering parries and thrusts from spears and swords, his khaki tunic becoming mottled and moth-eaten as drops of acid spit burnt themselves away against the thick serge. Chatts swarmed around them, like ants on jam. Again and again he stabbed, countered, swung the stock of his Enfield into the horned and nubbed carapaces, blocked blows with the barrel. As one Chatt fell, another took its place. Under his gas hood, Atkins howled with frustration and rage, and the muscles in his arms began to burn with the effort.

The Fusiliers advanced past Big Bertha and Big Willie. Arcs of electric energy blistering the air around them as the Chatts' lancers found their range.

The left flank of the line began to weaken and the Tommies were pushed back, but wheeled round to protect the straining battlepillars.

BELOW, IN THE crater, the sound of gunfire and screams echoed off the walls. The working party paused.

"Jesus, what the hell is going on up there?" said Mitchell. "Sounds like an attack."

"I don't know. But I'm not going to be stuck down here," said Cooper. He scrambled up the scree slope, stones slipping out from under his feet as he climbed.

"Cooper, who said you could leave your post? Get back here!" ordered Corporal Talbot.

Cooper ignored him, reached the vine rope by which they'd descended, and began to climb, hand over hand.

"What are you going to do?" Owen asked Talbot.

Talbot's shoulders dropped in defeat. "Nothing," he said. "Leastways, not yet. I've got his name, and he's climbing towards a fight, ain't he? He's not deserting."

"I don't know what's going on, but maybe we should all be up there, Corp," said Fletcher.

The tank groaned and clanked, clawing its way up the scree, like a faithful hound attempting to scramble up to help its master.

"Maybe we should, but our orders were to see to the tank. That's our job."

WOOLRIDGE JABBED THE driving spikes between the segmented plates behind Big Bertha's head, urging the beast forward.

"Come on, girl, come on," he urged, willing the larval creature on.

It wasn't lost on Woolridge that even as the others were forced back, he was slowly advancing towards the enemy, as the battlepillars hauled the twenty-eight-ton tank up the steep incline of the crater wall. To stop now would be disastrous. He knew that whatever happened, he must keep hauling the tank. But he also knew he'd need another fifty or sixty yards to do it. Yards that were slipping away as the Chatts advanced, although the Pennines were making them fight for every inch.

In front of him, in the forward machine-gun basket, Ferris swapped out the last circular forty-eight-round ammo canister from the forward Lewis gun and swore.

"We're out of ammo!"

Woolridge dug the driving spikes in again, pulling on the reins. Big Bertha reared up off the ground as the advancing wave of Chatts rushed towards it and Big Willie, before crashing down again, crushing half a dozen Chatts, their smashed carapaces crackling under Bertha's bulk like brittle sheets of cellophane.

Several Chatts sprang up onto Bertha's panniers, and from there scrambled up the sides of the beast.

Ferris was hit by a bolt from an electric lance. He went into spasm, lost his balance and slipped down Big Bertha's face. His webbing caught on one of its barbed mandibles; as he struggled to free himself, the battlepillar's mandibles scythed shut.

COOPER HAD ALMOST reached the top. Even Talbot found himself willing the man on. There was a blue-white flash from beyond the lip, and the rope he was climbing dropped into the crater. Cooper's body plummeted down the crater wall, hit an outcrop and pinwheeled out into the air.

"Cooper!"

He hit the top of the scree slope with a sound like a wet sandbag. His limbs flopped at sickening angles. The broken body tumbled down the crater side until it slid to rest against the port track horn of the *Ivanhoe*. The track plates rolled implacably forward, crushing the body beneath its port track before anyone could reach him; the sound of splintering bone and bursting organs was mercifully lost amid the creaks and screeching of shifting iron plates.

THE CHATTS ADVANCED along Big Bertha's back towards the driver's howdah. Woolridge cycled the bolt on his Enfield and fired, sending the first Chatt spinning off to the ground. And the second.

There was a loud wrenching and tearing followed by a snap as the load bearing fibre of the tow ropes finally tore, under assault from Chatt mandibles. Released from tension, the ropes snapped through the air, hurling Chatts from the battlepillar's back.

Free of its burden, Bertha lurched forward. Woolridge almost lost his footing. He grabbed the side of the howdah to steady himself. He caught sight of the Chatt with its electric lance a second before his world was filled with an agonising white light that faded into a consuming blackness.

LEFT TO BEAR the entire load alone, Big Willie began to lose the battle. The weight of the tank dragged the battlepillar back towards the edge of the crater, leaving a great furrow in the ground.

Electric lance fire burnt through the great ropes and Big Willie was suddenly released from its harness, but its freedom was short-lived. Stray electric lance bolts licked its armoured sides, earthing through it, burning carapace and scorching soft tissue. Thrashing in pain, its rear end crashed against the stock of fuel drums, sending them toppling over the crater edge, like skittles, where they bounced down the side in a succession of hollow, discordant notes.

TALBOT WATCHED AS the tank reached the top of the scree slope and abutted the crater wall. The track horns caught the camber of the wall and began to creep the chassis up the steeper slope.

There was a lurch and the tank rolled back several yards, sending the Fusiliers scurrying out of the way. A huge length of rope dropped, piling up on the driver's cabin between the track horns like a great fibrous stool.

The tank remained still for a moment, and then with a despairing groan of tortured metal, the *Ivanhoe* rolled back down towards the jungle, picking up speed in a cloud of dust and chippings.

Watching with horror, Talbot flinched at every sound.

With their arms windmilling, the salvage section ran down after the runaway ironclad, as if they had a chance of stopping it.

EVERSON HEARD THE grating, metallic crash and the rumble of the tracks, and knew that the tank was gone again.

And with it, the Pennines' resolve. They found themselves pushed back by sheer weight of numbers until they had their backs to the crater's edge. They were surrounded. Trapped.

The Chatts closed in around them, bristling with spears, swords and electric lances, mandibles clashing. But they didn't move in to drive them over.

"I think they want us alive," said Atkins.

"Works for me," said Porgy in ragged breaths.

Pot Shot eyed their scything mandibles. "Probably prefer their food live, knowing our luck."

A large scentirrii stepped forward. It wore a blood-red silk surcoat and its mandibles seemed larger and stronger than any Khungarrii. Its antennae waved. "You are prisoners of the Zohtakarrii."

The Fusiliers didn't move, but waited on a command from Everson. He knew they would fight to the last if he ordered them, but what would they be fighting for? Perhaps Bains had been right. This world wasn't about King and Country and Duty. It was about survival.

"Lower your weapons," he said, his voice laced with regret. He stepped forwards and offered his sword in surrender.

TALBOT AND THE others strained their ears. It had gone quiet up above. That wasn't good.

"D'you think they're dead?" asked Hume.

"If they are, then we're up shit creek," said Mitchell. "We're trapped down here."

"Maybe they've been captured."

Talbot cupped his hand round his mouth and called up. "Sir! Lieutenant Everson!"

There was no reply. Fletcher grimaced and shook his head.

"Anyone! Hello?"

"We can't just stay here."

"Doesn't look like we have a choice. We were ordered to watch over the tank and that's what we'll do until an officer tells us otherwise. It'll give us shelter, and maybe there are rations and ammo in there."

With many hopeful, but unfulfilled, glances to the top of the crater, they walked back into the tank's bower. It was dispiriting to find the ironclad embedded in the vegetation pretty much as they had first found it.

"Might as well be on the bloody Somme. A day's misery and no ground gained to show for it."

"Home from home, then, ain't it?"

"Corp!"

"What?"

Banks pointed into the undergrowth. Something was moving. They backed away, raising their rifles.

An officer, sallow-faced, unsteady on his feet, stumbled out of the undergrowth, his hand out searching for support to steady himself, but the branches and saplings bent under his weight and left him staggering. His skin and uniform were grey, dusted with a powder, motes of which swirled about him in the air as he moved.

"I recognise him," said Walker straining his neck as he peered into the gloom. "It's Lieutenant Mathers, the Tank Commander." He lowered his rifle and stepped forward "Are you all right, sir?"

Mathers lurched forward as if concussed and suffering from commotional shock, his mouth moving as he tried to speak.

Walker and Mitchell dashed to help him. "It's all right, sir, we've got you."

Mathers looked up at them. They could see, now, his eyes were rimed with grey powder.

Mitchell saw a gaping hole in Mathers head, filled with something soft and spongy extruding from the shattered cranial cavity. Not brain. He'd seen men with their brains hanging out, and this very definitely was not that.

Mathers' mouth still moved, as though he were trying to dislodge some obstruction in his throat.

"Here, Corp, I don't think 'e's well."

Walker slapped him on the back to see if it would help. Clouds of powder billowed into the air. Walker and Mitchell coughed thick phlegmy coughs as they inhaled it, drawing it deep into their lungs.

Hardiman backed away. "That ain't dust, it's growing on him. Look. He's covered with it."

A network of fine grey filaments had spread across Mathers' pallid skin and uniform, like a gauzy shroud.

Walker and Mitchell's coughing fit dissolved into desperate asthmatic gasps as they clawed at their throats, eyes wide with panic.

Mathers stepped clumsily toward the others, his mouth opening and closing like a goldfish, as something swelled inside it. There was a soft pop and a cloud of spores exploded from his mouth, enveloping the soldiers.

They tried very hard to scream.

CHAPTER TEN
"A Fear That is Weird and Grim..."

THE AIR OF the Croatoan Crater was humid and thick with cloying scents and the heady smell of decay. Under her coveralls, Nellie's skin was slick with sweat as they moved through the jungle, following Napoo in Indian file.

"Wherever Alfie is, he can't be far. Why, this crater can't be more than a mile wide," she said, more to convince herself than anything.

"If he's still alive," said Norman, avoiding her gaze.

Nellie's eyes narrowed. "Of course he is. He must be." But there was a note of uncertainty in her voice.

A string of muffled cracks reached them through the jungle foliage.

Reggie cocked his head. "Is that gunfire?"

Norman listened for a moment. "No," he said dismissively. "That's them whip things up in the trees, is that. Gave me a heart attack first time I heard them. Thought we were being sniped at."

They pushed on, ignoring the faint firework crackle. Cecil approached Nellie, barely able look her in the eye as he mumbled, "I got scratched," and held out the back of his hand to her.

She suppressed a smile. When she took his hand to inspect it, his face flushed with embarrassment. She cleaned it, bandaged it and packed him off to rejoin the others.

"If the rest of them get cuts or scratches, tell them to see me immediately," she said.

Cecil nodded dumbly and hurried off to lose himself in male company.

Over the next few hours, Reggie and Wally came to her individually with cuts, grazes and sheepish glances. Cecil regarded them jealously. Nellie knew the smallest cut on this world could lead to Lord knows what kind of infection. She patched them up from her dwindling medical supplies and they were pathetically grateful for her ministrations. Without their commander, without their petrol fruit juice, without the *Ivanhoe*, they seemed a little less than themselves. A little lost.

As Napoo followed the trail, the jungle folded in on itself, forming a living labyrinth, as if to protect itself against the parasitic creepers that spread everywhere and sought to engulf it.

They threaded their way through the labyrinthine alleys of giant trees, buttress roots and tangled undergrowth, sharing them with things that scuttled and oozed briefly across their path. In there, the air was close and stale.

They eased gingerly between groves of giant thorns where the high pitched whines of insects made them flinch and duck just as much as any whizz-bang or Hun bullet.

"Reminds me of moving up communications trenches to the front," said Jack without a trace of irony.

Here, however, the revetments reached to the sky. The sunlight, such as it was, came in momentary shafts of light, or glittering chinks in the leafy cover high above.

Even used to the cramped space in the *Ivanhoe*, the jungle was getting to some of them. Their petrol-fruit madness may have faded, but there remained a lingering paranoia. That could be a healthy thing on a world where everything was out to get you, but it didn't do much for your peace of mind. Cecil whimpered, his eyes darting about in terror.

Jack laid a large hand on his shoulder, offering comfort, but even that made him jump. "Easy, lad."

Napoo led them on between the trees and thickets, following a seemingly invisible trail, at times clambering over huge boughs or ducking under trailing creepers until, eventually, crawling through a spiny bower, they came to the end of the labyrinth and stepped out into open jungle.

A slight breeze rippled through the undergrowth.

"Fresh air!" declared Reggie with the manner of someone stepping off a train at a country station. He mopped his face with a handkerchief and puffed out his cheeks, before taking off his turtle helmet to wipe his balding head.

A rushing gurgle through the trees told of a river nearby, its cold current sucking the air towards it. They headed down towards the sound over damp rocks. The air felt cool and refreshing against Nellie's clammy skin.

Cecil cried out and tugged at the sleeve of Jack's coveralls. Jack turned.

Standing behind them was a figure both familiar and horrifying.

Jack frowned at the apparition. "Lieutenant Mathers?"

The others stopped their scrambling and looked back, drawn by the impossibility of its existence.

Bewildered, Reggie lost his footing and slipped on his backside.

"It can't be."

Mathers was covered with a fine cobweb of grey filaments. The hole in his head bulged with some sort of soft, grey puckered growth. His left arm had begun to lose its form as man and uniform were being absorbed by the malevolent mould.

Wally, stepped forward, hand extended. "Lieutenant?"

Norman pulled him back. "Wally, don't."

"But it's the Sub!"

"No, no it isn't. Look, man."

The figure moved its mouth as if trying to speak, or draw breath. It stumbled towards them, clumsily, its arms outstretched to counterbalance its awkward leaden gait.

Nellie stood transfixed, as from its mouth a spongy growth began to swell. Stretching the jaw open unnaturally, it emerged obscenely from between grey cracked lips.

Cecil fired his Enfield twice, hitting the mouldering cadaver in the arm and chest. Plumes of dust puffed from the dry wounds. It reeled with the bullets' momentum, but continued towards them.

Filaments, questing mycelia, spread out from Mathers' feet towards them. The threads probed outwards, creating an expanding carpet of living fibres.

This was no longer Mathers. His cadaver was merely a host, ambulated by whatever foreign fungus now possessed him, seeking nothing more than to reproduce and spread its spore. If they succumbed to it, their fate would be that of Mathers himself, and right now that thought horrified Nellie more than anything else she could imagine.

"Back!" called Napoo, dragging Nellie away. "Back! It is Dulgur. Evil spirit!"

She stumbled away, unable to tear her gaze from it as the fruiting pod extruding from Mathers' mouth continued to swell, its puckered skin now taut and shiny. As Mathers lumbered towards them, the pod burst, like a puffball, ejecting a cloud of spores.

The tank crew backed away from the drifting spore cloud, tripping over roots and dragging each other in an effort to remain out of its reach. Even as the breeze snatched the spores away from them, other pods were fruiting across Mathers' body.

"Keep away from it!" yelled Nellie.

Mathers advanced, his lumbering steps pulling the spreading filaments behind him, like a bridal train, a counterbalance to his unsteady gait.

Norman fumbled in his haversack, pulled out a Mills bomb and slipped a finger through the ring of the safety pin. Jack's powerful hand closed round his.

"Don't. If it goes off it'll scatter that stuff and put us all in more danger."

Fire wouldn't work for the same reason, spreading what spores survived on currents of hot air. There didn't seem to be anything they could do to stop it that wouldn't make the situation worse. Nellie felt a nauseous wave of panic rise like bile.

Then she heard the rushing susurrus in the background.

"The river," she ordered, in a tone that brooked no dissent.

Wally and the others didn't need telling twice. She was startled at how readily they obeyed her.

Their hobnailed boots slipped and skidded on exposed roots and rocks, damp and slick with reddish algae as they headed down toward the sound of rushing water.

Mathers followed at a plodding but relentless pace.

Nellie could feel the moisture in the air and the greasy wet stones beneath her feet. Flat, wet leaves slapped against her face as she raced on to the river's edge.

She was brought to an abrupt halt as Jack thrust out an arm to stop her. She looked down. Another step and she would have tumbled headlong into the river. Half-hidden by foliage, the rocks dropped away into the torrent.

Powered by the waterfalls that plunged into the crater, the river rushed past below, foaming and tumbling as it roiled over smooth, waterworn rocks.

"It's too fast and deep to cross," called Norman above the water's roar. "We're trapped."

Nellie looked around. Humid spray hung in the air, a rainbow struggling to materialise within it. It would dampen the spores, stick them down. It gave them a fighting chance.

"We have to get it into the river!" she yelled.

They hunted round for anything they might use. Jack pulled experimentally at a thick green branch growing across the path. He hauled it back to the side of the trail and let it go. It sprang back into the path with a satisfying whip. He grunted with satisfaction.

Norman pulled a long length of fibrous creeper from the undergrowth. Unspoken, a plan materialised.

Mathers, his grey dusty pallor glistening with a dew of condensation, came on, step by jerky step, having built up a stumbling momentum, a fruit pod swelling and ripening on his gnarled arm, like a blister.

Jack watched it from the shadows of the undergrowth, his muscles aching, his teeth clamped together as he held back the supple branch. "Come on, you bastard, hurry up," he hissed.

Wally stepped out of the undergrowth by the river's edge just long enough to shout, "Oi, Sub!"

Jack watched as Mathers turned his head and took a step past him towards the sound, another spore pod fruiting from his mouth.

Jack let the branch loose. It whipped forward, hitting Mathers in the small of the back with enough force to wind an ordinary man. Mathers stumbled forward. Reggie and Napoo, hidden either side of the trail, pulled the length of creeper taut, catching him just above his calf-length boots.

Mathers toppled forward, but there was nothing for him to catch hold of. Arms flailing, he tumbled forwards through the thin foliage and down into the raging torrent below.

The spores were instantly drowned by spumes of water as the current carried him spinning slowly out from the bank, the train of filaments billowing out around him like some obscene Ophelia. His mouth opened and closed, one arm raised above the water as he was swept along into the white water rush.

Nellie hurried along the bank, following his progress until she reached a rocky promontory. Below them, the water tumbled recklessly over a lip, not into some pool but into a huge crack in the rock, a fault in the ground that swallowed the torrent whole; she could hear its roar echo as it fell away into blackness. She watched with a mixture of pity and horror as the figure of Mathers, half-lost in the churning waters, rushed over the edge and into the yawning dark.

The men took it hard, losing Mathers again, and it was all Nellie could do to chivvy them on as Napoo picked up the trail of Alfie's abductor.

MOTES OF GREY mould danced in the air as spore-rimed eyes followed their movement.

With an unsteady, barely coordinated gait, the fungus-ambulated things that had been Corporal Talbot and his party set off in slow, inexorable pursuit as a filigree of mycelia spread across the ground at their feet.

SERGEANT DIXON LOOKED up at the canyon wall. He was less than impressed with the results of the demolition blast. It had cleared perhaps another twenty feet of scree, exposing only more wall of the same featureless metal. Not a scratch, not a dent. No sign of a hatch or window.

He scrambled up to inspect his handiwork with Lambert and stood at the base of the wall. The newly exposed metal was the same colour, same smooth texture. Whatever this stuff was, it was like nothing he'd ever seen before.

They could blast all week, but he suspected the result would be the same, even if they cleared all the scree.

"We could try knocking," suggested Lambert.

"What do you think we just bloody did, Private?" said Dixon curtly, surveying the scattered scree and newly-exposed metal. "Where's the Iddy Umpty bloke?"

Lambert fetched Buckley to the top of the scree, loaded down under the weight of several wooden boxes and haversacks.

"You're next on the bill. Show us what you can do, lad."

Buckley produced two copper plates each about a foot square, connected by wires to a listening set in one of the boxes. Normally they'd bury the plates in the ground to listen for German telephone communications, but now he set the plates against the metal wall.

"I need quiet," he said.

Dixon glared at him, took in a lungful of air until Buckley thought he'd pop the buttons on his tunic and bellowed, "Quiet!"

The order found itself repeated several times as it echoed off the canyon walls. Below them, the men stopped what they were doing and stood in silence.

"Quiet enough for you?"

Buckley smiled weakly. "Much obliged, Sarn't."

He put the earphones on his head and his forehead creased as he strained to listen...

NEWS OF THE armistice between the Pennines and the Chatts who'd plagued them for the last four months spread, and the air of relief in the trenches was palpable. Jubilation broke out in spontaneous displays of bonhomie as the soldiers celebrated in their own meagre ways; rousing choruses of *When this Bloody War is Over,* the more generous breaking out what little luxuries they had managed to save; tins of Ticklers, once despised, now prized; some shared their last hoarded gaspers, passing each one out as far as it would go, every inhalation so cherished and savoured they might have been the best cigars from the most exclusive gentlemen's club.

Even Sister Fenton, as stern and taciturn as she was, cracked a smile, so her patients claimed.

Impelled by his newly-remembered vision, Padre Rand anxiously made his way through the trenches looking for Lieutenant Tulliver. It was frustrating, therefore, to find himself stopped and congratulated every other fire bay or so; his shoulder patted, his back slapped and his hand shaken, even though he protested with all modesty that really he'd had nothing to do with the current situation and had merely been an observer. But they would have none of it and he was forced to bury his impatience deep down, for in their faces he saw the respite from their tribulations that he had long prayed for and took comfort in it. How might his vision shape their future? If it came true, could he shepherd them back to the Promised Land that was England?

The padre eventually found the pilot in the Command Post with Lieutenant Palmer, sharing what they called mock coffee. It was hot, brown and came from some sort of bean, which was about all it had in common.

Tulliver raised his tin mug in salute, as he entered.

"The man of the hour," said the young pilot.

The padre shrugged it off with a brief smile. "The Lord works in mysterious ways, Lieutenant. I believe you're due out on another reconnaissance flight."

"That's right, Padre, up with the angels. Want me to put in a word for you?"

The padre smiled. "That won't be necessary. I want to accompany you. I need to get my report to Lieutenant Everson. There are things he needs to know. I'm sure he'd want to be apprised of the situation on the Chatt front."

Tulliver drained his tin mug and put it down. "Well, I've no doubt you can patter out the prayers, and God knows a spare few might come in handy, but how good are you with a machine gun? There's something up there, and it's hunting me. I need someone who can watch my back."

"I've done a little hunting in my time," the Chaplain said. "I really must insist, Lieutenant. I don't want to have to take it up with a higher authority." He glanced at Palmer.

"I think you'll find I'm the highest authority round here," said Tulliver, tapping the RFC patch on his breast, a wry smile playing round his lips.

"Mine is a little higher, I think," retorted the padre.

Tulliver glanced at his dog collar and grinned. "Touché, Padre," he said, scraping his chair back and standing up. "Very well. I'll be wing, you be prayer. Because God knows, we'll probably need both."

THE SOPWITH 1½ Strutter climbed away from the trenches.

Wearing a leather flying helmet and goggles and an army warm he'd borrowed from Lieutenant Palmer, the padre—who had never been up in an aeroplane before—experienced the exhilarating terror of take-off and marvelled as the world fell away and he saw the landscape spread out below him. He briefly wondered if this was the view that God had of the world, before remembering with a flush of shame that this wasn't God's world. It wasn't their world. It was no man's world. He turned around to look out across the veldt towards the great forest in the distance where he knew Khungarr lay, and took a last look at the small island of humanity dug in on its circle of Somme mud. How tiny and frail it looked. And how all the more remarkable it was for that. The experience would have been quite serene, were it not for the loud, determined roar of the engine and the fine spray of lubricating oil, hazing both pilot and passenger.

Tulliver banked the aeroplane and they flew beyond the hills sheltering the camp towards the plateau and the scar running across it that was the canyon. The two sections of Fusiliers waved as Tulliver and the padre flew over. Tulliver waggled his wings in response. He pointed down over the side of the plane. The padre peered over nervously. A bright glint momentarily blinded him as the sun caught the metal wall.

THE AEROPLANE DRONED on out over the Fractured Plain. Tulliver was constantly vigilant for landmarks. This was one. On a world where compasses didn't work—the damn thing just spun in circles—landmarks were vitally important to flying.

Thirty minutes later and he could make out the Croatoan Crater in the distance. He flew low over the surrounding forest, the whipperwills snapping away from the canopy, and suddenly there it was, the sunken world.

He'd judged his approach perfectly. The discoloured strip of vegetation in the crater aligned. In fact, from a landmark point of view, it was as good as a compass. It pointed perfectly towards the plateau and the canyon with its metal mystery.

He banked round and found the ruins of the ancient edifice and clearing where he'd left the tank crew and where the rescue party should be camped. But he could see neither.

He came round again, lower. He noticed one of the battlepillars grazing idly and he knew it by the crude roundel daubed on its side. He made out scorch marks on the earth, and small craters left by grenades. Here and there were dead bodies in khaki, one being torn at by a pack of small creatures. A battle, then. One that didn't go well for the Pennines, by the look of things.

He came round again and let off a burst with his forward machine gun, the line of bullets stitching the ground. The creatures scattered back into the forest.

What had happened here? First the tank was lost, and then the party sent to salvage it, and Lieutenant Everson along with it. Had it been Chatts? He had to head back to camp and inform the others that the rescue party had been lost.

He pulled up and caught sight of a small shadow rippling over the face of a mountainous cloud. Was that the creature that had been shadowing him like a hungry shark, or just a phantom, a fleeting shift of cloud? He wanted to be sure.

He pulled back on the stick and climbed up into the canyons between the clouds, looking for his elusive prey. He glanced back. The padre had turned round and was gripping the Scarff-ring-mounted machine gun as if his life depended on it, which it very probably did.

He'd played games of hide-and-seek like this for fun in the French skies over Fine Villas, and with altogether more deadly intent over Hunland. He flew through bottomless passes and towering white rifts. Ragged wisps of cloud blew past like minute-old Archie, but there was no sight of his nemesis. It could, of course, be hiding inside the clouds. That was always a possibility. But he wasn't tempted to look.

He heard the abrupt chatter of the rear machine gun and turned to look over his shoulder. The padre pointed up and behind the aeroplane. Tulliver banked to get a better look.

Jabberwocks, fiercely territorial flying raptors with long necks, wings like a stingray and razor sharp talons and teeth, had spotted his bus and seen it as potential prey. They could shred the Sopwith, with its wooden frame and doped canvas, in a minute.

Tulliver pulled the nose up sharply. The world dropped away as the bus climbed. The jabberwocks pursued tenaciously, but their raucous cries were soon lost and they fell away, seeking easier quarry.

Tulliver pushed the bus higher. The air up here was cold and clear. Flocks of cloud lay below them, like grazing sheep. He'd never flown at this altitude here before; twelve thousand feet, close to the bus's operational ceiling. He looked down at the ground and felt that delicious thrill of flight, of being this high with nothing between you and the ground but the wooden seat you sat on.

And then he frowned. What the hell? What was that? He tried to rub his goggles clean of their mist of oil then, frustrated, pushed them up. He felt the altitude's cold bite into the exposed skin and the sting in his eyes. He had to squint against the cold, the air speed and the oil.

From this altitude, things always took on a different perspective, a bigger picture. The patchwork of fields over Kent, say, or the blasted pockmarked landscape of the Somme. But he'd never seen anything like this. What the hell was that? Below them, the landscape was—

The engine spluttered. He adjusted the throttle and the mixture, but it coughed and died anyway. There was a brief silence and then the weight of the nose pulled the plane down into a dive. The wind began to shriek through the wires.

The Sopwith started to corkscrew as Tulliver struggled with the stick. He had to pull out of the spin, level it out. If he didn't, the speed would rip the wings off and they'd fall the rest of the way in a folded mess of wood and wire.

Slowly he regained control of the aeroplane and brought it down in a long slow spiral, losing height and speed. The whole thing left him shaking and exhausted. He tried the engine again, but it coughed and spluttered, reluctant to catch.

"If you've got a good prayer, Padre, now's the time!" he yelled as he tried to restart the engine again.

He began looking for a place to land. Two thousand feet, now. Over to his left he could see the crater several miles away. The landscape below was filled with forest, with here and there little oases of meadow and heathland offering hope of a safe landing, but he was still too high and too fast.

Ahead loomed a towering hill of earth that Tulliver recognised as a Chatt edifice, like that of Khungarr. Unfortunately, the large managed clearing around it was also now the nearest landing space. After what had happened to the salvage party, it wasn't his preferred course of action, but there was no choice.

The engine caught. It coughed and spluttered, one of the cylinders missing intermittently, but with life enough for Tulliver to control his descent over the tree tops into the clearing. It was a bouncy landing and even before they had stopped, Chatt scentirrii were racing toward the Sopwith in their curious springing gait. By the time they had taxied to a stop and Tulliver had switched the engine off, they were surrounded.

Ignoring the agitated Chatts, Tulliver sat in a state of utter funk, still shaking, his heart pounding, and tried to compose himself. That had been a bloody close thing. No need to let the padre know, though. He pulled off his helmet, goggles and scarf, and left them in the cockpit as he climbed out.

"Sorry about that, Padre," he said brightly as he helped the pale-faced chaplain clamber shakily from the aeroplane.

"I think we have other more pressing concerns now," said the padre, eyeing the nervous-looking Chatts that had now ringed the aeroplane, armed with spears and electric lances.

"Really? Right, then." Tulliver turned and addressed the suspicious Chatts. "Take us to your chieftain," he said in a loud, slow voice. He turned to the nearest Chatt. "And make sure you take damn good care of my bus, or there'll be hell to pay."

If it knew what he was saying, it gave no sign.

As they stepped away from the Sopwith, the Chatts closed in about them. Tulliver put his hand down and checked the reassuring weight of the Webley in his waist band under his tunic before allowing himself and the padre to be escorted into the edifice.

They were conducted through dark passages illuminated with niches of luminescent lichen. One of the scentirrii exhaled on the barbed circular plant door and it shrivelled open.

"I've seen places like this before," said the padre quietly. "It's a gaol chamber."

"Ah," said Tulliver, and then he scowled. "I thought I told them to take us to their chieftain."

They were ushered through the dilated doorway. The barbs around the rim of the contracted plant looked like fangs around an orifice—he had seen too many ugly things on this world to call it a mouth. Once inside, the door cycled shut.

They stood inside while their eyes adjusted. There was no luminous lichen here.

"Tulliver?"

It was a voice the pilot knew and often resented, but he was more than happy to hear it now. "Everson!"

"What the bloody hell are you doing here?" said Everson, stepping forward. "And more to the point, what the hell are you doing bringing the padre?"

"That was my idea, Lieutenant. I twisted his arm, as it were."

"Well that was a bloody stupid thing to do, Padre, if you don't mind my saying." His voice softened. "I trust your mission was a success, then."

"Yes," said the padre. "Although as to the exact nature of the armistice, that will be down to you and Chandar to negotiate."

Everson gestured at the earthen wall of the chamber. "Well, looking at the sterling job I've been doing here, we'll be in for a rough ride, then." He changed the topic. "How did you—"

"We were forced down, Lieutenant," said the padre, patting Tulliver on the shoulder "Took some skilful flying to find somewhere to put us down in one piece."

Tulliver shrugged. It was actually a brilliant piece of flying, even if he did think so himself.

"What happened to you?" the padre asked.

"Ambush," replied Everson. "They seemed to know we were coming." There was a shuffling and the odd cough in the gloom behind him. "Corporal Atkins and the men from his section are here, along with Hepton and Jenkins, Tonkins and Riley from Signals. The others are in chambers nearby. We can shout. Well we could, until the Chatts got wise and got one of their dhuyumirrii to douse them with that benediction of theirs. We've not heard a peep for hours."

"So what next?"

The door began to dilate open again.

"I think we're about to find out," said Everson.

EVERSON, TULLIVER, THE padre, Hepton, Atkins and his section were escorted under guard up a spiralling inclined tunnel that led them up into the heights of the edifice. They came to a large plant door, with scentirrii guards either side.

"About bloody time," murmured Everson. "Now maybe we'll get some answers."

The guards turned and breathed on the door in unison. It shrank away from their breath and opened.

Everson and his men were ushered into an airy chamber. Light came through a large window at the far end.

Silhouetted against the light was the figure of a man. He was standing by the window looking out over the unfamiliar forest landscape, his hands clasped behind his back, master of all he surveyed. This was no Urman. This man was at ease in his surroundings, in control of them. This man wielded power, but what kind of man could wield power in a Chatt edifice?

Everson made out the familiar outline of a fitted tunic and fitted calf-length boots.

An officer.

He must have known they had entered, yet still chose to stand there. There was only one officer he knew audacious enough to do something of this kind, one man who had the absolutely bloody gumption to treat them like this and expect to get away with it.

Jeffries.

Jeffries, wanted for the double murder of two debutantes back in Blighty. Jeffries, the infamous diabolist. Jeffries, the man who claimed he was responsible for bringing the Pennines here with some black magic ritual, using the Somme as a blood sacrifice. Jeffries, who had almost set them to war against the Khungarrii the moment they arrived. And a man for whom they had been searching for the past four months in pursuit of a way home.

Everson snorted with derision as anger boiled up within him.

The man turned.

"Gentlemen, welcome."

CHAPTER ELEVEN
"He Shook Hands with Britannia..."

IT WASN'T JEFFRIES. "I have been waiting for this meeting for such a long time. It's good to see some familiar faces. Well, I say faces," said the stranger with a dismissive wave of his hand. "I mean uniforms. I don't suppose you have any cigarettes? I would kill for a cigarette."

Atkins felt his fingernails bite into his palms as he clenched his fists in frustration. He could almost weep at the injustice of it. For a brief moment when he saw the silhouetted figure, hope burned bright hot and white within him, like a star shell illuminating No Man's Land and casting shifting pools of light on the darkest parts of himself, parts he would rather remain hidden beyond the barbed wire of his conscience.

When he and Everson faced Jeffries down in the Khungarrii edifice before he escaped and vanished, Jeffries claimed they couldn't kill him as he was the only one who could return them to Earth.

Earth. Just the mere thought of the word was enough to make his eyes sting with tears. Not because of Earth itself, but for what it held. Flora. His love, his shame. Seven months pregnant with his child, by his reckoning. Although that wasn't why he was ashamed. He loved her. She had been his brother William's fiancée. But William had gone missing on the Somme. His betrayal wasn't just of William, but their families, and God knows, every bloody soldier in Kitchener's Army. He was the man they all despised, the unknown man who'd take their sweethearts while they were at the front. *"You were with the wenches, while we were in the trenches facing an angry foe..."* That was how the song went. He'd sung it in the dugout enough times, and each recitation twisted the knife more.

The thought of her made his very being ache at their parting. His one driving thought was to return to her, to do by right by her, to make up for all the wrong he had done.

But it wasn't Jeffries. He had wanted it to be true, but then he would have to face the possibility that Jeffries might have lied. He was terrified the truth would leave them marooned on this world forever, like the Bleeker party. Those twin urges, wanting to find Jeffries and *not* wanting to find him, kept his hope alive.

It wasn't Jeffries. And some small part of him was relieved.

"AND JUST WHO the hell are you?" asked Everson, angry for letting himself be duped, if only for a moment.

The man stepped away from the glare of the window and into the chamber. Two stately red-surcoated Chatts stepped out of the shadows to attend him, their antennae waving in agitation at the Tommies' arrival. The man, however, seemed quite at ease with their presence.

Everson could see him clearly now. He, too, wore a uniform. It was grey.

"How is this possible?" wondered the padre in hushed tones.

Everson shook his head.

"Jesus!" muttered Gutsy in astonishment. "It's a bleedin' Hun."

"A bloody Alleyman, here?" said Mercy, shaking his head. "And I thought we had the worst of it with Jeffries. Aren't we ever to be rid of the bastards?"

The Alleyman ignored them, addressing himself to the officers. He had a proud bearing, born of Teutonic aristocracy. His uniform was immaculate. His hair was black and slicked into a centre parting, and he had a peculiar little bow of a mouth that gave him a petulant look. He clicked his heels together. "My name is Oberleutnant Karl Werner, late of the Jasta Bueller." He held out a hand.

"You're a German pilot." Tulliver's eyes lit up and he shook the hand enthusiastically. "Lieutenant James Tulliver, 70 Squadron." Then he studied his host, somewhat aggrieved. "And, if I'm not wrong, I shot you down when we first arrived here."

The German laughed and clapped his hands on the top of Tulliver's arms. "Yes. Yes, you did." He smiled broadly. "You're a good shot," he said. "But not too good, I think. As you can see, I am still here."

The silent Chatts observed the polite introductions intently. Their antennae waved as they communicated with each other using senses beyond the ability of the Tommies to understand. Everson found himself unnerved by their scrutiny.

Reluctantly, Everson put out his hand and introduced himself. "Lieutenant Everson, acting commander of the 13th Battalion of the Pennine Fusiliers. Your English is very good."

Werner shook his hand. "My aunt married an Englishman. He has a leather goods business in Suffolk. I used to stay there. Before the war."

"This is Padre Rand, our chaplain."

Werner nodded and shook his hand, "A pleasure, Father."

Padre Rand returned a polite smile. "I must say, you're the last person we expected to find here."

Everson turned and indicated the Fusiliers behind him.

"And this is Lance Corporal Atkins and his Black Hand Gang."

Werner's glance swept up and down the NCO, unimpressed. "Yes, I did ask to see the officers only, but obviously the *insekt menschen* can't tell you apart. Never mind; you're here now, Corporal."

"Bloody cheek," muttered Mercy.

Pot Shot rolled his eyes. "Officers, same the world over."

One of the flanking Chatts spoke in its peculiar breathless, halting way. "What is Black Hand Gang?"

Werner pursed his lips as he searched for an appropriate term that they would understand. "I suppose you would say 'dark scentirrii,'" he suggested, looking to Everson for confirmation.

Everson nodded irritably.

The Chatt seemed satisfied and resumed its silent conversation.

Atkins felt a knot tighten in his stomach, and shot an accusing glance at Pot Shot. The lanky Fusilier's eyes widened and he spread his hands in protest.

Hepton pushed his way forward, an obsequious grin on his face, and grasped Werner's hand in both of his without being offered.

"Oliver Hepton," he said, pumping the pilot's hand. "Official War Office kinematographer, at your service. Pleased to meet you, Oberleutnant. What a moment! If only I had my camera."

"A photographer?" Werner pulled Hepton to one side. "You have a camera? Equipment?"

"Well I did until your Chatts took it from me after they captured us," replied Hepton. "I hope it's being taken care of, that's all. It's very expensive." This last remark was addressed rather loudly at the uncomprehending Chatts.

"My what?"

"Chatts. It's what the men called these insects. Chatts, after the lice that infected their uniforms in the trenches. Lice? Pop, pop, pop?"

"Ah, yes. Tommy humour, no? We must talk more."

Hepton beamed in triumph.

He was interrupted by Everson, irritated at Hepton's derailing of the conversation. "Look, this isn't getting us anywhere. What do you intend to do with us, Oberleutnant?" he demanded.

Hepton scowled but kept his eye on Werner.

The German took a deep breath and smiled at them, the expansive genial host. "All in good time, Lieutenant. All in good time. You're the first human company I've had in a long while. I'd like to savour it. Can we not converse as gentlemen? Perhaps your men are hungry."

He turned to the two inscrutable Chatts and mimed eating. Moments later, several Chatt nymphs with translucent carapaces came through from adjacent chambers, carrying gourds and platters.

Mercy leant over and whispered loudly to his mates. "So how come we're still living in trenches and he's living it up like a bleedin' lord? There's no fucking justice in the world."

"Have I not been telling you that?" said Pot Shot wryly.

There were no tables in the chamber. Mercy was considerably less impressed when the nymphs poured the contents into two long chest-high troughs set into the curved walls of the chamber, one of water, the other now containing some kind of sloppy fungus.

Gazette watched the Chatt servants retire from the chamber, his sniper's eye mentally fixing them in his sights.

"Please, don't stand on ceremony. Help yourselves," said Werner to the Fusiliers. "It is *insekt futter*, foul stuff, but nutritious nonetheless. I'm sure you've eaten worse in the trenches."

Atkins glared at the Hun and then at the troughs. "No thanks to your lot—and never like animals."

Werner laughed, amused. "It's how these creatures eat," he explained, throwing off the accusation. "They don't use crockery and cutlery. They don't even use their hands. They eat directly with their mouth parts. They have the manners of pigs, these *insekt menschen*. Have you seen them eat? They slice with their mandibles and scoop it straight into their mouths with their—what do you call them?" he put the back of his hand to his lips and waggled his fingers.

"Palps," said Everson.

"Ah. Palps, then. Yes."

Everson gave a weary nod to Atkins, dismissing him, while the officers continued their conversation at the other side of the chamber.

The men went over to the troughs. They were at an awkward height, too high to eat from comfortably, even if they felt like it.

"A Hun," said Tonkins in awe, as they huddled round the troughs, glad to have some space away from the officers. "I've never actually met a Hun before."

"Never met a live one, you mean," said Riley.

Gutsy grumbled. "Just let me at the Bosche bastard."

"Keep your voice down," said Atkins. He picked absent-mindedly at the fungus, but kept his eyes on the officers across the chamber. "What the hell was all that about dark scentirrii?"

"Ignore it," said Pot Shot. "It doesn't mean anything."

Atkins wasn't so sure. He remembered Mathers' prophecy, and tried to dismiss the unwanted implications.

"What do you think they're talking about?" asked Riley, watching the officers.

"A way out of here, with a bit of luck," said Mercy, through a mouth full of half-masticated fungus. He looked up to see Gazette staring at him. "What?"

"God, doesn't anything put you off eating?" asked Gazette.

"Gutsy's farts?" Mercy shot back, spraying him with a soggy shrapnel of fungus. "Besides, do you know when we're going to get another meal?"

It was this attitude, of getting what you could where you could, that made Mercy such a useful asset to the section, not to mention the platoon, but in this case, Gazette was prepared to make an exception.

"Suit yourself," said Mercy.

EVERSON HAD BEGUN to tire of the social niceties. "What are you going to do with us, Werner?" he asked.

Werner looked affronted. "Me, Lieutenant? Nothing." He waved a hand at the two Chatt attendants. "My hosts merely extended me the privilege of a little company. After all, I did let them know you were coming."

"You told them about us?" repeated Everson.

"Of course. They might have killed you all otherwise. After the unique manner of my arrival, the *insekt menschen* were on the look out for more like me. I told them of your existence and I told them you were coming. What are you even doing out here, Lieutenant, so far from your nice cosy trenches?"

"We lost... something. In the crater," said Everson. Ironclads were still supposed to be secret; tankers often referred to themselves as the Hush Hush Crowd, such was the clandestine nature of their training. However far they were away from Earth, Werner was still a Hun, and he didn't want to give any information to him that might profit the enemy.

Werner looked rueful. "Ah, the crater. Then I'm afraid it is gone for good. The *insekt menschen* are very zealous. They do not allow anything out of the crater and they certainly do not let anything in. They believe it is an evil place. When they knew you were headed towards it, they became very agitated, hence their attacking you like that. You were looking for some lost men, I think?"

"Yes," said Everson, warily. "Have you met a man calling himself Jeffries? An English officer."

Werner tapped his lips with a finger, frowned and shook his head. "I think I would have remembered an officer."

"You'd have certainly remembered him," Everson admitted with a grimace.

"What about soldiers?" asked the padre.

Werner shrugged. "The *insekt menschen* have brought in one or two patrols, or deserters, maybe? I had to question them, see if they were useful. But to be honest, even if they were, the treatment of the *urmenschen* they keep as slaves here is brutal. I wouldn't hold out much hope for them, Lieutenant."

Werner shuffled uncomfortably, noticing black looks from the men by the troughs.

"There was nothing I could do," he said diffidently.

"So that's why we're here," said Everson, scarcely able to maintain an even tone, nodding towards the inscrutable Chatts watching them silently. "So you could tell them if we're useful or not?"

There was an embarrassed silence.

"And what will you tell them?" asked Everson bitterly.

Werner lowered his head. "I regret, Lieutenant, that I cannot save you."

"Cannot, or will not?" he demanded. "Surely you can't side with these Chatts against us? We're human."

Werner shook his head, heaved a sigh and corrected him. "You're British, Lieutenant," he said. "These *insekt menschen* may be uncivilised, but they do understand the nature of a territorial dispute. I told them you were my enemy when they found me. Your battalion is your downfall. These creatures see your numbers as a threat to their territory and resources."

"So you're working with them?"

"Don't be so high and mighty, Lieutenant," said Werner with disdain. "You had your battalion. I was on my own. These creatures saved my life. They raised me above the *urmenschen* that cling so desperately to existence here, and I agreed to help them. They are searching for something. I merely offered my services."

"As what?"

"A *Luftstreitkräfte*."

Werner ushered them out onto a balcony beyond the window. Looking down, Tulliver noted that the Urmen shanty town that existed on the slopes of the Khungarrii edifice didn't exist here. The edifice was fortified, as if they expected a siege. Below, he saw a large courtyard, still under construction, judging by the Chatts scurrying over the partially built walls. There within it, tethered, patched and inflated, was a silver-grey German kite balloon.

Tulliver remembered seeing one when they first arrived on this world, its winch line severed the moment they vanished from Earth. He had a vague memory of it drifting off when they appeared here. He'd thought nothing of it at the time, having an Albatros to deal with, and a world of strangeness since then.

"They might not understand our flying machines, but it didn't take long for them to grasp the principle of the balloon. Even now they are constructing their own."

"For what purpose?" asked Everson. "Are they at war?"

"In a manner of speaking. I told you they fear the crater. To them it represents some great evil, and they seek to arm themselves against it. They see the balloon as a useful instrument in their eternal vigilance. They stand guard at the edge of the crater like the angels at the gates of Eden, no, Padre?" he said, turning to the chaplain.

Before the padre could reply, they were interrupted by a creaking sound and the fibrous door to the chamber shrank open. Werner's disappointment was evident. Even more so when two armed scentirrii stepped through. Four more waited outside. "No," he protested to his attendants. "They've only just arrived."

"Come," ordered the scentirrii. It waited for a moment then repeated the command, belching the word out. They were a lot less articulate than the Khungarrii. The scentirrii motioned towards the door with their spears, while guards outside wore clay battery packs and held electric lances similar in design to those of the Khungarrii.

"Come." It hissed again, raising itself up on its legs threateningly.

"Food was lousy anyway," muttered Mercy, spitting a half-chewed gobbet at Werner's feet as they passed. "Hope it chokes you."

Werner wore a look of pained exasperation.

Everson was still trying to finish his conversation with Werner, glean what further intelligence he could. "What happened to them, to the men they captured, damn it?"

Werner shook his head and waved his hand dismissively. "I do not know, but I'm very much afraid you will find out."

"No. Not me, I can be helpful," cried Hepton desperately, as a scentirrii prodded him with a spear.

Atkins looked at him with disgust. When another scentirrii manhandled him, he took the opportunity to accidentally plant his elbow into Hepton's solar plexus.

Hepton doubled over, winded, struggling to draw breath as he glared at Atkins through watering eyes.

"Sorry, Hepton," said Atkins.

A scentirrii attempted to seize Tulliver by the arm.

Werner stepped forward. "No, he stays," he said, appealing to his two Chatt attendants. "He stays. He flies—like me." He stuck his arms out like wings and mimed flying, as you might to a child.

The scentirrii waved its antennae towards the Chatt attendants, then shoved Tulliver out of the pack toward him, causing the flying officer to stumble.

"Hey!" Tulliver brought his arm back, preparing to swing for the Chatts.

As the others were being herded out of the chamber, Everson stepped forward, appearing to help Tulliver, although it was more to gently restrain him from fighting back.

"No," he said in a low voice, looking over Tulliver's shoulder to where Werner stood. "Stay here. Find out what you can. And if you get a chance, escape. Get back to camp, let them know what's happened."

Tulliver's eyes flashed at the Chatt that stood over them, but he nodded imperceptibly. He stood up and swept back his fringe as Everson allowed himself to be taken from the chamber with the others.

WERNER CLAPPED TULLIVER on the shoulder. "Don't worry, my friend. They'll be taken back to their cell," he said. "But come. We have so much to talk about, you and I."

At first Tulliver had been elated to find another flyer, someone who understood what it was like to be up there. He'd longed to talk shop, as if he were back in the officer's mess, but now the feeling had soured.

"I should very much like to see your machine. A Sopwith 1½ Strutter. Yes? With synchronised gears for your forward machine gun. You finally caught up with us."

"Maybe I'll take you for a spin," said Tulliver bitterly.

They moved round the chamber, unconsciously circling each other as if they were two thousand feet over the Somme, looking for the advantage. The Chatt attendants watched, conferring with each other.

Tulliver looked up with a dawning realisation. "Your aeroplane," he said. "It still flies, doesn't it?"

Werner's broad smile was all the answer the pilot needed. It hadn't been his imagination. There *had* been something up there. Not a creature at all. It had been Werner keeping an eye on him all this time. He must be a damn good pilot.

"Yes. I have been watching your progress for months," admitted Werner. "Flying high over your trenches, catching glimpses between the clouds. And I shadowed you of course, discreetly. Tell me, with your squadron, did you ever play hide-and-seek in the clouds?"

Tulliver knew the game well. Every flyer did. It was good practice for dog fighting. "You're not too good at it," said Tulliver. "You became careless."

Werner shook his head. "Careless? No. I got lonely. I think part of me wanted to be spotted."

He wandered back to the window, and stepped out onto the balcony beyond, beckoning Tulliver to join him

It was easy to believe, standing high on the side of the Zohtakarrii edifice and looking out over the forests and the plains beyond, that you were Master of the World. It felt like you were flying, until you looked down.

"Magnificent view, isn't it?" said Werner with a sigh. But he wasn't looking at the landscape. He was looking up. "A whole new sky, new horizons." For a moment he seemed lost in melancholy. When he spoke again, he had recovered his bravado. "My Albatros is far superior in speed and performance to your heavy Sopwith, Tulliver. Had I not been so disorientated when we appeared here, then the story might have been very different, no?" He mimed planes with his hands, his right swooping up under his left, towards its palm, illustrating some manoeuvre. "I think you took advantage of the situation, my friend. After you shot me down, Herr Tulliver, I barely managed to pull out of the spin and make a safe landing.

"At first I was furious. I couldn't understand what had happened. Can you imagine my amazement to find that I was no longer in France? Yes, what am I saying? Of course you can. But you had men and defences at your disposal. I was a downed airman in a foreign land." He made a sweeping gesture at the forest surrounding them. "A foreign *world*.

"A patrol of *insekt menschen* found me. They saved my life and I repaid them with the only thing I had to offer."

"Your Albatros."

"They had never seen a flying machine before. They were amazed. And they have been able to produce a passable petrol substitute. Not long after, they found the kite balloon and I was able to direct their repair of it. They have done a fine job, do you not think?"

"It's hardly an air force, old chum," said Tulliver. "If that's what you promised them, then they're in for a surprise."

Werner turned and appealed to the pilot. "Ah, but they have constructed their own; and now they have your machine, too."

"Maybe, but they don't have me," said Tulliver.

"Pity. I should have liked to fly with you."

"You could leave them at any time," challenged Tulliver. "Why stay?"

"Why does the falcon not leave the falconer? Certainly I may leave, Lieutenant, but where to, and to what? I have seen you in your trenches. I have watched your vain attempts to tame this planet, watched your little huts go up, seen you grub fields and grow crops. And I have seen it all ruined. Here at least, I am safe. Here, I am—"

"Kaiser?"

Werner clucked his tongue in reprimand. "Able to fly. Able to fly, Tulliver! And I have flown high and far." He lowered his voice and stepped closer. "And I have seen things, Tulliver, up there where the air is thin and cold. There is a mystery to this planet." Werner stepped back and examined Tulliver's face. "You have seen it also, I think, have you not? It is what the *insekt menschen* search for. You and I might be the only people on this world to have seen it."

"Seen what?" asked Tulliver. He remembered his own brief glimpse of the world spread out below him, before his engine cut out.

"Marks. Marks on the landscape. Intersecting lines, miles long." He waved a hand towards the watching Chatts. "You can tell them this, you can confirm what I have seen."

Tulliver wasn't sure what he had seen, it had been so brief, but his reaction now was one of scepticism. Markings on a geographical scale? And then he was struck by a thought. Wasn't that how Jeffries was supposed to have performed his Somme ritual, within a pentagram scored across the front lines by artillery fire? Tulliver should know. It was he who unknowingly took Jeffries up artillery spotting for it. He'd just been another anonymous spotter at the time.

Tulliver shook his head "I'm not sure what I saw. It was only for a brief moment. I couldn't confirm anything."

"The *insekt menschen* are searching for proof of their god's existence. I think I might have seen it. They believe it created this world for them, and that its mark upon it might be visible. The Albatros is only a single-seater. I cannot show them what I have seen. I have been trying to use a camera salvaged from the observation balloon, along with a number of unexposed plates, but I can't develop them."

"Then why on earth did you take them?"

"I thought perhaps someday..." He waved a hand. "That's why I need your help. You are the answer to my prayers, Tulliver. You can verify my findings." Werner paused, searching Tulliver's face. "You don't believe me." Werner shook his head. "You should see for yourself."

"Why, what was it, what did you see?" urged Tulliver.

"Fly with me. I will show you."

Tulliver was almost taken in by his earnest plea. "Free my friends and I'll consider it."

"I can't do that."

"Those are my terms. You have influence with these Chatts. Let the Fusiliers go free and I'll help."

Werner's whole posture sagged. "It is not possible."

"Why?"

"Because they are earmarked for the pits!" he declared. "They're dead. If you won't help me, then perhaps your kinematographer, what was his name, Hepton. Perhaps he will help. He seemed very eager to save his own life. If you care so little about yours, you can join your friends!"

That was when Tulliver saw the truth. Across the side of the edifice, all the other balconies were scentirrii watch posts. He glanced back into the chamber. This wasn't a private chamber with its own balcony, like some hotel in Paris. It was unadorned and functional. The Chatts weren't his attendants, they were his gaolers. This chamber was as much a cell as the one Everson had been kept in.

Tulliver's eyes narrowed with suspicion. "The Chatts didn't save your life, did they? They spared it. In return for what? What do you owe these creatures?" he asked.

"Nothing," said Werner. But his face told a different story. The mask of geniality and charm had slipped to reveal someone who had been playing a game for far too long and had grown weary.

"But I am afraid, Tulliver. If I am right, then this world is a hell like no other, and no human god created this place."

INTERLUDE THREE
Letter from Lance Corporal Thomas Atkins to Flora Mullins

5th April 1917

My Dearest Flora,

Today I spotted someone I thought knew. It would have been nice to catch up again, but it wasn't them. Still, maybe we'll meet up somewhere down the line. I remember bumping into William once down the reserve lines, when he was stacking artillery shells and I was on a ration party. We both had to do a double take.

We haven't made it to the tank yet (story of my life, that). We made some new friends along the way though, and took a bit of a detour. Still, I suppose we are still getting to see quite a bit of the local countryside, and at least we've got a roof over our heads for a while.

However, as Pot Shot will keep harping on, someone will have to pay the piper soon, so expect us to have to sing for our supper. They won't get much of a song for it though, because the food is nothing to write home about, so I won't. That never seems to stop Mercy. He'll eat anything (and he did). You should have seen Gutsy's eyes light up when he found out. "In that case, I've got some nice calves' trotters and scrag end of mutton I could sell you!" says he. What larks.

Ever yours
Thomas

CHAPTER TWELVE
"Keep Your Head Down, Fusilier..."

ALFIE HAD HEARD estaminet tales about the poor buggers found guilty of desertion and sentenced by court-martial to death by firing squad.

He had a mate who had stood guard with one on their last night. 'Prisoner's friend.' Filthy job, he said. You needed a heart of stone. Young, he was, too; barely nineteen. Only been at the Front for a month before he funked it. But he wouldn't sleep. Couldn't sleep, probably. The lad's moods would swing wildly. Sometimes he'd sit with quiet resignation, constantly asking the time, for they all knew that when dawn came he was to be shot. Other times he wept and cried and wailed and begged and pleaded, every shred of dignity gone, dissolved in streams of tears and snot. In the end they got him drunk. So drunk, as it happened, that he could barely stand the next morning when they led him out to the firing squad. They literally had to drag him. When they tied him to the post, blindfolded him and pinned the white rag over his heart, he'd pissed himself.

Then again, half the firing squad were more than a little squiffy themselves, having been given tots of rum to stiffen their resolve. Didn't do much for their aim though, his mate said. Sergeant had to come over and finish the bugger off with his revolver.

Sat here in the dark of the Urman hut, the pain in his leg flaring and a great knot of anxiety and terror churning in his belly, Alfie knew how the poor sod felt. He could feel the vomit burn up his throat, but he swallowed it again. He wouldn't give them the satisfaction of knowing he was afraid.

The Urmen were going to kill him. They'd said as much. He was to be sent to converse with their dead or some such. Bit of a one-way conversation, he thought.

He never reckoned he'd end his days as a ritual sacrifice, even if that was what Jeffries had planned for them with his diabolic battlefield rite back at Harcourt Wood. Funny, he thought. Perhaps that's all they'd been all along; sacrifices. The top brass seemed willing to sacrifice everyone on the altar of Victory for a few hundred yards of muddy corpse-ridden field. Ah, the good old days. He let out a bitter laugh. Jesus, who'd have thought he'd be longing to be back on the Somme.

His thoughts turned to Nellie Abbott. He smiled to himself, but it was wistful, full of regret for the time they would never spend together. He thought of her out there, with the others. At least she'd be safe. Oh, bloody hell, what was he thinking? She didn't just sit still. She'd come halfway across the planet to find him before. What on Earth made him think she'd stop now? He didn't know who to feel sorry for most: him here without her, or his crewmates with her cajoling and barracking them into action.

But what the hell could he do? How far did he think he could get with a broken leg, even if he did escape?

Ranaman entered the hut with Tarak, interrupting his thoughts. "The time of Croatoan's Torment approaches," the clan chief said. "We must ease his suffering with your passage."

Alfie pushed himself back up against the wall, and his broken leg protested with another burning jolt of pain. He clenched his teeth and sucked air in through them, hard. Not because of what Ranaman had said, but what the Urman was holding. It was a rifle. No, not a rifle; an old-fashioned musket.

"Where did you get that?" he asked in spite of himself.

"It is a holy relic. It is the Key. Our ancestors said it opens the door to the underworld."

"Well that's one way of bloody putting it," said Alfie under his breath.

He brandished the ancient firearm at Alfie, who flinched, half expecting it to go off, until he realised that Ranaman was holding it all wrong. He was holding it like a swagger stick, something with which to point. His finger was nowhere near the trigger.

Besides, Alfie found himself thinking, wasn't sacrificing done with a special sacred knife or something? What did they do, cut your heart out and hold it aloft, still beating, dripping with hot blood?

All of a sudden, a firing squad didn't seem that bad.

He determined to look for any opportunity to escape. At least then, if he were going to die, it would be on his own terms.

But no, if he did, the boy Tarak would pay the price. There had to be another way. If there was, though, he couldn't see it.

Ranaman nodded and Tarak took Alfie's arm, pulling him up without concern for his beside manner, or the suffering of his patient. Alfie sucked down the pain again as the young Urman put Alfie's arm over his shoulders and helped him out of the hut.

He stepped outside into a small stockade settlement of wooden huts, flanked by Ranaman and Tarak, and a collective gasp arose from the rest of the clan as they saw their sky-being. They stood around swaying gently and muttering chants and litanies under their breaths, or making signs. They were elated. A litter stood adorned with great fragrant blooms.

He'd seen scenes like this several times, with the rest of the *Ivanhoe* crew dressed in their raincapes and chainmail splash masks, pretending to be priests, servants of Skarra the dung-beetle god of the underworld, as they tricked gullible Urmen clans. He'd always had a bad feeling then, but he'd never expected to bear the full brunt of their come-uppance. That just wasn't bloody fair.

What Alfie wouldn't give for Norman and one of his music-hall magic tricks, or for the *Ivanhoe* to come crashing through the undergrowth like a wrathful god.

As the rest of the clan watched, eyes wide in awe at the sky-being, Tarak helped him onto the litter. This was his doing. He was responsible for bringing this fortune upon the clan. The pride was evident in the young Urman's face.

"For me? You shouldn't have," said a resentful Alfie.

Four Urmen picked the litter up to a great shout from the rest of the clan.

"So," said Alfie, though clenched teeth and pain. "Where are you taking me?"

"To Croatoan's Heart," said Tarak, as if that explained everything.

"Right," he said, none the wiser.

Holding his useless musket aloft, like an army band major, Ranaman led the procession out of the stockaded village. Two Urmen with burning torches joined him. Behind them came Urmen with metal-tipped spears and metal swords, then Alfie in his litter, while the rest of the clan fell in at the rear, blowing horns and banging hollow gourds.

The Urmen in front chanted as Ranaman led them along a narrow, but well-worn path. Tarak walked proudly beside the litter, where every misstep of the litter bearers transmitted itself to Alfie's broken leg, amplifying every jolt and jar.

"Oi, take it easy," he berated the litter bearers. "Bloody hell, I got a smoother ride in the *Ivanhoe,* and that was with bleedin' Wally driving!" Another jolt of pain seared up his leg. "Jeeeesus!"

The Urmen with spears cut their way through the writhing lianas crossing their path. Great fleshy plant pitchers turned as they passed, as if watching them.

Tarak pointed above the trees ahead of them, where a tall minaret pierced the sky. "There. The Heart of Croatoan," he said, proudly.

"Great." Alfie smiled weakly, his mind racing, as every jar and jolt of the litter carried him nearer to his death. If he closed his eyes, he could see Nellie standing, feet astride, hand on hips, scolding him. *"Alfie Perkins, don't you dare sit there and accept your own death. You've got a brain. Use it."*

There had to be a way out that would save him and the lad.

The procession filed into a clearing, dominated by an ancient domed building, from the centre of which rose the minaret, a hundred feet into the air. Worn and weathered, the building had seen better days and had fallen into some disrepair. It had been built from clay brick, which lay exposed where the painted clay daub had crumbled away. Only a few stubborn patches remained. Around its circumference, small, regularly-spaced, unglazed windows were set into it; like loopholes, Alfie thought.

The men carrying his litter placed it on the ground and Tarak hauled Alfie to his feet.

Ranaman's warriors unbarred the great wooden door, while Urmen holding torches entered ahead of the chieftain, their chants echoing round the space within.

Tarak held onto Alfie's arm tightly, as if aware that his life depended on him. Alfie tugged it experimentally. The youth did not look at him, but his grip tightened, perhaps fearing Alfie was about to fall, or escape.

Ranaman reappeared and approached the pair. He placed a paternal hand on Tarak's shoulder and spoke to Alfie.

"You fell, as Croatoan once did. It is a powerful omen. Today you will talk with our dead. And from you we will learn their will."

Alfie blanched. How would they do that, exactly? Through some sort of divination? Perhaps it wasn't his still-beating heart they were after; maybe it was his entrails. Alfie felt his stomach lurch. The day just gets better and better, he thought.

They escorted him inside. It was gloomy and bare, lit by a circle of flaming sconces. At the centre of the domed temple, beneath the minaret, was a boulder the height of a man, a fracture down its middle cracking it in twain. There was enough space between the two halves that a man might walk between them. This was the Heart of Croatoan, Alfie assumed. A broken heart, as Ranaman had told him.

Alfie's heart felt like breaking, too. It was beating hard, loud, and far too fast in his chest. He could feel its pulsing echoes in his neck, his leg and his ears. He could feel panic tightening its grip on him, but it was a fear he knew. It was an old friend to a soldier.

The clan filed into the temple behind him, moving out around the edge of the space, encircling the broken rock in the centre, their shadows dancing on the floor beneath flickering sconces.

His chances of taking them on and getting out of there alive were slim now. Even Alfie could see that. Nonetheless, he strained his ears, hoping to catch the clanking rumble of the *Ivanhoe*, but heard nothing.

Just him, then.

Damn.

Two Urmen stepped forward and took him from Tarak. The lad smiled at him as they took his arms and began to drag him towards the fractured rock. He cried out in pain, but his agony was lost in the rhythmic chants echoing around him. Shafts of light from the minaret focused on the rock, like spotlights on a Zeppelin.

He struggled to look back over his shoulder at Tarak who, not comprehending his situation, looked on proudly, his chest falling and rising as he joined in with the chant.

Ranaman waited for him in the space between the rocks.

"No, wait..." said Alfie, seeing reddish stains on the surface of the boulders, thinking they were signs of previous sacrifices. Then he realised the rocks, the Heart of Croatoan, were composed of iron. This must have been where they got their knives and spearheads. The lad Tarak thought the ironclad *Ivanhoe* was the same thing. Another sky rock. Alfie groaned. Hoisted by his own petard.

Ranaman walked between the two halves to the back of the temple. Two warriors held Alfie by the arms, his back to the rock. He couldn't see what Ranaman was doing. He had a sudden urge, a need to know. He tried to twist his head to see over his shoulder, but all he could see was the rock.

Panicking now, Alfie was turned round so he was facing the narrow gap between the rocks. As he was turned, he caught sight of Tarak watching with a fierce pride. The flanking warriors took Alfie's arms and held one hand on each half of the shattered boulder.

Ranaman returned through the cleft towards him, carrying a large ornately carved wooden box; the kind, Alfie thought grimly, that you would keep a ceremonial dagger in.

The chanting rose to a crescendo and then ceased.

"The time has come," Ranaman called out.

He opened the box and Alfie steeled himself for death.

GAZETTE HAD HIS ear to the wall of the gaol chamber by the door. Denied the use of his keen sniper's eye, he'd resorted to his hearing. He'd had his ear there for a while and his greasy ear prints stained the gritty hardened earth of the wall. "They're taking another lot," he said.

The others rushed to the wall of the chamber, pressing their own ears to the hardened earth.

Everson heard sounds of scuffles and angry protestations as scentirrii dragged other Fusiliers from their chamber.

"Get your hands off me, you filthy Chatt!"

"Knocker, no!"

There was a charged crackle, a stunned groan and a heavy thump.

"You bastards!" yelled Mercy, thumping the side of his fist against the wall.

The Tommies vented their anger with shouts and threats, but at length turned despondently from the wall, as the padre offered up an Our Father, the quiet liturgical tone calming them. Porgy and Tonkins joined in quietly.

Everson looked around at them. If there was any bunch worth being stuck with, it was Corporal Atkins and his Black Hand Gang. They'd had more experience of this planet than most others had and were still alive to tell the tale, which gave them the edge.

Right here, right now, they could do nothing but wait. Wait for the right moment, the right opportunity to act.

They had examined the cell from top to bottom. There was no air vent through which they could escape. The only light came from the garde l'eau in the floor that projected out over the wall of the edifice. Even if they could enlarge the hole, there was a hundred-foot drop to the ground.

The living plant door was cultivated for the purpose by the Chatts. Barbed thorns covered its surface, its roots bedded deep in the walls round the chamber's circular opening. They knew from experience in Khungarr that it could fire its barbs in defence. There was no hiding place within the round bare chamber from them.

To pass the time, the padre told away at his Rosary in a Morse code of *Hail Marys* and *Our Fathers*, like a spiritual Iddy Umpty man seeking Divine orders from HQ.

Hepton, sensing the hostility from the rank and file, had removed himself and sat across from the men, from where he shot them the morose glances of a beaten cur.

Riley kept up a cheery disposition, keeping young Tonkins' mind occupied with a series of trench anecdotes.

Gutsy picked his teeth with the point of a sharpened Lucifer he had saved for just this purpose. There seemed to be nothing else to do in the gaol chamber.

"Pity we haven't got that pet Chatt of yours, Only," he said as he winkled out a nub of chewed fungus and flicked it toward Hepton, who glared at him. "He could have talked to them for us."

"He was never my pet," said Atkins with more bitterness than he meant. "And I don't think it works that way. These Khungarrii and Zohtakarrii, they're like rival colonies or something. Like Britain and Germany."

"And we're in Germany?" said Porgy, trying to get his head round the analogy.

"Ain't that just our bloody luck?" chipped in Porgy. "And a bloody Jerry in charge, too."

"Bugger me if that's wasn't a turn-up for the books. Makes you wonder who else is wandering about out there."

The door puckered and shrivelled as it opened. The Fusiliers stood, tensed, fists clenching, glancing from each other to their NCO and officer for the order.

Two scentirrii armed with electric lances stepped through the door, with four more outside, scotching that idea. Everson shook his head and indicated with a hand down by his hip that they should stand down. They were ready for a fight, but with the release of an alarm scent, the whole population of the edifice would come down on them. Now wasn't the time.

Werner walked through the door.

"What do you want, Fritz?" rumbled Gutsy, slapping a meaty fist into the palm of his other hand.

"Private." Everson's rebuke stilled the stocky butcher, but his eyes still burned with contempt.

Werner waved the insult away with a magnanimity he could well afford.

Everson greeted him curtly, the same question on his own mind. "Well, Oberleutnant?"

"Nothing from you I'm afraid, Lieutenant. I wish to speak to your kinematographer."

"Me?" said Hepton warily, adjusting his glasses on his nose and risking a shufti at the Fusiliers.

"Yes, it appeared you were worried about your equipment."

Hepton glanced cautiously at Everson, who just scowled, then stepped forward hesitantly, expecting a trick.

"Yes. Is it all right?"

"As far as I know. There is, however, something you can do to secure its continued safety."

That caught Hepton's interest. "Yes?"

"You see, I need your expertise, Herr...?"

"Hepton. Oliver Hepton."

"Herr Hepton, I need you to help to develop some photographic plates."

"Plates?" Hepton looked from Werner to Everson.

Everson watched the exchange impassively. Hepton was an odd cove. On the one hand, the man was a coward and a cad. On the other, he was prepared to take the most outrageous risks to get his precious moving pictures. The canisters of undeveloped kine film he carried around, of the Pennines on this world, were his fortune. If they got back to Earth, they would make him tremendously rich. He needed them. He also needed Everson and his men to keep him alive until then.

But Hepton was a survivor. He hedged his bets and covered his arse. His only loyalty was to self-preservation, and now was no exception.

Hepton turned to Everson and tapped his nose. "Don't worry; I'll keep my eyes peeled. See what I can find out," he said in a conspiratorial whisper loud enough for those Fusiliers nearby to hear.

He didn't fool Everson. Still, the chances were that Hepton would procure some information as security against his own survival. That might prove useful.

Hepton didn't wait for Everson's permission but stepped forward to join Werner, who nodded curtly at Everson before turning and leaving the chamber. Hepton followed, looking back as he stepped through the door to give a shrug and sheepish grin, as if to say, 'What else can I do?'

"Be seeing you—Kamerad," growled Gutsy.

Hepton looked away with a guilty start as he followed Werner from the gaol chamber.

The Scentirrii retreated and the plant door shut again.

"The jammy bastard," was all Pot Shot could say.

TULLIVER WAS DISMAYED to see Werner return with Hepton. The kinematographer sauntered into the chamber with the air of one whose fortune had turned at the expense of others and who didn't care.

"Lieutenant!" Hepton said brightly when they met again. "It seems I have a commission." He clapped his hands and rubbed his palms together. "Shall we get started?" He turned to Werner. "Where is my equipment? You said it was safe."

"It is being held by their apothecaries," said Werner.

An escort of scentirrii took them up an inclined passage to the higher reaches of the edifice. A faint thrumming sounded through the passages as the ventilation system sucked fresh air deep into the core of the colony.

Despite his revulsion at the situation, Tulliver felt a rising sense of expectation. He was, he hated to admit, intrigued by Werner's mystery. Perhaps, he reasoned, there were bigger things at stake here than political enmity.

The scentirrii brought them to a small, unassuming chamber. They ushered them inside, going no further themselves. Werner strode past them with all the confidence of one who has rights and access.

Beyond was a succession of further chambers, occupied, Tulliver found, by a different class of Chatts. These had plainer, pallid carapaces, as though they had never left the dark recesses of the edifice. They wore plain white silken tabards that almost touched the floor. Each wore a small pouch at its hip, slung across its thorax by silken rope. They were clearly akin to the dhuyumirrii caste of the Khungarrii.

There was a groan of despair from Hepton, as he spotted his precious equipment in the corner of one chamber. He dashed over and fell upon it, with all the fear and relief of someone inspecting a child for injuries after an accident, checking the camera box, his tripod, his haversack of film canisters, wincing at each scuff and scratch.

He pulled out a wooden box from a haversack and swore under his breath. The brown glass bottles that had contained the remains of his photography fluids had cracked and one had shattered completely. The chemicals had drained away, staining the wood. There was precious little remaining. Certainly not enough to develop anything. Hepton sat back on his heels, crestfallen, sure his fate would now be to join the rest of the Fusiliers below.

"It's cracked. There's nothing left," he rasped. "Not a drop."

"Let me see," said Werner brusquely. He took a bottle from him, held it up to the faint lichen light and peered through the brown glass. It was empty apart from a residue at the bottom. He unstopped the bottle and wrinkled his nose, recoiling from the lingering acrid smell of the chemicals.

Hepton flinched. "It—it's not my fault. You can't blame me. We were attacked by your Chatts..." His voice trailed away.

Tulliver caught sight of the Chatts, who stood regarding them, as they themselves might watch ants. He had been in the officers' pow-wows and briefings about the Khungarrii. There was no reason to believe these Zohtakarrii were much different.

"If *we* can smell it," he said, nodding towards them, "then what could *they* do?" He strode toward them, belligerently. "Here," said Tulliver, holding out the bottle toward one of them.

The Chatt inclined its head in a questioning manner.

"Smell this. Can you make more? You know, more?"

The creature looked to Werner, who nodded his assent.

It hissed, reached out a long-fingered hand and took the cracked glass bottle with some reluctance, as if the act were beneath it, as if Tulliver had spoken out of place and dared to call their skill and sacred calling into question.

The Chatt returned to its fellows and, holding the cracked bottle with its precious residue, they gathered round it, like Macbeth's witches, their heads bowed, their segmented antennae waving gently over the opening.

They were like the alchemists of old, thought Tulliver. Although their main occupation was the protection and interpretation of the sacred scents and prophetic perfumes, they could turn their skills to other things. After all, they had manufactured a fuel for Werner and his aeroplane. Developing fluid shouldn't be beyond them.

The Chatts withdrew from the chamber and Werner followed. He beckoned Tulliver and Hepton. "Come."

In chambers beyond lay endless niches of stone jars and amphorae filling the walls, each containing scents and odours, elements and compounds, the contents of which Tulliver couldn't even begin to guess at, arranged by some system he could not comprehend.

Ranks of similar Chatts worked on unfathomable tasks at rows of solid clay tables rising from the floor.

"It's like a scriptorium," whispered Werner. "Medieval monks making illuminated manuscripts, but with odours, aromas and scents."

The three Chatts approached another, standing at a clay lectern, like a chief clerk or overseer. There was a brief consultation. The bottle produced much agitated waving of antennae and, in a disconcerting moment, all four turned their heads in unison to glance at the three men.

The clerk went over to the wall of the chamber, summoning an acolyte nymph with a few judicious clicks and hisses. The creature returned to the niches and carefully selected various amphorae, jars and pots.

The men had nothing to do but wait nervously as the Chatts attempted to concoct an ersatz developing fluid.

Then they would see if it worked.

THE CHATTS CAME for the Fusiliers several hours later.

The plant door dilated open. The moment it did, the men were up on their feet. This was it. They had come for them as they had come for the others before.

A moment's luck, to a soldier on the front line, could be a matter of life and death. They all had their good luck rituals, however idiosyncratic. Gutsy quickly kissed his lucky rabbit's foot. Porgy had a collection of girls' keepsake photographs, his 'deck of cards.' He quickly selected one to be today's lucky Queen of Hearts and put her in his top pocket. Atkins' was no more ridiculous than most. He pulled out his last letter from Flora. For better or worse, he had come to believe that if he could still smell the perfume on the last letter she sent, he would be safe, and it had worked. Now the letter was months old and her perfume had faded. Mathers, with his petrol-fruit-enhanced senses, was the last to smell it. With a heavy heart, he slipped the fragile letter back into his tunic as the scentirrii herded them down the passage, past gaol cells once occupied by men of the rescue platoon, now ominously open and empty.

PENNINE FUSILIERS

CHAPTER THIRTEEN
"Our Little Hour..."

UNARMED, APART FROM contemptuous glances and an anger that bristled like the scentirrii spears around them, the Fusiliers found themselves marched like POWs along a passage that spiralled down into the subterranean depths of the edifice.

"Another long bloody walk," Porgy muttered.

"It's not going to be Fritz machine guns and barbed wire at the other end, though, is it?" said an indignant Mercy.

Atkins took the feeling of fear expanding in his belly and, by a controlled application of hate, compressed it into a small hardened ball of dull nausea, as he had done many times going over the top to advance across No Man's Land.

The passage took them down into the bowels of the edifice, and Atkins became aware of a soft roar building on the persistent low hum of the air currents, beyond the padre's muttered Rosary.

Gazette had heard it, too. "Sounds like a carpet slipper bastard."

It didn't make any of them feel easier. As they continued their descent, it rose to a crescendo, punctuated with a clashing rhythm of carapaces, a rhythm that they had heard before, albeit to a Khungarrii beat.

The scentirrii guards stopped and ushered them into a side passage off the main incline. It was dark and small, and they had to go Indian file, the scentirrii bringing up the rear.

"Anyone else feel like we're going up the commo?" said Gazette.

Nobody answered. They didn't have to. That's exactly what it felt like; the long march from the reserve area up to the front line along the shallow, narrow zigzag of the communications trenches. Each man retreated into his own world, his own private space, preparing himself as best he could for whatever was to come.

Atkins thought of Flora. Denied his usual ritual of the letter, he plucked a memory to savour, as Porgy might select one of his photograph cards; that last night, the memory of Flora naked in the firelight, in her front parlour, her skin suffused with a rose gold glow, her saintly smile full of wonder. He froze the moment, before the smile slipped and welling tears distorted the scene, before the memory of William tainted it. He couldn't have one without the other. The memories were entwined.

They emerged from the cramped dark tunnel into another chamber. Once in, Atkins heard a creak and turned to see a barbed plant door contract shut. There was no way back. There was only one other exit from the chamber. It was in front of them and another barbed plant door blocked that, too.

There, piled on the floor were their confiscated weapons; webbing, haversacks, gas hood bags, steel helmets, rifles, bayonets, Mills bombs, trench clubs and even Everson's sword, along with the kitbags containing the modified electric lance packs and Riley's Signals gear.

Atkins and the others looked to Everson.

"Arm yourselves. Take everything you can. I've a feeling we won't be coming back this way," he said.

The men set about putting on webbing and packs, a sense of anxiety and foreboding building as they did so, ameliorated by small personal victories. Gazette was reunited with his sniper's rifle. Gutsy found his meat cleaver; he picked up the instrument and hefted it, comforted by the familiar weight in his hand.

He took the startled and frightened young Jenkins under his wing, checking his equipment and webbing. "Stick to me like glue, lad. You'll be fine."

Jenkins tried to force a smile through his fear and only partially succeeded.

Everson found and holstered his Webley and picked up his sword.

By the time they had readied themselves, there was not much left on the floor; a bayonet, the odd battle bowler and several pieces of webbing lay unclaimed.

Mercy went through the webbing pockets pulling out spare ammunition and the odd grenade and redistributing them.

By the time they were fully and correctly attired, they felt whole again, each item adding a little to their fortitude.

When they were ready, Everson instinctively looked at his wristwatch. "Stand by," he said, for no other reason than habit. Whatever they were about to face, they were as ready for it as they would ever be.

Atkins felt he could almost be back in the trenches, staring at the hated ladders, waiting for zero hour. He stood by the living door, through which they could hear chanting and carapace-beating. It began to recoil and open, shrivelling back towards the walls of the circular opening.

A breeze blew down the tunnel towards them, carrying on it the sound of massed Chatts... and something else: the smell of blood and shit and cordite.

For a few seconds, the men hesitated, though not from any sense of wind-up or funk. Atkins and the others turned their eyes to Everson, who stepped forward to the van. If they were going to go 'over the top,' they would go when he gave the order and not before.

Instinctively, Everson put his whistle to his lips and blew. Holding his sword and drawing his pistol, he began to walk down the tunnel and his men followed.

IN THE CANYON, Sergeant Dixon balanced on a block of unstable scree and glared at the ruddy-faced Buckley, hunched over his precious wooden box of tricks by the metal wall, a hand cupped over one of the earphones clamped to his head.

They had tried repeatedly, at different times of the day, with the same result. Dixon shifted his weight. The rocks clattered under his feet.

Buckley turned and shot him a dirty look. "Shhh."

Dixon glowered but bit his tongue.

The signalman finally pulled the earphones down around his neck, looked up at Dixon and shook his head.

"I've not heard a peep, Sarn't. But maybe that just means they're not doing anything the equipment can pick up."

"Is there anything else we can do?"

"Well, I could try sending a telegraph. If there's anybody inside listening, they might pick it up. Unless you have any better ideas, Sarn't."

He couldn't see the point of trying, but Lieutenant Everson would want a full report on his return. It wasn't as if they had anything better to do. The mystery of the wall was fast beginning to lose its allure.

Dixon frowned. "No, I haven't. I just blow stuff up. Frankly, if I can't bomb it, mine it or call a barrage down on it I'm at a loose end, and any more cheek from you and I'll have your name."

Buckley looked up at the sergeant, unsure if that was an order or not.

"Well hop to it lad, hop to it," said Dixon impatiently. "We haven't got all day."

That, though, was exactly what they did have, so Buckley busied himself connecting up a field telegraph to the wall and began tapping on the Morse key.

EVERSON AND HIS men walked warily from darkness into twilit gloom, until the tunnel opened out into a deep trench leading out in to a large arena. It was surrounded by a wall some twelve feet high, beyond which were stands of Chatts, mostly scentirrii. So large was the space that, unlike any Chatt chambers they had seen, it needed columns and buttresses to support the roof.

At the sight of the Tommies in the mouth of the tunnel, the carapace-beating from the assembled Chatts quickened aggressively. On the wall above, Chatts armed with electric lances urged the soldiers out into the killing space.

The spectating Chatts grew quiet with anticipation.

The bodies of Fusiliers and Karnos lay strewn about the arena, twisted and broken. Rifles lay scattered and discarded, along with several limbs, and shallow blackened grenade craters dimpled the arena floor.

The centre of the arena was dominated by a large striated outcrop of rock thrusting up through the floor at an angle, creating a small incline about twenty feet high with an overhang beneath its peak.

Lieutenant Everson, sword in hand, led the advance into the arena. Atkins, Mercy, Porgy and Gazette spread out in a line either side of him. In a second line, Riley and Tonkins advanced with their kitbags of electric lances and backpacks, flanked by Gutsy and Pot Shot. The padre was unarmed and while refusing to carry weapons, had loaded himself down with the Signals gear and brought up the rear with Jenkins, the Linseed Lancer, with his small medical knapsack and more Signals gear.

As they headed for the outcrop, they saw, round the other side, the body of a huge pale toad-like beast, larger than an elephant. It lay slumped by the rock, glassy-eyed, its side torn open by shrapnel, its rib cage shattered, allowing its viscera to slop out onto the ground.

As Atkins watched, an Urman stepped forth from the bloody cavity, stripped to the waist, covered in encrusted blood and gore. To the accompaniment of hundreds of scissoring mandibles, the warrior hefted the creature's heart above his head and threw it to the ground. Covered as he was with blood and viscera, it was hard to make out details, but Atkins could see that the warrior was bare-chested apart from some sort of harness. Around his neck, he wore a collar hung with small round adornments. The only clothing he wore were trousers tucked into knee-length boots, and he carried two long knives, their straight blades dripping with a dark ichor. He glared up at the watching Chatts with contempt as he wiped the knives clean on his trousered thighs before thrusting them into loops hanging at his waist.

"Bloody hell," said Gutsy, aghast. "And I thought I was a butcher."

"We could do with a few men like that," said Pot Shot. "Let's hope he's friendly."

The warrior ignored them and began searching the bodies of the dead Fusiliers nearby.

"Oi, mate, fuck off!" warned Gazette, lifting his rifle and sighting him as they edged towards the outcrop.

Crouching over the body, the bloodied warrior turned his bloodgrimed face towards the Fusiliers, white teeth clenched in a snarl as he glared at them with undisguised contempt. He continued to search the dead man, going through his pockets and webbing, extracting a paybook, bullets and a grenade, before ripping the identity disc from his neck, like a trophy.

Atkins' brow furrowed. Despite the warrior's savage appearance, there was a familiarity to the man's actions, and Atkins saw with growing horror that he had been wrong. They weren't knee boots. They were puttees. They weren't knives, they were bayonets. It wasn't a harness, it was webbing. This was no savage Urman warrior. Dear God in heaven, this man was a Fusilier.

ABOVE, IN THE apothecary chambers, Hepton supervised the conversion of a small chamber into a makeshift darkroom. He filtered the diffuse blue-white bioluminescent lichen light by using the large translucent petals of a red flower. A dull amber glow now filled the room.

Chatt acolytes had laid out shallow bark bowls to use as makeshift developing trays on a plain earthen work counter.

Tulliver watched as Werner entered the dark chamber, accompanying a handful of Chatt alchemists holding up an amphora, like a Eucharistic sacrament. They were followed by acolyte nymphs bearing a shrine the size of an ammo box. To them this was as much a religious ritual as a chemical reaction.

"Have they done it?" asked Hepton, the dull red glow lending an aptly Faustian cast to his features.

Werner merely shrugged his shoulders. This was out of his hands now.

THE CHATTS CARRIED the portable shrine to one end of the chamber. There, they removed three exposed glass negative plates from within, each held reverently by a nymph. They were about eight inches by five and wrapped in several layers of black silk cloth, like relics. These plates, the Chatts believed, would provide physical evidence of the existence of GarSuleth.

"What are they?" asked Hepton.

"Aerial photographs," said Werner. "Taken from fifteen thousand feet."

"And what is it that they think they're supposed to show, exactly?" asked Hepton, a faint but supercilious sneer playing round his mouth.

"That their god created this world."

"Tall order," quipped Tulliver.

"And what happens if it proves nothing of the sort?" pressed Hepton.

"Then we're probably dead men."

The Chatts no longer stood before a counter, but an altar. It had become not a darkroom, but a chapel. The senior Chatt stood holding the amphora before the counter with its shallow trays. The nymphs approached in procession behind it, each holding its silk-wrapped glass plate like an offering.

"Right, let's do it," said Hepton. "Then I can get out of here." He went to take the amphora, but the Chatt reared up on its legs, hissing venomously. Realising he had misjudged the situation, Hepton backed off.

"You must guide them only," said Werner.

Hepton was horrified at the thought. "Guide them? But look at 'em. How can I get proper results—and proper results is what we're after, if we want to live—with those things?"

"You will die if you try to do it yourself, Herr Hepton. It is a heresy. They are quite insistent on that," said Werner.

Hepton curbed his belligerence, but it still simmered beneath the surface as he directed the Chatts to pour the sacred 'balm' in the shallow troughs, and then have an acolyte nymph uncover the first plate and place it in the solution.

There was a slight delay when Hepton suggested that they agitate the troughs and swill the liquid over the plate. Well, not so much a delay, Tulliver observed ruefully, as a complete theological debate. Was this merely a task that could be performed by an acolyte, or did the very transformative nature of the ritual require a greater degree of initiation and honour? After all, if this 'ritual' worked, it would make manifest the hidden hand of GarSuleth itself.

By now, Werner had to restrain Hepton to stop him interfering.

"But don't you see? If you leave it too long—"

Tulliver felt just as frustrated.

By the time the Chatts had discussed the matter and decided that this was no work for a mere acolyte but an Anointed One, and with Hepton unable to intervene, the plate had been in the fluid too long.

It had turned black.

THE BLOOD-ENCRUSTED WARRIOR strode over to the Tommies.

"God damn it, Everson. This is all your fault!" he screamed as he threw out an arm at the bloody aftermath around them. With his other he ripped off the necklace about his neck and thrust it out at the officer accusingly. Hung from it were the collected identity discs of too many dead men.

Shocked, Everson took them and stared at the man, whose face was so streaked with blood and dirt that he couldn't place him immediately. It didn't take him long, though; he hadn't exiled many men. "Rutherford? Dear God, man. What's happened to you?"

Rutherford looked at the officer with disbelief, his rage and invective spent. "*You* happened, sir. You exiled us, sent us out to die, that's what happened. We'd only been out a few days when a Zohtakarrii patrol captured us. Bains, me and the rest of them bought the Urmen time to escape. Our uniforms saved us." He shook his head in bewilderment. "They said they were looking for us."

"Werner," Atkins realised.

Everson pressed the point. "The Chatts saved you?"

"For this," spat Rutherford as he gestured towards the bloody carnage.

"Where are Bains and the others now?"

"Dead, for all I know, but that's what you wanted, isn't it, sir? You were too cowardly to sentence us to a firing squad, wanted to spare your conscience, did you? Well, just because you didn't order anybody to pull the trigger, doesn't mean you're not responsible for their deaths," he said with rancour.

Everson looked at the filth-encrusted Tommy, sure now of his actions. "This is the mutineer that hit you, Padre," he said sourly.

The padre studied Rutherford's face. "No, no it isn't, John. He was there. He tried to stop the other fellow."

Everson reeled as if he had been dealt a physical blow. He looked at Rutherford aghast.

"Yes. Wilson. He framed me," said Rutherford simply, as realisation dawned on the officer's face. "I won't lie, I took part, but I wasn't guilty of the crime you punished me for. But that's Army justice for you."

Padre Rand stepped forward. "Son, this is not the time for recrimination—"

"Sir!" yelled Mercy, directing Everson's attention to the far side of the arena, where another gate opened.

"There's no time," said Rutherford. "Prepare yourselves, sir. God knows what the Chatt bastards'll send out this time."

All enmity was swept aside in that moment. Survival was all that mattered.

"Make for the rock," ordered Everson. "It's our only defensible position."

The section advanced towards the outcrop, rifles pointed at the opening gate and void beyond.

Atkins deployed his men, using the outcrop as cover. He sent Gazette up the incline to its peak, where they could use his sniper skills. "What the hell is this place?" he asked Rutherford. "Is this their sport, pitting men against monsters?"

"After a fashion," Rutherford said. "They think it their holy calling to protect their world from the spawn that rises from the crater. They bring 'em here, and force Urmen to fight against them so they can study the creatures, the better to defend against them in the future."

A high-pitched screech echoed round the arena and Atkins watched, tensed, as a huge squat creature lumbered out of the tunnel behind the open gate. A sulphurous stench accompanied it as it plodded into the ring. Moving on four pairs of short, thick legs, each wreathed in folds of tough leathery skin, it walked with a graceless movement, as if it were completely out of its element. Atkins could see no eyes, but the head bristled with long twitching hairs arrayed around a large maw. Scabrous growths covered its leathery back, and a heavy fanlike tail dragged behind it.

At the sight of the demonic thing, Padre Rand made the sign of the cross and offered up a hasty prayer.

The Chatts wrangling the beast took their electric lances to it and it bellowed with pain and rage as they herded it into the centre of the arena.

It looked slow and clumsy, but Atkins didn't let his guard down. Some of the deadliest things on this world barely moved at all. He had no idea what defences this creature might have. None of them did. Neither, it seemed, did the damn Chatts, which he supposed was the whole point of the exercise.

"Fire!" barked Everson.

A volley of rifle fire slammed into the creature. It screeched and retreated. The electric lances of the Chatts behind it crackled pitilessly, driving it forward again. It bellowed in pain and confusion, its maw opening to reveal a gullet easily big enough to swallow a man and filled with inward-pointing spines.

Everson gazed round at the stands of Chatt scentirrii. "They expect us to fight for our lives," he confided to Atkins. "They want us to fight. They've pitched us against this monster to study our strengths and weaknesses, but we're not going to give them the satisfaction."

"Then may I ask what you intend to do?" said Atkins, keeping one eye on the beast as it lumbered round the amphitheatre, snuffling blindly at the dead bodies.

Everson grinned. "Something they won't expect, Corporal. Escape."

The creature charged towards the outcrop with a territorial roar, building up a surprising momentum until, head down, it butted the rock. The outcrop shuddered under the impact.

"If you've got a plan, Lieutenant, I'm all ears."

"We need a diversion. We have to get the wall down, get that thing among the Chatts."

"We've got Mills bombs."

"We'll never throw them that far."

From a trouser pocket, Rutherford produced a braided length of rope with a bark cradle. "Sling," he said.

Everson glanced at it. "Good man. Evans, give Rutherford a bomb."

Mercy handed over a Mills bomb from his webbing. "I've used a trench catapult to throw bombs, but a sling? Jesus. Isn't that a little dangerous?"

Rutherford just laughed as he fitted the bomb into the cradle, pulled the pin, whirled it around his head, and then let it fly. It arced up into the darkness and was lost until the wall of the arena exploded in a fireball and the faint whistle of red-hot iron shrapnel. The blast flung Chatt bodies into the air, briefly silhouetted against the fireball.

Caught by the blast, a supporting column began to crumble, bringing down a section of the chamber's dome.

The section fired again, this time concentrating their volley to one side of the creature driving it away, towards the rubble-strewn breach. It scrabbled over the debris to escape the gunfire, causing panic among the Chatts, their acid spit proving ineffective against the creature's thick hide.

In the confusion, Everson ordered Atkins and the Tommies across the arena towards the beasts' entrance. Going back the way they came would only lead them back into the edifice. Everson reckoned they must get these creatures in here through a dedicated entrance somewhere, without endangering the general population. Perhaps that way lay an exit.

Pot Shot hurled a Mills bomb at the gate. The explosion ripped the toughened gate from its root hinges in a plume of dirt and resinous sawdust.

Atkins and his section walked through the cloud, smoke billowing down the tunnel and swirling round their feet. Bayonets caught the pale blue lichen light as they advanced in trench clearance formation, ingrained in them at the training camps in France. They'd swept through Hun trench systems time after time, and it was reassuring that their training and tactics suited battle in a Chatt edifice so well.

This was something they knew how to do, and do well.

TULLIVER'S MOUTH WAS dry with anxiety as they watched the third and final glass negative plate reverently slipped into the solution by the acolyte, almost as if it was being anointed or baptised. After a second failure the Chatts seemed to decide that what the process lacked was prayer and began a clicking, smacking chant, almost as if they were counting: *one elephant, two elephant.*

The air of tension was palpable. Werner rubbed a finger inside the stiff Teutonic collar of his uniform.

Hepton fidgeted impotently as he watched the Chatts wash the chemicals over the plate.

"I just wish they'd bloody well let me do it," he whispered. "I just wish—"

An image began to form.

Hepton, in an effort to preserve the image on the plate, stepped forward, only to be warned off by the Chatts.

"Wash it!" he said. "Wash it. The other tray!"

The Chatts understood and slipped the plate into the other tray to stop the process.

When the Chatts saw the image, the chanting stopped. They stepped back in awe, touching the heels of their long-fingered hands to the bases of their antennae and then to their thorax.

"What is that?" Hepton asked, squinting at the negative image that had appeared. The man might be a photographer, but he had no experience in aerial photograph interpretation. The composition was odd, the angle oblique.

"Look. Lines radiating out across the landscape from two central points." Werner was triumphant. "I knew I was right."

Tulliver, too, saw the images he'd glimpsed all too briefly as his bus spiralled down out of control. "You were right, Werner. But what are they? The scale of those things; they're miles long. What does it mean?"

"They are the Threads of GarSuleth," hissed the Chatt, beholding its new relic. "Divine proof that this One never thought it would see. These Ones are truly blessed. Our scentures tell us that GarSuleth came down from his Sky Web to spin this world for his Children, the Ones. You have seen them and by GarSuleth's Will have brought us this holy glyph. This is a most miraculous spinning. The elders must be told."

The discussion was interrupted by the arrival of several scentirrii, one of whom addressed Werner.

"The Urman like you and its dark scentirrii have escaped. You know what you must do."

Werner looked shocked.

The news shook Tulliver as well. Not so much the fact that Everson and his men had escaped—that much he expected of them—but the fact that he was now stuck here, alone. No, not alone; with Hepton, which frankly was less preferable.

However, Hepton took it the worst. The man was torn. He didn't know what card to play. Where did his best chance of safety lie, with the Fusiliers or with Werner and the Zohtakarrii? Confusion and alarm washed across the man's face like a rip tide.

Tulliver looked at him in disgust. He had no sympathy for the man.

"You are to come with us," the scentirrii urged Werner. "You are to be the acid on the Breath of GarSuleth and strike down those who defy his Will."

Tulliver stepped forward and grasped Werner's forearm. "Werner, you can't do this."

"I don't have a choice," Werner said, averting his eyes as he pulled his arm free of Tulliver's grip.

"You always have a choice."

"And I choose to fly. I am sorry, my friend. I truly am."

Tulliver looked the German pilot in the eyes and saw that his decision was not without cost, but it was one he was willing to pay. Service to the Chatts for the chance to fly.

"Fly with me," Werner appealed to him. "You and I, up there. The Zohtakarrii have only kept you alive because you are like me."

"I'm nothing like you, Werner. Nothing," said Tulliver vehemently.

After Werner had been escorted away, the two remaining scentirrii moved in to seize him and Hepton.

"Don't take me," Hepton wheedled. "I helped you. I can still help you. I helped reveal the Threads of GarSuleth. That must count for something!"

The feeling of impotence welled up in Tulliver again, summing up his whole time here on this world. It left him feeling grounded. Useless. He'd had enough of that with Everson. He'd never liked being helpless. That's why he joined the RFC. By God, not any longer.

He pulled the revolver from his waistband and shot the scentirrii.

Hepton looked on in horror as he saw his chance for salvation dissipating with the cordite smoke before his eyes. "What the bloody hell are you doing, man?"

"My duty," snapped Tulliver. "Move."

Waving the Chatt apothecaries back with his revolver, Tulliver picked up the glass plate negative, wrapped it in its cloth and backed out of the chamber, Hepton accompanying him only with the greatest reluctance.

One Chatt raised itself up on its legs and hissed venomously. Tulliver put a bullet through its head and it dropped to the floor before it could exhale its soporific benediction.

The others hesitated and sank back down again in a submissive posture, unwilling to risk their new relic.

Tulliver glanced at Hepton. "Come on. We're leaving."

"But my equipment!" begged Hepton.

"You want it, you carry it," said Tulliver still covering the Chatts, who looked as if they were just waiting for a moment to strike. "But I'm not waiting."

Hepton hastily loaded himself up with the canvas bags of film canisters, and picked up his tripod and heavy wooden camera box and shuffled as close to Tulliver as he could.

Tulliver raised the wrapped plate to the Chatts as a final warning. "Try to stop us and I'll smash your precious 'holy glyph' to smithereens."

PENNINE FUSILIERS

CHAPTER FOURTEEN
"To Face the Stark, Blank Sky..."

EVERSON KNEW THAT the creature attacking the Chatts would have set off their alarm scent and the rampaging monster would command their attention for only a short while. They had to take advantage of that.

He moved his men swiftly but cautiously up the tunnel, into a larger chamber with numerous broad tunnels leading off. The stench of urine, dung and musk hung heavily in the air. The space was filled with roaring, snarling and unearthly sounds that churned his insides and made him want to vomit. He felt glad that they didn't have to face what was down those passages, but they might slow the Chatts down. He signalled to Evans and a couple of Mills bombs rolled down the passages. The tunnels shook and bloomed with a brief hellish light and a chorus of inhuman shrieks.

The section pushed on quickly, picking off any Chatts that challenged them.

"Atkins, they must get the creatures in here somehow. That's our way out. Find it. We'll hold here. But we can't do it for long."

"Sir. Mercy, Pot Shot, Porgy: with me. We're looking for a big fucking entrance. Something you can drive a tank through. Put some jildi into it."

The phrase brought a smile to Everson's lips. It was one of Sergeant Hobson's little sayings from his time in India. Atkins could do worse than pick up a thing or two from his platoon sergeant.

Any major attack would come from the direction of the arena. Gazette, Gutsy, Riley and Tonkins covered the exit to the chamber. The padre and Jenkins huddled against a wall.

"What about Tulliver and Hepton, sir?" asked Jenkins.

"Oh, I shouldn't worry about Hepton, Jenkins," Everson said, his lip curling. "As my father would say, he's one of life's floaters, that one. And as for Tulliver..." He let out a sigh. "Hopefully he can take advantage of our diversion."

Everson shot another Chatt. "Come on, Atkins," he muttered impatiently.

Rutherford sloped up the tunnel, panting, his bayonets dripping.

Without warning, a Chatt appeared from a side tunnel. Jenkins, in a move so uncharacteristic it must have been from terror, roared to mask his fear and charged with a rifle at the thing, plunging his bayonet into it, cracking and splintering its chest carapace.

"Face, Jenkins!" yelled Everson in warning.

"Sir?" Jenkins turned as, with its dying breath, the Chatt spat its acid. It seared the side of Jenkins' face with a sickening sizzle, blistering his cheek and ear, as skin and muscle burnt and dissolved. Turning, however, had saved his sight. He staggered back, screaming, as the Chatt slumped to the floor.

Corporal Riley was first to reach him, emptying the contents of his water canteen across Jenkins' face, flushing away the remaining acid. "Stay still, lad." He cradled the man as he whimpered. "Tonkins," he called. "Morphine."

Tonkins fished in his haversack and came up with a tablet of morphine. Jenkins quietened down.

The others took the opportunity to pull their gas hoods on.

There was an explosion.

Mercy came haring down the tunnel, skidding to a halt.

"Sir, we've found it! Corp's holding it now."

"Move!" yelled Everson, waving his men past him up the tunnel.

The padre led the way, and Riley and Tonkins took Jenkins between them, whimpering in pain.

It wouldn't be long before the place was swarming. Scentirrii were already running down the tunnel towards them as the dust settled.

Rutherford charged, screaming, bayonets in hand, and thrust them into the throats of two scentirrii before they had a chance to spit acid.

Gutsy swung his meat cleaver, Little Bertha, and split the head of another.

Everson ran the next Chatt through with his sword.

Rutherford fought off two more scentirrii, swinging Jenkins' rifle, smashing in one facial plate with the shoulder stock, leaving the large black eye bleeding from its orbit, like a yolk from a broken shell. The other he caught against a wall and drove his hobnailed boot into its chest once, twice, three times to crush the carapace, driving shards into the vital organs.

Gazette knelt in the shelter of the tunnel giving covering fire for their retreat and picked off several more Chatts with characteristic accuracy.

Atkins, Pot Shot, Mercy and Porgy were covering the exit into a large partially built courtyard. It may have been used for wrangling demonic creatures from the craters, but today it held something else. Something even bigger, tethered by ropes to the courtyard walls.

Atkins was elated and despondent at its discovery: the German kite balloon, patched, mended and inflated, with a new larger basket fitted below, a cradle adapted from a battlepillar. It floated above the courtyard in a serene silence, its mooring ropes reminding him of tentacles and its great grey bulk of the aerial Kreothe.

It called to mind Mathers' prophecy. *'The Kreothe, made, not tamed.'* If that wasn't a description of a balloon, he didn't know what was. What the hell did it all mean? What was the next line? He couldn't recall and grimaced.

Tethered by anchor lines it floated, giving them some cover from the battlements above. There was a large drum of rope for winching it up and down. That would have to go. A swift blow with Little Bertha saw to that. The huge sausage balloon rose slightly, tugging at its moorings.

Already Chatts were rushing along the walls above. Bolts of white fire crackled down from electric lances, pinning them in the entrance. Behind them, Everson could hear the crack of rifle fire as Gazette held the rear.

Pot Shot picked off one or two Chatts on the battlements. They tumbled to the ground, hitting heavily with wet cracking noises, their broken clay batteries shattering with blue flashes.

Porgy dashed out to secure the long basket. "All aboard!" he yelled.

They clambered into it. It was a tight squeeze and even Pot Shot complained as Gutsy eased his stocky form into the wicker-work cradle. Riley and Tonkins helped Jenkins in, the right side of his head livid and blistering, and sat him on the floor in a morphine stupor, where the padre comforted him.

"Christ, we're never going to take off with you in it," said Porgy.

"You have to think good thoughts!" Gutsy declared.

"Bloody hell, then we really are in trouble!" Porgy said with a grin.

From the basket, Atkins called to Everson, who was sheltering in the doorway with Rutherford.

"We have to go, sir. Now!"

"Come with us, Rutherford," said Everson.

"In that thing?" Rutherford shook his head with a regretful smile. "Not a chance. Besides, I can't. My clan is out there somewhere."

"We're your clan," Everson replied earnestly.

Rutherford shook his head. "Maybe, once, but I'd made my mind up long before the so-called mutiny. We're marooned here for good. You're on a fool's errand, sir. The sooner you realise that and start to live in the here and now, the better it'll be for you and the men. And even if there was a way, I can't go back home, sir. Not to Broughtonthwaite. Not after all I've seen; all I've done. I can't go back to some quiet little redbrick terrace after all this. No. I'll wish you the best of luck, sir. I hope you find what you're looking for. I intend to find my Urmen."

The man had gumption, Everson had to admit that. And maybe there wasn't a way home—the Bleeker party certainly suggested that—but he wasn't willing to accept it until he had exhausted all the possibilities. He owed *that* to the men. Nevertheless, he held out his hand. Rutherford took it and shook it firmly.

"Good luck, Rutherford. I was wrong about you."

Rutherford held his gaze. "Yes, you were."

Everson ran for the cradle. Several pairs of hands helped him over the lip.

"Whoops-a-daisy, sir."

Once Everson was in, Rutherford untied the last of the mooring ropes. The large sausage-shaped kite balloon began to rise; Rutherford caught hold of the rope as the kite balloon drifted up over the courtyard wall. He planted his feet against the side and ran up the courtyard as the balloon rose.

Chatts swarmed along the wall to stop it. One raised an electric lance. Rutherford kicked away from the wall as he reached the top, swung back and knocked the Chatt off the wall as the balloon drifted over.

It continued to rise, edging towards the trees. Rutherford slipped down the rope and hit the ground. He turned and gave a brief salute before racing for the tree line.

Mercy shook his head in exasperation. "Bloody hell, who does he think he is, Peter bleedin' Pan?"

TULLIVER, REVOLVER DRAWN, the glass negative under his arm, followed the first passage he could find heading down. He knew he had to get off the main thoroughfares as soon as possible. He had their sacred relic under his arm, but he doubted that would keep them alive for long.

"Wait for me," demanded Hepton, staggering under the bulk of his kinematic equipment.

"If you can't keep up, get rid of it!" barked Tulliver sharply.

Hepton glared at him as if he'd asked him to leave behind his own grandmother.

"Suit yourself," said Tulliver, perversely satisfied to have earned one of Hepton's black looks.

He kept his eyes peeled and saw an Urman slip into a small side passage. He followed. It seemed to be a series of 'belowstairs' passages, exclusively for Urmen. That made things a little easier. Their scent would be lost among the throng, or so he hoped. The fact that Hepton was loaded down actually helped them. With Urmen hurrying this way and that on various errands and with assorted loads of their own, none of them gave Tulliver or Hepton a second look.

They reached the ground level and the Urman passage opened out into a larger tunnel filtering into the cavernous entrance chamber. Tulliver pressed his back against the wall and watched for a moment. It was obvious an alarm scent had spread. They were sealing the edifice. Scentirrii herded the Urmen out of the vast space, leaving baskets and bundles of harvested foods abandoned. Tethered to their loading quays, battlepillars rippled nervously.

Scentirrii urged Urmen to close the great bark doors.

"Just our rotten bloody luck."

Hepton had just caught up with him and was panting hard and trying to shift his load into a more comfortable position. Too bad.

Tulliver scowled at him. He'd have a better chance alone, and he was almost prepared to leave Hepton to his fate, but for the fact he needed someone to start the propeller. "They know something's up, they're battening down the hatches. It's now or never. As a favour to you, we're going to walk up there. That should allow you to catch your breath, but once I start running you'd better keep up."

Hepton swore under his breath.

Tulliver crept out, using stacks of abandoned foods and battlepillar jetties for cover until they neared the great bark doors. Hepton scurried along behind him, struggling to hold the tripod under his arms while lugging the camera box and knapsacks of film canisters. They had barely got two thirds of the way across the space when the two Chatts at the door stepped forward with spears raised to challenge them.

Tulliver carried on walking, pointed his revolver and shot the pair of them.

"That's your cue," he said to Hepton, sprinting towards the closing doors.

As the kite balloon drifted up over the surrounding forest, Atkins spotted the Sopwith, with its unmistakable British roundels, and two figures running towards it, chased by Chatts. "Tulliver!"

"I've got it," said Gazette. Resting his rifle on the basket and taking aim, he picked off the Chatt scentirrii around the aeroplane. The figure of Tulliver looked up and waved his thanks.

Tulliver fired his last bullet into the body of a wounded Chatt that rose to stop them, then stepped past and climbed up into his cockpit, yelling at Hepton.

Hepton staggered up to the Sopwith, as quickly as his forty-a-day body would let him. It hadn't been forty-a-day for a while, but the damage had been done and he was gasping and coughing like a mustard gas victim. But he still had all his equipment. Just. He stepped up and stowed the tripod and camera box into the observer's cockpit and was about to climb in himself.

"No," said Tulliver.

"What the bloody hell do you mean, no?"

"I mean I need you at the front to turn the prop over."

"I'm not a bloody air mechanic."

"No, and you're not bloody dead yet either, and you will be if I don't get my bus off the ground." He pointed towards the edifice, from where a number of Chatts were running and leaping towards them. "Prop. Now."

Swearing, Hepton stepped down off the fuselage and hurried round to the front of the machine.

"Contact!" yelled Tulliver over the roar of the engine.

Hepton swung the propeller with both hands. It caught, and Tulliver ran the engine up. The bus began to move, pulled by the propeller's traction.

Hepton raced round the wing and heaved himself into the observer's cockpit as the plane picked up speed, bouncing along the uneven ground. He had barely strapped himself in when the Sopwith took to the air.

"OH, NOW THAT's not bloody fair," said Porgy, peering over the edge of the basket in dismay.

Three smaller balloons of the Zohtakarrii's own manufacture rose out of chimney-like buttresses around the walls of the edifice. They were spherical and of some translucent skin stretched taut with gas. The balloons were tethered by long lines that played out as they rose into the air to meet the kite balloon's escape. Each carried a basket holding eight Chatts, armed with electric lances.

Atkins remembered the line of Mathers' prophecy now, '*Other Ones will travel on the Breath of GarSuleth, the Kreothe, made, not tamed.*' The Breath of GarSuleth was a Chatt phrase that could mean the wind. How did Mathers know? How could the Nazarrii, who made the prophecy and who died hundreds of years ago, possibly know?

Atkins looked back over his shoulder, to the open meadow, but could no longer see Tulliver, although he could hear the determined putter of the aeroplane's engine.

As if that wasn't bad enough, they were drifting back towards the edifice on the prevailing wind. The kite balloon was about as manoeuvrable as a bloody Kreothe, thought Atkins, his blood running cold.

The great earthen walls drifted past, too closely for comfort, and they passed by the great hollow buttresses from which the balloons had been raised; one of the balloons was above them even now. Pot Shot dropped a grenade down the chimney. The cap of the open buttress blasted apart, flinging rocky shrapnel and Chatt body parts high into the sky and raining down against the sausage balloon.

The men in the cradle ducked and covered their heads as it pattered down past them. Then the concussion wave hit, buffeting the cradle and sweeping them clear of the edifice.

Even as the gap widened, one scentirrii leapt from a watch balcony across the void towards them, striving to catch a trailing rope. It missed and fell, its body racing its shadow down the edifice side until the two collided against the incline, where it slid for a second before tumbling off towards the ground.

Driven by an impulse greater than self-preservation, two more Chatts made last-ditch leaps from the edifice as the kite balloon drifted beyond it

One leapt for the basket. Its long fingers closed about the lip, and it began to haul itself up. The moment its face appeared, Gutsy smashed it with his rifle butt, and it fell, flailing, to smack into the ground.

As the kite balloon drifted out over the forest canopy, the second Chatt, hanging from a trailing mooring rope, attempted to pitch its spear into the balloon. It struck the skin a glancing blow before falling harmlessly away.

Tonkins cut through the rope with his bayonet. "Thank God the bastards haven't got wings," he said as he leaned over and watched the Chatt drop. "They haven't, have they?"

The falling Chatt didn't even have a chance to hit the ground. Its shadow, falling across the forest canopy below, triggered a whipperwill, which lashed up into the air, caught the body and snatched it out of sight.

After that, Atkins watched the shadow of the balloon nervously as it sailed over the forest, a trail of hungry whips snapping far below.

A crackle alerted Atkins to more danger. He looked up. A Chatt balloon, its mooring now a smoking ruin, was now adrift. It was higher and floating in the same direction as the kite balloon, out towards the crater. The Chatts fired their electric lances.

Atkins couldn't get a sight on the Chatt balloon's occupants. The balloon itself made a better target.

He heard the roar of an engine and raked his eyes across the sky, looking for the source, but couldn't see anything. Then he heard the sickening stutter of twin machine guns and saw the Albatros diving towards them.

It was virtually impossible to move in the cramped basket now, as everyone crouched for what blessed little cover they could get. From the other end of the cradle came a shout. Atkins craned his neck.

Another aeroplane, this one theirs.

KNIGHTS OF THE air, jousting in single combat. It sounded romantic; Tulliver had thought the same when he volunteered. His flight commander had quickly debunked that notion. It wasn't a game. It was kill or be killed. There was no fair play. No chivalry. Shoot them in the back, from behind. Whatever it took. Up here, he owed Werner nothing.

Push forward on the stick, dive.

Werner's Albatros was in his gunsight. He fired.

Werner banked away sharply. The Albatros was faster and more manoeuvrable than the Strutter, but with its front-mounted twin Spandau machine guns, the Albatros could only fire head on. If they were to stand any chance at all, Hepton would have to use the observer's Lewis machine gun, mounted behind him. It would even the odds a little.

Seeing the two tethered Chatt balloons rising above their chimneys, Tulliver pushed his stick to the side and banked, coming down on them from above. He strafed them with brief bursts of machine-gun fire. You were supposed to wait until you were almost on top of them, but he wanted to keep out of range of their electric lances. The petrol tank was between him and Hepton, and the whole plane was doped fabric and wood. He didn't fancy going down in flames.

As he pulled up, he saw the punctured balloons begin to deflate and sink towards the edifice on their leashes.

He heard the *pop-pop-pop* of machine gun fire. The threat of death spurred Hepton into action. The man had found some gumption. He was firing off at the Hun as the Albatros dived down on them from behind.

Left stick and rudder, Tulliver side-slipped away. Both planes were now trying to turn inside each other's circles so they could bring their forward guns to bear on their opponents. Diving and climbing, they spiralled, each pilot desperately trying to thwart the other, seeking the advantage for himself.

Werner levelled out and swept towards the kite balloon, firing incendiaries at it as it drifted out over the crater.

Tulliver pushed forwards on the stick and followed him down, all the while trying to centre him in his gunsight. He needed to be as close as possible to avoid hitting the kite balloon, but it was looming up fast.

Werner flattened out at the last minute and roared so low over the top of the kite balloon that it looked as if he might set down on it.

Tulliver could see the men in the cradle shouting and waving at him frantically. He was on a collision course. Wiping the fouling oil spray from his goggles, he nudged the nose forward, steepening his dive, sweeping under the kite balloon's cradle.

He hauled back on the stick and the bus raced up in a long climb. He swivelled his head about him, looking for the Hun. He tipped his wing and, looking down, saw him below, readying for another run at the kite balloon.

Tulliver watched in horror as the balloon crumpled, flames consuming and shrivelling its skin, as it sank towards the crater.

RANAMAN STOOD IN the cleft between the two halves of Croatoan's Heart, holding the box. He nodded at the two warriors holding Alfie's arms and they released him. Alfie tensed himself for the inevitable. If they were going to sacrifice him, then he would go with as much dignity as he could muster. He wouldn't give them the satisfaction of screaming, or at least, he'd try not to.

"Now you are to commune with the ancestors," Ranaman demanded.

The Urman withdrew another smaller box from the first and offered it to him.

Alfie's resolve collapsed in confusion. Would it spring open and douse him with a poison? Or did it contain some sacred creature that would kill with a lethal sting? If they wanted to kill him, he wasn't going to make their job any bloody easier. He refused to touch the box, and glared at the chieftain.

With a nod, Ranaman offered the smaller box again. "It is time. Channel the spirits of the ancestors."

Alfie looked again and saw that it wasn't a box: it was a large book, spine on. He almost laughed. It was the last thing he expected. It had been an easy mistake to make in the dim light of the temple. It was an old book by the look of it, too, a large leather-bound tome with iron clasps. Its cover had some sort of symbol cast in iron set into it. Water damage had wrinkled the page edges and there was a faint smell of mildew about it.

Seeing no alternative, he reached out and closed his hands about the book, trembling. What could be so bad about a book?

There was an audible sigh of relief from Ranaman as he let go. It was as if he had transferred some great responsibility and was now absolved of any further expectations.

Alfie turned to face the gathered clan. Ranaman had stepped back and joined the others, looking on with an awed, expectant gaze, expecting some miracle to occur.

He's going to be severely disappointed, thought Alfie as he frowned and turned his attention to the book. He opened it and riffled through the pages, a murmur of expectation rippling through the waiting clan. They watched him in amazement as he turned the pages.

Why the hell didn't they just read it themselves?

And then it struck him. They couldn't. He didn't even think they knew what a book was, let alone writing. They seemed to think it was some arcane object, imbued with great supernatural powers, a vessel through which someone with witchcraft could communicate with the dead. In fact, this book looked old enough for their ancestors to have written it. If he could read it, then he supposed he *would* be communicating with the dead, reading their thoughts. He'd never thought of it like that before, and now that he did, it sent a shudder down his spine. No wonder they thought it a great magic.

There was nothing else for it. He thumbed through the pages and stopped at random. Illegible, close, handwritten text filled the thick parchment pages. It hadn't occurred to him that the language might not be English.

He flipped through the pages, becoming anxious. He tried to look serious and portentous. He glanced up over the top of the book at the clan, who shuffled uneasily. Two men had stepped up behind Tarak, as if to make good on their threat, should Alfie fail.

He could brazen it out. Make something up. If they couldn't read, they wouldn't know, would they? Is that what Jeffries did, make something up?

He stopped and squinted at the writing. Something familiar. A word. Was it a word? He traced the writing with his finger, trying to spell it out. C, O, M. Something long. A, N. Something long, similar but not exactly like the other long letter. Company? Company, that was it. With that, the whole page seemed to unlock. He glanced over the page. It was English. Very old English, the *s*'s were *f*'s and the handwriting was hard to decipher, but he could read it. He breathed a sigh of relief before the thought, *how was it English?* crossed his mind, but the Urmen were becoming restless. That was a question for another time. Here and there, he made out words: *White* and *Virginia* and *Roanoke*. On one page there even looked to be a date, *1588*. But that couldn't have been right, for any schoolboy who knew his dates of kings and queens knew that was the reign of Queen Elizabeth I.

Flanked by the broken halves of Croatoan's Heart, he began to read aloud to the assembled clan, hesitating as he tried to make sense of the unfamiliar script. Perhaps it had no more significance than the Bible readings he had heard the padre give during Church Parade. He tried to sound solemn and authoritarian.

"The rituals are complete. One has gone ahead to scout the way for the company. They will go to seek the mouth to the underworld, there to descend to the enclave of the dead and petition for our Lord and

Master, Croatoan, or else seek to destroy the false god and free him, restoring the Fallen One to his rightful place. Those that aid him, we have been told, will be granted great boons, and this new world will be theirs to dwell on, in the sight of Croatoan."

It wasn't merely the words that sent a chill down Alfie's spine. It was the fact that they were there at all. It was both an exciting and a horrifying discovery.

All at once, he was out of his depth. He had never felt at ease with Mathers' duplicity in pretending to be messengers of the gods. He was just a mechanic from Nottingham. All this occult stuff was fine, if fanciful, contained between the covers of Cecil's adventure story magazines. Give him his tank any day, its one-hundred-horsepower Daimler engine, its six-millimetre steel plate. He understood that. But this?

His brow creased as he gazed out over the pages of tightly-written text at the clan watching him beyond. Was it possible that these were the descendants of other earlier missing people? He looked up again at the people in shock, the book slipping from his hands, as the enormity of what he had just read sunk in.

It seemed a magical transformation *had* occurred with his reading. The tables had turned. He was no longer the magical being. They were.

"Who *are* you?" he asked, his voice barely a whisper.

Ranaman cocked his head and answered as if it were plain for all to see.

"We are the sons and daughters of Ruanach. Worshippers of Croatoan. We have long sought to ease his pain and we have been promised that Croatoan will return."

"Promised? Promised by who?" he asked, though he feared he knew the answer.

"The one who came before. Jeffries," Ranaman replied.

Ranaman stepped forward and took the closed book from Alfie, replacing it in its box, taking the responsibility from him once more, his part in the ritual done.

The hair on the back of Alfie's neck began to prickle. "But if we're not the first..." He tried to marshal his thoughts. "Your ancestors, did they not leave? Go back to where they came from?"

"Leave? Why? They sought a new world and were led to this place. They came a great distance seeking Croatoan, invoking his name. But he was tricked and defeated by GarSuleth and bound below in Skarra's realm and they were lost, our new world taken from us by GarSuleth and its children."

It wasn't just his neck that prickled now; it was the hairs on his arms, too, as if an electric charge were building.

The air grew warm.

The men groaned, the women wailed, and Ranaman cried out.

"The Torment of Croatoan begins!"

CHAPTER FIFTEEN
"I Feel Once Again as of Yore..."

THE ACRID SMELL of burning rubberised canvas filled Atkins' nostrils as charred scraps of material from the burning balloon swirled round the cradle, leaving a greasy grey smear across the sky as they sank down into the crater. Right now, it was a moot point as to which would meet them first, the fire or the ground.

"I'm not sure I like the Royal Flying Corps," Porgy confided to nobody in particular. "Have I got time to put in a transfer back to the Poor Bloody Infantry, sir?" he called over to Everson with a smirk.

"I think it'll be granted sooner than either of us would like, Hopkiss," said the lieutenant grimly, gripping onto the sides of the cradle as they plunged towards the ground.

They were passing over the strip of discoloured vegetation. As the cradle twisted in the air, Atkins turned his head to keep it in sight, in an attempt to keep his bearings. Rising just above the treetops, near the centre of the crater, was some sort of narrow tower.

"Sir!" he said to Everson, pointing.

"I see it, Corporal."

The balloon's passing shadow triggered small explosions, like gunshots, as whipperwills snapped hungrily at it, like sixty-foot bullwhips. As they lashed into the sky, sections peeled back at their tips, opening like fleshy petals, to reveal flayed-red lamprey-like mouths, each one ready to tear and strip, snapping one after the other at the deflating balloon like chained dogs, before recoiling into the trees beneath.

Tonkins, the signaller, squeezed off several rounds at them, but they moved too fast and the bullets vanished harmlessly into the canopy.

"Never mind, lad," said Corporal Riley.

The burning balloon was out of reach for the moment, but as it continued its inevitable descent towards the crater's jungle canopy, it was clear it wouldn't stay that way.

Several of the ropes suspending the cradle from the balloon burnt through, and the cradle dropped a few feet with a jerk and tipped precariously, causing yells of alarm and consternation from every quarter.

Porgy's gorblimey slipped from his head.

"My cap!" groaned Porgy. "Bloody hell, the Quarterbloke'll never give me another one."

"Aye, the only excuse he'll take for losing it is if you lost your bleedin' head along with it!" agreed Mercy as they clung to the side of the swaying and now spinning cradle.

"Yes, well there's still a chance of that," retorted Gazette, as burning scraps fluttered down around them.

The canopy was rising up to meet them fast now. Something struck the underside of the balloon's cradle, and again, and again, and they realised that they were now within reach of the whipperwills. Sensing wounded prey, the things began lashing out with greater ferocity, tearing at the wattle cradle, their fleshy petals opening as they snapped their small razor-sharp teeth.

Gutsy swung his meat cleaver at them. Everson slashed out with his sword, severing several whipperwills' heads and sending them tumbling down to the treetops, only for their hungry brethren to snatch them out of midair.

A bigger specimen cracked up out of the canopy like a seaborne leviathan and tore at what remained of the blazing gasbag above. The flames licked at it and some sap or aqua vita within it ignited, fire consuming its entire length. It thrashed about the air like a fiery lash, until with a thunderous *crack*, it extinguished the flames and the scorched whipperwill crashed back into the leaves, leaving behind the faint smoky ghost of it hanging in the air.

Unable to keep the cradle aloft any longer, the remains of the balloon flapped and guttered, streaming ineffectually above them as men and cradle now hurtled down. They skimmed across the treetops, the drub of branches and leaves against the bottom of the cradle sounding like sticks against a railing.

"Brace yourselves!" shouted Everson.

Atkins hunkered down into the cradle as best he could. He looked at the wan faces around him. Eyes met his, the unspoken communion of the soldier about to go over the bags: "We'll be all right," "Stick by me," "See you in the Hun trenches." But they all knew it was every man for himself.

The cradle hit the canopy with a crash and capsized.

Atkins' world tumbled, like a broken kaleidoscope, a whirl of limbs and wattle, of green, russet, khaki and daylight.

Boughs slammed into his limbs and trunk, knocking the wind from him as he fell, buffeted and pummelled from bough to branch, towards the ground as he dropped through the trees. Thick broad leaves slapped and scratched him. He plummeted through an angry buzz of insects, sounding like the whine of bullets, hands and face stinging as he passed through. For a brief, blissful moment, as if in the eye of a storm, all sensation ceased.

A flare of heavy floral scent burst around him. Perfume. He thought of Flora. Lily of the Valley. Oh, Jesus, Flor—

Atkins slammed into the ground.

NELLIE ABBOTT HELD up a hand, halting the rest of the tank crew. Underneath her short mop of unruly hair, her nose wrinkled and her brow creased with concentration.

"What is it, Miss?" asked Cecil.

Irritated, she flapped her hand in his direction. "Shh!" she hissed, a little more harshly than she had meant to.

Cecil flinched like a scolded puppy.

Above the rustle of the leaves and the faint rush of water, a distant purr caught her attention and held it, as no other sound could.

Wally cocked his head and listened.

He sniffed. "An engine," he said.

"Two," corrected Nellie. "Aeroplanes."

"Two?" said Jack. "Are you sure? But we've only got the one."

"Well, there are two now," said Nellie, her mood defiant.

"Friend or foe?" asked Reggie.

"I don't know," she said thoughtfully. She looked up at the sky, shielding her eyes and squinting against the glare.

Ablaze and drifting down over the crater, the kite balloon was hard to miss.

She soon spotted another smaller balloon, higher and partially hidden by the smoke from the first, drifting in the same direction.

Above them, she saw what she was looking for, the small shapes spiralling higher and higher. She could just make out Tulliver's Strutter, but the other—was that a Hun? Her eyes widened with surprise before her forehead scrunched with doubt. But how?

By now, the others had gathered around her and the air filled with theories and observations.

"There's men up there," said Reggie, pointing at the balloon.

"It's a Hun observation balloon," said Wally. The bantam cockney driver clenched his fists, and his lips contorted into a snarl.

It was spiralling down rapidly into the crater. It was going to come down not a quarter of a mile away. She felt a surge of pity for the men trapped on it. The smaller, higher balloon was sinking too, but that would come down further away.

"Where the hell have they come from?" wondered Jack.

"Perhaps it's a way home!" suggested Norman.

Nobody spoke out in agreement, but nobody would gainsay it.

Nellie felt a blossoming of hope in her breast at the words. Home. Could it be?

There was only one way to find out.

A PALL OF smoke stained the air above the trees. Expecting Germans, the crew of the *Ivanhoe* approached the crash site cautiously.

"Stay by me," Jack told Cecil in a low voice, as he drew his Webley.

The young lad stepped closer, his eyes darting about as if he expected picklehaubed Fritzs to leap from every bush.

Norman and Reggie watched their flanks and Wally. Wally wasn't to be trusted around Germans. It was frightening that such a little man could have such a fury bottled up within him. They didn't want him killing them before they got whatever information they needed.

Nellie wasn't happy about bringing up the rear.

"I can kill if I have to," she told Jack, petulantly.

He studied her face.

"I don't doubt it," he said. "But we're soldiers. It's what we have to do." He bent his head and spoke quietly. "You shouldn't kill unless you have to. Knowing you've killed a man changes you." He tapped his chest. "Inside. It breaks something in you. Something that can't be mended. Bad enough it has to happen to lads like Cecil; I wouldn't want that to happen to you. I don't want that on my conscience," he said. He straightened up and added firmly, "You'll stay in the rear."

Nellie had no answer and relented. This was one area where she was relieved to forego responsibility. The weight of the revolver in her hand began to feel like a poisoned chalice, but she gripped it firmly nevertheless.

Ahead, somewhere through the undergrowth, there was a sound like a groan. Jack held his hand up and the rest of the party crouched down. He signalled the crew to spread out in a skirmish line, then stood and, looking right and left, waved them on with his revolver.

LIEUTENANT EVERSON LAY dazed against the bole of a tree, a large lump forming on his forehead, waiting for the world to stop spinning and his body to stop hurting.

The last thing he expected to see was Nellie Abbott walking out of the undergrowth with a look of shock on her face.

"Lieutenant Everson! What happened? How did you get here?"

He looked up and saw the coverall-clad tankers beside her. "The crew of the *Ivanhoe*, I presume," he groaned. "Don't you salute a senior officer?"

Jack shrugged. "Generally not, sir. Mr Mathers said it usually gets 'em shot."

"And where is Lieutenant Mathers?"

"Gone west, sir."

While not a shock, it was unwelcome news. There were precious few surviving officers as it was without losing another.

"Then who's in command here?" he asked. The men looked sheepish.

"I guess that would be me," said Nellie, stepping forward in her coveralls.

Now it was Everson's turned to look shocked. "You?" he said. He looked to the awkward tank crew. "You're taking orders from a woman now?"

Nellie's eyebrow arched.

Reggie intervened. "Begging your pardon, sir. We were in a bit of a state for a while, the fumes from the tank engine and all that. Some sort of neuralgia. We weren't quite ourselves. Miss Abbott saw us right. Showed us how we'd let Alfie down. We owed it to him, to find him, sir. We only did what was right. Orders or no orders, right is right. We were on his trail when we came across you."

"We saw you come down. How on earth did you end up in that thing, Lieutenant?" asked Nellie.

Everson's tone hardened. "We arrived at the crater. You weren't there," he said. "We were captured by Zohtakarrii and escaped in a captured observation balloon."

"So there are no Huns?" said Wally, disappointed.

"No," said Everson. "Well, one. I expect Tulliver's on his tail this minute."

Now fully aware of his surroundings, he looked around. "Where are the rest, Atkins and the others? They were in the kite balloon. Are they all right?"

Jack waved his arm. "Spread out, find them."

THE TANK CREW came back in ones and twos, with bruised and battered Tommies and scattered haversacks, gasbags, battle bowlers and rifles.

Corporal Riley and Tonkins had found themselves stuck in adjacent trees, having slid down a succession of broad flat leaves as though they were slides. Their electric lance kitbags were found nearby, their fall broken by the undergrowth.

Gazette had twisted his ankle and ended up entangled in a thicket, as if he'd been left hanging out on the old barbed wire.

They came across Pot Shot groaning in shrubbery.

"Bloody hell, I haven't taken a beating like that since the police set about us during the transport strike!" he moaned as they hauled him out.

Gutsy had got away relatively unscathed, having had the benefit of the unfortunate Mercy as a soft landing as they came hobbling in together.

"Well, if it isn't Wendy and the Lost Boys," Gutsy said in clipped, bitter tones when he saw the tank crew.

Nellie threw him the kind of haughty look she usually reserved for her brothers. Gutsy, who had contended with Mrs Blood's occasional wrath for over a decade, baulked nevertheless.

All were maps of contusions, scratches, bruises and livid welts from whip-thin branches, and all had run their gamut of swear words until there was nothing left but a weary acceptance of the discomfort and pain.

They found Padre Rand kneeling over Jenkins, the signals gear hung from various branches around them. The livid, raw acid burns on Jenkins' face were the least of his worries now. He screwed up his eyes in pain as he snatched short ragged breaths. Padre Rand barely had time to read him the Last Rites before Jenkins' breathing became softer and then, with one last gasp, stopped altogether.

ATKINS CAME ROUND, his head hurting, every limb throbbing and aching. He eased himself into a sitting position against a tree trunk, resting uncomfortably against the jumble of gear in his knapsack.

He was amazed to find himself still alive. His first thought now was of Flora, just as his last thought had been. He was still alive. He could still get back to her. But to do that, he would have to move.

He saw his rifle some yards away, and levered himself to his feet. The action set off a ferocious pounding in his head. Spots danced before his eyes as he steadied himself. He heard voices calling. He tried to call out, but his mouth was parched and he couldn't find his water bottle, so he started towards the sounds.

Ahead, white petals drifted down from a tree bough, spinning round in eddies and carpeting the ground beneath the tree. Limping towards it, he realised they weren't petals, but pieces of card. He could see photographs on some. A slipknot of fear tightened round his stomach. He dropped to his knees and brushed his hand through the fallen photogravures, turning them over. They were photographs of girls, every one, some smiling, some demure, full figure, portrait, occasional French nudes and music hall singers. He knew them all.

Several more fluttered down from above.

Not wanting to, but needing to know, he looked up. He dearly wished he hadn't.

Fifteen feet above, a body lay face down, splayed awkwardly across a couple of boughs with an arm outstretched, as if reaching for the fallen cards. Pallid whipcord creepers had wrapped themselves around the neck, biting deeply into the skin. The eyes were wide and bloodshot; the fleshy parts of the face were dark purple and bloated with settling blood, distorting the once pleasant features into a grotesque caricature as it stared down through the foliage at him.

Atkins' voice was quiet but heavy with sorrow, regret and guilt, all bound up in a single word. "Porgy."

Try as he might, he couldn't reach his mate's body. Unwilling to abandon him, he set about collecting up the fallen photographs, Porgy's 'deck of cards.' As he did, Atkins felt the tears come, stinging the welts on his face as they tracked down his cheeks. Being alone, he let them fall.

He wasn't sure how long the voices had been calling. He cuffed his eyes dry and shook off his despondency enough to call out hoarsely, "Here!"

The rest of the section and the tank crew arrived in short order. It took five of them to cut Porgy's body free and lower him gently to the ground, as Atkins watched, numbed.

Nellie sought to comfort him, putting a hand on his arm.

"Only—"

Atkins shrugged it off, rounding on her.

"Where the fuck were you?" he spat at her. Shocked at his own vehemence and anger, he watched Nellie open her mouth to say something, but he wasn't listening. He didn't want to listen. He knew it wasn't her fault. But he couldn't stop himself. As if Porgy's pointless, stupid death had given him permission, all the pain and self-doubt he had kept bottled up over William, over Flora, welled up in a way he hadn't felt since Ketch died. Atkins' brutal words had opened a sluice gate, and the rage and pain poured out in a torrent. "I told you to stay where you were. If you'd stayed at the top of the crater, like I said, like I ordered you to, we wouldn't be in this bloody mess and Porgy wouldn't be dead! But oh, no, Miss bloody high-and-mighty knew better. This is all your fucking fault!"

The tank crew gathered protectively behind Nellie, and Jack stepped up to Atkins.

"Are you looking for trouble, chum?"

"Jack, Only. Stop it," said Nellie as the men glowered at each other. "I have four brothers. I can fight my own battles, Jack. I don't need you to do it for me."

Atkins balled his hands into fists. He didn't care. He deserved it. He would take anything the burly tanker dished out; after all, he thought to himself bitterly, wasn't he the penitent Fusilier?

"Come on, then," he said.

The longed-for blow never landed. Everson stepped between them.

"That's enough," he said. "I've already had one mutiny. I won't have another. Is that clear?"

Jack lowered his fists and allowed Nellie to escort him back to the others, berating him as they went and giving his arm a solid punch.

Atkins continued to glare at the gunner's broad back.

"Is that clear?" repeated Everson.

"Sir," said Atkins, grudgingly, his hands relaxing.

EVERSON BREATHED A sigh of relief and gestured Gutsy over.

"Blood, take Lance Corporal Atkins over there, calm him down. Otterthwaite, get Hopkiss' identity disc and divide his ammunition and food. Then we need to organise a burial party."

Everson noticed the tank crew in a brief huddle. They pushed Jack from the scrum towards him. The gunner looked awkward and embarrassed.

"We don't think it's a good idea to bury them, sir. We should burn them."

"Burn them?"

"It's just that the Sub—Lieutenant Mathers, sir—"

"I thought you said he was dead?"

"He was, sir."

"Was?"

"Some sort of fungus reanimated his body, sir."

Everson pinched the bridge of his nose and sighed. Was nothing ever straightforward in this place?

"And where is Mathers now?" he asked wearily.

"Sucked into an underground river, sir."

"Well then, problem solved. Private, we haven't the time to cut down wood and build a pyre to burn them. We bury them and move on."

Jack shuffled, unsure.

"That's an order, Private."

"I DON'T LIKE any of this, Corp," said Tonkins, as he stood by the fresh shallow grave with his entrenching tool. "I wish I was back in the dugout, making repairs."

"Well, lad," said Riley, stood by another, ready to dispense his customary wisdom. He really wished he had a pipe to draw on. These things always sounded better when punctuated by puffs of shag and wreathed in a fog of fragrant smoke, but needs must. "It's like my old father always said: 'Hope for the best, expect the worst and take what comes.' After all, I put in for extra staff in my unit and Battalion sent me you. And look how that's turned out!" he said, slapping Tonkins heartily on the back.

Tonkins smiled broadly, nodded with relief, paused as a penny dropped and then frowned. By then, Corporal Riley was already halfway across the glade.

AFTER THE PADRE led a brief funeral service for Hopkiss and Jenkins, Everson called Atkins and Riley together, along with Nellie who, although he didn't like it, seemed to speak for the crew of the *Ivanhoe*.

Hopkiss' death had hit the Black Hand Gang hard, Atkins most of all. Everson needed something to keep them occupied other than mere survival.

As he waited for them to arrive, he fished in his tunic pocket and retrieved the scrap of bloodstained khaki serge cloth, and the Pennine Fusiliers button that had once belonged to Jeffries. He played it through his fingers, rubbing a thumb idly over the raised Fusilier badge cast on it as he pondered. With his petrol-fruit-heightened senses, Mathers had been able to divine Jeffries by some sort of psychometry. He had said Jeffries' trail led into the crater. And here they were. If so, what did that make this, some kind of talisman, some sort of fetish? Did that mean it had some kind of eldritch connection with Jeffries? He shuddered and found himself stuffing the button away in his pocket again, as if to be rid of it, or at least put it out of sight.

"We need to decide our next move," he said as the others turned up. "It's clear we have several objectives. One, to find Private Perkins. Two, to see if we can pick up Jeffries' trail."

Nellie spoke up. "Napoo believes Alfie has been taken by Urmen."

Hesitantly, Atkins chipped in, "If we're looking for Urmen, sir, there was the tower we saw, towards the centre of the crater. That looked man-made. It should be easy enough to find."

Everson nodded, relieved that Atkins was engaged. "It's a start," he said.

Corporal Riley nodded in agreement. "Don't like leaving a man behind, if I can help it," he said.

Twenty minutes later, they moved off, heading for the centre of the crater and the tower.

TULLIVER SAW THE remnants of the blazing kite balloon crash slowly into the treetops, then lost sight of it as the bus continued to turn into its climbing spiral. There was nothing he could do for them. He silently wished them luck, pulled back on the stick's spade handle, hauled the nose up and raced after the Hun.

The Strutter was no real match for the Albatros as it was, but now Werner had the advantage of height and extra speed. And he used it.

The Albatros was now diving steeply on them from above. He would wait until he was almost on top of them before he opened fire. Tulliver had only moments to act.

He slide-slipped and plunged through an indolent cumulus as the mountainous cloud drifted by. The bright blue of the sky faded, and he found himself enveloped by a diffuse grey space. He kept his rudder as level as he could, or thought he had. He felt the negative plate at his feet slide across the cockpit. He was drifting, banking. Straighten up. Straighten up. The fog thinned to a mist and, through that, the ground gradually resolved itself.

He'd lost sight of the Albatros. Tulliver pulled up, climbing parallel to the great shifting white slopes of the cloud, the Strutter's shadow rippling over its bright surface.

The Albatros burst out of a cleft between two cloudy peaks above and he climbed after it, contour-chasing though the misty canyons of a morphing landscape, landing wheels scudding along their insubstantial surface, leaving whorls of mist in their wake.

He's leading me on a wild goose chase, thought Tulliver, as the Albatros stayed tantalisingly out of reach above.

They left the cloud behind as they continued to climb in a spiral. His ears crackled as the pressure changed, and the air got colder with the altitude. The sharp bite of the wind whistling through the wires was clean and exhilarating, at least to begin with. At this height, and at speeds of eighty to ninety miles an hour, the cold started to numb his extremities. Chances were his machine gun would freeze up, too, not that he had much ammo left. Still, he climbed hard on the Hun's heels. Now, if he could just settle the bastard in his gunsight.

There was a brief burst of tracer bullets across his top plane. Werner roared overhead, and waggled his wings once—twice. When he came round again, he was pointing down insistently.

Tulliver banked and chanced a look. Eleven thousand feet below, crisscrossing the landscape, were vast intersecting lines, scoring the landscape. He had seen a few of them in reverse on the negative plate down by his feet, but they didn't do the scale or the number justice.

Helped by the petrol fruit fumes from the engine, they were even harder to miss. The lines, however, weren't continuous. They were broken and faint in places, sometimes marked only by a slight change of colour or thickness of vegetation, sometimes vanishing under forests or hills and valleys, reappearing fractured, miles away, half-hidden but concomitant. They seemed to run for miles, disappearing off towards the horizon until they were lost in the haze of aerial perspective. On the ground, they would have been invisible, but Tulliver knew that the new aerial photography could reveal geological features that had long lain undiscovered. What they could be, he had no idea. Were they evidence of ancient earthworks or geological processes?

There did seem to be unpleasant associations with Jeffries' perverse appropriation of artillery to plot a pentagram on the landscape. Was this a pattern, too? There looked to be a geometric aspect to it all. Was this, as the Zohtakarrii claimed, proof of their world's creation? Were these the strands of the world as woven by GarSuleth for his children? From their reaction to the plates, they certainly thought so.

But the sheer scale of it. It beggared belief.

As he and Werner circled each other, it was clear now that the Strip in the crater was part of it, too, an exposed part of a line.

This was what he had glimpsed before. This was what Werner had tried to tell him about. There was more to this world than met the eye, the German had said. Tulliver had thought it mere hyperbole at the time.

Werner hadn't been trying to shoot him down at all. He'd lured him up here to show him, to let him see for himself, in order to corroborate it.

He turned to Hepton. Hepton had to see it, too. He couldn't fail to. But the kinematographer was sat huddled in the observer's cockpit, shivering, his hands cupped round his mouth, trying to blow on them to warm them. Tulliver pointed down, but Hepton wasn't interested.

Out of the corner of his eyes, Tulliver thought some of the lines shimmered. He couldn't be sure. Frustrated, he lifted his fouled goggles and looked again.

No, there it was. With his fuel-sharpened acuity, he could see an ephemeral energy flowing along the lines like water, towards intersections, building in intensity until a vast spastic column of lightning blasted briefly up into the sky. Across the planet's surface, lightning bolts jagged up into the atmosphere in an inverted lightning storm, with a noise like an artillery barrage.

The Strutter's rigging wires began to hum and sparks started arcing from one to another.

That wasn't good.

Then, with a roar like Wotan's furnace, a tremendous column of brilliant white lightning punched up from the ground into the sky between the Strutter and the Albatros, in a searing blast of heat and noise. It filled Tulliver's world, obliterating everything, leaving his ears ringing and his eyes blinded.

The concussive shockwave smashed into the fragile machines of wood and wire and fabric and sent them spinning out of control.

They were going down.

CHAPTER SIXTEEN
"Each Flash and Spouting Crash..."

TOSSED ABOUT BY the repercussing air, deafened and blinded by the brilliant flash of the blast, Tulliver struggled with the controls. It seemed a hopeless task. He could hear Hepton screaming incoherently behind him.

Dragged by the traction of the engine and the weight of its nose, the Sopwith fell from the sky. The struts groaned. The wires shrieked. Loose cotton drummed. Violent vibrations threatened to shake the bus apart.

Dear God, the engine was still going. He'd rip the bloody wings off at this speed. Hampered by a fog of afterimages, he groped around the dashboard and cut off the engine.

As his vision cleared, Tulliver was terrified to see the ground all around him, spinning like a dervish. He had to pull out of the spin; it was death if he didn't. He played the rudder bar with his feet and gradually brought the spin under control, praying the bus would hold together a little longer. He pulled back on the stick. The vibrations eased and the ground began slipping away beneath him; a flash of horizon and then everything was sky. He was out of the dive and gliding, several hundred feet up.

It was quiet without the engine. His hearing returning, even above the persistent ringing, he could hear the distant crumps as, far off, bolts of energy continued to strike skyward. Trembling and nauseous, he started the engine again and gripped the stick tightly in an effort to stop his hands shaking, biting the inside of his cheeks hard enough to draw blood in order to stop himself sobbing with relief. Not trusting himself or his bus to do anything else, he flew level for a while, to get his bearings.

Searching the landscape for the crater, he saw a telltale trail of smoke hanging in the sky and caught sight of Werner's Albatros spiralling down at the bottom of it.

He pushed the stick forward and dived after it, following it down; there was nothing else he could do but bear witness. It looked as if Werner had been trying to head back to the Zohtakarrii edifice, but lost control. Tulliver watched as his machine plummeted into the crater. Whipperwills snapped around it as it hit the tree tops. The Albatros stood proud on its nose for a moment before toppling over on its back. The canopy gave way beneath it, breaking its wings as it swallowed the machine in fits and starts, sucking it down out of sight beneath the waving boughs.

Tulliver felt a twinge of regret as the machine disappeared. Werner hadn't been a bad man, just trying to do his best with what he had. Tulliver suspected that under different circumstances, they might even have been friends.

As the terror drained from him, an almost divine elation at his survival replaced it. Had he not been flying at such an altitude, he would surely have crashed. Werner had been damned unlucky.

What was causing those vast electrical discharges, he couldn't say, but flying in these conditions was asking for trouble. Still shaking, he flew over the crater, the whipperwills snapping like ineffectual Archie as he looked for somewhere he might put down. He would have preferred landing outside the crater, but he didn't want his bus to fall into the clutches of the Zohtakarrii again.

He noticed the spindly tower poking through the tree canopy, swung round it and turned towards the Strip. After what Tulliver had just witnessed, it wasn't the best place to land, but it was the only place. Vegetation was thinner there. There were fewer whipperwills as well, and he couldn't yet see any build-up of energy along it.

Loath as he was to admit it, he would be glad to have his feet on solid ground again.

THE DIFFUSE FLASHES that lit the sky, and the loud but distant reports, startled the Fusiliers at first.

"Christ, they put the wind up me! For a moment it sounded like a barrage going off," muttered Mercy.

"Must be a lightning storm," said Gazette glancing up, unconcerned. "Good job we're in this crump 'ole of a place, if you ask me."

"It is the time of the lightning trees," growled Napoo. "It will pass."

They heard the putter of an engine and caught sight of the Sopwith as it flew low overhead.

The sight of the red, white and blue roundels cheered them, and several waved, glad to see it.

Everson was relieved to see Tulliver had survived. As the aeroplane came round again, he pointed in the direction of the minaret and, having seen him, Tulliver waggled its wings in acknowledgment.

*   *   *

THE TANK CREW and the Black Hand Gang still regarded each other with suspicion, neither fully trusting the other after the events at Nazarr.

"Well, they seem a little more normal to me," Gutsy said to Atkins. "Now they haven't been in the tank for a week, and those fumes of theirs have worn off. Maybe we'll get a bit more sense out of them. If you don't keep trying to punch them, that is, you dozy mare."

"Hmm," said Atkins, his mind elsewhere. The fumes had caused many problems, but part of him wished the tankers still suffered from its effects, and then maybe they might tell him if they could still smell the remnants of Flora's perfume on his letter. It was selfish, he knew, but since Porgy's death, it felt like a matter of self-preservation. Since he could no longer smell it, a sense of fatalism settled over him and he fought to shrug it off.

In the background, the star shell flashes of the electrical bolts continued beyond the rim, their thunderous crashes following more quickly in their wake.

EVERSON WAS STIFF and sore from his fall and still reeling from the shock of meeting Rutherford, as he watched the tank crew and Fusiliers anxiously. If he couldn't persuade these two sections to get on, what chance had he with the whole battalion? Maybe he was wrong, trying to hold the whole thing together. Maybe Rutherford was right; he should just let them all go their own ways and seek their own fortunes. He shook his head. Hadn't that been what he'd wanted to do in defying his father and volunteering? And look where that had got him. It might work for some, but for those that did prosper, dozens more would die. No, he had a responsibility to the battalion, the whole battalion. He couldn't afford to doubt that he'd done the right thing, otherwise what was the bloody point? No. He'd chosen his course. Onwards and upwards. There was no looking back now.

THEY HAD TO cross the Strip. Here, the soil was thin and dry, exposing weathered sandstone beneath. Networks of shallow roots laced the ground as plants tried to leech what nutrients they could from the poor shallow soil. Overshadowed by more fecund flora, the pale, hardy scrub clung stubbornly to the niche they had carved for themselves.

Napoo stooped, brushing sand away from the ground where the sandstone had weathered. He grunted, sat back on his haunches and rubbed his stubbly beard, perplexed.

Nellie noticed the Urman's unease and walked over. It was worth taking notice of anything that caused him concern.

"What is it, Napoo?"

In reply, the grizzled Urman swept his hand over the ground, brushing aside the shallow sandy soil to reveal a hard surface underneath.

Nellie's mouth formed a small 'o' of surprise. "Lieutenant! Only! Over here," she called.

Everson came over as she knelt by Napoo. Her forehead knitted to a frown as she swept her hand to and fro, brushing away further sand as she sought to clear more of the surface. She sat back on her heels, looking at the results of their work. A large, perfectly flat, brushed silver metal surface lay before her. 1 Section and the others drifted over to see what they had discovered.

"Well, I'll be damned!" muttered Everson. He looked up, abashed. "Sorry, Padre."

Padre Rand shook his head, dismissing the apology as unnecessary, seeming just as flabbergasted.

"I've seen this before," said Nellie.

"We all have," said Atkins. "We didn't make any sense of it last time, either."

"We haven't," said Reggie. "Where?"

"The canyon," said Nellie, "before the Fractured Plain, when Corporal Atkins came looking for you. Only that one was set in the canyon."

Norman shook his head. "We didn't see it."

"You must have," Nellie insisted. "You couldn't miss it."

Wally shrugged. "My eyes were on the road."

"And I was pounding away at some bastard insect men high up on the—" Norman paused. "The canyon wall you says?" A penny dropped. "Oh."

"Do you think there's a link then between that one and this one?" asked the padre.

Here, Nellie was on less certain ground. "Well, it does seem... odd," she admitted. "Don't you think?"

"Oh, it's that all right," agreed Jack, stamping on it with his hobnails, with a sound of metal on metal. It was solid; there was no hollow note. "But everything about this place is bloody odd."

Almost as a reflex, Atkins swung his right foot, scuffing the hobnails against the metal surface with the memory of sparking clogs on cobbles. He'd done it since he was a child, running through the streets with William, and later with Flora, too. There were no sparks here, though.

Beyond the crater, another bolt of lightning crazed into the sky with a thunderous clap hard on its heels. Whatever it was, it was getting closer.

"Riley, what do you make of this?" Everson asked the signaller.

Riley pushed his cap back on his head, and then rubbed his palms together with relish. "Tonkins, get the listening kit out."

The kit was one of Riley's own devising, based on a captured German Moritz set, used to listen in on British communications. He placed copper plates against the exposed metal and connected the wires to the boxed listening apparatus.

Tonkins put the earphones over his head. After several minutes his eyes narrowed, then slowly widened. He beckoned Riley urgently. "Corp!"

Riley rolled his eyes in exasperation and held his hand out. "Well, hand 'em over, lad." Tonkins gave him the earphones and Riley placed them over his own ears.

"What's going on?" asked Norman as they gathered to watch the sideshow.

"The Iddy Umptys reckon they can hear something," Gazette whispered back.

"What, down there?"

Gazette nodded.

"Jesus!" Norman leapt back as if he'd stepped on a hot plate.

"Relax," said Gazette, unperturbed. "If it's like the one in the canyon, it's built like a brick shithouse."

"Quiet, back there!" hissed Everson.

Turning his attention back to the signalman, Everson looked on in frustration as a similar look of bafflement washed over the corporal's face.

"Well, I'll go to the foot of our stairs!" exclaimed Riley. The NCO pulled the earphones down around his neck and looked up at Everson, baffled. "It's Morse code, sir."

"Morse—"

Riley scowled, held up a finger to shush him, and put the earphones back on.

His wide-eyed gaze met that of Everson's. "It's us, sir," he declared.

Everson was perplexed. "Us?"

"It's young Buckley, sir," said Riley.

Everson let this sink in for a moment. "You mean back at the canyon. How?"

"Same way we eavesdropped on German communications, I expect. Electric induction of some sort. There's a low electric current runs though the earth, a telluric current, you might say, but it should be too weak to transmit the signal this far, unless..." His voice trailed off as he deliberated.

"Unless what?" asked Everson impatiently.

"Unless these two places, this oojah, the strip, and the canyon wall are connected somehow, transmitting the signal like a cable."

Beside him, Tonkins nodded in eager agreement.

"Is that possible?"

Riley raised an eyebrow. "Have you taken a look around, lately, sir?"

"All right, point taken, Corporal," said Everson, taking it in his stride. "Can you send a message back?"

Corporal Riley gave him a black look for even doubting it. He hauled over a kit bag, set up the telegraph apparatus as best as he could and began tapping the Morse key on top of the wooden telegraph box. Then they waited.

"C'mon, Buckley..." muttered Riley, frowning intently as if trying to draw the message through the ground by willpower alone.

There was a tense minute until Riley yelled and punched Tonkins in the arm, before sobering up and reporting po-faced. "Sorry, sir. I mean, message has been received and understood, sir."

Everson was bewildered and surprised, but relieved. "So we have a line of communication."

There was a loud howl of interference. Riley let out a yelp and ripped the earphones from his head. "Jesus, Mary and Joseph!"

A moment later, a magnesium white light flared briefly, lighting up the jungle as another bolt of lightning ripped up into the sky beyond the crater, followed a couple of seconds later by a peal of thunder, causing the men to flinch and duck.

"Right, well, we'll try again after this damn freak storm has passed. Pack up again, Corporal, and prepare to move out."

AS THEY HEADED towards the centre of the crater, Nellie caught up with Atkins and tried to set her stride to his, but he didn't slow his pace and she had to compensate by jogging intermittently to keep up with him. He might not want to talk to her, but she had one or two things to say to him. She glanced back over her shoulder. The tank crew were watching her, though trying not to look as if they were. Sweet, really. She turned her attention back to Atkins.

"How's it feel to be commander of a tank crew, then?" he muttered darkly.

"Don't be like that, Only. They're not bad men. They haven't been themselves; the fumes affected them. You should know that better than most."

"You disobeyed orders. You went looking for him."

"You'd have done the same," she said, scurrying to keep up.

"Yeah, well, I only hope you find him alive, that's all."

The resentment in his voice surprised Nellie, but he had just lost a good mate and she put it down to that. "I'm sorry about Porgy. Edith will be, too. She liked him."

"He isn't the first mate I've lost, and he probably won't be the last," said Atkins.

There was another flash and thunderclap, almost on top of one another. Atkins sighed heavily.

"I feel like my life's not my own anymore," he said. "I've had prophecies thrown at me, deciding my future. I've had that bloody Chatt, Chandar, treating me like some kind of saint for saving its life and telling me I'm something of great significance. Half the men believe me to be some kind of St George, the rest think I'm a glory hound. It feels like everyone else owns a piece of my life but me. Nobody asks what I want."

"It's not just that, though, is it?" said Nellie. "There's something else troubling you."

"It's no business of yours."

"I'm not saying it is. But whatever it is, it's eating you up. It might help to talk to someone."

"You, I suppose?"

"No, but you need to talk to somebody. One of your mates, perhaps."

"No!" he said curtly. Then in a softer, reconciliatory tone, "They wouldn't understand."

"The padre's a good man," Nellie suggested.

"I'll think about it," he said, head down, eyes fixed ahead, drawing the topic to a close. He stomped along in a sullen silence but, she noticed, his pace had slowed to match hers. It was enough.

THE DOMED BUILDING, with its narrowing finger of a tower, dominated the clearing. From within the structure came the sound of chanting.

Lieutenant Everson beckoned the men to remain in the cover of the undergrowth at the clearing's edge. There were sixteen of them, all told, but their ammunition was severely limited. He didn't want to get into a skirmish if he didn't have to.

He ordered Gazette to cover the doors to the building. A little persuasive fire might keep those within from breaking out, if necessary.

But he needed to know with what he was dealing. With another gesture, he ordered Atkins and Gutsy to advance and scout out the building.

Crawling on their bellies, they crossed the open space until they reached the wall of the building. Crouching with their backs to the wall, Atkins beckoned to Gutsy to stay where he was. Keeping close to the wall and below the loopholes, he made a circuit of the dome, checking for other entrances. He made his way round and came to the only entrance they had seen. The wooden doors were shut as he crawled past. The sound of chanting from within rose and fell like a liturgy.

When he got back round to Gutsy, Atkins jerked his thumb up. "Take a dekko through t'loophole."

Gutsy stood cautiously and peered through the hole. "Urmen.

They've got the tanker," he hissed. "He's still alive, but I don't know for how much longer. There's loads of the buggers. Fifty, sixty maybe. Most of 'em had their backs to me, couldn't see much past 'em. Looks like some sort of temple. It's not looking good for Alfie. They had him by some altar thing."

"Bugger," said Atkins. "Stay here. See if you can tell what they're saying."

Atkins headed back to the cover of the undergrowth on his elbows. He slithered down by Everson.

"There's a large mob of Urmen in there, all right, sir. Gutsy—I mean Private Blood—thinks they might be getting ready to sacrifice him. From my experience they have a tendency to do that," he offered, before nodding with respect towards their Urman guide. "Napoo's mob excepted, that is."

Everson chewed his lip, looking at the building, considering his next move. "It's a defensible position."

"Only if they know how to defend it, sir. There's only one way in and out," said Atkins. "Seem to me that we have surprise on our side, and those loopholes can act just as much in our favour as theirs. Depends who gets to use 'em first."

Everson nodded approvingly. "I see your point, Corporal." He patted Atkins on the shoulder as he crawled back to where the rest had laid up.

"Jack and Pot Shot, take the door with me. Gazette, cover us from here. Riley, Tonkins. Miss Abbott, Padre, stay with him."

"What, we don't get to try out the electric lances, sir?" asked Tonkins, disappointment clear on his face.

Everson smiled. "Not now, Private. I can't take the chance." He looked back at Mercy and the tank crew. "The rest of you, fan out and take up positions below the loopholes. Make sure you keep the next man along in sight and on my signal, stand to arms and cover the interior. Fire only on my orders. Napoo, you're with me."

They crept up to the edge of the undergrowth and Lieutenant Everson drew his Webley, its cord lanyard hanging round his neck as he ran across in a stoop to the doors. Napoo followed. He reached the entrance to the building and stood with his back against the wall by the door, and listened for a moment. Inside, the chanting continued unabated. Jack and Pot Shot joined him either side of the door. He watched as the rest of the section and tank crew slipped from the undergrowth to take up their positions at the loopholes. He could hear the familiar but faint jingle and clink of equipment, of men moving and trying to be quiet. He waited for it to stop.

Gazette signalled him from the undergrowth. Everyone was in position.

Everson looked across the doorway at Pot Shot, who nodded his readiness.

He took several deep breaths, steeling himself. He could order the men to do this from the rear, but he was too much the subaltern. He'd always led his men over the top. This time wasn't any different. Neither were the nerves.

NELLIE LAY IN the undergrowth with Gazette and the signallers. Although she had her revolver, Jack's words still reverberated in her head. She checked her First Aid bag again. Field dressings, iodine, and morphine. It took her mind off Alfie, if only for a moment.

She thought she heard something in the jungle behind them. Or rather, she didn't hear anything. The background jungle noise, which seemed so ubiquitous it barely registered at all. She only noticed it once it had stopped. Why had it stopped? She glanced back over her shoulder, eyes and ears straining.

EVERSON BLEW HARD. The shrill pea whistle split the air.

Pot Shot and Jack put their boots to the wooden doors, which crashed open. The large Tommies stood in the doorway, silhouetted in the rectangle of light, before stepping to the side and covering the Urmen with rifle and revolver.

With a rattle of equipment and a cycling of bolts, the men outside stood to, the barrels of their rifles at the loopholes, as they had done hundreds of times before in the trenches, pointing in and covering the Urmen inside.

The chanting churned into a jumble of screams and shouts of anger as the Urmen turned to face the intrusion, raising swords and spears, ready to defend their sacred space.

Lieutenant Everson stood in the doorway. A couple of Mills bombs in this space and the Urmen would be taken care of, he found himself thinking coldly. Instead, he fired his revolver into the roof.

The shouting and screaming died down to a ripple of sobs and muted wailing.

"I want our man and I want him unharmed. Do you understand?" Everson demanded, loudly and slowly. He indicated the loopholes around the circumference of the building and the bristle of rifle barrels and bayonets thrust though them. "We have you covered."

The Urmen muttered darkly, restrained by uncertainty and fear, shooting nervous glances at the gun barrels.

"Where is Private Perkins?" he demanded again.

* * *

THE COMMOTION STARTLED Alfie as much as the Urmen, but when he heard the barked orders and the cycling of Enfield bolts he at least knew what was happening, even if he never expected it. He felt a flood of relief to know that he hadn't been forgotten, and that they had come for him.

"Here, sir," he called over the heads of the Urmen.

Alfie limped towards the lieutenant. The crowd of frightened, angry Urmen parted, allowing him to pass.

Alfie took in the rifle barrels at the loopholes. "I've not been harmed, sir. In fact," he said, "just the opposite." He hobbled forward on his splinted leg. The cheery grin of mustered bravado twisted into a grimace as pain lanced through him.

"Alfie! Thank God!" blurted Jack as he saw his crewmate.

Alfie hadn't parted on the best of terms with his crewmates. The last time he saw them they were so paranoid, they'd forced petrol fruit down his throat to try and make him see things their way. He hadn't expected to see them again, and now that he had, he wasn't sure how he felt about it. Anger, relief, and a bright flare of hope. Nellie. Was Nellie with them?

Everson shot a glance at the gunner over his shoulder and the man clammed up. It looked as if Alfie's answers would have to wait.

"It's all right, sir," said Alfie. He turned to face the Urmen, who were looking from Alfie to Everson in muted awe. "You can put your weapons down," he told them. "I know these men. They are like me."

"Perkins, what's going on here?"

Alfie glanced back at the Urmen. "Long story, sir,"

"Quick précis, then," said Everson, brusquely, eyeing the restive savages.

Alfie raised his eyebrows. "They worship Croatoan, sir," he informed him. "Seem to think he's condemned by that Chatt god to the underworld to be punished. They believe the earthquakes and this storm, something they call Croatoan's Torment, are signs of his hellish punishment, sir."

Everson arched an eyebrow. "All right, Perkins, you've got my attention."

"Apparently it attracted Jeffries' attention too, sir. He's been here."

"Jeffries? How do you know?"

"They knew him. I thought they'd killed him, but now I'm not so sure. They wanted him to communicate with their ancestors, sir, the way they did me."

"Spiritualism, Perkins?" said Everson archly. "I hope you haven't been up to Mathers' tricks."

"No, sir!" Alfie protested. "They wanted me to read them something," said Alfie. "Only they can't read. Forgotten how, I daresay. To them it's like magic. So when I read it, they thought I was channelling the voices of the dead, as it were. I suppose in some way I was."

"Read?" said Everson. "What did they want you to read?"

"A book, sir. They claim their ancestors wrote it, like. And there's something else, sir. This book, if it was written by their ancestors..." he started, indicating the Urmen standing around him. They wouldn't believe his next words. He was not entirely sure he did either. "If that's the case," he said, "the Urmen aren't native to this world. I think their ancestors came from Earth."

He pulled back, steadying himself, studying the officer's face, expecting some shared disbelief, that it came as a big a shock to Everson as it had to him, that there was, in all probability, no way home. That they were marooned here. But the revelation barely seemed to register with the subaltern. Everson's shoulders sagged, and a sigh escaped his lips, as if it was not the bad news he had been expecting.

Alfie looked at him in a disbelief that turned swiftly to anger. He felt the bitter betrayal of the soldier denied the full facts. "You knew!"

OUTSIDE, ANOTHER BOLT of energy crackled skyward with a flash and thunderclap. This time, there were scant seconds between them.

Croatoan's Torment had begun.

CHAPTER SEVENTEEN
"And Assemble the Engine Again... "

TULLIVER PUT THE Sopwith down on the Strip. To avoid any damage from whatever energies ran through the lines, he and Hepton pulled the bus into the lush undergrowth bordering the Strip and camouflaged it with large fronds.

Tulliver pulled off his helmet and goggles and leaned against the wing. The elation of survival was fading. He felt like he was going to vomit. He looked at his hand. It was still trembling, and his legs felt shaky.

Hepton walked round the machine in a fury. "What the bloody hell do you think you're playing at? You nearly got us killed up there. When I see Lieutenant Everson, I'll—"

"Mr Hepton."

"What?"

Tulliver's fist connected with Hepton's jaw, and the kinematographer went sprawling. The immense satisfaction it gave Tulliver far outweighed the pain that now ballooned in his knuckles, but at least his hand wasn't shaking anymore.

"I just saved your life. I won't feel obliged a second time."

Something the size of his leg, with nasty-looking pincers, scuttled towards the prostrate Hepton as he glared back up at him, rubbing his jaw. Tulliver swore under his breath, grabbed the man's arm and yanked him to his feet, while drawing his revolver with the other hand and shooting the thing.

Their eyes met and each could see that the other resented the action. Hepton yanked his arm from Tulliver's hand, straightened his glasses and tugged his officer's tunic down with nary a word of thanks. Tulliver didn't care. He wouldn't have accepted it anyway.

Hepton held his peace, and after retrieving his camera, kit and tripod from the aeroplane, let Tulliver lead the way towards the centre of the crater and the tower he had seen, where he hoped to find Everson.

As they pushed through the undergrowth, Tulliver felt things splinter and crunch beneath his boots. Occasionally there was a squelch or a pop. He didn't look.

They stepped through a curtain of hanging vines, and Tulliver stopped. There, hanging in the trees before him almost vertically, as if it were a carcass in a butcher's shop, was the burnt and broken wreckage of the Albatros. The top wing had been sheared off and Tulliver could see scattered sections higher up in the trees. The tail had been ripped off, and its lower planes hung awkwardly in a tangle of wire and snapped spars. Oil and petrol dripped and pooled on the ground beneath it. The engine casing and fuselage showed signs of recent fire, charring the struts and scorching the fabric. Tulliver ran up to the shattered machine. The engine had been driven back into the fragile space behind and he peered into the impact-crumpled cockpit. It was empty.

Tulliver felt a pang of pity, quickly subsumed by horror. Werner had been closer to the lightning bolt than he had, and now his machine had gone down in flames. The military hierarchy on both sides had decided, in their infinite wisdom, that fliers should be denied parachutes. It would, they thought, lead to cowardice and the abandoning of their machines in the face of the enemy. There were two stark choices faced by pilots in those situations. Jump or burn.

Tulliver, himself, had never been faced with that decision, but he'd seen men who had. He'd watched them slowly burn to death as their machines spiralled laconically to Earth and he'd seen them leap and tumble through the air to escape the ghastly pirouetting pyres that would have consumed them.

Jump or burn.

It looked liked Werner had opted to jump.

"One less Hun, then," said Hepton, appraising the wreckage.

Tulliver's eyes flashed with anger. Hepton avoided his gaze and clamped his mouth shut.

The feeling of the loss surprised Tulliver. He'd barely known Werner, but he had been a fellow pilot more than he had been an enemy. For a brief moment, he'd had someone else who could understand, someone with whom he could have shared his experiences.

The empty chair in the mess, the empty bunk in the hut, were constants in the life of a pilot, it seemed. Before, there would always be replacements. But not here. Now, with Werner's death, he felt the ache of loneliness again.

But Werner had wanted his secret shared, and the mystery of the planet penetrated. Tulliver felt the wrapped negative plate under his arm. He could do that much, at least.

* * *

"YOU KNEW?"

Everson shook his head emphatically. "Suspected," he said, fending off Alfie's accusation. He studied Alfie as the man glared at him. The revelation had obviously come as a shock to Alfie, as it had to him when he found out about the Bleeker Party. The man knew that others from Earth had been stranded here, but this new disclosure was a dark thought to which he had hardly dared give voice.

"For how long?" asked Alfie, aghast.

"Honestly? Not much longer than you," he said, aware of the Urmen's constant scrutiny and that Alfie's own crewmate, Jack, guarded the door. "We'll get your leg looked at." He turned to the door. "Jellicoe, ask Miss Driver to step inside, would you. She has a patient. Order the rest inside, too. Leave two men outside on guard."

"Sir."

Ranaman stepped forward, holding his musket. There was a rattle of rifles from the loopholes as they targeted him.

"No!" said Alfie, hobbling in front of the Urman. "He doesn't know what he's holding."

Ranaman bowed his head and offered the musket to Everson. Looking uncomfortable, Everson took it.

"Tell your people I need them to sit down on the floor," he said. "We won't harm them."

NELLIE ENTERED THE temple, the tank crew and Fusiliers filing in behind her and fanning out around the walls, covering the now seated and kneeling Urmen. The padre helped Riley and Tonkins dump kitbags containing the adapted Chatt weapons and the knapsacks full of Signals equipment against the temple wall. Mercy and Pot Shot remained outside as sentries, along with Napoo, who wasn't happy about entering another clan's sacred space.

Unable to contain herself, Nellie rushed forward. "Alfie!" She honestly didn't know whether to hit Alfie or hug him. Oh, dash it, of course she did. She hugged him, briefly, aware of the eyes upon them, then stepped back and tried to assume some semblance of public propriety, all thought of the troublesome silence outside pushed from her mind.

As if her reaction had given them permission, the tank crew surrounded Alfie and Nellie both, covering up their emotions with hearty slaps and bonhomie.

Alfie met their gaze. Their eyes were free of the black oil-slick glaze of petrol fruit fuel. He looked around at his crewmates, and knew them all. Days without constant exposure to the petrol fruit fumes had restored their natural selves. He breathed a sigh of relief. These were the men he recognised, the men he trained with at Elvedon, the men he fought with in France, the crew of the HMLS *Ivanhoe*. These were the men he was glad to see now, not the paranoids that they had become under the influence of the alien fumes. "Thanks for not giving up on me," he said.

"If we're being honest," said Reggie, taking Alfie's hand in both of his with sincerity and speaking for them all. "We could say the same. We weren't ourselves."

Wally coughed politely, and the rest of the crew began to drift away. Jack put a large hand on Cyril's shoulder and steered him across the temple. "Come on lad, let's give them a minute."

"What for?" he asked.

Jack whispered something in the lad's ear and Cecil blushed fiercely. Alfie and Nellie stood awkwardly for a moment.

Nellie punched his arm. "You idiot," she scolded. "You had us worried half to death!"

"Ow. We have to stop meeting like this," said Alfie, scowling and rubbing his bruised bicep. He took her shoulders in his hands, pushed her to arm's length, cocked his head and looked at her in the dark blue tanker coveralls. She looked more at home in them than she had done in the brown uniform of the FANY.

"There's something different about you," he teased. "New hair style?"

"Oh, you," she said, giving him a playful shove.

"Whoa!" he yelped, pivoting round his splinted leg and overbalancing. She caught his sleeve.

"Better let me have a look at that leg," she said.

ATKINS WATCHED ALFIE and Nellie as she ministered to his injuries, envious of their reunion. Then, unable to look any longer, he turned away, seeing Jack approach. Judging from the tank gunner's bearing, this was trouble.

"Did you hear, Alfie? These savages are descendents of people like us from Earth. Can you believe it, that there were others marooned here before us?"

Atkins looked around at the tank crew. They were looking for reassurance, but the Fusiliers nearby didn't return their looks of confusion. Their glances slipped away. Embarrassed. Guilty. The solidarity of the two sections, which had been fragile at best, began to fail. Whether it was lingering paranoia from the petrol fruit fumes, or justified outrage at being lied to, Atkins wasn't sure.

Norman turned to Atkins, a dangerous edge to his voice. "What, this isn't a surprise to you, either?"

"Not exactly," he mumbled.

"You knew? You fucking *knew*? How long have you known?"

"A few weeks. Since the Nazarrii edifice," said Gutsy.

"But we were there. You kept it secret?"

"You see?" said Pot Shot. "I knew this kind of thing would happen."

Mercy's brow furrowed with annoyance. "Come on, you lot weren't exactly playing with a full deck out there, now were you?"

Norman ignored the barb. "Who the fuck else knows?" he demanded.

"Nobody," said Atkins. "Everson ordered us not to say anything to anybody."

"You're all missing the point," said Wally. "Everson knew, they knew. What else aren't they telling us?"

Everson, noticing the altercation, marched over sharply, his face stern and resolute. "Nothing. I just wanted to avoid exactly this kind of situation, until I was absolutely sure."

The crew of the *Ivanhoe*, subdued by the presence of an officer, were reduced to sullen glares.

"You would have been told," said Everson, "along with everyone else, when the time was right."

"When?" demanded Norman.

Nellie looked over from where she was resplinting Alfie's leg. "For goodness' sake!" she said in exasperation. "You know about it now. This is why Lieutenant Everson is searching for Jeffries, to find a way home. We're all in the same boat, so stop it, all of you."

There was a stunned, shamed silence.

"Miss Abbott," said Everson. "I'd be thankful if you stopped telling my men what to do."

"I'm sorry, is it bad for their morale?" she asked in a scathing tone.

"It's bad for mine."

RANAMAN STEPPED FORWARD, a religious joy flooding his face, to address the Urmen sat before him, like a congregation at a Sunday service, eager to bear witness to the unfolding events. He threw his arms wide and high.

"This is a day long to be remembered; that so many of the sky-being's brethren should appear together at such a time is an omen of great fortune not witnessed in generations. The words of our ancestors are fulfilled before our eyes. Did they not say that at the time of Croatoan's Torment a party would gather here to enter the underworld to abate his suffering? Already one has gone before to confer with the ancestors, those who dwell in the Village of the Dead in the hinterlands of the underworld. They who petition Skarra for mercy and await the day of Croatoan's release, when the Fallen One would be reunited with his broken heart once more. And now, my kin, the time of Croatoan's salvation is here!"

All around him, the Urmen wailed in a ritual response.

Atkins heard the words with something akin to despair, and let out a low moan. He felt the weight of another prediction bearing down. It seemed that the more he struggled towards his goal of returning to Flora, the more the damned skeins of fate drew tighter in around him. Was there no way he could escape them? Besides, they promised only vague generalities, never specifics. Where was the one that could have prevented Porgy's death?

There was another flash. Atkins glanced up out of a loophole. Another discharge. Nearer, this time. He saw the perverse lightning bolt punch up, writhing restlessly into the sky. Then came the *crump* of thunder.

The Urmen flinched as one, and some wailed and ululated, as if in grief.

"It's another—" Atkins groped for the word.

"Telluric discharge," Riley offered.

"—Telluric discharge, sir. Nearer, this time, by the looks of it."

"They are the Anguish of Croatoan as he is punished in the underworld by Skarra on GarSuleth's decree. His cries made manifest," declared Ranaman.

"Tell me what you know of Croatoan," asked Everson.

The chieftain's face beamed with pride as he spoke, white teeth against a tanned weathered skin. "We are the devoted servants of Croatoan. We have kept the faith of our forefathers." He turned and beckoned towards the fractured rock. "Come, I will show you."

Everson's eyes flicked around, "Atkins, with me. Perkins, you'd better come too. The rest of you, stay alert. Keep them covered."

Ranaman led the Tommies to the huge split boulder that dominated the sacred space. Crepuscular fingers of light shone down upon it from the slits up in the tower above. With its blood-coloured rust stains, Atkins could well believe it was the heart of some giant.

"Behold, the Heart of Croatoan. Long has it been in the care of the Ruanach. His heart was broken when he fell and will only be healed when Croatoan is released from his prison in the underworld. And now, with your presence, as foretold by our ancestors, that time is near."

"This temple marks the centre of the crater," said Everson.

"The very spot where Croatoan fell," declared Ranaman catechistically.

Everson stood close to Atkins and Perkins and, leaning in, spoke in a low voice. "This thing is composed of iron. Probably the remains of a meteor that hit the planet hundreds of years ago. It would seem that Chatt and Urman myth has some basis in fact." He looked up into the minaret above. The domed temple, with its thin, tapering minaret, might be a representation of the ancient event, the dome being the impact of the meteor, the minaret its fiery tail.

"Iron?" said Atkins, touching the boulder.

"The reason I suspect Perkins was spared," said Everson. "They mistook the crash of the *Ivanhoe* for another sacred rock falling from the sky." He raised a sardonic eyebrow. "You're the Man in the Moon, Perkins."

"Come," said Ranaman, leading them through the narrow cleft between the two halves of rock, towards the back of the temple. They could have walked round, but there seemed to be some implied ritual in passing between them, a significance of which they were unaware. There, from a niche in the wall, Ranaman retrieved the wooden casket.

"This great magic was left in our keeping also. Through it, our ancestors who sought out Croatoan communicate with us from the Village of the Dead. It has been a long time since our ancestors spoke to us. Then came the sky-being, Jeffries. He said he came from the place of our forefathers in search of Croatoan. He spoke to our ancestors and then passed beyond, following them into the underworld."

As he spoke, Ranaman opened the casket, revealing the leather-bound book. Everson lifted it out of its resting place and set it on a shallow facet of the rock so that it was illuminated by a pool of light from the minaret above. It was definitely older than the Bleeker journal, with heavy binding and thick wrinkled vellum pages.

His anticipation grew as he traced a finger over the Croatoan Sigil, cast in iron embedded on the front. He licked an index finger and proceeded to turn the pages. The book was another journal of sorts. Many early portions were in a script he couldn't read, but one that he recognised.

"It looks like the code in Jeffries' occult journal," said Atkins.

"Hmm," said Everson thoughtfully. Here and there, he recognised the Croatoan symbol again. He felt the hair on the back of his neck stand on end.

Near the beginning, there was a manifest. Those sections he could read spoke of a new Virginia colony and of Croatoan. It seemed that whatever befell the missing colony, stranger and more deadly things had befallen them here.

"So they *did* come from Earth," said Perkins.

"It appears so," said Everson uncomfortably. "They'd gone looking for a new world. It seemed the one that they found wasn't quite what most of them expected."

Other pages spoke volumes, more so because they weren't there. Someone had torn them out. Jeffries again, no doubt. All of which served to convince Everson that he was on the right track. He speculated on what information they might contain. There was no doubt that this book contained a factual account of the colony's day-to-day survival, among other, more esoteric, matters. He would have liked to study it more closely, but Ranaman took the book from him and clutched it to his chest.

As the Urman led them back through the cloven rock, Everson wondered wistfully if the battalion's own War Diary would become such a relic in the future. He had a vision of some other snatched and stranded band of people, some decades or a century hence, arriving on the strange world in strange machines, coming across the Pennine Fusiliers' official account. He imagined them finding the remains of the trenches, reclaimed by the veldt, long overgrown and forgotten. Skeletons occupied the firesteps, standing to for eternity, their khaki uniforms rotting and their bleached bones intimately entwined with wireweed. In his mind's eye, he saw his dugout, half-collapsed and empty, a memorial, like Scott's Antarctic hut, and envisaged the strangers coming across the mildewed and foxed Battalion War Diary and looking at it in wonder and fear. He shook his head and dismissed the maudlin fancy. He didn't want that to become their reality.

TULLIVER CAUGHT GLIMPSES of the tower through the trees before him. The only sound breaking the silence around him was the crack and slap of the undergrowth and Hepton's inveterate cursing as he lumbered along, carrying his bags, boxes and tripod.

He squinted through the thinning canopy overhead. His petrol-fruit-enhanced eyes caught an area of the sky that seemed to shine a little brighter than the rest, as if it had been polished and worn through wear. Another bright flash arced its way into the sky. Interesting. It seemed his heightened senses could pick up a building discharge.

It was followed a few seconds later by a rolling boom, and in the distance, he could hear whoops and howls of alarm. However, around them, but for the persistent creep and creak of the parasitic creepers that pervaded the jungle, they were cocooned in an area of silence.

As they pushed on, Tulliver, curious, exercised his newfound skill, spotting other shiny patches of sky and finding that each built to a lightning bolt. So intent was he on honing this new skill that he stepped out of the undergrowth and almost onto the end of a bayonet, as Mercy and Pot Shot spun round to meet his unexpected arrival with cold steel.

"Halt! Identify yourself. Friend or—fucking hell, sorry, Mr Tulliver, sir!"

Something came crashing through the undergrowth, huffing and snorting. The two Tommies swung their rifles towards the sound.

"Christ, no!" said Tulliver, his hand pushing Mercy's rifle barrel down. "That's Mr Hepton." Then he sniffed and waved his revolver in the general direction of the noise. "Then again, kill him if you want. I shan't bloody blame you."

Hepton stumbled into the clearing and, upon seeing the Fusiliers, proceeded to divest himself of his baggage and equipment, dumping it on the ground at his feet.

"Where the bloody hell is Jenkins? He can carry this stuff now," he said, straightening up, arching his spine and pushing his hands into the small of his back as he recovered his composure.

Mercy and Pot Shot looked at each other.

Hepton stood there, waiting. "Well?"

"Jenkins is dead, sir."

Hepton threw his hands to the heavens and rolled his eyes in exasperation. "Bloody typical!"

"Where's Everson? I've something he needs to see," Tulliver asked, patting the wrapped package under his arm.

"This way, sir," said Mercy, leading him into the temple.

"Are you going to help me?" snapped Hepton at Pot Shot.

"Can't sir," said Pot Shot, straight-faced. "I'm on guard."

Muttering and huffing, Hepton glared darkly after the pilot before shouldering his load, unaware of the gossamer-fine white threads spreading silently through the damp soil and leaf mulch at his feet.

INSIDE THE TEMPLE, Tulliver saw Everson, standing at the centre along with Atkins, a tanker and an Urman, lit by shafts of sunlight converging from slits in the tower above. They served to illuminate two halves of a huge boulder. Around them, a host of Urmen sat or knelt, watching them with rapt attention as if trying to burn the moment into their memories.

The doors of the temple crashed open behind him as an irate Hepton dragged his equipment inside, almost tripping over an Urman, who shuffled out of his way.

"Bloody fuzzy wuzzies!" he muttered.

Tulliver shook his head and ignored him.

The Lieutenant looked up from his rocky lectern. "Tulliver! Thank God. Is your machine safe?"

"As safe as it can be around here," said Tulliver, irritated that Everson's first thought was for his bus.

"What about the Alleyman?"

"Werner?" said Tulliver. "Crashed, but not before he showed me something I think you ought to see. It concerns the wall we found in the canyon. I've reason to believe that it may be part of something much bigger altogether." Tulliver unwrapped his package. "Werner told me he'd seen a pattern etched across the landscape. I think the canyon wall and the crater strip are part of it."

Everson raised an eyebrow. "Interesting. We've managed to send a Morse signal along the Strip back to the canyon earlier. They seem to be made of the same metal."

"Really? Thanks to Hepton, unbelievably, now you can see, too. Werner took this negative plate from thirteen thousand feet. We got the Chatts to mix up some sort of developing fluid."

"It's not perfect. We didn't have anything with which to fix the image," said Hepton. "It's not my fault."

Tulliver passed the negative plate to Everson, who held it up in a shaft of light.

He frowned with concentration as he studied the image.

"What am I looking at?"

Tulliver took him through it, pointing out the tracery of geometric lines across the landscape, clearer for being reversed.

"They look like some kind of roadways across the landscape, or some sort of sacred geometry, perhaps; see how they radiate out from various points," he said.

"Reminds me of Jeffries' pentagram on the Somme, sir," said Atkins, peering at the pattern.

"That occurred to me, too," admitted Tulliver. "It's more than that, Everson. If you are right about the wall and the Strip, it would seem to indicate some sort of superstructure underpinning the landscape. The Chatts believe it to be a kind of geomancy, divine proof that GarSuleth wove this world for them. And another thing, these reverse lightning bolts—"

"Riley calls them telluric discharges," said Everson.

"—these telluric discharges seem to emanate from points where these lines converge and intercept. Here and here, for instance," he said quickly pointing out nodes on the rapidly darkening glass plate. "If you ask me, there's a much bigger mystery at the heart of this than mere Chatt theology. I'd stake my life on it."

"Hmm." Everson nodded thoughtfully. "The Urmen believe these telluric discharges are the agonies of Croatoan, imprisoned and tortured in some Chatt version of Hell."

As they studied the image on the plate, Tulliver felt a faint tingling in his hands. He lifted his arm, inspected his palm, and turned it over. The hairs on the back of his hand stood on end, as if a static charge were building. He looked at the rocks and noticed out of the corner of his eye, in the cleft between them, the same kind of peculiar shine; as if the air had been polished to a high patina and worn thin in the process. He couldn't think of any other way to describe it.

"John," he said in measured tones, "I think you should step away from the boulders."

A faint intermittent buzz started to issue from the two halves.

"He's right, sir, better step back," said Riley, foregoing military conduct and grabbing Everson's braided cuff.

By now the other Urmen were moving back, all except Tarak, who watched the proceedings with growing concern. Ranaman held the metal-clasped book, mesmerised by the sudden activity, as small writhing threads of white-blue energy began to spit between the two halves. As they built in a crescendo of power, crackles of energy leapt from the rock to the walls of the dome like Tesla arcs.

"The Heart of Croatoan begins to beat!" cried Ranaman, his voice filled with wonder and triumph, his hair now billowing out with collected static.

"No!" cried Riley, dropping to the ground. "Get down and for gawd's sake take off yer battle bowlers if yer wearin' 'em!"

Bolts of energy, attracted by Ranaman's proximity, leapt across the space and earthed through him, jerking him like a crazed marionette. He let out a strangled scream that cut off abruptly as the bolt vanished. He dropped to the ground, a broken puppet, as if it had been all that was holding him up. The book skittered between the two halves of rock.

There were moans and screams from the Urmen, who got up and stampeded for the temple doors, knocking the crouching Fusiliers and tankers aside.

Tendrils of blue-white energy spat out from the split rock to lick the inside of the dome before dying down as if someone had turned a dial, leaving one or two stray arcs that still sparked and spat intermittently between the halves.

Everson looked back past Ranaman's body to the rocks. The fallen book lay in the cleft between them.

Everson made to go back and get it, but Perkins grabbed him.

"It's too dangerous, sir."

"We need the book, Private!"

Tarak hesitated for a second, and then bolted past Ranaman's body towards the sacred rocks.

"No, son!" yelled Perkins.

Tarak knelt low by the rocks, stretching his hand out to reach the tome. Fingers flexed as he strained to reach for the book. Small arcs of energy snapped angrily about it, like electric teeth. Undeterred, Tarak edged into the cleft and grasped the book firmly. As he retrieved it, clasping it to his chest, a bolt of energy arced out and struck the book, propelling him back across the chamber.

Perkins began to drag himself on his belly and elbows across the dirt floor towards the Urman.

Then, from outside, the shouts and screams began, accompanied by the sound of rapid rifle fire.

INTERLUDE FOUR

**Letter from Lance Corporal Thomas Atkins
to Flora Mullins**

6ᵗʰ April 1917

My Dearest Flora,

Still no blessed tank. Would you believe it? We did meet up with the RFC chap, though. Not blagged a go in his aeroplane yet, then again, I've been a bit busy. Still, when all is said and done, we had a grand ride in a hot air balloon. You could see for miles. Who says the Army is all hard work and no play?

Having said that, we've come down to earth with a bit of a bump now. The place where we are now is completely overgrown, it's worse than your dad's vegetable patch. I think we might have to do a bit of weeding.

Mind you, we do actually have all the modern conveniences— and your Mama worries about us poor lads at the Front. We have Electricity at the moment. All I need is a smoking jacket and an armchair while I read my book and look at photographs and I'll be right at home. I know my Grandma doesn't hold with it, and I can see why. I very nearly did have a smoking jacket! The Company Quartermaster Sergeant wouldn't have been too happy about that.

*Ever yours
Thomas*

CHAPTER EIGHTEEN
"The Sullen Ghosts of Men..."

ON THE FLOOR of the temple, Alfie shook the prostrate Tarak by the shoulders, as the indoor lightning played over his head. Splayed on his back, Tarak still clutched the book tightly to his chest.

"Lad? Lad!"

The youth groaned.

"He's alive. Nellie. Nellie!"

Nellie came over on all fours, the medical knapsack swinging at her side from one shoulder as she sought to avoid the tendrils of energy that spat from the rocks. Needing to do something, Padre Rand went with her on all fours.

Nellie checked Tarak's pulse and breathing. He was still alive, but unconscious.

She gently prised the book from the lad's grasp, and as she did so, she gasped.

The padre made the sign of the cross. "Dear Lord, the poor man," he said under his breath.

Seared into Tarak's chest, from the iron design on the front of the tome, was the Sigil of Croatoan.

STAYING LOW, TULLIVER scrambled over to the temple wall and, with a wary glance back at the arcing rock, raised his head to look out through a loophole.

The clearing surrounding the temple was white, as if someone had draped a fine muslin sheet over everything. It was like a thick white cobweb. Through it, taut, swollen bulbs had fruited. It seemed as alien to the surrounding vegetation as that did to the flora of Earth, and that, thought Tulliver, was saying something.

The Urmen, fleeing the electrical discharge in the temple, had run straight into the deadly carpet. The fruiting bulbs exploded, enveloping them in yellowish clouds. They coughed and choked, gasping for breath in the noxious plumes, clawing at their throats.

"Christ! Gas! Gas! Gas!" cried Gutsy, peering out of a loophole in the wall.

"It's not gas, it's spores," yelled Nellie.

By now, the Tommies were at the loopholes, peering out as stray bolts of energy crackled out at the wall of the temple around them. They fumbled at their chests for their PH gas hoods, pulled them over their heads and tucked them into their collars. With their circular mica eyepieces and short red rubber non-return valves, they looked as alien as anything else there.

The Urmen of the Ruanach succumbed to the spore clouds and fell to the ground, where the gossamer fine carpet of mycelia advanced inexorably over their bodies, and the spores that they had inhaled sprouted from their mouths and noses, choking them.

The fast-spreading network of living threads made short work of their bodies. It desiccated them before the Tommies' eyes, and the mummified remains split open with dry cracking noises as more fruiting bodies rose from them.

Atkins hurried from one loophole to another. The carpet of threads was creeping towards the temple. "Whatever it is, it's surrounding us," he called out.

"I knew this was a bad place," said Napoo, a bandanna of cloth round his face against the spores.

Everson stood at the temple doors, revolver in hand. "Evans, Jellicoe," he called out. "Fall back! Get inside." Everson turned to the others. "The rest of you, stand to!"

Mercy and Pot Shot hared through the doors, slammed them shut and rested against them with relief.

"One minute it wasn't there, the next it's sprouting up through the ground. What the hell is that?" heaved Mercy through his gas hood.

Pot Shot turned towards him with an exaggerated movement so he could see him though his eyepieces. "Don't you ever get tired of asking that question?"

"Around here?" queried Mercy. "Half the time it's the only sane question worth asking." He arched his back, pushing himself off the door, and ran in a low stoop along behind the rest of the section and the tank crew at the loopholes, stopping only to duck and yelp as a venomous electrical tongue lashed out from the rocks, snapping indolently at the wall above him. He took his place next to them, and Pot Shot appeared by his side.

Outside, drifting in from the jungle, a yellowish spore mist was rising and a vague shadowy shape moved with it, coalescing into a ghost-like grey figure that stepped lethargically from the trees.

"Huns!" yelled Cyril, glancing back into the temple from the loophole. "It's bloody Huns!"

Risking a whiplash of energy, Jack launched himself up to the loophole and peered out across the shrouded clearing. "Huns?" Then he saw. It had been an easy mistake for Cyril to make. Too often, in a pale dawn, they had seen the grey-clad Huns creeping towards them.

This, though, was no Hun. Thin and cadaverous, its skin was grey and sunken, its ill-fitting serge uniform scarcely visible beneath a dusting of fine threads. Wrinkled, puckered growths, like some sort of cankers, distorted the shape of its head and right arm and half its chest. The figure moved clumsily, as if trying to maintain its balance was an effort. This was a misshapen travesty of a man, an obscene mockery of a Tommy.

Nellie recognised the sight, too.

"Mathers!" she cried though her gas hood. "But that's impossible. We saw him swept away."

"It's wearing puttees. It's not an officer," said Atkins, peering out. "That's Talbot, one of the tank salvage party."

"Jeffries has woken the dead to do his bidding!" cried Tonkins.

"Can he really do that? Bring back the dead?" asked Cecil, his voice tremulous with fear.

"It's the kind of diabolical thing he probably would do," said Mercy.

"Well, the last time we saw Talbot, he weren't actually dead," said Gutsy.

"Maybe so, but he doesn't look well," admitted Mercy.

"I'll give you that."

Mercy and Pot Shot fired at him. The bullets tore through Talbot's body, the initial force throwing his shoulder back and twisting him off balance momentarily as he recoiled from the impact, but he remained standing. Motes of grey spore dust swirled in the air around him from the impact.

Mercy looked back over his shoulder. "Well if he wasn't dead then, I'd say he is now."

"No!" came the muffled cry from one of the tankers. "It does no good. You'll just spread the spores. We tried it. You can't bomb them, shoot them, or burn them without spreading spores. There's no way to stop them!"

The gaunt, grey-faced soldier turned towards them and watched implacably.

"He's possessed by the same thing that Mathers was," said Nellie.

From out of the spore mist, other emaciated forms appeared to surround the temple, each one a shambling mockery of a Broughtonthwaite Mate, each one laced with a fine filigree of mycelia and deformed by cankers. It was the rest of Corporal Talbot's salvage party.

"Talbot, stand down!" cried Everson through his gas respirator.

The cadaverous corporal and his grey men stood immobile. From their feet, thin, pernicious threads began to advance across and through the soil, joining with the carpet spreading from the dead Urmen, weaving its way toward the temple.

ATKINS LOOKED ON with revulsion. Since he'd volunteered and been shipped over to France, death was something he'd lived with daily. For Christ's sake, his own pal had just died. On the Somme, you couldn't escape from death and decay; everywhere you looked there were bodies, English, Belgian, German, French. The stench of rotting corpses filled the air, but there was at least some comfort in that. As the old trench song went, '*When you're dead, they stop your pay.*' Dead was dead. But this? This was abominable. It appalled him. The fact that they knew these men repulsed him even more. There was Hume, Owen, Fletcher, Banks, Preston, Mitchell, Walker and Hardiman. It was like some sick joke Jeffries might play, reanimating the dead to serve his own evil ends. In some way he wished it were. But this was just nature, some kind of hellish mould that animated their bodies. It had taken them over, while all the time feeding on their flesh in order to sustain itself, even as it used them to migrate to look for new hosts, new food.

Now it had found them.

STANDING WITH HIS back to the wall, beside a loophole, revolver in hand, Tulliver glimpsed the shine in the centre of the temple again between the rocks. It grew brighter, shining as though the air was threadbare and worn.

"Down!" he warned.

Behind them, the two halves of the meteorite spat out bolts of energy.

"Jesus!" Mercy ducked as another buzzing arc of energy whipped the wall over his head and dragged itself upwards towards the apex of the dome. "Talk about a rock and a hard place—no offence, Padre."

The padre, hunched against the wall, clutching his Bible, shook his gas-hooded head. "None taken."

"By George! It's stopping!" said Reggie, peering through his loophole at the surrounding white carpet.

The creeping deathly white shroud had slowed and petered out six yards from the temple, like melted snow. The grey mould-ridden men waited.

"Why, what's holding it back? They've killed enough Urmen. What are they waiting for?"

Tulliver barked another warning. "Stay down!"

The Tommies hugged the earth as, overhead, bolts whipped and snapped.

"Bloody hell, it's worse than a barrage of whizz-bangs!"

Mercy shrugged. "It's all just stuff in the end," he said as he hunkered down on his haunches, his head under his arms as if he expected a rain of dirt and shrapnel, the default position for a soldier under barrage.

"Bloody good job we aren't wearing our splash masks," said Wally, as an arc of lightning brushed the wall above his head.

Outside, another flash went off. This time it must have been very near. The thunder was almost on top of them. Atkins felt it reverberate through the walls of the temple.

"Jesus, that was close!"

"Quite takes me back to the Somme," bellowed Gazette through his gas hood. "Ah, the good old days!"

Atkins saw the field of fungus convulse and shrivel in the presence of the lightning, and the grey men recoil. He looked at where the carpet of mould stopped, in a circle around the temple. He turned around and glanced at the Heart of Croatoan, the space between the two halves sparking half heartedly, as if the discharge was dissipating.

"It's the telluric energy," he said. "That's what's holding it at bay."

"And if we stay in here, the same energy might kill us," said Everson grimly.

AT THE CANYON, having sent, and received, a message from Lieutenant Everson in the crater, Buckley found himself regarded in a new light. The ability to press some technological advance on this world seemed like a triumph of sorts, as though they had managed to bend this alien nature to their will.

As a reward, Sergeant Dixon had him manning a permanent, if precarious, listening post atop the scree slope at the base of the exposed wall. For a job that required quiet, the last few hours of distant booms from beyond the canyon didn't make his job any easier. They echoed off the canyon's walls, rebounding in a constant barrage of noise and flashes.

Dixon tramped loudly and carelessly up the scree slope, hoping for more news. Buckley frowned at him and held up a finger for quiet. Dixon curled his lip and said nothing, waiting impatiently.

Without warning, Buckley ripped the earphones from his head with a yelp of pain as a high-pitched howl threatened to burst his eardrums.

Arcs of energy began to lash from the metal, rolling over the surface of the wall, spitting and hissing like an angry cat, until they danced and flickered out over the top of the scree slope, sending Dixon tumbling back arse over tit.

Buckley disconnected his equipment, lugged it behind a boulder, and prayed.

A bolt of lightning burst up the wall and exploded through the top of the canyon with a clap that echoed round it for what seemed minutes. It crazed briefly up into the sky, starkly illuminating the canyon, causing the blue-green lichen blisters scattered across the canyon rocks to burst in showers of glutinous acid that hissed as they etched speckled pits into the surrounding rocks.

Dixon looked up at Buckley, apoplectic with rage. "What have you done, lad? What the bloody hell have you done?"

"It wasn't me, Sarn't," said Buckley, looking down at the sergeant in alarm. "It wasn't me."

THEY HAD TO leave the temple. Atkins watched the telluric energy flicker and spit round the walls above them, the arcs becoming weaker and fainter.

"Isn't there any way we can channel this telluric energy, direct it somehow?" he asked.

"I don't see how," said Mercy. "Even if we could get near the rocks, how do we move them?"

"We don't even know what generates it," said Pot Shot.

"Oh, that'll be you and your books again, will it?" snapped Mercy.

"This isn't getting us anywhere," Nellie snapped at them.

Tonkins said something, but the thick flannel of his gas hood muffled it. Riley jabbed his elbow into Tonkin's ribs. "Speak up, lad. They didn't hear you through your gas hood."

Awkwardly, Tonkins raised his hand, cleared his throat. "It's only electricity," he said, emboldened by Riley's encouragement.

Fifteen pairs of blank mica eyes turned to stare at him. Their unblinking glares unnerved him until Riley urged him on, kicking his foot. "We—we don't need the rock for that," he added quietly.

Everson clapped his hands and pointed at the signalmen. "You're right, Private. Riley. Tonkins. You wanted to test those electric lances in the field. Now's your chance."

"Well done, lad," muttered Riley with pride.

"They will work, won't they?" asked Tonkins.

"Our bits I'm sure about," said Riley shrugging heavily for effect to compensate for his gas hood as he dragged the kitbags towards them. "The Chatt stuff, not so much."

They pulled the two jerry-rigged Chatt backpacks from the kitbags, along with the electric lances attached to them by insulated cable.

"You can't be serious!" said Hepton. "You're putting our lives in the hands of a pair of Iddy Umpties?"

Everson turned on his heels. Even through his gas mask, his tone was hard. "Mr Hepton. Entire divisions have often depended on Signals. The lives of every member of this battalion have depended on Signals. Their work, under dangerous conditions, has saved countless lives, so if you have any complaints I suggest you keep them to yourself, if you get *that* message."

Tonkins ran a hand over the smooth clay battery backpack, checking for damage.

"You ready?" asked Riley, setting his pack between his legs and gripping it with his knees.

Tonkins nodded and did the same.

"Good lad."

They began cranking the magneto telephone crank handles set in the back; the clay battery packs whirred as the charges began to build.

"How long?" asked Everson.

"We're going as fast as we can, sir," said Riley, frantically turning the small crank handle. "Some Chatts generate a natural bioelectrical charge that they can store. We have to do it manually."

Atkins peered out of the loophole and watched as the Urmen bodies beyond desiccated further, crumbling to dust before his eyes.

Outside, the telluric discharges no longer preventing their advance, the grey men shuffled closer, dragging swathes of white filaments along with them as they moved. They stopped at the boundary where the mycelia had stopped, unable or unwilling to advance further. The inert carpet of fungus at their feet began to grow once again, its mycelia threading its way towards the temple.

"It looks like we're out of time!" said Atkins.

"Tulliver, anything?" asked Everson.

Tulliver glanced out of the corner of his eye at the boulders. He shook his head. "Nothing."

Without the telluric discharge from the meteor to hold it in check, the web of fungus continued its relentless advance towards the temple.

"Whenever you're ready, Corporal," said Everson impatiently, as he watched Riley.

The fevered whirr of the magnetos filled the air with an insect buzz as the two men wound the handles for all they were worth. Tonkins resorted to short bursts of frenzied turning, stopping once in a while for a few seconds to catch his breath.

"That should be enough," said Riley, standing up and trying to shake some life into his cramped hand. Beside him, Tonkins eased himself up onto unsteady legs, like a newborn foal.

"Right," said Riley, picking up the attached electric lances. "I'm going to need four volunteers, two to fire and two to wind the crank handle and recharge the battery. It's a bit like a Flammenwerfer, you see, where you have to keep pumping."

Everson flicked out a finger. "Atkins, Evans, Tonkins, Blood."

Mercy and Gutsy shouldered their rifles and fell in by the signalmen, taking Atkins' and Tonkins' knapsacks for them.

Riley lifted a clay backpack and slipped the webbing straps over Atkins' shoulders, and helped Tonkins follow suit. Atkins hefted the unfamiliar lance, connected by cable to the backpack.

"Atkins, Evans, I want you at the van," said Everson. "Tonkins, Blood, you'll have to bring up the rear."

Both men nodded with slow exaggerated movements from under their gas hoods to show they understood.

Nellie wrapped bandages round the face of the young injured Urman to protect him from the spores. She called to the Urman guide huddling sullenly against the wall. "Napoo," she asked. "Can you help the padre carry this young lad?"

"His name's Tarak," said Alfie, through his gas hood.

Napoo, seeing the brand burn on Tarak's chest, shook his head and backed away.

"Napoo, it's not his fault. It was an accident."

"He is cursed!"

"He will be if we don't help him!"

Nellie gave the book she had prised from Tarak to Everson, who told Mercy to pack it in his knapsack.

The padre and a reluctant Napoo lifted the now semi-conscious Tarak between them.

Either side of the temple door, the tank crew and the Black Hand Gang readied themselves.

"Walk and keep walking." said Everson. "Stay close, don't get separated. Hold your fire. Don't shoot at them, don't use bombs."

Mercy stood by the doors with Atkins.

"Check you can turn the crank handle," said Riley. "Never really tried it in battlefield conditions."

Mercy glanced around in his hood, and Atkins smirked under his. He could tell Mercy was embarrassed. He gave the handle a tentative crank.

"You'll have to do it faster than that!" scolded Riley.

There was a peculiar hacking from under Pot Shot's gas hood. He was laughing. "It's what your right arm's for!"

TULLIVER PULLED OPEN the temple doors. The sky outside, just beyond the crater, had worn through and seemed almost black. If he shifted his eyes, its normal colour reasserted itself, as if some after-image danced in the corner of his vision. "Wait!" he called out.

A tremendous flash of light and a deep sonorous boom that he could feel in his bones drowned out any response. It set off a frenzy of whipperwills somewhere overhead as a concussive blast of wind swept over the jungle.

Before them, the advancing carpet quivered and almost seemed to ebb, and the grey mould-ridden cadavers cowered from the harsh flash.

As the skyward bolt dispelled, the fungal carpet was briefly dormant.

"Now!" commanded Everson.

Atkins stepped from the temple and aimed the electric lance at the edge of the fungus now covering the clearing. He squeezed the Chatt trigger pads and felt the lance kick and jerk in his hand, as the untamed bolt of lightning bucked and writhed, vaporising a patch of fungus. Fruiting pods had no chance to spore and surrounding mycelia shrivelled. He soon found that by varying the pressure on the trigger pads, he could vary the strength of the electric bolt.

"It's working!" yelled Mercy into his ear.

The Talbot-thing waved a hand and the clearing began to blossom with more swelling fruit pods.

Atkins fired again, moving forwards to clear a path out towards the surrounding jungle, sweeping the lance from side to side like a Flammenwerfer.

Following them, the rest of the party edged nervously along a narrow causeway of cleared ground through the deadly garden. Bringing up the rear, Gutsy turned the crank handle as Tonkins' bolts licked away at the ground, repelling the fungus threads trying to close in behind them, lapping at their feet like a rising tide, cutting off their path back to the temple.

"Keep cranking!" yelled Atkins to Mercy over his shoulder.

The grey fungus-possessed corpses kept their distance. The electric lance wasn't a useful long-range weapon, but it was enough to keep them at bay.

The tight knit group shuffled forward behind Atkins as he cleared a path, edging past the Urmen bodies smothered by the thick blanket of mycelia, like the cobweb-cocooned bodies of flies in a spider's web.

But the time between recharges was getting longer, and the strength of the electric bolts weaker. Gutsy and Mercy were tiring at their crank handles, leaving the Tommies vulnerable. Everson ordered Pot Shot and Gazette to take over the cranking.

With a fresh charge, Atkins' lance spat another convulsive stream of electricity into the growing fungal mass as the Talbot-thing watched impassively, out of range.

Tulliver stumbled, and several hands caught him up before he fell. "Wait!" he cried.

Another telluric discharge, somewhere within the crater this time, ripped up into the sky with a blinding flash and a concussive wave of thunder that Atkins felt roll through him.

Around them, the fungal mat convulsed and the advancing mycelia shrank back involuntarily.

Atkins pressed home their advantage, white bolts of energy carving a path through to the forest. From there, with Pot Shot behind him cranking the magneto handle, he covered the rest as they made it to the comparative safety of the tree line; the padre and Napoo helping the semi-conscious Tarak, Alfie hobbling along, aided by Nellie, followed by Jack and the tank crew; Cecil, Norman, Reggie and Wally, leaving Hepton to struggle alone, weighed down by his equipment. Mercy and Gutsy came next with Riley, who kept his eyes nervously on the backpacks. Everson followed them in and Gazette and Tonkins brought up the rear.

Even here, gauzy curtains of fungal threads hung from the trees, but they were thinner, as though the fungus had been conserving its energy for its assault.

"More spore pods," called Cecil as huge great plum-pudding-sized balls swelled in the fungus-covered undergrowth nearby. Atkins turned and swept a jagging electric bolt across them.

"It's at times like this I really wish we had the *Ivanhoe*!" cursed Alfie.

"I agree. But it's out of fuel and ditched," said Reggie.

"Fuel?" said Pot Shot. "I saw a stack of fuel drums go over the side of the crater during the Zohtakarrii attack. Rolled right over the edge, they did."

"Why the bloody hell didn't you tell us before?" asked Norman, aggrieved.

"I had other things on my bloody mind, all right?"

Atkins squeezed the trigger pads of his lance. The lance tip fizzled. "Pot Shot, stop gossiping and get cranking."

"You know I've already got a wife, don't you, Only?" he sniped as he set about the magneto handle with a will.

They advanced through the jungle. Shrouds of fungus hung from the boughs above them, where more fruit pods began to balloon.

"Overhead, Atkins," cautioned Everson.

"I'm on it, sir." Atkins brought his lance up. Behind him, Pot Shot's handle turning began to slow and he stopped again, shaking his wrist to try to bring some life back into it.

Jack pushed Cecil forward. "Take over, lad; give the mud-slogger a break."

Cecil stepped past Pot Shot, who nodded his thanks, and the young gunner whizzed the handle round. Hearing the hum build, Atkins held the lance firmly, squeezed the trigger pad, and played the arc of electric energy across the trees. Super-heated instantly to high temperatures, wood and sap exploded above them like Woolly Bears, even as the gossamer veils and fruit pods were vaporised. The Tommies ducked as hard wood shrapnel exploded around them like Whizz Bangs.

"Jesus! Watch it, Only. It's not us you're trying to kill!" yelled Gazette.

"Sorry!"

Atkins looked back and saw that the mycelia had reached the temple; the path by which they had made their escape was lost again under the tide of alien filaments that now covered the entire clearing.

Watching them, the Talbot-thing lifted its feet from the tightly knotted fungus fibres around it and, dragging a train of them behind it, began to lumber after them, the other grey reanimated Fusiliers turning to follow.

"Go on with the others!" Atkins ordered Tonkins, "I'll follow."

Atkins waited. Behind him, Cecil kept cranking the handle, building the charge. "Keep going, Cecil. I want to teach this thing a lesson." The whirring upped its pitch as Cecil redoubled his efforts.

Atkins fired. The lance kicked violently in his hand as a bright bolt of electrical fire snapped out at one of the grey mouldering dead, incinerating the puckered growth on its chest and flinging the creature backwards, where the carpet of corpse-fed filaments cushioned its fall.

The others halted their advance.

From under his hood, Atkins curled his lip with grim satisfaction. "That ought to buy us a minute or two. Come on, Cecil."

As he turned to leave, Atkins heard a whirring.

"Cecil, it's all right, you can stop cranking now."

"But I have," said the young tanker, standing by his side in his coveralls and gas hood.

The whirring noise continued. Was something wrong with the backpack? Atkins twisted his neck in alarm, trying to look over his shoulder for signs of damage, but couldn't see any, and with his gas hood on it was difficult to tell where the sound was coming from.

"Then what the hell is that... noise..." His voice trailed away as he turned.

Hepton stood with his box camera set on its tripod, cranking the handle and panning it across the shroud-covered clearing and its fungus-animated corpses.

Atkins didn't know what was worse, the fate of those Fusiliers or Hepton's exploitation of them. Did the man only have eyes for the main chance? Those were men out there, dead men who deserved better. Perhaps he should have left him to them.

"I can see the caption card now," bellowed Hepton cheerfully from beneath his gas hood. "Attack of the Crater Mass!"

Atkins shook his head in disgust and deliberately barged into the kinematographer with his shoulder as he pushed past, jarring the camera.

"I say, there was no call for that," said Hepton, looking up from the viewfinder. "I'm only doing my job!"

Atkins strode off after the others without looking back. Cecil followed, leaving Hepton alone.

Alarmed, the kinematographer hoiked his tripod and camera box onto his shoulder and hurried after them.

"Wait, don't leave me!"

CHAPTER NINETEEN

"What Dead Are Born..."

RAGGED WHEEZES AND dry gasps filled the air as men collapsed against tree trunks and rocks to catch their breaths; all except Napoo, who looked at the rest of them impatiently, as if they were dawdling children. Slowed down by Alfie and a dazed Tarak, Everson had let them rest only when he felt they were safe. Although here, safe was always a relative term.

Atkins' lungs burned with effort. Running and breathing in his gas hood, sucking in air through the thick layers of flannel and blowing out through the red rubber-titted non-return valve was hard work at the best of times. Couple that with your limited vision, the stink of the chemical-impregnated cloth and the stifling heat of the whole thing; it was a relief when he dragged the thing from his sweat-drenched head, before shucking off the clay battery backpack and lance.

They might have put some distance between them and the fungus, but neither could he hear the usual sounds of the jungle. They weren't out of the woods yet.

Riley and Tonkins began inspecting the Chatt weapons, fussing over them as if they were old family heirlooms.

"They worked. We did it, Corp. We saw the buggers off!" said Tonkins, flushed and ecstatic.

Riley carried on checking the clay battery backpack. "I don't think so, lad. I think they're just moving at the pace of a Hom Forty, a bit like Buckley. Even he gets there in the end."

Keeping a discreet distance from Atkins, Hepton laid his camera and tripod down carefully, and then ripped his gas hood from his head before doubling over with a hacking cough.

Atkins eyed the man, his resentment smouldering like a moorland peat fire. "I can't tell whether the man's a coward or a cad," he muttered.

"Saved his neck again, eh, Only? You're a better man than me," admitted Gutsy, following his gaze.

717

Atkins felt his cheeks flush with shame and guilt. He knew he wasn't, and if he told Gutsy about Flora, he'd know it, too. He brushed the compliment off. "I don't intend to make a habit of it but, like it or not, he's one of us. Besides—"

"—it was the right thing to do, I know," said Gutsy. "You'll have to watch yourself. You'll put the padre out of a job."

Hepton began patting his pockets, idly at first and then with increasing desperation. "Oh, for fuck's sake," he panted. "I've dropped my gaspers!" He looked around at the disinterested Tommies, a haunted look in his eyes behind his wire-rimmed spectacles. "Has anyone got a fag? Anybody? I'll pay."

If they had any gaspers left, they were keeping them to themselves.

"Bastards," muttered Hepton.

"Only." Mercy nudged Atkins and with a wink, nodded down at his tunic pocket. In it was a packet of Woodbines, crushed but serviceable. "Lifted them from him back in the temple."

Atkins shook his head. However incorrigible Mercy was, he took some small pleasure in Hepton's distress and allowed himself a smirk of satisfaction.

"See," said Gutsy, joining him, "there's hope for you yet." The large man nodded towards Everson. "Eh up, the lieutenant wants you."

Lieutenant Everson was talking to Nellie and Norman from the *Ivanhoe*. He beckoned Atkins across.

"No rest for the wicked," groaned Atkins.

"Or NCOs," grinned Gutsy, tapping the stripe on Atkins' upper arm.

Atkins heaved himself up with a groan and walked over, smartening his tunic as he went.

"Lieutenant Everson, sir," Norman was saying, "me and the lads want to see if we can get the tank running. If there's fuel down here, then we're in with a chance."

"It'd offer us some protection from those things, at least," said Nellie.

"Possibly," said Everson. "Splitting up might make some sense. There's no point staying all together to be all caught in a spore cloud."

Atkins wondered whether it was really the tank or access to the petrol fruit fuel they were more concerned about. They'd become quite animated since they heard about the fuel. "Sir, we're down here looking for Jeffries. We're so close; we can't give up now."

Everson studied him for a moment, and then shook his head. "Yes, but I don't see how, Corporal. There's nothing we can do to those things that won't make the situation worse. I can see no other option other than to fall back. The tank would be useful. It would give us more protection down here."

Atkins knew Everson couldn't afford to lose either the tank or the aeroplane. Both were major advantages in their survival on this world. From what Miss Abbott said, the tank crew had overcome their addiction, and it would take a while for the substance to build up in their bodies again. It was a risk he seemed willing to take, at least in the short term.

Atkins, however, couldn't just cut and run. "But Talbot and his men, sir. Those things, those men, they should be... in their graves. Dead is dead. You're their officer, sir. We can't leave them like that. It isn't proper. It isn't right. It's an abomination worthy of Jeffries himself. We owe it to them to see that they're put to rest. They shouldn't be walking round like some... mouldy Lazarus. It ain't natural. What about their immortal souls?"

Everson looked to the padre. The Chaplain raised his eyebrows, pursed his lips and shook his head. "They didn't say anything about this kind of thing in the seminary, but yes, if these poor souls can be put out of their misery and lifted to their Reward, then I think it behoves us to act, Lieutenant."

Atkins nodded. "It's the right thing to do, sir."

"Atkins, we can't defeat these things, we can't shoot, bomb, or burn them without spreading those spores and facing the same fate ourselves."

"I think I can help," offered Tulliver. "Those things don't react well to those telluric blasts and well, to be brutally honest, John, the petrol fruit fuel has sharpened my vision in some way. I can *see* where those charges will build."

Atkins saw the dark look cross Everson's face. Tulliver waved it away with an air of indifference.

"Yes, yes, I know you don't trust this petrol fruit stuff, but I'm the least of your problems. If I can get to my bus, I can lead you towards the next telluric discharge. This bizarre land storm is practically on top of us, so there should be another one or two from within the crater, somewhere along the Strip, surely? If we can lure them there, they'll be vaporised instantly."

Everson frowned and chewed his bottom lip. "That's a lot of *ifs*, Lieutenant. By all accounts, you barely survived one of those blasts."

Tulliver shrugged his shoulders. "But I did, and I've got the measure of them now; I know what I'm looking for. If we don't move soon, these telluric geysers will pass beyond us and we'll be back to square one. You have to make your mind up."

Everson considered for a moment. "Do it."

Tulliver grinned, and then paused. "I'll need someone to fly with me. I can't start the engine on my own."

"Take the padre, I can't spare anyone else," said Everson.

"Come on, Padre. We'll make an angel out of you yet."

"You may well have your wings, Lieutenant. I'm not quite sure I'm ready for mine yet," said the padre archly.

Tulliver tutted. "And you call yourself a sky pilot."

The tank crew and Nellie nodded and headed off into the jungle with Tarak, who had offered to guide them back to the tank, while Tulliver departed with the padre, leaving Everson, the Black Hand Gang, Riley, Tonkins, Hepton and Napoo to await the coming of the grey men.

Mercy watched the two groups go off.

"So," he said cheerfully. "We're the bait, then."

WITH TARAK'S HELP, the crew of the *Ivanhoe* stuck to the edge of the Strip for as long as possible and avoided the labyrinthine groves. In the distance, through the trees, they heard the muffled roaring of the river as it headed for its underground fall.

Alfie felt an odd mixture of joy and anxiety when they finally came upon the *Ivanhoe*, like meeting an old sweetheart with whom he'd parted awkwardly. He barely remembered the crash over the edge of the crater, and didn't recall Tarak rescuing him at all, but there were many other memories, not all pleasant, that stirred at the sight of the ironclad.

Looking at his crewmates, the old concerns rose unbidden. For almost two weeks they had been without the balm of the sense-altering petrol fruit fumes, and until he saw the tank, he thought he, too, was over them. Now it sat there, he could feel the dull need deep in his bones.

The *Ivanhoe* was quite hidden, at first sight. The ubiquitous pale strangling creepers had overgrown and entangled themselves round the machine. Thin tendrils entwined the great six-pounder guns, quested their way in through the gun slits and loopholes and tried to force themselves between the iron plates.

The lidded eyes of the drivers' visors peered out of the fast-growing foliage as if it were some ancient forest spirit, waiting to be invoked and awoken.

Tarak started to bow before the tank, until Alfie hobbled over on his crutch to stop him, catching his arm under the Urman's armpit.

"No," he said quietly. "We've had quite enough of that."

Tarak stood, confused, but obeyed. He touched the still-livid scar on his chest with bewilderment. "My clan..."

"They were killed," said Alfie softly. "I'm sorry, lad."

Tarak looked at him, uncomprehending. Alfie shuffled uncomfortably, at a loss for something to say.

Nellie interrupted the awkward silence. "Right," she said, rolling up the sleeves of her coveralls and taking charge. "We need to start cutting back this undergrowth and find those fuel drums. I do hope they're intact. Jack?"

"We'll find out," said Jack. "Norman, Cecil, with me. Let's hope that Fusilier was right."

Nellie, Wally and Reggie set to work hacking at the liana with the fire axe from the tank and their entrenching tools, while Tarak set about it with his short sword.

Even as they cut it back, the insidious pale growth sought to regrow. "Watch it," said Wally, ripping a thin stem as it sprouted along the track plates. "I reckon if you stand still long enough it'll have you an' all."

"What the hell is this stuff?" said Reggie as he tore his hand away from a few grasping feelers. "It spreads like some pernicious weed."

"We don't know. It appeared many spira ago," Tarak answered bitterly, punctuating his answer with savage swipes of his sword. "We call it GarSuleth's Curse. Ranaman believes"—Tarak faltered and swallowed—"*believed* that it was sent by GarSuleth in revenge for our faith in Croatan. It chokes the trees we live off. It kills the animals we hunt. It poisons those things that eat it. It is of no use, yet it spreads like a plague and nothing is able to stop it."

There was a dull metallic rumble as Norman, Jack and Cecil herded five recalcitrant fuel drums towards them.

"We found these caught in the shrubbery," said Jack. "A little dented, but none the worse for wear. A few others were split, worse luck. Still, we have these. We have fuel."

"So the show will go on!" said Norman, clapping his hands together.

Jack and Cecil set about refilling the petrol tanks in the front track horns, either side of the driver's cabin, with the salvaged fuel. Alfie, his splinted leg proving something of a liability in the tank's cramped interior, directed Wally, Norman and Nellie as they set about restoring the compartment and stores to some semblance of order and checking the engine.

They were soon ready to depart. Alfie clambered in through the starboard sponson hatch. Tarak made to follow him, but Alfie held up his palm.

"You can't come with us," he said shaking his head. "There isn't room. You must make your own way now. You saved my life and now I've saved yours and where we're going you can't follow. But thank you for all you have done for me. For us."

The Urman put an arm across the hatchway, blocking his way.

"GarSuleth has killed my Clan, the Ruanach," Tarak said. His eyes narrowed as his voice hardened. "He has snared them and cocooned them in that living cobweb for *food*." He looked down as his hand traced the raw, tender brand on his chest.

A voice called out from inside. "Alfie, get a move on!"

Alfie shook his head and was about to speak, when Jack's great arm brushed Tarak's hand aside. Alfie caught the Urman's eyes. "I'm sorry," he mouthed as Jack pulled the sponson hatch shut. Alfie was quietly grateful that the decision to abandon Tarak had been taken out of his hands. He wasn't sure he'd have been able to go through with it.

He heard the Urman bang on the iron plating. "I have been spared and marked by Croatoan to bring vengeance upon the children of GarSuleth," he declared. "Take me with you."

Alfie closed his ears to the pleading. He was doing the lad a favour. "Cecil, you'll have to be starboard gearsman, I'll tell you what to do," he said quietly.

Cecil's eyes lit up and he looked to Jack. Jack jerked his head. "Go on, lad, do as you're told."

Inside the cramped white compartment of the ironclad, Wally edged forward and took his place in the driver's seat. "When you've got it started, come up and sit with me," he told Nellie as he squeezed past her on the gangway. "I need a co-driver."

"Me?"

"You can drive ambulances, can't you?"

Nellie grinned, despite herself. Driving a tank. Since she had seen one, it was all she had ever wanted to do. She felt the same delicious thrill she'd felt when she rode her first motorcycle.

First, they had to start it.

Norman spat on his hands and grasped the giant starting handle at the rear of the compartment with the others. Norman had never quite accepted her as the others had, and held some deep-seated resentment to her presence. The great Daimler engine coughed and spluttered into life and settled into a steady roar. Nellie clambered forward to join Wally in the drivers' seats and tried to ignore the dried blood on the gangway and walls of the starboard bulkhead.

Wally ran the engine up and signalled the gearsmen at the back.

Norman and Cecil put their tracks into gear.

The crew exchanged wary glances as the fug of the petrol fruit fumes began to fill the compartment. Nellie held her breath for as long as she could, then took a deep breath, followed by a second, more contented one.

LIKE A BLIND and bound Samson, once the source of its power had returned, the *Ivanhoe* roared like a territorial beast, belching smoke from its roof exhaust as its track plates began to move tentatively, slapping the ground. The ironclad gained traction and rumbled forward, ripping itself free of the remaining tangle of undergrowth, shrugging off its now insubstantial chains.

Tarak watched the tank for a moment, touched the brand upon his chest once more in a silent oath, and then, as the iron behemoth moved off, he ran lightly up the back of the port track to crouch behind the raised driver's cab, like a barbarian astride a prehistoric mount.

"THEY'RE COMING!" ATKINS heard Pot Shot's warning shout. "They've bought it, they're following us." His gangly form came racing along the path, his lanky legs dwarfing Gazette's strides as the sniper tried to keep up with him. "And I bloody wish they weren't," he said as he passed Atkins.

"Shut up, you daft 'a'porth. They're just walking mushrooms."

"I hate mushrooms."

Atkins shrugged his shoulders in an attempt to make the electric lance backpack sit on his back more comfortably. It didn't work. Behind him, Mercy wound the crank handle to build the charge. Atkins could feel the whirr of the magneto in his chest as Mercy's efforts pressed it against his back. Atkins hefted the lance in his hands, his fingers fidgeting over the trigger pads. The end of the lance sparked. Mercy patted him on the shoulder. "You're good to go, Only."

The tide of grey filaments crept silently towards them, over the rocks and through the jungle floor detritus.

The grey dead men followed, their halting advance accompanied by the soft puffs of bursting fruit bodies and the muffled falls of creatures as they succumbed to the choking spore clouds, and whose desiccating bodies fed the ineluctable advance.

"Gas hoods!" ordered Atkins, pulling his own down over his head. He was soon cocooned inside the damp, close flannel hood once again, his vision, hearing and breathing impaired, the metallic copper tang of the return valve in his mouth.

He had a moment of doubt as the hooded soldiers with their blank eyes and red proboscises began to stumble forward in their masks. Napoo, bandanna tied over his nose and mouth, fixed him with an accusing glare, and Atkins felt abashed. Perhaps this had been a bad idea. Still, it was too late now. His repugnance for this stuff, and what it had done to decent men, drove him on. And, beyond all of that was the persistent thought of Jeffries, and above it all, Flora.

"We should be able to keep ahead of it," warned Everson, as they moved through the jungle ahead of the slow wave of mycelia as it burrowed through the decomposing humus beneath their feet. "But not so far ahead that we lose them," he reminded them.

"Shouldn't be too hard. They move like they were wading through Somme mud anyway," said Mercy.

Gutsy turned and watched their slow, implacable advance. "Still gives me the willies."

The Fusiliers moved on at a fast walking pace, checking every so often to make sure the things were still following them and that Hepton was still with them, refusing as he did to give up any of his equipment. They needn't have worried.

Atkins caught sight of something out of the corner of his eyes. He couldn't be sure whether it was really there or just a smudge on his mica eyepiece. He stopped and turned his whole head. Something grey slipped between the trees to their left.

"Blood and sand. They're trying to outflank us."

More glimpses of grey to the right.

He listened for the drone of the aeroplane, but it was difficult under the hood. They just had to stay alive until the next telluric discharge occurred. Atkins had eagerly acceded to Tulliver's plan since it meant Jeffries' trail would still be within reach. Now he was beginning to doubt the wisdom of it.

More grey figures appeared to their right and left, and with them came the grey-white carpet, as more fruiting bodies burst around them like a barrage and yellow-white clouds of spore blossomed like subdued trench mortar explosions. The cloud of spores billowed and settled, the turbid mist drifting around their legs in whorls and wakes as they passed.

It was the silence of the advance that unnerved Atkins. It lent an air of unreality to their predicament, as if he were watching it unfold in a picture house. He could almost imagine the melodramatic piano accompaniment.

Atkins heard the crackle and caught a brief flash against the tree trunks as Tonkins fired his electric lance. For a moment, the spore cloud parted and the creeping white carpet was repulsed, as if he had dropped soap into oily water.

He forged on, trying to stay ahead of the rising tide of spore cloud. "Have you charged me?" he bellowed at Mercy.

"What do you think I am?" retorted Mercy with a good-natured bawl. "A Lyon's Tea Room Gladys?" Mercy walked straight into Atkins' back as he came to an abrupt halt. "Oi! Watch it, Only!"

Atkins raised his electric lance. "We've got company."

"Bloody hell, how did they move fast enough to get in front of us?"

"Does it matter? They've got us surrounded."

Ahead of them, two more grey ambulated corpses emerged shambling from the woodland, a carpet of grey filaments laying itself down before them. Even with the cankerous growths and the blighted features, it was with horror and dismay that Atkins recognised one of them and let out a groan.

"Porgy!"

THE STRUTTER ROARED into the air, the landing wheels clipping the tree tops as Tulliver continued to climb. A few whipperwills cracked and snapped after it, but he left them behind as the aeroplane banked away.

Tulliver circled round the crater at a couple of hundred feet, out of range of the whipperwills. He could see the tower of the temple and the cobweb shroud of fungus threads draped over it. He pointed down for the padre to see. It looked like a cobweb-covered bride cake. From the air, the extent of the fungus became clear, draping through the trees. The extent of its growth was far worse than it looked from the ground. He was glad the Fusiliers didn't know. In his head, he was already calling it the Havisham Effect.

In the distance, beyond the crater, great plumes of telluric energy blasted into the sky. He saw the shiny patches in the air, far off, as distant energies built, but nothing over the crater. He circled over the Strip again.

Every now and again, through thinner canopy, he'd catch flashes down below as the Tommies' electric lances flared. At least he knew where they were.

Oil spattered from the engine and built up on his goggles. He pulled them off as he scanned the crater jungle for any sign of imminent telluric build up.

As he banked round again, he saw it, out of the corner of his eye: a patch of air that shimmered as though worn through. It was on the Strip's edge.

ATKINS COULDN'T BRING himself to disassociate the thing before him from his friend. To him, this shambling grotesque was in some way still Porgy, and therein lay the danger.

"Porgy, it's me, Only," he shouted though his gas hood.

"Then do him a favour and fire!" yelled Mercy from behind him as the things that had been Porgy and Jenkins lumbered towards them.

The mould-ridden men showed no sign of recognition. Anything that was Porgy was long gone. The advancing carpet of fungal threads forced Atkins and Mercy back.

EVERSON HEARD THE drone of Tulliver's engine overhead, and could see him circling above through the leaves and waggling his wings. He'd found a telluric build up. If they were to have any chance of defeating these things, of staying alive, they had to follow him.

"That way!" he bellowed though his gas mask. "Atkins, Tonkins, break out, follow Tulliver! We may only have one shot at this."

Atkins tore his attention away from the shambling things that were once Porgy and Jenkins, and joined Tonkins as they concentrated their electric fire. Blue-white bolts danced and flicked across the white-carpeted ground, vaporising a path through the thick fungal shroud that surrounded them.

Behind them, fruiting bodies began to swell as the Talbot-thing and the others followed, now keeping their distance beyond the range of the electric lances, paralleling their advance as they spread out in a skirmish line behind them. Like beaters, thought Everson bitterly.

"There!" said Pot Shot, pointing in the sky, where Tulliver was circling tightly.

The Tommies forged towards the spot beneath him, and broke out of the trees onto the scrub-covered Strip.

As they set foot on open ground, Everson waved the aeroplane away. Tulliver waggled his wings in acknowledgement and side-slipped out of the turn.

"I guess this is the spot, then," said Everson.

From the edge of the wood, the Talbot-thing and its ghastly grey section appeared and staggered silently towards them.

Something in the air changed. Even under his mask, Atkins could feel it. At their feet, the thin rocky mantle began to crack, exposing the metal beneath as the telluric charge began to build.

Napoo, trusting to his nature and innate sense of survival, would not stay. He fled to safer ground beyond the Strip.

The grey-faced Fusiliers shambled towards the small group. The creeping wave of mycelia stopped, its advance stunted by the discharge, but the twisted Tommies kept coming. The fungus that animated them was drawing on more and more of their tissue to fuel itself and the bodies shrivelled with every step as it sought to reach fresher hosts.

"Hold your positions," yelled Everson.

Atkins and his Black Hand Gang shuffled nervously. They'd been here before, repelling German attacks on the trenches; you hold your nerve, try not to funk it. It didn't get any easier.

Small crackles of energy flickered about their feet.

"Hold it."

Hepton danced a jig as ribbons of energy snapped and flared around his boots. "Christ, talk about out of the frying pan and into the fire!" he said. "Are you trying to get us killed?"

"No, just you if we're lucky," muttered Mercy.

Discharges of blue-white energy rolled across the ground, building in strength.

"It's coming!" hollered Riley. "Hold steady, son," he said calmly to a fidgeting Tonkins.

Hepton broke and ran, lugging his tripod, camera and film canisters.

Energy began arcing up from the exposed metal around them, striking out at trees.

"Hold it," Everson called.

The Talbot-thing stopped and the others lurched to a halt alongside it. It wasn't falling for it.

Atkins wasn't going to let this happen. This had been his idea. These things had to die, if only so the men themselves could rest in peace. He pulled off his gas hood and stepped from the defensive ring.

"Atkins, what do you think you're doing!" bellowed Everson.

Atkins ignored him and walked towards the grey men.

"Porgy. Porgy, it's me. Only! You remember me? Porgy!"

The ashen-faced soldier turned its head and stepped towards Atkins, pulling free of the mycelia that wove into the ground around it. The others began doing the same. The fungus, overcome by an imperative for survival, lurched towards him.

As energy began to build beneath his feet, Atkins could feel the thrum of it through his boots. About him, tongues of lightning lashed out at the trees.

The Tommies could hold their position no longer.

"Run!" yelled Everson. They didn't need telling twice. Atkins took one last look at the fungal effigy of Porgy staggering towards him, its grey skin almost shrivelling against his skull as the fungal canker that possessed it sought to extract every morsel of energy from its decaying host.

A huge bolt of telluric energy roared up from the ground, shattering the thin shell of rock over the metal below. The concussive wave threw Atkins and the others off their feet as a blast of heat washed over them. It threw everything into sharp relief, like all the Very lights in the world going off at once.

Atkins turned his head and squinted through his lashes against the light. He saw the silhouettes of fungal Fusiliers caught in the blast, consumed as the huge white beam jagged up into the atmosphere, like some electric beanstalk. Their faint outlines grew fainter and more indistinct against the increasing brightness until there was nothing left but a painful angry white light, spitting and crackling.

Suddenly that, too, was gone.

Ears ringing with the blast, half-blinded by the brilliance, the Tommies staggered to their feet. They wandered round dazed, waiting for their senses to return.

Where the blast had erupted, there was now an exposed circle of metal, one of those nodes Tulliver had talked about, a planetary junction, an intersection of geometric alignments.

Of the animated corpses, there was no sign. They had gone. Beyond the metal, the fungal carpet lay blackened and charred. It crumbled to dust with a soft satisfying crunch beneath the boot.

For minutes afterwards, the decaying afterimages of the men haunted Atkins, but eventually, they faded, too, as the ghosts of the dead ought to.

Atkins blinked away the last of the images and the tears that came with them.

"Goodbye, Porgy."

CHAPTER TWENTY
"Hellfire Corner"

AFTER THE TELLURIC blast, it took a while for Atkins' senses to return. His vision was mottled, and his ears buzzed with phantom swarms. Temporarily deaf and blind, he was not in the best condition to go stumbling round a cruel, capricious jungle. None of them were.

Gutsy, Gazette, Mercy and Pot Shot sat quietly, each lost in his own thoughts, waiting on orders and watching the exposed metal warily, as if no longer trusting the ground they stood on.

At least here, at the seat of the blast, the thunderous flash had panicked the animals into flight. It should be a while before they picked up the courage to return. The Tommies would be safe for the moment.

EVERSON LET EVERYONE take a breather while he took stock and decided on his next course of action. He turned his attention to the book they had taken from the Ruanach temple, as best he could with the fading afterimages obscuring and distorting his vision; the book that had come from Roanoke, all the way from Virginia.

He traced his fingers over the iron sigil of Croatoan on the book's cover. The crater had been caused by a meteor impact, and he had seen the proof for himself in the broken Heart of Croatoan. It had clearly inspired the myths that had been woven into both Chatt and Urman mythology. For all the Urmen's belief in Croatoan, the underworld and some Promethean punishment by a dung-beetle god, he couldn't bring himself to believe it, although some small part of him began to wonder. It was certainly enough to bring Jeffries all this way.

How many other groups of humans had been displaced from Earth? There were stories and legends of mass disappearances throughout history. What if all the Urmen were merely descendants of displaced survivors, subsisting like Adam and Eve cast out of the Garden of Eden? And if they were, what did that say of the Pennines' chances? He coughed and dismissed the thought as best he could. There would be plenty of dark, lonely nights in which to dwell on thoughts of that nature.

He looked around at the jungle-filled crater and idly fingered the scrap of khaki and the Pennine Fusilier button. If he had petrol fruit liquor, could he, too, see Jeffries' trail as Mathers had done? He withdrew his hand quickly, overcome with an irrational fear that Jeffries might somehow sense him through it. If the Chatts were insistent that nothing enters and nothing leaves this place, then returning might be problematic. Then again, so could leaving. They might as well try to find Jeffries' trail while they were down here.

RILEY AND TONKINS wandered idly over the metal, newly exposed by the telluric blast. The storm, or whatever it was, seemed to have passed now, and although the blasts continued, they had rolled into the distance beyond the crater.

Thinking aloud, Riley held forth on various electrical theories, wondering whether he could stabilise such power, to charge not just an electric lance, but also perhaps an electric cannon. Tonkins' only contribution to the discussion was, "I reckon you could have powered all the electric lights in London from that."

Riley mulled that over for a moment, before going to check over the electric lance packs.

HEPTON SAT BY himself, ignored by the others, his hands shaking, two fingers extended by force of habit as if holding a cigarette he wished he had, but didn't. He caught himself doing it and clenched his fist. It still trembled.

TURNING HIS MIND from Porgy, all Atkins could focus on now was Jeffries. Whatever Jeffries was after, whatever he wanted, he had come down here by himself to get it. By himself. Atkins held that thought for a moment and shook his head in disbelief as he recalled the men they'd lost getting this far. Jeffries had done it by himself. Whatever else he hated about Jeffries, the man possessed a self-belief and determination that he found hard not to envy. Whatever it was he was after, Jeffries was a driven man. But now, so was Atkins.

His mind turned to Flora. He would go to hell and back for her. Now it looked very much as if he would have to do just that.

Unfortunately, it meant taking his mates with him.

Talk to someone, Nellie had said. There was no one to whom he could talk. No one that would understand. His mates wouldn't. They thought he was a decent, honest chap. He'd gone out of his way to show that he was, to himself if to no one else, to prove himself penitent.

Silently, he renewed his vow to return home, and thought of those who wouldn't. Jessop, Lucky, Ginger, Nobby, Prof, Chalky, Jenkins, Porgy and, yes, even Ketch; he wanted their deaths to mean something.

He feared Everson might get cold feet. He hadn't come this far to give up now.

He approached Lieutenant Everson. "Sir, we shouldn't stay put too long," he advised, glancing warily at the surrounding scrub. "We're still going after Jeffries, aren't we?"

Everson was leafing through the ironbound tome.

"This mission has been a complete shambles, Atkins," he sighed quietly. "We've made peace with one colony only to start a war with another. Quite frankly, if I go back to the camp empty-handed, I think the men will lynch me."

"It won't come to that, sir. We have our second objective."

"Are the rest of the men up to it?" he said, glancing over to the weary Tommies. It seemed that he had asked much of them, over the past few months. Dare he ask more?

"They will be, sir. The Black Hand Gang hasn't let you down before. If that man knows the way home, I'd follow him into Hell itself."

"Well, it looks as if that's were we're going. But I don't think we need worry. We've been there before. Remember Wipers?"

Atkins shuddered at the memory. "That I do, sir."

THERE WERE ENTRIES in the book that, if they weren't allegorical, very clearly pointed to a gateway, an entrance to the underworld and the Village of the Dead.

They moved off out along the Strip, that the Ruanach clan referred to as the Road of the Dead, heading towards the crater's far wall, every so often marking their route with a chalked 13/PF on a rock or tree trunk, for the *Ivanhoe* to follow.

Wearing the Lightningwerfer, as Mercy had christened the electric lance pack, Atkins took the lead with Mercy as his winder; Everson followed, with Napoo occasionally scouting ahead. Pot Shot and Gazette eyed the jungle either side of the Strip, while Riley and Hepton struggled along like pack mules under knapsacks and kitbags of gear, but at least the going was firm, and Tonkins with the second Lightningwerfer brought up the rear with Gutsy.

Knowing now what was beneath his feet as they walked, Everson thought about the wider context of the mysterious lines on the landscape. He knew there were megalithic roads that scarred the landscape of Britain, but nothing there suggested any kind of giant structure beneath the surface like here. Who built it, and what was it for?

TREES TOWERED HIGH either side of the wide ribbon of scrub, spreading their thin spindly foliage out over the Strip and dappling the scrub beneath with dancing shadows. The tough shallow-rooted plants clung fiercely to the thin soil, reinforcing the image of an ancient, overgrown, long-disused road.

As the crater wall rose up before them, the vegetation became thicker. A grove of gnarled scab trees stood in their way, choked with the pallid creepers that infested the crater.

Mercy and Gutsy whirred away on the magneto handles, making sure that Tonkins' and Atkins' electric lances were fully charged. Atkins would rather have his Enfield in his hand—he trusted it more than this alien device—but knew as long as the magneto didn't wear out and there were hands to wind, he didn't have to worry about ammunition. Here, though, the electric lances came into their own: they spat and burned through the snarl of plants, sending small ugly creatures scurrying for new cover.

As Napoo slashed away at the last of the lianas and vines and they broke through the last of the undergrowth, they saw the far wall of the crater, towering six hundred feet above them. They clambered over moss-covered boulders down into an old stone-strewn dell, where huge buttressing tree-roots supported trees that must have been centuries old. At the base of the crater wall, a vast yawning crack split the rock, its mouth barred by a writhing mass of the pallid creepers that reached out to choke the surrounding vegetation. The size of the cavern mouth dwarfed the Tommies; it could have taken three or four battlepillars abreast.

A single valiant shaft of sunlight shone down through the scab trees behind them, attempting to penetrate the gloom beyond the entrance, but it fell on nothing within that it could illuminate. The light was swallowed whole and snuffed out, engulfed by the immensity of the black void beyond, a void that seemed to brook no examination from without, forcing those who gazed into it to take what lay beyond on faith.

Looking into that black gulf for too long gave Atkins an unsettling sense of unease and nausea. There was nothing within the obsidian darkness on which to focus, and strange unearthly shapes and colours swam in his vision, until he was no longer sure whether they were a trick of the mind or not. It was only when he looked away that reality reasserted itself.

Impressive though the entrance was, it was certainly more natural than their imaginations had led them to expect. Atkins had envisaged demons with flaming swords guarding it, perhaps, or giant lintels carved from the rock face and inscribed with unspeakable glyphs, standing on weathered, ruined Doric columns of great size. Or something darker, exuding great age and malevolence: vast forbidding blackened doors of charred bone, and niches of skulls.

"So that's it?" said Mercy. "The gateway to the underworld? Can't say that I'm impressed. I was expecting something a little more—"

"Fire and brimstone?" suggested Gutsy.

Mercy shrugged. "Well, yes, I suppose. A little less woodland dell, more *Welcome to Hell*, as it were. Although I'm not complaining. To be quite honest, I'm a little glad it ain't."

"Evil has a banality all its own," said Hepton, eyeing the entrance warily. "I wouldn't let your guard down." He made the sign of the cross and, a little self-consciously, Tonkins followed suit.

"Well, we're not getting through that stuff without a little help," said Gutsy, watching the slow-writhing creepers. He had a hand on Little Bertha, but knew it would be of little use against the mass of choking plant tendrils before them.

A bolt of blue-white energy blasted Pot Shot off his feet.

"Another telluric blast," yelped Tonkins.

They dived for cover. Atkins grabbed the dazed Pot Shot by his webbing and hauled him behind a buttress root.

"What hit me?" he asked.

"Lightning," said Atkins, his attention focused on the undergrowth around them. "Lucky for the rest of us you're the tallest. Makes you a natural lightning rod."

"Good job I wasn't wearing me steel helmet then," he said with a dazed smile.

Another blast followed, but it wasn't the thunderous concussive heaven-bound telluric bolt, nor was it the half-expected blast of sulphurous hellfire.

"What the hell is it?" asked Everson, his back to a boulder for cover, as he checked the chambers of his Webley.

Mercy peered over the top of a fallen tree, behind which he'd taken cover.

Another bolt of energy arced out from the undergrowth. It was the writhing, spitting Tesla arc of an electric lance. Another licked out across the open space, scorching the undergrowth in which they'd taken cover.

"Chatts!"

"Blood and sand!" cursed Atkins. "How? I thought they were afraid of this place. What the hell are they doing here?"

"One of their balloons must have come down, like us," said Gutsy.

"Nothing must enter. Nothing must leave," Gazette quoted, laconically. "They've been abandoned. They know they're not

getting out of the crater, so they've got nothing to lose. Makes them dangerous."

Another arc of energy spat across and hit a fallen log, vaporising sap and moisture in an instant and exploding the bole into a thousand fire-hardened shards of wooden shrapnel.

"Christ, you think?" yelped Gutsy, ducking as low as he could.

Gazette settled against a rock, nestled the stock of his Enfield into his shoulder and targeted the shadows in the grove of scab trees to the side of the cavern entrance. He squeezed the trigger.

Another bolt flashed from a different direction.

"How many of them are there?" bawled Pot Shot, pinned down behind a buttress root.

"I can't tell, they're leaping around, keeping us pinned down," replied Gazette.

"Where's Napoo?" asked Everson.

Atkins looked around. The Urman had vanished. Gutsy jerked his head upwards; Napoo was edging round a scab tree, trying to get a better vantage point to spot the Chatts.

Hepton flinched as the brief flash of another electric bolt threw his shaded funk hole into sharp relief.

There was a gunshot and a Chatt fell from its perch, in a tree overlooking their position. Gazette cycled the Enfield's bolt and looked for another target.

There was another gunshot. A Chatt staggered through the undergrowth towards them, its electric battery backpack spitting and fizzing. It stumbled a few steps before the pack emitted a brief whine and exploded, engulfing it in a ball of white heat that left its carapace charred and smouldering as it collapsed.

"That wasn't me," said Gazette.

There was a snap of dry wood underfoot and the shade of a grey ashen-faced man stepped into the dappled shadow of Hell's dell.

"It's another fungus-man," said Hepton, shrinking into the shadows as far as he could.

The figure stepped into the light.

"Fuck me," said Mercy. "It's the Alleyman."

"Werner," muttered Everson.

The German pilot looked the worse for wear. His smart uniform was scorched and his tunic unbuttoned, his face blacked with oil and soot; oil-filmed goggles sat atop his flying helmet and his smart polished boots were now scuffed and dulled by dust and mud.

"We meet again, gentlemen," he called out jovially.

"If you think we're surrendering to you and your Chatts, you have another think coming," called Everson.

"On the contrary," Werner called back.

Another electric white-blue flash arced towards him out of the undergrowth, interrupting him. He flinched and ducked as it earthed yards away from him, blasting a chunk out of a young Japheth tree. The trunk gave way slowly with a creaking tear. Werner began running towards the Tommies. The tree crashed to the ground and Werner flung himself into the dirt. Using the fallen tree as cover, he scrambled over to them before peering back out at the undergrowth where the rest of the Chatts were concealed. When he looked back, it was into the points of several rifles, fixed with bayonets.

Slowly Werner put his pistol down on the ground and raised his hands to shoulder height, not wanting to present more of a target to the remaining Chatts.

"Tulliver said you crashed," said Everson.

"My machine crashed. I survived, which is more than can be said for my uniform," Werner said, indicating his torn and scorched tunic. "My tailor will be furious."

"They were firing at you."

"I knew my alliance with the *insekt menschen* was at an end when I came down in the crater, that I would be outcast and untouchable to them," he said with a shrug. "I no longer have my machine, so I am of no further use to them. They will not let me out of the crater now. They let nothing out unless it is to kill it. They would leave me here to die, and I do not want to die, Lieutenant."

"None of us do," said Everson.

"I am alone," admitted Werner. "You have your battalion. I wish to put aside our enmity. I wish to be... human again."

They ducked as another flurry of electric bolts crackled through the air. The remaining Chatts had moved to cut the Tommies off from the cavern entrance.

Werner snatched up his pistol. Nobody stopped him.

Gazette squeezed off another couple of rounds. Normally, he'd look for a muzzle flash and target that spot, like any good sniper, but here the blue-white brilliance of the electric bolts left irritating afterimages blotting his vision. The Chatts fired and moved, springing across large spaces with inhuman speed, never firing from the same place twice.

"You know what?" said Gutsy, shouting over the miniature thunderstorm that raged briefly around them, "I'm beginning to look back on the days when I could kill Chatts in the hundreds using just a candle with some nostalgia!"

He pulled a safety pin from a Mills bomb and lobbed it into the writhing tangle of creepers that contorted around the cavern entrance. The explosion ripped and shredded it like barbed wire, throwing Chatt limbs up into the air in graceless arcs.

"They will not let us go," said Werner. "Nor can they leave

themselves. They are dead to the colony. All they can do is carry out their overriding chemical decree; nothing must enter, nothing must leave. They will die to fulfil that precept."

"Well I'm sure we can oblige," said Everson through clenched teeth.

"Are you really going to trust a Hun, sir?" asked Mercy, eyeing the German with deep suspicion.

"No, Evans," said Everson firmly. "I'm going to trust a gentleman."

TULLIVER CIRCLED THE crater, looking for signs of another telluric blast, but it seemed that the land storm was moving away.

He hadn't known about Werner's Albatros for long, but the sky seemed an emptier, lonelier place without it. As he spiralled down, he could see a haze of smoke hanging above the Zohtakarrii edifice. One of their balloons still floated above it on a winch line, on watch.

As he flew lower, he turned round and jabbed down with a gloved finger. He wanted the padre to keep a look out for the Fusiliers. Behind his goggles, the padre nodded in acknowledgement.

Tulliver spotted the deflated remains of a Chatt balloon hanging ripped and torn in the boughs of a tree below. Then, out of the corner of his eye, towards the crater wall, he noticed faint patches of air shimmer briefly. They erupted with the brief short crackle of electric lances. It looked like the balloon's passengers had survived.

He flew lower, risking the whipperwills, but they seem to have been shocked into sluggishness by the sheer violence of telluric storm. He flew along the Strip towards the crater wall. There he saw more polished patches of air shine amongst the overgrowth round the mouth of a fissure, birthing more crackling arcs of electric fire. As he circled, Tulliver saw the Fusiliers pinned down by constantly-shifting fire. They couldn't get a fix on their enemies, but he could.

He brought the bus lower and flew along the Strip towards the fissure in the crater wall, waiting for the patches of strange air to appear again.

"Come on, come on," he muttered as the Strutter closed on the crater wall. Areas in the undergrowth began to shine, and he fired. From deep within the undergrowth, there came a brilliant flash and a rising puff of white smoke like a photographer's flash powder.

He pulled on the stick and banked away sharply, climbing away from the looming crater wall.

The padre patted him on the shoulder and pointed down to the Strip. Tulliver followed his finger and then put his thumb up and let out a whoop of triumph.

* * *

BARELY HAD THE roar of Tulliver's Strutter receded when Atkins heard the slow, squeaking creak and rumble of the ironclad as it clattered along the Strip. As it approached, it ground the hardy growth beneath its tracks and ploughed over the shallow-rooted trees that had clung so tenaciously to life; surviving all that the alien world could throw at it, only to be crushed by something not of this world at all. To Atkins, right now, that felt like tit-for-tat.

The roar of the ironclad behemoth dropped to a throaty growl as the tank came to a halt, but it didn't stop completely. One track continued to run, turning the tank until it faced the cavern entrance. Astride the tank's roof, Tarak crouched defiantly behind the driver's cabin, at least until a belch of smoke from the roof exhaust set him coughing. He stepped sprightly onto the starboard sponson and leapt to the ground.

Napoo glared at the scorched brand on Tarak's chest, greeted him with a sullen growl of disapproval and turned away, wanting nothing to do with him. Not that Tarak seemed to care. He only had eyes for the cavern entrance.

"The way to the Village of the Dead," he said, brooding. "My clan passed this way not long since. Soon I will be reunited with them."

Werner witnessed the arrival of the *Ivanhoe* with a face that registered first horror and then incredulity as the land ship hoved into view and clanked to a halt.

"*Mein Gott*, is that what I think it is? I have heard of such a thing, but never have I seen one before. It looks like some kind of primordial beast."

"It is the hell hound of Croatoan," declared Tarak proudly, patting the sponson like the flank of a prized animal.

Looking at the ironclad in the confines of the jungle, Atkins had to agree. It was just as much at home here as on the battlefield of the Somme.

"That's what's going to beat the pants off your boys in the War, Fritz," said Mercy with a sneer.

The starboard six-pounder rose, paused and then fired, the report echoing off the crater side and the shell exploding in the middle of the writhing mass of pale creepers, sending a spume of shredded plant matter into the air.

"Now we'll show those Chatt bastards," said Gutsy gleefully.

In the end, they didn't have to.

As they watched, the Chatts revealed themselves voluntarily, stepping out of their concealment, surprising even Napoo, who had not known where they were. The tank rumbled closer, rolling past the Tommies, who came out from behind the shelter of their buttress roots and logs, falling behind the tank for cover, just in case the Chatts were of a duplicitous bent. Even Hepton managed to unclench himself from the bole under which he had hidden in order to witness the scene.

The Chatts divested themselves of their clay battery backpacks, put down their lances and weapons, and stood immobile before the tank. They performed a sign of reverence towards the *Ivanhoe*, touching the heels of their hand to their foreheads and then to their thorax.

"The Skarra thing still works, then," said Atkins with relief. "I still find it hard to imagine—a dung-beetle god of the underworld. They must think their time has come."

"Felt that way myself, sometimes," said Pot Shot.

Atkins grunted in agreement. They all had, at one time or another. It made the Chatts seem a little more human, albeit not enough for him to feel pity. Right now they were all that stood between him and Jeffries, him and a way home to Flora, for he felt sure that Jeffries had been this way. How could he have resisted?

As the tank brought its guns to bear on the Chatts, they turned and, without looking back, walked on of their own volition and disappeared into the cavern, entering their underworld as ones already dead, almost as if it were an honour to be escorted into the underworld by Skarra himself. Dwarfed as they were by the scale of the entrance, their bodies looked more insect-like than ever and Atkins watched as the Stygian blackness within swallowed them,.

"Blood and sand, who would have thought it was that easy?" he said.

"They had us bang to rights, but they just gave up," said Riley, shaking his head, nonplussed.

"Well," said Gutsy, "they met their god of death, they must have—"

High pitched squeals of terror and agony rang from the cavern, the unearthly screams prolonged, magnified, iterated and reiterated by the vast chamber beyond.

"What the hell was that?"

"Sounded like the Chatts," said Everson.

Something moved in the starless black expanse beyond the entrance. It was impossible to tell what, or how big it might be, or whether it was one thing or many, from the sound alone.

The tank engine revved, snorting like a territorial beast, and lurched forward, like a hound at the leash.

If they were expecting a demonic gatekeeper, they weren't disappointed. From the mouth of the cavern scrabbled a savage-looking creature of gigantic size, part insect, part reptile with razor-taloned feet and a wide mouth filled with sharp needle teeth for shredding and tearing. Caught between some of them were the mangled, crushed remains of the Chatts. It took a mouthful of the writhing creepers and tore them from their roots. A heavily segmented carapace covered its back, and when it roared, a warm foul stench assailed the Tommies. Atkins felt his stomach heave at the smell.

"Well at least it's only got one head," said Pot Shot. "I was half expecting Cerberus."

Gazette let off five rounds rapid at the creature. They hit its carapace, but they didn't stop it. It turned in the direction of the petty annoyance and roared. The Tommies scrambled back for their recently-vacated cover.

The tank's six-pounders fired. One missed, hitting the crater wall, and the other glanced against the beast's carapace, blasting a hole in its side. It roared in pain. Now it was wounded and roused to anger.

From out of the sky, Tulliver's Strutter dived on the creature, incendiary bullets streaking through the air. The beast shook its head as if trying to rid itself of vicious insects. It reared up after the Strutter and swiped the air with its talons, but Tulliver had pulled the machine away beyond its grasp.

In that moment, Everson saw their chance: the belly of the beast wasn't armoured. The tank crew had noticed too, for the *Ivanhoe*'s guns spoke again, carrying a message of death as two six-pounder shells hit their target squarely this time, in the soft underbelly, ripping open the flesh of the beast, disintegrating bone, eviscerating cavities and vaporising organs as the creature fell forward through a mist of its own atomised blood. Its jaw hit the ground, slamming its teeth together, and it released its last foul breath.

INTERLUDE FIVE

Letter from Lance Corporal Thomas Atkins
to Flora Mullins

6ᵗʰ April 1917

My Dearest Flora,

Today I walked a Road of the Dead that leads to Hell. I thought I had walked one before. I thought it was in Belgium on the Menin Road to Ypres, paved with mud, corpses and crump holes.

But I was wrong. This is different. This is a more personal torment. Sitting here now, with this yawning abyss of darkness before me, I can't help but feel that with every step I have taken, my own good intentions have brought me here. Mea culpa.

I always told myself that you were the kind of girl that I would go to hell and back for, and I know William had said as much to you, too, the night before we left for training.

I have lived through hell on Earth once and not returned. Neither did William. For that, I am truly sorry, but now I have a second chance, a second hell. I hope with all my heart that this time I shall return to you.

Ever yours
Thomas

CHAPTER TWENTY ONE
"A Forlorn Hope..."

HAVING LANDED THE Strutter on the Strip, just beyond the trees, Tulliver and the padre walked in the dell, trusting that it would be safe now that the telluric storm, Croatoan's Torment, had passed.

Tarak was roasting meat over a fire. Napoo was still keeping his distance, not approving of the Ruanach's worship of Croatoan. Atkins' Black Hand Gang and the others sat round the fire eating, Everson and Everson mucking in with them, while Pot Shot and Gazette stood on sentry duty. The tank crew sat together by the *Ivanhoe*. Old habits were hard to break, Tulliver guessed.

Tulliver sniffed the air. "Smells good! What's cooking?"

Mercy was about to open his mouth when Atkins spoke up. "Don't ask; just eat it. You'll be better off."

Tulliver caught sight of the slain beast and was about to venture a query when he was distracted by someone calling his name.

"Tulliver!" cried Werner, striding towards the pilot and shaking the man's hand. Tulliver was taken aback. This was truly a day for dead men.

"Werner? How the devil did you survive? I saw your bus crash, I found the wreckage."

Werner shrugged with false modesty. "I managed to slow my airspeed almost to a stall, so when I crashed, the tree canopy cushioned the impact. I was lucky; I was able to climb out and down a tree while those whip creatures tore my aeroplane to bits. Still, any landing you can walk away from, am I right?"

"Well, yes," said Tulliver, still stunned at the sight of the German.

"Did you see, up there?" he asked earnestly. "I was not trying to kill you. Did you see what I wanted to show you, the *Heilige linien*? It is a big mystery, is it not?"

Tulliver nodded. "Yes it is, we both saw it," he said, indicating the padre and getting caught up in Werner's enthusiasm. "The scale of it! It's unbelievable."

Everson patted the Roanoke journal resting on his lap. "We've learnt a lot about this world, and yet there is so much more that we don't know." He shook his head, daunted by the sheer scale of the task. "What is this structure that's buried in the ground, which covers hundreds of square miles and discharges telluric energy?"

"Well, I've no answers," said Tulliver, shaking his head, "but I do know we can use it to navigate by. It means I can fly further and higher. It gives us a network of landmarks, a vast geometric web, like roads or canals, to fly by. If one gets lost, one can simply follow one of these to a crossroads until you come upon some other landmark. We can map these lines, use them to explore."

Riley joined in. "We can send telegraph signals along them, carried on the telluric current that flows through them. That gives us lines of communication. We can stay in contact with patrols and exploration parties at much greater distances. There might even be a way we can tap the telluric current itself."

"All very admirable, gentlemen," said Everson, bolstered by their enthusiasm, "and with an armistice in place with the Khungarrii we may be able to do just that—if we can avoid colonies like the Zohtakarrii, that is. But I don't intend that we should stay here if there is a way home. We've come this far and discovered a lot about this world, but dare we go further?"

Everyone knew what he was talking about. It was hard to avoid it.

"It appears that Jeffries has descended into the Chatt underworld to free the imprisoned demon, Croatoan."

"Tartarus," muttered the padre, glowering at the pitch-black cavern. "The great pit, a hell for fallen angels."

"Quite. The point is—"

"We have no proof," said Alfie. "I know what the Ruanach say, but you pointed out that it's all just myth based on fact. This search for Jeffries could be a wild goose chase."

Everson nodded, frowning. "But surely we have to be certain?"

A high-pitched scream interrupted them.

"Nellie!" said Alfie in alarm.

"Yes?" Nellie said from behind, where she was applying a salve to Tarak's raw branded flesh. They had all been surprised that Tarak had hitched a lift on *Ivanhoe*, although Alfie was secretly relieved. Tarak was already proving himself invaluable.

"If it wasn't you, then who?"

"Over here!"

The cry came from a grove of trees by the side of the cavern entrance. It was Hepton. He staggered towards them, throwing an arm out towards the grove. "I was just, you know, call of nature. I think you ought to see." Something had clearly put the wind up him.

Pot Shot went to investigate; Atkins grabbed his rifle and caught up with him. They moved up past the body of the beast. Something glinted over to the side of the entrance, amongst some large boulders. Atkins nodded to Pot Shot and, cautiously, they made their way over.

"Ah," said Pot Shot. "Well, that's not nice,"

"Better call Everson," said Atkins.

BACK AT THE trenches, under Doctor Lippett's watchful eye, Edith had begun administering the first medicinal doses of petrol fruit liquor to a group of five Chatt-blinded volunteers. For a couple of days now, they had been taking a measure three times a day at a controlled dilution.

Sergeant Warton, blinded in the Khungarrii siege, was one of the first to volunteer; the bandages were still round his head, covering his eyes. Edith took him for a short constitutional walk around the parade ground. She held onto his arm while he tentatively shuffled along, one arm out to warn him of any unexpected obstacles.

The weather was warm, and across the veldt, in the distance, there was a peculiar lightning storm. Edith could swear the lightning flashes were zagging up, not down.

The tattered Union flag fluttered from the flagpole in the centre and Warton turned his head towards the sound.

"How are you feeling?" she asked.

"Not as peculiar as I expected," he said, a trifle amused.

He stopped and cocked his head. "I thought I saw something."

"Don't tease," said Edith, "it won't be working yet. And there's no promise it will," she added sternly.

"No, really," he said. He turned blindly and pointed out across the veldt, past the Khungarrii siege workings and their scattered grave balls. "There," he said.

Edith was glad he couldn't see the disappointment on her face. "There's nothing there," she said gently.

A second later there was. A bolt of lightning struck up into the sky, followed a few seconds later by a soft, muted rumble.

"And there," he said again, turning round and pointing elsewhere.

Moments later, another bolt struck skywards from the spot. Another muffled timpani roll.

Edith's eyes widened and she clapped her hands. "Again!" she demanded gleefully.

Warton smiled, bowed theatrically, and then correctly predicted several more flashes.

It was working. Already, the petrol fruit liquor was allowing him to sense the lightning bolts before they happened.

With time and training, wondered Edith, what else might Warton and the other volunteers be able to see?

EVERSON STARED AT the find. It was a totem, the body of an Urman lashed with vines to crossed posts in the form of an 'X,' a warning to bad spirits. The man had been dead for about a month, from the look of him, although there wasn't much left after the jungle creatures had been at him. From what clothing remained, he seemed to be one of the Ruanach. The men stood around in solemn silence as it stared at them from empty sockets, its jaw hanging open in mockery of their slack-jawed surprise.

"Dear God," said the padre, making the sign of the cross.

"It is Garam," said Tarak, reaching out to touch a scar on the arm. "He was Jeffries' guide. He was supposed to guide the sky-being on the first leg of his journey to the Village of the Dead. Garam never returned. We thought he had gone on ahead with Jeffries." Tarak's face twisted with fury at the sight of his kinsman. "That he should be placed here, like this, it is *jundurru*, bad magic."

It wasn't crucifixion that killed him, however, but the bullet hole in the centre of the forehead. But the most marked thing about it was the British Army Officer's cap that it wore, complete with a Pennine Fusilier cap badge. Someone was sending a message, and they'd hung it round Garam's neck to make sure it was received, scrawled on a flattened piece of bark; *"Everson, the underworld is mine; the rest is yours—for the moment. Do not attempt to follow me—Jeffries."*

Everson gave a guilty start. How did Jeffries know he would find it? Almost on impulse, he reached up to the tunic pocket where he kept the fetish of Jeffries' button, but thought better of it and let his hand drop.

"Looks like we're on the right track, then," said Pot Shot.

"So it would appear." Everson took no joy in the fact, but at least now he had his proof. Jeffries had descended into the underworld to free his demon.

Everson knew what he must do. They should go after him. They had suffered the worst that War-torn Europe and this place could throw at them; how could this be any worse?

"And if indeed Jeffries has gone into the underworld, then that's where we're going. To Hell."

He was surprise by how certain he sounded. Still, that's what officer training was for. He summoned the signallers.

"Riley, I want you to see if you can send a message back to the canyon. Let them know what we're doing."

Riley nodded and went to collect the kitbag that contained the Signals equipment.

"Tonkins, stop stuffing your face. We've got work to do!"

Tonkins, who hadn't gone to view the grisly find, hastily finished chewing, wiped the grease from his mouth with his cuff and followed Riley out towards the Strip.

AT THE CANYON, nobody was eager to go back up to the wall after it had lit up like a star shell, least of all Buckley, and certainly not Sergeant Dixon, but the lightning flashes and the thunderous booms were receding, and somebody had to do it.

Sergeant Dixon pushed out his chest and looked at Buckley with the curdling contempt that only an NCO could muster. "You will go up that scree slope and set up your Iddy Umpty equipment again. I don't care what might happen. So you can either have a thousand volts up your arse, or my boot; which is it to be?" he bawled, warm, thick spittle speckling Buckley's face.

Buckley grunted and heaved as he hauled the kit bag of equipment up the rocky slope to the base of the metal wall. Below, he heard the work party, building a defensive breastwork around the camp, break out into song in sympathy, relieved it wasn't them. *"Send out me muvver, me sister and me bruvver, but for gawd's sake don't send meeee!"*

At the top, Buckley touched the metal tentatively. It was warm, but then it always had been. There was no sign of melting or burning. It looked just as it always had, despite the lightning that had erupted from it.

With a sense of relief, he began setting up the telegraph again. At least he knew now that he'd get a few seconds warning if anything were to happen again, and to be honest being up here it was no worse, or more dangerous, than being in a listening sap out beyond the front lines. At least Sergeant Dixon wouldn't be looking over his shoulder every five minutes.

He put the earphones over his head and began listening.

He had been up there a few hours when the clicking began. He hastily scrawled out the message on a scrap of paper with a stub of blunt pencil.

He stumbled down the scree side, calling for Sergeant Dixon as he went.

He found Sergeant Dixon waiting for him as he reached the bottom. The NCO waited impatiently while he took a moment to catch his breath.

"Message, Sarn't," said Buckley handing the scrap of paper over. "From Lieutenant Everson, Sarn't."

Dixon studied the paper and fixed Buckley with a steely glare. "Is this your idea of a joke, Buckley? 'Go to hell'?"

Buckley looked alarmed. "What? No, Sarn't. No. It reads, 'Gone to hell.'"

ATKINS AND THE rest of his men got ready to move out. Atkins found himself both scared and elated. This was everything he'd been wanting for the past five months. At last, they were hard on Jeffries' heels, and perhaps a way home. It was a desperate hope.

"Mathers said this would happen," said Pot Shot, casually.

"Are you bringing that up again?" said Mercy.

"He did, listen," Pot Shot put on a solemn face, as if he were about to give a church reading. "*'Other Ones will travel with the breath of GarSuleth, the Kreothe, made, not tamed,'*" he said. "Well that's them Chatt balloons isn't it? *'Then shall Skarra with open mandibles welcome the dark scentirrii.'* Well, Werner said our Black Hand Gang were like dark scentirrii to them Chatts. And Skarra welcomes us. These Nazarrii knew we were going into the underworld centuries ago. Don't you find that just a little bit spooky?"

"Blood and sand, Pot Shot. Will you shut up about that? Just for once, just once, I'd like to think that something I did on this hell of a world wasn't 'fated.'" Atkins threw down his knapsack and stormed off.

"I was joking!" protested Pot Shot. "Only! It's just a bloody cave!"

If they really were going into Hell, or Tartarus, or whatever, then perhaps Nellie was right; he needed to talk to someone.

Padre Rand sat quietly by himself, reading from his bible.

Atkins felt awkward interrupting him. He seemed lost in some private contemplation. "Padre, have you got a moment?"

The chaplain looked up, smiled, and lifted the small book. "Trying to find a little guidance," he said with a smile. "Atkins, isn't it? What can I do for you?"

Atkins approached the padre, his hands wringing the bottom of his tunic. "I want to make a confession."

And it all poured out of him: his big brother William, his brother's fiancée Flora, and his own love for his brother's sweetheart, and the strength and companionship they'd found in each other when William was declared missing during the Big Push on the Somme. He told of the last few tormented months, of his guilt and shame, and of Flora's last letter and his hope for a return and reunion.

"Some men see this as a hell world, Padre," he said, in a voice almost devoid of hope. "I see it more as a purgatory planet. Once I have paid for my sins, then maybe I can leave."

Padre Rand listened quietly. "Do you truly love this woman?" he asked.

"With all my heart, Padre."

"Then so long as you seek to make it right, it seems to me that you are truly penitent and wish to do the right thing. God could ask for nothing more. I could give you a few Hail Marys and a bunch of Our Fathers to say in penance, but I can see you've been a lot harder on yourself than that. I can forgive you, Atkins, but more importantly, you must learn to forgive yourself. Go, and sin no more," the chaplain said in calm, measured tones.

Atkins didn't know quite what he was expecting. A lifting of a great weight, perhaps, and a buoyant and happy heart. What he felt, however, was the relief of sharing his problem and having someone actually listen, and that was enough for now. As the padre said, the rest was up to him. At least now he could look forwards, knowing that he was doing the right thing, and not torment himself with the past.

On his way back to his mates, Atkins saw Nellie.

"I talked to someone," he said. "It helped. Thank you."

Nellie smiled. "I'm glad."

THE PADRE WATCHED Atkins go and felt a little ashamed. He wanted to promise Atkins that he would get back, but he just didn't want to make a promise that *he* might not be able to keep, and for that he was sorry. He felt a connection to Atkins. They were both, in some sense, lost; alone. They both carried a terrible private burden they felt they couldn't share. At least he had been able to help there. As for himself, that was a different matter.

The vision he'd first had in Khungarr revisited him now in all its glory. He'd wanted a sign that out here on this alien world, so far from His creation, God could hear him, and God did hear him. He had prayed that he might save his flock, the battalion, and see them returned safely home, like any good shepherd. God had answered and the padre had accepted God's beneficence with tears of joy. But the price God was asking for their salvation would cost him every ounce of faith he had, and he had blocked it from his mind, shut it away, but the still small voice would not be denied, and it tormented his sleep. Seeking his vision a second time, it was now clear to him, although there were times when he wished it was not, for God had told him that in order to save the souls of these Pennine Fusiliers, then he would have to trust in God, and die a martyr's death. Only then would their souls be saved from this purgatorial world. It was a task worthy of any minister of God, but when that day came, would he have the strength, and the faith, to suffer the ordeal? That was the thought that haunted his quiet moments now.

EVERSON SAT, TRYING to appeal to the tank crew. "I really could do with the *Ivanhoe*," he said. "It's a scouting mission, nothing more."

"I'd like to help sir," said Jack. "But I'm sorry, we can't go in there.

It's not practical. We don't know what's in there. I don't want the tank getting stuck or driving into an abyss."

"No. No, you're right, of course," said Everson. "I just thought I'd ask."

"Well, if you ask me, you should just let us blast the thing and close the cavern entrance off for good," said Wally.

"It may well come to that, but not today," said Everson.

Wally *hmphed* his disapproval and went back to greasing some engine part.

Jack tried to be a little more conciliatory, "Look, if it'll help, we'll come in as far as we can. Just to make sure there are no more of those creatures, if nothing else," he said, looking at the carcass of the giant beast. "But that's it. We'll wait for you."

"The Ruanach enclave is stockaded. We can hole up there," said Alfie.

"Fair enough," said Everson, getting up. "Thank you." He reached out and shook Jack's hand, before turning his attention to Tulliver.

"I need you to fly back to the camp and let them know what's going on. Tonkins is going to stay here with the tank crew at this Ruanach stockade. He can keep in contact with the canyon, and if there's any chance that we can use these telluric paths to communicate, maybe we can send messages, too."

"Are you sure this is the right thing to do, John?" asked Tulliver.

"No, but we've come this far. Do you want to come with us, Oberleutnant?" he asked the German.

Werner smiled politely. "What use is a pilot without a plane? No, I will stay here with Tulliver and soar with the angels, not consort with demons."

Everson nodded. "Very well."

He noticed Hepton skulking uncomfortably, like someone on the horns of a dilemma. The sight of the totem had put the wind up him. He knew the plan and wanted no part of it.

The kinematographer edged up to Everson. "I'm not a member of your battalion, Everson. You can't make me go. This may be an officer's uniform, but it carries no rank."

"Got some demons you can't face, Hepton?" Everson asked wryly.

"I don't want to go," repeated Hepton. "Tulliver can fly me back to the camp."

"The aeroplane only seats two. Werner is flying with him. If you want to go back, you'll have to walk."

"Go to hell," said Hepton,

"Oh, I intend to," said Everson.

THE PADRE WAS offering the Last Rites to all those who wanted it. Considering their destination, it seemed a sensible precaution. Pot Shot was first in the queue.

"But I thought you weren't religious?" said Atkins.

"Look, if I'm really going to Hell, then I'm going to hedge my bets. I want to enter in a state of grace, all right? All my sins forgiven. That way the devils have got nothing over me."

In preparation, Tarak had gathered some of the same sort of bioluminescent lichen that the Chatts used, and he, Nellie and Alfie made torches for them, while the rest of the tank crew checked over the *Ivanhoe*.

When the hour came, the tank gunned its engines, belched smoke and lurched forward, slowly and implacably rumbling forwards to guard the entrance. If Skarra really existed, it was about to meet its mechanical match.

Everson drew his sword, took a deep breath, blew his whistle and began to walk past the slain beast towards the cavern entrance. The padre had joined the scouting party, arguing that he was uniquely qualified.

Atkins and the Black Hand Gang fell in behind him, Atkins and Mercy carrying the Lightningwerfers. Riley followed, pulling a makeshift litter loaded with equipment. He turned and waved at Tonkin, who stood watching some distance off, alongside the *Ivanhoe*, with Tulliver, Werner, Hepton and Napoo, the Urman guide refusing to have anything to do with the venture.

Tarak, however, would not be denied. He accompanied them, a look of grim determination on his face. He had a clan to avenge, and if he failed in that, he would join them in the Village of the Dead.

Close up, the size of the cavern entrance staggered Atkins; it was larger than he had thought. Staring into the vast starless space within, he felt gripped by a sudden wave of vertigo, but he carried on, one foot in front of the other. *If in doubt, walk forwards* was always the advice, and he clung to that now; that and the thought of Flora.

The padre clutched his bible to his chest and spoke the words of the twenty-third psalm under his breath, *"Yea, though I walk in the valley of the shadow of death, I shall fear no evil..."*

Everson took a deep breath as they stepped beyond the threshold into the Stygian blackness beyond.

"'Abandon all hope, ye who enter here,'" he muttered.

THE OTHERS WATCHED the cavern entrance until the figures of the Fusiliers were lost from sight, swallowed by the obsidian blackness beyond. As they began their vigil, Nellie wondered if they would ever return...

THE END?

GLOSSARY

Ack Emma: From the *Signalese* phonetic alphabet; AM, Morning.

Albatros: A single-seater German fighter biplane.

Alleyman: Mangled by the Tommies from the French, *Allemand*, meaning a German.

AM: Air Mechanic; ground crew in the *RFC*.

Archie: Slang term for anti-aircraft fire and for its aerial shell-bursts.

Battalion: Infantry Battalions at full strength might be around a thousand men. Generally consisted of four *companies*.

Battle Police: Military police assigned to the Front Line during an attack, armed with revolvers and charged with preventing unwounded men from leaving the danger area.

BEF: British Expeditionary Force. Usually used to refer to the regular standing army who were the first to be sent to Belgium in 1914. Kaiser Wilhelm called them a 'contemptible little army' so thereafter they called themselves 'The Old Contemptibles.'

Black Hand Gang: Slang for a party put together for a dangerous and hazardous mission, like a raiding party. Such was the nature of the tasks it was chosen from volunteers, where possible.

Blighty: England, home. From the Hindustani *Bilaiti* meaning foreign land.

Blighty One: A wound bad enough to have you sent back to England.

Boojums: Nickname for tanks, also a *Wibble Wobble*, a *Land Creeper*, a *Willie*.

Bosche: Slang for German, generally used by officers.

Brassard: Armband.

Breastworks: Temporary, quickly-built fortifications, consisting of low earth walls usually about chest height.

British Army Warm: An army issue knee-length overcoat worn by officers.

Bus: RFC pilot's slang term for their aeroplane.

Canteen: A water bottle.

Carpet Slipper Bastard: A heavy artillery shell passing high overhead, and thus with little noise.

Chatt: Parasitic lice that infested the clothing and were almost impossible to avoid while living in the trenches. Living in the warm moist clothing and laying eggs along the seams, they induced itching and skin complaints.

Chatting: De-lousing, either by running a fingernail along the seams and cracking the lice and eggs or else running a lighted candle along them to much the same effect.

Commotional Shock: Contemporary medical term referring to the physical short-term concussive effects or 'shell-shock,' from a shell blast and viewed as a physical injury, which qualified soldiers for 'wound stripes,' possible discharge from the army and a pension.

Comm Trench: Short for *communications trench.*

Communication Trench: Trench that ran perpendicularly to the *fire trench*, enabling movement of troops, supplies and messages to and from the Front Line, from the parallel support and reserve lines to the rear.

Company: One quarter of an infantry *battalion*, 227 men at full strength, divided into four *platoons*.

CQS: Company Quartermaster Sergeant.

CSM: Company Sergeant Major.

Emotional Shock: Suffering from 'nerves.' Unlike *commotional shock,* those suffering from mental stress were merely seen as sick and not entitled to a 'wound stripe.'

Enfilade: Flanking fire along the length of a trench, as opposed to across it.

Estaminet: A French place of entertainment in villages and small towns frequented by soldiers; part bar, part café, part restaurant, generally run by women.

FANY: First Aid Nursing Yeomanry. The only service in which women could enlist and wear khaki, they drove ambulances, ran soup kitchens, mobile baths, etc. in forward areas.

Field Punishment No 1: Corporal punishment where men were tied or chained to stationary objects for several hours a day for up to 21 days. At other times during their punishment they were made to do hard labour.

Fire Bay: Part of a manned *fire trench* facing the enemy. Bays were usually separated by *traverses*.

Firestep: The floor of the trench was usually deep enough for soldiers to move about without being seen by the enemy. A firestep was a raised step that ran along the forward face of the *fire trench*, from which soldiers could fire or keep watch.

Fire Trench: Forward trench facing the enemy that formed part of the Front Line.

Five Nines: A type of German high-explosive shell.

Flammenwerfer: German fire projector or flame thrower.

Flechettes: From the French, meaning 'little arrow.' Used early on in the war, they were large pointed darts that were dropped from an aeroplane over trenches and were capable of piercing helmets.

Fritz: Slang term for a German.

Funk: State of nerves or depression, more harshly a slang word for cowardice.

Funk Hole: Generally, any dugout or shelter, but often referring to niches or holes big enough to shelter one or two men scraped into the front wall of a trench.

Gazetted: All military promotions and gallantry awards were officially announced in *The London Gazette*. To be the subject of such an announcement was to be gazetted.

Gone Dis: Short for 'gone disconnected.' Originally used by Signallers to mean a telephone line was down, usually from shelling, and that they were out of communication.

Greyback: A soldier's regulation grey flannel shirt, with no collars and tin buttons.

Guncotton: A service explosive commonly used for demolition.

Hard Tack: British Army biscuit ration, infamously inedible.

Hate, the: Usually a regular bombardment by the enemy made at dawn or dusk to forestall any attacks; the Morning Hate and the Evening Hate.

Hitchy Coo: Itchiness caused by lice infestation and their bites.

Hom Forty: A French railway goods wagon, used for moving troops up to the front line. Very slow. Named after the sign on the side, *Hommes 40, Chevaux 8.*

Hush Hush Crowd: Nickname for the Machine Gun Corps Heavy Section, or Tank Section, owing to the secrecy that surrounded their training.

Iddy Umpty: slang for Morse Code and, by extension, the Signallers who used it.

Jack Johnsons: Shell burst of a 5.9 or bigger, know for its plume of black smoke and nicknamed after famed black boxer, Jack Johnson.

Jildi: From the Hindi; get a move on, quick, hurry.

Kite Balloon: A blimp-shaped observation balloon, carrying a basket for an observer but attached to the ground by a winch.

Land Ship: A tank.

Lewis Machine Gun: Air cooled, using a circular magazine cartridge holding 48 rounds each. Lighter and more portable than the *Vickers*.

Linseed Lancer: Slang for a stretcher bearer of the *RAMC*.

Look Stick: Slang for a trench periscope.

Luftstreitkräfte: The German Airforce formed in October 1916, previously known as *Die Fliegertruppen des deutschen Kaiserreiches*, or the Imperial German Flying Corps.

Maconachie: Brand of tinned vegetable stew. Made a change from endless Bully Beef, though not by much.

Mills Bomb: Pineapple-shaped British hand grenade, armed by pulling a pin and releasing the trigger lever.

Minnie Crater: Crater formed from the explosion of a *Minniewerfer* shell.

Minniewerfer: German trench mortar shell.

MO: Medical Officer.

Mongey Wallahs: Cooks or chefs, from the French *manger*, to eat.

Napoo: All gone, finished, nothing left. Mangled by the British from the French phrase, *il n'y en a plus*, or 'there is no more.'

NCO: Non Commissioned Officer; a sergeant major, sergeant or corporal.

Neurasthenia: Contemporary medical term to describe emotional shell shock, less charitably seen as a 'weakness of the nerves.'

No Man's Land: Area of land between the two opposing Front Lines.

OP: Observation Post.

QM: Quartermaster.

Parados: Raised defensive wall of earth or sandbags along the rear of the trench to help disperse explosions behind the line.

Parapet: Raised defence of earth or sandbags at the front of a trench to provide cover for those on the *firestep*.

Part-worn: Clothing previously worn by another soldier, either deceased, ill or otherwise having no further use for it.

PH Helmet: Phenate-Hexamine Helmet. Early type of full-head gas mask. Not so much a helmet as a flannel hood soaked in neutralising chemicals, and a mouth tube and distinctive non-return red rubber valve for exhalation.

Picklehaub: German full-dress helmet, ornamented with a spike on top. A very desirable souvenir.

Pip Emma: From the *Signalese* phonetic alphabet; PM, afternoon, evening.

Platoon: A quarter of an infantry *company*, commanded by a *Subaltern*. Consisting of 48 men divide into four *sections*.

Plum & Apple: Much derided flavour of jam because of the cheap and plentiful ingredients used by jam manufacturers on government contract.

Plum Pudding: Nickname for a type of British trench mortar round.

Poilus: Nickname for a French soldier, like the English 'Tommy.' From the French *poilu*, or 'hairy,' as French soldiers were often unshaven, unlike the British Tommy who was required to shave every day.

Port: The left side of a vessel or ship.

Pozzy: Slang for jam.

Puttee: Khaki cloth band wound round the calf from the knee to the ankle.

RAMC: Royal Army Medical Corps, often summoned with the well-worn yell, 'stretcher bearer!' Uncharitably also said to stand for Rob All My Comrades.

Reading Your Shirt: The act of *chatting*.

Red Tabs: Slang for staff officers, after the red tabs worn on the collars of their tunics.

Revetment: Any material used to strengthen a trench wall against collapse; wooden planking, brushwood wattling, corrugated iron, etc.

RFC: Royal Flying Corps of the British Army.

SAA: Small Arms Ammunition; rifle and revolver ammunition.

Sally Port: Small, hidden passage out under the *parapet* of a *fire trench* used for sorties into *No Man's Land*.

Sans German: Village of Saint Germaine, five miles from Harcourt Wood, behind the British lines.

Sap: A *communications trench* that runs out from an already existing trench to an emplacement, kitchen, latrine or stores.

Sappers: Generally, a private in the Royal Engineers. But in this case, a small dedicated unit formed by Everson from those men with a trade—bricklaying, carpentry, etc.—to perform a similar function.

Scran: A general term for food.

Section: A quarter of a *platoon*, usually consisting of 12 men under the charge of an *NCO*.

Signalese: A phonetic alphabet.

SMLE: Short Magazine Lee Enfield. Standard issue British rifle, with a 10-round magazine.

Sponson: The side-mounted gun turret of a tank, taken from the naval term. The Mark I 'male' tank had no central-mounted roof turret, like later tanks, but two side-mounted sponsons, one on either side. Each sponson was armed with a six-pounder gun and a Hotchkiss machine gun.

SRD: Supply Reserve Depot. The initials were stamped on official army issue stone rum jars issued to platoons, although the initials soon came to stand for other things like Service Rum Diluted, Soon Runs Dry or Seldom Reaches Destination.

Stand To: Stand to Arms. Highest state of alert when all men should be ready for immediate action, weapons at the ready. Occurred regularly in the trenches at dawn and dusk to repel any attempted attacks. See also *Hate, the*.

Starboard: The right side of a vessel or ship.

Star Shell: An artillery shell consisting of a large magnesium flare and a parachute. Used for illuminating battlefields at night.

Subaltern: Or *sub*; a commissioned officer under the rank of captain; first or second lieutenant.

Tankodrome: A tank park and workshops behind the lines where maintenance and repairs can be carried out.

Toffee Apple: Nickname for a type of British trench mortar bomb.

Traverse: Thick sandbag partition built in trenches to prevent *enfilading* enemy fire and to limit the effect of any explosions. In *fire trenches* they were used to create *fire bays*. Also; purpose-built changes in angle of direction in any trench to achieve the same effect.

VAD: Voluntary Aid Detachment, women volunteers providing auxiliary nursing assistance to the Red Cross and registered nurses.

Very Light: A white or coloured flare fired from a Very Pistol. Used for signalling or illumination at night.

Vickers Machine gun: Water-cooled, belt-fed machine gun. Heavy and bulky, but more accurate than the Lewis.

Whizz-Bang: A German 77mm high velocity shell.

Windy: Or *to have the wind-up;* apprehensive or anxious about a situation.

Wipers: Tommies' name for the town of Ypres, in Belgium.

Woolly Bear: The distinctive smoke burst of a German high explosive shrapnel shell.

BONUS CONTENT

THE BROUGHTONTHWAITE MERCURY

FAR FROM THE Front and the fighting, in the northern mill town of Broughtonthwaite, the *Broughtonthwaite Mercury* was the main organ of information.

The newspaper kept the local population up to date on the war's progress, alongside the seemingly banal incidents of everyday local life.

It charted the formation of the Broughtonthwaite Mates from their early patriotic recruitment and followed their movements, publishing lists of the wounded, the dead as well as the honours. However, in 1916, the paper broke the news of the Battle of Harcourt Wood to a disbelieving community as the true scale of the tragedy became apparent.

Broughtonthwaite Mercury 15.09.1914

A BROUGHTONTHWAITE BATTALION.

PENNINE FUSILIERS REGT.

War Office Accepts Mayor's offer.

1,100 men to be raised.

RALLY TO THE FLAG.

Your King and Country need you.
How will you answer to your Country's call?

JOIN THE BROUGHTONTHWAITE & DISTRICT BATTALION TODAY!

RECRUITING OFFICE ... TOWN HALL

Broughtonthwaite Mercury 24.02.1915

AU REVOIR TO THE "MATES"

A now familiar sight, the men of the Broughtonthwaite and District battalions of the Pennine Fusiliers have trained and drilled on the moors above the town for the past five months.

Yesterday, the men of the new Broughtonthwaite battalions left for new training quarters in North Wales amid scenes of hearty farewells and good wishes.

Work at the mills and brewery was suspended until after the "Mates" departure, that the workers might show their enthusiasm and admiration of Broughtonthwaite's Own. Proud families and sweethearts gathered to wave off the battalions of "Broughtonthwaite Mates". Tears did not hide the pride the townsfolk felt at having risen to Lord Kitchener's rallying cry in raising several battalions to fight the Hun.

The men paraded at the Broughtonthwaite and District tram sheds where the Mayor's rousing speech in bidding "au revoir" to our brave volunteers, stirred the blood and fervour of the assembled throng.

Then, led by the Broughtonthwaite Brass Band, the "Mates" then proceeded to march through the town, as crowds lined the way cheering and wishing 'God speed" as they proceeded to the station, where they boarded trains for their new camp.

Broughtonthwaite Mercury 02.11.1916

BRITISH ENGAGEMENT

-------------- · --------------

HARCOURT

BRITISH OFFICIAL.

FRANCE. 1st NOVEMBER. THURSDAY.—Yesterday at 7.30am, following a short bombardment, British battalions advanced on the German stronghold position at Harcourt Wood on the Somme.

With only sporadic German machine-gun fire, the initial advance proceeded as planned until it met with a German gas attack. The wind being in the enemy's favour, the first wave of the advance was driven back to the British Front Line, when a German mine of great size was detonated.

In the face of the face of the German counter-attack, the advance faltered, but no ground was conceded.

Broughtonthwaite Mercury 03.11.1916

HARCOURT

'MATES' TAKE HEAVY LOSSES

Unofficial reports that the 13th Pennines took part in the Battle of Harcourt and suffered heavy losses are beginning to make themselves known.

Last night, with no further official statements issued, shocked and angry townsfolk desperate for news marched on the Town Hall demanding answers.

The mayor has appealed for calm and has sent to the Government for more details.

Broughtonthwaite Mercury 04.11.1916

BROUGHTONTHWAITE BATTALION LOST

BRITISH OFFICIAL.

General Headquarters today released a communiqué:

"On the morning of November 1st, an heroic enterprise was directed towards the German stronghold holding the higher ground at Harcourt Wood, where the enemy had been offering stubborn resistance, negating the gains of the Summer Offensive elsewhere on the Somme. The 13th Battalion of the Pennine Fusiliers were in the vanguard of the assault.

The new British heavy armoured cars or 'tanks' were of great assistance in the initial stages of the advance. Aeroplanes were also active in co-operation, protecting the kite balloons directing our artillery.

A spell of fine, cold weather favoured our preparations but, in the morning, a light wind allowed the enemy to disperse poison gas in an attempt to thwart the British progress.

Within moments, the German gas cloud entirely obscured the advance across a thousand yard front. The offensive was thrown into disarray as the poison cloud dissipated, exposing a crater on a scale not seen before.

Some hundreds of yards in diameter, it had completely obliterated a portion of the British front line and battlefield. No further news has been yet received of the nine hundred men of the 13th Pennines who occupied the ground and trenches within its radius.

The crater is ascribed to the mining and the subsequent detonation, by the Germans, of a new and experimental high explosive of hitherto unknown power, the nature, composition and discharge of which are currently unknown."

Broughtonthwaite Mercury 06.11.1916

GERMANY REFUTES HARCOURT ATROCITY

BRITISH HEADQUARTERS, FRANCE, MONDAY.—Following the tragic events at Harcourt on All Souls' Day, Germany yesterday issued an official communiqué:

"The German High Command refutes, in the strongest possible terms, the accusations with regard to use of any experimental explosives in relation to the British offensive at Harcourt Wood. It is entirely possible, however, that the incident was the result of a failed British tunnelling endeavour that detonated a mine under their own men."

Broughtonthwaite Mercury 07.11.16

MARCH ON TOWN HALL

MAYOR TO PETITION WAR OFFICE

Confusion still reigns regarding the fate of the 13th Battalion of the Pennine Fusiliers in the action of November 1st.

With no information beyond confirmation that the 13th Pennine Fusiliers took part in the Harcourt attack, during which the Germans were reported to have detonated a mine beneath the British lines, the lack of Official Lists only serves to inflame the situation.

According to those with relatives aboard hospital trains and ships or receiving wounded at London railways stations, there has been no arrival of wounded from the 13th Pennines.

Reports from Harcourt itself are mixed and contradictory. Accounts of a handful of survivors being treated at the Casualty Clearing Station in St. Germaine have yet to be confirmed.

Broughtonthwaite Mercury 10.11.1916

DEVASTATING NEWS

912 MISSING

TOWN MOURNS

Following earlier official statements, and the recent posting of the Official lists naming over nine hundred men of the 13th Pennines as missing in action, with no dead or wounded, the War Office remains resolutely silent.

Disbelieving of the losses and desperate for news of loved ones, the whole community is in shock.

Mills closed and the church bells tolled all day.

There is not a street in Broughtonthwaite unaffected by the great tragedy. Groups of women gather in the street to give such comfort and solace to one another as they can. Men congregate in front of the Town Hall in the hopes of further news. At the railway station, travellers and soldiers on leave are pressed for any scrap of news. Families write letters enquiring of anyone they think might have information.

Rumours of a handful of unnamed survivors of the attack have done nothing to lessen the anguish of the waiting families.

However, according to early unofficial reports of the battle, no mine detonation was heard, no plume of earth seen, no earth tremor detected, nor concussion wave felt.

One eyewitness said the Mates advanced into the German gas cloud and, upon its dispersal, had vanished.

Aviators, during a course of reconnaissance over the area, reported no movement within the crater's perimeter, and that of the 13th Pennines there was no sign.

With no more official news forthcoming, rumour and hearsay concerning the fate of the "Mates" circulate through the community. Many seek to assign supernatural explanations to their disappearance, while others talk of Boche Zeppelins and death rays, or "dissolving gases".

The mayor has demanded answers and Broughtonthwaite MP George Ball has promised to raise the issue in parliament.

George Everson, twice mayor of Broughtonthwaite and owner of Everson's Brewery, whose son, Lt. John Everson, is among the missing, has also vowed to bring his considerable influence to bear on the government in pursuit of answers as to the fate of the missing battalion.

HARCOURT SECTOR MAP

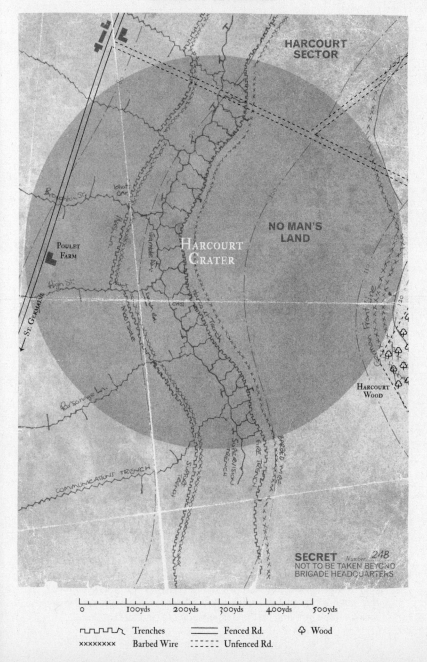

HARCOURT
SECTOR

NO MAN'S
LAND

HARCOURT
CRATER

POULET
FARM

HARCOURT
WOOD

SECRET *Number* 248
NOT TO BE TAKEN BEYOND
BRIGADE HEADQUARTERS

| 0 | 100yds | 200yds | 300yds | 400yds | 500yds |

⊔⊓⊔⊓⊔⊓ Trenches   ——— Fenced Rd.   ♧ Wood

xxxxxxxx Barbed Wire   ┈┈┈ Unfenced Rd.

HARCOURT HOAXERS EXTRACT

Arthur Cooke, whose childhood fascination with story of the missing Fusiliers grew into a lifelong passion, wrote one of the most popular books on the subject of the Harcourt Event, *The Harcourt Crater: Hoax or Horror?* Over the years, he amassed a large private collection of original documents and letters and memorabilia concerning the tragedy.

The book itself, long out of print, looks in depth at the original War Office cover-up, examines the numerous conspiracy theories surrounding the mystery, and covers the relatives' campaign for the truth, that continues to the present day, the files of the Committee of Enquiry into the Harcourt Event having been closed for an unprecedented one hundred and fifty years.

In the section below, Cooke looks at some of the swindles surrounding the mystery, perpetrated by con men who claimed, amongst other things, to be Fusilier survivors or returnees, some of which were spectacular, others petty and despicable.

An extract from *Harcourt Crater: Hoax or Horror?* by Arthur Cooke, published by Albion Amalgamated Press Ltd, 1973

Reprinted with permission

With the discovery of the Lefeuvre Find and the subsequent picture house showings of the Hepton Footage in 1926, the story of the Pennine Fusiliers once again ignited the public imagination. With the tantalising possibility of the missing soldiers being alive on some other world, here on this world the story of the Heroes of Harcourt took a darker, more sordid turn.

Those that came back from the war faced some tough choices. The post-war period was hardly a land fit for heroes. Unemployment was high and many were forced to make a living in whatever way they could. However, there are always those willing to take advantage of people more vulnerable than they are. For those that had turned to a life of crime, the resurgence of the myth of the Pennines was a golden opportunity.

If the film footage, documents and letters of the Lefeuvre Find had appeared from nowhere, then why couldn't the men reappear, too? It was certain that a great many relatives wanted to believe that such a thing might be possible. Unscrupulous men used this forlorn hope, preying on the desperation of grieving families.

Most were opportunistic chancers, trying their luck. They would turn up on a doorstep claiming to know something of one of the missing, citing amnesia or shell shock as the reason for their inability to come sooner. Eliciting sympathy by pretending to be down on their luck, they would claim to know the whereabouts of some magically reappeared letter or memento that, for a small remuneration, could be acquired. Many desperate folk were happy to give to them, only to find the money and the man vanished never to return. It was an old trick, but one that had found a new seam to mine. Many of these con men were minor crooks with no ambition beyond the next mark. Others were more calculating.

Duncan Thorpe turned up on the doorstep of Dorothy Ashworth in Kendal in September 1920. Née, Farley, she had been brought up in Broughtonshaw and had once been engaged to Joseph Knowles a Private in 'B' Company of the 13th Pennine Fusiliers who had been listed among the missing in 1916. Upon hearing that Thorpe had known her fiancé, she invited him in. Thorpe, who had lost a hand during the War, would claim that he lost it at the very moment that the Pennines vanished. It had been severed, he said as he reached out as Knowles and the other Fusiliers were abruptly transported to another planet before his eyes along with his hand, leaving the rest of him behind.

He inveigled his way into Ashworth home despite the initial objections of Mr Ashworth, and became a lodger, preying on Dorothy's feelings for her first fiancé. He stayed there for many months, working his way into Dorothy's affections. Only when Dorothy discovered she was pregnant by him and that her savings were gone, along with Thorpe, did she realise the truth.

Thorpe was caught some months later, attempting a similar fraud on another woman.

But perpetrating a hoax on one person at a time only brought small rewards. Some hoaxers had loftier ambitions. One such man was Ernest Naylor. After the war, Naylor made a comfortable, if disreputable living as a spiritualist medium, claiming that since a shrapnel injury to the head during the war, he was now able to hear the voices of the dead. To that end, he could 'help' the grieving contact those who had died in the conflict. He made a good living and achieved a certain reputation.

Now, with the sensation of the Hepton Footage, he decided to modernise his act and turned to 'science' to do so. He claimed to have invented a radio device which he could use to communicate with the distant world upon which the Pennines had found themselves.

After the sensation of the Hepton Footage swept Britain, playing in picture houses up and down the country, Naylor said that he had presented this device to the War Office to allow them to communicate with the men. They, apparently, declined his offer. Having done all he could to help, he now felt it was his patriotic duty to offer the same service to those engaged n a personal search for the missing – for a small remuneration of course.

In many ways, he used exactly the same tricks as he used as a spiritualist. However, instead of channelling spirits himself, he claimed his device did the job for him. Following in the footsteps of Nikolai Tesla, who back in 1899 said that he had received radio signals from Mars, Naylor said that after years of painstaking scientific research he had succeeded in constructing an extraordinary machine through which he could receive "cosmic radio" transmissions. The machine itself was said to have consisted of a large brass and walnut veneer cabinet full of valves and tubes, a great horned speaker, and great lengths of aerial. As his reputation grew, so did the size of his "cosmic radio."

Heard though the contraption, the voices were faint and crackly and their content hard to decipher, but they were definitely northern voices that sounded as if they had travelled a great distance. Those that heard them were thankful for even that.

In the early days, he travelled around in a van purchased specifically for the purpose. He declared that it contained equipment important to the reception of the cosmic radio signals. Driving from house to house, he performed his service for those who wanted it. It wasn't cheap. With a great deal of theatre, he would set up his cabinet in the house making a great show of plugging in cables that he would run out through the door to the van in which he had yet more "equipment." On top of the van, he would erect a large aerial.

Inside the motor van, he had an accomplice sat hunched in the box that he claimed to be the cosmic radio receiver. One of the cables would be a small tube through which the accomplice would speak, his distorted voice emitted from the speaker horn. He could have half a street paying money to gather in a front parlour, straining to listen to barely audible voices, while he fiddled with dials and made other adjustments to capture the interplanetary signals.

Later, he expanded his act to take in musical halls. His equipment became bigger and more impressive. He began to use specially prepared gramophone records, along with accomplices to deliver "messages" from the Fusiliers. He soon began claiming that he was experimenting on transmitting "cosmic radio" signals, too and inviting volunteers to take part in his experiments by speaking into a large, specially constructed microphone.

His luck ran out when, during a performance at the Tiverston Empire, the theatrical electrics of his great "cosmic radio" caught fire. The assistant within the "machine" (who turned out to be double-amputee invalided out of the army after losing both his legs, and was therefore small enough to fit inside the box) broke character and shrieked as the fire spread and the audience evacuated the theatre. Although the damage to the theatre wasn't severe, in the aftermath Naylor's machine was discovered to be a fake, containing no great scientific equipment and certainly none capable of receiving or transmitting any kind of radio signal.

One of the most audacious hoaxes, however, occurred in early 1927 in Piccadilly Circus, London. On the night of Friday February 18th, London was smog-bound, choked by a thick acrid cloud of smog. Around half-past ten at night, a huge flash of light, diffused by the sickly yellow smog, briefly lit the area just as the theatres were emptying and the crowds were hurrying home. It was accompanied by a loud bang, followed by what onlookers described as a scream. From the direction of the display staggered a man in a soldier's uniform, the uniform of the Pennine Fusiliers. Wearing a gas hood, and armed with a rifle, its bayonet fixed, the soldier staggered about as if drunk or disorientated, approaching alarmed theatre goers, his voice indistinct beneath the gas helmet.

A crowd soon gathered as the soldier took cover by the statue of Eros, warning people to stay back and refusing all offers of help. When the police arrived, Constable William Higson, who had served with the London Rifles, diagnosed the signs of shell shock in the man, eventually calmed the soldier down. Convincing the mysterious Tommy that he was indeed in England and safe, the man surrendered his rifle to Higson. Taking off his gas helmet and standing to attention, he gave his name and rank as Dewhurst, Cecil, Private, 'A' company 13th Battalion, Pennine Fusiliers, before collapsing. Although Dewhurst was indeed on the list of the missing, he had no known living relative to confirm the fact, his mother dying of tuberculosis some years earlier and his father in a tram accident a short time after.

His dramatic appearance caused a sensation and the newspapers clamoured for interviews. Initially, Dewhurst was put up in a police cell and seemed happy with the arrangement before the London *Illustrated Graphic and Chronicle* paid for him to be moved to a comfortable hotel. They also paid him for his story.

For several weeks, his tales of survival on the planet Oordia and the peoples that the Fusiliers met there gripped readers. Even those suspicious of his story, devoured the account for any information they might possibly corroborate; familiar names or facts they knew about the "Mates." Some people even wrote to the papers saying that they recognised him and he was indeed Cecil Dewhurst. Three weeks later, the hotel room was empty but for a note, stating that, with regret, Dewhurst had to return to Oordia. The paper proprietor's suspicions were immediately roused since the money, too, had gone.

It was only when an old lag recognised a photograph and later identified "Dewhurst" as one Arthur Rees who he had known in prison, describing a particular tattoo on the man's back, that the truth was revealed. Constable Higson recognised the description of the tattoo from the soldier's time staying in the police cell and "Dewhurst's" real identity was confirmed. The paper put out a reward for Rees, but to no avail. He had gone to ground, probably fleeing to Europe.

FREDRICK DWYER WANTED POSTER

IN 1914, THE Lambton Grange murders were the subject of much morbid curiosity. Fredrick Dwyer, aka "Dwyer the Diabolist" was forced to go on the run. With the outbreak of war some months later, it was assumed he had evaded capture by volunteering for the army under an assumed name.

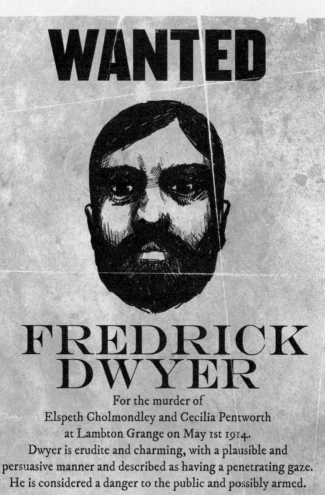

ABOUT THE AUTHOR

Pat Kelleher is a freelance writer. He has written for magazines, animation and radio. He served his time writing for a wide variety of TV licensed characters, translating them into audio books, novels and comics. Yes, he's written for that. And that. And even, you know, them. He has several non-fiction books to his credit and his educational strips and stories for the RSPB currently form the mainstays of their Youth publications.

Somehow he has steadfastly managed to avoid all those careers and part-time jobs that look so good on a dust jacket.